# THE
# STARS
## OF THE
# SOUTH

# By the same author from the same publishers

The Distant Lands
(*a novel of the antebellum South*)

Paris
(*essays — bilingual*)

South
(*a play*)

The Apprentice Writer
(*essays*)

The Green Paradise
(*Autobiography Vol I, 1900–1916*)

The War at Sixteen
(*Autobiography Vol II, 1916–1919*)

Love in America
(*Autobiography Vol III, 1919–1922*)

Restless Youth
(*Autobiography Vol IV, 1922–1927*)

The Publishers gratefully acknowledge the generous
editorial assistance of Euan Cameron, the translator
of Julian Green's autobiographies.

# JULIAN GREEN

# *THE*
# *STARS*
## *OF THE*
# *SOUTH*

a novel
translated from the French by
Robin Buss

**Marion Boyars**
**New York • London**

First published in the United States and Great Britain in 1996
by Marion Boyars Publishers
237 East 39th Street, New York, N.Y. 10016
24 Lacy Road, London, SW15 1NL

Distributed in Australia and New Zealand by
Peribo Pty Ltd, 58 Beaumont Road, Mount Kuring-gai, NSW 2080

Previously published in France under the title *Les Etoiles du sud*
in 1989 by Editions du Seuil, Paris

Library of Congress Cataloging-in-Publication Data available

British Library Cataloguing in Publication Data
Green, Julian
Stars of the South
I. Title II. Buss, Robin
843.912 [F]

ISBN 0–7145–2985–0 Cloth

Typeset in 10.5/12 Times and Garamond by Ann Buchan (Typesetters), Middx

# Contents

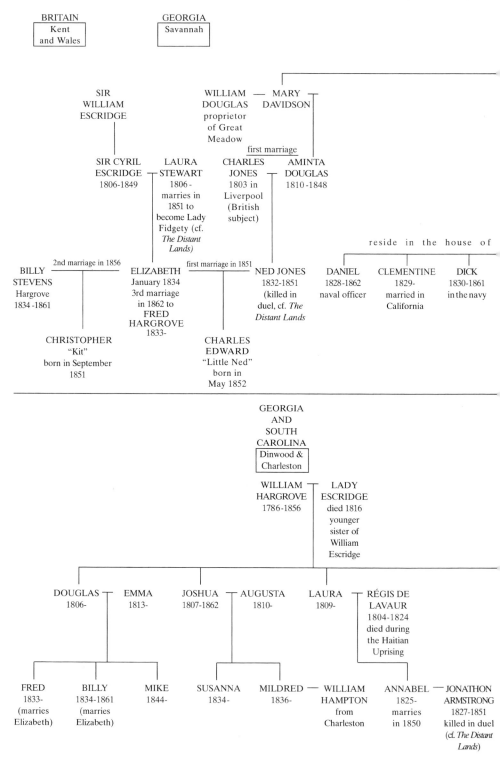

BRITAIN
Kent
and Wales

GEORGIA
Savannah

SIR
WILLIAM
ESCRIDGE

WILLIAM — MARY
DOUGLAS DAVIDSON
proprietor
of Great
Meadow

first marriage

SIR CYRIL
ESCRIDGE
1806-1849

LAURA
STEWART
1806 -
marries in
1851 to
become Lady
Fidgety (cf.
*The Distant
Lands*)

CHARLES
JONES
1803 in
Liverpool
(British
subject)

AMINTA
DOUGLAS
1810-1848

reside in the house of

2nd marriage in 1856

BILLY
STEVENS
Hargrove
1834 -1861

ELIZABETH
January 1834
3rd marriage
in 1862 to
FRED
HARGROVE
1833-

first marriage in 1851

NED JONES
1832-1851
(killed in
duel, cf. *The
Distant Lands*

DANIEL
1828-1862
naval officer

CLEMENTINE
1829-
married in
California

DICK
1830-1861
in the navy

CHRISTOPHER
"Kit"
born in September
1851

CHARLES
EDWARD
"Little Ned"
born in
May 1852

GEORGIA
AND
SOUTH
CAROLINA
Dinwood &
Charleston

WILLIAM
HARGROVE
1786-1856

LADY
ESCRIDGE
died 1816
younger
sister of
William
Escridge

DOUGLAS
1806-

EMMA
1813-

JOSHUA
1807-1862

AUGUSTA
1810-

LAURA
1809-

RÉGIS DE
LAVAUR
1804-1824
died during
the Haitian
Uprising

FRED
1833-
(marries
Elizabeth)

BILLY
1834-1861
(marries
Elizabeth)

MIKE
1844-

SUSANNA
1834-

MILDRED — WILLIAM
1836-       HAMPTON
           from
           Charleston

ANNABEL — JONATHON
1825-       ARMSTRONG
marries     1827-1851
in 1850     killed in duel
            (cf. *The Distant
            Lands*)

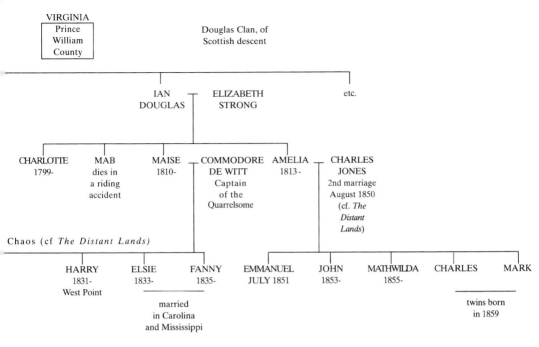

VIRGINIA
Prince
William
County

Douglas Clan, of
Scottish descent

IAN
DOUGLAS — ELIZABETH
STRONG

etc.

CHARLOTTE
1799-

MAB
dies in
a riding
accident

MAISE
1810-

COMMODORE
DE WITT
Captain
of the
Quarrelsome

AMELIA
1813-

CHARLES
JONES
2nd marriage
August 1850
(cf. *The
Distant
Lands*)

Chaos (cf *The Distant Lands*)

HARRY
1831-
West Point

ELSIE
1833-

FANNY
1835-

EMMANUEL
JULY 1851

JOHN
1853-

MATHWILDA
1855-

CHARLES

MARK

married
in Carolina
and Mississippi

twins born
in 1859

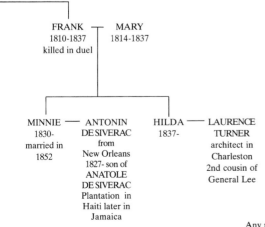

FRANK — MARY
1810-1837   1814-1837
killed in duel

MINNIE — ANTONIN
1830-        DE SIVERAC
married in   from
1852         New Orleans
             1827- son of
             ANATOLE
             DE SIVERAC
             Plantation in
             Haiti later in
             Jamaica

HILDA — LAURENCE
1837-     TURNER
          architect in
          Charleston
          2nd cousin of
          General Lee

Any resemblance to real persons or names is entirely accidental.

To the soldiers of the South and the North
who fell in a war between brothers

# 1
# THE LITTLE
# CONSPIRATOR

# 1

*T*he child was on all fours at his mother's feet, pretending to gather roses from a Persian carpet. As he explained quietly to an invisible companion, he was making a bouquet to present to the person he loved most in the world. His tiny fingers, more like living flowers than those in the multicolored woolen garden, pointed first to one rose, then to another, lingering over his choice.

Elizabeth watched him out of the corner of her eye, but, for a moment, her attention was directed elsewhere, to the open door. A woman was standing, somewhat hesitantly, at the entrance to the gold and green drawing-room.

'Well,' said Elizabeth, 'how much longer are we going to stay gazing at one another and saying nothing? What are you waiting for, Miss Llewelyn? Come in and sit down.'

The Welshwoman was wearing a gray dress and a little black flat-rimmed straw hat that gave her a false air of middle-class respectability.

She came in and sat down on the edge of an armchair.

'I can see,' she began, 'that my visit has taken you by surprise . . . I dare say not a pleasant surprise.'

For a few seconds, she seemed to expect a protest that didn't come.

For Elizabeth, she had appeared like an apparition from a past that had ended with a bullet in the heart . . . The visitor did not seem to realize this.

'After more than four long years of silence . . . ,' she sighed.

Her sea-blue eyes alighted on Elizabeth, who did not flinch. The Welshwoman continued:

'I have words in my heart that will not rise to my lips . . .'

'Excuse me,' Elizabeth interrupted, 'but if you find it embarrassing to say them, don't you think it would be better to let them stay where they are until some other time?'

Suddenly she got up. Unable to bear Miss Llewelyn's gaze, she went over to the window as if to observe the passers-by. She envied the fact that they were able to walk freely under the trees.

Intrigued, the little boy went over to her and pulled at the folds of her skirt:

'Mama,' he said.

'Leave me alone, my love,' Elizabeth murmured. 'I'm with this lady.'

'I love you,' he said.

She stroked the boy's head, then, turning to Miss Llewelyn, made an effort to smile.

'I didn't mean to hurt you,' she said quickly. 'Tell me all the news from Dimwood — I haven't set foot there for years. Mr Charles Jones hardly ever mentions it. It's almost as if he didn't want to.'

She tried to sound as natural as possible and, in doing so, she managed to reassure herself and make the presence of this woman, so shrouded with intolerable memories, less alarming.

Miss Llewelyn sighed:

'Mr Hargrove is no longer the same person, but Dimwood hasn't changed. Dimwood doesn't alter. Miss Minnie has married and lives in New Orleans. You remember that she was engaged to that gentleman from Louisiana just before . . . before the event . . .'

'I know,' said Elizabeth impatiently, 'that's enough'.

She sat down in her armchair again.

'Terrible, terrible,' Miss Llewelyn muttered.

Now quite pale, Elizabeth hugged her little boy tightly to her.

'And Susanna?' she asked.

'Miss Susanna has declared that she will never marry. When people ask her why, she just says that she has her reasons. I know what those reasons are.'

'Really? And Mildred? And Hilda?'

'Both engaged to young officers, but how everything drags on endlessly. The others are well, but they're bored. You'll be very welcome there. People miss you. They talk about you. The gardens are more scented than ever. There are masses of flowers as far as the edge of the woods.'

For the space of a second, Elizabeth saw herself back there, by the magnolias at the bottom of the veranda steps, and she closed her eyes. Suddenly she came to herself again, as if she had received a shock.

'There is someone you haven't told me about,' she said.

'Yes, Mr William Hargrove. Did you know that he was ill?'

'Mr Jones said something rather vague about it.'

It was as if a gleam of triumph shone through all the wrinkles of the face that observed her.

'Three days ago, as he awoke, Mr Hargrove's doctor told him that he had only a month to live.'

'Oh! How did he take it?'

'As badly as possible. He started shouting that he had not been looked after properly, he accused his doctor of not being conscientious and decided to make a new will. Mr Charles Jones tried to calm him down. Nothing could be done.'

'I can understand how you must have felt, Miss Llewelyn.'

'If you'd been there, if you could imagine what I have seen and heard . . .'

Suddenly she got up and appeared to grow taller, as if some inner strength had given her the dimensions of a giant, and the room with its delicate gilding grew dark. The blood of her people suddenly manifested itself in that woman with all the violent inspiration of her native land. She began to speak like a visionary, her eyes on some distant horizon, far beyond the young Englishwoman who was listening to her despite herself, in the magical grip of a hallucination.

The boy looked up, his eyes shining, his ecstatic face framed by a mass of black curls tinged with red. All his attention seemed to be concentrated on the Welshwoman, who, for him, had become monumental.

'The Dimwood you knew has not changed, because nothing alters at Dimwood, except in the minds of its inhabitants, and there, what a commotion! Do you remember the big dining-room, where everybody gathers for every meal? Well, picture the long table, without its cloth. At one end, a gaunt old man is sitting on a chair, the back of which rises well above his bald head, for the appalling illness that is eating him away is robbing him of his last white hairs and he is now no taller than a little boy. Well, you are avenged of that man who tormented you with his desires. William Hargrove, once master of the house with white columns which is now out of reach of his skeletal hands.'

'Uncle Charlie didn't tell me that Mr Hargrove was as ill as that,' Elizabeth cried out, 'I'm sorry for him, with all my heart — in spite of everything.'

'He's afraid of death and he won't let go of anything,' she continued implacably. 'And all the people that surround him! He has hardly any voice left, but he fills it with all his fury and, gasping for breath, he argues with the men in black, the lawyers, the bankers. On either side of him are his two eldest sons. Granddaughters and daughters-in-law stand aghast, at the far end of the room. The terror that William Hargrove inspired in them was no more than an instinctive recoiling at confrontation with death, whose presence they sensed, for it was a presence that reigned everywhere, from top to bottom of the house, awaiting its hour. You mentioned Charles Jones. He is there, standing, in a gray frockcoat beside the sick man, and, in front of them, on the table, among a mass of papers, is an open book, a notebook bound in red cloth. That book, Mrs Jones, was me.'

Her hands, the fingers bent like claws, moved to her breast as if to tear at it. The woman was apparently mad and she terrified Elizabeth, who hugged her little boy close to her.

'Calm down, Miss Llewelyn,' she cried. 'You can tell me all that later.'

The Welshwoman did not even hear her.

'My accounts book!' she roared in a fit of rage. 'They had examined it for a good half-hour beforehand, page by page, line by line, gone over it with a fine tooth-comb, while I was present, sweating with anger and indignation, in agony. . .'

Elizabeth ran over to shut the drawing-room door, for a moment leaving her little boy, who stood motionless, as if fascinated by this thunderous individual. Mouth agape, he stared at her, dumbstruck, with a mixture of astonishment and interest, but quite unafraid. His mother came back at once and held him tightly again.

'They also shut the doors,' Miss Llewelyn sniggered, 'but that didn't stop all the Blacks in the house glueing their ears against them so as not to miss a syllable, and I was glad to know that they were there. Suddenly the chief accountant interrupted old Hargrove, who kept repeating obstinately that the accounts book was worthless, proved nothing, that there had been extortion: "Speaking on behalf of my colleagues, I declare that I have never seen an accounts book kept so strictly. It's a model of accuracy." Hargrove then started to shout, as best he could, for his voice no longer carried. All we could hear was a raucous noise: "That woman practised extortion for years. . ." At these words, Mr Charles Jones grabbed the accounts book, which he brandished with one hand, while, with the other, he struck the pages on which the rows of figures were written. "Where are the extortions in this book, William? You've had it right in front of your eyes every evening for twenty years and you've never seen anything irregular in it. Each page is marked in the same bottom right-hand corner with your initials, your approval." His voice resounded in the stifling air. He looked splendid with his pink cheeks and his fine, unruly hair over his forehead. ". . . for you were suspicious, William Hargrove, but the law forbids you to accuse without proof the most devoted of housekeepers." Mr Hargrove put his hands to his head and began to moan: "You don't know, you don't know anything. That wretch has nearly ruined me. Proof, proof. . . ," he repeated. "What proof?" he repeated again. "What proof?" "You're talking nonsense, William Hargrove!" I yelled at him. We then saw this gentleman who had once been so respected shed tears like a child. I felt sorry for him. "May God forgive you," I said gently. He made an effort to raise his head and look at me. "Go away," he muttered. There was then a long silence. What a moment that was for me. . . I went to the door. Thrown out of Dimwood, I nevertheless sensed as I left the respect of almost everyone and I savored it as I would the exquisite scent of our camellias. Oh! The sweetness of knowing that one is the object of general esteem!'

She spoke with an almost religious gravity, then, suddenly changing tone, she went on:

'When I got to the door, I pushed it open, scattering some fifteen Blacks who fled in every direction.'

She fell silent and sat down.

'What a beautiful child you have,' she said after a few moments.

'His name is Charles Edward,' Elizabeth said quickly, as if to cut short the comments that she expected. 'His resemblance to his father is already striking. You seem tired, Miss Llewelyn. Your account has distressed me.'

'Mama!' cried the little boy, with the disappointed look of a spectator who has seen some exciting performance end too soon.

'Sshhh!' said Elizabeth, sitting down again in her chair.

With animal agility, he jumped onto her lap and tried to embrace her.

'Do you love me?' he asked. 'Why isn't the lady saying anything?'

'Be quiet, darling. Stay still and be good.'

He snuggled up against her and, turning toward Miss Llewelyn, he favored her with a smile. Grudgingly, the Welshwoman returned it.

Retreating into a silence interrupted only by sighs, she did not seem disposed to take her leave of Elizabeth, who sought in vain for some courteous, kindly way of getting her to go.

After a few minutes, which seemed interminable, she asked rather awkwardly:

'I am grateful that you have confided in me, but why have you told me all these things?'

For the Welshwoman, those words were like the crack of a whip announcing that the race had begun again. Indefatigably she raised her head and resumed where she had left off:

'I went up to my room and packed my bags. I then went off to find Azor — you remember Azor, the coachman? A few coins persuaded him to take me in the tilbury to Sister Laura's convent. She saw me at once and kept me there for an hour, urging me to be patient and giving me all kinds of practical advice to help me out of my difficulties. . . At her insistence, I decided to come and ring at your door.'

'And so?' Elizabeth asked, already alarmed.

'The words that a moment before I was stifling in my heart. . .'

The young woman could not contain herself:

'Please, Miss Llewelyn, let's get to the point.'

'Oh! You have nothing to fear, Mrs Jones.'

A request for money, thought the young woman.

Miss Llewelyn read Elizabeth's thoughts on her face.

'Oh! Do not be afraid, Mrs Jones. Providence has been generous to me and I have my savings, but, no longer being housekeeper at Dimwood, I am free to offer you my services. . .'

Elizabeth nearly recoiled in horror and, in a toneless voice that she did not recognize herself, she replied.

'I already have a housekeeper, Miss Llewelyn.'

The words fell into a heavy silence, then, half-screwing up her eyes, the Welshwoman whispered, as if it were a secret:

'There are no two housekeepers like Maisie Llewelyn, Mrs Jones.'

'I'm sure, believe me, and I regret. . .'

'I too,' said Miss Llewelyn, as she got to her feet, 'I very much regret it, for you as well as for me. I think we shall be seeing one another again.'

A wide, but cold smile, spread over her face, and she went over to the door, which she opened suddenly, out of habit, every closed door being suspect for her, but there was no one there.

Elizabeth did not see her out. She waited for the front door to open and close again. Then, putting her arm around her little boy, she hugged him with all her strength.

'The lady isn't pleased?' he asked.

'Yes she is, she is. She's always like that. Don't tell anyone you've seen her. Promise?'

'Promise.'

She covered him with kisses and whispered in his ear:

'My Jonathan.'

'Zonathan! Zonathan!' he repeated quietly as he laughed.

Elizabeth put her finger to her lips.


# 2


S tanding by a corner of the window, she searched in every direction, but the Welshwoman had already disappeared and, anyway, what was the use of watching her go? Whatever her intentions, good or bad, she was taking them away with her as well as her irritating mystery.

That woman hates me, she thought.

She rang and stood there, waiting. The child clung to her and she stroked his head.

A servant appeared, dressed in black, a tall boy with the face of a pale yellow half-caste.

'Sam, tell Betty to come and see me.'

Alone with her son once more, she took him by the shoulders. His white linen jacket and open-necked shirt made him look rather like a little cabin boy, but the short trousers and striped stockings proclaimed the young town-dweller. She looked at him, kissed him, looked at him again attentively. Was he as much like his father as everyone said? With those round cheeks and wide-apart brown eyes perhaps. What she was really looking for was the reflection of another face that haunted her memory, but that was only a sick imagination at work. Did she not know that herself? What strange game was she playing with the complicity of implacable memories?

'You are my Jonathan, you hear,' but she said it quietly, without ever saying Jonathan aloud. He threw himself into her arms laughing:

'Yes, Mama.'

At that moment the door opened and Betty, dressed in a green and red shawl, ran up to them, apologizing.

'I was with Miss Celina in the lumber-room.'

'That's all right my sweet Betty. Now that it's cooler you can take Charles-Edward out for a walk. Put on his big straw hat and don't let him let go of your hand.'

'No, Miss Lizbeth. Massa Cha'leddy is my t'easure.'

She threw herself on her treasure, who struggled as his fingers caressed the black mask that time had ravaged pitilessly as if to rob it of any human appearance. The huge dark eyes, which alone had been spared, swam in an immense tenderness.

Charles-Edward jumped for joy at the idea of going out and immediately put his hand in Betty's. Watching them leave the room, Elizabeth could not help smiling. Betty, in her red camisole, did not have to stoop far to hold the hand of the young gentleman entrusted to her. The light coming through the blinds was already weaker, spreading over the walls great splashes of pale gold, suddenly transforming the room into a place that was quite unlike America. It was the time of day that the young woman dreaded because it was then that she felt overcome with an irresistible melancholy that slackened the bonds with real life. The charm of that moment frightened her, but she looked forward to it as an escape. She then had to make an effort to shake herself free of her daydreams and pick up once more the thread of the insignificant events that made up her life.

As she left the room, she came across Sam, who bowed and handed her a visiting-card on a tray. Major Alexander Brookfield, she read and raised her eyebrows.

'I shall always be out for that gentleman.'

'*Yes*, Ma'am.'

The young half-caste looked at her. She glanced back at him in such a way as to make him look down. He bowed and disappeared.

A winding staircase led upstairs. On one of the first steps, she stopped, her hand on the polished wooden banister. The name that she had just read with its rather over-large letters was certainly not the one that she had wanted to see on that card.

She ran quickly upstairs to her room. With its half-closed shutters, her bedroom, bathed in half-light, closed around her like a shelter against the outside world and the young woman stayed there for a long time, lying on a mahogany sofa. A tall, tilted mirror reflected furniture that looked as if it were about to slide around the room, as if on board a ship in a rough sea. Despite herself, the name of Alexander Brookfield began to whirl round in her head. Indeed, she called him her number one scourge. Forty years of age, a handsome man and an artillery officer, he was in the first rank of her admirers. Received everywhere, he deprived the young and far too pretty widow of any hope of escaping him. By means of a subtle strategy, he succeeded sooner or later in cornering her in the drawing-room and inflicting upon her the torture of his compliments, which he possessed in large number. He administered them to her as one might offer sweets to someone of modest intelligence and on whom one might have designs. The special voice reserved for women then went through its various modulations until his victim could bear it no longer and suddenly escaped. This earned her his gentle reproaches on successive evenings and established between them a sort of false, bellicose familiarity, but until now he had never been so bold as to call on her.

Suddenly she began to think of someone else.

The thought of Ned out walking with Betty suddenly drew her from her thoughts and she ran over to the window and pushed open the shutters. Leaning out to left and to right, she scrutinized the avenue, which he knew he should not leave and, not seeing him, she felt a sudden terror come over her.

She rang. The door opened almost immediately and a young white woman entered. Tall and thin, she wore her dark blue, long-sleeved dress with a certain elegance. A starched collar added an austere note in keeping with her serious, regular features. Her calm, gray eyes implied a natural good humor that was effortlessly reassuring.

'Madam,' she said.

'Miss Celina, I'm worried about Charles-Edward.'

'I'm not, Madam. He has just come in.'

'But he went out scarcely a quarter of an hour ago.'

'No, Madam, you've been here almost an hour. Night is falling. Anyway,' she added, 'I can hear him coming upstairs with Betty. There is no need to worry.'

'I can't help it. When he is not here there is always a moment when I can no longer see him; I'd like. . .'

Her words were cut short by joyful cries. Running up to her, Charles-Edward tried to splutter out an account of his walk that had become an adventure full of surprises. He was still wearing his hat and its black ribbons shook at his slightest movement.

Betty followed, laughing out loud, and provided the commentary:

'All de ladies want to kiss him, but Massa Cha'leddy no want and he struggle.'

With wild enthusiasm, Elizabeth seized him in her arms and held him so tight as almost to smother him. The little hat had rolled on to the ground. Miss Celina laughed as she picked it up, and for a few minutes there was an eruption of happiness between the four walls of that room, usually devoted to silence. Elizabeth ran her fingers through the dark curls of her son's head, whispering words of love in his ear almost as confused as those of her little boy.

Betty interrupted this secret dialogue:

'Massa Cha'leddy,' she said firmly, 'Betty's going to give you your bath.'

'Yes, he's dripping with sweat,' Miss Celina remarked. 'After a bath, his bowl of soup and then to bed. Isn't that right, Ma'am?'

Elizabeth let him go regretfully.

'I'll tuck him up myself,' she said, 'Miss Celina, come and help me dress.'

With an air of tender devotion, she watched the child being pulled away by Betty.

Alone with Miss Celina, she looked at her gravely.

'What do you think, Miss Celina? Is it right to worship one's child as I worship mine?'

'What can I say, Ma'am? I'd have to have a child of my own, but my mother loved me like that, madly. She called me her trembling joy. It's an expression we have.'

'Trembling joy,' repeated the young woman thoughtfully. 'Have I ever known anything else?'

'What will you wear this evening, Ma'am?' Miss Celina asked in a detached tone of voice.

'My violet taffeta dress.'

'If you'll allow me to say so, won't it look rather sad? Rather like very prolonged mourning?'

'Parma or whatever you like. This evening I don't care what I wear. I shall be just as bored in all the colors of the rainbow. I'm dining at the Steers'.'

The Steers' house was among the oldest in the town and prided itself on being one of the simplest. Tall and narrow, the windows gave it an austere look, which was softened by the elegance of the door with its delicate Ionic columns.

As soon as Elizabeth arrived, she could see from the look on everyone's face that her housekeeper's choice had been the right one. Dressed entirely in white and without a single piece of jewellry, the young Englishwoman was dazzling. The freshness of her complexion withstood the climate of the country, still preserving the radiance of those first years at Dimwood. A closer examination would reveal in the eyes a shadow of anxiety that made her a different person from the young lady who six years before had climbed the plantation steps for the first time. Now her hair alone, which spread out around her face with well studied negligence, was enough to give her an air of supremacy. Not without a slight smile of irritation, the local beauties recognized in her the charm of her native land — 'a rather rustic charm', they murmured behind their fans. The men had no such reservations. She ruled over their desires still more with her sentimental enthusiasm which they took to be a murmur of the heart.

To feel oneself the object of such desire seemed to her to be unworthy of the idea that she had formed of herself. So she cultivated an air of polite indifference before these gentlemen who rushed up as she passed. She felt as though some of them, with their langorous looks, were sullying her face and what they could see of her breasts. The older ones especially. The young officers, in their tight uniforms, seemed less cynical and confined themselves to wild glances from eyes as silent as sapphires.

The tyranny of custom required that she should finally accept the invitations of a certain number of families and, of these, the Steers were in the first rank. In their drawing-rooms one admired pictures by famous painters in gilded frames, in which baroque art indulged in its most audacious contortions. Huge chandeliers with crystal pendants spread a generous flow of soft light that flattered the complexion and gave a more mysterious brilliance to the stream of precious stones that adorned the women's fingers and necks. With all the shrewd skill of their sex, these women stole up to the dangerous rival and shielded her from her admirers who ceded to this superior force of grace and, for a moment, Elizabeth was assailed with compliments and subtly indiscreet questions. One scarcely ever saw her and it was such a joy to welcome her, to hear her delightful, pure English once again, was it not. . . She replied with a touch of — charming — awkwardness, which she had never been able to lose since her arrival in Georgia. Wasn't it precisely this that had bewitched first Jonathan, then Ned? Now a prisoner of those jewel-bedecked women in their aggressively elegant silk and taffeta dresses, she felt naked and furious. She suddenly felt a strong dislike for everyone around her. Through the great doors with their dark gold moldings, she watched the groups of guests arrive and, to add the final touch to her inner turmoil, Alexander Brookfield appeared in uniform. Not without a certain military energy, he made his way toward her, provoking indignant looks all around him. He nevertheless came up to her and she caught sight of the look, twinkling with stupidity, as it fell upon its prey.

Panic-stricken, she fought her way through the ladies surrounding her, apologizing as she went. They moved back, rather shocked, allowing her to reach a free space, which she crossed without hesitation. She had her reasons for going in that direction.

In fact, she had just noticed the beautiful Mrs Harrison Edwards, then similarly surrounded, but managing to move around, mistress of the situation that she was, in the middle of a circle of respectful admirers, whom she held at a certain distance at the end of her fan. Her proud head remained erect at all times as if to affirm her power over the world, but nevertheless she distributed around her the smile whose indefinable charm had become famous, for it meant almost anything one cared to see in it, a yes, a no, a perhaps or a nothing, and she played upon it as a virtuoso plays upon his instrument. From a distance, thanks to the acuteness of the female eye in such situations, the young Englishwoman noticed that her face, once liable to plumpness, had become ever so slightly thinner.

Without being particularly drawn to this woman, whose regal manner embarrassed her, she decided that at that difficult moment she was the only one who could come to her aid and, with agile steps, she covered the few yards between them.

Catching sight of her, Mrs Harrison Edwards let out a drawing-room cry, a polite cry, for she had been well aware for the last quarter of an hour that Elizabeth was there and she was only moderately pleased by the fact:

'Elizabeth! What a surprise and what a pleasure! You here! . . . And more beautiful than ever.'

With an elegant about-turn, she left her disappointed admirers and joined Elizabeth, whom she embraced:

'Darling,' she said, 'we hardly ever see each other any more since . . . since that terrible thing.'

'I know, but I've never much cared for big society evenings like this.'

'Like this! But we have them all the time at Savannah. How could we live otherwise? We would die! Staying at home is one long martyrdom. The important thing, you see, is to kill time in good company. But who is this character who seems to be marching straight toward you?'

'Oh, Lucille, we must flee! A frightful soldier who persecutes me with his amorous declarations. Do something to get rid of him, please.'

'I've never trusted the compliments of a handsome soldier, but this particular one is depressingly ugly.'

As he approached with a conqueror's air, she suddenly turned such an imperious look on him that he stopped in his tracks. Never had this woman who was helping her out of trouble seemed more attractive in Elizabeth's eyes. The heavy mass of her hair shone in dark waves around her little curved forehead and brought out the delicate velvety whiteness of her skin. In their infinite depth, her large eyes seemed to contain all the secrets of the night, and that was how she presented herself when she felt minded to repel an enemy. At such moments she was wildly attractive and almost as fearsome.

Perplexed, the major stood there, for a brief moment lost for words. Quite evidently, his admiration vacillated between the young Englishwoman and the magnificent creature whose burning gaze was fixed upon him. She did not allow him to get in a word.

'Major,' she said in a firm voice, 'we have not been introduced and I am in conversation with this lady.'

He bowed.

'Oh! I should not have taken the liberty. . . I simply wanted. . . .'

'Why don't you go over to the buffet? Some exquisite ladies are already besieging it.'

As she spoke these words, she gave him what she herself called her tigress smile, which finally confounded him and he beat a retreat.

'You see, Elizabeth,' she said, when they were some distance away, 'that is how we must train men.'

'But I have never tried to do so,' the young woman exclaimed, 'nor even wanted to!'

'I'm afraid you overestimate them. They are sometimes welcome, I agree, but it gives one splendid satisfaction to see them at one's feet.'

'Frankly, I didn't see love in that way when I had my. . .'

'Dear Elizabeth, do not dwell on the memories of what will not come back. Personally, I accepted my widowhood with serenity. Enjoy the present, Elizabeth. Life, look at life. . .'

She made a gesture toward the drawing-room crowded with chattering guests. The loud rumble of conversation was becoming deafening.

'Listen,' she said, in a sort of rapture. 'What music to the ear! That is life, the delightful life of society. . .'

Elizabeth nodded and tried to smile.

'You know,' she said, raising her voice to be heard, 'I think I shall go home, but thank you for what you did just now.'

'Always ready to help, for, without wishing to give offence, your education as a young widow leaves room for improvement, darling.'

A long, caressing smile softened the sharpness of that remark. Elizabeth did not feel in the least hurt.

Her eyes began to shine with a sudden brilliance and, thinking she could see tears there, Mrs Harrison Edwards took her in her arms:

'Forget what I have said,' she said, 'I shouldn't. . . I was wrong.'
Her lips skimmed Elizabeth's cheek and she held both her hands:
'We're friends, aren't we?'

Like a ghost, a smile spread over her features that was impossible to categorize, but it nevertheless came from the heart.

# 3

*I*n the carriage that was taking her home, Elizabeth gave full vent to her disappointment. Someone she had wanted to see had not appeared or perhaps in that multitude she had been unable to find him, but it struck her nevertheless as highly improbable that, dressed in white, she would not have caught and guided his attention. There again perhaps, he had not come, unless his shyness, which usually got the better of him, had stopped him going up to her. After all, they had never exchanged more than a few words, but he must have known, the exasperating young man, he must have guessed. She sighed impatiently, almost angrily, as she threw herself back in the corner of her carriage.

She had come away from that evening in society with an impression of brilliance and boredom. One suffocated in those exalted circles . . . Mrs Harrison Edwards and her ever so slightly cynical views disconcerted her, despite the show of friendship at the end. Among the men about whom the great lady spoke with such disdain, there was not a single memorable face, for that still mattered to her, in spite of her memories.

Her house awaited her, wrapped in a silence that gradually calmed her. The familiar setting of the pale blue drawing-room, where she spent pleasant hours with friends who visited her, full of town gossip, had a similarly soothing effect on her. That evening, a lamp on a low table illuminated the happy little room with a sort of tenderness. Curled up in a large armchair, like a bird that had escaped from a storm, she reflected that she had acted stupidly throughout that evening . . . She had gone out in order to be seen, spoken to only one person for a few minutes and then taken flight. Where was the sense in that? She had noticed the hostess at a distance and could easily have joined her, but since she was also the prisoner of a group of guests, she had turned her back on her. After all, why not admit honestly that she had gone only to see a young gentleman whom she hardly knew. He was a redhead. Darkish red, she corrected herself mentally, as if to apologize, red with a glint of bronze. And shy too . . . Usually redheads . . .

Her restless meditation was cut short by the appearance of a rather calm Miss Celina.

'Back already,' she said with a smile.

'Yes, I was bored. Society bores me stiff, Miss Celina.'

Miss Celina looked serious.

'The little one took a long time to get to sleep. He said that you had forgotten to tell him a story before turning out the light. I found it hard consoling him. He cried a little.'

Elizabeth leaped to her feet.

'It's true, Miss Celina, for the first time I forgot.'

Forgotten Jonathan, she thought, both irritated and ashamed; forgotten that every evening, in a soft voice, she told him a story about someone called Jonathan. That moment was almost as important in her daily life as it was in her son's. The ritual would brook no variation.

So as to have him undressed, washed and put to bed, Elizabeth first made way for Liza, the boy's black nanny. Liza was a strong girl, and still young. Plump to the point of heaviness, she was attractive even though she waddled; in her coffee-coloured face, her great, beautiful eyes rolled from left to right when she walked. Nevertheless, she enjoyed a reputation for seriousness in all situations. Charlie Jones himself had recommended her to his daughter-in-law. Like so many women of her race, she breathed love, concentrating her ardour on the little creature that she had convinced herself belonged to her, so much so that she called him *my baby*. That love was returned. The great black mass that fell upon him, growling like some amorous ogress, did not frighten the child, who was already smothered in his mother's overwhelming love.

Elizabeth did not witness these rather monstrous effusions, but her time came later, in a quite different style.

She had to be left alone with the beloved, who sometimes had to wait. He quietly and patiently waited in his four-poster bed with its white canopy, passing the time by telling himself aloud stories in which his mother constantly appeared. In the flickering glow of the night-light, the room seemed to him bigger, invaded by large shadows that his imagination peopled with strange characters that made faces at him. He had a name for each of them, but best of all he liked to watch the door: soon it would open. Then the wonderful person would come to him, with all that gold that shone gently around her head. And for long moments she would cover him with kisses, calling him her Jonathan. He then had to say: 'Yes, Zonathan!' And she would take him in her arms. Her kisses were dotted all over his little face, not on his lips, but often on his neck, or behind his ear, which tickled him and made him giggle. When the gaiety had subsided there came the moment awaited with an impatience neighboring on over-excitement, the moment of the story, which always had to be new, full of mysteries, giants, chases, escapes, thieves. There then followed a short silence and, in a voice that was not her usual voice, his mother made him recite a very simple prayer in which he asked the 'Dear Lord' to make him a 'good boy' and to bless his Mom.

That evening, however, the evening of the Steers' party, he felt his eyelids grow heavy as he waited for his mother to come. Tired from his walk with Betty, he drifted obliviously into sleep.

# 4

*A* little later Celina came in quietly. She went over to the bed and gave the child a long, attentive look, as if she were trying to read a secret. He was sleeping with one hand on his chest and his curls spread out around his head in a great black pool on the whiteness of the pillow.

After turning the night-light down, thus plunging the room into shadow, the governess left as quietly as she had come.

In the drawing-room, where she went to await her mistress's return, she settled into a comfortable, well-cushioned armchair and picked up a newspaper that was lying on the floor. Adorning the tall, narrow chimney, a beautiful French clock chimed eleven o'clock. The thin, restless sound reminded one of a small, impatient person.

Miss Celina read the front page: 'Renewed rioting between Blacks and Whites in Kansas.' She yawned. Every day it was the same news from Kansas. Why didn't the government do something about it? Speeches, always speeches . . . She crossed her hands over her stomach and sighed, looking very dignified even in her sleep.

A cry made her wake up with a start. In less than a minute she was on the first floor in Charles-Edward's room.

The child had woken up in the middle of the night.

The night-light did little to disperse the mass of shadows and the child was clearly quite petrified. For him, waking up meant daytime or the light from a lamp. He had never in his short life opened his eyes in the dark. Terror was everywhere at once. At the top of his voice he was shouting for his mother and, not seeing her arrive immediately to help him, he called again. The door finally opened, but the sight of Miss Celina merely made his condition worse. It was not her he wanted to see. In his distress he began to sob, calling for his mother. The violence of his distress began to worry the housekeeper. Much more than an explosion of sadness, the child's sorrow was more like that of an adult.

She did her best to reassure the little lost creature.

'Your Mama will come back and you'll see her, she's had to go out.'

'Why didn't she come before?'

'She was in a hurry, you see, in a very big hurry, they said that her coach was waiting for her so . . .'

He stopped crying and in the darkness she felt that he was fixing her with a terrible look, like the look of a man.

'So what?' he asked.

'So she simply forgot . . . But she'll be here soon.'

'Forgot?'

'Well, yes, she thought about it when it was too late.'

The child, who was now half sitting up, fell back, his face buried in the pillow, and she thought that he was going to suffocate. Slipping her arm beneath his shoulders, she tried to make him sit up, but he struggled, shaking with sobs and she was afraid. Muffled speech reached her ears, she could make out the words 'forgot, Mama' which constantly recurred and suddenly, in an incomprehensible murmur:

'Zonathan . . .'

She thought that she must be mistaken, but something told her that this was not so and she was tempted to ask him what he meant, but she suddenly had the overwhelming feeling that she had no right to do this, that if she did her conscience would reproach her later.

She decided instead to sit down on the chair at the bedside and wait until this disturbing attack calmed down; to relieve his horror of the darkness, she turned up the night-lamp a little and, still crying, the despairing little creature went back to sleep.

When Elizabeth realized that she had forgotten to kiss her son goodnight before going to the Steers', she stood there speechless and could do no more than look at Miss Celina and repeat:

'I forgot.'

'It's quite natural, there was the party.'

'The party.'

She repeated the words as if it would help her to understand.

'You say he was crying.'

'Yes, Ma'am.'

Standing opposite one another in the little drawing-room, the two women looked at one another, motionless.

'He was crying? Did he say anything?'

'He called out for you.'

'Nothing else? He didn't say anything else?'

Miss Celina was one of those women whose determination not to tell a lie caused a moment's embarrassment.

'What else would you expect him to do except to call out for his mother?'

Elizabeth then realized that Miss Celina was hiding something from her. She also knew that it was impossible to make her say what it was, but she read a great deal of the truth in those dark, unblinking eyes. She had made the child love her like a lover and he saw her absence as an infidelity.

'I'll go up and kiss him goodnight.'

'He's asleep. If I were you, Ma'am, I'd let him be. He found it very hard to calm down.'

Confronted by such a solemn look, the young woman hesitated. It was as if everything had changed in the world around her.

'Everything will be all right tomorrow,' said Miss Celina as if reading her thoughts.

And she added at once:

'If you like, we can go upstairs and I'll help you undress. You seem tired.'

'Tired, yes.'

She gave in. That would be best, she thought. She dared not admit that she felt guilty and preferred not to confront the disappointed beloved who had not had his share of tenderness, or his story, or that mysterious repetition of the magical name of Jonathan that she spoke in his ear, and which he whispered back, instantaneously becoming a fabulous character in an enchanted world.

Suddenly the idea occurred to her that her life was split in two and that the child would no longer believe her. He would no longer be the one she secretly called her little conspirator.

She looked blankly at Miss Celina. 'Let's go up,' she said in a tired voice. 'I want to try to sleep.'

With a skill that Elizabeth never failed to admire, the housekeeper undressed her, then put her to bed in less than ten minutes. With her reasonable, reassuring voice, she brought peace to her mistress by reducing Charles-Edward's little attack to a mere whim of growing up, and those words, which meant practically nothing, seemed to the mother to be wisdom itself. Miss Celina moved silently to and fro, sorting out the clothes, turning out the lamp, leaving the door that led into the next room, where the child lay asleep wide open, then, gliding through the shadows like a fairy, she disappeared.

Alone, Elizabeth lay there, her eyes open, exhausted, ready for a long insomnia. The child was sleeping next door and she overcame the desire to tip-toe over to him and at least listen to his breathing, but the little fellow was so sensitive that he would have sensed her presence, and then the tears would surely have flowed, followed by reproaches, unleashing a new attack.

Out of the darkness, in which at first she could make out nothing, there emerged one by one the familiar pieces of furniture, all the things that made up the setting of her solitude, the bulbous chest of drawers, surmounted by a mirror, the desk at which English ladies of the time of Queen Anne had no doubt scribbled their love letters, the rocking chair in which one could endlessly spin out one's dreams. The night breeze from the door gently rustled the net curtains in front of the half-opened window.

From time to time she could hear the distant rumbling of the carriages from the other side of the gardens, where Ned had gone walking with old Betty that same afternoon. At that moment she felt, if not very content with her lot, at least at peace with herself. And now there was this anxiety . . .

Fortunately, Miss Celina was with her in a house that was really rather large for one person.

# 5

*E* lizabeth did not know as well as she would have wished what she really thought of Miss Celina. Certainly she respected her, but the woman practised the art of silence to a degree that sometimes made her presence embarrassing.

Charles Jones had known her for a long time. Long before Elizabeth arrived in Georgia, he had explored, without ever saying anything about it, the most neglected parts of the town. It was part of his nature to interest himself in those who were known, with a disdain that he found appalling, as White Trash. His wealth enabled him to extricate many of them out of abject poverty. Celina was the daughter of a small craftsman, a toy-maker, who had gone bankrupt. A Protestant, he was descended from those whom the Most Christian Emperor of the Holy Roman Germanic Empire had expelled from his states.

Taking charge of the fate of that man and his family, Charlie

Jones made the father a clerk in one of his offices and put Celina in a boarding school at Macon.

Fifteen years of age and having known hunger, she was, moreover, much too sensible not to grasp the opportunity life offered her. It was like a wager. Without belonging to high society, her more privileged companions might well wonder where she had come from. Her foreign origins made this all the easier. Coming from elsewhere gave her the right not to be quite like everyone else. Pleasant, rather than pretty, she made up for it with a smile that she did not use to excess, but which could attract. Early on she had made up her mind not to marry.

When the time came to find her an occupation, Charlie Jones placed her as a lady's companion with venerable persons who were dying of boredom in luxurious widowhood. She read delightfully with a metronomic regularity that induced sleepiness, which was praiseworthy, but, once this result had been obtained, she had nothing left to offer. She had no conversation. After a year, she was thanked for her services.

Charlie Jones had her do the rounds of society in Macon, then in Atlanta, and she discreetly saved a little money, hoping one day to achieve material independence, but she was far from that.

However, after the tragic duel that robbed him of his son, Charlie Jones did not often experience a desire to visit Elizabeth. While, deep down, he felt sorry for her, he secretly held her responsible. Faithful to Ned, she would have kept him alive beside her. He saw her punished in a terrible way and gradually pity took its course.

One day in 1855, he had gone to ring on his daughter-in-law's door.

It was the child who won the fight for Elizabeth. It was as if he knew this and that all the infallible little ruses were inspired by it. When he saw that tall individual in a black frockcoat bending over him, he began, with a broad smile, to pull on his side-whiskers. His grandfather then picked him up and held him in the air at a terrifying height, which produced cries of inarticulate delight from young Charles-Edward. Nothing more was required; victory was assured. Putting him back on his mother's knees, Charlie Jones said in a rather unsteady voice:

'He already has our Ned's gaiety . . . and his eyes.'

Elizabeth looked down, so that he would not see that she was blushing.

'Yes, the eyes,' she said.

The reconciliation effected, he came back to earth at once and wanted to know if Elizabeth had a good cook. The cook was a chef. Did she have able, devoted servants?

'Four in all, very conscientious, plus the valet who opened the door for you.'

'He has style, it seemed to me. And for the boy?'

'A splendid black nanny whom he adores — and, of course, my dear Betty.'

'Good, I am reassured on that side. A caretaker, I hope?'

'An Irishman who is taller than you, something of a gardener, too, and a boxer when necessary.'

'So everything seems to be all right. Order above all. And the housekeeper?'

'I don't have a housekeeper.'

'Why not?'

'A principle . . .'

He knew that she was thinking of the Welshwoman.

'Let's forget it. I have one for you. I would ask you not to say no before seeing her.'

There followed a brief but complimentary description of Celina.

'She was brought up in conditions bordering on penury. But don't let that put you off.'

'Why would you think it would? If you think I've forgotten the winter months spent in London with Mother . . . I still have the taste of poverty in my mouth.'

She could see the rows of black and red houses in the mist, the dark and freezing room, the vile little restaurant . . .

He said nothing for a moment, then continued:

'Rather as they were for you, circumstances proved favorable to Celina and got her out of trouble.'

At that moment, circumstances, embarrassing ones, produced a slight hiccough.

'Boarding with very well brought up ladies, she was given a good education and today she is more than presentable. A foreigner . . .'

'A foreigner?'

'Don't look so worried. What is not English is not necessarily suspect. Her family comes from Salzburg in Austria, but she is a real Protestant.'

'And so?'

'I can already see her as a model housekeeper.'

'You have better eyes than I have. For my part, I can't imagine her here at all.'

'I would ask you simply to see her.'

'How old is she?'

'In her forties, well-preserved.'

In the end she gave in, almost instinctively.

'Send your good woman to come and see me, but I can't promise anything . . .'

He thanked her with a smile and for a few minutes they said nothing.

'You will save her,' he said simply.

In the gentle light of that late afternoon, his features revealed something of the man with the fine English face who had welcomed her at his home five years earlier. Elizabeth made a gesture with her hand as if to sweep aside the moral turn that the conversation might take. He understood at once and declared:

'I admire your taste in the choice of colors for this sitting-room. That sky-blue watered silk looks wonderful.'

'Do you think so? I am getting a little tired of it by now.'

'It is true that habit makes almost everything seem ordinary, one no longer sees things in the freshness of their novelty.'

The sententious tone reminded the young woman of the Charlie Jones she had once known, but what followed disturbed her.

'I have a question to ask you,' he said, 'a question that might seem rather indiscreet, and so it's up to you whether you answer or not.'

'Well, let's skip the fine oratory. It's like the prefaces in books. Whoever bothers to read a preface?'

'Since you are putting me so much at ease, this is what it's about. In one way or another, I am doing my best to ensure Celina's future in an honorable way.'

'Celina, again?'

'Yes. The day will come for her when she will have no more worries and that terrible fear of what the next day will bring.'

'And you're counting on me for this fine dream.'

'On you or someone else, for after all there is Providence, but she'll know the happy time when she can finally breathe a deep sigh of relief, when the weight will be lifted from her chest. Without wishing to compare her fate with yours, you, too, must have breathed a great sigh of relief.'

'How strange you are, Uncle Charlie!'

'But no, no, there was a time when you must have said to yourself: I was poor, I'm poor no longer; I'm rich.'

'What vulgarity! I never spoke to myself like that.'

'Ah? My case is different. As a youth I felt the tooth of poverty sink into the hollow of my stomach. You understand?'

'Not being utterly stupid, I do.'

'The years have passed like the wind. America, youth, work, ambition, connections, calculations turning out right. The day came when I was thirty-five, at the high point of my life, when I realized that I was already among the richest men in the country. I was one of those who had more money than everybody else.'

Elizabeth assumed an air of indifference:

'And then?'

'And then I was afraid. Money makes you afraid. In a way, too much wealth can be a trial.'

'I've known gentlemen who put up with that trial with magnificent courage.'

'You can be as sarcastic as you like, you incorrigible Englishwoman, but if you saw before you a huge pile of gold coins, you might wonder where it came from: from God or the devil.'

'From both perhaps.'

'My word, there's an answer. Let's go into the details. One day, you'll go traveling in the old country. You'll be invited into the finest palaces of the kingdom. You will be dazzled by their wealth.'

'I, dazzled? Do you take me for a village girl?'

'Not at all. I myself — and I think I know what I'm talking about — have always been struck by it. The pile of gold has become a collection of furniture and pictures to take your breath away. It is, if I may say so, its culmination. Lords painted by Raeburn or Gainsborough look at you with indescribable disdain as you pass — it's enough to make the ground open up and swallow you.'

'Rest assured, they've almost all got the gout.'

He ignored this poisoned remark and went on.

'Outside, through the high casement windows, you can see meadows and woods stretching to infinity. Those in high places are very fond of nature.'

'I didn't know you were a revolutionary, Uncle Charlie.'

'No more than Mr Dickens, who has revealed to the world the scandal of children working in English factories — even in mines.'

Suddenly she stood up, red with sudden anger.

'There we are beginning to disagree,' she said, 'and you know as well as I do that the North also gets rich with the labor of children.'

In her emotion, she let young Charles-Edward fall from her grasp and roll, laughing, on the floor. Thinking that this was a new game, he tried to climb up his grandfather's legs. Uncle Charlie picked him up like some precious object and sat him on his knees. He then found he had to protect his side-whiskers, the sight of which fascinated the young boy. There followed a silent struggle with the assailant and Charlie Jones could not help bursting out laughing.

'My dear Elizabeth,' he said, 'I am well aware of those things that the North could not hide, but what amuses me, apart from a personal battle with your son, is to see how we are completely in agreement, even when our conversation has so little to do with the delightful blue silk of your little sitting-room.'

Far from joining him in his merriment, she gave him an angry look.

'Do you think I am not aware of it at certain times? It all began the day I first came here and saw in a Savannah suburb men, women and children almost in rags, who watched us in silence as we passed in front of them in our carriage. White trash.'

'Elizabeth, there are good works.'

At this point, Charles-Edward tried to stand on his grandfather's knees in order to make a final assault at the prestigious side-whiskers. Seizing his adversary with both hands, Charlie Jones pretended to offer him to Elizabeth. Irritated, she took the child and put him on a chair. He looked up at her with eyes full of reproach. Neither she nor Charlie Jones heard him humming to himself:

'Mama . . . I love Mama . . . Mine . . .'

'You say money makes you afraid,' she exclaimed. 'It makes me ashamed when I see the eyes of the poor. It is that which has more or less kept me apart from social life since the end of my mourning. The balls above all, everything that glitters.'

'One can very well look after the needy and still go to the ball. I can make any number of suggestions, if you like.'

'Thank you,' she said, 'I know the right addresses.'

In an almost shy voice, he asked:

'Would it seem indiscreet if we talked about them?'

'Certainly. One must keep such things to oneself . . .' she hesitated. '. . . like secrets of the heart . . .'

These words, which she spoke with a sort of modesty, made her blush and, for a few seconds, she was the very young English girl she had once been, as if her entire childhood had risen from her heart to her face.

Charlie Jones observed her in silence, struck with admiration.

'Elizabeth,' he said at last, 'I wasn't aware . . . You are no longer the same person.'

He added in a confiding tone, 'This moment does something to wipe out my sad memories. I am happy, Elizabeth. I could almost embrace you.'

'I have no objection,' she murmured before they took leave of one another.

He moved closer to her and his lips brushed her blushing cheek.

'I shall be leaving shortly for Dimwood,' he said hastily. 'I have to attend to some wretched business to do with wills, but Celina has been warned and you can expect a visit from her tomorrow.'

# 6

*N*ow, in the solitude and darkness of her room, she relived that whole scene from the previous year with the perspicacity of a pitiless memory.

Why did this man, who was usually so self-confident, claim to be frightened of wealth? Was it a matter of soothing a conscience, as in the case of William Hargrove, who made his wealth his hobby? Absurd. Charlie Jones's generosity was well known, but, although he had saved hundreds of families, there was still a disturbing number of poor to be provided for. Good works were not enough. They all depended on the person who had founded them, but there was a proliferation of apparently irresistible poverty.

There remained the mystery of that ruinously extravagant Tudor-style construction. Almost completed, at once massive and precious, it looked oddly like an English castle, right down to the smallest details. If there were any purpose behind that rather uncolonial architecture, Charlie Jones kept it to himself.

Tired of going over these pointless questions, Elizabeth got out of bed and quietly walked over to the door that opened on her son's room, but dared go no further. A moonbeam, as thin as a line, cut across a black floorboard. For no particular reason, the white curtains of the little bed took on a disturbing brightness in that other-worldly light.

Elizabeth did not move, convinced that she could hear the breathing of the person whom in her heart she called Jonathan, but, after several long minutes of waiting, she had to admit that not the slightest breath disturbed the silence.

She did not want to be afraid. She was somewhat reassured by the fact that the bed was too far out of hearing to be able to catch the child's almost imperceptible breathing. Nevertheless, she looked at the curtains, swathed in ghostly whiteness, with horror.

Back in bed, she remembered what Celina had said: 'The crisis is over.' He had had a crisis. A crisis to do with her, a lover's crisis. Should she not go over and, very gently, draw him from his sleep? The dramatic turn her imagination took provided an immediate answer: 'You might kill him. A shock is always possible.'

She saw him dead. She had never been a woman given to prayers, but, in hours of danger, terror suddenly gave her back her faith. Her consuming love of the child was adulterous. God would take her present-day Jonathan from her just as he had taken her Jonathan of yesterday, because adultery continued to live inside her. This monstrous reasoning seemed to her like the revelation of a truth that she had always hidden from herself.

In her distraction, she hid her head completely under her blankets to stifle a cry.

'Oh dear Lord, no!'

Her heart was beating too fast and it hurt her. Tearing off the blankets, she listened. No sound came from the next room. She had not woken him, but then can the dead be woken?

Slipping out of her bed, she felt that she was becoming the prey of one of those instinctive forces that she could not control. Like a beast, she began to crawl over toward her son's bed. In this way, he would not hear her if he was asleep. Her hair loosely fell over her face and brushed the floor and rugs, like a mane shimmering with golden highlights.

At the end of that strange journey, she lay flat on the floor, facing downward, her forehead in her folded arms, and she waited, believing that she could make out the rhythm of the light sound, the almost imperceptible beat of life. What she heard above all was the continuous murmur of blood in her own head, which she took to be the voice of silence.

She did not weep, but she despaired. Suddenly sleep overcame her.

She was awoken by the sunlight, piercing the folds in the curtains and sweeping over half the room. Birdsong was greeting the day with an almost hysterical emulation. Immediately she got up and knelt by the bed. The child was asleep, his face buried in the pillow.

Suddenly snatched from his dreams by the light, he saw his mother and leaped into her arms with a cry of happiness.

'Mama!'

She pressed him to her, smothering him with kisses. Laughing, he ran his fingers through her hair, pulling it gently:

'Mustn't forget Zonathan,' he said, placing his cheek against hers.

She shut her eyes.

'Never, never again, my love,' she said.

# 7

*T*he next day wiped out all memory of that night of anguish. With one smile the child had made everything normal again. How could she think she was unhappy when Jonathan was not? Brought back to day-to-day life, Elizabeth tended at first to see everything in the best light. Uncle Charlie knew what he was doing when he had introduced her to Celina, who became more and more reassuring, despite the indefinable hint of mystery that still floated around her.

In her blue cotton dress with its white collarette and sleeves, she moved around with a natural grace that seemed above her station, even though her bonnet with its lace curtain declared her to be a housekeeper. One might have wished that her regular shaped face would relax sometimes, for it almost always retained an expression of imperturbable rigor. Only her dark eyes were animated on occasion with a sudden intensity, for a word or a look, betraying depths of secret violence. To the servants under her command, she spoke with a gentle authority that did not brook the slightest contradiction and, with the ancestral instinct of slavery, all the Blacks felt it. She showed Elizabeth the respect due to her mistress, no more. Her main virtue in the young woman's eyes was to make perfect order reign in her house from top to bottom, and above all never to be around when she shouldn't be. One might like her or dislike her, depending on one's tastes, but she was in a sense a personality who was beyond contradiction.

October advanced in an exquisite mildness, still full of the odors from all the gardens in the town. Even in the avenues, the air went to one's head at the whim of the sudden breezes. It was not yet the season for big parties, but the drawing-rooms were beginning to prepare for the first receptions of late summer, the signal having been given by the Steers.

With her widowhood already distant, Elizabeth felt a certain attraction for the social life that she had never seriously cultivated. The evening at the Steers' had been an unfortunate experience. Her conversation with Mrs Harrison Edwards had rather disconcerted her by its cynicism, and she was revolted by the unsavory admiration that she aroused among the men. No doubt she would have done better to have been accompanied, but no, she preferred to remain alone. Alone in order to be freer in her movements.

It had served no purpose. She had not seen anyone she had hoped to meet there. In fact, she did not attach much importance to it. She had not fallen headlong in love. She had fallen in love at first sight only once in her life, at the end of a veranda, in the heavy air of a summer's night. All that was far, far away, and yet sometimes cruelly close.

He had not turned up, quite simply.

She repeated that little phrase of humiliating vulgarity to herself, without suffering on account of it apart from her pride as she returned from the Steers', but, in the dreadful night that had followed, the absurd memory had vanished of its own accord.

And now that peace reigned once more in the charming house at

Oglethorpe Square, and that her Jonathan smiled at her as he made his eternal declarations of love, why should the face of this man who did not turn up rise up in her mind with impudent obstinacy? Elizabeth was defenceless against the tricks of an inflexible memory. She could never forget certain faces. For her, every man revealed himself in his face. It was an idea that even withstood her experience of marriage and her passion for Jonathan, and that idea would not go away, fixed and false, defying the passage of time.

She had met him at the end of a late summer's day in a place little frequented by Southern nobility, during a meeting of simple, but interesting people. Charlie Jones had taken her there with the notion of encouraging in his daughter-in-law a tendency to good works. It was not a question of performing acts of charity, as they say. Those people lived modestly, but a circle around them still remained to be broken, because they were not invited, as if their lack of fortune was ill fortune. Almost all were descendants of Protestant exiles and, without actually being in need, they did not have the means of shining in the eyes of the world. If a few members of Society visited them, it would gradually reduce a moral ostracism: this was Charlie Jones's reasoning; whereas in reality those exiles preserved a caste spirit and would never have admitted that people came to see them out of condescension. In such disastrous good gestures, Charlie Jones imagined that he could encourage a small group that in the end would rise and be socially respected, as if two such different worlds could merge. On the part of ordinary folk this could produce only unspoken indignation and envy and, from the rich, deep incomprehension. The ditch was more difficult to fill than that of the town's old fortifications.

Charlie Jones's protégés lived together in a fairly large ochre-colored house, situated in a once elegant district near the river, since abandoned by the rich, near one of the ancient fortresses, in the middle of gardens whose trees were now covered in dust, as if the abandoned houses had cast the shadow of poverty upon them. The great house, built in a style that flourished at the end of the previous century, retained a certain allure. It was called the Old Schmick House. It had known days of grandeur. Parties had been given there, lines of carriages had waited in front of an imposing porch, while the casement windows glittered with the chandeliers that could be seen between the heavy, draped curtains held back by gold clasps. The music from an orchestra could be heard in the street against the background of laughter and all the merry, carefree noise. With the financial crash of 1830 and the great upheaval in fortunes, this prosperous district emptied. Time passed, soberly dressed people took up residence in the old house and, to the consternation of those who remembered former days, a grocery store appeared on the ground floor.

Absolute silence was observed in the drawing-rooms on the subject of this decline, especially as, by a collateral line, the grocer Schmick was distantly related to one of the best families in the South. Five years passed and he went bankrupt. The unfortunate grocer's shop closed down a few weeks later and old Schmick died, though not without leaving numerous progeny in residence at the house. The tribe gathered, determined to stand their ground, and a taste for work, together with the generous, secret complicity of Uncle Charlie, solved the most urgent financial problems.

The whole inside of the house was renovated in an unpretentious style. However, a visitor might consider the simplicity of the lightwood furniture, the tablecloths embroidered in peasant style, the big vase of flowers that always stood in the middle of the long table, the marquetry clock with its slow, grave tick-tock, as forming a pleasing whole, expressive of a quiet confidence in life.

Taken there one September day by her father-in-law, who had left her there almost on arrival, Elizabeth was sensitive to the rather rustic happiness that the house seemed to exude. The discomfort that she sometimes felt in the presence of luxury gave way here to a feeling of inner peace that delighted her, like the unexpected discovery of a new world. An old lady wearing black and two young women smiled at her in welcome. Their unexaggerated politeness made it seem all the more sincere. Introductions were soon made: the widow of Johann Schmick and her two granddaughters.

Frau Schmick's head was wrapped in a lace bonnet the fringes of which were so large that, from the depths of this head-dress, she seemed to be looking at you from a window. Her face was hardly wrinkled, but huge dark eyes dominated that old, authoritarian face. Flora, the older of the two granddaughters, had a round pink face, topped by brown hair combed back as if to contain curls about to escape, and her blue eyes shone brightly. Engaged to be married a month ago, one felt that she was determined to seem as serious as possible, but her good humor kept erupting from her rather ample person. She was not trying to hide the fact that she was happy, and she looked forward in her imagination to the expected paradise of marriage as her innocence presented it to her.

Quieter and prettier, her fair plaits reaching down to her shoulders, Ida, her sister, smiled. Her little, upturned nose was still that of a very young girl, though she was now seventeen. But her observant, chestnut-colored eyes were more telling.

'Welcome, Mrs Jones.' Frau Schmick's voice was both thin and warm. 'We are expecting a few friends to come after work to congratulate our Flora. She is engaged to a fine boy.'

The two girls shook Elizabeth's hand vigorously.

'We saw you at the store in Broughton Street,' said the younger girl. 'It was quite a long time ago . . .'

'Unfortunately,' her sister explained, 'we were not at the counter where you had stopped to talk to Mr Joshua Hargrove. We are salesgirls in the fine leather department.'

'He guided your choice a little, except for the underclothes,' Ida remarked delicately.

Both girls laughed so heartily that Elizabeth, to her astonishment, joined in.

'Yes, I remember, it was very warm . . .'

'You have a pretty English accent,' said Flora, 'we don't speak so well.'

'That is because I am English,' said Elizabeth with a smile and, not knowing what to say to keep the conversation going in a tone with which she was so unfamiliar, she asked: 'Your family is not from here, I believe?'

'No,' said Ida, 'from Salzburg, expelled from our home by the bishop . . .'

'. . . the bishop on orders from Rome, the scarlet woman of the Apocalypse,' Flora added with unexpected intensity.

'That is true,' said Ida, sticking her nose in the air, 'we are descendants of the Moravian Brethren. And what about you? You wouldn't be a Methodist, by any chance?' young Ida asked, her cheeks blushing.

'No, I'm an Anglican . . .'

'In any case, that's better than Roman . . . Roman Catholic,' she added firmly.

Frau Schmick clapped her hands:

'Children, that's enough of that,' she said firmly. 'Mrs Jones, they become quite furious whenever religion crops up. Here are the guests and the fiancé isn't here yet.'

Five or six young people came in, their shoes making a great deal of noise on the floor. Dressed in gray or black, they were all wearing a white shirt and a tie. Quite obviously, they had found time, after work, to dress carefully, not forgetting the parting in their hair, executed with rigorous precision. The group exuded a strong smell of wax and coarse cloth. The most noticeable of them held in his hand a bunch of forget-me-nots and, walking straight up to Flora, held it out to her. No doubt he had been chosen as being the most personable of them and he did not lack a certain rough beauty.

'Never could pay compliments,' he said, 'but these flowers . . . these flowers . . . they give me the right to a kiss?'

Flora took the bunch of flowers and held it to her breast without answering.

'Bravo, Willi,' one of the boys called out cheekily. 'Make the most of it while the fiancé isn't there!'

Everyone laughed and Flora offered a cheek flushed with emotion. Willi applied his lips over most of the girl's face and neck.

'Hey, that's enough!' Frau Schmick called out. 'That's enough!'

'And what about us?' his companions then asked in chorus.

'You behave yourselves!' the old woman ordered. At that point, Willi caught sight of Elizabeth, who was trying to hide behind the two sisters, but, giving in as usual to the temptation to admire a handsome face, she had imprudently glanced at the young man, who stared back at her, mouth gaping, and she thought that she saw in his eyes that stared at her attentively that sudden eagerness that she knew so well, the furious desire that revealed the whole man in the windows that were his eyes. In her confusion, she had to lean against Ida, who did not flinch.

'Willi,' said Ida severely.

He did not hear.

In one of those dazzling hallucinations all too familiar to her, Elizabeth felt that the façades of an entire street were covered with thousands of faces, their searching eyes like monstrous flowers. Young though he was, the idea took shape in her mind that for this man she was not so much a person as a thing, a body that he wanted, and she felt a sudden disgust, not so much for this inept fellow as for the person she was in his eyes.

She decided to go and wondered how she could take her leave without hurting anyone's feelings, when suddenly the door opened to reveal the fiancé and all her embarrassment left her.

He was tall, slim, and dressed like a gentleman. He was wearing a frock-coat, for he was an assistant head clerk in Charlie Jones's large cotton-exporting firm, and it beat against his calves as he walked. He was not a gentleman, but where he ran no risk of rejection, he assumed the appearance and manners of one. In his well-fed face, the little upturned nose seemed to set out to conquer the world. A pince-nez on the end of a thick black ribbon compensated for an excessively youthful appearance that might not go with his position, for he was twenty-five and others, older than he, had their eyes on his job, but his ambitious, quick-thinking mind had brought him rapid promotion among Mr Jones's favorites.

Responding to the little chorus of welcome, he gaily waved his top hat and went over to take his betrothed in his arms. Flora let herself go without restraint. The pince-nez flew into the air and the kiss, though legitimate enough, was judged by Frau Schmick to be rather too long.

'Walter,' she said curtly, 'the banns have only just been put up in the church. So let's have a little moderation!'

Mocking laughter accompanied this necessary recommendation, but Frau Schmick added:

'You don't seem to be aware that Mrs Jones, your employer's daughter-in-law, has done us the honor . . .'

Suddenly he turned right round, caught sight of Elizabeth and performed the obligatory bow in her direction.

Then the door opened again and, with a great burst of laughter and shouting, there erupted a dozen very excited young ladies. They had left their workshops a little later than the men and were furious that they had missed the betrothed couple's first great kiss. But, as the lucky man delicately remarked, it could be repeated for the pleasure of unfortunate latecomers!

This rather heavy bantering did nothing to dimish the embarrassing joy that Elizabeth felt. Among the newcomers there were some charming faces, which betrayed intrigue, malice, and annoyance, too, for there was marriage in the air and the boys' hands were already very busy as they introduced themselves among the ranks of young ladies.

No true elegance was to be seen; the simple dresses differed only in their colors, but these were of such variety that they seemed to light up the austere walls of the entire room, like an enormous bunch of flowers. Only one of the seamstresses from 'Bon Ton de Paris' stood out by virtue of a touch of originality in a lilac dress with scalloped flounces, but she was younger than her companions and a touch of haughtiness prevented her from throwing herself wholeheartedly into the festivities.

Lastly came the inevitable parents, all wearing the kind of assumed gravity that kills youthful pleasure dead and sends young people mentally on to the barricades. However, they could do nothing and, suddenly, the gaiety faded.

Other people came in, soberly dressed however, and smiling in the expected way. Of different ages, they were all unknown to her and, feeling slightly alarmed, Elizabeth watched this methodical invasion, filling the room and warming the air minute by minute. She felt more and more as if she did not belong there. The doors were left open.

It was now a good opportunity to slip away. Since no one seemed to notice her presence, what was she doing there? She was making her way to the door as best she could, when her path was inopportunely blocked by a young man in black velvet.

He seemed as put out as she did by this sudden confrontation. With a scarcely perceptible smile he said quietly:

'I see we are going in opposite directions. I am endeavouring to come in, you to leave . . . May I be of assistance?'

Elizabeth needed only a glance to take in what she saw of the stranger: a face of extreme delicacy, handsome certainly, even very handsome, dark reddish hair, almost black in places, green, or rather aquamarine eyes and, on top of all that, a face oozing pride.

He must have been aware of her very attentive gaze, for, to Elizabeth's surprise, he blushed.

'Please excuse me,' he said.

Taken aback, she protested:

'For what?' she asked.

In a rather cowardly way, she added, for she felt ashamed in front of him:

'I admit that I feel rather surprised to be here.'

'I don't, but then I'm only here because Mr Charles Jones particularly wanted me to be. It all looks rather boring, doesn't it?'

He laughed gently.

'Mr Charles Jones has such ideas!' he said with a touch of mockery.

To stop him going any further, she said quickly:

'Mr Charles Jones is my father-in-law.'

Bowing as best he could, for there was very little room, he said, 'Mrs Edward Jones?'

'Yes, sir.'

'Allow me to introduce myself: Algernon Steers.'

She felt a slight shock. The name had a ring about it.

'Mr Jones and I are distantly related,' he added. 'By his first wife, Miss Douglas, I am myself a Douglas, and therefore also by the second, as you know.'

It was now his turn to examine her attentively. He did this, without the slightest embarrassment, like a connoisseur.

'We could talk more easily over by the window, don't you think?'

Talk . . . with what assurance he said that! She was on the point of refusing.

'Yes, of course,' she said.

They both went over to a corner of the room where a breath of air slipped like a knife blade through the surrounding heat.

'Ah, we can breathe a little here,' she agreed, in order to say something, irritated that she had given in to this handsome boy's whim.

'A little, yes,' he said, 'but can you imagine a more boring way of killing an evening than spending it among these people?'

'No,' she said.

She lied as she had never lied. She lied because he had eyes of a sea-like transparency, both empty and deep, because those eyes caressed her, but without passion. He thought her good-looking enough, a little different from the other women on account of her hair, which made one want to plunge one's hands into all that gold.

'You don't go out very much,' he said. 'You were not seen at the ball or at the big parties . . .'

'Oh!' she said, striking back, 'they're probably all as boring as this is.'

'Perhaps, but life is boring anyway with all the time one doesn't know what to do with from morning to evening. So one pretends to enjoy oneself. Sometimes there are surprises. You ought to try.'

Suddenly she was overcome by a mad wish to strike him. She held back. What could he do, except withdraw with his slap still warm on his statue-like cheek? Better to insult him in some other way.

'Anyway,' she said with a smile, 'I can safely say that I have not really been spoilt today.'

Again he blushed a little. The rebuff had been well applied and his long black eyebrows formed imperceptibly into a frown . . . His well-known charm had not worked this time. She noted a gleam of fury in his eyes which, until now, had been expressionless. Suddenly he seemed to be very angry with her.

'The next season looks like being brilliant, as they say,' he resumed amiably enough. 'It opens in our house, as usual, at the beginning of October. They do things well enough, the parents, they can do anything, you understand.'

This allusion to the huge family fortune struck Elizabeth as the height of vulgarity. Suddenly he seemed a little less handsome to her. 'Upstart,' she thought. How could she find out? She would put the strange question to Uncle Charlie.

'Mr Charles Jones begged me to make an appearance here,' said Algernon with a laugh. 'Out of his sense of equality, I suppose. Well, I'm here. I kept my word. I have been seen. Should I stay any longer?'

'That is for you to judge,' she said.

A little old man in black had just made a discreet appearance and raised his hand to request silence.

'I bet there are going to be prayers,' said Elizabeth.

'Oh, no, really!' Algernon cried. 'If they start praying, I'll smash the windows and jump out.'

She gave a hollow laugh.

'It's embarrassing,' she said, 'I agree.'

Suddenly she looked down in shame. As in a flash of lightning, she saw little Betty again, kneeling before a holy picture but this evening, in the Schmick House, she lied continually because of this boy who looked like a model in a drawing-class.

Suddenly she was struck by a thought of irresistible violence: naked, he must be like all the rest, horrifying. Miss Llewelyn's words still echoed in her head. 'The face, the face . . . and the rest, will you bear it?' Was she not doing much more than bear it, now that she knew? But the contrast struck her as no less ignoble. The soul was in revolt against what the body wanted.

'What's the matter?' Algernon Steer asked, taking her hand. 'You look quite pale.'

'It's the air,' she said, 'the bad air . . .'

'Shall we go outside? These people are unbearable.'

Yes, she had had enough of asking herself questions about herself, of trying to find out why her repulsions turned into desires, and something in her threw out a distress call.

Outside, he suggested taking her home in his carriage, but she had her own waiting for her a little way off and she refused.

He seemed disappointed, insisted almost shyly, which surprised Elizabeth and again she said no, for she no longer felt the same woman, she was now mistrustful.

In the shabby, silent street, all the windows were dark. Nobody lived in these tumbledown houses any more. Whole rows of façades were crumbling away, and a gray vegetation was mounting an assault on the bricks and ruined canopies. The evening softened the peeling walls but even in the half-light they seemed to be hiding shameful sores; financial collapse had struck that part of the town like a burst of cannon shot. Shoots of honeysuckle were coming up through the wooden veranda floors.

They stood there, facing one another, under a street lamp of neo-Gothic style, a relic of the prosperous years. At their feet spread a pool of pale yellow light and, in that lighting, which fell directly over them, she could see him with a more coldly critical eye, but there too lay a trap, for in the gaslight a sculptor's talent was revealed, enhancing the perfections of that disdainful mask. The great arc of the black eyebrows lent a nobility to the whole upper part of the face, down to the slight projection of the cheekbones, but the rim of a sullen lip was bordered by a dark line as if to indicate a greedy, cruel nature, however admirable the shape of that mouth might be. Taken as a whole, those perfect, regular features lacked something irreplaceable, the splendid authority of youth. Barely twenty-five years' old, the man fascinated without dazzling because something inside him was dead.

Elizabeth sensed this and felt a sort of horror at it. In spite of herself, she remained conquered, but furious too, and suddenly overcome with a need to deal with this creature who was so full of himself; everything inside her was revolted by that self-sufficiency.

Nevertheless, he wanted to appear amiable. In that drawing-room tone that she so hated, he suddenly asked, with a smile:

'Would you at least agree to a walk beneath the trees?'

With anybody other than him she might well have accepted, but he added with an attempt at social affectation:

'The night is so beautiful . . . with all these stars.'

The night, the stars! He had no right to touch them, the night was hers, with its stars . . .

'No, really.'

She guessed that he was angry. Usually, when he played the poet with women, it produced results. At present he wanted this stubborn little English girl.

'Let me hope,' he said, adopting a honeyed tone, 'that we shall see each other again.'

She said nothing, as if to reflect on the question. Together they took a few steps and, in the softened light, she stole a glance at him and found in the face that was turned toward her a little of the charm that had attracted her a moment earlier.

'As I told you, I go out very little,' she said. 'A party or two each season.'

'The seasons follow one another, it looks as if we shall have an Indian summer.'

'You don't imagine that I shall stay here. In a few days I leave for Warm Springs.'

Standing very close to her, he touched her hand and looked at her. The face of the ancient god became human, became fascinating as it had in the room at the Schmick House.

'Does it displease you so much if someone loves you?' he murmured.

'You're crazy, Mr Steers, I shall not allow you to speak to me like that.'

'The heart dispenses with all permissions, Madam, I can do nothing about it.'

He said this with such convincing humility that she felt herself weaken.

'I think you would do better to conduct me to my carriage,' she said gently. 'Will you?'

'Will you at least promise to come to the next ball at our house? I shall be there, I shall wait for you — from the first minute.'

She took her time to reply: according to all the rules of the game, she should keep him waiting a little. They walked slowly toward the carriage. The silence of the deserted street was so deep that they could hear the sounds of their shoes on the uneven paving stones and, from time to time, a muffled noise from the Schmick House.

'Answer me, I beg you.'

She waited until she was by the carriage.

'If nothing keeps me away, yes, I shall come, I'll come.'

# 8

*A*nd she did come. He didn't. These few stark, cruel words said it all. It was because of him that, for the first time ever, she had forgotten to go upstasirs and say goodnight to . . . to whom? To her son Ned or to Jonathan? In her pretty blue sitting-room she could freely reflect on this fascinating problem, but deep within her someone was trembling. Someone, herself, an Elizabeth that she didn't quite know.

To begin with, there was this: Algernon Steers had not turned up, and why? She had worn white in order to appear more beautiful, but also to be seen more easily among the crowd of guests. It was a very naive thought. He would have been waiting near the entrance to welcome her, on arrival, as he had himself said. But no. She had stayed at least an hour in that drawing-room, which Algernon Steers's absence transformed into a desert. No doubt her dreary admirers of all ages concealed her behind a hedge of black suits, but she had escaped and, as she moved around the room with Mrs Harrison Edwards, she had made sure that she was seen; he could not have failed to notice that white dress that was looking for him . . . In the end, she had left, shame emblazoned across her forehead. He had lied. He had not come.

Had he done it on purpose? This opened up a whole field of suppositions, all of them painful . . . He was taking his revenge on her coldness, on her resistance to his compliments and entreaties. He wanted to teach her a lesson.

She tried to convince herself that he had quite simply been unable to come, but what could have prevented him?

Suspicions arose, but she dismissed them at once. At her feet, Charles-Edward was playing with the toy soldiers borrowed from a chess set that had come from England. It was rather unusual, that chess set. Instead of the usual white and black pieces, gilded Cavaliers were opposed dark gray Roundheads. It was a reenactment of the English Civil War: the soldiers of Charles I against the soldiers of Cromwell.

The child knew nothing about that part of history, but he knew that there had to be a battle and he preferred the Cavaliers with their plumed hats to the iron-clad men who seemed to him to be evil . . . He busily drove the combatants against one another, pell-mell, over the squares of the chess-board, a strategy that was accompanied by little shouts of victory when a pile of Roundheads fell before the splendid Cavaliers.

From time to time, his pretty curly head was raised in an upsurge of adoration toward his mother. The question that he then asked never varied:

'Mama, do you love me?'

In that little clear voice, she perceived a tone that she knew very well. A false anxiety, an innocent ruse intended to obtain in response as much love as possible.

'Of course, my love. Be good. Don't send the soldiers under the furniture.'

He gave a little smile, which quite overwhelmed her because he knew how to inject it with everything that he could not yet express. In the bitterness of her experience at the Steers', she wondered whether she would die for that pure smile, so utterly devoid of all lies. What it offered her was the total abandonment of a four-year-old soul.

Was he, too, aware of a mysterious presence? Looking around to make quite sure that both doors were closed, he picked up a gilded Cavalier and whispered:

'Zonathan, Mama.'

She was frightened and put a finger to his mouth.

'No, darling, not here, this evening . . .'

The look of understanding that he then assumed was that of someone much older. He shook his head.

'Very well, Mama.'

Suddenly she got up and ran to one of the doors, which she suddenly opened, then to the other, which she also opened, but her fears were groundless. Anyway, she was sure Celina did not listen at doors. Almost sure . . . Sam perhaps, but he would not have dared.

She rang. After a moment Celina appeared.

'Celina, tell Betty to take Charles-Edward for a walk in the park in front of the house.'

'A walk without you, Mama?' asked a sad little voice.

'You can go with me another time, my love.'

Bending down toward him, she picked him up and held him tight. Laughing with happiness, he stroked her face with both hands.

'Mama,' he repeated, 'Mama.'

# 9

As soon as she was alone, she went up to her room and examined herself in the tall rectangular mirror that at all hours of the day reflected an image of an Elizabeth who was sometimes radiant, but more often worried.

That morning she had not come to admire herself. Severely and anxiously, she examined her features in detail, right down to the texture of the skin, for there above all she awaited the appearance of the wrinkles that announced the end of true youth, but the large, fiercely scrutinizing eyes failed to discover the slightest mark left by the years.

So why did she see herself so differently from what she had been at her wedding? To answer that question she would have to look elsewhere and that she dared not do. Yet the mirror repeated it to her with unfailing obstinacy. The look in the eye was no longer the same. The eyes were as brilliant as ever. Yet something was missing. What? Something quite indefinable. A freshness of the soul and of the heart, the blessed ignorance of life, everything that she could read in her son's large brown eyes. Just to gaze at them was to drink at a fresh spring.

In the distance, she could hear the call of the steamer in the harbor, reminding her of Jonathan's name. Could she ever forget it at any moment of the day or night? Often, when she was with her son, she would take the little loving face in her hands hoping to discover in it some vestige of the *other*. Was it possible that the brief embrace by the waterside had left a trace? She counted the number of days on her fingers, but Ned's honest face replied in silence, saying: 'No!'

She did not give up. 'All that love that comes welling up out of my little boy is Jonathan's, he got it through me.' At certain moments, as dusk was falling and she was alone, that thought brought her up with a start. What ghost had she introduced into their lives? How could they now rid themselves of it? She could not, because she did not want to. Sometimes it crossed her mind that she might be losing her reason. The word that she hated kept recurring in her mind: adultery. Absurd. He had taken her by force on the river bank, and she had loved him. The most that could be said was that her heart remained adulterous. Who was going to accuse her of that? What woman had ever been able to control her heart and prevent it beating at the mere sound of her beloved's name? And, anyway, apart from her son, her little conspirator, who knew anything of the existence of the myth of Jonathan?

The sound of a carriage in front of the house interrupted her train of thought and drew her over to the window. She saw a pink parasol in a carriage. Who could that be, she wondered, at eleven o'clock in the morning?

After a few minutes, a discreet knock was heard at her door and Celina appeared with that serious air that never left her.

'Mrs Harrison Edwards wishes to see Madam. She is waiting in the sitting-room.'

'Mrs Harrison Edwards! Good, I shall be down in a moment.'

She looked at herself in the mirror once more, but with no particular aim in view, just long enough to give her hair a brush and to throw a shawl around her shoulders before she went downstairs.

Standing in the middle of the little blue sitting-room, resplendent in a dapple-gray satin dress with wide lace flounces, the tall, elegant woman cast a curious eye around her. As if to offset this rather formal dress, a huge straw hat, its broad brim artistically turned down, was adorned with a long mauve ribbon and hid her face as if under a roof. She looked like a peasant woman who had suddenly come into a fortune and gone mad.

Greeting Elizabeth with a joyous burst of laughter, she cried, 'Yes, I know, it's quite outrageous. I arrive at your house without warning and carry you off.'

'Carry me off, Mrs Edwards?'

'Exactly. We are going to Bonaventure to chat about things, for the newspapers are full of bad news, but let's not bother about that. You seemed worried at the Steers' and I like you too much not to have felt for you. I regard it as my duty to give you back your zest for life.'

'But I'm not ready. I'd have to dress . . .'

'You're charming as you are. Throw anything on that glorious hair and get yourself a sunshade.'

Caught off balance, Elizabeth succumbed. Suddenly she felt like a schoolgirl on holiday. What a wonderful opportunity to banish the gloomy thoughts that had been besieging her a moment earlier! To forget all that, forget it quickly. Exceptionally, fate was offering her the opportunity to escape with this rather eccentric lady who was taking her off to a place whose name said it all: Bonaventure.

In a very stylish black carriage, she took her place beside Mrs Harrison Edwards, and the two parasols, one white, the other pink, were already leaning toward one another in the friendliest way when the whip cracked, setting in motion a team of four thoroughbred horses that plunged into the avenue as if they were attacking an enemy.

Somewhat alarmed, the passers-by drew back on the pavements, but they soon recognized Mrs Harrison Edwards's carriage and, since the eccentric noblewoman was one of the most prominent people in Savannah, they just smiled. Suddenly Elizabeth let out a little cry.

'What is it?' Mrs Harrison Edwards asked.

'Is Bonaventure far?'

'I'd say a little more than three miles.'

In her mind's eye, Elizabeth saw her little boy, mad with anxiety, calling out to her on his return from his walk with Betty.

'You'll be back at home for lunch, about two o'clock,' said Mrs Harrison Edwards. 'Will that suit you?'

'Unfortunately not. I'm expected at home. How can I explain?'

An emerald-laden hand was placed on hers and a very gentle voice murmured into her ear.

'You do not have to explain anything, my dear, I understand everything, especially what is not said. And I want you to be happy. We'll drop the whole idea. James, to the big park. Are we agreed, my friend?'

'Absolutely. I think I know Forsythe Park.'

The name brought back the distant memory of a conversation with Aunt Amelia, who revealed her a family secret in a rather isolated place of her choosing.

'There are some particular places there that only I know,' said Mrs Harrison Edwards, as if she sensed Elizabeth's reluctance. 'James, full steam ahead.'

James interpreted this order in his own way, slowing down as they crossed the squares, but his mistress had too many things to say to Elizabeth for her to notice.

'You must be wondering, dear Elizabeth — you will allow me to call you Elizabeth? Yes?' she asked, without waiting for an answer. 'It helps to break down the barriers, don't you think? Anyway, you must realize that, if I have dragged you out of your home, it was to be able to speak to you more freely than in your adorable blue sitting-room, which has no fewer than two doors, and I don't trust doors . . . James!' she suddenly cried out, 'you're slowing down on purpose and I know why.'

'Excuse, M'am, I'll go faster.'

'James, I hate you,' she added.

'Yes, Ma'am. Yes, Ma'am,' he said in the most natural way in the world.

His whip skimmed the rear of one of the horses and they set off at a fast trot.

'He's trying to catch a snatch of conversation,' said Mrs Harrison Edwards under her breath. 'These people are so thirsty for gossip, but I wouldn't lose him for the world and he knows it. He drives beautifully and he looks too splendid in his red frock coat and gold buttons, don't you think?'

'Oh, yes,' said Elizabeth, who blushed pink under the muslin veil that covered her head. She had noticed James's face: a handsome young half-caste.

'People admire him and that is important in Savannah. But we're nearly there. By the way, my name is Lucile. Do remember that, dear.'

The carriage stopped at the park gates and, leaping from his seat, James opened the door, hat in hand. His mistress got out first, followed by Elizabeth, who had just taken off her veil. Dumbstruck with admiration, the young half-caste could not help looking her straight in the eyes, and she looked down.

A fierce sun licked the rows of small, dark red houses and the sidewalks paved with pink brick, but, as soon as they had entered the great avenue, the two women felt as though they had been plunged into a deliciously cool bath. With rather studied grace, Mrs Harrison Edwards took off her wide-brimmed hat and threw her head back as if to show off her haughty profile, celebrated in every drawing-room.

Under the vault of giant oaks whose branches met high above them, the two women walked slowly and the shade caused them to lower their voices. So different from one another, they both experienced the same feeling of existing outside the world. Solitude favored that agreeable illusion, for it was not a time of day when people went for walks. From the lower branches of those century-old trees that watched them pass by hung long curtains of verdigris moss the edges of which were constantly stirred by the slightest breeze.

For Elizabeth, she might have been in one of those dreams of the South that she had known at Dimwood. All that was lacking was the song of the birds, which fell silent as noon approached.

She hardly said more than a few words to her majestic companion, who was not short of them, but who spoke to her as if confiding to a friend. The setting produced exactly the effect she desired. Her bare arms emerged from the broad lace sleeves. They were described in Savannah as models of perfection and she made use of them at every possible occasion in broad gestures that caught everyone's attention, whether she was pointing out some remarkable object or expressing a sudden emotion, of surprise or joy.

'Elizabeth,' she murmured, in a grave tone that she considered appropriate to the solemnity of the place, 'I have a message for you. It is from an unfortunate woman. But let's walk on a little further,' she added with a mysterious air.

They walked on for another twenty paces in silence, then left the avenue for a mossy path.

'Nobody comes here,' said Mrs Harrison Edwards, 'it's a little place I discovered myself. I love wandering in the wild. There is a great, lonely savage within me.'

Elizabeth nearly burst out laughing, but controlled herself. A moment later, they found themselves in a place surrounded by a pool from which sprang a little jet of water. The young Englishwoman immediately recognized the isolated spot where, five years previously, Aunt Amelia had revealed to her a family secret, the failed marriage of Aunt Charlotte. Once again she admired the willows whose long branches filtered the rays of the sun as they curved above their heads. The same rather rusty metal chairs awaited them and, like a lost traveler, a wild magnolia grew nearby, spreading its heavy, languorous scent.

'Isn't it charming?' Mrs Harrison Edwards asked, with a splendid gesture of her immaculate arm.

'Charming,' said Elizabeth, her heart full of memories — her Jonathan was alive then . . .

They sat down.

'Yes, my dearest,' Mrs Harrison Edwards began, 'a message comes to you through me from a very unhappy woman.'

She added quickly, as if to dismiss the irritating idea of a request for money from someone in distress:

'Very unhappy, but phenomenally rich.'

'That should make her a little less unhappy,' Elizabeth remarked.

'Ah, my dear, money does not bring happiness.'

'Very well.'

'Beautiful as a goddess of antique art, witty, attractive, and yet shunned by society, as if she were a leper. Isn't it horrible?'

'Horrible.'

'I am referring, of course, — but you have already guessed — to Annabel.'

'Ah!' said Elizabeth.

'Yes, and she wants to see you.'

'Are you sure? She has never expressed any wish to since . . . Since four years ago.'

'For many reasons. Out of tact perhaps. She does not ask for very much. Simply for you to visit her so that she may resume contact with society.'

'But I'm not society!' Elizabeth protested.

'Oh yes you are, by birth. Just think. You can go anywhere, whereas society erects a sort of wall against her. On account of a drop of black blood, of which no trace remains except a detail in the hands, all doors are closed to her.'

'But you are society, Lucile. It is you who represents society in the eyes of the world and with an authority that only you possess.'

'Oh! I . . .'

'Yes, you, far more than I, who hardly ever go out. Invite her yourself.'

'But, my dear, between you and me, there is no shadow of kinship, whereas you . . .'

'I!' exclaimed Elizabeth, blushing deeply. 'Lucile, you are quite wrong. I have nothing against Annabel, but we do not belong to the same family.'

'A little, after all, through the Hargroves.'

'No, no. Such a kinship is mere speculation. There's absolutely no proof of it.'

The women stood up, both trembling with emotion. The conversation threatened to turn into a quarrel. Their voices were rising too quickly, their heads thrust back in anger and, as happens in such cases, they looked, without knowing it, like two hens about to peck one another.

The magnolia scented the surrounding air with the perfume of forgotten loves, and from between the interweaving branches of the willows the light played over the shadows on the grass at their feet, but they went on tearing at each other with words that they no longer believed and, suddenly, in one of those unpredictable reversals of the soul, Mrs Harrison Edwards hid her face in her hands.

'I give up,' she said, 'because I am ashamed. I'm fighting for a woman I feel sorry for and I have failed to make you share that pity.'

An astonished Elizabeth stepped back.

'Lucile . . .,' she said.

Mrs Harrison Edwards dropped her hands and looked at her:

'I cannot blame you, Elizabeth. You are still too young. You will never grow out of the childhood that remains within you. One must suffer in order to understand.'

'But I have suffered!' cried the young widow indignantly.

'I know, but suffering can close you up in yourself or it can open your heart. I've said enough. Let's talk of something else and let's embrace, shall we?'

So dazed that she was struck dumb, Elizabeth proffered her face to this woman, who had become miraculously human, and felt on her cheeks lips still warmed by the fever of argument.

They exchanged a smile. Still as impulsive as she was at sixteen, Elizabeth had to struggle to contain feelings that now drew her toward that woman, but the latter resumed her normal composure with extraordinary self-control.

'Since we are now reconciled, let's speak frankly,' she said. 'We have been rather ridiculous. It's merely a question of nerves and quite unimportant. Please don't misunderstand me.'

'No, Lucile, I assure you.'

'Bah! The role that I perform in society is one that the world expects of me. You will not escape from the rules of the same. But, deep down, I feel a revulsion against the injustices of our etiquette. Annabel is a victim. She is an exceptional case. The world refuses to admit it. For my part, I can no longer see her suffering in the solitude of her great house, visited by nobody. It is you she wants to see. If you refuse, I shall invite her to my house and the world can think what it likes.'

'You must tell her that I shall see her, Lucile.'

'That is the answer I was expecting an hour ago. By the way, I think it's getting late. Let's go back to the carriage.'

'Is it late?' said Elizabeth, suddenly worried at the thought of what awaited her at home: a scene, in truth, that would be very like a scene between husband and wife . . .

They quickly left the park.

# 10

*T*here was no scene. It was worse. Instead of a little boy leaping for joy at her arrival, she saw a silent Ned looking deeply upset. Already a master of every ruse, he knew how to reach her. The lover played his role well. Instinctively, he knew the art of making others suffer.

As usual, he had his lunch at table with his mother. That day she did not manage to make him speak, and it troubled her. This silence disturbed her as a harsh, revengeful lesson might have done. What future lay in store for both of them?

When the dessert arrived, she was so exasperated that she pretended to refuse the blackberry tart.

'No dessert for a Mama whose little boy no longer loves her.'

At these words, the child jumped from his chair and ran up to her, his face streaming with tears. 'It isn't true, Mama! It isn't true!'

The inevitable, passionate embrace took place.

I've won, thought Elizabeth, but I'm lost. If we're already playing those sorts of games, there's nothing more to teach him. It's a short step from sentimental scheming to lies, and then . . .

By the time evening had come, he had resumed all his rights and showed her no mercy. With all the doors shut, in the soft intimate light of the lamp, he demanded his Jonathan, a substitute Jonathan, replacing the one who had mysteriously disappeared the day before. Again she had to set her imagination to work and dispatch the ghost of the man she had loved astride his black horse through unknown lands. In spite of herself, a lump in her throat, she was taken in by this macabre fantasy. The boy wanted to know what Jonathan looked like, demanded details. She was making it all up as she went along, not very well, as one might lie before a judge. She broke off. With the infallible memory of childhood, Ned, a stickler for literal truth, rectified the contradictions. She obeyed and, in the dizziness of memory, resuscitated her Jonathan with his eyes flaming with love. Ned clapped his hands together. That was what he wanted, the Jonathan with the fiery eyes, the valiant, the irresistible, for that Jonathan was himself.

Suddenly, at her nerves' end, she collapsed and began to sob into the bed-clothes, very near her son's shoulder. Her body shaking with pain, she gave in to her feelings. Frightened, the boy placed his hand on her head:

'Mama!' he moaned. 'What's the matter? Is it me? Is it me?'

She made an effort to sit up.

'No, darling, it's not because of you,' she said, in a strangled voice. 'Your Mama is very tired. That's all.'

She wiped her eyes with her handkerchief.

'We must go to sleep, Mama,' said Ned, stroking her face. 'You mustn't cry. Do you love me?'

'I love you too much, my love. Put your hands around my neck. Say your prayers with me and then go to sleep. Promise?'

He promised and, kneeling in his bed, he put his head on Elizabeth's shoulder. Together, they recited the sentences. The child muttered without really understanding what he was saying, but with his mother he found himself suddenly in regions, still obscure though the young woman's heart gradually grew calmer. She kissed the little boy and turned out the lamp.

'It's over,' she thought. 'I'll find something. I shall make Jonathan go away on a long journey and Ned will forget. I shall stop tomorrow.'

With the door shut behind her, she repeated the words aloud:

'I'll stop tomorrow.'

Quite distinctly, a voice answered her:

'No.'

She stood stock-still, trembling. She could have sworn that a voice had spoken, quite near her.

'Yes,' she said, 'I must.'

Just at that moment, Celina appeared and asked:

'Do you need me, Madam? I thought I heard . . .'


# 11


Next day things were not easy. Yet young Ned behaved well enough, almost too well. Elizabeth suspected him of guessing something of what was going on in her head. It was altogether too much like a rupture, and would she find the necessary courage?

Leaving the little boy in Betty's hands, he gravely watched her go, without asking any questions. She had decided to devote the morning to shopping in town, buying all sorts of things that she did not want: French lace handkerchiefs, when she had a drawer full of them at home, four or five silk scarves, which she did not really like; but, that morning, it amused her to spend money. She was well aware that it was one of the well-known whims of the rich, a way of killing time when one has nothing to do.

By a sudden twist of conscience, she acquired an Indian doll for Ned, in the hope that the Indian might console him to some extent for being robbed of Jonathan.

She was already anxious. In the carriage that brought her back to the house, she wondered, 'Why was I born?'

A surprise awaited her at home. Charlie Jones, dressed in black from top to toe, was walking up and down in the little blue sitting-room.

His pink face seemed to shine with renewed youth. Never had he seemed to Elizabeth so like the portrait of him that she had once admired so much.

However, he was not smiling and he came up to her, his hands extended, in a cloud of Russian toilet water.

'Yes,' he said, kissing her, 'it's me again. Time flies. Our little world changes quickly. I have some news to announce, which will not surprise you.'

'Oh! What is it, Uncle Charlie?'

'Three days ago, destiny laid its hand on the brow of my old friend William Hargrove. His hour had come. The grim reaper passed at dawn.'

'You mean he's dead?'

'In rather crude language, yes.'

'Ah!'

'I wanted to tell you myself for all sorts of reasons. If you have a luncheon engagement, cancel it . . .'

'What do you mean?'

'I mean that, at certain moments of this short, fleeting life, one must be stoical and carry on, with heavy heart, but a clear head. I'm taking you out to lunch at the De Soto, the only restaurant where they serve a champagne worthy of the name. For we must react, my dear girl, react.'

'I shall do my best.'

'Bravo! Bravo, little English violet!'

'Ah, no!'

'What's the matter? That was what he called you. I shall have things to tell you about that.'

'I must warn Ned that he will be lunching alone. He'll be upset . . .'

'Dear little Ned.'

'I don't know if I'm dressed properly to go to the De Soto. Perhaps I should . . .'

'Rubbish! You look madly elegant in that gray-blue silk and that hat with its ostrich feather behind the ear.'

Celina appeared at the open door. She was holding a recalcitrant Ned by the hand.

'He heard you,' said Celina, coldly. 'If you give him a kiss, it might help matters a little.'

'You're going away, Mama!' cried the boy, running up to Elizabeth. She threw herself on him.

'My love, I'm going out to lunch with your grandfather. Say hello.'

'Hello, grandfather,' said Ned, without moving.

'Hello, Ned. Ah, I can understand why you adore him so, your Ned,' Charlie Jones exclaimed. 'He's already the picture of his father. It's wonderful to see you together. But he can pull my sideboards another time. I have a ship arriving from Europe this afternoon . . . Elizabeth, as they say in Paris, *filons*!'

He now looked very jovial, as if a great weight had been lifted from his mind. In a strange way, Elizabeth rediscovered the Uncle Charlie she had known years ago, before the terrible days. She followed him, feeling vaguely happy, without really knowing why, and climbed into the carriage which was waiting in front of the house.

Ned and Celina stood in the doorway. The child looked at his mother with that air of unspeakable distress that disturbed her more than any of his cries. From the carriage, she threw him kisses, then suddenly called out:

'Celina, there's an Indian! Give him the Indian!' The whip cracked. The horses moved. Neither Celina nor the child made the slightest gesture. Never again would she feel so guilty.

# 12

*I*n Bull Street, the finest and longest avenue in the town, which it crossed from north to south, from the river to Forsythe Park, stood the De Soto hotel, an imposing mass of dark red brick. Surrounded by a spacious veranda, it offered the choice of luncheon in the open air, under gigantic sunshades, or inside, in one of the halls, whose painted ceilings and gilt were worthy of a palace in the Old World. Because of the heat, Uncle Charlie thought they would be better indoors, both for Elizabeth's complexion and to be more private. However, he did not consult his guest on any of these points. Out of an unconscious nostalgia for the past, he persisted in seeing her as the same girl who had once so impressed him with her charm, and he led her forward politely, as he felt entitled to, with a firm hand.

A rather isolated corner was declared to be the best place. They sat down on resilient, well-buttoned banquettes. Why did something have to come and spoil the picture quite so quickly? An enormous bunch of violets adorned the middle of the table. Uncle Charlie immediately had it replaced by roses, then, turning to Elizabeth without a word, made a movement of the chin by way of emphasizing the delicacy of his gesture.

'A little heavy,' she thought, and she gave him the smile that he was expecting.

The menu that Charlie Jones had planned the day before was accepted without resistance by Elizabeth, who would later find everything delicious. The champagne was and could not be anything other than the best.

'Krug, 1845, note, a new champagne, but it will be memorable.'

She promised to take note of the fact and the conversation soon degenerated into a monologue from the mouth of Charles Jones

'What you don't know,' he began, 'is that beneath our feet are over a mile of underground passages. Once they were used against the Spanish, now they contain row upon row of the best wines in the world. This bottle we are drinking represents only a drop that has escaped from an intoxicating sea; but that's enough of that. Let's get down to business. Dreamer that you are — and your day dreams are part of your charm, yes, yes, do not protest . . .'

She did not protest, the Krug worked faster on her than on him. They had only reached the truffles cooked in embers, but her voice had already taken on an uncertain tone:

'You're too kind, really.'

'So,' he resumed, 'Daydreamer that you are and prisoner of your dreams, you know almost nothing of the world in general or of Savannah in particular. Now that you have your own house and are a part of the town, I shan't subject you to a history lesson . . . However, you should know the main points. In 1819 and 20, a triple scourge ravaged the town. First a financial crisis, such as the South had never known, sowed panic and, as if that was not enough, the following year fire swept through Savannah, reducing most of it to ashes, particularly the port. Yellow fever, probably from Cuba, then found its way among the ruins, striking the population at random. One saw men standing in the street, talking to one another, suddenly drop dead. Their bodies took on a deep orange color, with bluish stains . . . They had to be buried as quickly as possible.'

'Oh!' Elizabeth cried out, horrified, as she put her hand around the champagne glass. 'I suppose the whole country flew to the aid of the stricken city.'

This eloquent turn of phrase was so unlike her that it surprised her and warned her to go easy on the champagne. She put her glass down again without drinking anything.

'Never mind that,' Uncle Charlie went on. 'Savannah, relying only on her own resources, set to work immediately to repair the damage. A young architect, one of our own people, William Jay, had come in 1817 to build Richardson House, a wonderful building which was fortunately spared by the fire. This time he helped the town in the most sensible way by making the most sensible and tasteful suggestions for the rebuilding of the private houses. His idea, which was of striking simplicity, was an immediate success: a sober style, not too many windows, just what was needed, perfect symmetry, façades without useless ornaments, beauty triumphant in balance and elegance. The splendid trees and the profusion of flowers would do the rest. After over ten years of effort, it produced the town that we see now. However, in '34, prosperity having returned to Savannah, a great Irish actor visited the town that had returned, he thought, to its early splendor. Remember the name of this illustrious artist: Tyrone Power.*'

'I shall never forget it,' murmured Elizabeth, in a pleasant haze.

'Well. He had agreed to give a few performances and he was taken to the theater, one of William Jay's masterpieces, but he was deeply disappointed when he saw the sorry state of the auditorium. Nevertheless, he did not refuse to go on stage and was applauded in several plays, by, it has to be admitted, a rather meagre audience, for the seats were expensive and money was still scarce. Some of the splendid houses in the town were still being used at the time as cheap boarding houses . . . Thank you, thank you.'

He paused as the wine waiter served him, drank to little Ned's health and continued:

'At the end of his visit, Tyrone Power delivered a great rhetorical speech on stage, expressing his sorrow at the misfortunes that had befallen the noble city, which he compared to Niobe. He then remembered that glory awaited him in England and went on his way. It was about that time that the great merchants girded their loins for one great effort to revive their humiliated town. Three or four years later, in '38, Savannah was resplendent once more. Gold began to roll on the counters again and the waltz took the newly decorated drawing-rooms by storm. Nothing changes. War was at our gates and the South was waltzing. I hope you like the leg of lamb, which is served here in the London fashion, accompanied with braised lettuce.'

* Ancestor of Tyrone Power, the screen actor.

Elizabeth declared that she was delighted with everything. Look-ing around, she was astonished to see that the huge dining-room was almost empty. Two or three diners in the distant corners were bent over their plates, but the noise of their forks could not be heard. It was like a dream. Separated from one another by an array of tables, covered with white cloths, all laid and decorated with bunches of violets, they ate in silence, beneath a blue ceiling in which troops of chubby-cheeked, garlanded cherubs chased one another through a profusion of snowy clouds. Already rather distracted, Elizabeth observed them absent-mindedly.

However, the inexhaustible Uncle Charlie resumed his speech, now adopting a slyly confidential tone that obliged the young woman to pay attention.

'You see over there, through the trees, on the corner of Madison Square, a light red house?'

'But of course, Uncle Charlie, it's yours.'

'There is still scaffolding on one side and, as you see, the roof isn't finished yet, but in eighteen months' time it will be finished. Parties will then take place there that will be talked about, I swear, as far away as London. And do you know to whom I have left it in my will?'

Instinctively, she moved away from him, but he immediately drew closer and she could smell his breath.

'To your little Ned, of course. Hadn't you guessed?'

'No,' she said, 'no, no.'

Uncle Charlie looked at her in amazement.

'But it's a splendid present I am making to your son!'

'Thank you. Oh, thank you, for him — and for me! I wasn't expecting it.'

As if the child were there before her, on the other side of the table, she saw his great eyes staring gravely at her, dark and still. 'So far away from me?' they were saying to her with intolerable gentleness, 'why don't you come back to your Jonathan?'

For a few seconds she was in the grip of an illusion that he was really there and she could no longer hear anything that Uncle Charlie was saying. A strange, demanding, urgent thought occurred to her; it was no longer necessary for Mammy to bath the child. The long black hands would no longer touch her Jonathan's body: she would wash him herself.

Charlie Jones's voice suddenly reached her.

'My dear girl, what's the matter? I hope it isn't something you've eaten. You're quite pale and you seem miles away . . .'

She came to her senses at once.

'It's nothing, I assure you, a slight discomfort . . . It happens to me sometimes. Here, pour me a little champagne . . .'

In order to reassure him completely and to cut short any indiscreet questions, she began to say the first thing that came into her head:

'So few people . . . in so well-known a restaurant . . .'

'People seldom lunch in restaurants in the South, but try getting a table in the evening. You won't succeed. It's the smartest place in town. In other places there are only fixed menus!'

'Ah! how interesting!'

'Yes, isn't it, but I wonder if you followed me when I spoke to you of my modest personal origins. What do you know about me? Don't answer: nothing. In brief, I come from an honorable Shropshire family, recently ennobled.'

Elizabeth was only half-listening, as she brushed the tips of her fingers against the roses. Petals fell where the reflections from her glass glittered on the tablecloth.

'My grandfather Josiah,' he went on, 'was — would you know it? — a corsair!'

She was suddenly paying more attention.

'A corsair! As in Lord Byron!'

'A real corsair, but less romantic, in the service of George II. His Majesty didn't even speak English and he let America go. But he needed real corsairs and, in return for the French and Spanish ships sent to the bottom of the sea, he gave land and a title to his faithful sailor. With a coat of arms, of course. Having made his fortune, my grandfather went home, laden with honors.'

'Home . . .'

At this point, Charlie Jones thought he could see the whole of England in Elizabeth's dreaming eyes.

'My father Joshua left the little half-English, half-Welsh town where I was born and set himself up in Liverpool. It was there that the importers of American cotton prospered. He decided to join them and, before long, became almost as rich as they were. For him, as for many men of his generation, America was the future and he sent me here when I'd reached my twentieth year. I left for Savannah, the greatest cotton exporting town in the United States. In order to teach me to earn my living the hard way, my father had given me only a very small sum of money. When I got there, I set off on foot to the offices where I was to offer my services. On the way, I was stopped by a poor man. There were a lot of them in the country at that time. Georgia was only just recovering from the disasters of the twenties. "Here" I said to the man, "here's half my fortune." And I put a dollar in his hand.'

'Oh! Bravo!' Elizabeth cried.

'I didn't make such a bad deal with Heaven, for that silver coin was paid back to me a hundredfold and in millions. That's how the Lord does things!'

'Because your beggar was God,' Elizabeth said timidly.

They suddenly looked at each other, as if they had just exchanged improprieties.

'Ah, what a lot of nonsense we talk,' said Uncle Charlie.

'It's the champagne,' said Elizabeth, in an attempt to dispel the embarrassment that had come between them.

'With your English irony, you've spoilt a good story,' said Uncle Charlie, a little sadly. 'But let's get back to earth. Where was I?'

'On your way to some offices.'

'Ah yes . . . The offices! The port . . . What poverty! It was the time when our chivalrous neighbor, South Carolina, thought fit to take over our town's wealth. Since the merchant ships could no longer use the port of Savannah, they sailed up the river as far as Augusta, the main cotton center. Charleston seized the opportunity to do a deal with Augusta and cleverly built a railway linking the two towns. A real masterpiece, that railway, the longest of its time. In 1833, it won the admiration of the world and was called the wonder of its day. In this way Charleston was able to supplant the port of Savannah. But what have I got to do with all that? You may well wonder.'

'Not at all, Uncle Charlie. Faithful to the town that welcomed you in its distress, you bravely stayed with her.'

'Not quite. How the devil would I have earned a living? As a young man of good sense, I offered my services to Charleston, where I lived for some time.'

'*Very* chivalrous!'

'Don't be silly. Life is one thing and fine feelings are something else. It was at Charleston that the portrait you saw in your room, in my house, was painted, do you remember?'

Did she remember! The champagne was playing tricks on her again. She was falling in love with the twenty-year-old Charlie Jones and, just recognizing him, as if through a fog, in the Charlie Jones of today, she forgave him everything.

'Very well,' she said, with a rather sad smile.

'So you'll be interested to learn that the young man of the portrait met at Charleston a young Scottish lady, Miss Douglas, fell in love with her and married her.'

How well he knew that English girl, still so innocent, still so easily won by any handsome face! How much would he tease Elizabeth to hurt her? For, despite his natural kindness, he still retained a little rancor at the bottom of his heart. That woman, so ready to be infatuated, had caused his son Ned's death. In the end, he had learned the truth about that mysterious challenge to a candle-light duel — or at least he thought he had. That adventurer Jonathan had not been provoked for nothing.

Suddenly sober, Elizabeth felt those words like a contemptuous insult. Is that why he had asked her to come to this vast, almost empty room? To take his revenge? She could not believe it and tried to convince herself that she was wrong. She stared at him in silence. On those sensual, firmly drawn lips, she clearly read the word that he would not speak and which sometimes haunted her at night: adultery.

One by one the tears that she was ashamed of being unable to hold back rolled down her cheeks.

What was taking place in Charlie Jones's heart? Without even being aware of it, she was beating him at his own game, with the most unfair weapons in the world and the most irresistible in the memory of man. He took her hand and held it prisoner in his. Anyone passing at that moment might have believed that he was witnessing a love scene.

'What is the use of talking?' he said at last, his voice made heavy with emotion. 'There are times when words don't mean anything any more. I've suffered perhaps as much as you have. People will tell you so. Don't cry, Elizabeth. You will always be one of those people who never learn from life and who preserve an inexperienced, I was going to say, innocent, soul to the end.'

'Oh no!' she cried, shaking her head.

'Well,' he said, smiling and letting her hand go, 'let's leave it at that and order dessert.'

She dabbed her face with her handkerchief.

'Frankly,' she said, 'I don't want any dessert.'

'I don't either and I'll drive you back home, if you like. It's a bit too warm for a walk at this time of day, but before we part, I have something to say to you that you may find difficult to listen to.'

'Something else?' she asked anxiously.

'Oh! It's nothing very terrible. As you know, William Hargrove is no longer of this world.'

She said nothing.

'He had an indescribable fear of death. The Presbyterian minister who had come to his bedside simply terrified him all the more. His son, my friend Josh, then had the idea of fetching an Anglican priest from Savannah. So they sent him a sort of elderly angel who heard the tormented old man's — what do they call it? — confession, and he put his mind at rest. Then William Hargrove declared that he wanted to die in the Church of England. The funeral service will therefore take place in Christ Church, your church.'

He paused for a moment, then added:

'You are earnestly requested to attend.'

Elizabeth jumped:

'Oh no, never! I don't have to . . .'

'The whole family is asking you to go. You can't refuse. It will almost be a scandal.'

'What a strange dessert you are offering me there, Uncle Charlie! I'll go, under duress.'

'A little champagne to chase away the gloom?'

She shook her head.

Leaving the De Soto, they got into the carriage, which was waiting for them at the door.

'I'll take you home, but, if you don't mind, we'll go the long way round. I still have some things to say that will be of interest to you — nothing very dreadful, on the contrary . . . Tommy, we'll go to the end of Bull Street.'

Curled up under her sunshade in a corner of the carriage, Elizabeth felt mistrustful despite the reconciliation at lunch. Never had she seemed more beautiful in the shade of the tall sycamores whose thick foliage filtered the dazzling light. The parasol that the young woman was holding hid her face as far as her mouth, and the tresses of her long hair shone over her shoulders.

Charlie Jones could not hide his admiration.

'I don't know what you do to preserve your youth so well, but you look as you did when I first saw you.'

'You're too kind.'

'That's enough of compliments,' he said, as if she were ready to pay him back in kind. 'I forgot to ask you for news of the party at the Schmicks's. Without wishing to appear so, they are people of extreme sensitivity. They were really touched by your presence, your simplicity, your smile.'

'That surprises me. They didn't say a word to me.'

'That's their way. At once proud and shy.'

'Well, if everyone is happy, I'm delighted.'

'I hope that young tearaway Algernon behaved himself. It's him I want to hear about. Did he pay court to you?'

She shrugged her shoulders, irritated.

'Men are all the same.'

'I understand and that's enough for me. But let me draw his portrait for you. Physically, to begin with . . . He's a work of art: pretty as a girl.'

'Oh! Please, the gentleman does not interest me at all.'

'Fine, but you must understand. He has broken hearts by the dozen. Here they call that *assassinating*: assassinating the ladies is his main, I would say, his sole occupation. Need I make myself clearer?'

She tried to repel the thoughts that assailed her: being assassinated by Algernon . . .

'Uncle Charlie, please, let's talk about something else.'

'The end is in sight. Since he is very careful, he avoids showing himself in public too often, for he has an unhealthy fear of angry gentleman seeking him out to insult him in front of Society and challenging him. He has a phobia of challenges. It's what they call here — excuse the vulgarity of the term — a cocktail. You understand?'

She was furious, and thinking that he was jealous, she turned away and said:

'No, and I have no desire to understand.'

'A cocktail,' Charlie Jones continued knowledgeably, 'is someone who has all the appearances of a gentleman but is not one at all. Algernon Steers with his dazzling name is nonetheless, on his mother's side, the great-great nephew of Schmick the grocer.'

Her heart beating with emotion, she suddenly felt a burst of pride.

'Well, Uncle Charlie,' she said icily, 'allow me to tell you that I don't care in the least and that you are getting very boring.'

'I know, my dear girl,' he said humbly, 'but you had to be warned. That scoundrel was at the Schmicks's on my instructions, for, on one side of his family, he is related to my wife, to represent, after a fashion, what is pleased to call itself Society. Did he stay till the end?'

'I don't know what you mean by "the end". I wasn't there to observe him.'

'Forgive me, Elizabeth, I felt compelled to talk to you about him for your own good.'

'I would be very obliged if you left me just as I am. I think we've arrived.'

'Yes,' he said earnestly, 'but that is not all.'

'What else? Oh! Uncle Charlie!'

He had the carriage stop some twenty yards from Elizabeth's house.

'I'm overcome with apologies, dear, dear Elizabeth. I nearly forgot this.'

Taking a letter out of an inside pocket, he said solemnly.

'A letter for you. I don't know what's in it, but I can guess it's important and worthy of reflection.'

Elizabeth took the letter without a word.

'That isn't all,' Uncle Charlie added and, pulling out of another pocket a flat, long box covered in violet silk, he said simply: 'Open it when you're alone, in your room.'

She took the box more politely, but said nothing.

'Now,' he said quietly, 'tell me that you forgive me.'

Taking off his panama, he looked at her so affectionately that she forgot her irritation.

'Just say yes.'

'Uncle Charlie, yes, but what have I to forgive you for?'

'Everything. The whole of lunch. I behaved appallingly. Sheer mischievousness. It's because of Ned — they will tell you . . .'

She could only make a gesture of protest.

'It's true. But you have behaved perfectly,' he said, then added, raising his voice: 'Tommie, proceed.'

In front of the house, he took Elizabeth's hand and placed a long kiss on her cheek. And suddenly, with the laugh of a smiling boy, he said in her ear, 'That wasn't Uncle Charlie kissing you, but the young man in the portrait.'

She blushed and tried to laugh.

# 13

*C*elina opened the door and, without waiting, Elizabeth asked: 'Where's the boy?'

'For the moment, he's asleep. It's the heat.'

'Yet it's cool in the house.'

Celina remained impassive.

'Silent all morning, silent since. Very well behaved.' She took her mistress's hat and parasol.

'I hope enjoyed your lunch, Ma'am.'

'Very much. I'm going up to rest. I don't want to be disturbed.'

'No, Ma'am.'

Alone on the stairs, she leaned against the banister. Algernon. Great-great nephew of a grocer. And what of it? Is one talking about an ancestor who died a hundred years ago or a lively, very handsome young man?

And supposing the letter was from him? And the violet silk box?

To prolong the heady uncertainty, she valiantly struggled against a mad desire to open the envelope. A horrible idea occurred to her: supposing the letter and the violet silk box were from Charlie Jones? He joked so strangely about the portrait . . . It would be monstrous, truly. Whereas Algernon . . . Suddenly she admitted it: she wanted Algernon.

It was the first time in her life that she had dared to admit to herself so clear a truth. She had the unsettling impression that as she went up the staircase she was descending another.

'No longer the same person,' she thought.

On tip-toe, she went into her room and very quietly closed the door of the next room, in which her son was asleep.

An exquisite scent floated in the air around her, and there was a tightening in her throat. A magnolia . . . Heavy with too many memories, that perfume made her relive moments she was unable to contain. Because of that, she had banned that flower in her home. All the servants were aware of this. Celina, who had been there for a year, might not have known, for she alone could have brought the beloved enemy into the room.

The half-closed shutters darkened the room and the young woman had to let herself be guided by the so sadly familiar scent before she discovered the flower at last, faded in a glass dish, it's milk-white petals surrounded by dark pointed leaves . . .

Celina did not know. Elizabeth repeated the sentence several times in order to convince herself. She had not been told — and why should she have been? — that two years before, on her orders, the Irish gardener had dug up a magnolia growing at the bottom of the garden. Scandalized, Pat had complained bitterly and called all the magnolias of the South to bear witness against Madam.

To ring the chambermaid and get her to remove that flower seemed to her to be the only intelligent decision. But she could not do so. Standing near the console, she looked again and again at the petals, already wide open, and tears came to her eyes. She would explain to Celina that there must never again . . . The thought, which she had tried to banish in vain, gradually became clearer in her mind: Celina knew something and the flower had been put there on purpose.

It was an absurd suspicion, she told herself, in order to calm her feelings. There was only one person in the world who could have informed the governess: the Welshwoman, but Celina did not know Miss Llewelyn.

The Welshwoman, or Annabel, but, if she were not careful, such thoughts could drive her mad. She must take a grip on herself.

'Impossible,' she said out loud.

The word calmed her.

Banishing all cares from her mind, she opened the letter that she had kept in her hand and collapsed into the rocking chair to read it more comfortably.

At first she understood nothing. There were two almost indecipherable lines, hastily written, but she could read fairly easily a signature that froze her:

### William Hargrove

The letter fell from her hand and as the chair rocked, she groaned. What could she do? A man whom she could not bear had written to her, and that man was dead. A sudden disgust overcame her at touching that sheet of paper on which the hand of a corpse had impressed itself. That was how she saw a situation that was becoming more repugnant as the minutes passed. What did he die from? She did not rightly know. Was not death in itself contagious? She wanted to go and wash her hands. A scruple held her back. Supposing the dead man saw her . . .

Yet the letter was there, at her feet. She stopped rocking. She must read the letter, now she wanted to know. From a drawer she took a pair of gloves that she put on and picked up the sheet of paper, lying open on the red carpet.

The letters formed only one sentence and all the words were linked to one another so that they formed only one, endless word. With effort, she managed to make out at least the general meaning. With a hand over her mouth, in order not to absorb the miasmas that might be emanating from that paper that had come from another world, she succeeded in deciphering the message and, with a horrified whisper, she stammered:

*For the woman I have loved more than my soul and who has never known it.*

The violence of the shock almost made her fall off her chair. She ran over to the bed and threw herself, face downwards, her head buried in the pillow in order to stifle her moans.

She could not understand. There was a mistake. The letter was not for her . . . But the envelope said that it was. In a sort of mental tumult, she relived the strangest moments of her years at Dimwood. More frightening than any others were the hours spent with the dead man in his library, the mysterious remarks that he had made to her, in such a surprising way, the alternating gentleness and irritation, and the brutal way in which he had suddenly thrown her out, and later her refusal to speak to him, his efforts not to see her, those huge bunches of flowers that were thought to have been put on the table in order that he should not have to see her during meals. Mad, she thought. Mad and wicked.

How she hated him! In her rage and disgust, she began to beat upon her bed, her heels in the air, her fists beating down on the bolster. Had he not wanted to make fun of her, to punish her by trying to frighten her with this declaration from the grave? And what were Uncle Charlie's intentions in this funereal comedy?

Suddenly she remembered: 'The box. The violet box. Where did I put it?'

With a leap, she was at the foot of the bed and tip-toeing over to open the blinds. She looked around the room and, lying carelessly on a chair, was the object wrapped with such care in its violet silk. At first she had not noticed the color, but now the choice of that particular color was clear and it exasperated her.

'Your little English violet,' she muttered to herself. 'Well, no, Mr Hargrove!'

The parcel was wrapped with ribbons. Furiously, she tore them off and was about to subject the precious material to the same violence when she stopped. What did the box contain? What surprise? What trap? She did not believe at all in the letter's macabre declaration of love. What could that man, who probably hated her and was perhaps making fun of her on the other side of the grave, have hidden in that box?

With her still gloved hands, she picked it up, shook it and thought she could hear a barely perceptible sound. Her imagination suggested a thousand possibilities. A cloud of wasps . . . Some creature that would leap out at her . . .

To calm herself, for she was ashamed of her infantile fears, she sat down on a little sofa and placed the box beside her. Suddenly coming to her senses, she realized that the emotions she had felt enabled her, in a general reversal of the world around her, to see everything clearly. There had been no creature in that box. Uncle Charlie kept a watch over everything and would not have allowed her to be frightened to death.

Without taking off her gloves, she undid the folds of silk, which revealed a little cedar casket whose exquisite smell rose to her nostrils, as if to reassure her and, she carefully lifted the emblazoned lid.

She gasped with astonishment and stifled a cry.

With wide eyes, she saw shining in front of her a necklace of heavy emeralds to which was added, as a pendant, an emerald larger than any of the others, studded with diamonds. At first she dared not touch it, gazing at the regal jewelry as if it were some prodigy that might at any moment disappear. Each multi-faceted stone had been cut and polished to increase its brilliance. But the pendant outshone all the rest, as much by its size as by the fine crown of light formed by the diamonds. At last, throwing her gloves to the floor, Elizabeth took the incredible necklace in both hands and it came alive, gleaming and shining, as she moved it this way and that in her fingers.

Her head was spinning a bit and, without being able to help it, she began to laugh. She was overcome in turn by joy and a vague fear. She wondered if she were not going mad, for nothing in her mind could explain the appearance of this magnificent object, worthy of a queen. Never had she seen anything like it around the necks of the richest ladies in Savannah. Suddenly, she picked up the necklace and fastened it around her neck.

And now, standing in front of the tall mirror above the fireplace, she saw someone whom she hesitated to recognize, so much did those dazzling stones transform the everyday Elizabeth. The proud pendant fell to the cleavage of her breasts. Would she dare to go out so splendidly adorned? Was it possible to wear such jewelry with simplicity? Haughty and contemptuous, wearing the displeased look of a crowned head, that was how one would have to be. She tried looking like that and suddenly burst out laughing: she could not, but neither did she want to take off that necklace. She was already dreaming of wearing it from morning till night around her neck and not even being parted from it to sleep. She looked back at her proud, determined reflection.

The name of William Hargrove found its way gently back to her memory. In some inexplicable way, it too had changed its appearance. How could she put it? She thought hard and found the answer: it was less horrible.

It was not much. Her conscience began to react and, as she played with the pendant, she began to wonder whether or not she had behaved badly in her relations with William Hargrove, but she did not find an answer. In his short letter he had made it clear enough that she had not understood him. She had understood nothing. In silence, he had loved her with an impossible love.

It was then, as the years suddenly began to surge back, that she felt overcome by an immense pity for that gray-haired man driven half mad by a cruelly hopeless desire.

With a mechanical gesture, as if to console him, she stroked the emeralds and murmured:

'Poor Mr Hargrove.'

# 14

*A* sharp kick at the bottom of a door startled her out of her reverie. Young Charles-Edward could sense her presence.

She quickly seized the scarf and put it round her neck to hide the astonishing ornament, then let the little boy in. He immediately noticed the jewelry box and the violet material, and went over to touch them with his curious little hands.

'Leave them, my love,' Elizabeth said.

'Are you cold?' he asked. 'Are you cold? Why is that round your neck?'

Very busy, he ran from one side of the room to the other. He was interested in everything to do with his mother's realm. She belonged to him. Even when she was there in person, he seemed to be looking for her, and finding her, in the things that she used, in some clothes on a chair, in her toilet case, on her dressing-table. The cedarwood box was opened and closed a dozen times. She had to take it from him. What intrigued him most of all was the magnolia in the glass dish.

He had always known that scent. It was the scent of the South.

From the first weeks of his life, he had smelled it in the parks where Betty took him walking, but never before indoors. Usually, anything that caused the slightest disturbance to the order of things in his mother's bedroom would upset him and the questions would pour out; but the open flower in its ring of great, dark leaves made him cry out.

'Mummy,' he said, transported with joy. 'The big flower!'

Slightly worried by this enthusiasm, she immediately replied:

'Very pretty, darling, but your Mama can't keep it here. Celina will take it away.'

He looked concerned: 'Oh? why?'

'Why . . . because that scent gives me a headache. You can see I'm not well, can't you, darling?'

The child's eyes stared at her with a seriousness that she found embarrassing.

'Then put it in my room,' he said.

'Oh, no, it's bad for little boys. It stops them sleeping at night.'

'Not me. Give me the flower, Mama.'

Elizabeth rang her bell and did not reply.

There was a short silence, during which she felt young Charles-Edward's eyes on her. All over his attentive face, even in his brown ringlets, she thought she could already see an obstinacy that she would be unable to overcome.

There was a knock at the door and the maid appeared.

'Ask Miss Celina to come and talk to me.'

Once more alone with the child, she noticed that he was standing in front of her with an attitude which she called his little man's look: normally she found it touching, but today it bothered her. Neither of them said anything. Elizabeth tried to smile, but the big brown eyes did not leave her. A moment later, Miss Celina was there, calm, her hands folded in front of her.

'Miss Celina, didn't you know I don't like magnolias in my house?'

'No, Ma'am.'

'Who put that flower there?'

'I did, Ma'am. It was your neighbor, Miss Rumboldt, who allowed me to pick it from the tree by her front door. There are so many flowers . . .'

'Yes, but what is it doing here?

'I thought you'd like it,' said the tight thin lips.

Elizabeth sat down. 'Thank you,' she said, 'but I would still like you to take it away and get rid of it.'

She was shaken by a cry of anguish and anger.

'No, Mama!'

Miss Celina remained impassive even though Elizabeth looked at her, begging for help.

'What is to be done? Perhaps I'll let him have it for just one evening. It will go brown and he won't want it any more.'

'I do still want it,' the child insisted.

'Darling, we can't pick one for you every day. It's not allowed.'

'Celina did,' he whined.

'Never again,' said Miss Celina. 'I was only allowed to once.'

Yet, feeling sorry for the child, she gave a kind of smile which he did not notice.

Pulling his mother's skirt, he said in a voice close to tears: 'You don't love me any more.'

Without waiting for a reply, he ran to his room. They could hear him muttering there to himself for a while, then silence.

'Will you allow me one piece of advice?' Miss Celina asked. 'If you give in to his whims, you'll never stop giving in to him.'

'I expect you're right,' Elizabeth said, putting her hands to her throat. She felt as though the housekeeper's eyes were boring through the folds of the scarf hiding the emeralds.

'I realize I shouldn't spoil him,' she added humbly, 'but it's hard.'

'Shall I take the flower?' Miss Celina asked.

'Yes, for heaven's sake, do.'

Alone once more she was struck by the deep silence. Not a sound could be heard from the room next door where a four-year old heart was breaking.

'I shall never find the strength to tell him that Jonathan has gone,' she thought.

Like a guilty person begging for pardon, she walked slowly toward Ned's room.

# 15

*T*he reconciliation scene was bathed with consoling tears from both of them. The young tyrant asked for nothing more at that moment . . . Far from informing him of Jonathan's disappearance, Elizabeth swallowed her pride and, on the spot, invented new exploits which had recently come to light in the career of the mysterious personage. All this did not affect the inevitable story that would fill the last quarter of an hour before the evening prayer and the goodnight kisses . . . The sun was still shining and Betty would soon come to look for the well-behaved child and take him for a walk.

And so the day ended quite normally. Elizabeth gave in about everything. She did not even have the moral strength to insist that from now on it would be she, and not Black Mammy, who would wash her little boy.

'I am beaten,' she thought. 'I know it, and feel it. Lost. I can read my future like an open book. I cannot say no to a man. Shame on you, Elizabeth Jones! The child has found me out.'

That night her sleep was plagued by terrifying fantasies and she woke at dawn, bathed in sweat, her hands clasping her throat. Above her nightdress, the necklace was still around her neck.

'The price of a graying old man's passion,' she thought with horror. But at that, her whole being rebelled. In the dim light of dawn, she tore off the nightdress that was sticking to her, walked over to the large mirror, and stood naked in front of it. The emeralds had never seemed more beautiful, nor had she . . .

'You are not alive,' she murmured. 'You are dreaming you are alive.'

A few minutes later, she took off the necklace and put it back in its box.

# 16

*I*n one of its moments of high irony, so-called 'real' life gave her a special surprise.

While she was taking breakfast with Charles-Edward, who had quietened down despite the removal of the magnolia flower, Elizabeth was wondering what the day had in store. For the sake of peace, she had been cowardly enough to promise the child that one day he would have another magnolia blossom . . .

The room where they were drinking their morning tea was almost round and had a slightly old-world charm: the narrow high-backed chairs stood out against the pale green of the woodwork and a heavy silver teapot with an ebony handle gleamed on the white tablecloth. A still soft light filtered through the yellow shutters and enhanced the atmosphere of tranquil happiness.

With instinctive stubbornness, Elizabeth dismissed from her mind all that Charlie Jones had told her about a funeral which, most definitely, she would not be attending; but the large silver teapot and the Queen Anne chairs seemed to saying: 'Oh, yes, little Mrs Jones, you will go with the rest of society, because that's what society expects.'

At that moment, a white-gloved hand held out the morning post to her on a silver platter together with the daily newspaper which was never unfolded.

Two letters . . . She immediately recognized the writing on the first: Aunt Charlotte was writing to tell her of her forthcoming visit to discuss some important matters. Dear Aunt Charlotte: she came to Savannah once or twice a year and the important matters always concerned religious matters and good advice on reading the Bible.

The second letter was already in Charles-Edward's hands. He had seized it and was delighted by the size of the envelope, offering to open it with the butter knife. Elizabeth snatched it away from him. She knew beforehand what it would be. Tearing the envelope open with her fingers, she pulled out a card which left her in a cold sweat. It was a formal invitation to the funeral of William Hargrove, on October 12 next, in the Episcopal church, Christ Church, at eleven o'clock precisely. She was also invited to attend the burial in the town cemetery, her presence being urgently requested according to the express wishes of the deceased in his last will.

These final words, added in handwriting, leaped out at Elizabeth like the claws of a wild cat. She recognized the imperious handwriting of Charlie Jones and knew that there was only one thing left for her: to die before next Thursday.

Pushing aside her still half-full cup, she rang and called for the housekeeper, who appeared almost instantly. With a gesture and without opening her mouth, Elizabeth showed her the lavishly printed page with its disturbing handwritten postscript.

A glance was enough. 'Sad news,' the housekeeper said calmly. 'The whole town knows, but don't worry, Ma'am. I know your wardrobe. You have all the black dresses you need. I shall look after everything. It will be no trouble . . .'

Her flat voice spoke these remarks with a precision that made them unbearable to listen to, but Elizabeth did not keep up with her. The only words that struck her were: 'mourning dress, only used once.' She looked at the woman, her expression like that of one of the Fates of classical mythology, and she thought confusedly: 'Now you are no longer dreaming . . . All this is true . . .'

The child looked on without understanding and said nothing, but his wide, anxious eyes remained fixed on Elizabeth's face, and above all, the slight trembling of her silent lips.

Terrified, he held out his hand and said: 'Mama, I'm here.'

She stroked his cheek and muttered: 'Hush, my love, everything's all right.'

She thought she was about to burst into tears, but with a rush of energy she managed to control herself, and said sharply to the housekeeper: 'That's fine, Miss Celina. We'll see about that later.'

Celina bowed and smiled.

That same afternoon, Elizabeth received Miss Charlotte. Time had been kind to the venerable old lady who still had the same pink cheeks, surmounted by a large bonnet, worn at a crooked angle. Everything about her spoke of bygone innocence. A bunch of keys rattled in the folds of her dress and most of the time she chattered on in a sharp, but kindly voice.

However, this day Elizabeth had the feeling that some almost imperceptible shadow had come between them.

'My dear girl,' Miss Charlotte said, 'in this pretty drawing-room one hardly likes to speak of serious matters. The life of man is like the flower of the fields: the wind blows and it vanishes, Psalm 102.'

'I know,' Elizabeth said, with a hint of impatience. 'The grim reaper. Mr Hargrove is dead.'

'Are you not afraid that such serious talk might frighten your child?'

The boy held his hands up to her with a wide smile.

'You see how much he adores you,' said Elizabeth; 'and he is not interested in what he does not understand. In any case, Betty is coming to take him for a walk.'

'Miss 'Lotte, a sweet,' said Ned.

Miss Charlotte felt in a pocket of her dress and took out a box which she opened, saying: 'A honey sweet for a good boy.'

The huge bonnet bent down toward him and she kissed him, then gave him the sweet.

'Now, remember that honey, together with milk, was the blessing of the people of Israel . . . Your Mama will tell you about it.'

'This evening,' Elizabeth said. 'Meanwhile, dearest, sit over there and send the Cavaliers after the Roundheads, without making a noise.'

He settled down behind his mother's chair.

'A fine young lad,' said Miss Charlotte, sitting up in the rocking chair. 'He's coming up to five, isn't he? You can't imagine how little we know of what's happening over there in our dear Great Meadow. Neither Amelia nor I read the newspapers. The news gets too confusing up and we don't understand it any longer.'

'Nor do I, and I feel no need of it.'

'You may be wrong. For myself, I prefer to read my Bible, but when I arrived here, I had a shock. Everything I'm about to tell you comes straight from Uncle Charlie. When I am at his house — but I'll come back to you when Amelia is there this winter — Charlie insists on keeping me up-to-date with politics . . .'

'He's given up where I'm concerned: he knows I'm bored by such things.'

In no way discouraged, Miss Charlotte went on: 'That's a pity. There comes a time when politics arrives on our doorstep and, if it must, breaks in through the windows. Two new States are to enter the Union.'

'What! Aren't there enough already? What an odd country, to be constantly changing shape.'

'Yes, it's a bit like the Promised Land when the Jews entered it. A piece added here, another there, but it was still the Promised Land.'

'This is no Promised Land.'

'That's where you're wrong. Many immigrants are coming from everywhere, from the Americas and the old continent, to settle here and make themselves rich. And, like the Jews in Palestine, the Whites are settling down in territory that doesn't belong to them. Kansas and Nebraska are Indian lands — and the Indians, I might add, keep slaves. My dear Elizabeth, I feel so knowledgeable that my head is spinning.'

'We could speak about something else, especially if you feel unwell.'

'No, you shall have your history lesson. Well, then, Kansas and Nebraska. The latter is to the north of the line separating North from South, so it will be admitted as a free State. On the other hand, in Kansas, the people will vote and choose if they want slaves or not.'

'And will the Indians vote?'

'What an innocent you are! The Indians don't count. In the end they will be driven out and put into reservations, somewhere else . . .'

'But that's dreadful!'

'You think like Uncle Josh. Meanwhile, the Sons of the South are invading Kansas and grabbing as much land as they can in the best region for growing cotton . . . everything will be ready for the planters who come with their slaves. But as you can imagine, the North is not standing idly by. It is sending as many people as possible to occupy the land, so that they will be in a majority when it comes to a vote. There are already clashes, insults, fights and civil war.'

'What about the Missouri Compromise, Miss Charlotte?'

The older woman sat upright.

'It's in shreds, my girl. Wakarusa, an Indian village, was rechristened Lawrence by the Northerners. The Sons of the South captured it, burned the army post and a few buildings. And then,' she lowered her voice, 'the Devil appeared.'

'Oh!' Elizabeth cried.

The little boy, who had sat silently throughout this informative and mysterious conversation, leaned against his mother's leg and pressed his Indian rag doll to his chest, wide-eyed. Betty had told him about this wicked gentleman.

'A rabblerouser, a religious fanatic who thinks that Heaven has ordered him to free the Blacks by force. At Pottawatomic — another Indian name, note — with a band of eighteen rogues, he came after nightfall, seized five Southerners, dragged them outside in the darkness, butchered them and cut them in pieces with cutlasses. As he was making his escape, he also killed some Indians on the pretext that they kept slaves. His name is John Brown. The North will put its own construction on the events and make a hero of him.'

This frightful story produced a wave of horror in the little blue drawing-room. The child gave a cry and clasped his mother's dress. She went pale and said:

'That was last May and we've heard all about it, Aunt Charlotte. In fact we've heard too much about it already, and you shouldn't frighten the child.'

'You may be right, but he's always clinging to your skirts, and I gave way to an impulse. I felt obliged to tell the truth. You will know how to comfort him.'

Tears were running down Charles-Edward's round cheeks and he looked at his mother like someone appealing for help.

'Don't you be afraid, now,' she said, kissing him. 'Think no more of all that, it's a long way off, it's over. Aunt Charlotte, would you call for Betty?'

On the rocking chair, Aunt Charlotte's feet didn't even reach the ground, but with a single leap she was standing up and ran to pull the bell.

Little Charles-Edward had climbed on to Elizabeth's knees and was clasping her desperately in his arms. Miss Charlotte gave an affectionate laugh.

'You two are too fond of one another, you know.'

'There are no limits to love, Aunt Charlotte.'

'I know that as well as you do: I too have loved someone. But you must make a man of that child.'

At that moment, Betty appeared, her head wrapped in a green scarf.

'Take Ned for a walk under the trees in Bull Street. And listen to me now: don't you ever talk to him of the Devil.'

'Oh, no Ma'am!' Betty exclaimed, with that gesture which seemed so bizarre to Elizabeth as though she were wrapping her face in an invisible veil. 'I tell the li'l darlin' about his guardin' angel.'

'That's a good idea. Off with you, Ned, be good and go for a walk with Betty.'

There was a short struggle and heavy sighs, then he gave in, grabbing his Indian doll by one leg and giving it a good shake, as if it was the Devil.

'You're tearing your Indian,' said Miss Charlotte.

Betty raised her eyes to the ceiling.

'Betty spend her whole time a-sewin' Massa Ned's Injun.'

When they had gone, Miss Charlotte set off once more on the galloping rocking chair.

'You may be surprised to hear it,' she said, 'but I feel sorry for that frightful man John Brown . . . There is a devil in him like the possessed in the New Testament. Everyone knows about his family. His mother and maternal grandmother died insane. Five of his cousins were also mad. He has twenty children, two of them died mad. How could he escape? He is not responsible.'

'Then they should put him in an asylum.'

'First they have to catch him. He has a band of fanatics who obey him like soldiers. It must be said that he gives them a lot of money,' she gave a little laugh. 'It's a blessing for the North.'

'What is the government going to do?'

'It will wait for the result of the elections, because they are voting like crazy in Kansas and cheating on both sides.'

'You have no illusions, Aunt Charlotte.'

'None at all!' she exclaimed, rocking so fast it took her breath away. 'Now you know what's happening in this country.'

Elizabeth was seized with a burning anxiety and wondered if she would dare to ask the unbearable question that was on the tip of her tongue.

'Do you think there will be war?'

Miss Charlotte grasped the edge of a nearby table to stop the racing chair and her piercing eyes fixed on the great blue pupils of Elizabeth's, which still displayed some of the unspeakable terrors of adolescence.

'You're behind the times, my girl,' she said, gravely. 'The way things stand, that's not a proper question: the answer is too obvious. So we must pretend that all's well. According to Charlie Jones, people have never thrown so many balls or had more magnificent parties. The world is disintegrating and the South dines, dances and plays the guitar. Have you read *The Last Days of Pompeii*? No? You should, it's a masterpiece. Charlie has it in his library in Great Meadow. I could bring it for you one day, when I next come.'

Elizabeth made a gesture as if pushing aside some pestilential beast.

'Too bad,' said Miss Charlotte. 'The one time I do offer you some entertainment . . . Today, I've been forced to tell you the whole truth: an inspiration from On High. One should not fight against it. But I love you dearly and I have a piece of advice: if your mother comes back here and suggests . . . Why not? England is your country.'

Elizabeth shook her head. A whole part of her lived and breathed in England and for a moment she saw herself there, her hair ruffled in the wind, in a field red with poppies, beside the sea; but she was ashamed to run away. She thought she could hear Ned's plaintive, dying voice: 'Stay with us . . .'

'You are young and very beautiful,' Miss Charlotte went on. 'I missed my chance in life, Elizabeth; don't you miss yours.'

# 17

*T*he next day was made more difficult by young Charles-Edward, who had not recovered from Miss Charlotte's story. Against her better judgement, his mother had to tell him that it was all untrue and that John Brown was only an ogre from a fairy story, with an invented name. There was still the Devil to deal with. Elizabeth said that he only ever appeared to very disobedient little boys, but the child was so disturbed that, like Miss Charlotte, he saw him everywhere. The rag doll, which he strongly suspected of being the Devil's creation, became his favorite scapegoat. He used him to vent his anger, hitting the ground and the furniture, or else, in a whim of his uncontrolled imagination, called him John Brown and thumped him with his fists. In the evening, Betty tended the victim's wounds with needle and thread.

Elizabeth was disturbed by her Ned's behavior. She was discovering in this still young creature a violence akin to that of adulthood. She decided that the only advantage of this disturbing discovery was that she thought she would be free of the eternal Jonathan each evening, but soon learned better. The phantasmagoria inside that over-active young brain must have been overwhelming. The horseman on his black horse had to gallop as usual, braving unexpected dangers, always the victor, always handsome. To dispose of him by sending him off on a long journey was unthinkable.

Overcome, she was able to assess the madness of the game which had entranced her as it had the child. She had tried to bring her beloved back to life with the complicity of an innocent creature; and now he had grown and matured.

You might almost have said that he suspected his mother's unease. Indeed, that very evening, when he was going to bed, he asked her a question as disconcerting as it was apparently simple.

'Mama, in the daytime I'm Ned, aren't I? But who am I now?'

In a flash, Elizabeth realized she had to take the plunge.

'Now, darling, you'll pretend to be someone else, called Jonathan.'

He cried out and clasped her arm.

'But I am Zonathan, Mama, I want to, I want to.'

'Of course, my love; and this evening, in your dreams, you will get up on your black horse and gallop through the trees and you will be Jonathan.'

'With my sword?'

'Of course, to frighten off the robbers. But you know, it's our secret. You won't forget that, will you?'

'Oh, no. But in the daytime with Betty, I'm still Zonathan.'

Elizabeth controlled her feelings as well as she could.

'For Betty, you are Massa Ned. Don't you like that?'

'Not Zonathan?'

'Not for her. She doesn't know our secret, you see? Ned was the name of your father who went away.'

'Away,' the child repeated. 'Where to?'

'I told you before, darling. To heaven.'

'Zonathan didn't. I like Zonathan better. I am here, I'm Zonathan.'

'Yes, yes,' she said, exhausted. 'You are . . . You are my . . .' something stopped her saying: *my Jonathan.*

'My dearest,' she exclaimed, suddenly clasping him in her arms. 'Dearest! Jonathan is a long way away and I can't see him any more. Your mama is very tired, my little man. You must go to sleep.'

'Will Zonathan come back?'

'Of course, darling.'

They exchanged a last kiss and the night light was turned down to a faint glow.

Alone in her room with the door shut, she dropped on to her bed.

'What have I done?' she wondered. 'My God, what have I done?'

Only then did she realize that she had forgotten to say her prayers.


# 18

Next day, Celina came to say good morning with a ceremonial air that immediately cast a black veil over the golden October light.

'May I remind Madam that Mr Hargrove's funeral is tomorrow.'

'Tomorrow already? But I've got time to think about that.'

'A black dress?'

'Certainly not. I'm not a member of the family.'

'Then we have a good choice of dark outfits.'

'I'll see, Miss Celina.'

'A very fine dress in purple silk.'

'No, it ages me and will seem like semi-mourning.'

'Then perhaps a splendid dress in plum-colored taffeta?'

'Plum-colored taffeta . . . I'll see, I'll see later. Tell Ned's Black Mammy to look after him.'

Celina bowed and went out.

When Black Mammy appeared, Elizabeth could not find the words she wanted to say to her. Nounou was standing, looking even more enormous than usual in Elizabeth's eyes, blacker and as if inflated with love in her vast white apron that made her look like a cloud. The young woman would like to have told her that from now on she herself would give Little Ned his bath, but the ecstatic smile on the ebony features prevented her.

'Me go wash Massa Ned,' Nounou said, brandishing a large cake of mauve soap. 'Massa Ned like that a lot.'

'Very well, dear Mammy, give him a good wash — behind the ears and everywhere.'

'Yes, Miss Lizbeth. Me do everytin' verra well.'

Elizabeth returned her smile and, with a slight tug at her heart, followed the white cloud which seemed to float into the room where Ned was still sleeping.

Everything was making her suffer today. Why didn't she dare tell Black Mammy what she wanted? She did not dare admit it to herself. She had never truly looked at her son's body, his naked body, and suddenly she wanted to, she wanted to stroke his little shoulders and his chest, and at the same time she was afraid of it. Afraid of what?

'I don't want to upset Mammy,' she said aloud.

This explanation would have to do and settle the matter for once and all; but it concealed the truth.

The hours passed one by one and now she was sitting at table in the green dining-room beside her little boy, fully dressed and prettier than ever in his white cotton sailor suit. His lovely brown legs hung out of his short trousers; she felt proud of him. One day he would be a fine man, but she made up her mind, if there ever was a war, not to let the Army have him. She already had a plan.

For the time being he was chattering away, constantly turning toward his mother. Nothing was left of the terrors of the day before. Or was there? Suddenly, a piece of toast in his hand, he cried:

'Mama, I don't want anyone to talk 'bout Zohn Brown any more. I want stories 'bout nice people.'

In their innocence these words almost brought tears to Elizabeth's eyes, but she thought that this was ridiculously sentimental of her and merely stroked the child's velvety cheek.

She liked the room around her for the feeling of happiness that the light green walls and the darker green curtains at the windows gave her. She also liked the table, with the silver gleaming on the white tablecloth, and the bowls of flowers and the pots of marmalade around the heavy black teapot all the way from England. Sitting next to a talkative little boy in these friendly surroundings, she found she could forget the dark thoughts that had plagued her over the past few weeks. She was cheating the menace of the future by forgetting it. Nothing existed except the sound of a teaspoon against a saucer and the clear voice of a child getting muddled telling the story of his rag doll's misadventures.

As soon as breakfast was over, feeling lighter at heart, she decided to go for a walk in the garden. Ned clapped his hands. In the garden, he entered a different world.

Much longer than it was wide, the garden gave an impression of narrowness, like a tunnel of greenery. Banks of flowers with aggressive scents bordered a grassy path which led under a vault of slender young sycamores to a wall laden with a thick curtain of honeysuckle. Here, in a corner, was a brilliant white garden house. The green shutters gave this modest dwelling a rural appearance, although it extended into the street. The front door was as big as a barn's.

Elizabeth called out imperiously:

'Pat!'

There was no answer. Young Charles-Edward added his own voice to hers to call out a second time:

'Pat!'

Now, from the inside of the house came a commotion of crashing furniture, accompanied by barely suppressed swearwords; then the huge door opened and a bronze-haired giant appeared. The first impression, however, was of a smile, and behind the smile was Ireland — Ireland with its freckled face shining with irrepressible merriment in eyes of a celestial blue full of mischief.

'Yes, Ma'am,' he said. 'Lovely day, don't you think?'

'What I think, Pat, is that the garden is pining because the gardener is sleeping. Don't deny it.'

Pat raised a huge hand, emerging from a checked shirt.

'Ma'am, as Heaven is my witness, I was in the street talking to people, and that's the truth.'

'People! You're making fun of me.'

'I'd rather die than do that. There are people going past and we say hello. You have to: we must stay friends with our neighbors to keep peace in the world, Ma'am.'

'That's just what I've come to talk to you about. I've had a complaint from our butcher. He doesn't want to deliver here any more because you beat his boy.'

'That's not my fault, Ma'am. As soon as he saw me at the door, he put the meat down and tried taking to his heels. He's a yellow-belly. I caught his leg and said: "Get up and put up your fists! Defend your honor" — because I'm fair, Ma'am. All God's holy angels can bear witness to that. I always give due warning and never hit below the belt. First of all, a good hook to the chin.'

'Pat, I'm sick of hearing about your heroism. We'll have to get rid of you if you can't stop causing trouble with the trades people.'

'But Ma'am, they only have to send delivery boys who are capable of arguing with me man-to-man, with their fists.'

Drawing herself up, Elizabeth spoke so loudly that Pat raised his eyebrows in astonishment.

'I want your word of honor that you will obey me, Pat, or else you must go this very day. No more trouble with the trades people and no more fights. Is that understood?'

'Ma'am, I promise you on the head of my patron saint, Patrick, who drove the snakes out of Ireland as he will one day drive out the English.'

Elizabeth could not help laughing. She said:

'The English are not afraid of Saint Patrick, but I'll let that pass and I hold you to your promise, which must be definite.'

A huge, winning smile appeared once more.

'Ma'am, I swear it on the head of your little boy. If I may say so, I can already see him at fifteen able to take on anyone, with his boxer's legs and arms . . .'

'Be quiet, Pat. I'm not very happy with your flowers, and the lawn needs watering.'

She continued to reprimand him, interrupted by the 'Yes, Ma'am', 'No, Ma'am' of a momentarily subdued Irishman, and they went to look at the flowers. There were a lot of them, but the young woman wanted more.

'Your garden is boring. Put a little fantasy in it. Enough is not enough, I want too much, I want people to die of pleasure as they go past, do you understand?'

'Yes, Ma'am. Die of pleasure . . .'

'More heliotropes, more seringas, more tiger lillies! Jasmine until it stuns you, color, more and more! I want the impression of a riot.'

With his powerful hands, Pat ruffled his thick crop of hair, as if to start a riot there too.

'Yes, Ma'am,' he said. 'When you talk like that, I can see what your pleasure is, Ma'am.'

As he spoke, he came closer to her and a suspicion of tenderness entered his eyes. Elizabeth quickly moved away.

'Very good, Pat. That will be enough for today.'

'I'm sorry about that, Ma'am.'

She pretended not to understand.

'Don't apologize, but remember I'm watching you. I want work, and a garden I can be proud of. Come on, Charles-Edward.'

She walked toward the house, then suddenly turned.

'And leave the butcher's boy alone.'

'Yes, Ma'am. You have my word on it.'

'And the rest of them. No more brawling in my garden.'

'Yes, Ma'am. On my word, as an Irishman.'

Ned had followed this scene without saying a word, his hand in his mother's, but with his eyes wide open. Pat upset all his ideas about human beings, whom he saw as either good or bad. The gardener was unclassifiable. His size and rough appearance were frightening, but his smile made it all better, in a way that Ned could not understand, because his mother seemed displeased; so he preferred to say nothing.

That man is unbearable, Elizabeth thought. At one point I really thought he was going to start making what mother calls 'calf's eyes' at me, like a lover. I don't want to dismiss him, because he's an ideal watchman, and . . .

And she did not dare acknowledge that even in this brute of a man she could vaguely sense that 'damned Irish charm'. He was attracted to her and he was on the point of saying so. That is why she was angry, less with him than with herself.

Once back in the pretty blue drawing-room, she was suddenly repelled by this room where she had already suffered, and did not want to suffer any longer. As usual, she glanced in the mirror over the chimney. How well anger suited her! The slightly disordered gold tresses on her forehead seemed to be the result of coquettish design. At the worst moments, what remained was her simple joy in being very beautiful.

'Do you still love me, Mama?' Ned asked, pulling her arm.

'You? Oh, yes, I do, dearest; but go and play with your Indian for a while.'

'Betty took it away to mend. I tore it in half.'

'Why did you do that?'

'It was Zohn Brown.'

At this moment, Miss Celina appeared and held out a tray with an envelope.

'A gentleman called just now, Ma'am. I thought you had gone out.'

'I was in the garden . . . Very well, Miss Celina.'

'You've thought about tomorrow morning, Ma'am? You must try on your plum-colored dress.'

'No need. I haven't changed my mind. Now please leave me.'

Miss Celina bowed and left.

The envelope contained Algernon Steers' card, with a few words in a large, aristocratic hand:

*'Apologize most profoundly for my entirely unavoidable absence.
Beg your forgiveness . . .'*

She broke out into a nervous laugh. After what Uncle Charlie
had told her, she no longer much wished to be assassinated by
Algernon. With bitter irony, she imagined an impossible encounter
between Algernon and Pat, ending with the demolition of the aristocrat . . . Yet what handsome features Algernon had!

'Mama, why are you laughing? Are you happy?'

'Happy to have such a good little boy as you, darling.'

'Will you tell me about Zonathan this evening?'

She put her fingers to her lips.

'Ssh! Not so loud, but yes, of course, I'll tell you a story.'

# 19

*A*nd so night came and there was Jonathan galloping like a
madman through dark forests where owls screeched. The ride
was exhausting for her, who slept fitfully, pursued through cem-
eteries by the prickly bearded spectre of Mr Hargrove, while the
owls in the woods screeched: 'Little English violet!'

And then, as ever, the new day broke.

She was up at dawn, impatient to have done with the dreadful
day before her. The horrors of the night were dispelled and her
looks were as rosy as ever thanks to that indefinitely extended miracle which the women of Savannah were unable to explain. Even
she sometimes shuddered at the idea that, like so many other beauties, she would eventually have to face the dreary day when she
would need powder and make-up.

Now, however, she was afraid of nothing. She had resolved to
consider the day's events as a kind of solemn ceremony, undoubtedly a grave one, but amounting for all that to the fact that someone
was dead, while she was alive. Who has not felt some secret satisfaction at that notion? She would not make herself look ridiculous
by feigning sorrow. What genuine kinship was there between her
and Mr Hargrove? She denied everything.

By eight o'clock, she was dressed and rang for her housekeeper.

'I've been thinking, Miss Celina. I don't like the idea of the plum-
colored silk. Get out my purple taffeta dress.'

'But, Ma'am — for a funeral?'

'Miss Celina, I don't feel like discussing it. Find my taffeta dress

in the big wardrobe and lay it carefully on my bed. I'll dress myself, after breakfast.'

Miss Celina gave her usual nod and went out.

Hating slovenliness, Elizabeth took breakfast in her most elegant
navy blue dressing-gown. The taffeta dress could wait, lying in her
room like a princess in a faint.

Charles-Edward, sitting next to her, started telling her about his
dreams and said that he had met Jonathan. She gently told him to
be quiet: 'Darling, you know all that is our secret. You must only
speak of it upstairs when you're going to bed.'

She was wasting her time. The child seemed over-excited.

'But I did see him, Mama, I did.'

'Of course, in your dream.'

Ned waited for a moment. Everything in his face seemed to freeze,
his mouth half-open, his eyes staring blankly.

'No,' he said. 'Not in my dream, Mama. He was there.'

In the soft morning light that bathed the room, the words took on
a disturbing echo for Elizabeth. She made an effort to dispel this
unpleasant sensation.

'My dearest, what we think we see in dreams doesn't exist. So
let's think no more about it, or I shan't be able to tell you any more
stories. There,' she said laughing, 'that's all over.'

The sharp little voice persisted:

'But he was in the room, Mama.'

Throwing her napkin on the table, Elizabeth exclaimed:

'My little boy is annoying me. We must have no more of this
talk, because I can't eat my breakfast.'

Trembling all over, she read an anxiety in Ned's face at that
moment, which suggested terror and swiftly taking him in her arms,
she smothered him with kisses.

'It's nothing, darling. Tell Mama you love her.'

Ned was crying so much he could not speak. She tasted the tears
that were running down his flushed cheeks.

'I love you. I love you enough for two, my sweetest.'

At last, he smiled; then asked in a whisper:

'Am I still your Zonathan, Mama?'

She felt a chill on the back of her neck.

'Yes,' she said, controlling herself. 'yes.'

Back in her room, she began to walk up and down, her head bowed
so that she could think more clearly. For the first time, she perceived the full enormity of her mistake. The frenzy of a love that
had not been driven out of her heart by death, had brought this kind
of presence into the life of the child: it refused to go away, as if it
were really there in this unsullied soul.

For a short time she was afraid: her memory was assailed by

recollections of fantastic stories. Her whole adolescence cried out to her: 'Suppose it is true: what if Jonathan has returned?' The fairy-tales were full of dead knights coming back from the dead . . .

She stamped her foot in rage, then went to stand in front of the large mirror.

'Idiot!' she cried at herself.

This verdict on herself relieved her, as if it shifted everything back into reality. She would act, she would cure her child of this ridiculous lie in which she had immersed him and (but how much doubt there was of this . . .) she herself would recover all her English common sense.

Turning, she saw the taffeta dress at the back of the room and gave a little cry of delight. At once sober and ornate, the purple color with its reddish sheen offered itself to her admiration, with the sleeves extended and the flounces carefully unfolded.

At ten o'clock, after dressing and doing her hair herself, she was ready. Her hair was not plaited and drawn up as it should perhaps have been, but slightly bouffant and almost free under a charming little fur hat in a dark violet which provided a discreetly funereal note.

She still had some time left. She locked her bedroom door, then stepped up on a chair to take down the jewel case which she had hidden behind a row of books on the top shelf of her bureau.

Two minutes later, the emerald necklace was around her neck and the young Englishwoman, standing in front of the long mirror, was admiring herself unreservedly. The serious tone of the dress marvellously brought out the magnificence of the proud stones which split the daylight into shafts of lightning. Before this image of herself in the mirror, Elizabeth could only exclaim: 'Oh!', and suddenly felt as if royal blood was coursing through her veins from head to toe. Precious stones went to her head, as they do to many women. This ecstasy had lasted for some time when a knock on the door caused the infatuated woman to start. The first time she had tried on the magical necklace seemed like nothing compared to the supreme pleasure of this morning.

There was a second knock.

'One moment!' Elizabeth cried, coming out of her dream. 'Who's there?'

'Celina,' said a voice through the door. 'Mr Charlie Jones wants to say that he will take you to the church himself in his carriage. He'll be here in twenty minutes.'

'Very well, Miss Celina.'

Uncle Charlie, the church, the painful ceremony, the people: all that was still to come. She must take off the stones and, entirely disenchanted, carry on living like those whom she called The Others. In spite of everything, she was touched by to the attentions of the one man who could politely bring her back to earth.

# 20

*T*he only daylight inside the church came from the dark colors of a huge stained glass window covering almost the whole of the back wall. Round lamps hanging from chains on each side of the altar threw a dim light that seemed to call for silence. The verger in his black robe showed new arrivals to their places, but in Elizabeth's case, it was Charlie Jones who performed this function.

At first she saw nothing; then she started to distinguish the rows of long box pews to right and left of the center aisle. Sitting at the end of one of these rows, she was wondering who her neighbor could be when a delicate, black-gloved hand came to rest on her own, which was bare. Turning to her left, she recognized Susanna in full mourning.

'It was kind of you to come,' she whispered.

Elizabeth replied with a smile. Already ill at ease, she felt as if she were dressed for a ball, but everything was enveloped in a half-light, and she had the feeling that she was hiding there, as if in a cellar.

It was very hot, because the church was now full, but not a murmur was to be heard. The silence was only broken by the soft noise of fans, undulating discreetly, like fluttering wings.

A further five or ten minutes passed in this stillness before they heard the doors of the church being thrown wide open. The congregation stood up and Elizabeth turned round to see, in what appeared a blinding light, a priest dressed entirely in black, walking behind a large cross, made of smooth copper, that shone like the sun, while the cleric slowly intoned, in a deep, resonant voice:

'I am the resurrection and the life, saith the Lord. He that believeth in me, though he were dead, yet shall he live. And whosoever liveth, and believeth in me, shall never die.'

The words resounded in the young woman's ears with the force of a thunderclap. For a moment she closed her eyes, and thought that she saw her whole life pass in front of her. Then the sound of footsteps made her open them again and she saw the heavy coffin, draped in black, pass by her, in which lay the body of William Hargrove, carried on the shoulders of six men toward the choir.

Overcome with an insurmountable weakness, she fell backward, but two powerful, braided arms caught her and she fainted. Smelling salts were immediately waved under her nose and she regained consciousness with a start, throwing her head back like a rearing horse. Still reeling from the shock of the words she had heard, she felt all the religion of her adolescence flood through her, bringing terror much more than hope.

'Lost,' she thought. 'Lost because of the child I have driven mad.'

A few steps away from her, in a box, the flesh of a man who had loved her, without ever having been able to confess it, was dissolving. Like ribbons in old engravings, the words of a psalm unfolded around him, as if to tell him of his adventure in the land of the living:

*'And at the last I spake with my tongue: Lord, let me know mine end and the number of my days, that I may be certified how long I have to live.'*

She was cold, despite the oppressive heat around her.

'Lost because I did not believe strongly enough that I was saved . . . Because of the child.'

At once vast and very soft, the sound of the organ filled the church with its song of sad love. It was the dead man's favorite hymn: 'Abide with me . . .'

'It's over,' Susanna whispered in Elizabeth's ear. 'The farewells and long prayers are for the burial, which you need not attend.'

Her mourning dress gave off a faint smell of mothballs. She leaned over to Elizabeth and gave her a quick kiss. Meanwhile, the priest, turning to the door, was walking out, behind the copper cross, reciting the prayer for the dead, and the six men were carrying the coffin at a pace and with a care that made it seem huge.

In a great shuffling of shoes on the stone floor, the congregation left the church, leaving behind the palm fronds on the benches.

Outside, many stopped under the porch and on the steps. Men in frock coats and top hats, and women in shawls, the long fringes of which covered the ruffles of their dresses, black from head to toe, seemed from a distance like a splash of ink against the whiteness of the six Grecian columns. While the plumed hearse was being loaded and the family was dispersing in the carriages, voices, delighted at being able to resonate through the air while another voice was forever silent in its coffin, were exchanging views on the latest political rumors.

'Whatever they say, it's war already in Kansas.'

'There's opposition to foreigners and Catholics. You know: they are all suspected of being ruled by Spain.'

'It's a plot that goes back to the founding of South Carolina . . .'

'Pay no attention,' said Charlie Jones, who had taken Elizabeth's arm to lead her to her carriage. 'Go home and lie down. I'll drop by later. For the meantime, I have to accompany poor Will Hargrove.'

'The South will never accept,' said a slightly drawling voice; but the tone was unmistakeable.

There was an immediate response, because the object of the attack happened to be the all-too-celebrated journalist Garrison, a great scoundrel of the sort that always turns up in time of trouble. In his newspaper *The Liberator*, with the persistency of a madman, he was pursuing a campaign against the South inspired by the delirium and much of the indefatigable eloquence of the age. That bogeyman John Brown was, as it were, the personification of his dreams, activated by hatred, and he stood firmly behind him. Finance was needed for the huge enterprise of freeing the slaves by massacring the plantation owners.

Unfortunately for Garrison, he was not only hated in the South but also despised in the North. The rich refused to give him the huge sums that he requested. But he knew how to talk: this was undoubtedly his most powerful weapon. Where his pen failed, his tongue would eventually succeed. Wendell Phillips, an idealistic multi-millionaire, was an easy victim. Like many in the North, he was opposed to the Constitution which declared the right to own slaves, but as the virtuous old Mr Phillips remarked, conscience is above the law; so, by virtue of that principle, the dollars finally made their way into John Brown's pockets.

In front of the white colonnaded portico, Garrison was being tried from the top of the steps, before a court of stovepipe hats.

'The Devil is in all this,' said a long-faced gentleman, pale with fury. 'His latest article in the *Liberator* is an incitement to murder. What more do they need before banning the paper?'

'Alas, there is such a thing as freedom of the press. There's nothing that one can do about these rogues.'

A voice piped in, sweet as the note of a flute.

'They say he's a cocaine addict.'

'That's a sin, not a crime; that's not how you'll get him,' said a little old man with a malicious look.

This was old Mr Robertson, whose silver curls framed a smooth pink face, and who wore an air of admirable candor despite the twinkle in his gray-blue eyes.

'You keep on about that reprobate — but at least he doesn't disguise what he's up to. What would you say if I told you that, in front of a huge congregation in a church in Brooklyn, I saw the Reverend Beecher get into the pulpit . . .'

A chorus rang out:

'Beecher! Head of the gang of Beecher, Stowe and company!'

'The very same, in his surplice with that famous angelic smile on his lips that you may have heard about.'

There was mocking laughter and cries of: 'Keep quiet!'

'At the feet of this Minister of the Gospel, or rather, at the foot of the pulpit, there was a virgin.'

'A what?' a young man's voice called out cheekily.

Paying no attention to this interruption, Robertson continued:

'Very beautiful, with long white veils as if to guarantee the authenicity of that title of virgin, a young half-caste, sitting down, her eyes lowered and her hands neatly folded: for sale!'

'For sale! A virgin, a pretty half-caste!'

At this, conflicting feelings produced a dull murmur in the crowd. Old Robertson waited, then went on:

'Those of the congregation who wished to contribute to the purchase of this dangerously beautiful creature and give her the freedom of a Child of God, could put their alms in the great copper plate on a chair beside her. Reverend Beecher himself described this as a holy procession of generous donors . . . The total amount gathered in this way was judged stupendous and received a blessing from the pulpit accompanied by grateful tears. From here on, the story becomes confused. The half-caste and the dollars disappeared simultaneously. Silence, gentlemen, this is not the end. Time passed, and the Reverend reappeared, this time with another colored virgin wearing a white veil. One must suppose that the holy man had several beauties at his disposal and swapped them around, giving each to the highest bidder for a considerable amount. This same religious auction took place, I must tell you, in another town, but with no less success, thanks to the famous preacher's talents. Do not sit in judgement; but if anyone tells you this is not so, then send them to me. Everyone knows where I live. Goodbye, gentlemen.'

He firmly replaced his broad-brimmed hat on his head. Everyone stood aside respectfully to let him pass and, in utter silence, he came down the stairs and disappeared.

Usually so talkative, the congregation dispersed in silence and, five minutes later, the square in front of the church was totally deserted, like a person who has lost his memory.

# 21

*E*lizabeth could hardly hear what was being said to her. In a state of semi-stupor, she took a hand which was held out to her from inside the carriage by a woman whom she did not recognize. Never before had such a strange terror swept through her. Slumping into a corner of the carriage, she tried to understand what had happened, but her memory stumbled against the very second when she lost consciousness. The fear of Hell had torn her away from the world.

Having somehow recovered, she could only think of the certainty that she would be reproved, and constantly saw Ned's little face in front of her eyes.

A parasol opened above her; then, a long time afterwards, she became aware that a voice was trying to reach her; but an infinite distance seemed to separate her from the sound of these words. Where she was, space was limitless and vanished into nothingness.

Someone was shaking her so hard that she once more felt herself alive, alive in her body, but inert. Then she was being slapped and, through half-open eyes, she saw the gesture, as her head went this way, then that, and suddenly she started back to life. Her cheeks were burning and a voice was saying: 'At last!'

Between one kind of stupor and another, she thought she saw Miss Llewelyn.

'I don't understand,' Elizabeth stammered.

'You don't understand? About time! It's something at least that you understand that you don't understand. You scared me. Another fainting fit and I would have taken you to hospital.'

'To hospital . . .'

'Do stop repeating everything I say. It's annoying. You are Mrs Edward Jones and your carriage has just drawn up in front of your house.'

The Miss Llewelyn who was speaking had a large black hat which made her almost as imposing as a duchess. But it really was Miss Llewelyn.

'Come, now, have some guts, Mrs Jones,' she said. 'Don't let people see you like that.'

Elizabeth made an effort and almost managed to stand upright, but she was trembling.

'Come, now, Mrs Jones,' said Miss Llewelyn. 'Get down.'

The order had the same effect on the young woman as pride and a new hail of blows made her rise to her feet.

The coachman had got down from his box and, taking off his hat, respectfully held out his arm to Elizabeth, but she pushed it aside.

'On my own, thank you,' she said.

In spite of that, she had to be supported going up the steps to the front foor. The Welshwoman did so, with imperious solemnity, curtly issuing orders to Miss Celina, who opened the door:

'Go and prepare Madam's bed and send her up a strong pot of tea. Is that understood?'

At the top of the staircase, Ned clasped the bannisters and called out: 'Mama! What's wrong? Have you hurt yourself?'

She motioned to him and said, 'Be a good boy, dearest, and let me be. It's nothing.'

'Don't try to come down,' said Miss Llewelyn. 'You'll fall.'

When they at last came up to him, he grasped his mother's skirt.

'I'll hide, I won't say anyfing.'

'He'll sit quietly at the foot of the bed,' said Elizabeth. 'Let him come in.'

The Welshwoman did not object. Taking off the large hat which spread like a roof around her skull, she at once began to undress Elizabeth with a speed which astonished the young Englishwoman. In less than three minutes, she was under the bedclothes, with her head on a pillow, if not happy, then at least vaguely reassured by the unexpected, almost maternal kindness of someone whom until then she had considered as rough as a peasant. Now she saw her going back and forth around the room, plunging it into darkness by lowering the blinds on the windows.

Ned had already grabbed a stool and taken up his place on it with the gravity of an adult who knows what is happening, but he still had his Indian doll on his knees. His eyes were wide open and did not leave the face of Elizabeth, who smiled at him without saying anything.

'That's not a little boy you have there,' said Miss Llewelyn under her breath. 'It's a lover.'

Elizabeth looked at Ned and smiled.

'In any case, a lover whose heart is pure,' she said.

'I don't deny it, I'm just sorry that he doesn't have a brother to scrap with.'

'Alas!' Elizabeth sighed.

The Welshwoman, who had been laying out Elizabeth's clothes, returned to her side and, putting her hand to her mouth in a theatrical gesture, merrily whispered:

'Remarry, Mrs Jones.'

'Oh!' Elizabeth said.

Suddenly serious, Miss Llewelyn continued:

'With all due respect, let me say that it makes me ill to see you alone in your beautiful house. You would have every young man in Savannah at your feet, if you went out a little more.'

'Miss Llewelyn, thank you for your advice, but let's leave it at that.'

'Very well, I'll do as you say, and I'll leave the talking to that fine mirror which I see over there which is telling you, in its way . . . do you know what?'

Elizabeth gave in to her natural curiosity.

'Tell me, it amuses me.'

'Every day it says: "Don't wait".'

A long silence followed this warning, given in deferential tones, because Miss Llewelyn never lost her sense of distance. At once, Elizabeth recalled her terror of the first wrinkles she had noticed that very morning in front of the same long mirror, and she shook her head with a forced smile.

'Perhaps you don't know,' the Welshwoman continued, 'that in the most fashionable salons you are referred to as the beautiful Englishwoman.'

Elizabeth blushed slightly.

Raising an eyebrow, Elizabeth waited with an indulgent air.

'You break people's hearts, Mrs Jones.'

For a few moments Elizabeth searched for the appropriate reply and finally said something which she intended to be ironic, but which was remarkably apt in view of what had happened in the past:

'Miss Llewelyn, it is always very educational talking to you . . . I think I shall try to rest for a while.'

'Would you like to take luncheon? It is nearly two o'clock.'

'I don't know. Later, perhaps.'

Throughout this conversation, Ned had remained motionless, listening with a concentration that made him simultaneously open his eyes and his mouth wide. He was disturbed at seeing Elizabeth in bed, as if about to sleep, when he had seen them laying the table downstairs. For him, lunch with his mother was one of the best times of the day, and he was upset by this hitch in the course of everyday life.

As soon as Miss Llewelyn had gone, he ran over to Elizabeth's bedside. At once, the eternal dialogue of love resumed, but from Ned's side with a note of alarm:

'Mom, I'm here.'

She reassured him as usual, but unable to bear the sight of his pained look, she added against her better judgement:

'Nothing has changed, darling, your Mama is going to have a few minutes' sleep and then we'll go down to lunch.'

He waved his Indian with a sudden burst of impatience.

She made an effort to calm him, but he guessed that something was being hidden from him which threatened his happiness and, as in a battle against the powers of evil, he whispered an appeal to a secret rallying of his own forces:

'Zonathan, Mama, Zonathan!'

'Oh, be quiet,' she begged. 'I've already said . . .'

The child was no longer able to keep quiet. Almost beside himself, he said aloud:

'But, Mama, I'm still Zonathan.'

Elizabeth felt her blood freeze. Putting a hand to Ned's mouth, she ordered:

'I forbid you, I forbid you . . .'

At the same time she heard the words forming in her mind:

'The adulterous heart cries out his name.'

She had thought she heard the strange phrase during the ceremony in Christ Church, but it was blurred and failed to reach her; now it was fearfully precise.

Her strength failed and she fell back on the pillow, while Ned sobbed and went to hide under the bed. She could not move, but wanted to call him back. In vain, for no sound came from her mouth and she felt as though struck dumb. She was terrified by the sounds of grief coming to her from beneath the bed.

' . . . for having loved too much,' she repeated to herself. 'Loved too much.'

Suddenly regaining her senses, she slipped out of the bed, then held out a hand to the child, who was curled up like a wounded bird, and tried to pull him toward her.

'No,' he said. 'No.'

'Forgive me, darling, I frightened you without meaning to. Ned, my dear Ned, don't upset your Mama.'

'Zonathan,' he repeated.,

She realized she was powerless against such obstinacy, at least for the time being. Shameful and desperate, she gave in.

'Very well, Jonathan, come on.'

He immediately stood in front of her with his hair tousled while she knelt by the bed. She had difficulty in recognizing her everyday lover in this boy who was looking at her in silence: with an air of determination, though not a look of triumph, he waited for her to get up . . . Where were the stormy emotions that sometimes tired her? He simply seemed different, as if in some indefinable way, something had made him grow up. He was grasping the Indian doll by the foot in his hand, like a fragment of childhood in the little man that Ned was now becoming.

She got up. A wave of indignation swept through her and she said, in a slightly trembling voice:

'Go and stay quietly in your room while I get dressed, then we'll go down to lunch. Do you understand?'

He nodded.

'But first, remember that you promised not to say anything about Jonathan. We must only mention him when we're alone. Do you remember that?'

'But I am Zonathan,' he said obstinately.

'When you're alone with me, not with other people. You promised.'

He did not reply, but left to go to his room. She felt a lump in her throat, realizing the extent of the disaster. She knew only too well that she had lost him. With that small figure, striding resolutely away, something irreplaceable was vanishing for ever, an affection that filled her heart, but which he perhaps no longer wanted. At that very minute, life was changing. Without knowing it, Ned was taking his childhood with him from one room to another.

She got back into her clothes, but instead of a dress she put on the navy blue dressing-gown she had worn at breakfast.

# 22

As he had promised, Charlie Jones came by to see Elizabeth after the burial, but much later than expected. In fact, he did not arrive until the moment of the dessert, a strawberry ice-cream designed to warm the heart of a small boy. It had failed to do so, however, and the meal had taken place in an unusual silence, which still hung over it, for silence can leave traces like wisps of invisible mist behind it.

Charlie Jones quickly sensed this indefinable mystery in the air. Even though he was in deep mourning, he had the rejuvenated look of a man who has just taken one of his fellow creatures to his final resting-place.

'My dear Elizabeth,' he said as he sat down. 'I guess this ceremony must have had a disproportionate effect on you. The Anglican Church has a feeling for pomp and ceremony. Everything is simpler among us Presbyterians. Could I have a little of that ice-cream?'

The young woman rang and a place was laid in front of Charlie Jones.

'I must say, the prayers at the tomb were interminable. Why do we have to remind the Lord that Will died and that, as a good Protestant, he deserves his place in paradise? Your little boy seems very silent today. Hello, Ned.'

The child did not reply. Elizabeth quickly intervened:

'He was upset at seeing me lying down in bed as though I were ill.'

'Sensitive, sensitive like the dear father whom he resembles more and more.'

'Doesn't he?'

'I don't know if you realize,' Charlie Jones said, helping himself to a large portion of strawberry ice, 'that all Dimwood was in Christ Church, even including our dear Souligou in a dark violet cap bristling with horns like those of a devil. Expect a few visitors, one of whom at least will dazzle you. By the way, I hope you have found a safe place for the packet which I gave you the other day in the carriage.'

'Of course, Uncle Charlie.'

'I don't want to be inquisitive and I won't ask if you've opened it, but you know that no one has any idea what Willy Hargrove left you, myself no more than anyone else. Like everyone, I'm longing . . .'

Taken aback by the eagerness in Charlie Jones's eyes, she replied without thinking:

'You'll soon know, because I want your advice . . .'

'Always at your service.'

There was an uncomfortable pause. Out of the corner of her eye she was watching her son who, with his hands on the table, seemed to be waiting for an opportunity to get up and leave the room. She thought that never before had she seen him so well-behaved, or so pretty; and she had to overcome a sudden surge of love for the little creature who had become solemn and self-absorbed in barely two hours. She noticed that Charlie Jones was also looking at his grandson and seemed as intrigued as she was.

Carelessly, she said, 'I so often think of the plantation that I sometimes imagine I'm walking there as I did in the old days, along the river by the pine trees.'

'You would be welcomed with open arms. Of course, not everyone is still there: Minnie is married in Louisiana . . .'

A name rose to Elizabeth's lips and she could not refrain from asking:

'Fred?'

'Oh, that's a mystery . . . A cavalry officer in faraway Colorado. We never have any news, fond as we are of him. But he changed after the accident.'

The young woman bowed her head. A punch in the chest would have seemed less painful. She could see the thin, passionate face bravely declaring his love for her.

She gave a little gasp.

'What is it?'

'Nothing,' she said. 'Memories . . . The great house with all its rooms, the long corridors, the balls . . .'

She said the first thing that came into her head, because suddenly she was frightened. For the past few moments, Ned had been looking at her too closely, as if he too wanted to walk through the unknown old house.

'Nothing has changed. It's all the same. In my opinion a few good licks of paint would do wonders for the fading walls . . .'

'I hope the garden hasn't been touched.'

'Of course not. The flowers are bursting out everywhere: gardenias, oleanders, rhododendrons and . . .'

She stopped him by rising to her feet. Charlie Jones and Ned followed suit. She suddenly had the feeling that she was going too far into her memories and wanted to stop there. In any case, there was no strawberry ice-cream left. However, her curiosity revived as they were walking toward the hall. She smiled to herself.

'Before you go, I'd love to know if the round room, the forbidden one on the top floor, is still there: the room where no one dare stay for a minute.'

Charlie Jones burst out laughing. 'The room where conscience spoke? Walled up. It knew too much.'

He was still laughing in the street as he put on his large black hat.

# 2
# REINVENTING LOVE

# 23

*T*owards the end of that afternoon, while Betty was taking an uncommunicative young Charles-Edward for a walk, Elizabeth lay down in her room and was on the point of falling asleep when Celina announced a visitor. For the first time, the housekeeper's face lit up a little when she mentioned that the person 'preferred not to give a name', but insisted on seeing Madam at once.

It must be Annabel, Elizabeth thought. So why the mystery?

Aloud, she said: 'Ask this person to be so kind as to wait for a moment.'

'In the little blue drawing-room, Madam?'

'Of course,' she said, resignedly.

'Let it be my little blue hell,' she thought, tidying her hair in front of the large mirror. 'If it is Annabel, it may be painful, but emotional. She has little affection for me, but she needs me to force her way into society.'

Her taffeta dress, which she had put back on, suited her wonderfully, as the mirror told her when she enquired of it one last time; and, with a confident step, the beautiful widow went down the stairs.

In the drawing-room, she thought she had lost her wits.

Before her stood the handsomest man she had ever seen, or so she thought: tall, broad-shouldered, his torso enclosed in a light red tunic with impressive frogging, while braided stripes were wrapped around the sleeves (she recognized the sleeves), his long legs pressed into dark blue linen trousers and, at the very summit of this human edifice, a slightly tousled head which she recognized with a cry of joy.

'Oh, Billy! It's you!'

Throwing herself at his chest, she wrapped her arms around him and clasped him like a tree. Without a second's hesitation, he took her head in his hands and placed his mouth on hers . . . Letting her arms fall to her sides, she felt close to fainting.

'How handsome you have grown!' she stammered at last, laughing.

'The uniform always impresses the ladies,' he said with false modesty. 'You haven't forgotten me?'

'Forgotten you? Not altogether! But how much has happened! You aren't still angry about my slapping your face on the stairs?'

'Elizabeth, when a boy gets a slap from a pretty girl, he doesn't flinch, he waits to see what will come next. And then, you came to do my tie up for me and make peace, you remember?'

She sharply interrupted this delightful flow of nonsense.

'Billy, I have reason not to like this room, and every door seems to me to have ears. Follow me.'

Leaving the little blue drawing-room in a swirl of taffeta, she led him down a corridor which went from one end of the house to the other, ending at the foot of a steep indoor stairway. Thirty steps took them up to a long veranda protected from the neighboring gardens by a green trellis. A lattice of thousands of wooden lathes allowed the soft light to filter through, and in this isolated spot, where one could see without being seen, one was sure of not being overheard.

There were rocking chairs, but Elizabeth and Billy instinctively preferred to remain standing.

'A splendid place for secret discussions,' Billy said with the laugh of a mischievous student. 'But it doesn't suggest the South to me.'

'It comes from Spain, via Carolina.'

'So let's say Spanish things, fiery, passionate words. Who'll start? Suddenly I feel idiotically shy.'

'And I feel that I am going to say things that I should not, but which, if I don't say them, will burst my heart.'

'Let it burst straight away to make things simpler.'

Once more, she threw herself against his chest, as in the little blue hell, and buried her face in the gold braid:

'Billy,' she sighed, 'why wasn't it you I married?'

To her great surprise, he answered gently, raising Elizabeth's face to the level of his own red lips.

'My beloved, there were two men in your life.'

She struggled free.

'What do you mean, Billy? There was Ned, and he was the only one at Great Meadow who asked for my hand.'

With unexpected urbanity, Billy dropped on one knee:

'Do you think I have come here for any other reason today?'

She leaned toward him and covered his face with kisses.

'Dear Billy, don't talk to me about other men, I have suffered too much from them.'

At once they both got up and clasped each other with all their strength as though each afraid that the other might be torn away. Ignoring the rocking chairs, they sat on a bench along the wall.

'The way things stand between us,' he said with sudden gravity, 'we owe each other the full truth. Perhaps you never thought that I was the only person in the world who knew the truth about that duel which is still a mystery for people in Savannah. When the man who I shall not again mention to you, spoke your name, I was so close that I could hear, but no one else apart from myself could understand.'

Without answering, she looked at him so sadly that even he was bewildered for a moment, trying to see what was in those limpid eyes from which all joy had vanished.

'Is anything wrong?' he asked finally in a stifled voice, as though some curse was already threatening the happiness they both glimpsed.

'Save me,' she said.

Immediately, he took her in his arms and said, in a voice which she did not yet recognize:

'I'm here to protect you against anything. Who would dare . . .?'

'Somebody knows the name that you don't want to speak and that name hurts him, the child, my little Ned. I told it to him. I couldn't help it. There, it's done, now you know.'

'But why?'

'How do I know. Death is powerless against love. I wanted the child to take the other's place.'

She was about to fall down at his knees, but he pulled her to her feet.

'No, never! You are mine. You love me and I love you. Nothing else matters. The child will forget and you, my Elizabeth, will see that in my arms I can make you forget the entire world and all its ghosts. When shall we marry?'

With delight and stupefaction, she stammered.

'I don't know, Billy.'

'Don't put it off because I'm in mourning. That doesn't matter much to me. There was a great gulf between me and my grandfather. We had nothing in common; but we must think of society and its primitive attachment to tradition. Let's say two months. Why not at Christmas?'

The word, full of light, made her smile.

'Christmas, Billy! Christmas!'

Suddenly, she was twelve years old and imagining Christmas in England, the countryside white as far as the eye could see, the bells ringing in the little Norman churches against the vast silence of the snow.

Billy stood before her with a smile that abolished everything and drew her out of herself. His impertinent, pugnacious nose and red lips were irresistible, like the windswept hair, at once reddish and brown — in short, the whole of this magnificent being in his splendid uniform sprinkled with gold by the sun shining through the lattice. Something in her saluted the vanquisher of all her fears, the exterminator of nightmares and, as a guarantee of all that, she noticed, a little above his waist, a short sword, suggestive of boldness . . .

With studied candor, she suddenly said:

'In any event, nothing can prevent us from announcing our engagement, because I suppose it goes without saying that we are engaged? I don't think you need to wait for that.'

'A few days, perhaps. Remember, the funeral was this morning.'

'Then a week, no longer. I don't want to wait.'

'Nor do I,' he said, with passionate urgency. 'Just think: a little cloth and some taffeta stand like a wall between us and the greatest happiness on earth . . .'

'A lot of taffeta,' she said, with a laugh.

'Don't even speak about it. All tonight I shall dream about the provocative rustle of your dress.'

Suddenly, he put his two hands round her waist and lifted her above him, laughing.

'Tell me you're mine,' he said.

'Are you mad? Haven't you understood? As soon as I saw you just now, I was sure of it.'

'And I have been thinking of nothing else since the slap on the stairs, six years ago. We were both sixteen . . .'

'We are sixteen again, but you had better put me down. Can't you hear? There's someone coming.'

'Someone's always coming, like in a play!' he said, putting her back on her feet as Celina appeared at the top of the stairs.

'I didn't call, Miss Celina,' Elizabeth said, coldly.

'Beg your pardon, Ma'am, but Ned is in the same agitated state as the night when you went out.'

'You should tell him that I have a visitor. You knew that. There was no reason to come up.'

'Pardon, Ma'am, but we were worried about him.'

'Very well. Tell him that I'll see him in a moment.'

Miss Celina left at once.

'She heard everything,' Elizabeth murmured. 'But I don't care. I don't care about anything now you're here.'

'What's wrong with your little boy?'

'Billy, I adore him, but he worries me. I'm relying on you to calm him down. He's just jealous. He's afraid I might go away. Billy, save me.'

She said the last words without thinking or knowing why. It was the sort of remark that sometimes came out inadvertently. Billy took no notice of it.

They went down to the drawing-room where Charles-Edward was waiting for his mother, the Indian hanging head downwards from his hand.

Frowning, he said nothing, but then, when he saw the officer coming toward them, there was an immediate transformation. Childhood seemed to leave his wondering face. In a sort of secret joy, he was revelling in his own astonishment. You could see that the world was changing shape around that little curly head, solely thanks to this presence which enlarged the blue drawing-room as if to open the way for a whole army. He was constantly asking for soldiers, and now he had one whose head seemed to touch the ceiling.

Just like his mother, he saw the uniform first and allowed himself to be dazzled by the gold braid on the red tunic and the gilded stripes that twisted around the sleeves, only later discovering the smile, at the top of this magnificent monument, addressed to him personally, acknowledging his existence. The Indian dropped from his hand.

'Mr Charles-Edward Jones?' asked the colossal presence, in a smooth voice.

And a hand reached out for him in which he gravely put his own.

At that moment, he noticed his mother, whom he had not at first seen, and gave her a little smile which might have been described as polite if not manly. Declarations of love were not appropriate when the armed forces were being deployed. However, Elizabeth bent down toward him and, very quietly, whispered in his ear — as if it were a secret — another secret:

'Be nice to Lieutenant William Hargrove, who has done you the honor of shaking your hand. One day he will be your Papa.'

Charles-Edward stared at her in an effort to understand and, to facilitate the operation, furrowed his brow, suddenly becoming someone who was not to be trifled with.

'Papa has gone,' he said softly.

As if caught in a trap, Elizabeth blushed.

'When a little boy's Daddy goes away, the Mummy asks some-one else to take his place. Do you see: so that the little boy is not without a Daddy any more? Only the Mummy can't be replaced. And you would be proud to have a Daddy in uniform. Most little boys have a Daddy in civilian clothes, but you, an officer . . .'

'Will I see him every day?'

'Perhaps not every day, but often.'

The private conversation must have seemed long to Lieutenant Hargrove, because he came and stood with his legs apart and his hands behind his back, next to these two people who were whis-pering like conspirators.

'Am I accepted?' he asked, in a mocking tone of voice.

Once more the brown eyes shone with admiration and a smile lit up the wilful little face. The uniform was once more exercising its power.

Elizabeth gave a merry little laugh: 'That looks to me like an unconditional yes,' she said, getting up. 'Say yes, Charles-Edward, and make your mother proud of you.'

'Yes,' he said.

'Yes *who*?' asked Billy.

To the surprise of them both, he replied:

'Yes, Lieutenant Hargrove.'

'Well answered,' said Billy. 'That's how we address one another among men.'

He took his shako and his cane that he had left on a chair.

'I'm keeping the Army for dinner,' said Elizabeth.

But she couldn't persuade him: custom demanded that Lieutenant Hargrove should be present at the family reunion at Charlie Jones's where, in memory of the deceased, one of those funereal meals was to take place that almost always turn into a happy gathering of survivors.

On the steps of the front door, they clasped one another passionately.

'Tomorrow morning at ten, I'll come in a tilbury and we can go out for a ride, if you wish . . .'

If she wished . . . Further unrestrained kisses, in front of an observant and attentive Charles-Edward.

When the door closed, Elizabeth turned round to see her son standing still, his large shining eyes brimming with questions.

'Won't I be Ned Jones any more?' he asked.

'You'll be Ned Hargrove-Jones, darling. It's a pretty name, don't you think?'

Once more he put on a sombre air of reflection, then in a firm voice declared:

'But I'm still Zonathan.'

# 24

*T*he next day before ten o'clock, the tilbury was in front of the house, harnessed to an apple-gray trotting pony. Billy had barely the time to jump down from his seat before Elizabeth was at the foot of the steps. Madly impatient and madly in love, she was waiting in a dove-gray taffeta dress which made at least as much noise as the one she had worn the evening before.

'You're late, you wretch!' she exclaimed gaily.

'You're early, you dreadful little English girl whom I adore!'

'At the first rendezvous, to be early is to be on time,' she said when she was by his side. 'Quickly, off we go — which paradise shall it be?'

'Bonaventure.'

'That name has been dangled in front of me for years.'

'It's a good omen.'

A festive sun was shining in the blue sky and Elizabeth had never felt more light in heart. She pressed herself against Billy, whispering sweet nothings to him, and he replied in kind.

'For the two of us, life is starting,' she said. 'Everything behind us no longer exists.'

'In my case, that's easy. I can forget years of idiotic contentment.'

'Dorcas?' Elizabeth asked, sniggering.

'What? You remember? A Lousiana millionaire took her away from me one evening, in a coach with a coat of arms on the door.'

They laughed so loudly that the pony itself seemed to catch their mood, pricking its ears and eager to break into a gallop. In less than a quarter of an hour, they were at the gate leading into the gardens at Bonaventure. The tilbury was handed over to black servants who looked after carriages, and two more lovebirds on earth drank in the romantic atmosphere under the century-old trees.

Endless paths of holm oaks criss-crossed beside a quiet little stream whose brown waters eventually joined those of the Savannah River.

Standing like rows of titans opposite one another, these gigantic pillars joined huge branches above the heads of those walking below to form a thick vault from which hung the fragile fabric of a gray-green curtain of Spanish moss: this strange vegetation, like torn rags, fluttered in every ocean breeze, until one eventually recognized the charm of its funereal appearance. Elsewhere, the sun beat on the cobbled paving beside the river, but in the cool of these tunnels of greenery, the most talkative of people naturally lowered their voices and gave in to the magic of the shade.

At this time of day, the gardens were empty, while at night they were the haunt of adventurous couples.

'Alone with you,' Elizabeth murmured. 'If this is a dream, I hope I never awake from it!'

'I'll give you better dreams than this,' Billy replied in the same hushed voice. 'You'll see.'

Reaching the end of the alleyway, they took another in the opposite direction beneath the same tangle of branches and leaves; at times the Spanish moss tickled their ears. At one point, Billy stopped.

'Look at those straight lines of bricks at the edge of the path. Inside you can see nothing but a large pile of trees, but once there was a huge house there, a palace: these bricks mark the outer walls. It's an interesting story. If you like, I'll tell it to you.'

She liked anything that would please this enchanting storyteller.

'Around 1760, a certain English colonel from Charleston was walking around this wilderness, when he came across the site. He fell in love with it and bought it. A lot of gold changed hands and Bonaventure rose from the ground. What feasts! What banquets! I can't describe things, but imagine, when the colonel's daughter was married. The nobility from all around, a free flow of imbecilities in the whirlwind of dances, jewels, beauties, intrigues, the procession of turkey hens and peacocks, in short, everybody, society! Can you imagine? Magnificent! Are you following?'

'I'm following, Billy. Carry on.'

'One evening when they were dining and making speeches, a lackey dressed like an admiral came and whispered in the ear of Tattnall, the son-in-law: "Sir, please forgive me, but there's a fire in the loft." "Very well, no problem. Have the table taken out onto the lawn by the river. We'll finish dinner there." So, getting up, he told his guests that he had had the idea of carrying on the meal at the water's edge, under the stars, and everyone, somewhat taken aback, followed him, continuing to chatter away as they did so. Liveried servants brought the tables and laid them with astonishing speed. No sooner said than done: they were dining by torchlight under the summer moon. This notion seemed so wonderfully fanciful to them that they were laughing and joking about it when suddenly someone noticed the flames licking out of the top-floor windows as if to watch them as they ate. Being light-headed and very brave — and much too far away from the house to be in any danger — they loudly praised their host's sang-froid. It is said that the flames shone from the glasses while they drank toast after toast to him. The house burned very acceptably until dawn, and nothing was left of it. Let's go and see the flower gardens; they're famous for their japonicas.'

Elizabeth was so struck by this story that she could not answer, but she nodded and he put his arm round her waist to lead her gently toward an isolated corner of the park where the flowers cascaded from the top of a little terrace.

'That's where you get the most famous view,' he explained.

They paused for a moment and the silence around them seemed so beautiful that they were unwilling to disturb it. In the distance, beyond the huge expanse of water and grassland, they could see the whole town with its white houses hidden among the trees, alive with joy and happiness beneath a radiant October sky.

Elizabeth was the first to speak, in a voice like a whisper:

'How far one feels from everything here,' she said, leaning against Billy. 'I don't want to forget this moment.'

'You'll never manage to count all the moments that are awaiting you with me that will be much more exciting. Just wait for the future I'm preparing for you,' he said, in a manly voice. 'And let's go and see the view from the top of this terrace. You won't believe your eyes.'

As they were walking toward a corner of the park, where some steps were hidden behind banks of flowers, she had the feeling that the rustling of her taffeta dress was scratching and chipping at the precious silence, and that it was getting on Billy's nerves. And he did indeed give a little laugh.

'If you knew the feeling that that skirt and that sound arouse in me, my dearest, you'd be afraid!'

'Afraid?'

'Oh, don't worry, I was only joking. It's just that I shall take a savage delight one evening in silencing it by tearing it off.'

'Oh, Billy, I won't wear it again.'

'Yes, yes, my love, do. But it drove me wild last night, because in my dreams you were there and I was clasping the void, but dying with happiness. Do you undersand?'

'No.'

'It doesn't matter. I'll explain, I'll explain everything. Now come. Can you see anything on the terrace?'

'A sort of summer house, with meshed windows . . .'

'A pagoda, with a rounded roof.'

'It's pretty, but a trifle odd.'

'A folly of Tatnall's: he wanted to take his coffee there and read his paper. We'll go inside for a moment and you'll see what a good place it is for admiring every detail of the view.'

The memory of the pinewood at Great Meadow flashed through Elizabeth's mind and she saw herself in Ned's arms.

'I'd rather go back now. I'm always a little worried about the child.'

He took both her hands and looked into her eyes.

'Tell me the truth, Elizabeth. Don't you trust your Billy?'

'Of course, if anything it's myself I don't . . .'

'What are you thinking? In public? And I in uniform?'

They took a few more steps and suddenly, grasping her head in both hands, he pressed his mouth to hers with the same hunger as Ned; and, as in the little wood six years earlier, she had the impression that she was being utterly obliterated, body and soul, dispossessed of herself, in these arms that supported her, preventing her from falling. She had only once before had this strange sensation with this same terrifying and delicious intensity. With Ned, the other times were only a feeble repetition of the first. The dizziness had vanished . . . Then later with Jonathan — but she put that memory aside.

'Must we wait much longer?' she asked, when he freed her.

'No. I've been thinking. I'm not prepared to let social convention stand in the way of nature and love . . . I'll arrange it all; but don't be afraid of me in this pagoda.'

They climbed up a dozen steps hidden in a mass of flowers; their scent, sweet, heavy and heady, was already turning the young woman's head more than that of her lover. The voice that she heard so distinctly in difficult moments insistently repeated to her not to stop here, but she was no longer mistress of her own actions.

The house, when they reached it, was larger than it had seemed from below. Built in the style of the pavilions in the gardens of a sultan's palace, with an onion dome, it had five or six little openings with trellis windows that could be opened or closed to give shade from the sun or to discourage the curiosity of passers-by. Inside, it was decorated with garlands of roses against a dark green background and broad padded seats lined the octagonal walls.

As soon as Elizabeth set foot in this exotic little parlor, she thought: 'I'm lost.'

But, contrary to her fears, Billy stood in front of one of the windows and in a calm voice pointed out all the buildings in the town, hiding in the ocean of greenery.

'Savannah, the forest town,' he said. 'Are you sure you'll be happy here, my darling? Because this is where we'll live, for ever.'

'Where wouldn't I be happy with you, Billy?'

'Do you see the port, there, where the tall masts of the ships are swaying?'

She nodded and, taking his arm, said in a strained voice:

'Billy, it's more than I can bear. I feel that we must leave.'

He drew her to him, stroking her face:

'What's wrong? Why are you so pale all at once?'

'Tired,' she murmured.

He kissed her and asked:

'Are you still afraid of me? Don't you love me?'

'Oh, Billy!'

She felt faint, and put both hands around Billy's neck to support herself.

'I love you only too much, but we must go.'

'One can never love too much. But you may be right: we must go.'

And he added simply:

'I am burning.'

Almost effortlessly, he lifted her off the ground and carried her in his arms to the flight of steps which he descended with the agility of an acrobat. Her head on his shoulder and both hands behind his neck, Elizabeth might have thought herself to be in one of those dreams that haunted her solitude.

'Happy?' he asked in her ear.

She didn't reply. Intoxicated by the flowers which brushed against her as they came down, she felt unable to open her mouth, but when Billy put her down on the gravel path, she came back to her senses and said, with a laugh:

'Another unforgettable moment!'

'And on a staircase, as once at Charlie Jones's,' he remarked.

They were still laughing and making their way to the gate, when a very distinguished voice hailed them from one of the vast alleyways of green oak trees. It was Mrs Harrison Edwards who was approaching, waving an arm bare up to the elbow. Dressed in mauve and topped by a wide shepherdess hat with black ribbons, she was striding quickly across with a mischievous smile on a face lit up by curiosity.

'What a wonderful surprise!' she called out from a distance. 'Our delightful Elizabeth, to whom I promised to show Bonaventure, has succumbed to the appeal of a uniform! Lieutenant Hargrove, I shall never forgive you, but I do find you magnificent in all that red.'

At every step, the reproaches and compliments multiplied. Relieved that she had paid heed to her premonition, Elizabeth did her best to appear composed and offered a cheek to the queen of society who was bearing down on them, shaking a mocking little finger.

'Traitress, I've caught you and I'm delighted. Lieutenant, what am I to imagine? Would my congratulations be premature?'

'Madam, imagine what is most obvious and you will be very close to the truth; but keep it to yourself, I pray you.'

'On my honor, mysterious young man. I was so looking forward to showing Elizabeth the delightful Turkish kiosk which is only two yards from here, but perhaps you've already . . .'

Elizabeth interrupted her:

'Alas, I'm already expected home. I must go.'

'Oh, what a pity! We'll arrange to meet another time. Miss Furnace tells the story of this architectural gem so well. She spent a month as a guest of the Sultan and he himself insisted on showing her the fairytale gardens of Topkapi and the marvellous little summer houses from which you can see the Bosphorus. It's one of that great travelers' best tales: she has captivated the town with her talent and the incredible richness of her memories. Her description of the harem in particular is a delight. But I'm keeping you. See you soon, dearest — and you, lieutenant: take care of our beautiful Englishwoman.'

With a fine sweep of the arm, she said farewell and left. Elizabeth and Billy looked at one another.

'She saw everything,' said Elizabeth.

'Everything,' he echoed. 'From that dark avenue she saw us when we came out of the pagoda into the sunlight and I was carrying you in my arms like a child. Whatever she didn't see, she will make up.'

'Billy, tomorrow the whole town will know.'

'No, my love, not tomorrow: this evening.'

'What a disaster!'

'On the contrary, the lady has forced my hand. Now, you must listen to Billy without trying to understand. I only ask you to obey me.'

'Anything, as long as we can belong to each other.'

'Then I'll take you straight home and leave Savannah as fast as I can . . . We must steal a march on them. Don't say anthing, don't ask any questions. Keep quiet. Do you think you can do that?'

'It's hard.'

'Our happiness depends on it.'

'Very well, but I shall not breathe . . .'

'Don't make a drama out of it, my love. Trust Billy.'

With long steps he marched her toward the tilbury. She could only keep up with him by grasping his arm and hopped rather than walked.

A little later they reached Elizabeth's house and there they said goodbye; but, seeing her anxious face, he felt a burst of tenderness.

'Look at me, my love. Do I look like someone who is unsure of himself, worried, defeated?'

She saw his eyes and his features light up and then the radiant smile of triumphant youth. Had she not made a huge effort to restrain herself, she would have leaped into his arms.

'You see,' he said, with a schoolboy's laugh. 'Happiness is winging toward us.'

Her eyes damp with tears, she also laughed.

# 25

*A*t home, everything was in turmoil. It was always the same when she went out, despite Celina's efforts. Once more the butcher's boy had been beaten by the gardener and, his nose bleeding, had vowed that he would never return.

As for young Charles-Edward, he was making the housekeeper anxious with his wild look and his refusal to talk. Elizabeth could see that for herself in the dining-room where he was waiting for the culprit. He was sulking brilliantly with the guile of a grown-up. Without quite turning his head away when his mother appeared, his sullen little face dropped.

'What's the matter?' she asked with exasperation.

'Why, nothing Mama, nothing at all.'

His voice was clear and calm. Childhood and tenderness had vanished from it.

She suffered for it. Nothing would be altered by her taking the child in her arms, nothing . . . She was dealing with someone who was jealous — jealous of the soldier whom he had nonetheless admired.

The clock struck two o'clock. A black servant came to lay the table for lunch.

'Only one place,' she said gently. 'Mr Ned will have lunch, and I'll just sit at my place without taking anything.'

The child was standing by the window watching people come and go in the square. Almost aggressively, his head turned and he looked at Elizabeth. The blow had struck home and she could read the words he was about to utter on the little, half-open mouth: he too would not have lunch; but she immediately outflanked him:

'Serve the corn pancakes first.'

Ned said nothing. Corn pancakes were one of his great weaknesses.

A few minutes passed in the still heavy silence of a passing storm blowing past. Finally, Ned was able to take his place beside his mother while she, sitting very upright in front of an empty plate, watched her adversary's behavior out of the corner of an eye. One pancake, then another disappeared. Elizabeth motioned for another to be served and a shy smile dimpled the round, pink cheeks of the defeated little boy.

'Aren't you hungry, Mummy?'

'No, darling. You can see: I'm giving you my pancake.'

Ned kept his thoughts to himself and polished off the extra pancake; after which, there were signs of an armistice. Elizabeth, still impassive, heard the cry of distress, delivered under his breath:

'Zonathan, Mummy.'

She did not move. She was resolved. Her heart beating, she finally put a finger to her lips and whispered in a firm voice:

'He has gone and he won't be coming back.'

A massive silence greeted this shattering news. She waited for a moment, but received no reply except a look of defiance.

# 26

*T*orn between her worries about Ned and the joy that her lover had brought into her life, she did not know what to do with herself, with her time. Ned, less and less her little boy, and more and more her son, was with Betty, who had taken him for a walk. As far as that was concerned, her mind was at rest, and then the memory of the hours spent with Billy obliterated everything despite the languid cravings of desire, a frightful and wonderful torture. Toward the end of the afternoon, she decided to go for a walk down the endless length of Bull Street. She seldom went here alone because at the end of the day this favorite haunt of society turned into a gossip-shop. However, she took the risk.

A light ocean breeze was stirring the leaves of the great sycamore trees, and the softening light cast little spots of pale gold on the ground. The number of strollers was increasing, making a sort of parade of little parasols and stovepipe hats: everything that Elizabeth most feared, for she remained a recluse; but she proceeded boldly, rather than remaining in her own company, to avoid thinking too much, alone at home.

In her light green dress which showed off her rich head of golden hair, she knew that she was very beautiful and pretended to admire the splendor of the centuries-old trees that hung above the heads of the elegant burghers of the town; but she could not help noticing that several people greeted her in a more emphatic way than usual. Among them, Algernon Steers gave a bow as he passed in which she thought she detected a hint of irony; or was she dreaming? She thanked him with an imperceptible nod.

What insolence! she thought. But how handsome he was.

She was struck by it and immediately drove away the untimely thought as though the Devil had whispered it to her. Yet she felt more and more disturbed by the interest aroused by her presence and quickly turned round and started to walk back homeward.

She had hardly gone a dozen yards before she found herself face to face with Mrs Harrison Edwards. More ostentatious than ever in a dress of bright yellow tussore, she was coming up the avenue toward her and cried:

'You! What an unexpected pleasure! Imagine: I was just thinking about you and, guess what, here you are!'

'Oh, I was only passing through on my way home. I must say that all these people . . .'

'Not so fast, Elizabeth, my dear. You must give me a minute.'

With a gesture of discreet familiarity, she linked their arms.

'All these people, you say? Don't worry, they are all looking at you.'

'It's precisely . . .'

'Precisely what, my dearest? You are noticed, people smile at you, they are happy that you are happy, because they have guessed everything.'

'Oh!' Elizabeth exclaimed indignantly. 'You gave your word!'

The splendid round arm drew back a little, but not altogether.

'What do you mean? I'm too fond of you to be upset by it, but your innocence does perturb me a little. Don't you know that Savannah is the most curious and the most inquisitive town in the South? And do you imagine that you can pass by unnoticed in a tilbury with a young officer, on your way out to Bonaventure and back again?'

Elizabeth suddenly blushed.

'I don't know what's so extraordinary about that. Billy and I have known each other since we were sixteen.'

'That's what makes it so appealing, my dear Elizabeth. Everyone is talking about an engagement, because everyone was sorry to see your widowhood prolonged. Why, they nearly applauded you in the street — both young, handsome and so romantic!'

Still pink with embarassment, Elizabeth searched desperately for something to say. She would have liked to drop Mrs Harrison Edwards and everyone else and flee as fast as she could; but the finely-molded arm holding her was surprisingly strong.

'Thank you,' she murmured.

'Thank me! Why on earth! What have I done? Let me kiss you. I want to be the first.'

And, without waiting for permission, she grasped Elizabeth in both hands and brushed her delicately painted lips against her cheek which still miraculously preserved some of its adolescent freshness.

She knew very well that the people who were stopping around her and Elizabeth, observing them as if on a stage, knew everything; but she had said nothing. Her word of honor, still more or less intact, might serve a later purpose.

# 27

*R*eturning home, the young woman felt more perplexed than ever. Alternately happy and anxious, she walked back and forth in what she still called her little blue hell, trying to understand Billy's mysterious behavior. Where was he? When would he come back? Would he really marry her? And suddenly she saw once again the wonderful smile that he had given her as he left, and she burst out laughing with happiness.

She rang for the housekeeper.

'Where is Mr Ned?' she asked.

Celina did not answer, but her eyes, which usually wore an absent look, filled with a wave of human tenderness. Had she too known the anxieties of love? What secrets lived within her? Almost nothing was known about her except that she came from a particular region in Central Europe and, for political reasons, had been driven out of her country. Like so many other victims of persecution, she had taken refuge in America. However that may be, she pretended to have misheard the question.

'Mr Ned is with his Black Mammy who is going to give him a bath.'

Caught off balance, Elizabeth remarked curtly:

'From today, I'm the one who will give him his bath. Go and tell Mammy that, Miss Celina. I'll be up in a moment.'

Celina bowed and went out, leaving her mistress astonished at her directive. Many women insisted on personally bathing their children when they were still quite young. Hadn't her own mother washed her, with a considerate if slightly rough hand, until she was seven? Without quite knowing why, Elizabeth refused to do the same. She did not want to admit that she did not dare and, this time, giving way to an impulse she had given the order to Celina.

Foolishly, she said to herself, and went upstairs.

The bathroom, next door to Ned's room, was small, with dark red tiles. It overlooked the garden through a window with white curtains. Porcelain tiles, decorated with flowers, protected the lower half of the walls. There was nothing dreary about this little room where the light fell on a bath with large copper taps, a tub and a towel rail.

Elizabeth strode in resolutely. On her knees, dressed entirely in white, the vast Black Mammy was taking off Ned's sailor suit. Turning her ebony face to look up at her mistress, her shining white eyes and teeth exposed by a wide smile, she said in an irresistibly soft voice:

'Yes, Ma'am, Miss Celina told me, but Mammy knows better how to wash children.'

'Mammy, I must be obeyed,' Elizabeth answered with a smile. 'Get me a big white apron.'

Celina who was standing by the door vanished at once.

'Massa Ned like Mammy to wash him with the soap,' the nursemaid continued, taking off the boy's trousers.

He remained silent but was watching his mother closely. She felt embarrassed: the lovely brown eyes seemed to be asking questions that the lips did not form. In his serious little face, the young woman could see no trace of the loving flame that had so often made her heart beat faster.

Now that he was undressed, he stood naked in front of her and, in a sudden fit of impatience, she looked round and asked:

'Why doesn't Miss Celina come? The child will catch cold.'

'Oh, no, Ma'am!' said the black woman, throwing a large towel around her 'tresha' and pressing him hard against her.

Celina came back at almost the same moment and offered Elizabeth a huge white apron, made to fit the Black Mammy. The young woman put it on as best she could, but Celina had to tie the cords as high as possible, because the apron was hanging too low.

It was easy for the housekeeper to see her mistress' difficulty and she tried to help. A sponge larger than a melon was waiting in the warm water of the tub where Ned, freed from her grasp, took his place. Standing in the light, his perfect little body radiated innocence and beauty, so much so that his mother was struck dumb by it. For a year, she had avoided seeing him undressed, because the young body was becoming more masculine as it grew and she preferrred to hand over to the black maid.

'Perhaps if you were to kneel down,' Miss Celina suggested.

But Elizabeth appeared not to understand. Her eyes involuntarily turned toward that part of the male body that she did not want to see because she found it deeply disturbing.

The next moment was painful. Ned looked at Elizabeth and, young as he was, could not avoid reading the expression of distaste that contorted his mother's face. In terror, he turned toward Black Mammy who was also observing the young woman. Without hesitation, the black maid dipped the sponge in the tub and squeezed the warm water across the boy's back and shoulders.

Elizabeth promptly stood up and called the housekeeper.

'Help me to get out of this apron,' she said, with a forced laugh. 'I think Mammy is right, she does it better than I do.'

The sponge dipped in and out of the water, running across the pinkish brown skin, which shone like marble.

'Mammy knows,' the nursemaid said, smiling like an ogress. 'Ladies don't know how to do it like Mammy.'

Now, with honey-colored soap in her huge hands, she was covering the soft, smooth skin with foam.

Rid of her white apron, Elizabeth fled.

In her room, she threw herself on the bed and hid her face in her pillow. She had covered herself in ridicule in front of these two women and was stifled by shame. Why had she given way to the stupid desire to show her authority? What could Mammy and Celina be thinking of her? And Ned? She didn't even want to consider it. She had frightened him. How could he guess what it was about his body that so strongly displeased his mother. She had wounded him with a single blow, she was killing love.

That evening, regardless, she went to say goodnight to him and say his prayers as usual, but he didn't hold her back for news of Jonathan. After squeezing him in her arms and covering him with kisses, she was about to leave when suddenly she started to cry at her own stupidity and heartlessness. Only then did he react in the way he used to do.

'Why are you crying, Mummy?' he asked, stroking her cheek. 'Do you still love me a little?'

'Yes, yes, darling, more than ever . . . Now you must go to sleep.'

By the light of the little lamp, she saw him smile with a look of good humor that consoled her, because it brought back the child he had been, and she went away reassured; but something inside told her that a secret world was being forever closed behind her. By removing the evening Jonathan from Ned's dreams, wasn't she also removing him from her own heart?

In her room, she paused before getting undressed, putting off the moment when she would slip between her sheets and face up to insomnia. From time to time she went to Ned's door and listened for his breathing. At last she heard it, light and regular.

Somewhat relieved, she sat in front of her mirror to let down her hair and gave herself over entirely to recalling her morning with Billy. Now her heart could indulge in a joy that wiped out every shadow. She returned over and again to the wonderful moment when he picked her up to carry her down the stairs from the Turkish summer house. Her head had been so close to his that she could smell his flesh. Suddenly, in the silence of night, she heard two knocks at the front door.

She waited for a moment, then came down just in time to see the servant open the door.

A woman came in, dressed in black from head to foot under a lace mantilla, also black. Quite tall, she carried herself very erect and her whole figure emanated out an almost regal grandeur.

'Elizabeth,' she said simply.

In amazement, she recognized the voice of Annabel. She was so astonished that she could do nothing except walk toward her, holding out her hands, and lead her into the little drawing-room. Only there did Annabel lift the veil and, in the light of the oil lamps, Elizabeth was finally able to see the face which she could hardly recognize at first, so much had it aged. What remained was the nobility of the features, the great arched eyebrows, the straight nose and the fine disdainful mouth; but behind the dark eyes lay a terrifying sadness. The cheeks had shrunk under the cheekbones, and the face had lost the glow that made it famous. Something else had replaced it which could be defined only as a sort of weariness with life, softening the natural pride with a hint of humanity.

At once, she let her mantilla drop, revealing shoulders that were still beautiful and a bust that suggested that the rest of the body had remained unaltered.

They sat down.

In a calm and politely controlled voice, she began:

'What should I call this unannounced visit? A friendly visit? What do you think, Elizabeth?'

'Call it what you like. It is so sudden that I haven't had time to think about it.'

'Might I help you? Let's be blunt: don't I have every reason to hate you? Did you ever ask what ties of love bound me to the man with whom you became infatuated? The fact that he was my husband did not stop you writing to him either in your own hand, or with the help of an accomplice whose name is still unknown to me. He tore the letters up, but not very thoroughly. Do you follow me, or do I have to be more explicit?'

'Madam,' Elizabeth said, her face paling. 'Might I know what all this is leading to?'

'To something very simple: I never doubted that your love was real and sincere, even though it was impossible. That is why I felt pity for you.'

'Pity?'

'Yes, because you were suffering. Did you feel any pity for me when through your fault my husband was killed in that absurd duel?'

The young woman, overcome with emotion, tried to speak, but the words stuck in her throat. She sat up and bowed her head.

A slight smile crossed Annabel's lips and she said, almost in a whisper:

'All the protestations in the world could not match that simple gesture.'

As she had leaned forward to say these words, Elizabeth's eye was caught by a ruby hanging between her breasts. The stone, wonderfully lustrous, was shaped strangely, like a drop of liquid. It shone at the end of a slender gold chain on the visitor's delicate skin.

'Elizabeth,' she said, 'do you want us to make peace?'

'With all my heart, Annabel.'

The words burst out, as if in a wave of joy. Everything that remained of the child inside the young Englishwoman was in that cry. She could not avoid seeing in Annabel's eyes the desperate sadness, bordering on despair, that she had noticed earlier.

Sitting on the same sofa, they were now so close that Elizabeth could feel Annabel's breath; it had a bitter smell.

Elizabeth felt a sudden wave of repulsion, but did not show it. This woman in mourning took on a new and frightening appearance in her eyes. The Annabel of former times gave way to a kind of apparition. She did not dare go further, but in her heart the words were there: she had the impression of being in the presence of death. A rush of common sense came to her aid. 'Don't be ridiculous,' she told herself. 'Annabel is not well, and she is full of goodwill.'

'Since the cloud has passed,' Annabel said, with a smile that stopped short of her eyes, 'we can talk freely. But I must add, under the seal of secrecy. First and foremost, can I be sure that these two doors do not have ears?'

'You take one, I'll look behind the other.'

Lowering her voice, Annabel whispered:

'Tiptoe over to it without making a noise, then open it quickly.'

'I know the system,' said Elizabeth. 'I'll be quick.'

'Be very quick.'

They each walked over to a different door. Elizabeth was struck by the majesty of Annabel in her funereal dress, its taffeta train muttering in some unknown tongue on the parquet flooring.

The young woman opened the door rapidly and found no one, but Annabel was luckier. With an expert hand, she swung back the door with lightning speed and saw the lackey, Joe, fall at her feet in his red livery. Without a word, he got up as best he could, glanced at Annabel and took to his heels, his face contorted with horror.

'He is incorrigible,' said Elizabeth. 'But now we do at least know we are alone.'

'Will you keep that man in your service?'

'First of all, I'll get him to explain himself to my gardener. He's the person who ensures order around here.'

Annabel raised an eyebrow but said nothing. They returned to their seats on the sofa.

# 28

W hile this scene was unfolding in the blue drawing-room, a quite different discussion was taking place on the first floor. Sitting on the edge of his bed, Ned refused to go back into it despite the insistence of Celina who was standing beside him. The weak light of the night lamp left both of them in a half-light in which only the boy's white pyjamas could be seen. He thus seemed oddly alone, the housekeeper's black dress making her fade into the darkness.

Ned shook his curly head

'No,' he was saying. 'I'm going to stay like this until she comes back.'

And at the same time he kicked two little bare feet which made one think of flowers.

'Your Mummy will be very angry if you don't sleep,' said the black dress.

'I'll go to sleep when she's here. Why is she downstairs?'

'I told you, she has a visitor.'

There was a long silence.

'Why are you staying, Miss Celina?'

'So that you won't be afraid all by yourself.'

'I'm not afraid. When she's not here, I can't close my eyes. First of all Mummy has to tell me a story.'

'A story? I can easily tell you a story myself. I know plenty.'

'Not my story. When Mummy doesn't tell it, he comes all alone, and it's not the same thing.'

'Who comes, Mr Ned?'

'Why, the story, as soon as I'm in bed. But you don't understand anything, Miss Celina.'

'Suppose you went to bed and I stayed near you?'

'Then he wouldn't come.'

'But where does he come from?'

'From over there, behind, next to the big corridor.'

He stopped talking and went on swinging his feet in the air. Celina looked around hardly able to make out the bedposts. Beyond them she could see nothing but darkness. She felt slightly uneasy because of the oddness of the situation and the mystery that the little boy was weaving around himself. Now she certainly didn't dare leave him alone.

'You tell me your story, Master Ned.'

'No, the story is our secret, I promised.'

'You say it comes from the back of the room. Is the story somebody? Just tell me that and I won't ask anymore.'

'I'm not saying anything. You can't understand. It's our secret.'

Miss Celina took a step toward the bedside table and lifted the lamp, moving it around her until she saw a chair at the foot of the bed. She went up to it, put the night light back in its place and sat down.

There followed a few minutes' silence.

'Go away,' said Ned.

'No, Master Ned, I'm not allowed to leave you alone unless you are asleep.'

'Go 'way, Miss Celina,' he begged.

'I can't.'

Suddenly he stood up on the bed, shaking with rage.

'If you stay he won't come,' he shouted. 'I'm not afraid. Go 'way.'

'I can't do that, Master Ned. I must stay until your mother comes.'

At this, he let himself fall on the bed and, burying his head in the pillow, began to weep with great howls of anger. Celina did not move, not knowing what to do, but she was certain that she should not leave her post.

The crying fit lasted a long time. In the darkness that made this violent outburst of frustration seem quite sinister, the housekeeper had begun to feel frightened, when suddenly there was silence around her and the bed. Exhausted, Ned had lapsed into sleep.

She waited for a long time until the sleeping boy's breathing had deepened. Then, leaning over Ned, she managed to draw the blanket very gently until it covered him up to the shoulders.

Conscience kept her there a short while longer; then, very cautiously, she crept toward the door and went out.

# 29

*I*n the blue drawing-room, Annabel was concluding the story of the great insult she had had to endure a few days after her marriage to Jonathan Armstrong. Her voice was lowered, but still as precise as ever, ringing out like a long chant of dull, violent hatred.

'Elizabeth, I would ask you to imagine the vast room dimly lit by candles and the most refined society of the region going in procession past my husband and myself, with their hypocritical smiles and all the bowing and scraping of their old-fashioned manners. It only took me a minute to realize that in this masquerade of courtesy, they were telling me that they did not want me, and I had the impression of being suspended on the rim of hell. Do I need to add that I did not receive the merest word of thanks or any visit? The door that I hoped would be opened to me was slammed in my face. Elizabeth, you have a rebel before you. My husband did not suffer from this insult as I did, because he knew that by birth he was far superior to these little provincial aristocrats, but he understood my indignation and when I told him of my decision to leave for Europe, he accepted without hesitation.'

This phrase was like a knife wound for Elizabeth and she could not help exclaiming:

'Without hesitation!'

There was no response, but Annabel looked at the young woman with silent compassion.

'Should I continue?' she asked.

Elizabeth nodded.

'I do not need to tell you that we lived for a time in Vienna: I don't know how you learned that, and having our address enabled you to encourage him to betray me. No, don't protest, I'm determined to let it pass. In that city, the finest in Central Europe, I had my moment of celebrity and I knew some happiness until the day when he managed to have our marriage annulled. All that, you knew. How joyful he was! What triumph! And you?'

Elizabeth's mouth started to open, but not a word came out. Annabel was content with looking at her and her lips shaped into a long sardonic smile.

'How I love that silence,' she said at length. 'How much you say, without saying anything! At that time, it was in the summer of 1851, you still had the naivety and impulses of a schoolgirl. I eventually forgave you, though without forgetting. Now, could I just make a small observation about the person you have become today?'

'Of course, Annabel,' Elizabeth said softly.

'Since the start of our conversation, you have been glancing from time to time at the ruby which I wear on my breast. It was a present from the betrayer. The stone, which is of unmatched beauty, was left to him by his mother. He gave it to me the day after our divorce as a sign of repentance, because he knew very well that he had behaved dishonorably. I accepted it and put it on my bosom, of which I could still feel very proud. Our separation was kept secret. The sight of me wearing this ruby was an embarrassment to him. That was my only revenge. I wore the ruby whenever I could, and all Vienna admired it. By Vienna, I mean the aristocracy, whose claim cannot be denied. Where are the lands, where are the titles, where is the sovereign of the one to which I, like you, belong? I am only a poor expatriate who remembers her origins in the way one dreams of a lost homeland, and lives by those dreams. But enough of that.'

With a courtly solemnity, she got up and took off the ruby from around her neck.

'I shall give it to you,' she said. 'Will you accept it as a token of reconciliation?'

The young woman also rose to her feet and endured a moment of torment. Everything in her cried out: 'No!' But a powerful wave of desire prevented her from refusing.

'Silence means assent,' Annabel said, putting the chain around her neck. 'You will never be more beautiful than you are today. It's a gift of Heaven. Enjoy it. There: it's fastened. Go and look at yourself in the mirror.'

Elizabeth did not move.

'I don't know if I should . . .' she muttered.

'Lovely child, don't think twice about it. Let me kiss you. You have lifted a terrible weight off me by relieving my heart of an unspeakable burden of resentment.'

As she said this, she leaned toward Elizabeth and pressed her cold lips to cheeks that burned with shame.

'Smile for me,' said Annabel, in a voice of near entreaty. 'Don't you see that I am trying to like you? Hatred is so sad. Let's sit down a moment longer.'

Too overwhelmed to reply, Elizabeth obeyed.

'When I learned that I would never see him again in this world,' Annabel went on in a soft voice, 'and when I finally realized that he was lost to me for ever, I felt at the same time — how shall I say? — destroyed . . . When I went back to Dimwood, I read in everyone's eyes a reluctance to recognize me. But let's end our conversation there. We shall no doubt meet again. Wear that lovely ruby, it suits you so well.'

They both got up.

'Annabel,' Elizabeth said.

'No,' said Annabel, taking her by both hands and squeezing them. 'No.'

She walked quickly to the door and vanished. Through the window, the young woman saw the tall, haughty silhouette sailing toward a coach that was waiting for her on the corner of the street.


# 30


Now, alone in the little drawing-room that was becoming more and more unbearable to her, Elizabeth, eaten up with shame, was about to tear off the ruby when she had an irresistible desire to look at herself beforehand in the long mirror over the fireplace, as if to savor her humiliation.

There, her turmoil gave way to unadulterated admiration. It had been undeniably beautiful on Annabel's dull, pale skin, but between the amber-colored breasts of the lovely Englishwoman the stone came alive and flared, happy to rediscover its glow and magic power.

She marvelled at herself, passionately, in love with the image that looked out at her from the golden frame. With both hands she let her hair fall on her shoulders, turning a little to one side, then the other, the tips of her fingers playing with this mysteriously attractive stone. One could go on and on looking at it, because it changed color according to the light, and the young woman soon found that there were certain translucid glows in its mysterious depths like a light wine disappearing into a heavy, rich red. She could not stop exploring the variegated colors in the rays from the lamp; then, suddenly, her hands fell and she gave a cry. What Annabel had put on her breast was a drop of blood.

The intent was clear to her. The ruby which Jonathan had offered Annabel recalled the death of the unfaithful husband. Between the two women, there was this crimson drop, the blood of Jonathan.

Horrified, she tore the ruby off her neck and threw it down on the carpet.

Back in her room, she anticipated a dreadful night. She was even unwilling to undress and instead of sleeping, which would be impossible, she considered a solitary walk through the streets; but would she not risk being approached by 'individuals'? There was always laudanum, but here too she hesitated. This was a desperate solution and she remembered her very first, unhappy experiment with it.

Uncertain what to do, she called the housekeeper. Perhaps she was sleeping at this rather late hour. Even so, she rang and then felt guilty about having done so; but she had to see someone, not to be alone with herself, even for a moment, and she would invent some story or other; she'd think of something.

However, she was delighted to see Miss Celina appear after only a few minutes, dressed as usual, but with a candlestick in her hand, because there was no light now downstairs.

'It's a little late to call you, Miss Celina,' Elizabeth said in a low voice.

'Quite normal, Madam.'

'Was Ned good?'

'No, Madam. He cried.'

'Because I wasn't next door. He'll have to get used to it.'

'I stayed with him until he went to sleep.'

'That's very kind of you. You didn't have to, Celina.'

'Yes, I did, Madam.'

'Why?'

'He imagines that when he is alone and you have not gone to bed something or someone comes from the back of the room.'

Eizabeth felt a cold shiver down her spine.

'That's all right, Miss Celina,' she said, in what she hoped was a calm voice. 'The main thing is that he did go to sleep.'

She went to bed feeling happier. The malevolent object had been driven away. From her bed, by listening carefully, she convinced herself that she could hear her little boy's even breathing. Everything was returning to normal and, thinking of Billy and the happiness which he said was winging toward them, she felt herself lapse into a contented sleep.

However, a little before dawn, she woke up with a start, overcome with such powerful and sudden anxiety that, without hesitation, she got up and went down to the drawing-room. Who could tell whether, candlestick in hand, the housekeeper had not taken a look around as she went back to her room on the ground floor?

The little blue room was still dark, but Elizabeth did not bother to light a lamp. After stumbling against one or two pieces of furniture, she got down on all fours and began to feel the carpet in every direction; suddenly, her hand touched the ruby which she grasped firmly, as though it might escape, and in her heart she felt ashamed at having secretly feared Celina might steal it from her.

Once back in her room, she hid it at the bottom of a wardrobe and went back to sleep.

# 31

*T*he morning post brought a letter which she greeted with a cry of joy. Dated December 5, 1856, it came from Fort Pulaski and said:

> Three cheers for my commanding officer, dear Elizabeth! I have just left his office where I went to inform him of our marriage, as I am obliged to do under Army regulations. He gave us his permission with all sorts of blessings. You don't know, perhaps, that I am his favorite thanks to my talent as a whist player: he loves the game. You can choose whichever church you like. As far as I'm concerned, it doesn't matter: any church is good if it will unite me with you for ever. My charming commandant begs you, however, not to marry in the 'Romish church', because he suspects all Catholics of being in the pay of the Spaniards. I can do what I will, but on that point he is adamant. So we can go to a dear little country church and no one will know anything until we want them to. We have to think of society, with its conventions and the time it allows for mourning . . . I shall be coming back tomorrow afternoon (there are formalities to be undergone, you understand) with a leave that can be extended according to circumstances. I bury my face in your golden hair.
> 'Crazy with happiness,
> 'Your Billy.'

Elizabeth sat down and closed her eyes, so overcome that she could not move for several minutes. Happiness had struck her like a bolt of lightning. She had what she had so eagerly desired for so many years. All the past failures, dramas and terror vanished down a great black hole. All that remained, sometimes as luminous as a ghost, at others as dark as a shadow, a little shadow sent by that shade from the regions of night, was the child.

Sobering up, she got to her feet and made a gesture as if pushing someone away, but she felt a stab in her heart.

'Billy will arrange everything,' she said. 'He'll know how to talk to him.'

But what could a man do?

At table and during lunch, Ned behaved perfectly. She would have liked him to be more talkative, but he was in one of those silent moods that overtook him from time to time. Let him shut himself in his mysterious little world: she accepted it now like a blessing from heaven, since it brought her peace. Her natural curiosity did, however, make her want to ask questions. When she looked at him, he smiled back merrily. At such moments, he looked disturbingly like his father. She briefly had the impression that the dead man was observing her through the eyes of his son, with the same gentleness as in the early days, when he had not yet plucked up courage to tell her that he loved her.

While they were waiting for dessert, the boy asked a question that made her start:

'Mummy, where is the officer?'

'With his regiment, but you'll see him tomorrow.'

The news brought a new smile.

'Do you like him, darling?'

'Yes, a lot.'

'Thank heaven for that,' she said, impulsively.

How considerately Providence was smoothing out even the smallest details . . .

<h1 style="text-align:center">32</h1>

*I*n spite of that, they had to wait until the next afternoon before seeing Billy, and the wait was unbearable. Others could wait, she couldn't. The only thing was to do something.

She had the buggy harnessed and decided to go and see Uncle Charlie to tell him her news and ask his advice on what she should do, because she suspected Billy of lacking in social polish. She loved him as he was, but having lived so long in Dimwood, that is to say in the country, he had something about him that was a bit rustic — deliciously rustic, of course, but even so . . .

In a state of extreme excitement, she whipped her horse and in less than five minutes was at the house in Jasper Square.

She halted the carriage in front of the sycamore where Charlie Jones, reminding her that he was her guardian, had often repeated his promise to look after her and her happiness. She gave a sigh and went up to ring the door bell. An old, gray-haired black man opened and told her that Massa Jones had left for his office. Elizabeth nearly stamped her foot on the marble doorway with impatience, but finally she just left a message: 'Mrs Edward Jones would like to see Mr Charles Jones as soon as possible.'

Now what should she do? There were hours and hours to kill. Why did Billy not come back at once since the Army had agreed to it? She whipped her horse and set off home at a gallop.

To work off her anger, she decided to give Pat a piece of her mind. Because of him, the cook had to fetch the meat from the butcher's herself.

Like a fury, she swept through the hall where a mirror stopped her just long enough to tell her that she had never been so beautiful. Anger suited her marvellously. What a shame Lieutenant Billy Hargrove was not there to appreciate it.

No sooner had she set foot in the garden than she was overcome by the wonderful abundance of greenery that braved the winter — though it must be said that even that is a very mild season in Savannah. The great cork tree extended its branches over her tousled head of golden hair and said: 'don't worry. Happiness is on its way, and waiting for it is a form of happiness . . .'

But she wasn't listening. She was looking for Pat and, as usual, he wasn't there. She ran over to the little house, opened the door and heard him chatting with the passers-by in the avenue. His cheeky Irish voice sang out over the slightly drawling accents of the South. At the top of her voice, she cried:

'Pat!'

He appeared at last, his straw hat in his hand, beaming in his checkered shirt.

'Yes, Ma'am. You only have to say Pat and Pat is there!'

'I've had enough, Pat. The butcher's boy's face is all swollen and this time he won't be coming back. You're dismissed.'

'No, Ma'am.'

'What do you mean: "No, Ma'am"? What insolence! You'll leave tomorrow morning.

'No, Ma'am, because you'll never find another gardener like Pat.'

'That's where you're wrong. I'll take on an obedient Black.'

'A Black wouldn't be able to tell a palm from a pine.'

'I'm not arguing about it. Get packed.'

'So you're sending Pat back to Ireland, where there's a famine, Ma'am.'

'Famine! The great famine of 1840 is over!'

'No, Ma'am. With us, when one famine goes, another takes its place. Today's is the worst.'

With a dramatic gesture he threw his hat on the ground, and his Gaelic inspiration started to work:

'The potatoes are rotting and all the cattle were eaten long ago. People are eating grass — where there's any left — or tearing the bark off the trees and chewing it, trying to imagine that it's bread. May the Good Lord and His Saints forgive you, Ma'am. You're sending Pat back to the land of hunger.'

This speech, delivered in a dull, sinister voice, struck Elizabeth with its tones of sincerity and she felt herself weakening.

'I find it odd that the newspapers have not spoken of it,' she said quietly.

The man rose up to his full height and thundered like a prophet:

'And what does the world care if Ireland is starving?'

'Very well, Pat,' Elizabeth said, embarrassed. 'That's enough for today.'

And she added quickly:

'You'll soon have a new master who will know how to deal with you.'

'A new master?' he asked, uneasily.

'You'll soon see. Meanwhile, clean up this garden a little for me and stop talking to people outside. I'm keeping an eye on you.'

'Yes, Ma'am,' he said calmly.

She hurried back, conscious of having suffered a humiliating defeat; but she was counting on Billy.

# 33

*B*ut what was happening at the barracks in Fort Pulaski? An uprising? A seditious plot? An attempt at secession? Night is falling and from the officers' mess can be heard wild cries and loud *hurrahs*. Sub-lieutenants, lieutenants and captains — thirty of them in red dolmans — are sitting around the long table, while a splendid lieutenant is on his feet, waving his arms. Why are they all shouting:

'Death! Death! He is stealing our beautiful Englishwoman!'

There can be no doubt that the man they want to tear limb from limb is Lieutenant Hargrove, nicknamed Beau Billy, in a uniform tailored by Slaughter and Carver, the leading outfitters in Savannah, in such a way that it shows off the hero's shoulders and his perfect waist.

'Woe betide whoever should touch the beautiful Englishwoman,' he shouts loudly.

'We may at least look at your goddess, I suppose?' asks another, equally powerful voice.

'Perhaps, but I forbid you to stare or make lovesick cows' eyes at her.'

'The rogue! Let's drink his health, for all that: to Beau Billy?'

Fists holding glasses rise toward the ceiling in an outburst of cries that makes the walls shudder.

'To you, Billy, and your belle! Give her fine children for the South. Long live the Secession!'

A unanimous cry:

'Speech, speech!'

A dramatic entrance; the door opens: it's the commandant.

Thickset, ruddy-faced and bow-legged, he gives a savage smile and the noise ceases at once.

'Gentlemen,' says a resonant voice. 'I am happy for you to celebrate, but I will not tolerate disorder. You can be heard on the parade ground and the men are becoming restless. Lieutenant Hargrove, get down off that table.'

Billy jumps down and the commandant leaps up to take his place with the agility of an athlete. His black eyes look round the room:

'Every collar undone,' he says. 'Button up, gentlemen. We are not in the North. Discipline is a trial, I know, but it bothers me and I have it in my blood. Now, back to happier matters. You have all drunk Lieutenant Hargrove's health, but I have still to do so. What are you going to offer me?'

A dishevelled sub-lieutenant cries out:

'The best beer in the country. It comes . . .'

'Directly from the North! I don't want it.'

Suddenly he is a different man. He bursts out laughing and stamps with all his might. The door opens. Four black men bring in cases of champagne. They are followed by two others carrying huge trays with crystal champagne glasses.

'Serve the champagne and serve it fast, before it becomes warm. It comes from France and the Emperor drinks no other.'

A wave of merriment flows through the room. Corks pop on all sides with the sound of a victorious burst of gunfire. As if by magic, the glasses are almost simultaneously lodged in each man's astonished hands.

'Billy,' the captain orders, 'get back on the table!'

Dumbstruck, the young man obeys, his glass is handed up to him and the commandant's is raised.

'Gentlemen, to Lieutenant Hargrove!'

A huge *vivat*. The fine glasses are lifted and almost immediately emptied. Suddenly, in the midst of the celebration, there is an oddly serious note. The commandant turns toward Billy, who has remained standing beside him on the table.

'Lieutenant Hargrove, I have something to say to you and I shall try to keep it short. You are about to marry the most beautiful woman in Savannah. Be faithful to her!'

'I swear it!' Billy cries.

There follows a short, meaningful silence. We are in church already.

'Though it is no secret,' the commandant continues, 'this marriage is nonetheless private. Your comrades will not attend.'

A dull murmur of disappointment in the assembly.

'No one will cross the threshold of the church except the couple and their witnesses.'

A new silence, this time of disapproval.

'Lieutenant Hargrove,' the commandant says in a serious voice. 'Give the South fine children and hurry up about it. Time is short and peace is shaky.'

Just as one can shout louder and louder, can one also be more and more silent, adding silence to silence? If anyone were to close his eyes, he would think himself alone in the room.

'Remember this,' the speaker goes on. 'When battle comes — and it will come — you will charge the enemy, sabres drawn, sitting upright on your horse, not leaning over its neck, as though behind a shield. A Southern gentleman charges straight ahead, with his shoulders back. Understood?'

From all parts of the room, a roar greets the words:

'Upright, sabre drawn!'

There is a bustle on the parade-ground where the soldiers are trying to discover what is meant by this commotion, of which only an echo reaches them through the mess windows. Against a black sky a crescent moon in its last quarter casts ripples of silence.

# 34

At that same moment, Charlie Jones was entering the blue draw ing-room where Elizabeth waited and fretted. He had the usual smile which he wore like a mask on his face, but he looked tired. There was a black shadow darkening the corners of his eyes. Per- haps it had been a hard day in the port offices. Even so, he put on a cheerful voice.

'Sorry to arrive so late, Elizabeth. It is the first time I have made such a charming lady wait, but you wanted to see me as soon as possible, and here I am. I suppose it's about Billy Hargrove.'

'How do you know, Uncle Charlie?'

'My poor child! General gossip. I'm delighted. My dreams are coming true and I haven't had to lift a finger. I wanted you to get married and give a brother to the son of the one I lost. I admit I never thought of Billy, but why not? He will adore you.'

'I hope he already does, but I've just had a very brief letter from him in Fort Pulaski. He was here on leave, but he had to go back.'

'So soon?'

'It seems he must inform his commandant and he is not coming back until tomorrow afternoon.'

'Well!'

'Yes, because of some formalities he has to carry out.'

'The devil! He calls it "formalities", does he?'

'Yes, but why are you laughing?'

'Nothing, it's just that I'm stunned with happiness — happiness for you and for him . . .'

'We're going to get married, at once.'

'Unfortunately, there is the period of mourning . . .'

'No, the marriage will be almost secret.'

' "Almost" is charming; but we can always find a way.'

He stopped and said sadly:

'As we did for you and my poor Ned.'

At once, he looked anxious, 'I hope you have not already done anything foolish.'

She gave a slightly melancholy shake of the head.

'Thank goodness! We don't have to rush things. You say he wrote a letter which was rather short, but passionate, warm, loving . . . No?'

'So-so. He said nice things about my hair.'

'Really? The charming shyness of the young lover.'

She burst into tears.

'He said he wanted to bury his face in it, that's all.'

'But that's love,' Charlie Jones exclaimed. 'Silly goose, he's a Romeo!'

'Do you really think so?' she asked, dabbing her eyes.

'I know what I'm talking about. Don't cry. An English woman doesn't cry.'

'Yes she does. We're human, after all.'

'Well, let's carry on. You need two witnesses. I will offer myself for Billy. And you?'

'I did think of Mrs Harrison Edwards, if she is willing.'

'If she's willing! She's counting on it. She considers herself the finest ornament of society. Where is the wedding to be?'

'I don't know. "In a darling little country church . . .", he says.'

'What nonsense is that? You'll get married here. In which church?'

'I'm an Anglican, like Mama.'

'He comes from a Presbyterian family. No matter. He'll become an Anglican. It will be in Christ Church. Very smart: the best socially. I don't mind one way or the other. I have other ideas. But hurry up, children. Life is beautiful, enjoy it. Now I've got something to tell you. But why are we standing like actors in a tragedy?'

'Oh, forgive me,' she said, sitting down on the blue sofa.

'May I sit beside you? I know it's not done . . .'

'In England it is,' she said, smiling.

He sat down.

'Between ourselves,' he said, 'this Southern custom presupposes that it is necessary to keep youth's fiery temperament at bay. We'll let that be. I came back from my office at around six o'clock, exhausted, ready to dine . . . and I was told that you had come and that you wanted to see me. I missed dinner . . .'

'What! You haven't dined? Would you . . .'

'No, nothing. My appetite faded with the passing of the dinner hour. I was putting on my hat to come out and see you when, at that very moment, the bell rang. Do you know who it was?'

'No idea.'

'Annabel.'

Elizabeth made a slight movement of revulsion.

'You don't like her,' said Charlie Jones.

'Not very much, no. It's hard to explain.'

'I know that there is something in her appearance that makes one uncomfortable, especially as you knew her before when she was so extraordinarily lovely, but the death of the man she loved broke her heart.'

'She hates me, Uncle Charlie.'

He did not reply, but went on:

'It was because of you that she came. She didn't want to dine. I had to shut myself up with her in the smoking room where no one comes. Entirely in black and wearing a mantilla over her gray hair, she told me about her visit to you.'

'Perhaps I didn't receive her as I should have done.'

'On the contrary. Everything you said touched her, but she is worried about you. She thinks you are very vulnerable.'

'That doesn't mean anything.'

'She is quite blunt. In her view, your first marriage taught you nothing about life and you are dangerously ignorant of the pitfalls of love. You are too easily led astray.'

Elizabeth stood up in indignation.

'I'd like to know what business it is of hers.'

Charlie Jones did not move but looked at her sadly.

'Listen,' he said, gently. 'When I saw you married to my dear Ned, I experienced one of the greatest joys of my life, but I was afraid for the two of you. Ned, a young student with no experience of women, and you . . . I was anxious at seeing two children entering into life, together, because of a mistake made by my son.'

'But we were in love . . .'

'A very mild love after the first passion faded. Do you think I wasn't watching you?'

'Uncle Charlie, please.'

'No, you must know. Your real passion, your wild love was for someone else. From the window of my office, while the crowd was waiting for the *Bonaventure* to arrive, you were beside one another. A single glance was enough. I didn't want to know any more and I turned away. I had understood.'

'But I wasn't yet married!' the young woman exclaimed, blazing with anger.

'I know, I know,' Charlie Jones said calmly. 'Marriage came later. Then there was the duel.'

'I don't want to hear any more,' she said firmly. 'Let me say that I consider it cruel of you to remind me of these things.'

With no change in his voice, he continued as if he hadn't heard.

'Do you remember that when I lunched with you at the De Soto, I told you that I had seen Ned when he was dying and you had just said farewell to him?'

Suddenly Elizabeth was motionless, her face hard.

'I remember,' she said in a dull voice.

'I was supporting him on my arm and he made a great effort to speak. I could hardly hear him: "My Elizabeth . . . Look after her, Papa . . . She's a child . . . I loved her . . . Tell her . . ." That was all. He didn't say anything more. He went.'

With uncertain steps, Elizabeth crossed the little room and sat down in a chair some way away from Charlie Jones, shivering a little, as if she were cold; the blood had drained from her face.

'I would like to be alone,' she said, quietly.

'I understand, my dear Elizabeth, and I will leave you alone, but

there is one more thing I must tell you. It is about Annabel. I beg
you to listen to me. It will not cause you any distress.'

'I am suffering enough of that already, Uncle Charlie.'

'I shall never forget the moment when she lifted her veil and
showed me those eyes, with their horror of being alive. Yet I saw
her at Dimwood a short while before, after the duel, and the change
that had taken place in her was terrifying; that evening, however,
she seemed to be coming back from another world.'

'I know,' Elizabeth said. 'Yesterday, I thought I saw death.'

'Oh, no! The flame that burned behind those eyes was frightening. Under the harsh light of the gas lamp, pitiless shadows streaked
her cheeks with vertical furrows. Struck dumb by this evidence of
disaster, I listened to what she had to tell me. In some strange way,
her voice still had some of its old intonations, like a muffled song.
She began speaking of you with more sorrow than anger: "I should
hate that young woman who deprived me of the only being I shall
ever have loved on this earth; but I cannot. She is an unconscious
victim of circumstances, but she makes me anxious and I feel sorry
for her. What fate can await her in a country where the first shadows of an absurd war are lurking?" '

He paused.

'There, I do not agree with her. War is still far from inevitable
and I am optimisitc, but Annabel was speaking like a mad woman.
Suddenly she cried: "I gave her the most precious thing I possessed and it was as though I was tearing it out of my heart: a
ruby that he gave me when he loved me, and which I wore all the
time. I saw that Elizabeth was looking at it, fascinated by the magic
beauty of that mysterious stone. Why did I give it to her? Does
one always know why one performs certain actions? Perhaps the
sudden and violent urge I have occasionally to give up everything
I have. I don't know. But I guessed that the ruby would make her
suffer as much as it attracted her with its brilliance . . . I asked
her to wear it always . . . I know her, she will do it, but that will
be her penance.'

'I shall not wear it,' Elizabeth said.

'We shall see,' said Charlie Jones with a smile.

There was a pause, then he went on:

'When she had finished what she was saying, she put her veil
back and said calmly: "That's the end. I have freed myself of a
great weight and you have been patient. I am leaving, and I shall
not often be seen in future in Savannah. Give Elizabeth Annabel's
love. I shall not say farewell to you, though it is unlikely we shall
see one another again . . . Who knows? Life is so odd, sometimes . . ." She made a rather formal little curtsey, in the old manner, and went out. That explains why I am so late. Now, I am listening. I think you have something to say.'

'No,' she said. 'Nothing. Nothing more. I wanted to tell you about the ruby.'

'I advise you to wear it. It was never seen, because she kept it under her shawl, but it is famous, ancient, almost legendary. It is called the Armstrong Ruby. See you soon, dear Elizabeth. I am tired and I'm going home to bed.'

# 35

*T*hat evening she did not dine. She had no appetite and went up to her room. To her great relief, she could hear the quiet and even breathing of her little boy, sleeping. Quietly, she closed the door and got undressed. She liked to imagine that all the worries of the day were slipping to the floor with her dress. The unsettling words of Charlie Jones and Annabel. Why had he needed to let her know her husband's last words on his deathbed? And that dramatic speech by Annabel, tearing a ruby out of her heart, to give it to her, Elizabeth, with her love . . . Had they both agreed to torture her conscience? She decided to be firm; and now, in her white silk dressing-gown, she walked backward and forward around her room, opening and shutting drawers, displacing the brushes and scent bottles on her dressing table, then went to lean out of the window. The air was a little chilly, but its softness caressed her face. Who would have thought it was only a fortnight to Christmas? Under the tall sycamores in the square, she noticed a man and a young women strolling, hand in hand, perhaps lovers . . . In the distance were the lights of the port where Charlie Jones saw her in the crowd with Jonathan. She turned away.

Once more, she walked around the room. Her mind was a confusion of thoughts, which she could neither get rid of, nor concentrate on. She thought of trying to get a good night's sleep by taking a little laudanum. She had everything she needed in a locked closet, but she was afraid that the next day, when Billy came back, she might be talking in a confused way, as had once happened before, so she decided against it.

In the same cupboard, under the linen, was the emerald necklace, a treasure which she did not know what to do with for the time being. At least she had to be certain that the jewel was still there. She was attached to it, but afraid of it. She thought it would be dangerous to mention it to Charlie Jones. Who was he? Odd question. Hadn't she known him for years? But she sometimes suspected that one could never really know anyone, and that one spent one's whole life among strangers, who said one thing and meant another.

She looked over at her bed, and thought, 'I am not going to sleep.' She sat down heavily on a chair and holding her face in her hands, sighed. 'If only Billy were here, holding me close to him . . .' She imagined his presence and her whole body hungered for that embrace, that suffocation. Shutting her eyes, she gave herself up to the sensation and suddenly leaped up and ran to the closet. A moment earlier, she had taken the key out of a drawer, without daring to admit why, like a thief.

Now all her ridiculous comings and goings around the room took on a meaning. She had done what she feared. The ruby shone in the cup of her hands with a victorious glow. With little sighs of joy, she put it to her lips. Jonathan had held this magic stone in his hands, turning it over and over. Holding it on her bosom, she shuddered with joy and terror. A hallucination swept over her and she felt a burning hand on her flesh.

Like a woman elated, she went to bed, the ruby around her neck, buried herself under the blankets and sank into oblivion until morning.

# 36

S he awoke with the confused feeling that she had ventured into some forbidden realm, but the memory was so vague that she could not have said where she had been or what she had seen.

It took a few second for her to notice someone standing by the bed. Her little boy, in his white pyjamas, was looking at her and smiling. His curls were entangled across his forehead. Love lit up his big brown eyes and she was as overwhelmed by it as if the child's father had been there in front of her, so strong was the resemblance between them. She quickly covered herself. The ruby had slipped between her breasts. Ned had not seen it.

'Good morning, Mummy,' he said simply.

She took his head in her hands and smothered him with kisses.

'Darling,' she asked, 'why are you up so early?'

'Not so early, Mummy. Look at the sun.'

He was right: rays of sunlight were shining through the shutters and falling on the carpet.

'You shouted something,' he added.

'I must have been dreaming,' she said, anxious.

Ned continued, in a serious voice, 'You said something, and you shouted. I had a dream, too . . .'

'Tell me! Tell me your dream,' she said, to stop him saying any more about what he had heard.

He looked at her maliciously.

'First tell me your dream, Mummy, then I'll tell you mine.'

'I can't remember it, darling.'

'Then I shan't tell you my dream.'

'You're not kind to your Mummy.'

'And you're not kind to me,' he said, in a singsong voice. 'Mummy had her dream, Ned had his.'

'At least tell Mummy if you were afraid.'

'No . . . Not any longer.'

'Before you were?'

'The first time he came, yes.'

'Who came, Ned?'

'The dream.'

She sighed. She would never be able to get anything out of this obstinate little creature. Did he enjoy teasing her, or was he hiding something?

She stroked the round cheeks of his innocent-looking face.

'Darling,' she said, softly. 'Go back to your room until Betty comes to look after you.'

'Yes, Mummy.'

He smiled sweetly and vanished with an alacrity which only made Elizabeth more anxious. His bare feet, which she had time to see running across the carpet, filled her with tenderness, but she was still worried.

Getting up, she felt embarrassed at seeing the suspicious disorder in the room, which reflected her disturbed night . . . Her dress thrown on a sofa, her underclothes, stockings and shoes cast aside . . . What haste to get into bed . . . She hoped that the child had not noticed anything, but she knew that children did see and remember everything, even if they did not understand. Ashamed and worrried, she did her best to restore the room to its usual order.

Banishing these dark thoughts, she took special care washing and getting ready. This was a great day. Time was racing her toward happiness with the prospect of Billy's return. A dress in a bold and unambiguous green seemed best to suit a young woman losing her head at the very idea of a first embrace. The ruby which she was still wearing vanished into the depths of her bodice.

Lunch followed its accustomed course. Just in case, obeying a mad ray of hope, she had three places laid, even though she knew that Billy had said he would not be there until the afternoon.

Ned seemed a little anxious when Elizabeth told him that the soldier would be there shortly and asked carefully thought-out questions about braid, frogging and the officer's defensive and offensive weaponry.

Around the end of the afternoon, the house (which up to then had been quiet) was suddenly filled with cries and the sound of footsteps, in a commotion that might have suggested the invasion of a whole Army corps; but it was merely Billy making his presence felt. Her feet hardly touching the steps, Elizabeth flew toward him in her green dress, like a giant parrot, chattering with happiness.

Billy caught her in his arms and lifted her to the ceiling, while she kicked and pretended to be frightened; then, without a word, he smothered her face with wet kisses.

In the fading light, he arrived like a late ray of sunshine bursting into the astonished house in full dress. The servants appeared from every direction to witness a scene that lost any sense of intimacy, while Charles-Edward junior watched the emotional outburst with astonishment and a powerful curiosity which made his eyes bulge wide. Celina stayed at some distance, and it was as if the ghost of a smile crossed her impassive face, while Joe, the black lackey, focussed his hungry look on the dishevelled Englishwoman. At the top of the stairs stood Betty, small, motionless and solemn.

'Billy,' Elizabeth said, panting. 'We are behaving badly in front of all the servants. Let's go to the drawing-room.'

He burst out laughing:

'Let's go to your room.'

'Wicked boy!' she exclaimed. 'Not yet. I'll take you to the drawing-room and we can close the doors.'

In the blue room, with its starchy, conventional appearance, so out of keeping with the times, he looked around him with the eye of a wild animal driven into a cage, glaring fiercely at the rather short sofa.

'Elizabeth,' he said.

'I know . . . I am suffering as much as you . . .'

She remembered the child's room, with the bed that was too short where she had given herself to the student, Ned; but the door did lock.

In a low voice, she continued: 'Suppose someone were to come in: can you imagine?'

'Then, let's go to the woods, let's go anywhere, in the colonial cemetery . . .'

'Are you mad? In a public place . . . A lady and gentleman . . .'

'Oh, no!' he exclaimed, in an exasperated voice. 'Not that old song, my beloved: "Remember you're a gentleman . . ." My ears have rung with it since I first wore long trousers. Am I shocking you? I'm talking like a soldier . . .'

'You can't shock me, darling. Society irritates me as much as it does you. When are we getting married?'

'Not until the day after tomorrow. So much wasted time for a formality that lasts ten minutes . . .'

She felt she must correct him:

'A little religious ceremony.'

'As you like. It's the same to me. What matters is for you to belong to me. Say you do, you wicked girl!'

She threw herself against him and hugged him as if to crush his bones.

'Smother me,' she said.


# 37

*T*ime, in its famous headlong plunge toward the abyss, will sometimes slow down cruelly for lovers who are waiting to marry.

Finally the great day came. As a widow, Elizabeth could not dress in white, but she opted for a pale pink dress and covered her head with a white lace mantilla.

At exactly eleven o'clock, she was standing at Billy's side before the vicar of Christ Church. Uncle Charlie and Mrs Harrison Edwards were close by, carrying out their duties as witnesses with impressive solemnity. Everything was very simple. There was only one note of ostentation: Billy's uniform and the fussy plume of feathers in Mrs Harrison Edwards' hat. The shadow of the great Wesley seemed to float in the half light of this venerable church and there was an emotional moment when the priest pronounced the couple man and wife, and the rings were exchanged. A discreet sniff emanated from the lovely Mrs Harrison Edwards, and Elizabeth suddenly thought of her mother, who would have done the same.

There was an elegantly phrased blessing from the vicar, and that was all. Trembling with joy, Elizabeth leaned on her new husband's arm for him to lead her out.

The fine winter sun dazzled the young woman as she took her first steps on the stairway outside the church, and she thought she could make out several dozen people on the square when suddenly a powerful voice rang out, making her start:

'Present arms!'

At the bottom of the steps, two rows of officers in red dolmans were brandishing their sabres, and the sunlight glinted on the steel blades. A great 'hurrah!' accompanied the movement. Trembling, she clung to her husband's arm.

'Stand upright, Elizabeth,' he said. 'The Army is saluting you.'

Cheers rose from the square and, her heart beating, she walked down the steps as if in a dream.

As she stepped beneath this glistening tunnel, she felt overcome by their bellicose fever, but she was much less intimidated by the sabres lifted up in the sunlight than by the look of all those men whose eyes followed her in a coordinated movement from left to right down to the end . . . It was a frightening yet delicious walk — one that seemed interminable to her, yet too short, such was the turmoil in her head beneath the white lace veil.

Emerging from this trial, she was suprised to see Charlie Jones in conversation with the commandant.

The sabres were returned to their sheaths and Charlie Jones announced in a loud voice:

'Commandant, a celebratory glass in my house. What do you think?'

'Do you hear that, gentlemen? Mr Charlie Jones is inviting us to his house. Quick march to Asper Square.'

A new 'hurrah!' while the crowd of onlookers scattered rice on the newly-weds.

'And don't forget,' the commandant said in a thundering voice, 'that this is a secret wedding. Keep the press away.'

This instruction was greeted with homeric laughter.

'Let's escape,' Billy said, hurrying Elizabeth toward a tilbury that was waiting a few yards away for them: Uncle Charlie had thought of everything.


# 38


*I*n the large, white and gold drawing-room the sight of these thirty officers in red dolmans had a strange effect on Elizabeth.

'War,' she thought. 'It's like war already.'

They were very young. Several had that Southern beauty in which good humor can combine with a certain unconscious hauteur in the carriage of the head and a gleam of defiance in the eyes.

The young woman felt too disturbed to understand the kind

remarks that they were making to her — cautiously tempered by the presence of a husband who looked as if he might be fierce.

'They are going to die,' she thought.

She had already had the same presentiment as she passed beneath the arch of sabres above her head. She listened in vain to their laughter and the carefree chatter of these drawling voices: she could not dispel the certainty that there were battlefields awaiting them from which they would not return.

One of them above all, a very young sub-lieutenant, struck her with his air of innocence and his wide-open blue eyes. His charming face blushed as did her own, so she was not very surprised when, pushing a way through his companions, he came up to her and said naively:

'I am English, like you.'

Having risked the remark, blushing a little more, he gave her a smile which seemed singularly like a declaration of love. Certainly, he was quite unaware of his boldness.

Touched, she stuttered.

'Where from?'

'Haworth, a small town,' he added, as if to apologize.

'But famous, even so,' an urbane voice said behind Elizabeth, who was surprised to recognize it as that of Mrs Harrison Edwards.

Her victorious feather rising above the heads of all these men, Mrs Harrison Edwards had arrived just in time to put an end to a situation that looked like turning out badly.

'Young man,' she said. 'You don't have a Yorkshire accent.'

'It was knocked out of me at Eton,' he replied, laughing.

'Eton! Interesting . . . Dear Elizabeth, you look tired,' she said, slipping between her and her incautious admirer. 'What does your *husband* think?'

The young Englishman understood immediately and vanished.

Struck dumb, Elizabeth looked at Mrs Harrison Edwards as if she had never seen her before.

'You are surprised to see me here,' she said, with a smile. 'As soon as we came out of church, I took my cabriolet and came here after paying a few calls . . . Mr Jones took me aside to say something to me about you. There is a rather delicate problem . . . You will say that I am interfering with everything, but no matter, we'll come back to that.'

She took Elizabeth firmly by the arm and led her into the empty little drawing-room, papered in almond green and overlooking a garden dominated by banks of azaleas and camelias.

The two women sat on a sofa of dark chintz which evoked an atmosphere of England and quiet conversations. But for some time now Elizabeth had felt far from everything. In the exhilaration, the people and things around her were losing a little of their reality.

However, she made an effort to understand what Mrs Harrison Edwards said, but it was useless. Her mind was more preoccupied with the face of the tall, elegant woman than with the words that poured out of it like water from a spring.

Looking closely at her, you could see the pretty girl she must have been before becoming the very attractive woman that she now was. Life had left its mark. As she approached thirty, her cheeks were filling out, threatening the charming oval face that was now taking on a look of nobility. Her youth was still to be found in her smile: and, in her violet-colored eyes, there danced an irresistible flame of gaity.

Sometimes Elizabeth caught a snatch of what she was saying. Soft, reasonable, the voice droned on and suddenly, with a light laugh, it uttered something which caught the young woman's attention:

'. . . without wishing to be vulgar, I must remind you that the first night of a honeymoon is not entirely given over to sleep . . .'

'Yes . . . No . . .,' Elizabeth said.

'You will be heard. Have you thought of that?'

'Oh, do you think so?'

'The child.'

Suddenly, Elizabeth understood everything

'With the door shut . . .'

'That won't be enough . . . I've often looked at your little Ned. He is thoughtful, attentive, inquisitive . . . When he was younger, it didn't matter, but now he is a little man. He will see that splendid soldier shut himself in with you . . .'

Taken aback, Elizabeth got up:

'I agree with you,' she said. 'But what can be done?'

'Don't fret about it, my dear Elizabeth. Charlie Jones has suggested you live here for a few days. There is a fine apartment for you on the second floor with a view over the garden. The child will be told you have gone on a journey.'

'It will make him ill; he won't believe it. I know him: he sees through everything.'

'Two black angels will watch over him: Betty and his black Mammy. Later you can alter the rooms around. Ned will sleep on another floor.'

'He'll never get used to it. It will be awful for him.'

As she was saying this, Charlie Jones came in quietly.

'Excuse me for interrupting, ladies, but Billy is looking for his beloved, like Orpheus for Eurydice.'

'He only had to open the door to find us,' said Mrs Harrison Edwards with a laugh. 'He's not very smart, your Billy.'

'Poor child, he loses his head where you're involved,' said Charlie Jones sarcastically. 'I hope Mrs Harrison Edwards has told you of my suggestion.'

'How can I do otherwise than accept?' the bride said, with a sigh. 'Thank you, of course.'

'You will be quite quiet in my house. I'll give fearful orders that no one must come prying around your quarters.'

'Their room will be a sacred place.'

Charlie Jones looked at Mrs Harrison Edwards and burst out laughing.

'What's come over you, Lucile?'

The society queen continued in a pompous tone:

'A smiling angel watches by the door of the newly-weds, with a finger to its lips.'

'Are you mad? Where did you find that?'

'I don't know. I plucked it from the future. An inspiration . . .'

'What mysterious and gigantic imbecile are you quoting? A poet, of course. One must be a poet to be so dully sublime.'

Suddenly, Elizabeth turned toward Charlie Jones and said emphatically:

'If I might be permitted to say something, since this is about me and my husband, you are saying things which I find more and more embarassing. Billy and I are not animals, we are not going to bellow and bleat and roar.'

Behind her back, Mrs Harrison Edwards was shaking her head at the same time as her feather, as if to indicate: 'Yes, you will!' — which did not stop her bursting into laughter with Charlie Jones.

'She is right,' they said together. 'We were behaving very badly. Forgive us, Elizabeth.'

Disarmed by this, she too began to laugh.

'Agreed,' she said, 'as English housekeepers say; but go and reassure my Billy.'

'Your despairing Billy is consoling himself at the most prodigious buffet this century. It was an architectural marvel before the Army set about demolishing it: pyramids of sandwiches and colonnades of cream cakes, caviar by the ladle, the champagne that they drink in the Tuileries . . .'

But the young Englishwoman was shaking her golden curls. She only wanted Billy.

Conspiratorial smiles were exchanged between the two people who were watching over her happiness, then Charlie Jones took her by the hand like a child and led her up to the first floor where she found her old bedroom, full of memories, dreams and daydreams. Nothing had changed except the narrow bed which had been replaced by a huge double bed, with white silk covers.

'There,' Charlie Jones said, slightly embarrassed, without knowing why: the circumstances were perhaps a little odd for a man like him. 'I am going to see what Billy is doing. Rest here, meanwhile,' he said, pointing to a chaise-longue piled high with cushions.

He was aware that he was playing the role of an indulgent guardian managing the love affair of two simple innocents, and he was strongly aware of how ridiculous the situation was. This was not precisely the case, but it looked like it.

'A little patience,' he said, before going down the stairs — but that too was an unfortunate remark . . . It reminded him of a brothel in New Orleans — dreadful!

Left alone, Elizabeth was suffering a different kind of torment. It was still bright daylight and she recalled the moment when she wanted to bathe her little boy herself, and her insurmountable revulsion at male nudity. She could not bear the idea of what she would shortly have to see in Billy's body. If she could shut her eyes, as she had done with her first husband, who understood . . . It would have been easier at night.

It was some time before Billy appeared.

Dishevelled, his face red and merry, like a man who has eaten and drunk well, he cried, loudly: 'At last!'

Through the door, which he had left open, she could hear the din of laughter and exclamations, together with more and more brazen remarks; suddenly, like the bursting of a shell, a wild 'hurrah!' which made her shudder.

She shut the door and turned toward Billy. For a few moments, she wondered if she was not going mad. Standing there, his legs apart, he looked superbly handsome in a uniform which showed off his powerful figure to the best advantage; but she did not recognize him. Was it that look, the serious and eager expression all over his face? She looked in vain for love, or for the tenderness of the first days in those staring eyes, and she was afraid. Somewhere deep inside her there was a sort of retreat. She wanted to undersand and could not. Only one word echoed over and over in her head: error. She muttered:

'Billy, listen, let's wait until it's dark.'

'Why?' he asked.

And, without waiting for her to reply, he grasped her in his arms and forcibly kissed her lips, while she struggled feebly.

'Why are you resisting?' he asked. 'Day or night, you are mine, aren't you? Don't you love me any longer?'

He began to unbutton her bodice and his fingers discovered the ruby which was hidden between her breasts. Astonished, he held it in his palm and looked at it:

'Who gave you that—'

'Annabel.'

'She's crazy, the halfe-caste! These things are worth a fortune!'

'Leave it,' she begged.

She took off the ruby and clasped it in her hand. The ruby was Jonathan.

'Why are you doing that?' he asked. 'Precious stones look pretty on a woman.'

Elizabeth had a sudden burst of inspiration.

'Aren't I enough for you without that?'

For a second he was overcome with delight; she took advantage of it to slip the ruby into the pocket of her dress.

'I adore you, Elizabeth.'

These words, spoken fervently, calmed her and the young bride managed to open the rest of her bodice herself. Mad with desire, he threw off his uniform without taking his eyes off her. She turned away her head.

# 39

The child said nothing. The housekeeper had laid the table as usual with two places and, since Madame was late, lunch was also delayed, at quarter-hourly intervals, until they finally served it at something closer to tea-time.

Ned dutifully ate up his plate of snow-white hominy. From time to time he looked up at Celina who was talking to him softly; but he wasn't listening. He just pretended so as not to upset her.

'This morning,' the housekeeper repeated, 'as I told you, your Mama married the handsome officer in his magnificent red uniform . . . Why aren't you saying anything, Ned?'

Spoon in hand, he was watching her, eating his hominy and not saying a word . . . This obstinate silence impressed Celina: it was not a child's silence, but that of an adult who was determined, after considering it, not to say anything. For that reason she felt a certain unease in his presence, but could not stop herself feeling a surge of affection for this little creature, devoid of all malice, with his touchingly sweet smile. The one thing that bothered her a little was the unhappy memory of the night when he had revealed that someone or something came from somewhere in his bedroom, which he called his dream. She preferred not to think about it. After all, it was not for her to watch over Ned while he slept and she had only been there because Elizabeth was away.

Meanwhile, sitting beside his Indian, which he had put on the chair next to his own, he was twisting the rag doll between his fingers, while waiting for dessert. Everything in him spoke of innocence, an innocence with an aura of mystery; but what child did not have little secrets which he kept from grown-ups, thinking they were not able to understand?

The day ended in the usual way. The walk with Betty, a little shorter than usual, took place without any other alteration, and at the appointed time Black Mammy gave a bath to a little boy who allowed himself to be soaped and rubbed without saying a word. The black angel, in her great white cloud, sang little songs to him about a rabbit who was cleverer than his brothers and escaped from every tight spot.

Finally, night fell in the house and Elizabeth's room remained empty. Without asking anyone's advice, old Betty came and sat by Ned's bed. Between the two of them, in long months of daily walks, a silent bond of love had grown up, a sort of complicity of the heart which was impossible to put into words. He felt that with her, nothing dreadful could happen. She was sitting on a stool and, in the light of the lamp, he saw her black face furrowed with lines, but radiating tenderness and driving away any fear.

'Betty,' he asked, after a few minutes' silence. 'Where is Mummy?'

'Massa Ned, I dunno; but she be comin' back.'

'Sure?'

'Yes. She was married today, and when folks gets married, they stays out all day.'

'Why?'

'Because they'm happy and have lots of things to say.'

This explanation must have puzzled the inquisitive child, because a moment later he said:

'Stay there Betty, don't go away.'

'No, Massa Ned, Betty no go away.'

And almost at once, he fell asleep.

# 40

At about nine o'clock in the evening, the doorbell rang, not once, but twice, impatiently. Slightly perturbed, Celina ran to open it.

It was Elizabeth and her husband, both smiling at the housekeeper's look of astonishment.

'You weren't expecting us,' said Elizabeth, and immediately asked: 'Ned?'

'I think he's asleep. Betty is with him,' said Celina.

Elizabeth took a step toward the stairs, but the housekeeper stopped her:

'Excuse me, Madam, but if you wake him, it will be hard to get him back to sleep.'

'Do you know if he cried?'

'No, I would have heard him, I was here. But he is nervous and he is asking questions.'

'In your place,' Billy said, 'I'd leave him be. You can see him tomorrow morning.'

'I won't wake him. I just want to look at him, I want . . .'

Pushing Celina aside, she went upstairs, lifting her skirt with one hand, her feet barely touching the steps. She paused in her own room before going next door to the one where the child was sleeping.

For a moment she stood motionless, looking around at the familiar scene. A streetlight in the avenue enabled her to see the commode and the brass handles of the drawers which glowed softly, and beyond it the great patch of pale green that was the blanket on her bed. Everything else had vanished into the darkness.

On tiptoe she went into Ned's room. Betty, perched on a chair, saw her at once and waved her hands around to beg for silence. The glow from the nightlight cast the shadows of her arms on the white curtains, enlarging her gestures with dramatic effect.

'Hush . . ., Ma'am,' she whispered. 'Massa Ned's sleepin'.'

Elizabeth nodded and bent over the child. He was in a familiar pose, with one hand on his heart, curled up, his breath barely audible. His curls were tangled on the pillow, black and tangled.

Elizabeth had to restrain herself from kissing the little head full of dreams. She bent toward the old black woman and whispered:

'It's going to be hard for me, not sleeping near him any more.'

'Yes, Ma'am,' Betty said.

She smiled, showing her last remaining four or five teeth.

'I'll be here, Ma'am.'

'Not all night?'

Betty's head, in its green shawl streaked with red, nodded vigorously.

For a moment the two women looked at one another and said nothing. Then Elizabeth went out.

Downstairs, Billy was waiting patiently with the housekeeper.

'Well,' he asked, 'what news?'

'Nothing. He's asleep.'

'Then you didn't need to stay so long,' he said laughing.

'You don't understand, Billy.'

'Yes, of course I do. A mother's heart . . .But if you want me to take you to dine at the De Soto as you asked, we have only just the time to jump into the tilbury and drive there. We haven't reserved a table and in the evening it's full.'

In less than a minute they were outside. Celina shut the door behind them and, in the once more silent house, gave herself over to the austere pleasure of meditation.

She remained standing in the hall for a moment, thoughtful, as though she had just witnessed an unusual sight. Her idea of Elizabeth had changed abruptly. Still beautiful, with that slightly over self-confident beauty, she had lost the worried expression which added an air of mystery to the freshness of her enduring youth. Now, radiant and merry, she gave the disturbing impression of no longer being Elizabeth, but her double.

# 41

*T*he sun was shining in a clear blue sky when they reappeared the next morning, with the preoccupied look of people who have just reached decisions and do not intend to lose any time in carrying them out. Elizabeth most of all. Everything about her proclaimed her married state. What she had lacked yesterday, she now possessed — that indefinable something: authority . . . She no longer leaned on her husband, but stepped out proudly, as if in her own territory (where, moreover, no one challenged her). The shyness of yesteryear, not without its charm, had vanished for ever. She was now Mrs William Stevens Hargrove.

Followed by her husband, she went into the drawing-room and immediately declared:

'Everything here must be changed. I am tired of this drab blue. I want something with character, something bold.'

'Red,' Billy suggested.

'Bravo. No more mawkishness. But what red?'

'Blood red.'

'Blood red!' she said, like an echo. 'Darling, you're wonderful.'

'Military, my dearest.'

'Society will be appalled.'

'Oh, no! Not any more.'

'Really? Then why not a crimson damask.'

'I'll leave the details to you.'

'Oh, I can see our red drawing-room!' she exclaimed. 'I can see it; can't you?'

'My darling, I'll see it better when it's here. Let's think about the new arrangement of rooms which we decided upon last night. You and I can take Ned's room, which will become part of ours.'

'Oh, Billy!' Elizabeth sighed. 'How can we tell him?'

'He'll have the fine room on the ground floor with his own bathroom. That is what we decided together at De Soto's.'

'I know, but I feel a terrible coward . . . Oh, if only you could  . . . You'll get him to accept it, with your presence and your uniform . . . If only you knew how much he admires you . . .'

'Very well, I give in. But let's strike while the iron is hot! Where is he?'

'In his room, I'm afraid.'

She stopped suddenly and struck her forehead:

'I've got an idea! Why not do it in the garden? He can be having a quiet talk with you. It will be easier than in his own room, the place he considers his territory.'

'Very well, agreed. I give in again, because it's a holiday to-day . . .'

'I'll go and fetch the poor love . . . You can see my garden, which you don't know very well yet and at the same time you might say a word to Patrick, the gardener; he is impossible. I'll tell you about it . . . He fights with the delivery boys. Do say something to him.'

'Let's call that task number three. Anything else?'

'Oh, Billy!'

'Oh, Elizabeth . . . Quickly fetch your boy. I'll go into the garden.'

A moment later he was walking down the steps and through the long, narrow garden; however, having been brought up in one of the finest plantations in Georgia, it only needed a glance for him to realize that the appearence of neglect in Elizabeth's garden disguised a deliberately cultivated impression of a wilderness. Hence the chaos of the tufted bushes which seemed to be competing for space in the corners, hence the trees growing here and there, their overgrown branches extending across paths of wild grasses and magnificent flowers growing at random, standing alone like queens in exile, amazed at finding themselves where no one had planted them; but on the whole there was a charm to this Eden and the narrow garden, long as a street, was an invitation to the simple happiness of peace and dreaming idleness.

Looking as out of keeping as possible in this muddle of vegetation, Billy marched across this false jungle and halted in front of the open door of the little house. There he called loudly:

'Is there someone here answering to the name of Patrick?'

Silence. From beyond the wall, in the avenue, whips cracked, carriages rode by and people were chattering.

He waited. Finally a tall man appeared, dressed in grubby white canvas clothes.

'Yassum,' he said simply, at the same time examining Billy from head to toe.

'Are you Patrick?' Billy asked.

His clear eyes shining with admiration and curiosity, the Irishman once more answered:

'Yassum.'

'Then you're my gardener and I'm your new boss. I am the husband of Mrs Jones, who is now Mrs Hargrove.'

Every line on Patrick's face melted into a wide smile and his open mouth presaged an important speech, but Billy quickly cut him short:

'Thank you for your congratulations. Now let's talk about gardens. Yours is a mess. I want the whole thing redone.'

He turned smartly round and saw Elizabeth hurrying toward him, leading Ned by the hand.

Billy seized the child and swung him up into the air. Little cries of fear and pleasure came back to him from mid-air.

'Do you recognize your new Papa?' Billy asked, putting him down again. 'We are old friends already, aren't we?'

Ned turned a shining face toward him.

'Yes, yes!'

'Yes, Papa,' Billy corrected.

'Yes, Papa.'

'Well, then, I'm going to make you a fine present. As you are not a baby any longer, you are going to have a room of your own, like a real man. Are you a man or a baby?'

Not sure what was coming next, Ned replied hesitantly:

'A man . . .'

'Then I'm going to give you, all to yourself, the fine room on the ground floor with a lovely big window, to look at the garden.'

Something crossed Ned's face, as though the baby were waking up with a start.

'And Mummy?' he asked.

'And Mummy . . . That's not how a man talks, my boy.'

Elizabeth bent over Ned and hugged him.

'Don't be afraid, Ned darling. Your door will be open, so will mine: you just have to call Mummy and she'll be there.'

'I won't be near you any longer,' he insisted, close to tears.

'Yes, you will. I can fly down the stairs faster than a bird and I'll be with you. If you don't want Mummy to be unhappy, then say: "Yes, Mummy."'

He didn't answer, but kept his eyes fixed on his mother's face and she could read in his wide pupils the distress of a lover being torn away from his beloved.

She murmured in his ear fearfully:

'I'll come and sleep beside you.'

In a flash, she saw everything: herself lying beside Ned until he fell asleep, then leaving him to go back to her own room and her husband.

Without answering, he put up his hands to stroke her face and she briskly lifted him in her arms, then put her lips to each of his damp eyes. Reassured, the little boy smiled.

Billy came over and, in a faintly ironic tone, said:

'I hate to disturb this delightful scene of maternal love, but since that problem is solved, let's turn to horticulture, darling: your garden.'

She put the child down and gave Billy a severe look:

'Try to understand,' she said.

'I do,' he replied, merrily. 'I understood everything the first time I saw you together.'

'Whatever you saw was entirely normal.'

'Let's say it was exceptionally normal and leave it at that. Elizabeth, how do you want your garden?'

'I want an English garden,' she said defiantly.

'Perfect. English gardens are the finest. Pat, come over here.'

Pat strode over.

'Your garden looks like a rubbish heap,' Billy told him with his hands behind his back and his legs apart. 'We're going to make it a paradise. So, I want color, you understand: roses, azaleas, hortensias; and for scent, enough seringas, honeysuckle, jasmin and heliotropes to stun you; and camelias, and above all magnolias. I can't see a single one, it's ridiculous, so plant four of them for me to besot the heart with tenderness. Elizabeth, do you agree?'

The young Englishwoman, standing bolt upright, had gone pale, as though expecting a blow.

'Of course,' she said coldly.

'Do you remember the two great magnolias beneath the porch at Dimwood? You loved them so much.'

'I still do,' she said.

'So, some magnolias, for the memory.'

'It will take a lot of work,' Pat remarked.

'Yes, a lot. I'm doubling your wages.'

Turning to Elizabeth, he took her hand to lead her toward the house and said under his breath:

'You must arrange the garden as you wish, my beloved, but do put some color into it, as at Dimwood. But your hands are cold: what's the matter? You are quite pale.'

There was so much love in his eyes and his voice that she dismissed the awful thought that had come into her mind. He wasn't thinking of Jonathan. In any case, who would have revealed the episode of the veranda to him? But she had been afraid.

'It's nothing,' she said. 'A momentary weakness, because of the child, but he's calm now, and all's well. I almost forgot to remind you to talk to the gardener. He keeps getting on the wrong side of our tradesmen.'

'Why's that?'

'He boxes and knocks the delivery boys down, just for fun; it's his obsession, he just loves fighting, so they don't deliver here any more. Yet, I would like to keep him because he guards the house like a mastiff. And then, I like him, in spite of everything.'

'I'll fix it straightaway.'

'Oh, I must see this,' Elizabeth said, suddenly amused. Then, turning to Ned who was standing beside her, she said: 'Darling, be good and keep quiet.'

Smiling at what he saw as the prospect of a golden future, the Irishman was on his way back to his house, when Billy's imperious tones stopped him in his tracks:

'Patrick, come here.'

The man turned round, still radiant, his sharp eye already calculating.

'Yassum.'

'It appears you beat up the delivery men.'

'All the saints in Ireland will be my witness, I don't do it on purpose. They have fists, they only need to defend themselves, but they only send me weaklings.'

'That's no reason to box with them.'

'It's not my fault, I can't stop myself. It's the noble art, don't you know?'

His face suddenly took on a sly look:

'If I dared . . .' he said. 'Supposing it would amuse you, you and I, like that, right here . . .'

'With pleasure,' Billy said.

He put up his guard. Pat, delighted, did the same. With incredible skill and the vigor of a young man, he lashed out his long, muscular arm in a blow that Billy only narrowly ducked; but the very same moment, and not without a certain affectation of nonchalance, he caught the Irishman on the jaw with a steel fist that laid him full out on the ground.

Ned gave a cry of terror and ran over to Pat shouting:

'He's killed Pat!'

He ran across to the defeated fighter, lying stretched out in the grass, bent over him and, timidly, touched the rough face. After a few seconds, the Irishman came to and, without moving, winked at the child.

This time, Ned gave a shout of joy.

'Mummy, he's not dead.'

The gardener got up, laughing.

'Well, is that it, Pat?' Billy said, merrily. 'Do we leave the delivery men alone?'

'It's a promise,' said Pat. 'As long as I'm not provoked.'

'I'll give orders that you won't be,' Billy snapped.

Pat watched him walk off with Elizabeth and Ned. He may have been struck with admiration by the figure of his conqueror, because he murmured:

'All the same, what a boxer he would have made . . .'

With Billy, plans were carried out in military fashion: quickly, summarily and definitively.

Appalled by upheavals that he could not understand, Ned hung on to his irritable mother's skirts, begging her to stop everything. Above all, the moving of his bed and its journey down the staircase filled him with horror.

'Look, Mummy!' he cried, seeing it vanish into a room with which he was not familiar.

Betty, who was returning from the market with the cook, arrived in time to calm him down. Drying his tears, she talked to him in that voice whose wild softness seemed to come from a world where childhood reigned, and its tender modulations eased the sorrow of the boy she called her 'treasure'. She stayed beside him in his new room and hugged him every time a piece of furniture was brought from the room he had left. Tables, chairs and armchairs seemed out of place and the former familiar setting was not recaptured.

Eventually, the black woman's tender affection soothed the little boy and he left for a walk with her, his heart eased somewhat.

# 42

*T*he new way of life soon established itself in the house. In appearance, at least, everything was for the best. Merriment was the keynote: Billy knew how to impose the schoolboyish good humor which he had never lost, and proved to have an inexhaustible fund of amusing anecdotes. Ned listened carefully and misunderstood everything in the most delightful way.

At bedtime, Elizabeth's stratagem was tested and succeeded wonderfully. She only needed to stay at Ned's bedside for a quarter of an hour, pretending to sleep, before she would hear him breathing evenly the whole night long.

At the beginning, she felt a slight remorse for this simple deception of innocence, but Billy laughed kindly at her scruples and praised her ingenuity in finding such a good tactic. Did he realize that this game of lies and love was strangely like a preparatory course in marital infidelity?

However, for the time being, nothing could be further from anyone's mind on the upper floor of the attractive, rather prim house on the corner of the street. Undoubtedly, the emphatic 'yes, you will!' of Mrs Harrison Edwards and her feather had been quite correct. Almost without restraint, Elizabeth abandoned herself to passions which she had patiently repressed since the death of Jonathan. Yet she still felt the strange disgust that made her close her eyes at a particular moment.

Billy could not cope with it and his male vanity suffered, because a woman's psychological labyrinth was a mystery to him. He comforted himself by saying that he had the main thing he wanted, and did not venture to enquire further.

Betty had still not had the opportunity to see Lieutenant Hargrove since the day of his arrival at Elizabeth's. Only a day and night had gone by, but instinctively the old servant showed her face as little as possible. She seemed to be determined to have herself forgotten, entirely dedicated to the service of little Ned and less often of his mother, even though the latter had an unreserved affection for her.

It so happened that, on his way to the dining-room to have breakfast, Billy noticed her in the hallway. Confronted with this person, who seemed enormous to her and intimidating in his splendor, Betty gave a cry like the tiny squeak of a mouse.

'Massa Billy!' she said.

'What is it?' said the colorfully dressed giant, glancing down at his feet.

'Massa Billy, it's Betty.'

At these words, he bent double and clasped the little old black woman in both hands, then lifted her to the level of his face.

'My dear Betty,' he said, 'Elizabeth didn't tell me. I thought you were still there, in Virginia, or else with Charlie Jones. But I see you haven't forgotten your little Billy, whom you used to bath twenty years ago.'

The idea that she had once run her hands over the body of this giant, filled Betty with confusion and she cried:

'Oh, Massa Billy! I'm shamed . . .'

'Why? I'm delighted to see my black Mammy again.'

Gently, he put her down. She came up to his waist.

'And what are you doing here, Betty?'

'I'm a-lookin' after Massa Ned. I take him walks.'

'And this is your home for ever. You are free, you understand? Not a slave: that's right, isn't it?'

'Yes, Massa Billy; thank you, Massa Billy. Miss 'Lizbeth done tole me, "you're free".'

'She was right. I'm going to dress you in new clothes from head to foot.'

'Oh, no, Massa Billy. I prefer my ole red'n'black skirt and blouse and my green bandana . . .'

'As you wish, Betty.'

'Thank you, Massa Billy. I'm goin' to see Massa Ned.'

In his honor, she clumsily attempted a little curtsy, like a lady, and sped off. He watched her running on her short, slightly crooked legs. Worn by age and work, she now looked like a very old doll, but her black eyes were still full of that almost superhuman goodness which had already won him over as a little boy.

# 3
# TROUBLES

## 43

Christmas was approaching quietly. In Savannah, the season was celebrated with a piety sustained in the Prayer Book by prayers of unequalled literary beauty. It was formal, even moving, but nothing more. There were not yet, as was starting to happen in the North under the influence of the Mother Country, fir trees with little candles or, above all, long and joyful feasts dominated by turkey and plum pudding, followed by crazy sleigh rides through the wintry landscape. In Savannah, the scenery still had the magic, hardly altered, of its leaves and flowers. Bells rang, carols celebrated the angels, the shepherds and the Child in his manger. What was missing was the snow and the magic of cold.

Late in the afternoon, three days before Christmas, the young couple had a visit from Charlie Jones, all smiles as usual. Pink, smelling of eau de cologne, and dressed with studied elegance in a black frock coat, he gave the impression of being extremely satisfied with life in general, no less than with himself, and a somewhat commonplace good humor erupted through the door at the same time as he did. After kissing Elizabeth and treating Billy to a sort of friendly thump, he announced:

'Children, my dear Amelia is arriving in Savannah on Tuesday to spend Christmas here, together with the little girl and two boys she bore me at our dear old home in Great Meadow. We shall celebrate the season at home in the quietest possible way, as a family. Both of you are invited to dinner.'

Billy and Elizabeth bowed two faces in resignation, yet armed with the expected smiles.

'Three children already!' Elizabeth said politely. 'Time goes so fast . . . I can hardly believe it.'

'Little Mathiwilda is still so tiny that you won't see her, but I am very eager for you to meet my two sons, Emmanuel and Johnnie, who are already very lively lads. Until now, I have always sent Amelia and the rest of my little family to spend the winter at Warm Springs. The remainder of the time, they don't leave our home at Great Meadow. Don't you miss Virginia a little, Elizabeth?'

'Yes, often,' she said, without conviction.

'This year, dear Amelia has decided to make an exception and come to Savannah for part of the winter. This was quite a decision for such an upright soul, because she has a low opinion of our town, suspecting it of depravity.'

Billy burst out laughing.

'She is confusing it with Louisiana. You have to go to New Orleans to really enjoy yourself.'

Charlie Jones raised an eyebrow.

'You don't sound to me like a responsible husband,' he said with mock severity. 'But let it be. The slightest thing alarms Amelia's moral rectitude. You will see for yourselves. Her inner life has become so deep that her face alone, without either moving or speaking, delivers a sermon.'

Elizabeth and Billy exchanged looks.

'I can see why you are surprised,' Charlie Jones went on. 'There is a mystery in this admirable woman, which I can sense without understanding. It conveys a kind of moral wellbeing which makes life pleasant for me and ensures peace in the home. Do you know what I am saying?'

'Oh, yes, Uncle Charlie!' they said, simultaneously.

'As in England, you will celebrate the birth of Our Lord by eating a turkey with cranberry sauce. This is not the usual custom in the South, but in my home you are in England.'

'Long live England,' Elizabeth said, softly.

'Bravo, Elizabeth: still loyal. I might add — and this is a pleasure which you must not refuse me — that on Christmas morning, the cream of Savannah society will see you in the wonderfully elegant Christ Church. This is important for you, my children. Dinner is at two o'clock.'

Returning to their room, Elizabeth and Billy did not comment on what was awaiting them, but, on one of those unfathomable whims of nature, they threw themselves into each other's arms, in an ecstasy of the senses.

On Christmas morning, in accordance with Uncle Charlie's express wishes, they went to Christ Church where they cut a very fine figure alongside one of the leading figures in town and his very imposing wife Amelia, who was dressed in plum-colored silk.

Many eyes turned to look at the handsome officer and the beautiful Englishwoman, and no one failed to notice the ruby hanging around her neck.

In truth, Elizabeth's appearance in church was a sort of event in itself, since she hardly ever went there. No one questioned her on that point; what could she have said, anyway? She did not understand it herself, but being seen at prayer embarrassed her like some impropriety. She felt that this aspect of her life should remain entirely private. No one should be part of it, not even — above all — Billy. So, in Christ Church that Christmas morning, she felt a profound unease.

The dinner went better than she had anticipated. Uncle Charlie himself carved the turkey, an overestimated fowl, tasteless apart from all the things that are stuffed into it; however, everyone persuaded themselves that it was delicious. A fine French wine helped to dim their judgement. Amelia pronounced herself satisfied and agreed to wet her lips on a glass of Saint-Julien. The years had hardly marked her expressionless face which struck one with the nobility of its expression and a dignity which did not incite to frivolity or confidences.

Elizabeth, observing her from time to time, admired the depth of the large pensive eyes which sometimes turned toward her, so that their looks crossed and suggested the start of some silent conversation.

Charlie Jones and Billy, both under the influence of the wine, were as talkative as each other and chattered away merrily. Uncle Charlie was reminded of his youth, listening to the jests of the soldier whose complexion was ruddy from the effects of the good fare.

As the meal drew toward its end, Charlie Jones said to Elizabeth, 'I shan't show you my little ones today. They are asleep, dulled by too much plum pudding, but I shall soon bring my Emmanuel to see you; he will be five and a half shortly. He could play with your Ned, who needs a companion to fight with. You and I, lieutenant, will go to the smoking room where I have some real cigarillos from Havana for you. Ladies, I very much hope to rejoin you in the little green drawing-room where large armchairs await you, just the place to digest a meal with one's eyes shut, for example . . .'

This abrupt manner of dismissing the usual courtesies was rather unlike the normal Charlie Jones, but the three bottles of his precious Saint-Julien 1835, which he had shared with the valiant hussar, were gently taking effect.

In the green and gold drawing-room overlooking the garden, the two women sat down, not in the wide armchairs designated by Charlie Jones but on a mauve satin sofa. Amelia was sitting a little too upright for Elizabeth to dare to slump back in the plentiful cushions. At first there was a fairly long silence. Amelia looked at a little square of sky above the green oak trees in the garden, as though searching for inspiration; then she turned to Elizabeth.

'My dearest, do you remember the conversation we had once in a corner of the colonial cemetery?'

'Yes, even though it was a long time ago. I think you talked to me about your sister, Charlotte.'

'I did. That unhappy broken engagement that nearly drove her mad . . .'

'Now I remember. Poor Aunt Charlotte.'

'Don't feel too sorry for her, Elizabeth. She did well not to get married. Now, at least, she knows peace.'

'She is very good.'

'With the heart of a child. Listen, my experience of life has been very different. You see before you the unhappiest woman in this town.'

Elizabeth looked up in astonishment.

'Please don't misunderstand me,' Amelia went on. 'Charlie is the best man in the world, but the misunderstanding between us is so vast as to be entirely insuperable. In a word, I have the faith and he doesn't.'

'And because of the faith . . .'

'You cannot understand the gulf that it creates in the long run. Although he does observe a few conventions, such as going to church on certain days, he does not truly believe in anything. He is not aware of it himself. He considers me simply as a bigot . . . He would never say the word, but I read it in his eyes and his indulgent and amused smile when he praises what he calls my serenity of soul. There is not the slightest doubt that he loves me. For him, I am the much caressed women who gives him children. He thrives on it, and everything suggests that my health also benefits . . . But I wish I was dead.'

'Oh, Aunt Amelia!'

'Let it be, I've finished. I could go much further, but you would be bored. It is almost impossible to speak of religion. All my life I've just wanted to hide myself in God.'

At these words, Elizabeth started to her feet, as if some other Elizabeth inside her were making a leap toward this woman who was watching her calmly. She wanted to say something, but couldn't. In any case, Amelia raised her hand to stop her.

'We must part,' she said simply. 'I am feeling very weary. I want to go up to my room. Even in silence we have said a great deal to one another. Yes, don't imagine I'm joking. You have talked to me, from the depth of your being, perhaps. Now, would you be good enough to pull the bell beside you.'

The young Englishwoman obeyed and a black servant shortly appeared.

'Tell Mr Jones I am ready.'

The servant bowed and went out.

'Charlie knows what that means,' Amelia said. 'He'll be here in a moment. I must say, he is very obedient.'

As she said this, her features took on a look of sovereign authority which had not been there a moment before. Elizabeth immediately recognized the provocative pride of the Highlands of Scotland, the consequence of a merciless war with England, though five minutes earlier the woman had exhibited charming modesty. The sudden transformation came from a change of mood which Elizabeth could not interpret, but it was quite evident that Amelia was the one who ruled in that house.

'We left rather abruptly,' Billy said to Elizabeth on the way home. 'I was beginning to enjoy myself. Charlie Jones was not at all shocked by my army stories. On the contrary, he wanted to hear more. Anyway, that's another Christmas over. These events bore me to death.'

Elizabeth paid no attention to this admission with its military frankness. She felt much too bewildered to think of anything except Amelia's odd confession. In some strange way, they had disturbed all the young Englishwoman's ideas about life. For this reason she would have preferred not to hear any of the astonishing monologue which Amelia, for reasons known only to herself, called a conversation. What would be the use of deciding not to see her any longer? What a misfortune it was that one could not will oneself to forget . . . Certain phrases, certain words buried themselves in the memory for a long time. One did not have the right . . .

'Mad,' she thought. 'My Billy puts everything back in place. He at least is straightforward. Happiness blots out everything.'

She pressed against him in the tilbury.

'Patience,' he said, gaily. 'I understand.'

# 44

*N*ed had stayed at home. Endowed with the tyrannical memory of childhood, he had forgotten nothing of the previous Christmas. Then, his mother's love had watched over his happiness at almost every minute. Now the world around his little person was oddly changed. No doubt he himself was to some extent responsible. His mother wanted to take him with her to his grandfather Charlie and he had said no. At that moment, the handsome officer said, with a big smile:

'Little Ned, you never say no to your Mummy, you say "Yes, Mummy" and you do as she says.'

'I don't want to go to Grandfather's.'

He had said this without turning his eyes away from the officer.

'You know that I am your Papa, and that you must obey me if I tell you to.'

Ned did not answer, because he had not understood anything about this business of one Papa replacing the first who had gone away.

Elizabeth and Billy looked at one another and shook their heads.

'After all,' Billy said, 'if he doesn't want to . . . That will be one complication less: children at table can be a real bore . . .'

'Even so, it is sad to leave him alone at home on Christmas Day.'

'He won't be alone: there's the housekeeper.'

'You don't realize, he doesn't like her.'

'Betty, then.'

'Oh, yes, Betty. It's still a bit absurd.'

'We'll come home after dinner. And he has all those toys you bought for him.'

'I think you're right, but I still feel bad about it. Really, I feel bad.'

The words made her feel better and she repeated them. Then she went to give instructions to the cook and Miss Celina. Ned had to be given a good, carefully prepared breakfast. Sweet potatoes would console him in his solitude and a good slice of chocolate cake.

After that, she went to find Ned and smothered him with affection. He accepted everything with the rather self-satisfied patience of those who feel that it is their right to be loved, but he got her to promise that at bedtime she would come and sleep next to him.

Slightly ashamed of the deception she had introduced into his life, she promised the child everything he asked and escaped to join Billy who was waiting by the door in the tilbury.

Ned's meal was quick. According to the housekeeper who kept an eye on him from time to time, he ate much too quickly, but that day he was in a hurry . . . Obedient to Elizabeth's orders, she insisted on him lying down for a quarter of an hour after eating, but he refused. With his mother and the officer away, he could defy anyone.

In his new room, a regiment of lead soldiers, some in red, the others in blue, replaced the Roundheads and Cavaliers, which had begun to bore him. The red soldiers represented the famous 'lobsters' of the English army and the blues were the republicans of the Revolution of 1776. Billy had chosen the best of their kind, but that morning the child cast a cynical eye on them and left them in peace, as he also did the astonishing little railway with its three carriages and locomotive, whose chimney puffed out a little cloud of black cotton smoke. All this was clearly displayed on a low table in the middle of this room in which Ned was still unable to settle. In vain did the housekeeper pretend to be delighted by these wonderful presents. She was no more successful when she tried once more to persuade him to lie on the bed. He turned his back to her and she went out, irritated. He waited for a brief moment, then followed her, making his way to the narrow staircase which led to the first floor.

There were thirty steep steps to climb. Without wasting time or thinking about it, he pulled himself up on the first by clasping his tiny fingers round the fluting of the little column that marked the point of departure. The next step proved less demanding, thanks to the slender bar which offered a better handhold for a brave little four-and-a-half-year old. After the third step, his legs, though still a bit short, managed to overcome the forbidding staircase, but when he reached the top of his climb, Ned sat down, panting.

No sooner was he in his old room than he shrank back in horror at seeing it so brutally changed by the introduction of furniture that was not his. He had anticipated this, but the shock came only with the first glimpse. His heart was heavy with grief. His own territory had been taken away from him.

With cautious steps, as though advancing through enemy lines, he walked from one side to the other, mentally restoring the old order and its mysteries: he had filled his old room with too many dreams, with the murky stories that his mother had invented to occupy the minutes before sleep every evening, month after month . . . Everything evaporated in this new decor. Now he was proceeding with cruel disenchantment to the back of the room, toward a dimly-lit corner. There, nothing had changed and here he stopped. Out of this chiaroscuro came the thing for which the child had no name. It did not frighten him; he was expecting it.

Soon he began to mutter to himself. Does anyone know in what unknown world children wander: who they speak to or what they see? Education would wipe out the memory of these explorations, closed to adults, in which may lie the secret of our destiny. Like a whisper in the ear, the vague syllables of a name emerged from the little mouth with its moist lips.

An instinctive caution told him not to stay too long.

When Elizabeth and Billy came back to the house, they found him in his new room, looking out of the window at the garden where the trees were casting the first shadows of evening on the empty pathways.

Standing near him, Betty was telling him off in a sad, soft voice:

'Betty not happy when she look for Massa Ned everywhere and Massa Ned not there . . .'

The child looked at her with a smile.

'Be quiet, Betty.'

He put a finger to his lips. The front door had just opened and Elizabeth's voice was already calling him.

Ned frowned and, without taking his eyes off Betty, said very quickly, 'Don't say anything.'

At the same moment, his mother appeared. In her pink dress, she seemed like an eruption of happiness. The gold of her hair was shining and her whole being radiated youth and silent exuberance. When she saw Ned with Betty by the window, she exclaimed:

'You had a nice walk, I hope? You're back very early.'

'Not go out,' said Betty.

'I might have guessed. Even though we prefer to stay with our toys, we must go out. In a moment it will be too late. Quickly, Betty.'

She ran over and kissed the little boy.

'Billy will explain to you about the war with the English. Tell Mummy you love her.'

'Yes, Mummy.'

Eager to leave and bound up the staircase to her room, she did not notice the child's solemn expression.

'Will you come back this evening?' he asked softly.

She only vaguely heard this imploring murmur. Casually, she said:

'Of course, darling.'

'Do you promise?' he cried.

But she was already far away.

# 45

There was no dinner that evening. The meal was cancelled by Elizabeth who told the housekeeper, through the door of her room, that she and her husband simply wanted to rest. Coming back from his walk with Betty, Ned knew nothing of this decision. His black Mammy in her white cloud seized his small body and gave him his bath with all the usual loving cooings. After that, the child was seated at a little table in his former room and served soup and fruit compote with a light glass of cold tea. Miss Celina thought it proper to let him dine in front of the window where the sight of the garden at night might console him for the loss of his former room; and, indeed, the cold light of the moon transformed a scene, that was in no way mysterious, into a vision of another world. The child allowed himself to be enchanted for a moment, his nature easily inclining him to the charm of the unreal.

The housekeeper kept him company until the end of the meal and then made way for Betty, who was always welcome. She tried, with rather clumsy enthusiasm, to interest her 't'easure' in the red and blue lead soldiers and the very modern railway. Ned had not touched them. In his eyes they belonged to this new room which he did not like, but he still kept his Indian rag doll close by him as a token of happy days.

Bedtime came when Betty lit the night-light. Usually at this moment, the person would appear whose presence alone gave a different dimension to everything. He didn't even need to see her clearly: it was her, and that was enough. He would have recognized her from the smell of her hair or the rustling of her dress as she gathered its folds to sit down on the edge of the bed; but most of all from that leap of the heart that he felt like the warmth of a flame.

'Mummy's going to come soon,' he kept saying to Betty, who was trying to make him sleep, because it was starting to get late. 'Mummy always comes.'

'I know, Massa Ned,' she said, a little uneasy.

To reassure her, he said:

'She promised.'

In the darkness at the back of the room, he tried to distinguish the shadows of the room they had taken away from him, but this one, the new one, seemed empty; nothing could come from the back to him, everything was hidden up there: the ride through the night on a black horse. Only Mummy knew about it, apart from himself.

Betty's shy voice broke the silence.

'Miss Celina said Miss 'Lizbeth very tired.'

'She always comes, Betty.'

'She sleepin', Massa Ned.'

'She will come, Betty.'

'Massa Ned, Betty goin' sleep too. Miss 'Lizbeth, she no come.'

'Don't go, Betty.'

'Very well, Massa Ned. Betty goin' sleep by you. Miss 'Lizbeth, she no come this evenin'.'

Hitting the bed with both fists, Ned shouted:

'She promised.'

And suddenly, seizing the truth like a punch in the chest, he burst into tears. In a second he learned all the bitterness of love betrayed.

He did not want to believe it and curled up in the bed, his head buried under the pillow, so that he could howl as much as he liked.

Terrified, the old black woman made a succession of signs of the cross and prayers for the dreadful crisis to end, but the mixture of sorrow and anger had to exhaust itself in a storm of stifled cries . . .

For several long minutes, Betty saw his little shoulders shudder at each wave of sorrow, and she had to wait for exhaustion to end his distress by suddenly casting the little boy into sleep.

The following morning, Elizabeth, still in her white-dressing gown, came down as usual to kiss her son. The housekeeper was standing next to him, helping him to put on his boots.

'Good morning, Celina. Good morning, darling.'

Ned looked at her and answered with a smile.

'Don't you say good morning to Mummy?'

'Good morning, Mummy.'

'How did he sleep?'

'Well, I suppose, Madam. I had difficulty waking him up.'

'That's a good sign,' Elizabeth said, stroking the child's curls.

Leaning toward him, she peppered his cheeks and hair with kisses full of the affection that came so naturally to her. She did not suspect what an effort he was making to contain himself and not say the words that were burning on his lips: 'You promised . . .'

However, he said nothing, for a reason that would have made her kneel in front of him and beg for forgiveness: he loved her too much to make her feel guilty, but tears shone in his brown eyes.

'My love,' she said, seeing them. 'Aren't you happy? Don't you like your presents? Mummy will give you others. I must say, I'd enjoy making the English and American soldiers fight, and I know who I would make victorious . . . And that funny little railway . . . You wind it up and its goes by itself. I hate traveling by railroad myself . . . All that smoke . . . Celina, I'm going back upstairs to dress. Breakfast in an hour, as usual. For Mr Hargrove, bacon and eggs with strong coffee. Darling, Mummy will have a nice surprise for you at New Year.'

# 46

Some news arrived in late morning and, although there was nothing alarming about it, it scared Elizabeth as though some dangerous future had taken a step toward her. By one of those tricks of fate that life habitually plays, an unexpected event made it still more disturbing. It was the young English sub-lieutenant who brought the message. He gave it to Billy while the latter was talking to Elizabeth in the drawing-room.

With a frown, Billy opened the letter and went over to a corner by the window.

'Excuse me,' he said. 'It's rather long.'

Elizabeth sat down at the far end of the room in an armchair. With a wave and a smile, she indicated a chair opposite her to the messenger, but he remained standing, his shako in his hand. She insisted. Looking faintly guilty, he sat down on the edge of the chair. His shyness was hardly consistent with everything martial in his costume. His complexion said it all. It was as if his cheeks, which grew redder and redder, were vying with the aggressive red of his frogged dolman.

Was it the magic of the uniform that affected Elizabeth, as it did so many women? Yet surely her husband provided her with an ample supply of that magic, from noon to night? So was it a surge of loyalty to Mother England that made the over-impressionable young woman's heart beat faster?

She stared at him; he looked down.

'Virginal,' she thought.

And, in a half-whisper, she ventured:

'Do you get homesick sometimes?'

Astonishment. As if launching an assault at the risk of his life, he stared at her with the look of irrespressible tenderness generally known as 'calves' eyes.' With exquisite charm, she bowed her head, while turning away a little, which can mean this, or that, as the onlooker wishes.

Billy's deep voice cut through this silent dialogue, which was becoming an idyll.

'Here's something new. We're leaving Pulaski. The fort was there to defend the coast, but we are going to occupy Fort Beauregard in South Carolina, not far from Charleston and Fort Sumter. This will put us a litle further away from one another, Elizabeth, but I can be here in three hours' ride.'

'Even so,' Elizabeth said, sobering up completely, 'you will be further away. I don't like this kind of news: it sounds like strategy and preparation for war.'

'You're imagining things. Pulaski is no longer any use and we are moving out. For that matter, one wonders what purpose Beauregard and Sumter serve. They had some significance when there was still a threat from England and Spain, but the federal government wants them. Who is going to attack Charleston? And then, if you want to visit me in Beauregard, there is the railroad.'

'The railroad makes me feel ill.'

'In that case, we must find some alternative. You know that I can always find a way. What does bother me a little is that I have to be there on January 2nd.'

Elizabeth gave a cry:

'January 2nd! But that's so soon!'

'We still have four days left, but don't worry. I know how to get the commandant to give me elastic leave, you understand?'

Suddenly terrified, she exclaimed:

'Promise me there won't be a war!'

He burst out laughing and took her by the shoulders, pretending to shake her.

'Don't listen to rumors and don't read the newspapers, because you don't understand anything about it. There is trouble a long way from here on the frontier of Kansas and Missouri, where anti-slavery fanatics are attacking the plantation owners — and even the Indians, because they too have slaves. Let's call them skirmishes. It will calm down.'

She put both hands on his chest.

'You reassure me,' she said. 'I'd die if anything were to happen to you.'

'Does it worry you that they've put me in a fort? I am going to fight, it's true, but over whist with the commandant!'

Elizabeth smiled.

'I hate forts because for me forts mean war and I hate war.'

'Don't start again. There are times when it has to be. In the West because of the Indians, in Texas because of Mexico, but it's so far away. If there is any place where you can be at peace, it's here in Georgia.'

'Darling,' she murmured.

For a trifle, she would have thrown herself on his chest weeping with joy into his braiding, but the presence of the young sub-lieutenant restrained her.

To tease her, he whispered in her ear:

'I thought that English women were not afraid of anything.'

She looked back at him provocatively:

'Englishwomen are afraid of nothing, but they are human and fear for what they love.'

'Lieutenant Charlton,' Billy said, anticipating some endearments, 'give my respects to the commandant and tell him I shall be in Beauregard before the evening bugle sounds.'

The sub-lieutenant put on his shako and went out, saluting.

'You see how simple it is,' said Billy.

'Darling, you're perfect.'

# 47

The New Year was welcomed in like its predecessors. Secret anxieties were drowned in champagne and whisky, and the custom of delivering visiting cards was carried out with the usual precision. Naturally no one was at home because everyone was performing the same duty, so absent friends greeted absent friends with calling cards turned down at the corner.

As for Elizabeth and her husband, they decided to forget the whole world in the intimacy of conjugal delight.

That left little Ned, who would have endured hours of unusual solitude had not his grandfather given him some thought. To celebrate New Year, Elizabeth had dressed her son in a very elegant suit of dark red velvet with a lace collar which, she thought, made him look just like a little prince. Thus transformed, the child felt ill at ease, but that was only one aspect of a nightmarish day about which he understood nothing and yet which he accepted with the patience of despair.

From the end of the morning, after he had taken a mortifying walk with Betty along the grand avenue, where he was pursued by the amused looks and derisive remarks of uncultured urchins, a carriage came to pick him up and take him to Charlie Jones's.

The latter greeted him with kindness, because he loved children and wanted to introduce him without delay to his two sons, but first of all to little Mathiwilda, a tiny creature only one year old. Carried in the arms of her black nanny, she could only wave a hand and roll her angel's eyes before being taken away.

It was a different matter with the two boys. Aged three and a half, Johnnie, the youngest, with his long, straight blond hair, already seemed the charming fellow he would eventually become. His blue eyes settled gently on the face of the visitor to whom he proffered a delicate, slightly soft hand. Ned took it and then let it fall as something of no interest.

Up to now, peace and an appearance of puerile civility had reigned. With Emmanuel, however, a major misunderstanding broke out. A year older than Ned, who was his nephew, this solid lad with his short red hair stood four square in front of the little prince and examined him from head to toe. Was it the velvet suit or simply the Bruges lace collar? Something provoked him like a red rag to a bull. Bearing down on Ned with joyous fury, he laid him out on the carpet and battered him with his fists.

Confronted with this barbarous assault, Johnnie, who could do nothing, took fright and started to cry. Ned, however, quickly recovered from the shock and, in a burst of anger, hammered his aggressor's face with both fists. The other got up with a cry of pain; a red stream was running from his nose to his half-open mouth.

Standing up, legs apart and hands in pockets, Uncle Charlie had watched this boxing match, which he had expected, with a connoisseur's eye.

'Short,' he said, 'but mainly satisfactory. Ned, you defended yourself well; you have your father's blood in you! Emmanuel, you should know that a surprise attack can be unfair if it is unprovoked. Go and tell your black nanny to wipe your nose, but first I want the two of you to shake hands. Come on!'

A moment's hesitation and the two boys held out their hands. They were shaken without conviction, then Emmanuel left.

'As for you Johnnie,' Uncle Charlie said, 'stop snivelling like a girl. I'm ashamed of you. Try to be a man.'

Johnnie swallowed back his tears and made an effort to be a man, but his long hair seemed to weep on his shoulders.

Lunch clarified the situation. Aunt Amelia appeared in a violet satin dress, her impassive face imprisoned in a monumental bonnet of fine linen decorated with a smoky gray ostrich feather. The indulgent look in her large eyes settled on one person, then another, and finally gave the impression of turning back inside. Despite this she gave evidence of a fine appetite and did due homage to a Virginia ham with pink potatoes.

Uncle Charlie behaved jovially, as befitted the personality he had adopted since his youth. To speed up the reconciliation between uncle and nephew, both young and only an hour earlier mortal enemies, he reddened their water with a light Médoc, which went slightly to their heads, and they exchanged smiles.

The dessert appeared, in the shape of a tower with battlements; made up of superimposed layers of chocolate, sugar-coated fruit, caramel, almonds and chestnuts, this construction was dressed in an outer skin of sugar which disguised the riches inside. The building collapsed under the knife of a black servant and they were each given a large slice which soon disappeared. Aunt Amelia herself was unable to resist a natural love of food which still kept her bound to this earth.

This was soon followed by a general sense of heaviness and a slowing down of thought which preceded a persistent torpor. Boredom reigned. Aunt Amelia had to get up and took her leave with dignity, her liver already starting to rebel.

It was at this point that Uncle Charlie had a brief moment of bewilderment, seeing himself alone with the three boys, because while he could send Emmanuel and Johnnie off to play by themselves, he was perhaps expected to pay a little attention to amusing his grandson, the guest. He was therefore much relieved when Ned, after thanking him like a little gentleman, asked if he could go home.

Go home? Charlie could not believe his ears. Nothing easier. The tilbury would be ready in five minutes. Grasping the little boy by both hands, he hugged him in a cloud of eau de cologne and put him in the carriage himself.

At Oglethorpe Square, the coachman lifted Ned out of the tilbury and rang the bell. Celina opened the door.

'Back already, Master Ned? I wasn't expecting you until dinner time, and it's still daylight.'

The child smiled and pushed her aside without answering. As soon as he had found himself at his grandfather's house, he had been hatching a secret plan. Without hesitation, he ran into the garden.

The light was fading gently as the first shades of evening were poised on the horizon. The clusters of greenery were darkening, but the trees along the walls still plucked some last rays of sunlight from the sky.

The tranquillity of the spot also had an effect on the child who stopped as if on the threshold of some unknown region. Yet he had been here many times, though never alone or so late. In the half-light of this transitional hour, everything seemed mysterious and he looked around in a mixture of delight and thrilling anxiety because he found something in this deserted garden that reminded him of his old room; and he began to follow the grassy path, as if it led to some country where everything is possible. Of course, it would lead to the gardener's house, but that did not alter what was on his mind. He was guided by intuition and under his breath he muttered stories that had to remain secret.

In front of the gardener's door, his heart began to beat wildly. Standing very still, he hesitated, then knocked. No reply. He knocked again, with no more success, but the handle offered no resistance to his hand and the door opened as if by itself.

The room was dark and in such disorder than at first you could see nothing in it: the disorder was well-established and destined to last. Four or five straw chairs piled one on top of the other barred the way to a window with closed shutters. Placed sideways in the center of this indescribable place, a long table covered with empty bottles made it difficult, unless one knew the way, to move from the door that opened on the street to the one that opened onto the garden.

Something that looked like a huge, long, deep chest occupied a more obscure corner and a torn mattress had been stuffed into it beneath a thin blanket of gray wool, darned and mended in red and green.

Apart from all this, the room was empty. Ned waited, then called. No reply. Getting impatient, he began to shout:

'Patrick!'

Almost at once the door at the end opened and the gardener gave his almost mechanical acknowledgement.

'Yassum!'

After that he looked left and right, but could see no one, until Ned repeated:

'Patrick!'

This time, lowering his eyes, the Irishman noticed the boy standing beside the oblong box.

'Is it you, little fellow?' he exclaimed. 'Welcome to Patrick's; but what do you want here?'

Ned, taken aback, said nothing.

'You haven't an answer,' Patrick said. 'But I know. You came for a trip to Ireland. For example, do you know what you're standing next to there?'

'Your bed?' Ned suggested.

'Bravo. But to start with, it wasn't a bed. You wonder what it could have been. I'll tell you. When I had to leave the old country because of the famine, my grandmother, seeing me going off with my pockets nearly empty, the same grandmother of mine who must now be somewhere in paradise with our saints, well, she gave me the most precious thing she had in the world, which was her fine wardrobe. "Because you never know," my grandmother told me, "if they even have wardrobes over there." '

'And then?' said Ned, slightly stunned by the whisky fumes which were pouring over him in abundance.

'And I kept my wardrobe for a long time, out of respect for my grandmother, who is now in paradise, and inside, in the wardrobe I mean, of course, I put everything I had and I slept on the ground and then I began to put my things here and there in every corner, because I was happier that way. But one evening when I had drunk a glass too many, I emptied the wardrobe and committed a sacrilege, for which the angels forgive me: I turned it over on its back and I took off the door. After that, I filled it with bundles and rags, and I lay down in it and slept as never before, and dreamed that I was up there.'

'Dreamed?' Ned asked.

'I dreamed as we dream at home in Ireland; you can't imagine. Then one day, I found in a rag dealer's hovel an old mattress that wasn't too bad, and I pushed the packages into the corners with the mattress in the wardrobe — and so I sleep and dream.'

'You dream?' the child asked.

'I am in Ireland, which is more a dream than a country, but you can't know that.'

'Do you see frightening things too?'

'Splendid things, my little lad. That's the best of all.'

Ned swallowed.

'Horses galloping through the night?'

At these words, the man drew himself up to his full height and appeared immense in the gathering darkness.

'You, my lad,' he said, 'you talk like one of us, from the old country. Your Mummy's not Irish, by any chance?'

'I dunno. I see a horseman on a black horse.'

'Galloping through the night? Oh, my fine little lad.'

'But you mustn't say anything about it,' Ned said, suddenly afraid.

'It's a secret. Mummy saw him too, every evening when we were up there in the house.'

'Up there, my lad?'

'Now they've put me downstairs and Mummy doesn't come any more. Don't ever say any of this to anyone.'

'I swear it, Massa Ned, on the word of an Irishman.'

This oath, sworn in a dramatic voice, made the child lose his head and he could not resist the need to confide in him.

'He came from the bottom of my room, up there, on a great black horse, black, black . . .'

'Were you afraid?'

'Yes, sometimes, but not always; and then the horseman was me. Mummy told me so.'

At this, the Irishman, delighted, exclaimed in surprise:

'Someone from our country had made you a present, my child, someone in the invisible world.'

'What are you saying?' Ned asked, once more anxious.

'Don't be afraid, it's wonderful.'

Without adding a word, he took a box of matches out of his pocket and soon the light of a lantern which Patrick was holding in his hand shone in the darkness. He bent down toward Ned, bending his huge body double, to have a closer look at the little pink face framed in its unruly curls. Ned did not recoil, but closed his eyes when the lamp reached the level of his head and, opening them again to show that he was not afraid, he saw the Irishman's eyes fixed on him, their pupils as blue as a limitless sea under a gray sky. He felt so strongly attracted toward them that they prevented him from seeing the rough features and the sunken cheeks bristling with reddish hairs . . .

'You, my little fellow,' Patrick said slowly, 'you are not like the rest.'

'The rest?'

'All the rest — not if you see a second Ned galloping toward you through the night.'

'No, not Ned,' the child said. 'I've got a different name, a true name . . .'

Suddenly terrified at what he was about to say, he put both his hands across the bottom of his face.

'What's the matter? Am I scaring you?'

Ned let his hands fall.

'No, but I promised Mummy not to say the name.'

'Then you must keep it to yourself,' said the mouth with its thick lips, next to the lamp. 'But my people would listen to your stories, because you see what others don't and you walk as in the depth of the woods, in another world.'

Ned looked at him, his mouth wide, torn between fear and the wish to know more.

'Come now,' said Patrick, 'it's dark. I'm going to take you home, or they'll be getting worried.'

He led him to the door and both of them started down the grassy path which ran across the garden. The moon was not yet up and it was pitch black. Patrick held his lamp in one hand and the little boy's hand in the other.,

'You would like it in the old country,' said Patrick.

This voice, coming down from on high, enchanted Ned.

'Take me there, Pat.'

'If I could, I would, my lad . . . But when you get bored, come and see me and I'll tell you stories from Ireland and you'll think you're actually there.'

They separated at the foot of the steps.

At the top of the stairway, framed in the door, Betty was waving her arms, groaning with anxiety.

# 48

*E*lizabeth knew nothing of this escapade. Her thoughts were elsewhere. She and Billy had to tear themselves away from one another when the time came to part, the day after New Year's Day, and that night she could not sleep. With no strength to bear the trial, she wept, seeking the body that was absent from the great deserted bed.

However, life had to resume its normal course and the young woman, though unhappy, pretended not to be, out of sheer pride.

On the subject of Ned, she asked herself questions that she preferred to keep to herself. How had he borne the absence of his mother for a whole day? Apparently he was still the same little boy whom she adored. On both sides, the urge to love was still there. He kissed her with the fervor that she had always known and needed. Nothing had changed — or had it?

She knew nothing of the new life that her boy was (more or less secretly) leading. In the daytime, when no one was looking after him, he ran around the garden. She approved of it; she did not like to see him in a corner of the drawing-room with his Indian, playing at knocking down Cavaliers and Roundheads. Now he would come and go in the open, often alone, but not always. Sometimes Patrick would appear with a rake or a spade, and then Ned would start to talk with him, even to chatter. It was charming to see the little fellow and the big Irishman. She approved of that. She did smile and wonder what they found to talk about, but she didn't breathe a word.

The essence of it escaped her. She did not know that at night, when Betty and the housekeeper, who took turns at watching, had left his bedside, thinking him asleep, he would get up after a short while and go to the window, where he would wait. Soon, at the very bottom of the garden, Patrick's light would start to shine discreetly in the corner of a window. Then, from his side, Ned would light a candle set in his copper candlestick on his own window-sill! It did not burn for long, because it was forbidden and someone would eventually notice that it was melting quickly. But this was the signal. The child and the Irishman greeted one another from afar, in the night. After a few minutes, they both put out the lights.

Elizabeth also lived in her dreams, but they were of a very different kind. They expressed themselves in love letters. She excelled at this craft which her nature had long prepared her to practice. In order to express herself entirely freely, she had adopted a style which might be called 'the torrential style', which could not be displayed at full power in less than four pages — though it must be said that the first words gave the meaning of the whole: 'My beloved . . .'

Leaning over her writing paper, which was almost covered by her long hair, she intoxicated herself with phrases; and these, for the moment, replaced the irreplaceable.

Billy, who did not possess his wife's ferocious gift for epistolary adoration, rewarded her only with short, masculine, martial notes: 'Patience, my lovely, hold firm. Reinforcements are coming. I have a piping hot leave for a newly-wed. You shall have your Billy in four days.'

Leave was frequent. The commandant being human, he made this concession to a partner who had no rival at cards. The latter would arrive home either by railroad or on horseback, and the delirium of the senses was resumed with a new frenzy. Once more, the ordinary routine of the household collapsed into a sort of disorder that had to be accepted. The married couple would appear at the two o'clock meal, but never at dinner. From the afternoon onwards, they would disappear until the next day. Ned observed these changes without asking questions. This was what intrigued the housekeeper most of all, but since she had entered into Elizabeth's service she had learned to keep her mouth shut.

However, one day, the lovers sacrificed an hour of their precious time to go and inspect the garden. The orders which Lieutenant Hargrove had given Patrick had been carried out: no doubt the gardener had remembered the magisterial lesson that his new master had given him, and four young magnolias were now standing, facing one another, near the house. Billy took more pleasure in this even than his wife did: she contemplated them with an odd look and was content to nod her approval.

'You see,' he said. 'From the first days of spring, they will start to grow and in the summer they will be beautiful with heavy white flowers . . . as in Dimwood. You must remember.'

'As in Dimwood,' she said, mechanically.

Despite all her efforts, she could not manage to look happy. Yet she loved her garden, and it was not so much the memory of Dimwood that bothered her, as the presence of Ned who was so happy at being with her.

'It's pretty, Mummy,' he said, pulling on her skirt.

How could he put so much love into such simple words? She lowered her eyes toward him with a smile. She was disturbed by his resemblance to his father: in some way that she could not explain, this resemblance was more apparent at some times than at others, especially when she felt there was more spontaneity in him.

She found an explanation for the mystery that soothed her and which she considered subtle: he was jealous of Billy who took his mother away from him every time he came to the house. Without realizing it, she was on the brink of a much more serious truth. What was she to make of the fact that the resemblance did not vary but that she saw it more or less plainly according to whether she saw Ned on his own or in Billy's presence? In the second case, the dead husband appeared in his son's face.

However, she did not pursue her reflexions beyond certain limits. She preferred to watch Billy preening himself as he walked back and forth around the garden. Very pleased with his appearance, he gave the impression of displaying it like an idol. This vanity did not shock Elizabeth; on the contrary, he had no more ardent admirer and she expressed her adoration to him without restraint.

When leave was over came the moments she found hardest to bear: the dreadful goodbyes in front of the house. The handkerchief, which she waved ceaselessly, could not halt the tilbury as it carried her happiness away. Normal life resumed.

# 49

Not far away, however, some interesting things were going on. Elizabeth knew all about them but, a prisoner of her amorous obsessions, she rather tended to forget about such matters.

A mysterious little plot was being hatched in one of the most sumptuous houses in town. On days when there were guests, Mrs Harrison Edwards' house, the grandiose ornament of Chippewa Square, looked like a palace. Instead of just one porch, it had three. The two side ones were remarkable for the elegance of their twin columns, while the central porch, huge in size, rounded out into a terrace behind high columns with ionic capitals.

Adopting the same shape as the terrace, the green and gold reception room was perfectly round. This was where the most sparkling balls took place as well as the social events that one had to attend if one was to keep one's place in aristocratic society. The finest jewels in the country sparkled, and crinolines, like a squadron of ships, sailed under a huge chandelier with a thousand pendants.

One evening, however, a long way from this ostentatious place, in a little drawing-room entirely decorated in pearl gray satin, six people had gathered and were sitting in a circle in large, straight-backed armchairs. Beneath their serious expressions one could sense the secret pleasure of playing at conspirators. Mrs Harrison Edwards, in a mauve taffeta dress, with her arms bare, was quite obviously presiding, as was plain from her bearing and her chair, which was higher than the rest. On her right, Charlie Jones was wearing a black coat, open to display a white waistcoat. Elizabeth, sitting beside him, had chosen to appear in light green, the color that she thought was most flattering for her on important occasions.

Had she deliberately been seated to the right of Algernon? The latter, in a waisted green jacket, was the very image of the beau, his face emerging from a huge lace ruffle like a meringue. His eyes continually roved over his neighbor's cheeks, ears, neck and bosom, and she allowed herself to be admired with a careful show of patience. Between the two of them, they represented youth and its habitual scheming.

In contrast, Major Crawford, his face bronzed from his campaigns in Mexico, was sitting stiffly in a high-buttoned black coat. His graying hair was flattened around a stubborn forehead which framed the strikingly forceful features of a soldier. Sitting perfectly still, he had not yet unclenched his teeth and seemed to be waiting for the first shots to ring out.

Near him, his Honor Judge Pilgrim exhibited a more affable kind of gravity. Pink and tranquil under his fine white curls, he sometimes smiled, but without moderating the steely look in his blue eyes.

In her most polished accents, Mrs Harrison Edwards opened the discussion with a charming smile that went round the table, so that everyone could enjoy a share.

'Since I have the pleasure of seeing you all gathered in my home, without anyone else knowing, we will be able to debate freely in this little room, where no inquisitive ears can overhear us. And first of all, with your permission, no politics.'

With one voice, they all repeated loudly:

'No politics!'

'Good, very good,' she said. 'The problem is a delicate one, namely the situation of Mrs Jonathan Armstrong, who has been unjustly barred from society and feels it deeply.'

'Unfortunately, tradition is adamant,' said Judge Pilgrim. 'We must ensure the purity of the blood that flows in our veins.'

'If you had seen her in the full pride and splendor of youth,' Major Crawford said suddenly, 'you would have been convinced that she was an honor to the white race.'

This humane attitude was an agreeable surprise coming from Major Crawford.

'The hands,' said the Judge.

'Oh, her hands were gorgeous, so they say . . .,' replied the Major. 'I only glimpsed Mrs Jonathan Armstrong when I was a captain. She turned every head, even those of the most serious men, in their youth.'

'Major Crawford, there is no secret about your admiration for the fair sex, but you say you only glimpsed Mrs Jonathan Armstrong, while I was among the guests at that disastrous reception which caused so much talk in the country. I held that half-caste hand in mine . . .'

'Poor woman!' Elizabeth exclaimed.

'No, not poor woman,' Mrs Harrison Edwards said sharply. 'She is a great lady who is conscious of her hereditary nobility.'

'We must make up for the insult,' said Charlie Jones, 'and I shall take charge of it. It was not our town which repudiated her.'

'It was mine,' retorted Judge Pilgrim. 'But the cause is common to both of us and we are in it together.'

'What a lot of fuss about a little shadow on the ends of the fingers,' Algernon suddenly exclaimed.

This protest, quite unexpected from a young man who seemed at best indifferent in the matter, made his Honor Judge Pilgrim raise an eyebrow.

'My young friend,' he said, 'before favoring us with your opinions, please take a look at the laws and customs of the State of Georgia.'

To everyone's surprise, Algernon struck back:

'That doesn't prevent public opinion from being outraged by the case of an unfortunate black man who demands his freedom in the courts because he has lived with his master in a free state . . .'

'That has nothing to do with it,' said the judge. 'His demand is meaningless.'

'The fact remains that according to the laws and customs of the State of Georgia . . .'

'Are you talking about that Dred Scott?' the Major interrupted. 'We've been hearing about nothing else for months; but what has that to do with Mrs Jonathan Armstrong?'

In a burst of self-justifying pride, Algernon confronted the Major, fixing him with his eyes:

'They are both being persecuted for a heredity for which neither of them is responsible.'

'Algernon,' Charlie Jones said gravely, 'you are not a fool, but this evening you're talking like one: you're confusing everything.'

'Dred Scott would never have considered going to court,' said the Major, 'if he had not been driven to it by the Northern abolitionists.'

As though afraid that Algernon might respond, Mrs Harrison Edwards gave the Major a winsome look and said in a gently pleading tone:

'In Heaven's name, Algernon, don't let's reopen this racial argument which has already brought us to the brink of war.'

Algernon merely smiled.

At that moment, Judge Pilgrim raised a hand to call for silence:

'The case of Dred Scott is not without interest for a man of the law. The North is trying to make him out to be a martyr of the Southern slave-owners. Let's look at the matter a little more closely.'

Elizabeth and Algernon exchanged looks of consternation.

The Judge went on, as if behind a pulpit:

'Born in Virginia in 1795, he became the house slave of a planter in this state. No planter can ever remember a case of a black servant who was tortured. I ask to all those present to confirm that.'

Charlie Jones replied at once:

'The status of house servant is a privileged one which every black aspires to when he is bought as a slave.'

'Sooner or later,' Mrs Harrison Edwards added, 'they become part of the family if they are obedient and hard-working. I think I can hear a chorus of Black Mammies and Old Black Joes agreeing with me.'

'And many others, young and old, male and female,' Judge Pilgrim went on. 'But let's continue . . .' (he continued without paying any attention to the heavy silence of the others). 'Dred Scott's master took him on a journey with him to Missouri and sold him to an army surgeon as a house slave. His new master took him to Rock Island in Illinois, then to Fort Shelling in Wisconsin. In both these states, slavery was forbidden. Dred Scott and his master spent four years there, subsequently returning to Missouri. Do you follow me?'

'Perfectly,' said several voices.

'Just as well, because this is where our Dred Scott went off the rails. In fact, he declared that having lived for four years in free states, he was now a free citizen of Missouri. This idea was put into his head by anti-slavery campaigners in the North who encouraged him to go before the courts to have his new status legalized . . .'

'You're taking us back to 46,' Major Crawford interrupted. 'And the Supreme Court . . .'

Judge Pilgrim ignored this interruption, being used to such incidents in court.

' . . . Scott was sixty-one, and in no fit state to work. His master was dead and the widow who inherited him was in a dilemma. She asked nothing better than to be rid of an unfortunate slave for whom she had no further use. Even justice was in a quandary. A black, a free citizen?'

'Ridiculous idea,' said the Major.

'Why not?' Elizabeth asked.

'Elizabeth!' Charlie Jones exclaimed, severely.

She fell silent.

'A quandary? But an eminent jurist decided . . .' Major Crawford began.

'Yes, the Attorney General Taney declared to the Federal Council that the slave Dred Scott should be given back to his master.'

Judge Pilgrim continued imperturbably:

'His view prevailed and, before the judgement was given, the North turned in fury against Taney. He had said that a slave belonged to his master wherever he was with him! This is the point we have reached. The judgement will be public as soon as the new president is in office.'

Mrs Harrison Edwards threw herself into the fray with a sharp-witted smile:

'The most amusing part of the story — if I may say so, because it could easily have turned to tragedy and taken on a much wider dimension — is that when for a moment poor Dred Scott thought himself a free man in a northern state, he realized suddenly that the Northerners would expect him to work for them to earn his living. At that, he was immediately overwhelmed with nostalgia for the good old plantation . . .'

The Judge bowed gravely, as if excusing himself for speaking again:

'By one of those unpredictable whims of the law in these great political matters, his freedom was suspended and he was given back to his master. In spite of everything, Dred Scott declared himself happy to return to the South. Anything rather than the specious freedom he was offered in the North. I have simplified in order to spare you tiresome details.'

'Elizabeth,' Mrs Harrison Edwards asked, 'do you now see more

clearly through the chaos of ideas with which our country is struggling?'

'No,' she said, 'but I find it disturbing.'

Major Crawford, who had not taken his eyes off the lovely Englishwoman, gallantly declared:

'What need is there to upset such a charming lady who has no
part in our quarrels, since she is not of this country?'

'Oh, oh, Major!' Mrs Harrison Edwards said. 'You are forgetting that her husband is a Lieutenant of Hussars in the United States
Army.'

'The devil he is!' the Major muttered. 'It had slipped my mind
for a moment.'

Algernon took the opportunity to assert himself after the insult
he had suffered a little earlier and, to show that he was not afraid,
he turned to the Major and pronounced, with a touch of malice:

'There, Major Crawford, that's what happens when we succumb
to the charms of the gentle sex.'

The Major's thunderous voice made everyone shudder:

'Young man, for less than that I have fought a duel in which my
sabre has passed right through the chest of a pipsqueak like you
and come out the other side.'

At once, Algernon turned as white as his tie and would have
slipped out of his chair under the table if Elizabeth had not grasped
his arm.

'Try to be a man,' she whispered.

His Honor Judge Pilgrim saved the situation with a gesture such
as he might have made in court. In deep, measured tones, he spoke
some resonant words.

'Let us forget our personal differences for the moment and, to
help Mrs Hargrove understand better, tell her that this trial, which
lasted no less than four years, helped to weld together the Republican Party, which claims to rise above all other parties by sustaining
the power of the central government and consolidating the Union.
A certain Lincoln, name of Abraham, if you please, has set himself
at the head of this movement.'

'He comes from Illinois,' said Mrs Harrison Edwards, to lighten
the tone. 'And he's no Adonis! A bit of a rustic, so it seems.'

'All of which revived the great debate about the right of every
state to govern itself as it pleases. Factions are arising and voicing
their demands. The 'Know Nothings' want no foreigners, especially Catholics. Others violently demand an American for the
Americans, and for them alone. As you may imagine, the Republicans will try to win over all this mob . . .'

'Oh!' Mrs Harrison Edwards exclaimed. 'Why can't we keep
our dear Franklin Pierce as President? He is the epitome of upright
common sense and has never been known to tell a lie. He is the

honor of the South. He wants peace in the country and would have found a solution to our problems, because he is not against the authority of central government when it matters. Alas, in a few weeks he will be giving way to that Buchanan, who inspires no confidence in me at all.'

'Yet he does seem favorable to the South,' Charlie Jones observed. 'He has a right to respect, as every President does, at the start of . . .'

'He won't have mine,' said Mrs Harrison Edwards, throwing her head back in defiance. 'He's a waverer, terribly easy to influence, with no authority, a ridiculous old beau, comic in his behavior. How will he stand up to the northern Democrats — for there are now Democrats in the North!'

'In any case,' said Charlie Jones, 'there is an upheaval in the political world, and that unfortunate black man was the pretext for it, even if he was not the cause.'

At that moment, Algernon tried to wipe out his shame and, on Elizabeth's advice, to show some masculine strength:

'So it's breaking apart, that tyrannical Union. And I, for my part, am glad. Their America is falling to pieces!'

At once, the Major was on his feet:

'My boy,' he cried, 'if you don't want to taste cold steel, you will take back those disgraceful words. It is my country as well as yours that you are insulting. Five minutes away from here is a place called the colonial cemetery. There we can cross swords and come to an understanding about your interesting ideas on the fatherland.'

'Major,' Charlie Jones said calmly, 'I take the views of our friend Algernon upon myself and you can consider all the usual apologies to have been made.'

Algernon, who had risen, dumb with horror and white as a condemned man, sat down at once and dabbed his forehead with a dainty lace handkerchief that he took out of his sleeve. Furiously shrugging his shoulders, the Major turned a look full of scorn on the young man and sat down again with a great insolent laugh.

'Note,' Charlie Jones went on, in a professorial tone, 'that his opinions on the present state of the Union do contain some elements of truth, though expressed without consideration for diplomatic niceties; but America is falling apart, and we have the threats of secession to prove it. The Union is not solid because it was founded on a badly constructed Constitution, which has already been repatched as well as possible with a good ten amendments. Unless it is seriously modified, as it will have to be sooner or later, the Union will remain vulnerable.'

The Major began to snort through his nostrils like a dragon and was about to bellow again, when Charlie Jones stopped him with a gesture full of authority.

'Listen to something that you may not know. When the Founding Fathers came to discuss the question of slavery and the principle of the institution, one of the authors of the Constitution declared himself opposed to slavery. He came from the South and his name was Thomas Jefferson. Another member of the same assembly strongly argued that slavery should be permitted. He came from the North and his name was Benjamin Franklin.'

'Correct,' said Judge Pilgrim.

'Ah!' said Algernon, coming dangerously close to exulting again.

'Algernon, be quiet,' said Charlie Jones.

The young man obeyed and made an effort not to lose face. In one of those almost maternal impulses so frequent in women, Elizabeth grasped his hand under the table.

'Honor is saved,' she whispered.

However, now that Charlie Jones had the floor, he would not give it up.

'All this is taking us a long way from the subject of this meeting. We have lost sight of Mrs Jonathan Armstrong, whose very name is a guarantee of nobility. Formerly one of the beauties of the age, she is now in the splendor of an Indian summer.'

'Charlie Jones, how finely you speak,' said Mrs Harrison Edwards.

Algernon was dying to add his word:

'I am for her!' he cried.

His thick eyebrows raised in astonishment, the Major turned to his chosen victim and said with a sarcastic laugh:

'Well, well, my boy, for once we agree. I salute in Mrs Jonathan Armstrong the one who yesterday embodied all the beauty of the South and today offers us its prestigious relics.'

'My word!' exclaimed Mrs Harrison Edwards. 'We weak women with our charms make you men into devilishly inspired poets.'

Elated by this compliment, the Major carried on:

'Madam, if you will allow it, by common consent, you are the ornament of what is so rightly called the fair sex. Any objection?'

'Not one,' said Algernon in a high-pitched voice.

Elizabeth turned a little away from him. Judge Pilgrim, who had maintained a ponderous silence, took the floor in turn, to say in a loud voice:

'Without being inspired like these gentlemen, I enjoy the company of great poets and, on the subject of Mrs Jonathan Armstrong and that confounded drop of half-caste blood, I would quote a famous phrase to you: "All the perfumes of Arabia . . .'

'Oh, no,' said Charlie Jones, 'not that!'

'" . . .will not sweeten this little hand."' continued the imperturbable Judge.

'I protest!' cried Charlie Jones. 'Mrs Jonathan Armstrong is not

Lady Macbeth and there is no possible connection.'

'I too protest,' said the Major. 'I don't know the noble lady about whom our friend Charlie Jones is speaking, but I protest. There is no connection. So, my boy, go on: protest too.'

'Oh, I do!' said Algernon. 'I protest!'

'My dear and most honorable friend,' Charlie Jones said, turning to the Judge, 'show the world that justice has a heart when needs be. Your principles will not suffer and poor Annabel, who has no thought of remarriage, will pass on without leaving any heirs; so who will remember the color of her nails?'

'You are a born advocate,' the Judge replied. 'And, put in that way, your case is acceptable. I am going against my opinions and giving way — giving way to a good impulse, which is always to be avoided as dangerous; but I do request that no legal trace be left of this discussion, and that it should never be invoked as carrying the force of precedent.'

'Agreed, agreed!' cried Mrs Harrison Edwards. 'All agreed — aren't we, dear Elizabeth, you who are the loveliest Englishwoman in the world?'

Like a flower dipped in water, the beautiful Englishwoman blossomed under the effect of this compliment, though she considered it belated:

'Agreed, of course.'

Mrs Harrison Edwards rose to her feet:

'This acceptance by society must be a celebration and I would ask for it to take place in my home, in the main reception room overlooking the terrace. Everyone agreed?'

All agreeing, she continued with increasing authority:

'I want this to be a memorable event in the history of our town, which our grandchildren will recall with feeling.'

'Will there be dancing?' asked Algernon.

'That goes without saying, young man. An orchestra of twenty or thirty musicians, there's lots of room.'

'And the buffet?'

'Algernon,' said Charlie Jones, 'keep quiet.'

'Let him be,' said Mrs Harrison Edwards. 'I find these naive remarks charming; but rest assured, dear Algernon, these delightful details are all in hand.'

'Allow me,' said Charlie Jones, 'to remind you that the unfortunate little stain owes its origin to a marriage on the island of Haiti during the revolution there, and that since Annabel's mother has retired from the world, only one person can enlighten us on the circumstances of that union.'

'What does that matter, pray? What concerns us is the unfortunate result.'

'For Annabel's honor, it is necessary to ascertain that her mother thought she was marrying a white man. Only one person, I repeat, knows about it: Mrs Llewelyn, who brought Annabel up.'

'The Welshwoman? Dear Charlie Jones, I can't really see that woman testifying in my drawing-room. My guests would not stand for it. Think: a woman of the people . . .'

'You don't know her as I do. She has the gift of the gab, which she gets from her race, and which would astonish you. In an instant, she will transport your whole drawing-room to Haiti.'

'That might be worth seeing,' said the Major.

'Absolutely the high point of your evening,' said Charlie Jones. 'What risk is there? A moment of astonishment, followed by an hour of wonderment. I take full responsibility for the daring notion. I shall introduce Mrs Llewelyn.'

'In that case, I cannot refuse. You alone are an army in battle.'

The army in battle bowed, with a slightly ludicrous air:

'Too kind.'

'All that remains is to settle on a date for this evening, which I want to be dazzling. Winter is coming to an end; I suggest April. Are we agreed?'

The agreement was unanimous.

'Perhaps,' said Judge Pilgrim, 'we should ensure that Mrs Jonathan Armstrong will agree to come — and not forgetting Mrs Llewelyn.'

'I will take care of that,' said Charlie Jones, with the self-assurance he found in difficult moments. 'They will come.'

'Women are apparently unable to resist you,' said Mrs Harrison Edwards with a malicious laugh.

'I never force anyone,' he replied, with a wide smile.

'Very well,' said Mrs Harrison Edwards, 'without counting our chickens, we can go away content. My dearest friends, the meeting is over and refreshments await you in the north dining-room, if you will excuse the expression; it is the coolest.'

The general rush toward the dining-room resembled a sort of polite bustle and the now empty little room began to look like an absolutely empty brain, barely disturbed by the buzzing of words which had now faded into silence!

# 50

*I*n Elizabeth's garden, Patrick was leaning on a spade and Ned had his hands behind his back, as they exchanged opinions on the world and mankind.

A lovely February sky spread its light over the heavy clusters of greenery and the young magnolias, freshly planted in the rust-colored earth. The breeze was toying with the boy's brown curls and Patrick blinked as he looked at the sun.

'My little fellow,' he said, 'sooner or later you'll have to learn to defend yourself with your fists.'

'Defend myself?'

'Yes, against people, because people are either good or bad . . . When things go wrong, straight to the jaw, and that settles it all. Sometimes even between friends. The other day, for example, your soldier father laid me out as flat as a pancake. but we're still friends. Your soldier Daddy is a darned good boxer.'

'He's not my real Daddy. My real Daddy went away.'

'We know that. But the replacement has a great little fist on him. He'll teach you. So will I, when you want.'

'I made my cousin cry like a baby with my fist at Grandpa's.'

'You told me that; but first he laid you out. A sneak attack: that's forbidden. Come to Ireland. You'll learn it all there. Everyone fights with everyone else, just for fun.'

The name Ireland worked on Ned like a magic charm. Thanks to Patrick, he already had his head full of fairies, giants, witches and ghosts.

'I'll go at the gallop, at night, on my black horse.'

'Your horseman will take you behind him on his horse.'

'No, you don't understand. The horseman gallops in my new room, but further away, like upstairs . . . In any case, I'm not sure how he comes . . . Perhaps through the window, I'm not sure.'

'That would make a lot of noise, no?'

Ned put a finger in his mouth and was thoughtful for a moment.

'I think he comes through the ceiling,' he said.

Patrick could not help laughing.

'You're right,' he said. 'That's more likely. It's none too clear, your story, but no matter. Come to Ireland.'

'Now, I only have to close my eyes and he comes . . . Tonight, I'll be galloping over there when I close my eyes, because at night I'm the horseman and I go out of the house, then I hear people calling my name in the woods. Mummy knows my name, no one else in the house does; but Mummy doesn't call me.'

'Something went wrong?'

'Yes, when the officer came.'

'Oh, women are like that, don't you know, but she still loves you, surely.'

'It's not the same thing.'

'I know that. Don't fret about it, Ned, it's life.'

Ned looked up at him with a pained expression.

'What is?'

The gardener took off his broad-brimmed hat and scratched his head.

'I don't know, but don't cry over it, young fellow. A man doesn't cry; he hits.'

'I don't understand . . .'

'No matter. Go back home, I have to do some digging; but you see, your Mummy still loves you.'

'I'll come back tomorrow, Pat.'

'Tomorrow, be sure to. But tonight, at home in Ireland.'

The child smiled.

'Tonight, in Ireland.'

At that moment, Elizabeth's voice reached him. She had just come home and was waiting on the steps.

'Mummy!' he called, and ran off as fast as he could toward the house.

Patrick burst out laughing and began to dig.

'We're all the same,' he said.


# 51

A week later, on March 5, 1857, Buchanan entered the White House. The event had been expected for four months, but it still caused a stir. A friend of the South, even though a native of Pennsylvania, everyone agreed he would have made an excellent stand in president in normal times, a figurehead, but it was felt that he was not the man needed in the crisis that was then sweeping the country. The battle for influence around him threatened to be formidable.

Since all business had stopped after February 28, Charlie Jones had taken the train for Washington. His income permitting him any indulgence, he was occupying a carriage reserved solely for his own personal use. The rawhide seats of the spacious compartments were heavily padded, while a bed and a table had not been left out of this design for complete comfort. Cooks and waiters in white jackets were all housed together in more modest, but in Charlie Jones's view, splendidly adequate quarters. Obedience and cleanliness were demanded and everything had been anticipated to the last detail in order to achieve this. Charlie Jones could not stand unpleasant smells, so a fragrance of eau de Russie hovered about him. He forbade himself tobacco during the journey, but allowed himself a considerable compensation in the form of a large walnut box lined in metal. Inside, on ice, were forty bottles of champagne — 'Krug, naturally,' he said.

There was a hint of ostentation in all this, but people did not hold that against him, because he knew how to be generous; and his black servants, far from complaining about their lot, thought of a journey with Massa Charlie as a kind of holiday. For that matter, he only wanted to see around him slaves who were as happy as they were devoted, so he spoiled them.

However, since he was not fond of solitude, he would choose one or two traveling companions. One did not refuse this invitation, but he could be awkward. Generally speaking, he thought of politicians as the most tiresome people on earth, apart from clergymen.

This time, the chosen one was none other than the thunderous Robert Toombs. The two friends had reached an agreement beforehand: because of the black staff, the word slavery would not be mentioned, but replaced instead by the official euphemism: 'private institution'. Dressed in black and with a gold chain across his white waistcoat, the colossus of the South shook Charlie Jones warmly by both hands with loud protestations of friendship. His reputation as an Apollo still stuck, despite some silver locks around his temples, but his face, that of an angry god, appeared scarcely touched by the last forty and more years. A supporter of abolition, but in his own way, he might have disconcerted an audience that did not know what to expect, had his fanatical attachment to the South not made him a celebrity. No sooner had he sat down opposite Charlie Jones than his black eyes began to blaze and he threw out a few vindictive remarks to put himself at ease:

'When we have sent back the devil's private institution to where it belongs, we shall be better prepared to roll up our sleeves and settle the score with those moralizing hypocrites in the North.'

'Calm, my dear Robert, things are not that simple. There has been strong opposition to the Blacks in some parts of the North and every day abolitionists are thrashed . . . What does it all mean? The Dred Scott affair seems never-ending. That little Black who wanted to become a citizen of Missouri will have shaken the Union to its very foundations, like an upside-down pyramid. It's civil war already in Kansas. So let's consider the coming man: Abraham Lincoln.'

'That Republican! He'll be swept aside in six months.'

'Don't rely on it. I have had the chance to see him. He has the build and solidity of a peasant — huge hands and the clear and direct look of a man who seems honest.'

This eulogy was greeted with a great burst of laughter.

'What a shame it is, Charlie, that he can't be sitting in the White House, instead of Buchanan.'

'Toombs, there are times when a dubious ally is more dangerous than an intelligent foe.'

'Do you already doubt the incoming President even before he has taken office?'

'Yes. There is no doubt about his integrity, he has the upright and serious look of a scholar, but he is totally lacking in self-confidence; he is irresolute, listening now to advice from one direction, then from another. We have a weak President.'

'In short, if I am correct, you would prefer a president from the North, in the person of Abraham Lincoln?'

'Lincoln didn't run.'

'And do you think that scoundrel hasn't considered it, with his wily look?'

'It's possible.'

Toombs began to get upset.

'And could you see him as President of the Union?.'

'I wouldn't wish it, but I think it's possible.'

'Lincoln president!' Toombs roared. 'That beanpole in the White House . . . Why not a monkey from Africa?'

Now it was Charlie Jones who began to get angry.

'If you want a decorative president, why don't you run yourself, my dear Robert!'

'Good idea. I would act, believe me. And firstly, all Blacks to Africa.'

'Not so loud, Robert, we don't want to incite them.'

Toombs lowered his voice:

'Our people are constantly saying that they will not rise up, so as to reassure themselves . . . Does the name John Brown mean anything to you?'

'John Brown is a zealot who belongs in an asylum.'

'Good. And do you remember Toussaint Louverture in Haiti?'

'There's talk of Haiti again, but thank heavens we're not there. Here, a new Louverture would have no chance.'

'But I think he lives in the dreams of every Black and sleeps in the heart of every one of them. There is a fearful: "why not me?" in the minds of all those men.'

As he said this, he stood up and he took on the tone of a prophet, raising his index finger toward the heavens.

'My word, Robert, anyone would think you were afraid of them!'

The famous Toombs thunder boomed out immediately, 'I'm not

afraid of anything and I challenge the world,' he exclaimed. 'But I want them out, all of them, down to the last pickaninny. At the first cry of "liberty!" I answer "Liberia!" and, if necessary, an entire fleet will take them there.'

'You could suggest that policy to Lincoln,' Charlie Jones said in a very calm voice. 'On that point, he agrees with you. I would find a different solution to the problem of the private institution. I talk to the Blacks not as equals, which they wouldn't understand, but as if to creatures, if not of the same race, then at least of the same species, and then they can feel that I like them.'

'And I like them,' Toombs bellowed. 'I like them as much as you do, but from a distance, from a long way away. I want them to be as happy as possible, with the Atlantic between us.'

'Let's have done with this, it's becoming tedious. I'm thirsty.'

Charlie pulled a bell-rope.

'And so are you,' he added.

Toombs's Olympian brow was suddenly calm.

'I admit . . .,' he began.

He had not time to say more because the door half opened and the head of a young black man appeared. Charlie Jones smiled and the black man smiled, then Charlie Jones raised a hand, with two fingers extended . . . The black head vanished and the door shut behind him.

'Telegraphy,' Toombs remarked.

'Telepathy,' Charlie Jones corrected him.

'An ear to the door, perhaps?'

'The tradition goes back to the invention of doors. Without doors and ears, how many chapters in world history would be missing. Just think of it!'

Two juleps arrived a moment later and restored their good humor.

'I don't know if you like Washington,' said Charlie Jones. 'As far as I'm concerned, it's the capital of boredom, like all serious capitals, with its dead straight avenues radiating out from the Capitol or the White House. I find its splendor melancholy. Even the shady walks don't redeem it in my eyes. It lacks a certain measure of disorder, which is that of old Europe . . .'

'It is still unfinished; in any case, you don't go to Washington for fun.'

'Where do you go?'

'Where do I go for fun? To New Orleans.'

'When I was younger, I went to New York for pleasure. Don't look so surprised. It's the most fascinating city, and then I'm English, I can go where I like, North or South. Since my marriage to Amelia — a saintly woman, by the way — my comings and goings have taken on a more serious turn and I have learned all sorts of interesting things. There is just as much a foreboding of war there as in the South. It's the civilians who plan it and young men who fight it.'

'You intrigue me,' Toombs said, between gulps of his julep.

A great cloud of black smoke engulfed the train and plunged the travelers into darkness for a minute.

'I am sorry for our fellow-travelers who have to cough and groan in their open carriages.'

Robert Toombs's voice echoed through the darkness:

'What stops them from rebelling?'

'The State, or the railroad companies.'

'Without intending any criticism, isn't your luxurious carriage an insult to the ordinary public?'

'This is my way of rebelling. Don't you enjoy rebelling with me?'

'Pretend I said nothing. It seems to me that the cloud is blowing away. So tell me what you saw in the North.'

'A lot of things that made me worry about our casual attitude, especially where armaments are concerned. There is not a single factory in the South, while the North is full of them.'

'That doesn't alter the fact that our young people are ready for a fight; what about those in the North?'

'They're far from unanimously in favor of war, many are against, but all will go, willy nilly. Remember this: you are against slavery for the Blacks. Every war is first of all a general levy of white slaves. Every soldier is a slave carrying a rifle . . . If he escapes, he will be captured, and hanged or shot.'

Toombs leaped to his feet.

'Well, that's original!' he exclaimed.

'Wrong: it goes back to prehistory. The child is brought up in an ideal of heroism. The politicians find excuses, journalists and preachers heat up the atmosphere and the multitudes of well-trained slaves march to the slaughter accompanied by the cheers of the men and women who will be staying at home.'

'What about you? What will you do if war breaks out?'

Charlie Jones replied calmly:

'As a British subject, I shall go abroad and do everything possible to assist the South.'

'And if the slaves in uniform rebel?'

'That's unlikely. They have war in their blood, it's as strong as the call of the flesh; but I would suggest a solution. Suppose they call up all those in charge, whose name is legion . . . All those gentlemen, without any age limit, could be armed and sent to fight their counterparts in the enemy camp. The losses would be great and it would be the end of all wars. But that's only a fine dream. Have no illusions, Robert. This absurd conflict is on the way and it will be frightful . . . What the North wants is the total subjection of the South.'

'And the abolition of slavery? That's all they ever talk about. *Uncle Tom's Cabin*, that ridiculous book, is beating all the current sales records.'

'That's just a screen. It is large enough to mask the real aim of a policy that they will not admit. The North wants the South. It's as simple as that. The policy is helped by the enormous naivety of the public, which swallows Mrs Beecher-Stowe's inventions like a child listening to stories of robbers. I have had a chance to talk to the woman herself. My being an Englishman encourages people to confide in me. All she knows of the South is Kentucky. Her information comes from people whom she "considers serious" — she herself has never put a foot in the South. Fanatical and stupid, that's what she is!'

'She does modestly declare that she is not the author of the book. "God wrote it," she tells us.'

'An interesting clarification, but let's leave it at that. The North wants at all cost to strengthen the Union by conquest. Your great Henry Clay stated forcibly that a real Union can only come about by a union of hearts. We are not going down that road. By the way, what can you see through the window?'

'Nothing very remarkable. Fallow fields and in the distance a series of swamps.'

'Details, Robert: the detail that gives life to the landscape. Over there, a little old man in a cart pulled by a donkey, going along that path.'

'You have eyes that would make a fortune for a spy.'

'North and South are full of them. They are the petrels that fly before the storm . . . And, as always in times of trouble, Washington is full of cartomancers and fortune tellers, who are favored by politicians who secretly go to consult them.'

The conversation took a frivolous turn and one julep followed another until lunch time. Lunch was served in a neighboring compartment where the family silver shone on the white table cloth covering a round table. The lack of space helped the illusion that they were in a private room in a very luxurious restaurant, and the meal, which was delicious, was so generously washed down with champagne that it was immediately followed by a prolonged siesta in the afternoon, so that the austere charm of the countryside passed them by. In any event, as they were following the coast, though at some distance, they would have seen nothing except huge marshlands stretching to the edge of the Ocean, deep green beneath a gray sky.

Night was falling when they awoke, in time to admire the battlements of a chain of mountains on the horizon.

Somewhat ashamed at having slept for so long, both were all the more ecstatic about the splendors of nature, but night cut their commonplace observations short. The soft light of the oil lamps calmed them and they reverted to exchanging political views, each in the end secretly finding the other slightly obstinate. So the evening was cut short as far as possible. The champagne flowed again and then they took to their divans, transformed into beds of the most refined comfort.

# 52

The following day, they were riding through North Carolina where the tobacco plantations offered new topics for discussion and gave them the means to revive a conversation that had been steadily faltering; for they found that they had already discussed the most important issues.

Newspapers which they bought in quantity at Salisbury station gave each of them a classic refuge behind a wall of paper. Juleps and glasses of champagne completed the process of making life tolerable. Meals brought a kind of truce, an effort to regain the comradeship of the earlier hours. Charlie tried to cheer up his companion with the help of a joke which was circulating in the bars of Savannah:

'Do you know what the governor of North Carolina said to the governor of South Carolina?'

Toombs shook his head. Charlie Jones leaned over the table with a confidential air:

'It's a long time between two drinks.'

Toombs burst out laughing and merriment was restored, more or less, bit by bit.

The last day of the journey was very different. Sitting in front of their morning coffee, they turned toward the window and their hearts swelled. On the left were the snowy peaks of Blue Ridge which seemed to reach back into the heavens and melt into the blue sky, while on the right a huge valley cut its way through the hills which undulated like waves.

'Virginia,' both of them said, like a whisper of love.

Confronted with the calm magnificence of these open spaces which reaffirmed the beauty of the world and spoke of peace and joy, they wondered in silence why they chose to live anywhere else.

In Richmond, the train stopped for ten minutes and they took a short walk round the station. The newspapers reported the start of Buchanan's term without much comment. Nowhere could one see the nervousness that one felt in Savannah. Even the voices, quieter and less singsong than in Georgia, were reassuring.

There was to be no further stop until Washington, but when they passed through Charlotteville, they could see in the distance the dome of the library, and the memory of the son he had lost, killed in a duel, cast a shadow over Charlie Jones.

'You didn't know him,' he told Toombs. 'He was a good boy, serious and affectionate. A model husband. I'll never know exactly why he died. They have kept something from me. He was not the sort of person to pick a fight with anyone, poor Ned. Only Annabel Armstrong could tell us, but she will never talk.'

'I know Mrs Armstrong. A great lady and an inconsolable widow.'

'You've summed it up in a phrase. But let's speak of something else. In a moment we are going to pass near to Manassas. The property where my wife goes to take a rest in the summer is only a few miles from there. I'd very much like you to come and see us there.'

'With pleasure.'

In a confidential mood, Charlie Jones could not resist a complicated need to speak ill of his wife, even though he adored her.

'Do you know Amelia well?'

'My dear Charlie, I know and respect her, if one may say so, down to the ground, for she is a woman of imposing dignity.'

'A saint.'

'Oh?'

'Yes.'

'Charlie, don't tell me she's a Catholic.'

'What are you thinking of? No one in the family has sunk so low. When I say a saint, I mean a pious woman.'

'You mean god-fearing.'

'Worse than that, dear boy. I venerate her, I cannot see her without falling in love with her each time like a young man. She's already given me two boys and a girl. But that doesn't alter the fact that this woman whom I think I possess, escapes me.'

'By gosh, Charlie, do you suspect her?'

'You haven't got it at all, but not at all. She would have her heart pierced and her throat cut rather than look at another man . . . It's something quite different. If I dare mention it . . .'

'Dare, Charlie, dare. I am as silent as the grave and you have my word of honor.'

'She breathes religion through every pore in her being.'

'I can see the torment.'

'You can't imagine it. She plunges into the Bible like an otter

into its lake and comes out dripping with quotations which are sometimes disturbing.'

'That's the very reason why I haven't opened the Bible since I
was a child. If you believe in it, you find yourself under attack on
every page.'

'You've hit the nail on the head. She does believe, but to a point
beyond reason. She is mad.'

'As long as she keeps quiet, why should you worry?'

'It's not a matter of that. She has this terrifying stillness about
her. Always ready to abandon herself, but always seeming to be
somewhere else.'

'Where? Can you be clearer, old man?'

'If I could, if I knew, but I know and feel that she is somewhere
else. I can't grasp her, do you see? Always consenting, but eter-
nally absent.'

'There's a shadow of moral infidelity there.'

'Metaphysical, Robert.'

'Good Lord, I feel sorry for you.'

'The holy woman in all her horror, but that's not all. I guess, I
can sense something else.'

'As if that wasn't enough . . .'

'She doesn't like it.'

'It?'

'Yes, try to understand.'

'Say no more, I understand, but you don't realize that the majority of married women in America have the same repugnance. There
are countless mothers of families who have never known pleasure.'

'It's different with her: everything is different with her. I have
the impression that she considers it as a profanation that she has to
undergo.'

'That's marriage. I don't want to criticize your wife, but she's
complicated.'

'Women who believe can be impossible to understand. Are you a
believer?'

'Oh, I go to church at Easter, because it's the done thing, but
don't assume anything because of that. I'm no fanatic.'

'Nor am I. There is a whole mass of abstractions and legends
that I don't accept. The wisest thing is to leave that to women,
because it makes them into model spouses, except for mine, who
had swallowed too much religion — just as one can take too much
laudanum. There's nothing to be done about it. She belongs to another.'

'Mystery!'

'You don't know how right you are. She doesn't stop me being
happy, but she poisons my happiness. Anyway, forget what I told
you and let's say no more about her. We have just passed Manassas,

a large and uninteresting village. Washington is not far off. One last glass of champagne, perhaps?'

'Certainly.'

Charlie Jones rang. The servant appeared immediately.

'Champagne,' said Charlie Jones.

'Massa Charlie,' said the black man in consternation. 'No more champagne.'

The forty bottles were empty. Forty bottles of laughs, of quips, of confidences, of curses, of good humor . . .

'Never mind,' said Charlie Jones. 'I know all the best addresses in Washington.'

This invigorating remark gave them strength until the moment when the bell on the locomotive announced the triumphant clamor of their entrance into Washington station.

# 53

On their way to the Capitol in the carriage which had been waiting for them, Charlie Jones furnished Toombs with a wealth of enlightening information, protesting that he did not like to set foot in Washingon even to attend the sessions of the Senate.

'They haven't finished building it, so what is the interest?' the Colossus of the South asked.

'Dickens calls it the city of sublime intentions, but he loses no opportunity of making fun of America, even though he was received here like a prince. This magnificent avenue lined with tall trees: surely no one can deny that it's beautiful?'

'You're joking . . . Beautiful in one sense, perhaps, but in another, its only a building site. I'm sorry, but I have eyes to see: huge piles of cement, a heap of bricks, countless pieces of columns in this indescribable chaos. Bravo! Yes, indeed, bravo! That's Pennsylvania Avenue!'

'Stop complaining and admire the fine proportions of the Capitol. You can't deny that the proportions of the colonnade are imposing.'

'And what about that scaffolding up there, across, behind, everywhere . . .'

'The dome has to be built.'

'In short, all of this is trying to set itself on its feet, just like the Union itself.'

Charlie Jones nearly lost his temper, but managed to contain himself.

The carriage drew up at the foot of the steps, which they climbed amid a tumult of festivity. The crowd, humming and over-excited, was rushing to enjoy the spectacle, laughing, shouting and braying noisily as it waved bunches of flowers and paper flags, totally overcome by a collective return of the anarchical instincts of childhood, elated by a joy that was close to getting out of hand. In the midst of this scruffy crowd, with men in shirt sleeves and women with their hair in a bun, a few black coats stood out in somewhat discreetly violent contrast, as if to preserve the official character of the assembly.

'Let's leave,' Toombs shouted in his companion's ear.

'Not yet, you'll see, it will be worth the effort. History is created out of disorder.'

Each as powerful as the other, they elbowed their way to the hall where gigantic statues stood between the columns. With blind eyes, Strength, Law and Fraternity, draped in marble, looked down on the mob which had been unleashed in the very heart of government. A cordon of good-natured guards held back the crowd, preventing it from entering the Rotunda. Toombs's critical eye quickly surveyed this huge space ringed by high columns with Corinthian capitals. The effect would have been magnificent, had it not been for the green tarpaulins disguising the work still in progress on the uncompleted dome. However, this improvised ceiling did not spoil the effect. There was a majesty about the whole setting which made the clamoring crowd lower its voice a little.

Standing in the center of a huge circle of men in black coats, Buchanan was reading his inaugural address. The persistent noise coming from outside overwhelmed his rather weak voice, and only scraps of sentences, like the feeble yapping of a dog, could be heard. The man was undistinguished. Everyone felt it. He was one of those unfortunate creatures who never manage to make themselves heard, however much authority they are given. With the tips of his fingers on the lectern, as if to support himself, he was made visibly unhappy by his obvious inadequacy. Seated on his right, President Pierce was modestly playing his role as a great man standing down in favor of a lesser one. He felt himself admired and was enjoying his return to being a private citizen, and the incompetence of his successor added a false air of victory.

Meanwhile, Buchanan was struggling through his laborious phrases and tasting the bitterness of a spurious glory that the presence of his embarrassing neighbor had managed to undermine.

Charlie Jones and his companion exchanged glances and shook their heads. For once they were in agreement.

Groups of onlookers, disappointed by the tedium of this dull inauguration in which nothing startling was going to happen, were already beginning to disperse. Polite applause was greeting the end of the speech when Charlie Jones said to Toombs.

'Let's go!'

They returned to their carriage as fast as they could.

'Before we go,' Toombs said ironically, 'do at least notice those two completed wings to the right and to the left. In one of them is the Senate, where many of my colleagues come to sleep or toss balls of paper at one another to pass the time, and in the other is the House of Representatives. They meet under the Dome along wide underground passages, where the public loves to walk. That's promising for big occasions! And now, let's make haste to the White House! We'll be there before the mob, who will be heading that way at full speed, because if the Capitol is the dreary part, the White House is the party. At least, let's hope so!'

They did indeed arrive before 'the mob', and great was Charlie Jones's satisfaction when he heard Toombs give an admiring grunt.

'Restored certainly, but tastefully.'

Low and long, this single-floor building would have suggested a country house, without the very majestic portico supported by ten Grecian columns and adorned by a triangular pediment, but a certain rural innocence persisted even so on account of a meadow which extended to the rear.

They went in to find the guests, in their frock coats, already surrounding the two presidents, yesterday's and today's, in a reception room where immense mirrors reflected the chandeliers with their countless pendants as though to infinity. The walls seemed to disappear under the massive gilding and here and there Louis XV armchairs gave the final note to an overwhelming feeling of luxury: there were just too many of them, too brilliant and too gilded.

'A little of the *Thousand and One Nights*, combined with a little of Versailles,' said Charlie Jones. But Toombs did not answer.

The public entered in its turn, in very different mood from the one it had been in at the Capitol, and visibly intimidated. Policemen in civilian clothes, recognizable from their searching looks, were moving around by the doors.

Toombs took Charlie Jones by the arm and guided him toward a corner of the room where the new president was greeting his guests.

'Watch this piece of play acting,' he said.

Buchanan and Pierce were both standing and expending a good deal of effort to appear polite and charming, with more or less equal grace, but in some indefinable way, Buchanan excelled at the game, while Pierce was smiling with a little more restraint. Now Buchanan was settling into his role as master of the house, puffed up and from time to time addressing a smile full of goodwill, with a touch of melancholy, toward the outgoing President, for it would soon be the moment for them to take leave of one another.

Pierce did not need a great deal of intuition to understand these fine nuances and suddenly, disregarding protocol, while the brand new Buchanan was frantically chatting with the ladies, he vanished like a cloud.

'Well played,' Toombs muttered to Charlie Jones.

A few minutes later, they both decided to leave as well.

Toombs remarked:

'What shadows there are lurking behind those shows of friendship and polite grimaces!'

As they were coming down the stairs, they heard their names called by someone behind them.

'Jeff Davis!' Charlie Jones cried, turning round.

Jefferson Davis burst out laughing.

'It's a real compensation after this deadly session to suddenly stumble across Charlie Jones and Robert Toombs. But what are you doing here?'

'What the American people are doing: we are taking part in an historic event.'

'Not a great success,' said Jefferson Davis. 'But I am not the one who chose the main actor. For that matter, look at the mood of the crowd: the public was expecting something else . . . Toombs, I heard you in Savannah when you were talking about slavery. We agree on almost everything, but then in any case, you are the Voice of the South.'

Charlie Jones quietly corrected him:

'The Thunder of the South.'

'Well, three cheers for the Thunder of the South!' said Jefferson Davis.

The same age as Charlie Jones, he wore a ceremonial dress cut with obvious attention to its appearance, and a thick silk cravat drew a black line beneath a fine, regular face in which the extraordinary gaze spat fire, even though he had trouble with one eye. You felt that fury might suddenly flood these bright blue eyes, however courteous his normal manner.

He invited the two visitors from Georgia to walk a little with him under the trees.

'I'm leaving the White House with no regrets,' he confessed, 'now that Franklin Pierce is no longer there. The South will not find it easy to replace such a defender of our rights.'

'What about Buchanan?' asked Charlie Jones.

Jefferson Davis shrugged his shoulders.

'Harmless,' he said.

'From the lips of a Minister of War, such an opinion makes one anxious for the future,' said Toombs.

'I am not Minister of War now that Pierce has gone, and there is no cause for anxiety, but I shall not be giving away any secrets if I tell you, in case you did not already know, that in the North the governors of several states are piling up large stocks of armaments in their arsenals.'

'Buchanan must know that,' said Charlie Jones.

'Buchanan prefers to ignore everything that might disturb his sleep. There are enough people in his entourage who have an interest in persuading him that all is well.'

Along the whole length of the avenues, the March winds were tossing the tops of the high sycamores without affecting those walking below. Soon they turned back toward the White House. Charlie Jones spoke:

'Everyone's eyes are turned toward the Capitol and on everyone's lips in the South there is the same question: "Is it war?"'

A flame burned in Jefferson Davis' eyes, but in a deliberately calm voice, he replied:

'I am not a prophet, Charlie Jones, but every day there comes a voice from the future which says to the South: "Keep your hand on the hilt of your sword."'

And, as if to temper the grandiloquence of that statement, he added with a broad smile:

'Be sure, my friends, that if our neighbors in the North want to visit us in uniform with guns in their hands, we shall be there to greet them.'

'My turn to cheer!' said Toombs. 'You should get up on the steps of the White House and say that as loudly as you can. You would be acclaimed by the crowd.'

'In Washington? Perhaps,' said Jefferson Davis, 'But we have not reached that point yet. The real cure would be a genuine union.'

'You are dreaming,' said Toombs.

'Perhaps, but it was the dream of Henry Clay: a Union of hearts . . .'

'Oh, yes,' said Charlie Jones, with a sigh . . . Calhoun found the naive formulation, but Clay was right. There will never be a Union, you understand, whatever happens, war or peace, if we do not finally achieve a Union of hearts.'

'So it's up to you to get up on the steps and announce that to the crowd,' said Jefferson Davis.

'I deeply regret, but I am English, I have no right.'

'English, you?' said Jefferson Davis. 'You are Welsh, as I am.'

'There you have a perfect Union of hearts,' Charlie Jones replied. 'But my passport reminds me that I am a subject of Her Majesty, Queen Victoria, and I assure you it's very useful.'

Toombs began to thunder:

'You're from the South, Charlie, the South has adopted you.'

'And it is as a Son of the South that I want to serve my adoptive country, but I want to work for peace by defending the great principles of Henry Clay.'

Carried away by his own eloquence, his voice grew louder and louder, and passers-by paused to listen to him. Far from being embarrassed, he felt inclined to harangue this chance audience:

'Peace through a Union of hearts,' he cried, 'a sincere, profound union, with fraternity triumphant, for without it America will collapse in blood and ruins.'

Jefferson Davis took his arm:

'Calm down, Charlie,' he said. 'With your English accent you might be taken for an agent of Queen Victoria.'

'Victoria is for the South,' Charlie Jones continued. 'It's that German, Prince Albert, who is for the North . . .'

'Come, let's go!' said Jefferson Davis.

He and Toombs led him through the group of increasingly attentive onlookers.

'At least you have something to say when you talk,' said a simple woman as they walked by. 'Not like the new President . . .'

A mocking voice was raised louder as they moved away:

' . . . the President with his Constitution like a frying pan tied to the tail of a cat!'

'Splendid! Subversive!' Toombs chuckled. 'Charlie, you are starting a riot. To our carriages!'

Jefferson Davis laughed with him:

'Firstly, there will not be a riot because I am still a senator and the mob respects the Senate. Secondly, I do not have a carriage: I came on foot, democratically.'

'Pooh!' said Charlie Jones, slightly calmer. 'I have no desire to cause a riot, but that great ninny Buchanan put me in a rage with his continual talk of justice and constitution.'

'Gently, now,' said Jefferson Davis. 'The South is supposed to be ready to fight for that Constitution. But let that pass. Toombs, are you staying in Washington?'

'Oh, no! I'm going back to Savannah.'

'And you Charlie: of course, you are also going back home?'

Charlie Jones looked grave:

'No, I'm going North.'

'An odd answer, but I will ask no questions.'

'It's very simple. I want to find out, because I am curious; I, too, have a thirst for knowledge.'

'Be careful, they are starting to get suspicious.'

'An Englishman can go where he likes and do as he pleases. An Englishman, my dear Jeff, is *un-touch-able*.'

At these enigmatic words, the three friends decided that the time had come to shake hands and part . . .

'One last look at that White House,' said Toombs. 'It will never make my heart beat faster, but I acknowledge that it is quite pretty, pleasant looking, even smart.'

'It didn't look very smart that day in 1814 when the English set fire to it, to teach the natives not to upset His Majesty's continental blockade by trying, without his consent, to resume their trade links with Europe. In fact, it became quite black, your White House.'

'Yes, but when the English left, it was repainted,' said Toombs. 'How irritating she can be, your England!'

'Very,' said Charlie Jones. 'She knows that and she will go on and on!'

A few chuckles and they went their separate ways.

# 54

*I*n the days that followed, a stream of speeches flooded forth and it soon became clear that President Buchanan would be a man who would do nothing, a sort of transitional president, as if history needed a moment's peace, a pause in which everything could ferment. The orators took full advantage of this, and there was a rush of finely fashioned sentences, as much on the lips of politicians of all shades as on those of preachers, and all the rhetoric and phrases and all those grand words wended their way across the pages of the newspapers in the North. However, the new President was sometimes accused of favoring the South and having advisers around him who would be ready to make any concession. This was playing on his weakness: he was a politician, nothing more, and he repeatedly put determined opponents of the celebrated Union of hearts in their place, in order to restore the balance.

Senator Douglas was already active in Illinois with a view to the forthcoming elections and in New York the Northerner Garrison was still breathing words enflamed by discord. And, thoughout the country, day by day, these great phrases, escaping from all these mouths, hung above the silent forests, the marshes, the rivers and the cotton fields, in the immense checkerboard of wheatfields, woods and towns, forming letters which were soon reassembled over those same landscapes of America into chants of war.

# 55

*I*n Savannah, spring was bursting out like a song of victory. In all the gardens of the red and white houses around the squares, the flowers were coming into bloom in a vast profusion.

In Elizabeth's garden, Billy's passion for magnolias was triumphing over his wife's hidden misgivings: she could only suggest a little moderation — because he wanted magnolias everywhere!

'You don't remember the magnolia at the entrance to the veranda, in Dimwood? You were crazy about it, you used to stop close by as if to speak to it . . .'

Yes, she did remember, she remembered very well. She just wondered if, in their own garden, they might not space them out a little, perhaps?

Then Billy, in the uniform which suited him so well and made him look almost embarrassingly handsome, took her gently in the crook of his arm and said with a wide smile:

'My darling, will you let me do what I want?'

She knew what he meant. He knew only too well how to bring her round to his point of view and, without answering, she smiled, indignant deep down at a weakness in which she no longer recognized herself. And these trees held out their flowers to her; these trees with their dark leaves glistening in their sensual splendor offered her these large flowers, heavy with scent and memories. Though still young, they almost touched one another. One day they would cover the wall right up to the top and all the way along, as far as the house from which Patrick, as usual, was absent.

Billy looked at Elizabeth's silent face.

'Happy?' he asked.

'Very happy.'

'You look thoughtful and you don't say anything,' he insisted.

'I'm admiring, Billy. There really are lots of magnolias! I mentioned it to Patrick one day, but he had your orders and I did not want to complicate things, so . . .'

He looked into her eyes.

'There's the Elizabeth I love,' he said, with the tenderness full of affection that he kept for certain intimate moments.

She tried to protest and in a teasing voice said:

'So there's an Elizabeth who is not always lovable.'

To her great surprise, he stopped smiling and slowly let go of her arm.

'You know very well what I mean,' he said.

She almost cried out, but contained herself and drew herself up to her full height:

'No,' she said.

The word gave her strength, as if reviving in her the young English girl of former days, proud and always ready to rebel, but her thoughts were milling around in her head and made her feel dizzy.

'Let's go away from here, shall we?' she said.

'Yes, yes,' he said in a reasonable voice, as if calming a child. 'It must be the scent of the flowers that is troubling you.'

She challenged him with a haughty look, but she could feel her heart beating in her breast.

'I just want to lie down,' she said.

Not without a slight affectation of gallantry, he offered his arm and they walked in silence to the steps.

As was their custom, they were served a buffet supper in the dining-room. Elizabeth hardly touched it, contenting herself with two cups of tea, but Billy ate voraciously. Not a word was exchanged in the course of this brief meal which dusk made even more solemn. It was lit only momentarily by the joyful entrance of Ned coming back from his walk with Betty. He hurled himself at his mother with cries of love, something which she needed a good deal that day. Dressed in white linen, his tousled head emerged from a wide sailor's collar and he laughed as he tried to talk and tell her a story:

'Mummy, I didn't tell you my dream last night . . .'

'Don't you say hello to Daddy?' she asked.

He looked at Billy and said simply:

'Hello.'

'"Daddy" will come later, when we know one another better,' Billy said, with a rueful smile.

'Has he been good?' Elizabeth asked Betty.

The woman walked over with a broad smile on a face which never seemed to have changed, the wrinkles deepening in her lean, shining cheeks.

'Massa Ned go on long journeys when he sleep,' she said, with a child's laugh.

'No, Betty,' Ned exclaimed. 'I'll tell Mummy what I dreamed last night.'

Elizabeth caught him in her arms and, with tears in her eyes, covered his face with kisses.

'Why are you crying, Mummy?' he asked, stroking her face.

'I don't know, my love; but go and have dinner, then to bed, and you can tell me all about it tomorrow. Betty, you take him.'

The child vanished with the old servant.

Elizabeth stood up.

'Let's go upstairs,' she said. 'I'm tired.'

In the bedroom with its closed shutters, the oil lamp burned gently on the table and the big bed with its sheets neatly folded back was waiting. This familiar scene seemed to wait in patient expectation for the great amorous disorder that never failed to follow within a few minutes. Yet nothing of the sort happened that evening. The night was exemplary.

Elizabeth went to bed first while Billy got undressed carefully and then, without hurry, without ardor, performed his conjugal duty. After which he wished his wife good night and, turning his back to her, fell asleep.

It took much longer for sleep to come to Elizabeth. First of all, she needed a full quarter of an hour to prepare herself and, once the light was out, she lay there, her eyes wide open, in what had only a short time before been the site of their lovemaking. Something very simple had happened: two people, beside themselves in love, had become husband and wife. Matrimonial order reigned, respectable as could be, but with no tumultuous convulsions, or bellowings of the sort that Mrs Harrison Edwards knew.

In the room, lit only by a street light on the avenue, the subdued Englishwoman considered some ideas that had just occurred to her:

'He knew. I might have guessed, since he was at the ball under the trees at Dimwood when Jonathan appeared. The moment was unforgettably horrible. The glass of champagne, full in the face . . . How could he have failed to understand everything? But he is so sly, so dissimulating. He wanted me, he has had me, but he's jealous, jealous of a dead man, jealous of this ghost whom my poor little Ned revives in his child's dreams full of sinister gallopings . . . And the vulgarity of that invasion of magnolias in my garden . . . That is a mystery. Who told him? No one could know. Did he spy on us? That's the only possible answer. The child faithfully kept his word and kept secret the name which will always make my heart beat faster . . . Shame, shame on me . . . What has happened to my dream of love? Lying next to a trooper who doesn't even turn toward me . . .'

And the trooper was snoring.

Suddenly, a name flared up in Elizabeth's memory: Miss Llewelyn. Something the Welshwoman had said rang in her ears: "Do you know what desire is, Elizabeth?" "Yes, love." "Not necessarily." Everything was in those two words. She had thought she loved this man, but she had only desired him.

Instinctively, she moved away from him. She didn't love him any more. But what was the use of fooling herself? She didn't love him, but how could she deny that she still wanted him with a passion she would never contain?

The night passed. Waking the next morning was hard. He rose and got ready with a haste that she did not understand at first. As he was finishing shaving, he said absent-mindedly:

'I forgot to mention it yesterday. I'm leaving shortly.'

She took the blow, without flinching, and said nothing. He added:

'They're expecting me there. I'll send you a message to tell you when I'll be back.'

'Very well,' she said.

Was he disappointed at seeing her so calm? He buttoned his jacket and put on a good-natured air:

'Try to be patient, my little Elizabeth.'

How sure he was of himself with this air of the complacent, handsome soldier . . . She soon found an answer.

'There's always something in Savannah to take one's mind off things,' she said with a chuckle.

He smiled indulgently. If anyone knew her well, it was he; and he would make her pay for it.

# 56

*A*s soon as he had gone, after breakfast (a huge one for him, a very light one for her), she ran to the drawing-room. There at a corner of the window, half hidden behind a curtain, she watched him leave, even though she had promised herself she wouldn't; but she was already starting to feel tired of the struggle and her eyes wore the wide, disappointed look of a child again. What he was taking away with his triumphant step, was her happiness, all her own happiness . . . How handsome he was! How could she have let him go away? It would have been easy to win him back, by throwing herself in his arms, and to make him give in; he was not strong enough to resist, she knew what to say; he burned with the same fire, the same desires as she did.

Leaning against the wall to prevent herself from falling, to allow the worst of the despair to pass, she finally ventured to take a few steps in the drawing-room. How she hated it now, this little blue room . . . It brought her misfortune with its ridiculous blue walls . . . Billy was right: what was needed was a blood red; but she had enquired of all the best suppliers in Savannah, and no one had the material she wanted. She had been told that she would do better to enquire in the North — since everything came from the North . . . And Uncle Charlie was taking care of it. Leaving the room, she walked over to the staircase and walked up, holding on to the bannisters.

Her room had been tidied while she was having breakfast with Billy. Here, everything was in order, wiping away the memory of that awful night. Now she rediscovered herself, determined not to complain any more. After locking the door to her room, she went into the bathroom, opened the little medicine chest and without having to feel around in it put her hand on the blue flask with its yellow label bearing all the instructions that she knew by heart: dosage, warnings . . .!

In Billy's cupboard, she found the port. She had all she needed.

Suddenly she felt the presence of her mother, counting the drops with her.

Someone knocked on the door, probably the housekeeper.

Elizabeth made a gesture of impatience:

'I don't want to be disturbed today,' she called. 'I'm resting.'

The sound of her own imperious tones comforted her.


# 57


*T*hat same day, at around three o'clock in the afternoon, there was a ring at the front door. The housekeeper opened, having been forcibly made aware of her mistress's instructions.

Instinctively she shrank back on seeing Miss Llewelyn crossing the threshold. Against the light, the Welshwoman, dressed in black, seemed even more imposing. Nevertheless, Celina tried to stop her coming in:

'Madam is alone in the house and wishes to rest.'

With a strong arm, Miss Llewelyn pushed her aside.

'Alone in the house means that her husband is away, I assume.'

'Yes, Madam, he left this morning.'

'I understand,' Miss Llewelyn said. 'I'm going up to see your mistress.'

'But, Madam gave orders not . . .'

'That's all right, Celina, go back to your work.'

In a few strides, she crossed the hall and went up the staircase, its steps creaking under her weight. Reaching Elizabeth's door, she knocked and, obtaining no answer, said aloud:

'Mrs Hargrove, you must open to me. I am Miss Llewelyn and what I have to tell you is important.'

Silence.

'I know very well what has happened. He has left, but if you take too much of that blue flask, you will become ill.'

A faint voice reached her:

'I want to be left in peace.'

'Very well, I'm going down into the garden, but I shall come back. You are entirely inexperienced. Remember the day you came back from the harbor.'

With the palm of her hand she knocked on the door:

'You can hear me perfectly . . . When you came back from the harbor, the day he left for Europe.'

Silence. Miss Llewelyn waited a moment, then shrugged her shoulders and went downstairs.

On the steps she stopped and gave a sigh:

'The garden has lost its shape with all these magnolias.'

Standing near the house, Patrick was chatting to Ned, who was waving a tiny spade while trying to tell a story, but as soon as he saw Miss Llewelyn, he threw the spade away and looked at the visitor, recognizing her immediately. That pale, but smiling face, under an odd sort of straw hat, recalled an exciting scene, so he smiled back and walked quickly over toward the Welshwoman.

At the foot of the steps, she bent double, picked Ned up in her arms, raised him up to her face and said with a laugh:

'Little lad, I am not pretty enough to be kissed, but I'd like it even so.'

It took Ned a few moments to understand, and brusquely he offered his round cheeks. She touched them with her lips, so moved that a tear hovered in her green eyes.

'I see that you have not forgotten the lady who came and spoke very loudly to your Mama. You weren't afraid?'

'No, I wasn't afraid,' he said.

She put him down gently.

'You are a nice little gentleman,' she said.

He thanked her with a smile.

'And that's the gardener, I suppose, near the house down there?'

'Yes, Pat.'

'An Irishman,' she said. 'You can tell even from here . . .'

Ned looked knowledgeable.

'Ireland,' he said. 'We both go to Ireland.'

Miss Llewelyn looked at him for a moment and said:

'Well, now!'

He shook his curls and answered:

'Yes.'

Flabbergasted, she asked:

'And just now, I saw you waving your spade while you were speaking: were you talking about Ireland?'

Ned suddenly felt very important.

'Yes. Last night I went there.'

How closely she was listening to him now. The intense pleasure of surprising a grown-up went to the little boy's head. He explained, without really explaining, like a real storyteller.

'I travel to Ireland, but,' he added with a superior look, 'you can't understand, so . . .'

Put firmly in her place, she smiled and said, leaning toward him:

'Ned, I think we're going to be friends, because you say some very interesting things. And how did you make that fine journey?'

Slightly self-satisfied, he said:

'On horseback.'

She was so surprised that she had to lean against the wall of the steps, but she was also too astute to let him see, so she decided to counter-attack by giving this mysterious little personage something to be surprised at in his turn:

'In my country,' she said, 'we women, we take a broomstick when we want to travel.'

'Oh!'

'As I'm telling you. It's very practical but, if you like, I'll sit on one of these stairs and we can tell about our journeys. Here, I can't find the right sort of broomstick, but there I had them all, and I went wherever I wanted to. I streaked through the skies in my youth.'

'I like my horse better,' he said.,

Slowly and cautiously, she sat down on the second step and adjusted her hat.

'I'm listening,' she said, quietly. 'You know lots of things. What color is your horse?'

'Black.'

'Black, that's splendid. And they go and get it for you from the stables, I suppose.'

'No, it comes by itself when the lamp goes out. But first I have to close my eyes.'

'Then?'

'Then it comes at a gallop.'

'At a gallop! But where from, my dear?'

'From the back of the room.'

'Of course, how silly of me. Ned, I like your story very much.'

'I don't tell everyone,' he said. 'Only Pat, because I go down there to see him and he shows me Ireland.'

Miss Llewelyn looked down, as if to hide her joy and her overwhelming curiosity.

'And do you think Ireland is beautiful?'

The reply was unexpected and unhesitating.

'It's like heaven.'

'Heaven,' she said, dumbfounded. 'Do you know Heaven, Ned?'

'Pat says it's like Heaven.'

Miss Llewelyn could not repress a smile.

Yielding to the temptation to reveal a little more of this secret which was making him so interesting in the eyes of this attentive lady, he added:

'Mummy also knows the story of the black horse, but she doesn't want me to talk about it, it's forbidden. Don't say anything, you mustn't.'

The Welshwoman felt she was on a track that would be worth pursuing.

'At first,' the innocent storyteller continued, 'the horse didn't belong to me, but to another rider with the same name as me.'

'Ned?'

He gave a cunning laugh.

'No, come on. Prettier than that.'

'So tell me.'

'No, no, never. No one must know it. I promised Mummy never to tell it, never, never.'

The Welshwoman's eyes narrowed as though trying to focus on something odd in the distance . . . In Elizabeth's life, there was only one name forever forbidden and it was certainly not that of her husband.

She felt how unjust it would be to pursue the questioning any further and hesitated for a moment or two. Ned looked at her, smiling in a teasing way, enjoying her disappointed curiosity.

'So,' she said. 'You have the same name as the rider.'

'Yes, and then I am the rider.'

'And does Mummy call you by the same name?'

'Only when we're alone and she says goodnight . . .'

A shadow passed across his face and he said sadly:

'But not now. Not any longer. When the soldier came . . .'

'But he is very kind to you, the soldier . . .'

'Yes, very kind. But it was better before.'

'You mean that, before, your Mummy gave you the name of the horseman and now the soldier doesn't want to?'

'Oh, he doesn't know! It's Mummy's secret and mine . . . But the soldier doesn't know, Mummy doesn't want him to . . . Never, never . . .'

Tried and tested by life as she was, the Welshwoman still felt her eyes moisten and she said nothing. Maisie Llewelyn, she thought, you are a wicked woman. You are drawing all this little angel's secrets out of him, with the cunning of a magistrate or a policeman. Now you know everything. Elizabeth is afraid that Billy is jealous of a dead man. It has happened, I know cases. The fact that Jonathan is rotting under a tombstone changes nothing. What killed him was his love for her, and because of that she will always love him. She would not be a woman if she did not betray herself unconsciously. Even a lad as simple as Billy must eventually sense something. Silence on that subject for ever.

She got up painfully. Her joints cracked and she bit her lips with a grimace of pain.

'My child,' she said, 'let's go and see Patrick . . . I also know Ireland.'

She took Ned's hand and they walked slowly toward the gardener's house. As she was passing beside the banks of white flowers, her dark shadow took on a huge appearance beside that of her young companion who came up to a point just below her waist, and they walked, pursued by those heavy perfumes, those which still troubled an Englishwoman who was unable to forget.

Patrick came straight up to Miss Llewelyn and respectfully removed his straw hat.

'Pat,' she said, familiarly, 'I'm an old friend of Mrs Hargrove's and I'm bringing you back her little boy who left you, if I understand him correctly, while you were telling him about your country. I know Ireland and I am Welsh, as you may guess from my accent.'

'Long live Wales!' he said.

'Long live Ireland, without the English!' she said. 'It seems that you consider your country as beautiful as Heaven.'

'Madam,' he replied, 'when you go to Heaven — but perhaps you are Protestant?'

'No, Catholic.'

'Then,' he said, reassured, 'when you go to Heaven you will look around and say: "But this is Ireland . . ."'

'And me?' said Ned. 'Aren't I going to Heaven?'

Miss Llewelyn winked at Patrick.

'Anglican,' she muttered.

His reply was instantaneous:

'Of course you'll go to Heaven,' he told Ned. 'But first, in the waiting room.'

'It's lovely,' Miss Llewelyn added. 'A big, big garden with flowers.'

The little boy's anxious face lightened a little.

'But I will go to Heaven?' he asked.

'Listen, my little fellow,' Patrick said, with a solemn air, 'you will go to heaven sooner than we will if you stay as you are today, with a pure heart and clean hands.'

'I'm surer about the heart than the hands,' Miss Llewelyn said, with a sly smile. 'They're always black.'

'He'll go and wash them and they'll be fine,' said Patrick. 'Don't worry, Ned.'

'Betty has black hands,' said Ned.

Patrick and Miss Llewelyn exchanged glances.

'We'd have done better not to talk about Heaven,' said the Welshwoman.

She leaned over toward the boy and said gently:

'Betty has black hands, but they are very clean because she has never done anything bad; and nor have you, and I'm sure that you never will. Be happy, don't worry.'

The look that he turned toward her thrilled her with the profound innocence of his large brown eyes. For the first time in her life, this woman had the experience of peering into a soul which had never been touched by evil and she suddenly felt a mortal anguish at the idea of the fate that awaited her on leaving this world. She turned her head away in fear and put her hand on the gardener's arm.

'Pat, I don't like what we have been saying to this little lad. I'm going to take him back to the house. It must be time for him to go for his walk with Betty.'

And brusquely she added:

'Your garden looks ridiculous with all those magnolias standing side by side like soldiers. It wasn't Mrs Hargrove who told you to plant them in that way.'

He shrugged his shoulders.

'Of course not, but she can't say no to her husband and he wants them like that.'

After a pause he added;

'He has his ideas, I don't know what they are, but he is attached to them. He's a strong fellow all the same. I can tell you about that.'

'We'll see what he's worth, Pat, if there is war.'

'There will be,' he said laconically.

Grimacing at the sun which was shining in his face, he pulled his straw hat down over his red boxer's nose.

'Take my advice, Pat,' the Welshwoman said. 'Go back to Ireland.'

'Back home, to live with the hunger? Not likely. I'm staying here, Ma'am, and I'll march with them.'

'It will be a dirty war.'

'All wars are dirty. Going to war is not like going to a wedding.'

'The South is not ready. There's not a single factory in the whole country! Come on, now, Ned. We're going back to the house.'

Hand in hand, they went off, but after a few steps she turned around and said to Patrick:

'Of course, if I were in your place, I'd do exactly the same. I'd go off with a song on my lips.'

# 58

*O*n emerging from a laudanum-induced fog, Elizabeth had slipped back into a heavy sleep which relieved her of her anguish, if not the sadness of a woman in mourning. Now she had to accept the indifference of a husband who no longer wanted her, and had to summon up all her self-respect in order to play her part properly as a deserted wife in the eyes of the world. She began at the very start of the day.

Sitting beside Ned, she took her breakfast with him as usual when Billy was away. She listened absent-mindedly to the boy. He was talking to her mysteriously about some tall woman in black; but, imagining that it must be one of his confused dreams, she smiled and shook her head without replying to his questions.

Meanwhile, Celina had brought her her mail as usual. There was a letter with no stamp which instantly cleared her mind. She recognized Miss Llewelyn's writing on the envelope and read as follows:

Dear Mrs Hargrove,
Your housekeeper will give you this letter tomorrow at the same time as your mail. By then, I assume you will be in a fit state to understand an important message which I was unable to give you today. For reasons which are not for me to know, but which I can guess well enough, you were under the influence of drugs and the dosage must have been strong. You must do as you wish, but please do not pass life by when you are still so young. It is imperative, it is urgent, that I should see you on Tuesday morning and I shall be at your house at ten o'clock. In the name of common sense, recover yourself and believe me to be, your humble servant,
Maisie Llewelyn.

'That tone!' said Elizabeth, slipping the letter into its envelope. 'At once respectful and authoritarian: "In the name of common sense . . ." How dare she! But she'll always be the same; and how can I refuse to see her?'

It was almost half past nine. The idea of a conversation with the Welshwoman in the accursed little drawing-room upset her more than anything. She rang for her housekeeper.

'Miss Celina,' she said. 'When this lady comes this morning, take her to the second floor where I shall be waiting for her on the veranda.'

Leaving her cup still full, she decided to go up to her room, followed through the hall by Ned, who was asking her insistently if she loved him as much as ever.

'More than ever, my love!' she called out from the stairs, 'but Mama is busy. Go and finish your pancake.'

Later, sitting in front of her mirror, she examined her face with the scrupulous attention of a portraitist studying his model. Were there any remaining traces of her crisis? Had the drug marked or dulled her complexion, made her features look drawn, or left any wrinkles — that female nightmare? In short, was she still the lovely Englishwoman, untouched by the years? Only youth made life bearable.

She stood up, reassured. Everything was as it should be. However, something indefinable had escaped her. How could she have seen it, since it was the very thing that she used for seeing? Her own gaze, coming as it did from the depths of those splendid eyes. A certain inexperience of life that could not be faked, the disturbing charm of prolonged innocence.

Having done her hair with almost fanatical care — the comb and brush were tireless — she only stopped looking at herself when she was quite satisfied with her appearance, and then went downstairs on to the veranda.

Sifted and softened by the wooden trellis, the light spread gently, and, arranged in a semi-circle, broad willow chairs with flowered cushions awaited visitors.

Protected from the sun by the sycamores in the square, Elizabeth walked back and forth casually waving a palm leaf fan, which was chiefly designed to support the slightly detached attitude which she had chosen to adopt for the occasion. In spite of that, she was impatient to know what this urgent message that the Welshwoman was bringing her could be. Soon she heard a heavy, very slow step which made her drop her fan and run to the top of the stairs leading to the veranda. Like a great dark mass with a hand reaching out of it to clasp the bannister, Maisie Llewelyn was coming up toward her without looking up, and suddenly Elizabeth felt ashamed.

'Oh, Miss Llewelyn!' she cried. 'How sorry I am for having thoughtlessly put you to such an effort . . .'

Red and running with sweat, the face finally emerged, like a message of suffering and anger.

There was a brief silence, broken only by heavy breathing.

'I'm pleased to see some signs of compassion in your heart at last, Mrs Hargrove. As for my own, it is beating so fast it seems likely to burst. Please excuse me.'

Elizabeth walked down to her and held out her hand to help her up the last ten steps, but the Welshwoman refused.

'On my own,' she said.

Both of them sat down in the armchairs but Elizabeth suddenly went to pick up the palm fan which she offered Miss Llewelyn. Without a word, the latter took it and waved it in front of her scarlet face in a kind of fury. Her breath, short and wheezing, made a strange sound in the silence that worried Elizabeth, but she could not bring herself to ask a question, feeling herself too obviously responsible.

'Since I am here to deliver a message, here it is without any further preamble.'

Elizabeth interrupted her:

'Can't I first get you something to drink? It's very easy. There is a gong here to call the servants.'

Miss Llewelyn shook her head.

'I have been informed of the little plot on behalf of Mrs Jonathan Armstrong whom you wish to bring back into society. Society, indeed, did not want anything to do with her six or seven years ago. Mrs Armstrong herself organized a soirée in her home near Macon. It was a memorable disaster.'

'I know all that,' Elizabeth said, a little impatiently. 'But that was merely a group of provincial families.'

'And are you so interested in Mrs Armstrong, despite . . .'

'I have good relations with Annabel,' Elizabeth said drily. 'She paid me a friendly visit which I shall not forget.'

'And you think that she will be more of a success in Savannah than she was with the country aristocracy? The insult may be less direct, less crude, but the so-called aristocracy of the coast is famous for its rigid standards.'

Here Miss Llewelyn's voice became more conciliatory and was accompanied by a slightly pitying smile. She added:

'Let me tell you that I find you just as ignorant of human nature as you were before your two marriages. Let's put aside these sullen looks, shall we, and try to talk to one another as we once did, in the time when you called on my help in writing certain letters . . .'

Elizabeth jumped to her feet, her face blazing:

'Miss Llewelyn, I will not permit . . .'

'Yes, yes, you will,' said the Welshwoman, very calmly, settling into her chair. 'You will permit Maisie Llewelyn to do anything, whenever her presence is essential to you.'

'Essential? I don't understand.'

'It's very simple. Mrs Jonathan Armstrong will suffer another rejection if I am not there beside her when she appears in that drawing-room.'

The Welshwoman's tranquil self-assurance exasperated Elizabeth, who sat down again and said, in a cold voice:

'Unless I'm mistaken, this is about Mrs Armstrong, not you.'

The reply came slowly, already prepared long ago.

'Mrs Hargrove, do you think that I ever entertained the hope of entering your society? You should know that there is not a drop of my blood which did not start to boil at the very idea of making a step in that direction. On what grounds, in Heaven's name, should I cross the threshold of your aristocracy? I should have as my coat of arms a sewing machine and a broom, and perhaps the pick and shovel which my cousins still use, over there, in my own country.'

Stupor and consternation were written on the face of the beautiful Englishwoman.

'That's all very well,' she said in her confusion, with all the dignity she could muster. 'Let's say that I must have failed to make myself understood clearly.'

'Very much so, Mrs Hargrove. Now, listen to me and try to understand. There is only one person in the world who knows what happened in Haiti where Mrs Jonathan Armstrong's fate was sealed. I say only one person, because the other, the first and main victim, is now beyond the reach of this world and its aristocratic carnival: Laura, the best, who will never speak. It is I, Maisie Llewelyn, a daugher of the people, who can open the door of your society to Lady Jonathan Armstrong.'

With what a hiss of contempt she threw the word society in Elizabeth's face! The younger woman shuddered and raised her hand as though to protect herself from the flood of words . . . But the Welshwoman had not finished.

'It is for you to do the most difficult thing, without which nothing is possible: to ensure the entrance into Mrs Harrison Edwards' great white and gold drawing-room, of fat Maisie Llewelyn, in the presence of those rows of upright and contemptuous people, hoist on their ancestral pride. It will be a moment of high drama.'

Elizabeth suddenly grew very pale and sat up.

'Miss Llewelyn, you are going too far,' she said in a slightly unsteady voice.

'I know,' said Miss Llewelyn, unmoved. 'I am going beyond the limits. It's so pleasant to do so . . . But I can see from your face that you will not dare to do anything.'

'Mr Charles Jones will take care of it,' Elizabeth retorted.

'I am not unaware of Charlie Jones's omnipotence in the town of Savannah, but there are limits that can only be crossed by force. I shall act alone, and on my own authority.'

'In that case,' Elizabeth said, in a softer tone, 'can I consider that our conversation is at an end?'

She stood up, expecting Miss Llewelyn to reply, but the latter merely looked at her in a silence that was starting to become awkward. Only a great sadness could be seen in the Welshwoman's eyes.

'Do you know why I left Dimwood?' she asked softly.

This unexpected question plunged Elizabeth into confusion.

'I suppose,' she said at length, 'that after the death of Mr Hargrove, who engaged you . . .'

Miss Llewelyn interrupted her at once.

'Would you be so good as to sit down?'

It was another woman speaking now, and a refusal seemed impossible. Without a word, Elizabeth sat.

'Mr Hargrove's absence changed nothing,' the Welshwoman said. 'I could have stayed. A Maisie Llewelyn is not easily replaced. I was the true mistress of the house. Everything worked wonderfully when I was there to look after it. I knew everything; I knew almost too much.'

She stopped for a moment to catch her breath.

'Do you remember Miss Pringle?'

'Yes, of course. I did not have any dealings with her, but we would pass in the corridors. She didn't interest me.'

'You, on the other hand, interested her, and a great deal.'

'Well, I never!'

'You would talk about England. She noted it down, everything. She was a spy for the North. What she could understand of what was being said, she noted. Mr Stoddard, who had fallen in love with her, was a tool in her hands. When she guessed that I had discovered what she was up to, she announced that she was leaving for Gettysburg where, she said, she owned a little country house.'

'What a base creature!'

'I agree, but that is not all. When she got home, she had to report what she had learned to the people who employed her and paid for her services. To that end, she wrote a letter, not to Mr Hargrove who had become almost irresponsible, but to one of his sons, in the hope of obtaining a reply which would be an accreditation to her employers.'

'So?' Elizabeth asked, increasingly attentive.

'Mrs Pringle's letter was addressed to Joshua Hargrove. He read it and, as a man of honor, tore it up and threw it in the wastepaper basket, without replying. I have that letter.'

'Excuse my curiosity, but how did you manage . . .'

'To get hold of it? Very simple. You know how inquisitive the Blacks are. Listening at doors and rummaging through baskets provides the most enjoyable entertainment in their monotonous lives. One of them found this letter, which had been torn in two. He read it and saw my name . . . To be on good terms with the housekeeper is an excellent policy for a Black. He gave it to me in return for a reward.'

'Am I mentioned in the letter?' Elizabeth asked.

'Not a word. But I am, and denounced as a dangerous Spanish spy. She had indeed learned that I am a Catholic, which means in the pay of Spain. This is a firm conviction in the North and, unfortunately, also in the South. In any case, here is her letter. Read the heading and the date.'

Taking the piece of paper, which had been glued together, out of her pocket, she handed it to Elizabeth. The writing was fine and meticulous. Elizabeth read:

Gettysburg, Pennsylvania. September 10.

The young Englishwoman at once handed the letter back to Miss Llewelyn.

'Take it,' she said. 'It disgusts me even to touch it and I am not used to reading letters that are not addressed to me.'

'Still so proud,' said Miss Llewelyn. 'But I understand. Doesn't the address seem interesting to you?'

'No, why?'

'Joshua Hargrove placed Gettysburg in Massachusetts, because he did not like Miss Pringle and he instinctively sent her as far away as possible. It must be said that Gettysburg is a small, very small town, the name of which means little to most people and nothing at all to Joshua Hargrove. I was careful not to breathe a word of this business, my status as a Catholic making me somewhat vulnerable, if not in the eyes of the domestic slaves, almost all of whom were converted by Sister Laura, then at least in the eyes of the Hargroves.'

'Not in mine,' Elizabeth said warmly.

Seeing Miss Llewelyn's astonished look, she hastened to add:

'My point of view has changed because of Betty. But please, carry on.'

'I have little left to say. Joshua Hargrove, who is a man of heart and good sense, never again mentioned Miss Pringle's name and nothing changed at Dimwood until the death of William Hargrove, followed by the reading of his will. You know what followed. I took advantage of the opportunity to justify myself against the deceased's accusations and left the plantation. I have no taste for spying and I have nothing against Spaniards, but I could not bear to be considered suspect.'

Leaning with all her strength on the arms of her chair, she rose and stood in front of Elizabeth who at once said:

'Let me call Celina who will help you go down.'

The Welshwoman's green eyes held her with a piercing look.

'On my own,' she said. 'I came up on my own and I shall go down in the same way. On that point, I have a question to put to you. I am getting old, Mrs Hargrove, as you know. So, seeing me painfully climbing the two floors up to your veranda, did you not consider that it would have been simpler and in a sense more humane to spare me that effort and receive me in your pretty blue drawing-room on the ground floor?'

Taken aback, Elizabeth stammered:

'For personal reasons, I loathe that blue drawing-room.'

At that, in a firm, slow voice, without taking her eyes off her, the Welshwoman replied:

'You have made me pay dearly for your whim, haven't you?'

These words finally overwhelmed the young Englishwoman who exclaimed:

'I was wrong, Miss Llewelyn, I accept that I was wrong and I knew it as soon as I saw you coming up. I beg you to forget . . . to . . .'

The Welshwoman cut her short:

'It's done. I have forgotten. I only remember this moment which restored to me the Elizabeth of former years whom I loved. So let us part good friends, if you do not consider that a breach of etiquette . . .'

Elizabeth cried out:

'Etiquette! One has to pretend to believe in it, but I refuse to see any difference between us.'

Seizing the Welshwoman's hand, she pressed it in hers.

Not another word passed between them. Maisie Llewelyn turned away and began to go down the stairs as she had said she would, on her own, followed by a chastened Elizabeth who looked vaguely like her servant.

At the foot of the steps, they restrained themselves from kissing one another. A look replaced the impulse they both felt.

# 59

*E*lizabeth took refuge in her bedroom, ashamed of everything she had said and done that morning. With the passing years, it seemed to her more and more obvious that she was becoming increasingly tactless, because she did not know how to behave with people. Little by little she came to realize that she was unable to escape from her childhood. As soon as a burst of energy made her act like a woman, it was sure to be disastrous. Everything was settled later, because life settled everything, but badly.

Rough, and sometimes crude, the Welshwoman had more heart than she did. In her presence, Elizabeth felt unable properly to play the role that her social standing demanded. At times she would be an arrogant lady, at others demean herself with unworthy humility, as had happened on the veranda in her conversation with Miss Llewelyn. Blushing, she recalled the whole scene and guessed that the Welshwoman despised her, even though she felt a condescending affection for her. The insult was hard to swallow, yet, despite everything, she liked this fat woman, violent, sly and greedy though she was, because of her courage and her constant defiance of the powers of this world.

The moment was hard to endure. Only one person could have comforted her in her humiliation, but there too she was defeated: Billy no longer wanted her. The failure was so serious that she wondered if it might not be better to return to her mother's home in England. At least there she would be protected from the bloody conflict that was about to break out in America. She was starting to feel frightened and she was no longer the Elizabeth she imagined herself to be. The proud Englishwoman was suddenly contrite at having deceived herself for so long. One day perhaps she would discover that she was a coward. Had she ever heard a canon being fired?

In her inner turmoil, she did what she always did at times of extreme uncertainty: she sat in front of her mirror and admired herself while combing her hair: combing her hair became a gesture of despair. A hundred times the little tortoiseshell teeth bit into the golden tresses which seemed to stream around this anxious face. Billy loved to plunge his hands into this hair, so full of light, to cover his forehead, his cheeks and his mouth as if washing in it. He adored the smell — he used once to adore so many things when he took possession of her and her body with a sort of barbarian savagery. Once . . . That is what she wanted, nothing more. What was the use now of throwing herself on her bed and crying into the pillow.

The crisis passed. She put her hair up again, went downstairs and had lunch as usual; and, as usual, Ned at her side spoke all about the little life he led in the garden with the magnolias, and the stories that Patrick told him. The inexorable tedium of existence closed around her, tearing her away from the turbulence of her desires, forcing her to be calm, like a wild beast reduced to obedience in a pretty cage.

# 60

*T*hat afternoon, she put on the pale green dress which suited her best and had her carriage harnessed. Sitting, head high, under a little white parasol, she gave the order to the coachman to take her for a ride anywhere, except down to the port.

React: she had to react, she told herself and rediscover a little self-respect, in the ruin of her damaged pride! Even if she had lost everything, she remained the indestructibly beautiful Englishwoman. Great waves of lifted hats that would have done honor to a queen reminded her of the fervent admiration of men of taste, and once more she found her smile.

Her black coachman, a little bewildered and having no imagination, took her round one square after another. She let her gaze wander around the rows of elegant white or red — and exquisitely simple — houses. Behind banks of flowers in which garnet, midnight blue, sky blue, purple, mauve and reseda battled against the dark green of the foliage, they gave an indefinable impression of keeping a certain distance. They maintained a tranquil dignity, not without a hint of disdain, which was a little intimidating for the world at large.

Miss Llewelyn's outburst against society came back in all its violence into Elizabeth's mind. How likely was it that she should be right, faced with that wall of patrician respectability? Yet, behind these silent barred windows, who could say if there were not women who suffered as she did from the long solitudes of night? She recalled a laconic remark of her mother's: 'One gets by.' The shadow of the sycamores gently swept across the haughty façades, as though to give them a semblance of natural life, but they remained impassive, standing apart from everything.

Finally, Elizabeth told the coachman to drive up Bull Street where the sight of people walking and riding might entertain her. It was not yet the time when the greatest crowds gathered, but one could already see ladies in lawn dresses competing in clarity and variety of colors. They were accompanied by gentlemen whose tail coats never varied, regardless of season. From her carriage, the young Englishwoman could only recognize a few people, having chosen to follow the avenue that lay parallel to the riding avenue.

Men rode by, trotting, mostly on slender-legged thoroughbreds: they were there purely to be seen. The young especially . . . Proud, arch-backed in their gray jackets with hanging basques, some were daring enough to salute the lovely blond lady, even if they knew her only by sight, because there was something irresistible about her which made their blood burn. She herself was very conscious of this since her marriage to Billy. It was as if the impetuous hussar had awakened dormant energies in her.

What fate was relentlessly pursuing her? A rider passed. Singularly handsome, he began to turn his chestnut mount toward Elizabeth's carriage when he saw her. Instinctively she dropped her parasol to hide her face from the self-confident look that was directed at her.

It was Algernon, the 'assassin' of the town's beauties. With an expert hand, he swept the air with his mouse-gray top hat. She raised her parasol and said:

'Good day.'

He wanted nothing more than that for the moment, but he took full advantage of it and the imprudent young woman soon saw him trotting beside her carriage.

'I am touched that you should remember the dreadful evening in the Schmick house. I couldn't tell you the other evening.'

'I try not to think about it any longer. I thought I would die of boredom . . .'

'Yet your humble servant has the most touching memory of it. A few words exchanged later . . .'

'Oh, in the street, sir,' she said, sensing the danger of going any further.

'The place is of little importance when I recall some of your words.'

He was all smiles as he doled out his nauseating commonplaces, but once more she felt the magic attraction of a handsome face. Even so, she struggled a little.

'I have no memory of what I might have said to you.'

The regularity of the features was perfect, the distance between the eyes and the shape of the mouth were sublime; and, as for the softness of the look and what it secretly implied, it would be better to turn gracefully away for fear of succumbing to it. She found that Algernon was ten times more agreeable to the eye today, in bright sunlight, than in the light of a lamp or in a drawing-room. In her bewilderment, she said:

'Sir, I am going home, I must part company with you.'

'Oh, then at least let me be allowed, one day soon, to present my respects to you.'

His respects . . ., his visiting card, no doubt. What could she do with that?

'Yes, yes; and . . . au revoir. Coachman, home!'

Throughout the journey to Oglethorpe Square, she meditated on her mother's mysterious advice: 'One gets by.' What did she mean? Elizabeth knew only too well. Now that Billy was, to all intents and purposes, neglecting her, she asked nothing better than to 'get by' with Algernon — though she didn't dare admit this to herself. In her mind she still retained the image of the red-hot iron which was once used to brand the shoulder of adulterous wives. It was a difficult problem, too difficult for a young woman who was still not properly informed of how customs had changed. In the last resort, she imagined what Miss Llewelyn would have replied on the subject of the scarlet letter, and almost at once thought she heard:

'Good heavens, Elizabeth, times have changed!'

A little calmer, she reached home and rang the bell. The house-keeper handed her a letter which a young officer had just brought to the house.

Her heart leaped. At first, she was frightened; in a flash of intuition she imagined that Billy was giving her his views on adulterous wives. She put aside that unlikely assumption and, mad with impatience, was already opening the envelope with her finger when she heard voices in the blue drawing-room. She hurried down there immediately and exclaimed:

'Minnie!'

Her cousin, whom she had not seen for five years, was standing before her, next to a very elegant young man dressed in light gray. Minnie threw herself into Elizabeth's arms.

'Yes, it's Minnie, come from New Orleans to see the family. My husband, Antonin de Siverac, who is dying to know you. We are going to live in Charleston from now on.'

The introductions were concluded, followed by the little storm of questions and answers that one would expect. Minnie radiated happiness. She had hardly changed. Her face, a little fuller, had all its former vivacity, her dark eyes still shone with the same calm and gentle gaiety as ever and she smiled continually, displaying teeth of whose whiteness she was visibly proud.

Handsome, tall, tanned and square-shouldered, her husband had wide black sideburns which seemed to put parentheses around a long face with attractive, fine features; and, as if to make his delicate looks more virile, his dark black eyes shone with audacity.

Elizabeth had slipped Billy's letter into her handbag and was pretending to feel delirious with joy in order to harmonize with this rather ill-timed visit. Yet she liked her cousin Minnie and memories began to flood back.

'That blue dress you lent me immediately after I arrived in Dimwood: do you remember?'

'Mildred's dress: I can see it now. It was — why, it was the color of your beautiful blue drawing-room.'

Elizabeth made a face which she immediately transformed into a smile.

'And that summer night,' Minnie went on. 'The one when we stood, all three of us, on an old stone bench to greet the new moon with three curtsies . . .'

'And on the third, we rolled in the grass, you, Susanna and I, all three at once . . .'

'What a memory!'

'And Susanna cried . . .'

'Heartbreak — but all that's a long way off . . . You must, you absolutely must come and visit us in Charleston, you and your husband. Where is Billy?'

'In Beaufort, quite near here, and not far from you. He is a lieutenant of hussars.'

'Hussars, you hear.'

She turned to her husband.

'The hussars! Bravo!' Siverac exclaimed in a ringing voice. 'I served for two years in the hussars at Bâton Rouge. And I'm ready to go back at the first sign of trouble.'

Minnie burst out laughing:

'Antonin is a real swordsman who only thinks of fighting. But there won't be any war, will there, Elizabeth?'

'Of course not. Billy is sure there won't.'

'You see. Above all, one should not read newspapers, because they print anything. Charleston is full of young hotheads who shout very loudly and insult the Washington government. The only word they have on their lips is 'secession' . . . I hope Billy hasn't forgotten his cousin Minnie. He doesn't write to me.'

'He never writes,' Elizabeth said, feeling her bag with a nervous hand to make sure that the letter was still there. 'He's like that.'

Minnie gave her a curious look.

'He loves you . . . very much, I'm sure,' she said, without conviction.

'Of course he does, Minnie.'

'Then everything's fine. We are here for a month. When you come and see us, you'll be interested in our house. Antonin inherited it from his maternal grandfather. Our neighbors are the Lows, who are related to you, I believe.'

'Perhaps . . . I'm not sure. Genealogy is not my forte.'

'In the South,' Antonin said gravely, 'everyone is related to everyone else — at a certain level in society.'

Minnie cut short the threatened tirade on the nobility.

'Elizabeth, we still have so many things to say to one another, but I hope we'll see each other often. This evening Antonin and I have still more calls to make. Our address is very simple: we're staying with Uncle Charlie, who is due back shortly. So do get in touch with us, won't you?'

She kissed her tenderly.

'See you soon, Minnie darling. You are just as you were in Dimwood, just as delightful . . . Au revoir, Antonin.'

Antonin gave a great bow.

At the front door, there were further kisses.

'You will always be the more beautiful,' said Minnie,

When the door was shut, Elizabeth slumped down on a chair in the hall and sighed:

'At last!'

Escaping from the blue drawing-room, she went straight up to her bedroom. It was there, alone, that she wanted to read Billy's letter. She took it out of her handbag and sank back into the rocking chair.

'If it's over,' she thought, opening the envelope, 'I shall not hesitate. I'll have Algernon.'

The large, clumsy handwriting covered the first page:

'My love, forget everything, I'm an idiot, as soon as I got back here I realized that I had behaved like a madman, don't ask me why, I can't say. There are times when I lose my head when I am burning with desire. Forget, forget everything. I am rolling in your hair, I have thought of some new things, you'll see. Forgive me, arrange the garden however you want, we will dig up the magnolias and replant them wherever you like, and we shall have breakfast downstairs like everyone else, and live like everyone except when we are up there, in our room, where we shall do things that others do not . . .'

A list of the things in question followed. From the first line she read words that made her think she was going mad. Never had she seen with her own eyes, in black and white, such crude details, and her astonishment made her drop the letter.

The idea did occur to her that he had lost his reason. She recalled the odd note in Minnie's voice when she mentioned cousin Billy and his love. It was as if she did not believe in it. And, suddenly transported back to the distant past, Elizabeth saw Billy once more in the dining-room at Uncle Charlie's, alone before a huge bowl of strawberries and cream, stuffing them into his mouth and cramming his cheeks in his haste to swallow all of them. The relationship between that gluttony and the contents of the letter were plain to her. She herself was only another source of greed for him.

Despite everything she picked the letter up and read a few more lines, then folded the paper, without finishing it.

'A glutton,' she said quietly. 'I've married a vulgar glutton.'

She had the strange feeling that, to him, she was not someone, but something.

Suddenly she saw Jonathan. For all their violence, his amorous frenzies left intact the image that she had of him and, in that sweet moment, she felt herself falling once more desperately in love with that man, beyond all the spaces of time that separated them.

She had given her heart, once and for all.

# 61

*T*he hours that followed were hard. As if in a waking dream, she heard little Ned talking to her and could only kiss and hug him, without saying anything; and, with no dinner, she retired to her room.

For the first time, she felt a distaste for life. Billy's letter had rent a veil. It showed her every gesture and every bodily impulse in a light that repelled and sickened her. Astonishment had calmed her and it was now in cold blood that she reflected on the brutal description of what she had managed to do in the delirium of desire. The words killed something. It was not a matter of shame or morality: in the circumstances, these words seemed to her ridiculous. Something else vanished: enchantment, the turn of the key in the lock, the secrecy, the fascination of what was never spoken about, never, as if it was a crime, which it wasn't, a forbidden act, when there was nothing forbidden about it: everything that shrouded in mystery an act of animal banality.

After some consideration, she slowly tore up the letter, with a hand that was both furious and assiduous, leaving the tiny pieces scattered around the carpet.

She undressed quickly and went to bed early, tired and disenchanted, in the bed which only the evening before she had called her desert. The occasionally faltering light of the street lamp in front of the next door house shone into the room from the avenue. Weak though this light was, it drove away the terror of total obscurity, of that element which children call the dark and which Elizabeth could not bear. The yellowish rays shone through the half-closed shutters and allowed her to distinguish the shape of the wardrobe, a chest of drawers and an armchair, which was enough to soothe her. She fell asleep suddenly, just as she was listening to the clock on a nearby church sounding the hour.

A little before dawn, when the darkness was deepest, a loud noise woke her up with a start. Downstairs, a door slammed, then some brisk steps on the stairs threw her into a childlike terror. She shouted. Someone came in.

Billy, but a Billy whom she did not know. In the light of the street lamp, she made out his tall outline, then a curt voice called her:

'Are you there, Elizabeth?'

'Yes. What is it?'

'I want that letter, Wake up and give it to me.'

'That letter?'

'Yes, mine of course. Have you had any others?'

She could feel the dull anger rising which had been grumbling inside her for some hours.

'Not today,' she said, drily.

There was a short pause and then, in an altered voice, he said:

'My love, give me my letter.'

She was so astonished that she did not know what to say. She had the feeling that these words were echoing in a sudden stillness that seemed to steal over everything: time, night, objects.

At last she said gently:

'If you light my bedside lamp, we'll be able to look for it.'

He came over to the bed, struck a match and lit the little oil lamp. His powerful hands were the first thing to appear in the light, then his face with its red cheeks and his tousled blond hair, giving him a schoolboy look.

Elizabeth waited a moment. Her throat was dry with emotion.

'Look,' she said, 'beside the rocking chair.'

He thought she was teasing him.

'I'm not joking, you know,' he said, without moving.

Raising her head, she looked up at him and their eyes met.

'Billy,' she said gravely. 'I'm not joking either. Why not do as I say.'

He hesitated with the shame of a child who does not want to believe what he is being told and is afraid of seeming ridiculous, but obeys even so, against his will; and he went over to the chair.

'Well,' he said, irritably. 'Where am I to look for the letter? There's nothing here.'

'Don't move, but look around, look everywhere.'

Raising his eyebrows, he searched the four corners of the room when suddenly his eyes looked down and he cried:

'On the ground!'

'Yes, that's your letter.'

'You've torn it into a thousand pieces!'

In two leaps he was at the head of the bed and kneeling in front of her. Once more she saw and recognized the love radiating from his face, and he began to talk in a rush of words, Elizabeth's two hands clasped in his, squeezing them until he almost crushed them in his over-excitement.

'You did the right thing. Oh, you did the right thing, my beloved Elizabeth! I have galloped for three hours through the night so that I could tear that filthy letter from you, hoping that you had not yet read . . .'

'I didn't read all of it, only the first page.'

'Not the end? Oh, God be praised! Listen. I wrote those pages in a moment of madness. You do not know what a man can suffer when he is deprived of what he needs with the full force of his body. At such moments just writing certain things is a sort of illu-

sory compensation, there are words that produce a hallucination . . .
I am ashamed, I am dying of shame before you, I am not at all as I
appear in that horrible letter, you must not judge me, Elizabeth.
Judge not. That's a phrase which is sometimes quoted. I don't know
who said it first, but he was right, whoever it was . . .'

Struck dumb with surprise, Elizabeth tried to pull her hands away,
but failed. A voice from deep inside her cried out: 'Tell him who!
Tell him the name! Don't resist!' She let her head fall backward
and her hair streamed down her back.

'Let me go, I beg you,' she said.

'What is it? You don't agree? You're judging me: do you think
one should?'

'No, no, but the person who said that . . .'

She could not speak the name. To speak it might change everything, change her life, change Billy . . . One could never know, but
the voice continued: 'Just say the name, Elizabeth.'

'The person who said that . . .' she said, and stopped.

'What does it matter who said it? What he said is still true. You
should not judge me because you don't know me — and that's true
for everyone, don't you think? Tell me that you believe it, my love.'

'Yes,' she said. 'Of course it's true.'

Inside her, there was silence.

Letting go his grip, Billy took Elizabeth's head in his hands and
pressed his mouth against hers. She closed her eyes, entirely absorbed in the ecstasy of rediscovered happiness.


# 62


When they were in a state to discuss anything apart from
their own pleasure, he revealed that he had persuaded the
commandant to give him this exceptional short leave by letting himself be beaten twice at whist and écarté. In ten more days, he would
be granted a longer leave.

She was conscious of the care that he took during the day to
appear more courteous and compliant. Together they made a tour
of the garden and he told Patrick to obey all Madam's whims in the
matter of horticulture.

At the same time, he set out to win Ned round by stunning him
with fantastic stories.

He departed the following evening, leaving her more in love than ever. She loved him even more, in fact, than when she thought she was about to lose him.

Some minor events helped her to bear the pain of separation. One day, Mrs Harrison Edwards called on her, beside herself with worry. Still extremely elegant and wearing a hat with a ruffled feather in it, she nevertheless showed signs of panic in her eyes. The scene was played out in the blue drawing-room which, according to Elizabeth, breathed disaster.

'My dearest,' the visitor said, 'our plans are crumbling.'

She sat down heavily in a chair and impatiently threw her handbag on the floor, before going on.

'Everything was ready for the great evening on April 16, the invitations had been sent out, received and all accepted. The musicians had been informed and were prepared to attend on the day. In short, every slightest detail was fixed, down to the most incredible buffet one could imagine, do you see, do you understand?'

'Perfectly.'

'And now Annabel is not coming.'

'Not coming!'

'In a letter couched in terms of already outdated politeness, she told me that one insult was enough and that, on reflection, she did not feel inclined to risk being exposed to a second one, more definitive and wounding.'

Elizabeth expressed consternation. Mrs Harrison Edwards stood up.

'Only you can save me, save my party.'

'Me?' Elizabeth said, with a hand to her breast — starting to be affected by the slightly theatrical turn the conversation was taking. 'The woman whom she considers responsible for her misfortune . . .'

'Heavens above!' Mrs Harrison Edwards groaned, attempting to wring her hands (which was difficult, for they were covered in lilac suede gloves). 'What are we going to do? Without formally accepting, she left me with the firm belief that she would be there, on condition that everything was done discretely, with tact. With tact, the wretch!'

'Not at all!' said Elizabeth. 'You can still appeal to Uncle Charlie who usually manages to arrange everything.'

'You do it for me, Elizabeth. You have before you a poor woman at the end of her tether.'

This was not entirely true. Mrs Harrison Edwards always kept a cool head, but self-respect would not allow her to undertake certain tasks which she considered humiliating. Already, Annabel's rejection stuck in her throat. She knew that by injecting a little emotion into her appeal she would touch the naive Elizabeth's heart and persuade her to undertake the begging mission.

The young Englishwoman had not yet seen the great society lady behave in this way and she took pity on her:

'Calm yourself,' she said, nobly. 'I shall speak to Uncle Charlie. It is in his interest for Annabel to be present, since he is the one who organized this special party with you.'

They embraced and parted; then, turning back again, Mrs Harrison Edwards embraced her once more, with fervor, as if they were two fellow souls. And suddenly, in a burst of gratitude, the visitor uttered this cry from the heart:

'You will save my party!'

# 63

On his return the day after next, Uncle Charlie showed himself to be far less devious. Elizabeth went to see him as soon as she could, and he received her in his little private drawing-room. This was a room of refined charm, furnished with copious gilded arm-chairs and a huge padded sofa in eggshell velvet, too voluptuous to be quite proper — though two busts of Aristotle and Lycurgus seemed to look down from the two high niches where they were placed, as if to dispel suspicion and silence gossip.

In this pleasantly ambiguous decor, he greeted Elizabeth with an entirely paternal affection, for in his eyes she was still his ward. Her beauty had something to do with it. As soon as he saw her in his drawing-room, he took her in both hands and drew her toward him, unaffectedly giving her a kiss on each cheek, country-style.

'Good news, my dear child,' he said. 'I found the material you need for your drawing-room in a shop in New York. Thirty rolls of light red brocade are on their way to your lovely house. You will have a room which will be the talk of the town, a real drawing-room for an officer's wife: furiously heroic. How is your Billy?'

She answered briefly in a good-humored way and went straight to the point of her visit. Emotion made her talkative and awkward, but she eventually managed to describe Mrs Harrison Edwards' anxieties and Charlie Jones listened to her patiently with an attentive air.

'Poor dear Lucile,' he said, with a broad smile. 'Always sensitive and compassionate, but the problem is not a very difficult one and I have long experience as a lawyer to inspire me. Tomorrow she will have a letter, not a letter presenting some unanswerably persuasive argument, but a letter that will break her heart, the kind that never fails. Now, my dear Elizabeth, a ship is due into harbor and I must leave you. In any case, we shall see one another again on the evening of April 16. It will be a great event in the history of Savannah, I guarantee.'

Going into his study, he sat down at a heavy walnut table piled high with papers and books. On a large white sheet of paper, several lines were written, crossed out, rewritten and crossed out again. At last he had the following:

> 'You who, for so many reasons, are so dear to us, Annabel: I am thinking of you this evening as a man life's raw experience has delivered from many illusions and cured of the lies and hypocrisies of society. So, by the quiet light of my lamp . . .' (the sun was shining out of a clear sky) ' . . . I see you as you are: pure in heart, noble in race and features, armed with a beauty that defies time. I can understand and approve of your rejection of the world; but in the silence of this April night, I appeal to your sense of filial piety. Think of your admirable mother, herself a victim of the inhumanity of man, who had to bear the burden of a false accusation and was treated as a guilty woman until disgust drove her into solitude. Annabel, make your appearance in society — a society that is ashamed of its own mistake, because it now understands the truth better, and is ready to welcome you with the respect you deserve; in that way you will lift the stigma of an unworthy suspicion from your mother and avenge her honor. For your mother's sake, come; I will guarantee the welcome that our aristocracy will give you, touched and impatient as it is to repair the errors of a few petty village aristos.
>
> Charles Jones.'

I may be going a little too far, he thought, folding the letter. But it is enough for Annabel to be there; I shall look after the rest.

An hour later, an errand-boy from the office took the letter and delivered it to Lady Jonathan Armstrong. The reply was not long in coming. The very next evening, the post brought it to Charlie Jones who opened it and read these words:

> 'Because of Mama, I shall be there, of course.
>
> 'But you are not straightforward enough, dear Charlie. You did not need a full orchestra to say a simple: "Come!" But we love you very much all the same.
>
> Annabel.'

# 64

*A* week before the great party at Mrs Harrison Edwards', important discussions took place at Charlie Jones' home. As it happened, he too, like Mrs Harrison Edwards herself, was feeling increasingly anxious as the 16th April approached. Both had accepted that the arrival of Lady Armstrong would be preceded by the appearance of Miss Llewelyn bearing evidence in the form of a testimony that would be essential, certainly, but the length of which might seem excessive. And this was nothing compared to the risk involved in letting an ordinary woman, not to say a woman of the people, appear in a society gathering. The principle of this unprecedented event had been agreed even before the invitations were sent out at the end of March. Viewed from afar, the occasion looked a trifle difficult, but possible. Now that it was imminent, however, Mrs Harrison Edwards went from mere apprehension to terror; she could no longer sleep and only managed to get by with the help of laudanum. As for Charlie Jones, he controlled himself, but was worried by the idea that some sort of scandal might be in store.

In a moment of cowardice which they did not admit to one another and which they preferred to think of as a burst of commonsense, they agreed to ask Miss Llewelyn to cancel what had been arranged and to stay at home that day. She was therefore asked instead to drop in at Jasper Square and the meeting between the three of them took place in Charlie Jones' private drawing-room.

The discussion was lively and soon became so noisy that at least four black ears were glued to the door. The risk was great but the pleasure quite exceptional. Miss Llewelyn refused outright on the grounds that she had revelations to make which alone could overcome the misgivings of High Society against the admission of a half-caste, even one who belonged to the highest ranks of English aristocracy. Her authority — her fury, even — made Mrs Harrison Edwards tremble at the prospect of her party degenerating into a disaster, but Charlie Jones, with all his authority, came up with an objection which he considered decisive: how could a woman without the necessary experience of speaking in public hold the attention of some forty ladies and as many gentlemen for a considerable period of time, when they had come to spend a pleasant evening?

'Telling a very long story is a difficult art,' he said at last, 'and one which requires formal training.'

At these words, Miss Llewelyn exploded and, in a deafening voice, hurled out a remark which would have pierced a brick wall:

'Asking a Welshwoman if she is able to tell a long story from one end to the other without hesitating, is like asking a nightingale if it can sing.'

'I agree,' said Charlie Jones, going scarlet in the face. 'But Mrs Harrison Edwards can always refuse to let you into her house.'

'I agree too, Mr Jones, but I still have the street and there, I promise you, I shall declaim my story, and in three minutes I shall have my audience.'

Slumped into a chair, Mrs Harrison Edwards was inhaling a bottle of smelling salts.

'Charlie,' she murmured, 'I don't see how we can refuse.'

He nodded in agreement.

'In that case,' he said, 'Miss Llewelyn will present herself at Mrs Harrison Edwards' on April 16th. At what time?'

'The invitation is for seven o'clock,' Mrs Harrison Edwards groaned. 'But we must allow for latecomers. So, at half past seven.'

'At half past seven on the dot, Maisie Llewelyn will be there,' said the Welshwoman in a firm voice.

With what was almost a sob, Mrs Harrison Edwards asked:

'Might I know — oh, good God — in what form of dress?'

The reply was instant and almost haughty:

'Appropriate to the occasion.'

She gave a satisfied nod of the head, which might be taken for a bow, and went out.


# 65

*I*n town, no one talked of anything but the great party on April 16th at Mrs Harrison Edwards', and already the evening overshadowed all political news. By listening at doors, eventually the names of all the guests were known: the complete list could have formed a directory of the entire aristocracy of the coast. A few proud but obscure families suffered at having been omitted and there were any number of plots to try and obtain the prestigious invitation, building up to a secret, undeclared war which at times reached tragic dimensions. Disappointments ended in floods of tears, for Mrs Harrison Edwards could be pitiless. She must, at all costs, have the nobility there and nobody else.

Sure of his own authority, Charlie Jones had recovered from his stormy scene with Miss Llewelyn, but Mrs Harrison Edwards was still a prey to dreadful uncertainty. She considered herself brave, but the Welshwoman frightened her. In her distress, she begged Providence to intervene and spare her the shame of too resounding a disaster; but Heaven did not answer. Preparing her laudanum, she told herself that if the worst did happen, she could leave the country and go into exile somewhere in Europe; London, of course.

Naturally, Elizabeth knew nothing of this raging drama. Everything for her was simple. An invitation had come asking her to attend the reception of April 16, and she thought of it from time to time, with some pleasure and much curiosity.

Worries of an entirely different nature occasionally came to trouble her. Admiring herself in the mirror, she was soon obliged to acknowledge that her waist was spreading, and she soon had to accept the evidence: Billy's furious attacks were bearing fruit and she was going to provide a brother or sister for young Ned. At Christmas, perhaps before, those awful pains which she had partly forgotten would come and torture her flesh. She constantly wondered about the inevitable event. She was repelled by the idea of pain; and, furthermore, how would Billy react? He had never shown any desire to have a child. What he wanted most of all was pleasure; love, to him, had no other meaning apart from that.

Days passed, and one evening she had an unexpected and disturbing visit. Annabel, in mourning, appeared after dinner and asked to speak with her in her room.

Night was falling quickly at the end of a brilliant afternoon and the gaslight was burning on the stairs.

In Elizabeth's room, the bedside lamp glowed with a peaceful light, but there was something dramatic about the arrival of this woman in a black dress which upset the tranquillity.

'Elizabeth,' Annabel said, without any preamble, 'don't be too surprised at seeing me, but we are now five days away from the reception which I have agreed to attend. You have in your possession an object which belongs to me and I beg you to return it.'

'An object?' said Elizabeth, disturbed.

'Don't try to evade the issue, you know perfectly well what I'm talking about: my emerald necklace. It is mine and I want it.'

The tone of voice made the young Englishwoman blush with sudden indignation.

'I'll give it to you at once, but it was left to me by William Hargrove and put into my hands by Charlie Jones.'

'I don't doubt that for a moment, but my father had given it to my mother as a wedding present and when she left the world to become a nun, she passed it on to her father, William Hargrove, who was to bequeath it to me at his death. The will that he made then did indeed state that the emerald necklace would be granted to me as a gift from my mother. Meanwhile, he had what he called a crisis of conscience and, in the name of morality, decided that these jewels, coming from a sinner (as he thought of my mother), could not be delivered to another sinner, namely myself. So the will was altered in your favor. Do you accept this treachery?'

In reply, Elizabeth went and looked for the key of the linen cupboard in a drawer of her dressing-table, opened it and took the emerald necklace out from beneath a pile of shirts. Still without saying anything, she handed it to Annabel, who took it in both hands, looked at it for a moment and put it in her bag.

'I feel no obligation to thank you,' she said in a gentler voice. 'But I do appreciate the fact that you believed what I said unhesitatingly. I am also aware that I must have seemed hard. Yes, I must. For that alone, I beg you to forgive me. Good night, Elizabeth. You are indeed just as I had hoped.'

As she was going toward the door, Elizabeth stopped her:

'Excuse me, I have one question to ask you.'

Annabel smiled:

'I think I can guess what it is. In your place I should have done the same, and sooner.'

She sat down and said, simply:

'I am listening.'

'Well, let's not beat about the bush,' Elizabeth said, also sitting down. 'How did you know that the necklace was here, in my room?'

'I like your directness very much. It saves time. You said just now that the necklace was given you by Charlie Jones.'

'Yes, I did.'

'He gave you this object which is of such value in the eyes of the world, in a case, and the case was in a box.'

'Precisely.'

'He himself did not know what the box contained and his curiosity was awakened.'

'That's putting it mildly. He was burning to know what William Hargrove left me.'

'And you didn't tell him . . . I know that because he confided in me one day. He wanted to know, but being too well-bred to persist with you, he asked me if I could tell him.'

'Now I understand. You told him.'

'Not exactly. I could not describe an object which I had never seen, but that emerald necklace, which disappeared during the revolution in Haiti, left a sort of legend behind. They said that it had been claimed either by the Queen of Spain or by the Queen of England. Everything is possible, even the improbable. Two living people were able to give a precise description of the necklace. One was Mama, who no longer thinks of such vanities, though I am certain that she had not forgotten the man whom she loved with all her heart. The other was William Hargrove, who had simply seized the necklace at the time of their flight from Haiti and kept it a secret until his death.'

'Why?'

'I can't tell you; but when I learned that he had left you an object, the nature of which he had not revealed, several people, including Charlie Jones and me, but especially myself, had the same thought: the emerald necklace.'

'Then it was merely a guess.'

'On my part, it was an inner certainty. I could not give you any proof, but I remembered what my mother had told me many years before. This too was not known, but I kept my secrets. Having said that, a memory is not proof. When I came to see you just now, I could not say anything definitely. I took a risk. I knew you. You might have shut me up with a single word: "Prove it" — when I told you the object was here.'

Elizabeth stood up and said in a very calm voice:

'So I yielded to intimidation.'

Annabel, who already had her hand on the door handle, turned back to Elizabeth:

'Yes, you did.'

'And do you find that fair?'

'No, but there are locks which one has the right to force in order to repair an injustice.'

'This is a quite new morality which I do not recognize. Without wishing to offend you, it would have been much admired by the late William Hargrove.'

Annabel looked at her for a long time before replying, then said softly:

'The day and the hour will come, Elizabeth, when you will regret those words; but you were provoked and I like you for reacting.'

Elizabeth said nothing and came down with her, accompanying her to the door of the house. On the front steps, Annabel stopped as if to listen to the birds in the sycamore trees, greeting the arrival of night.

'Do you like the South, Elizabeth?' she asked.

'Of course, a lot. Don't you know that?'

'Yes, and a new bond ties you to it, as strong as marriage. Do you understand?'

'But . . .'

'You are going to give the South another child.'

Distracted by the deafening song of the birds, Elizabeth said nothing. Annabel merely smiled and continued:

'I see you are still wearing my Jonathan's ruby . . . Would it irritate you to embrace me?'

Without hesitation, Elizabeth put her lips to the cold cheek which was offered to her. Annabel squeezed her hands.

'Until April 16th,' she said, going down the steps.

Her proud silhouette was soon lost in the shadows.

Back in her room, Elizabeth fell into one of those crises of despair which were becoming more and more frequent with her because she no longer understood the direction her life was taking. Trembling, she remembered the happy days in which nothing had seemed to threaten her personal future. She had been persuaded that there would not be a war, but far, far away inside her was the idea of escaping to England if things turned out for the worst, a ridiculous dream inspired by a fear that she did not admit to herself. And now Annabel had devastated her with a phrase that made her a prisoner of the South. A new bond attached her to it, as strong as marriage. The child that would be born, one day next winter.

And Jonathan's name, thrown into the last moments of that strange conversation. How could Annabel have taken the emerald necklace away from her in that imperious manner? 'I am not obliged to thank you . . .' No more than one is obliged to thank a thief when one finds her with her hand in your bag.

Blushing with anger and anxiety, she could only calm herself by thinking of the sudden gentleness of the tall lady in black who had asked her, on the steps, to embrace her. There was no further doubt: Annabel had gone mad. Perhaps from grief. The allusion to the ruby seemed to Elizabeth full of sinister undertones.

She regretted having allowed herself to be deprived of the emerald necklace by a madwoman. She should have said: 'No, no, and no again!' But she had lost her head. 'I took a risk,' this older woman had dared to say, using intimidation because she knew that she could impose herself. Her lovely emeralds! Elizabeth sometimes used to look at them, all alone, without showing them to anyone, not even Billy; and suddenly this half-caste had come into her room, saying that the emeralds did not belong to her, Elizabeth, but that they were hers, and that she needed them at once. And, without a word, like a simpleton, she had given them to her.

She went over these things again and again in her mind as if to convince herself that they were real.

The light from the street lamp, a garish yellow, was now seeping into the room.

Elizabeth sat down in front of her mirror and began to comb her hair assiduously, fascinated by the copper highlights shining along the tresses. And her hair crackled under the comb.

# 66

*T*here was nothing Mrs Harrison Edwards could do about it. By the force of circumstance, April 16th arrived, bathed in victorious light, scented with perfumes that assailed her from every garden bursting with spring. One could not have imagined a better day for a party.

On the terrace as in the drawing-room, rows of armchairs in gilt wood were arranged in semi-circles, waiting for the arrival of a hundred guests. A vast blind in cream canvas protected those who preferred the open air.

Blacks, armed with huge feather fans, in royal blue livery and silver braid, stood ready to do battle with the stifling heat of a warm evening.

In Chippewa Square, the carriages with the arriving guests were being parked as best they could. The doors were slammed insolently and the great wheels shone in the sunlight, in a splendid exhibition of disordered splendour. The carriages, arriving from every corner of the town and the coachmen in their gray top hats swore and quarrelled, but this was part of the general hubbub that accompanied high-class festivities.

Inside the house, garlands of leaves decked with flowers and fruits were festooned between the columns around the sumptuous entrance hall, and the gentle murmur of a serenade drifted from an adjoining room. Unfortunately the charm of this welcome was lost in the merry bustle of ladies appearing in dresses of elegance so refined that it could not help bordering on ostentation. Silks the color of champagne were mingled with variegated tafeta and satin in Parma or Indian pink. The older ladies took refuge in dark violets glimmering with gold or red sheens, but here and there pure black stood out with calm, proud authority. Fans, made of feathers or painted linen, flapped like the wings of captive birds, while like a heroine in the midst of an uprising, Mrs Harrison Edwards, in mauve satin, tried to put some semblance of order into this extravagant chaos. With despair she observed all these ladies sitting down anywhere, when the places of honor had been reserved for those of more venerable nobility; but nothing was more like a horde of unleashed schoolgirls than a crowd of society ladies who could hear nothing except the sound of their own chatter.

Finally, all the chairs were occupied and the latecomers courteously directed toward the terrace where the most comfortable of seats helped them to forget their wounded pride. Like a flock of crows, and with elaborate bows and compliments, the men in their black coats were seated at the very back.

Viewed now in its entirety, the whole assembly glittered with precious stones. Diamonds shimmered on flat or rounded bosoms and, through a process of slow strangulation, dog-like collars helped the septuagenarians to raise their heads and scoff at death. Rubies bled everywhere, sometimes on exquisite hands, or, as in Elizabeth's case, in a single scarlet drop deliberately half-hidden in the cleavage of a magnificent bosom. Elsewhere on so many necks, fingers, arms, ears or foreheads, in fact wherever that noble flesh could find space, sapphire reigned. The proud wealth of families had come to breathe the drawing-room air.

Outside, around the terrace, in the pink dusk, the birds were telling another story at the tops of their voices and flying from branch to branch as if disturbed by the conversations below.

This was the moment when Charlie Jones appeared. With the self-confidence of a popular tenor, he strode to the middle of the glistening parquet flooring that extended in front of the seated crowd. With the pink complexion of a well-nourished young man, he moved around in a cloud of eau de cologne which could be smelled from afar. His coat, tailored in London, gave him a sort of arched look at the waist.

'Ladies,' he said in a warm and resounding voice. 'And you over there, my good friends for so many years: the pearl of our city, Mrs Harrison Edwards, who is doing us the honor of gathering us here this evening, has asked me to say a few words to you. In the course of this evening, which promises to be interesting and full of surprises, we shall first meet a person whose friendship is dear to us, but who because of her particular situation is not accustomed to appearing among us . . . The welcome that you give her will be for me the proof of your esteem, which I hope I have always deserved.'

A polite murmur gave him to understand that he had never done anything to lose it and that whatever might happen, it was awaited with fortitude.

Charlie Jones bowed and retired to the back, on the terrace, next to Algernon.

The hall doors now opened wide and Miss Llewelyn came briskly in, stopping only a short distance from the first rows of ladies, who were already sheltered behind their open fans.

Dressed in an iron gray dress which left her black boots with their pointed toes visible underneath it, she had made just one concession to the exclusive nature of the gathering . . . Having taken her graying hair up into a bun on the top of her head, she had placed in it a large red and pink exotic flower which intrigued everyone present, much as they were expert in horticulture; and it was this flower that cut short any signs of possible protest. People wanted to know where it came from and the fans fluttered vigorously in general agitation; but there was also something aggressive and dominating in the appearance of this large, fat women which could also not but help create a certain unease. Her small clear blue eyes swept defiantly around the assembly, dressed as though for a ball, their jewels shimmering in the light from a huge chandelier. This light fell directly on her and the Welshwoman's forceful features were underlined with black, like the strokes of a charcoal pencil: the angry nose with its flaired nostrils and the square mouth seemed poised to launch a stream of invective.

No doubt she was unaware of the impression she could make without even saying a word, but she was imbued — and puffed up — with a sense of her own importance and she was savoring the joy of confronting society in the very heart of its place of assembly. Oddly, she felt herself to be the stronger, even though she was alone, but, too intelligent to give way to pride, she recalled that she was there to win by persuasion a cause that was almost impossible to defend.

In a sonorous voice that she did her best to soften, taking no notice of the men at the sides and back of the room, and considering them negligeable, she began:

'Ladies, you are astonished to see me among you. I, too, am astonished — at being accorded an honor which is perhaps not of your making; but let's leave that. During the past year or more, people in Savannah have started to speak again of Haiti, of Soulouque the First and of the troubles in the island, and this stirs old, dark memories. But do you know what Haiti is? Well, I shall tell you. Haiti is the azure, the emerald; it is passion, love and violence; it is blood.'

# 4

# LAURA
# OR PARADISE LOST

*"Pa'adis d'amou'*
*Pa'adis pe'du."*

# 67

*I*n the last minutes of this dusk which seems fixed in time, the sun drowns everything in reddish waves. As if seized by panic at the approach of night, birds of every size are flying and calling as they fly around the trees: blue jays, scarlet cardinals, parrots, humming birds, in a frantic whirl, are fleeing the darkness which will fall almost instantaneously.

Two men and a woman are standing in the field overlooking a huge plantation: William Hargrove is talking to Anatole de Siverac. A large American flag floats over a long single-storied house, the front of which has a veranda with a sloping roof.

Near the men, the woman, robust and full of self-assurance, listens and sometimes joins in the conversation: Maisie Llewelyn, Welsh. Even though she is young, she has been superintendant of the household since the death of Mrs Hargrove in 1816.

'I can't believe that a new misfortune is threatening the country . . . The days of Rigaud and Dessalines are so far away. This island was paradise, and it still is.'

Anatole de Siverac seems to be irritated by this naivety of Hargrove's. The master of the plantation, thirty-eight years old, is staring into the distance with a dreamy look. Tall, broad-shouldered, he is wearing a panama which reveals a face framed in black, neatly trimmed sideburns, with fine, regular features, though the black eyes are hard.

'Down there,' said Anatole de Siverac, 'can't you see that smoke rising, on the other side of the Artibonite? They're setting fire to the properties of the Spaniards again. They'll get themselves massacred as the French did in 1804.'

William Hargrove glanced at him from under the edge of his panama:

'Well, at least you no longer have any cause to fear, now that you've got an American passport.'

'No more than you do, since I hoisted over your house the one flag that the Blacks really respect.'

'Huh! In spite of everything, I think the worst is over. We saw the slave Christophe make himself Master of Haiti and rule the island like a despot.'

'He was emperor. A Black, emperor! It ended tragically as it did for the rest. He shot himself with a golden bullet. Now Santo Domingo and Haiti are one, we have a president and a republic.'

'Does Mr Boyer seem more reliable to you than Christophe?'

'A president of the republic is more reassuring than an emperor.'

'Don't believe it,' said Maisie Llewelyn. 'Blood attracts blood; and atrocities are always the same. But so is courage. There have been so many examples of it. In the time of Emperor Christophe, there was terror. The colored women were admirable. You know the story of the wounded White who took refuge with one of them. She hid him. A group of black soldiers were after him and wanted to break into her house by force to take him and finish him off. She hid herself in a dark corner behind the door and, when they came into the house, killed four of them with a machete. With the help of an old mulatto woman, she threw the bodies down off her veranda into the street. The crowd admired and applauded, but nothing more. And the massacres continued further on.'

'What a splendid woman!' said Anatole de Siverac.

'Wasn't she! Of course, the attackers fled as if they had the devil on their tails.'

There was silence. The dying day took on a heart-rending beauty. These three people suddenly found themselves watching as the whole plantation shone in a final burst of brilliance before being plunged into darkness. The green banana plants concealed their fruit in a tangle of long, light-colored fronds, illuminated in a huge red stain, the blazing conqueror of the dusk. Beyond them, the enormous tobacco leaves spread out, decorating the space that sloped gently down to the cotton fields which cast their snowflakes against a wood of burning red mancenillier trees. The golden fruit of the mango trees hung in the dying rays of the sun. This gaudy spectacle ran gently down to the banks of a tumbling stream, which suddenly calmed as it looped down to a cove, further on, where the mangroves intertwined their monstruous roots. Scattered here and there across this frenzied piece of land, palm trees, hungry for light, reached out for the last rays of the dying sun that was about to sink beneath the horizon. Suddenly all the birds fell silent.

'What a love song has ended,' William Hargrove murmured. 'What a triumph for the dusk!'

'You're a poet now,' said the Welshwoman sarcastically. 'In your place I should be seriously concerned about our means of defence in case of an uprising.'

'The star-spangled banner will protect us. And then we treat our Blacks far too well for them to rebel. They love us.'

'That remains to be seen,' said Maisie Llewelyn.

'William, you must take account of the revolutionary fever which is catching on little by little.'

'Not here. They don't touch American properties here. We have nothing to fear . . .'

There was one final vibration of the sun and all nature, the trees, the sky and those who were speaking, turned red. Suddenly a cloud of bats invaded the shadows around the three motionless people, passing between them, almost touching their faces, like searching black hands.

Servants carrying torches came to the assistance of their masters and led them back to the house.

The large room where they met for dinner gave a surprising impression of space and refinement. In point of fact, it was only furnished with a table and some chairs, Dutch style, with carved backs. The table, under a white cloth, weighed down by heavy silverware and crystal glasses, shone in the candlelight.

Contrary, no doubt, to all the customs of the Old World, Maisie Llewelyn sat between the two men, so occupying the place that had formerly been that of Mrs Hargrove.

Servants in white at once served a cold soup and the glasses were filled with an excellent dark red wine.

'Without wishing to appear pessimistic, ' Anatole de Siverac said, 'I must agree that this invitation from Don Diego de Serra y Atalaya, which enchanted us a week ago, seems less appealing to me today.'

'A farewell luncheon,' said William Hargrove. 'Their property is twenty kilometers from here, as the crow flies, behind the *morne* of San Raphael. They are not yet threatened, but they prefer to leave the country. It won't be a sad occasion, on the contrary. They are superb hosts.'

'Oh, the risk is not great, but counting the journey there and back and the time spent there, it means 34 hours away from here.'

'What are you afraid of?' asked Maisie Llewelyn. 'I shall be here, with Miss Laura and the boys — not to mention the servants.'

'Miss Llewelyn is quite right,' said William Hargrove. 'Douglas and Joshua are seventeen and eighteen, and they know perfectly well how to defend themselves. Even Frank is old enough to hold a gun. And then, what are you thinking of? With that great flag flapping in the wind . . . Your flag, my dear fellow!'

'Very well. When shall we leave?'

'The morning after tomorrow, at nine o'clock, perhaps.'

'That's not giving us much time. But there will surely be latecomers.'

'You can leave without feeling anxious,' said Maisie Llewelyn. 'It's not for nothing that I'm a Welshwoman.'

# 68

*T*he day after next, at the appointed hour, the carriage, drawn by four horses, was carrying William Hargrove and Anatole de Siverac along sandy roads, shaded here and there by palm trees. A haze of heat floated like a curtain in the far distance above the sea. Despite the creepers which often cluttered the roads, the journey seemed likely to be easy until the moment when a hillock, or *morne*, rose in front of them and they had to skirt round it, at the risk of tipping over. Then they drove up a rocky pass. The bunches of verdant palm trees in the hills always hid some solitary cabins. Great birds of prey circled in the empty sky. After that the landscape provided them with a more tranquil journey, but they were traveling through the heat of the day and wide parasols were opened. Soon they were passing beside woods so thick that they seemed impenetrable, and not an hour had passed before the travelers had the pleasant surprise of passing a few meters away from a waterfall, plunging directly down from a wooded height. It made them shiver pleasantly and reinvigorated them, so that they arrived free of tiredness at the giant pine wood that surrounded the residence of Don Diego de Serra y Atalaya, whose family could trace its aristocratic line back to the days of King Boabdil.

Surrounded by the coolness of these vast trees, Don Diego's home was not much different from the one they had left, though it was considerably more spacious and richer. Inside, on a table so large that you could not see where it ended, gold plates and cutlery shone with a mysterious sheen in a room which had deliberately been plunged into half-darkness since dawn.

Entering from the gardens, the scents of which permeated the house, the guests soon walked in to the sonorous buzzing of the Spanish language. Lackeys lit a few candles at the four corners of the room. William Hargrove and Anatole de Siverac, welcomed by Don Diego and his Duquesa, were shown to places of honor and the meal began in a merry din. The vowels tinkled loud and high in a torrential rolling of Rs and aitches. People discussed everything except politics and around the time dessert was served, the merriment reached its climax, when they saw, through the veranda which opened onto the plantation, a young Black gambolling around, very lightly dressed. In a very clear voice, he was spouting ditties, the words of which made the ladies blush a little, but soon laughter broke out from all sides, because the little rascal was quite witty and danced with the childish grace of his people.

'He's the local jester,' said Don Diego. 'He is amusing though unbearable in the long term.'

The guests cried out that they found him entertaining and were only sorry that he kept himself at a distance. Everyone stood up and left the table unceremoniously to gather on the veranda. Some bolder souls even ventured outside and soon, in an irresistible surge of curiosity, all the guests had gone to the front of the house to watch the clowning of the jester. He outdid himself in leaps and turns, showing considerable agility.

The gentlemen gave their arms to the ladies to lead them into the avenue and bring them close to the dancer, and beneath their parasols they indulged in unrestrained outbursts of crazy laughter which won over even the most solemn of the guests.

Meanwhile, the servants were clearing the table and it might have been as well to supervise them a little; but everyone was outside.

As the crowd moved toward him, the jester moved back. Then suddenly he vanished behind a tree, only to reappear at once at the other side, quite naked. There were some protests, but he began to sing, wiggling his hips:

'Oh, Madam, Madam, do dirty 'ting,
Mus' break a leaf and cover dat!
Ah, ha, break leaf, Madam,
An' not served, Madam,
Dat not served and cover dat!'

He was imitating their bows and suddenly, while the little group was rooted to the spot, he turned round to show his backside while shouting obscenities.

Don Diego, indignant, fired two pistol shots in the air to scare him and he took flight, jumping from side to side. A moment later, he reappeared ten meters further on. Though a little taken aback, the men went toward him, while the women stopped at a crossing in the avenue, intrigued and pretending to find it amusing. In a show of bravado, the joker turned round and launched a stream of new insults, making obscene gestures. The guests took up the sport and were beginning to follow, chasing after him, when suddenly great cries were heard. Behind all of them, in the middle of the plantation, Don Diego's noble house was blazing in a huge crackling which sounded like irregular bursts of gunfire. Gigantic tongues of flame were cutting through clouds of black smoke; the house was erupting.

There was an immediate panic in which all semblance of good manners, obligations of rank and etiquette were lost. Don Diego tried in vain to calm the shattered nerves of his noble guests. They would have trampled him underfoot to make their way more quickly to the carriages which, fortunately, were in the open; but here the terror was even greater. The horses, driven mad by the fire, were standing bolt upright like heraldic animals and the coachmen, hanging on the reins, could see themselves on the point of being carried away with the coaches in a nightmare cavalcade.

In these difficult circumstances, William Hargrove did not exhibit great heroism. His companion, Anatole de Siverac, had to shake him hard to force him to stand on his feet and not to let himself be hauled like a dying man to his carriage where the coachman was bravely struggling with four horses foaming with terror. The joint efforts of the coachman and de Siverac managed to overcome the madness of the animals which were dancing with horror, and William Hargrove, dumped rather roughly inside the carriage, was able to sit down on the floor. Three minutes later, the carriage was making its way more or less successfully toward a more tranquil spot. Seeing William Hargrove curled up in a corner, Anatole de Siverac simply snapped:

'Pull yourself together, dear fellow. You're out of danger.'

# 69

While this drama was unfolding, events of a quite different nature were taking place twenty kilometers away, in William Hargrove's house.

Hardly had the carriage departed than Maisie Llewelyn went into Miss Laura Hargrove's room, and found her writing a letter. The young lady was at this time aged a little over fifteen years old and, without being what is called a beauty, she was nonetheless quite delightful, with dark brown eyes rather too large for so small a face and a mass of auburn hair which spilled down on all sides, covering her rounded shoulders and what promised to be an ample bosom. In her dress of white muslin, she won every heart by the tenderness of her look and the natural elegance with which she endowed every movement of her arms and her whole body.

'Well?' she asked, as soon as she saw the Welshwoman.

'Rejoice, my girl, They have left for a whole day. You can send your nanny to fetch the handsome officer whom you may receive in a corner of the drawing-room. That will be more proper than for you to be seen with him in the park.'

Laura clapped her hands.

'Thank you, Miss Maisie, you arrange everything so wonderfully well. Alone in the drawing-room with him, of course?'

'Come, come. Everyone is agreed. We love your Régis, but don't do anything unwise: no giving way to impulses before marriage . . .'

Laura raised her eyebrows to indicate indignation.

'I was writing him a letter when you came in. Would you ask Betty to give it to him? I'll add a note to tell him to come at once.'

'If he is free . . .'

'He will make himself free. A lieutenant . . .'

She hurried back to her letter and scribbled two words on it, then gave it in its envelope to the Welshwomen.

'Quick, Miss Maisie, quick!' she begged. 'Every minute counts while Papa is away. Oh, I'm longing . . .!'

She almost pushed the large woman outside to make her move faster; then, left on her own, she didn't know what to do with herself, with her much smaller and less imposing body. In her room, where everything was white, the mosquito nets around the bed and the curtains on the windows, and even the walls, which were the color of snow faintly tinged with blue, she ran around senselessly, like a bird which has strayed into a room and cannot escape. A huge, leaning mirror watched her flapping around like that, distraught with joy and anxiety. Hanging inside an oval frame at a place where she could see it from her bed, a large picture of the Assumption of the Virgin Mary smiled at her gravely. This Spanish painting, in delicate colors, had been put there by Maisie Llewelyn after the death of Mrs Hargrove. The young woman had looked at it so often that she no longer noticed it. She merely knew it was there.

Now she was running from the window to the door, as if her lover would come at any moment. Sometimes she threw herself, for ten seconds, into a wide rocking chair which, like all the furniture in the room, was made of precious wood, black and shining, from the isles. Laura rocked, tossing her tiny feet with their red shoes in the air, then jumped down, then ran to a window and leaned out at the sound of a horseman riding up the avenue toward the house — it was always stewards from the estate or mulattoes who worked for their neighbor. Then, at last, it was him. She dashed to the stairs, leapt down almost without touching them, and there she was, standing in the drawing-room before the beloved in his dark blue jacket and white trousers.

Of medium height, he stood head and shoulders above her and seemed tall beside her. As soon as she was in his arms, she had to throw back her head to look at his face; for her, it was the most handsome one in the world — and perhaps she was not far out in that estimation, because one could not imagine finer features, which looked as if they had been lovingly drawn by an inspired artist. Only the impetuous look in the dark green eyes added a virile note to his extreme delicacy. What was most striking was the flat whiteness of the skin. Black, windswept hair was tangled with slender sideburns around his small ears.

Extricating himself, he took her hand, led her to a chair and sat down in front of her.

In the long room with its high windows and white walls, the sunlight shone through the orange shutters, and the dark wooden furniture lost its austerity as if to make this large, solemn drawing-room more welcoming.

'Well, what's happening, Laura?' he asked calmly.

'I love you,' she said.

'So do I, but you suddenly call for me to come here, as if something had happened.'

'Nothing. I just had to see you.'

'Laura, stop looking at me with those sweeping eyes as if I were a landscape, and speak to me seriously.'

'I am looking at you because each time I do, I find you more handsome.'

He gave a nervous laugh as if this kind of compliment, to which he was accustomed, irritated him.

'If only people would say something else to me: you look so intelligent, or: you seem so brave. And then, my little Laura, listen, I must explain to you, you know that I love you.'

She gave a cry:

'Kiss me, if you love me.'

Leaving his chair, he went across to a window.

'You make it difficult for me by getting me to come here when I begged you to be patient. We have taken the decision to get married. For the time being it isn't easy.'

'Why?' she asked, close to tears.

'You know very well, Your father is opposed to it because I am a Catholic and he hates Catholics, as almost all Englishmen do.'

'But I was converted six months ago by Maisie Llewelyn.'

'He doesn't know that. We can only get married in secret. On my side, it was hard to get permission. You are still so young . . . To avoid a scandal, we must wait until your father is away.'

'Then today, this very day!'

'Don't think of it. He may come back at any moment.'

'Oh, I'm dying for love and love doesn't seem to want me.'

This time he adopted a severe look that perturbed her.

'Laura, when will you behave like a grown-up? You oblige me to tell you that at this very moment I am struggling with an insane desire to clasp you to me. I have the hot blood of men of my country. If we were to do something foolish, all would be lost. The Church here is so inflexible. I am not saying that it is right, but I am forced to obey.'

She in turn got up and looked directly at him.

'You don't love me,' she said.

Without moving, he said in an imperious tone of voice:

'Come here.'

Amazed, she came forward a few steps, as though in a dream. The man did not seem to be the same as a moment before. A light was shining in his green eyes that at once made her afraid and him more attractive. When she was close to him, she felt the heat coming off his body.

'Laura,' he said, in an altered voice, 'tell me again that I do not love you.'

She said nothing. A strange desire suddenly overwhelmed her and she did not dare say anything, but her face went purple.

'You tried to trap me. Don't you know that it is dangerous to play that kind of game with a man like me?'

She was overcome with a sharp feeling of anxiety confronted with those eyes in which she thought she could read anger, and she turned away, but he grasped her by the waist and bent her backwards. It was then that for the first time she experienced the terror of the hunger that she had aroused and she wanted to cry out, but he closed her mouth with his own. Everything in her swooned before this voracity.

For a minute, he held her against him, a prisoner of the first kiss that she had ever had from a man, and she was stricken with terror. When he released her, she moved away from him and wiped her mouth with her hand.

In a softer voice, though his eyes were still enflamed with that incomprehensible fury, he asked her:

'Isn't that what you wanted, Laura?'

She could not answer. Her whole being rebelled against the man and she looked at him with horror, even though he had never before seemed so handsome to her. She could not understand how such a perfect face could be capable of such crudeness.

Suddenly, he intuitively felt what she was feeling and his look immediately changed. Now she had before her a being of indescribable sweetness who was smiling at her with a sadness full of love.

'I shocked you, my little Laura. I gave way to an impulse that was too strong for me. That is just what I feared when I realized that I was alone with you in this room, but love does not recognize any obstacle.'

'Love . . . ,' she said.

'Yes, love, that's it, that dreadful urge, that first savage, devouring kiss . . . which also devoured me . . .'

Instinctively, she shrank away from him.

'I didn't know,' she said.

He came closer and, with the shyness of a child, she stroked his eyes and murmured:

'Stay as you are now, handsome and calm. Don't ever frighten me again.'

With the tips of her fingers, she touched his forehead, his nose, and finally the lips of that mouth which had bruised her, and she was lingering endlessly there when he gripped her wrist:

'No,' he said.

She looked at him, wide-eyed with astonishment.

'Why not?' she asked.

His face softened by a great wave of tenderness, he whispered:

'I can't tell you why, but don't do that.'

She looked at him, dazzled, as though she had seen an angel and said nothing. He continued in the same voice:

'You are like a little girl, even more so than I thought. But we shall be married and you will see how happy we shall be.'

'Always be as you are now,' she murmured again.

He did not answer and the silence that followed told them everything that they had to say to one another that day.

A slight noise made them turn toward the door which opened slowly and cautiously. Maisie Llewelyn appeared.

'Am I disturbing you?' she asked.

'Not at all,' Régis said, good-naturedly. 'As you can see, in fact.'

They were standing face to face, both intimidated, but for different reasons. Miss Llewelyn did not understand. Yet she had listened conscientiously before coming in, as she felt she must, and she was expecting a pleasant love scene, instead of which . . .

'Well, I hope you are happy at least.'

This remark, though irreproachably commonplace, seemed inexplicably inept to her, and she wished that she had not made it. For the first time in her life she was disturbed and disappointed. The handsome young officer seemed to her the most eligible match for Laura. In the Army, as off duty, his conduct and strength of character were almost proverbial. One might even have understood if he had proved to be a little bit unruly, as his youth and his striking beauty would have allowed him to be, but there too it appeared, there was nothing to report — or, alas, to repeat. He remained as charming as he was enigmatic. What made him interesting despite this was his personal fortune, inherited from a dead relative who had been concerned for the happiness of a young man whom he considered to have a good future and who was dear to him. Now, money, in Maisie Llewelyn's view, was important. It had a strange effect on her, rather like magic. Wherever she sensed its presence, she made sure she was also present.

How could one know if he still intended to marry Laura? One must not ask any direct questions. She felt that some elegance of expression was needed.

'I wager,' she said, in a playful manner, 'that you have been saying important things to each other.'

'Very,' said Régis.

'Very, very,' said Laura.

'If there are any problems,' the Welshwoman said, 'I am here.'

'Miss Laura is not yet sixteen. What can be done about it? She is a minor.'

These words, spoken in a sad voice, had the effect of exciting Miss Llewelyn's combative instincts. Her little green eyes sparkled with daring.

'Her guardian will relent if I want him to. But have you made up your minds?'

'We have never wavered. I would marry Laura tomorrow if it were possible, but I don't believe in miracles.'

'Forget about miracles. You will see what a Welshwoman can do when she puts her mind to it. But, Lieutenant, remember this: you must come immediately I call.'

He bowed.

'You have my word, Miss Llewelyn.'

'Maisie!' the girl cried.

She could say no more, choked with emotion.

'I know,' said Miss Llewelyn, with a superior air. 'I experienced all this in the flower of my youth; but enough of that. Lieutenant, night is falling and you have a fair way to go.'

Once more he bowed and, after a last loving look at Laura, he left.

# 70

*A* little before three in the morning, a sound of wheels and horses' hooves woke Maisie Llewelyn, who slept badly. She looked out of the window and could see nothing. In the April night, the moon spread a milky light across the plantation, giving the familiar landscape the unreal appearance of a dream, despite the extraordinary precision of the details. Every leaf was outlined as though with black ink and shone like glass.

The Welshwoman did not admire the landscape for long. Slipping on a dressing gown (pink, verging on red), she descended to the ground floor and went out. Behind the house, she saw the coach and a Black who had been hurriedly woken to look after the team.

De Siverac came toward her, bare-headed with his coat unbuttoned.

'Help me carry your master into the house. We can go through the little door in the veranda.'

Saying which, he opened the door to the carriage and grasped William Hargrove by the shoulders, where he was lying on the bench, and dragged him outside. The Welshwoman took his legs.

'Fainted?' she asked.

'I don't think so, just exhausted with tiredness and fear. San Miguel has gone up in flames.'

Without asking any questions, she helped de Siverac carry the motionless traveler to the house, then into his room by the moonlight which flooded the room through the muslin mosquito nets.

When they had put him into his bed, Mr de Siverac said in a low voice:

'I hope no one saw us. I'm ashamed of him in his present state. No courage.'

'He never has had any,' the Welshwoman said contemptuously.

'In any case, he's home now and asleep. He was sick on the road and in the carriage.'

'He smells very bad. In a moment, I'll give him a wash, but is it true . . .? The Blacks set fire to it?'

'Always the same thing. They lure everyone outside the house and accomplices throw torches into the drawing-room. We took hours: the pass at San Raphael was full of coaches. Fire always attracts onlookers. I leave you now. Keep an eye on him. Say that he's resting and that he's well. Say what you wish. I am dying with exhaustion and must go home to bed.'

Left alone with William Hargrove, Maisie Llewelyn decided to let him sleep until morning. Meanwhile she undressed him, taking off his coat and trousers without him realizing it and leaving him only his shirt and underclothes; then, with a look of disgust, she covered him with a sheet and a light woolen blanket. Feeling some pity in spite of herself, she wiped his mouth and his sideburns, stained with vomit, with a sponge.

However, she did not leave his room without going through the pockets of his jacket and trousers which were lying on the chairs, but found only the bunch of keys and the pocket book which contained nothing that she did not already know about. This is what she called keeping an eye on her master. After that, she retired to rest a little until morning.

While they were serving breakfast, she appeared once more, this time fully dressed, in William Hargrove's room. He was still sleeping. She shook him by the shoulder. Painfully he opened his eyes and said:

'What?'

'On your feet!' she said.

He repeated:

'What?'

In her dark lilac dress, she stood next to him and dominated him like a statue of fate, while he thrashed around in his blanket.

'If you say what once again,' she said, threateningly, 'I'll lose my temper. Downstairs they can't understand why you have not yet got up.'

'The fire at the Spaniards' . . . ,' he stammered.

'We know about that, but Siverac is there like everyone else.'

He dragged himself out of bed and got up, leaning against one of the slender columns. His face had lost all dignity. With his dishevelled hair and his half-open eyes, he suggested a tramp who has felt a policeman's hand on his collar.

'I don't want to go,' he groaned.

Irritated she said:

'We'll see about that later. For the time being, get properly washed up in the bathroom. I'll be back in a quarter of an hour.'

'Maisie,' he begged.

She did not answer but left, slamming the door behind her.

In the dining-room, she found Douglas and Joshua, William Hargrove's two sons, at the table: big boys of seventeen and eighteen, drinking tea with their sister Laura; also Frank, the youngest, with a face as pink as a flower; and Anatole de Siverac.

She sat down next to him. Unlike William Hargrove, he seemed fresh and well-rested, and his dress indicated concern for his appearance.

'Pleased to see you, Miss Llewelyn. I have something to say that will interest you. Yesterday, after leaving San Miguel in the circumstances you know about, I almost stopped the carriage before reaching the hill that we have to drive round. As usual the spyglass was in the carriage. In times like these, it is essential to have an eye on the horizon. It was still quite clear and in the distance, in a corner of savannah where there was just a clump of trees, I could see a group of *papa-lois*. Dressed in ragged shirts which hung on their bodies like ribbons, and decked out in cock feathers, they seemed to be in a trance. There were other bunches of feathers in their hair. They were dancing in a frenzied manner and waving cows' tails in the air — with the idea of warding off I know not what danger.'

'All that could be clearer,' said Miss Llewelyn calmly. 'They were performing the dance that announces a threat to the country.'

'Well, now,' said Mr. de Siverac. 'I see that you are well-informed. It is fortunate that William Hargrove is not here to hear us. The story would terrify him.'

'Not at all,' Joshua said. 'Papa is very brave.'

'I can tell you that his mind is already made up,' said Maisie Llewelyn. 'He wants to leave.'

'To leave Haiti?' Laura exclaimed.

'He'll tell you so himself. I must go back to see him in a moment . . . He will explain his views to you,' she added sarcastically.

'On due consideration,' said de Siverac, 'I can't say he's entirely wrong.'

'Sir,' Joshua asked, 'what about the American flag flying over the house?'

'America is all-powerful and relatively near,' said de Siverac. 'But, when the spirit of revolution overtakes a country, violence exceeds all limits and flags serve only . . .'

At these words Laura gave a cry and hid her face in her hands.

'Don't be afraid, Laura,' said Douglas, putting an arm around her. 'We shall be here to defend you.'

Without even finishing her cup of tea, Maisie Llewelyn went out.

Back in William Hargrove's room, she found him putting on his trousers.

'We're very slow this morning,' she said drily.

He gave her a foul look, but said nothing.

'Clean at least, I hope,' she continued.

'Can't you smell the eau de cologne?'

'Eau de cologne doesn't prove that one has washed properly. At best it covers smells.'

'Maisie, there are times when I hate you.'

'And there are others when you need her, your Maisie. Come on, comb you hair, put on your coat and come downstairs. Try to behave like a man.'

Five minutes later, they were downstairs.

'Well, good morning, William,' said Anatole de Siverac. 'It seems you are thinking of leaving.'

'I've already decided,' Hargrove said, siting down. 'I've had enough of a country where plantations are set alight everywhere.'

'Not here, sir,' said Joshua. 'The American flag . . .'

'The star-spangled banner, Papa,' said Douglas in an earnest tone.

A mass of accumulated rage filled William Hargrove's chest and he said, in a determined voice:

'Boys, pack your bags. We're leaving tomorrow for Port-Haïtien and then for America.'

'That's definite,' Maisie Llewelyn remarked.

The two boys got up.

'Sir,' Douglas said, 'I don't understand.'

'I'm taking you to Louisiana and thence to Virginia, to the University. You are old enough.'

The two boys looked at other.

'The University of Virginia!' they cried, in a single voice, with radiant faces.

'A young university, but already famous throughout America. A university for gentlemen,' said Anatole de Siverac.

'At least, that's what they say,' said Maisie Llewelyn.

'And how long do you expect to be away?' Siverac asked.

'That depends.'

'Uncertainty and haste,' said Maisie Llewelyn. 'That's what your plans add up to.'

'Miss Llewelyn, kindly be silent,' said William Hargrove.

She bowed.

'I beg your pardon, Mr Hargrove,' she said insincerely.

Hargrove turned toward Siverac.

'Allow two full months, or two and a half,' he said. 'Miss Llewelyn, look after my bags. I want everything ready by this evening. Boys, get ready and forget nothing. We are leaving the plantation tomorrow morning at dawn, to avoid the heat.'

The clarity with which he pronounced these orders gave him an authority which surprised everyone, except Maisie Llewelyn.

'You will have a very short night then,' she said. 'And I predict you will not sleep. You will have your work cut out.'

'Miss Llewelyn, I am not taking any directions from you,' he said, withering her with a look that was greeted, on her part, with a knowing smile.

'Mr Hargrove, I am merely doing my duty.'

This fencing match greatly amused Siverac, who had grasped the situation a long time ago.

'Slaves sometimes have rebellious instincts,' he said. 'Even here we must keep watch on them.'

'Oh, since you're not leaving,' said Joshua innocently, 'we can count on you to defend the plantation.'

'And our dear Laura,' said Douglas, leaning toward his sister with a wave of affection.

'Don't worry, boys,' said Siverac. 'If you catch them early enough, they can be calmed and smothered, these little bursts of insubordination.'

In a flash, William Hargrove felt certain that this sly remark referred to himself and, white with rage, he swept quickly out of the dining-room.

'What about me?' young Frank said suddenly.

At fourteen years of age, his thoughtful young face under its mass of black hair showed no emotion, but his large dark eyes looked from one to the other with calm curiosity.

'You will stay with me,' Laura said very softly. 'We'll be together, brother and sister. Don't go away.'

As she said this, she looked at him, full of distress. He smiled and clasped her hand under the table.

# 71

*U*ntil afternoon, life went on more or less as usual, but that evening the whole house was turned upside down. Blacks came and went amid the chaos of a major departure, carrying suitcases, packets and sometimes suits on clothes hangers which they carried on one finger. Meals were served on trays and doors opened ceaselessly through which voices called urgently.

Maisie Llewelyn shut herself in William Hargrove's room: he was still overwhelmed by the events of the morning. She gave him some good advice:

'Pull yourself together, my friend. You seem quite distraught. Don't worry. You are being looked after — you, your journey, your comfort. The servants have their orders.'

He slumped into a chair.

'I anticipated this journey,' said Maisie Llewelyn. 'I felt a desire to leave coming over you . . .'

'I shall return, I shall return . . . It's for the boys; they will be better off over there than here.'

'Of course, of course. But time is passing and we have a lot to do.'

He muttered something in a grumbling voice which she did not catch, and was then suddenly seized with rage:

'I don't like the way Siverac talks to me,' he said, clenching his fists.

'Oh, don't start that again. Forget it, forget all that. In twenty-four hours you will be far away from one another.'

'The insolence of the fellow! He reckons he's some great nobleman . . .'

'Because his grandfather had some title which he dropped during the Revolution. What does it matter? He teased you a little this morning, but beneath it all he is very fond of you.'

'I'm delighted to hear it.'

He took a few steps with his hands clasped behind his back. The ceiling was high and the room so vast that large pieces of furniture seemed lost between its light green walls: the majestic four-poster bed hung with white curtains, the black rocking chair upholstered with plaited straw, and in the middle of the room, a huge work table surrounded by chairs with ridiculously high backs, carved in the Dutch style fashionable in England a hundred years earlier. All the casements were wrapped in white muslin mosquito nets. Only a floor of pink tiles added a note of bright, happy color to this deliberately austere decor. Nothing in it, even remotely, suggested a love nest.

'Are you hungry?' she asked. 'Do you want me to have a tray brought up?'

'Oh, no, Maisie. I have no appetite.'

'Nor do I, as it happens. And then we have work to do tonight, perhaps all night through.'

'Work!' he exclaimed horrified.

'One cannot just leave like that, on an impulse, without first putting one's affairs in order.'

'My affairs? I don't understand.'

'You will in a moment.'

He edged away from her as though she had become dangerous and sheltered by a window behind the muslin curtains.

As if in a sudden vision, he saw the plantation in the moonlight and never had it seemed to him so strikingly beautiful or so commanding in its allure. Far away, between two hills in their cloaks of greenery, you could see the sea, silver white, while on the far horizon some tiny red dots glimmered feebly: Port-Haïtien.

William Hargrove felt a lump in his throat. He realized that he was attached to this island, now so full of danger, but still so bewitching.

'Curses!' he exclaimed.

'What's the matter?' the Welshwoman asked.

Disentangling himself from the net curtains, he came toward her.

'I can't help it, but I'm sad to be leaving.'

'Huh! You'll be back.'

Tilting his head, he murmured:

'I'll be separated from you for weeks. This is the last night, Maisie.'

He tried to kiss her, but she pushed him away firmly.

'No, my friend,' she said, with a pitiless smile. 'Later, perhaps.'

'Later? When later? Why not now?'

'Out of the question.'

'Oh, you wicked Maisie!'

'Duty first, sweet nothings later. Follow me, you lazy man.'

She took his arm in a firm grasp and led him over to the big table, where she sat him down beside her.

Was she trying to make him more malleable by spurning his desires? She was wearing a lilac robe which was, very discreetly, open on her breast.

However that may be, they set to work. From a deep drawer in the table, she took out first one, then two, then a third folder, all three full of documents printed on a paper size known as legal format. One by one, so as not to discourage the poor wretch, they were given to him for signature.

A little oil lamp with a dark green shade cast a studious light on the columns of figures that had to be checked. Outside, cicadas scratched in the branches of the trees. Paying no attention to this irritating noise, Maisie Llewelyn's reasonable voice soothed the ear of the plantation owner.

'Here you have the account of Oreste Lepou, to whom you sold sixty bales of cotton and who only paid you for thirty-five . . . You are expecting the rest: there is a statement to that effect.'

She dipped the pen in ink and held it out. He signed with a clammy hand.

Then a sale of land. Signature.

More seriously, there was the protest of a neighbor who refused to knock down a wall which was impeding the cultivation of a tobacco field, at the far end of the plantation: thus, a summons to Népomucène Tuvache to submit to the requirements of the law. Signature.

In her patient hand, she gathered the great sighing leaves and put each one down methodically beside her on the table. There were dozens of them.

William Hargrove only glanced briefly at each of them because, since the death of his wife, who had been more attentive to the management of the family wealth than he was, he had relied on Miss Llewelyn whose financial expertise was well-attested. But she had never seemed quite so mindful of his possessions as she did tonight, and the disturbing thought entered his head that she might think him in danger of disappearing for good. Despite that, he admired her rectitude and obsession with detail where the interests of the plantation were concerned.

Pretending to be absorbed in this game of checking everything, he leaned forward and ran his eyes across the columns of figures, followed by paragraphs in copperplate handwriting; then, once the examination was completed, Miss Llewelyn would ask, 'finished?', and the sheet vanished.

An increasing weariness hung over William Hargrove's eyelids and he found himself saying 'finished' almost at the same time as the Welshwoman — who, for her part, continued to sit bolt upright, though she may have accelerated slightly as her wrist turned over each successive document.

Once the first folder was empty, the second was attacked with renewed zest as if the superintendent of the plantation had found her second wind.

At one moment, William Hargrove gave a little groan and said:

'I find something funereal about this procedure. I have the feeling I'm burying myself under these papers.'

'You're imagining things,' she said, smiling. 'But stay awake, because from now on I shall need more signatures. We are coming to more serious matters.'

'Are we?' he said faintly.

'This, for example, comes from the United States.'

'What did I do?'

'Nothing. Do you, as a British subject, accept the American law on property?'

'Yes, yes, of course.'

'Sign.'

He signed. The sheet was put to one side.

'In the event of a dispute, you have recourse to the United States consul.'

'Yes.'

'Sign.'

Other documents of the same kind were offered for his weary hand to sign. Miss Llewelyn, taking pity on him, read faster and faster, but always in a very clear voice: she articulated perfectly. The documents become more and more enmeshed in a mass of legal jargon; but Miss Llewelyn's set formula never varied:

'Agreed? Sign.'

'Agreed, sign,' he repeated mechanically, scribbling his name at the foot of every page.

'That's good,' she said, closing the second folder. 'You're working like an angel. Now let's start on the third and last folder. This time I want more legible signatures. Make an effort, please.'

He promised and she resumed her reading, with a clarity that would have been the envy of a great actress; and in this way, being so precise, she allowed herself to hurry on.

'Do you follow?' she asked, suddenly becoming scrupulous.

'Very, very well.'

In fact, he had not followed her for some time: the documents that she put before him were muddled in a sort of grayish cloud, yet he signed.

'Le-gi-bly!' commanded the authoritarian voice.

Drops of sweat ran down William Hargrove's brow and, grasping his pen with a fury, he managed to produce a perfect signature. Outside, the cicadas had fallen silent and from all around could be heard the dull croaking of the bullfrogs.

Over and over again he did his best to sign, but the Welshwoman no longer bothered to hasten the process. It was not necessary now. The last pages were unimportant. She left them in the folder, unsigned. William Hargrove, slumped on the table, was fast asleep.

# 72

*T*he last stars were fading in the heavens. It was the darkest hour when the night, reluctant to die, still hesitates to make way for the dawn. The Welshwoman reopened the last folder full of signed documents and took out one which she re-read carefully by the light of the little lamp. A broad smile helped restore to her face some of its youthfulness, lost through fatigue.

Unhurriedly, she walked across the room and double locked the precious paper in a drawer of her dressing table.

A pale light was creeping under the curtains and spreading like a pool on the pink-tiled floor. The woman put her hand on the sleeper's shoulder, He shuddered and turned a haggard face toward her.

'Now, quickly: go and shave, my dear,' she said. 'I can already hear noises in the house. Your sons are up. You have barely time to get ready before you must leave.'

'Maisie!' he exclaimed.

His hands tried to grasp her, but she easily slipped away.

'Later, when you come back,' she said, roaring with laughter. 'Console yourself with that, Willy, and leave with a clear conscience. You have done your duty.'

# 73

*W*hen the sun rose, the travelers were already far from the plantation. Now, free to do as she wished, Maisie Llewelyn set to work with a will.

A note was sent by her to Lieutenant Régis, begging him to come as soon as possible, and the following morning he was there. She immediately shut herself up with him and Siverac in a small drawing-room and addressed them as follows:

'After patient effort and long discussion with William Hargrove, who is now on his way to Louisiana with Douglas and Joshua, I obtained his signature to the following document:

"I, the undersigned, William Hargrove, proprietor of the plantation known as the New World, in the Republic of Haiti, being obliged to absent myself for an indefinite, but perhaps lengthy period, delegate to Anatole de Siverac, my friend and neighbor, and to Miss Maisie Llewelyn, superintendent of my possessions, the power and rights of guardianship over the person and goods of my daughter Laura, born in 1809 from a marriage to the late Lady Escridge. It will be their duty to celebrate her marriage in the Catholic Church, with Lieutenant Régis de Lavaur, on a date to be mutually agreed.

"Signed this 8th of April, 1824, on the plantation known as the New World, in Haiti.

"William Hargrove."

'Nothing remains for us but to sign this document in our turn, then for Mr Siverac and me to inform the priest at Saint-Michel, the parish church of Dondon.'

At this, she held out the document to Lieutenant Régis, who took it in a hand lightly trembling with emotion. His gaze fell on Siverac, struck dumb with admiration for this manner of proceeding.

The young officer's face radiated with a happiness that made him more attractive than ever, so that even the Welshwoman was affected by it. He came toward her:

'How can I tell you . . .?' he began.

She cut short these thanks, which threatened to be fulsome:

'Let's be brief,' she said. 'We must act quickly. A regular marriage cannot be improvised, even if it is to be a quiet one. The banns are not essential, but there are preparations to be made. This must not appear to be done hastily. In any event, I know Hargrove. He could easily come back, leaving his sons to manage by themselves with plenty of money in their pockets. And he will try to prevent it.'

'He will cause a scandal,' said Siverac.

She gave him a look that made him blink.

'Scandal!' she exclaimed, indignantly. 'I'd like to see it. I can put him in his place whenever I want, with a single word. Believe me,' she said, in a gentler tone, to Lieutenant Régis, 'I want all this to be done decently and simply, without a hint of mystery. Mr Hargrove will know about it when I decide that he should. Is that clear?'

The Lieutenant nodded.

'Do you know the priest?'

'A little. I go to mass every Sunday.'

Lowering his voice, as if out of modesty, he added:

'Can I forget that it was at Sunday mass that I saw Miss Laura for the first time . . .? She is there every Sunday with her nanny, dear, kind Betty.'

For an instant, Maisie Llewelyn seemed to be caught unaware, but she rapidly recovered:

'Oh . . . Ah . . . At mass, every Sunday. That's very good. I only go on feast days.'

'So do I,' said Siverac.

'The priest knows us,' Maisie Llewelyn added. 'Particularly since we do things properly when the collection comes round. Such details are important in relations with . . .'

She did not dare finish the sentence. Siverac came to her aid:

'The ecclesiastical authorities . . . You are right, by heaven. Either one is a Catholic or one is not. My family, for twenty generations . . .'

'Monsieur Siverac, we are straying from the point,' said the Welshwoman. 'Time is short. Lieutenant Régis, we shall devote ourselves to your happiness. As soon as necessary, you shall be informed. I dare say that we shall see you soon.'

The Lieutenant bowed again, and left the room.

Without delay, Miss Llewelyn set off with Siverac for the little Catholic church in a village close to the plantation. The priest, Father Chautard, received them in a fairly modest white house kept in exemplary fashion by an old servant. Its walls were covered with violet red clematis.

Old Abbé Chautard, a native of Périgord, was at once saintly and sly in appearance. He studied the document through his spectacles.

'A marriage with delegation of the powers of guardianship,' he said, at length. 'This is quite unusual, but since Mr 'Argrove's signature is on the document . . .'

The sentence was left in suspense and the two visitors waited patiently in silence. The priest carried on:

'I do not have the good fortune to count Mr 'Argrove among my parishioners, but the document is valid despite that.'

'As you say!' said Maisie Llewelyn.

The old priest continued in his old-fashioned French:

'On the other hand, I do have the advantage of knowing Miss Laura 'Argrove and Lieutenant Régis, both of whom attend church regularly.'

Maisie Llewelyn and Siverac turned absent-mindedly toward the trees that could be seen beyond the window.

'The wedding cannot be celebrated for a further three weeks, even without publishing the banns — since the author of this document does not require them.'

'Pooh! The lovers will be patient,' Siverac said in a playful tone. 'These venerable formalities need observing.'

'I beg your pardon, Monsieur, we are talking of a sacrament.'

The correction was given in a sharp voice that made the Welshwoman shudder.

'The Father is right,' she said, turning a fierce look on the bewildered man.

The visit ended with the gift of a considerable sum for the poor. The priest thanked them with great dignity.

'The poor will receive you in paradise,' he said, showing them to the door.

# 74

*L*aura and Lieutenant Régis were told the news, and the three weeks crept past with deadly slowness. They saw one another as often as possible, special leaves being granted to the model young officer. The bridge that had been carried away by the rain had been rebuilt over the Grande Rivière, so he was given another job which brought him still closer to the plantation: the road to Marmelade had been blocked by flooding in several places.

In his talks with his beloved, Régis was determined to reassure her that never again would he act with the savagery that had so shocked her. She believed him, all she wanted was to consider him as an angel. Had anyone unkindly pointed out to her that angels are sexless, she would have tried to believe it. The little she knew about male anatomy inspired terror mixed with disgust. She could not imagine that there was any connection between the face shining with purity and the indescribable horror barely concealed lower down. To calm herself and not to tarnish her image of Régis, she convinced herself that in any event he would spare her the crude brutality which some of her classmates had once mentioned to her, their faces shining with delight.

'Stay just as you are,' she sometimes told her bewildered fiancé.

For her part, Maisie Llewelyn endured agonies of anxiety, rushing to the windows when she heard the sound of a carriage coming up to the house. The idea that William Hargrove might come back unexpectedly kept her from sleep part of the night. If he should reappear before the wedding, she was determined to reduce him to silence by sheer terror. Lily-livered as he was in his heart, he was terrified that she might reveal what the world must never know about their secret relationship since the death of his wife, Lady Escridge. The Welshwoman did, however, hope that she would not have to use this dishonorable means of coercion.

Her fears were unfounded. One morning, the bell above the little church tinkled gently and the marriage was celebrated almost without the parishioners realizing it. The building, mean in appearance, with whitewashed walls, was decorated inside with statues painted in bright colors. One could see the madonna crowned with stars and the Archangel Michael in a breastplate thrusting his lance into the void (since the Devil did not have access to this holy place, even in defeat). It all gave an indefinable impression of modest grandeur which was moving in itself. Régis wore his dress uniform, but had left his sword in the barracks. Simply dressed in white chiffon — where could she have found a satin dress? — Laura had covered her head with a veil; but what aroused astonishment was the emerald necklace on her breast, in regal splendor. Supported by a gold chain around her neck, it glittered in the sunlight and must have caused some embarrassment to the young bride, because she tried to hide it under a light, white silk scarf, folded across her breast.

The couple came forward, hand in hand, toward the altar; and old Abbé Chautard himself could not disguise his amazement when he saw the almost supernatural beauty of this couple, radiant with joy and youth. He knew them well, but that morning they seemed to have come from another world.

Behind these two creatures, clothed in this strange charm, Maisie Llewelyn in her mauve outfit and Siverac in his dress suit, without knowing it, cut a rather poor figure, while little Betty, radiant with happiness, followed timidly behind and made herself smaller still, shrinking into a corner on a stool.

The ceremony did not take long. Abbé Chautard made a short speech to the couple that was full of feeling, for he was very fond of them. It was impossible for him not to have noticed the emeralds, but he did not comment on them. The same was not true of Siverac and the Welshwoman. Hardly had Abbé Chautard disappeared into the sacristy than they wanted to know . . .

The Lieutenant, overwhelmed by the occasion, was left speechless at hearing this question, while they were all still in church.

'It's my wedding present to my wife,' he said quickly. 'Come, Laura.'

Alone at the back of the nave, with Betty who didn't say a word, Siverac and Maisie Llewelyn looked at one another.

'I'll get the dear girl to talk,' she muttered, dipping her fingers in the bowl of holy water.

And she made the sign of the cross.

# 75

During the few days' leave granted to Lieutenant Régis, the newly-weds occupied William Hargrove's room. Laura knew nothing about the latter's relations with the Welshwoman but, standing in front of the huge four-poster, she said to her husband:

'This is the bed where I was born. Mama loved it very much; she had it brought from Virginia.'

He enveloped her in his arms and hugged her until she was gasping for breath.

'Oh! You're hurting me!' she cried, laughing. 'It's those lovely emeralds . . .'

He let her go, laughing with happiness himself.

'How odd they are, those two in church!' he said.

'I know! Especially Miss Llewelyn . . .'

'Listen, if they bother you trying to learn all about it, tell them that I inherited these jewels from my grandmother who received them as a present from the viceroy in Peru when she was living in Madrid.'

'A viceroy in Peru!'

'My love, I can't tell you any more because that's all I've been told. I only know that she was reputed to be beautiful, stunningly beautiful — but less stunning than you!' he cried suddenly.

And, with gestures of extraordinary tenderness, he took the necklace off her and unbuttoned her bodice.

She immediately felt frightened and said:

'No, not now.'

And, trying to find an excuse in her sudden panic, she said, 'They're preparing lunch.'

'I don't see how that affects us,' he said with a sad smile. 'But tonight, my beloved . . .'

'Promise that you will be kind and not frighten me, as in the drawing-room?'

'You must forget that, Laura. You'll see how gentle I can be.'

The table that day was spread with white flowers, jasmins intertwined with irises and amaryllis, which exhaled heavy and subtly intoxicating scents. They served champagne which William Hargrove had had brought from Paris . . . Maisie Llewelyn had thought of everything to give the meal a festive air. Blinds in faded pink ensured a pleasant half-light and the punkas moved slowly above the guests as if rowing in the warm air.

At her husband's request, Laura wore the emerald necklace. Maisie Llewelyn couldn't take her eyes off it and when the time came for dessert, as a sort of additional treat, Lieutenant Régis told them its history.

'From the Viceroy of Peru!' Siverac and the Welshwoman exclaimed simultaneously.

Their admiration was indecently close to barely disguised cupidity. The collosal worth of these dazzling jewels was being calculated in the depths of their greedy eyes.

'Your grandmother must have been beautiful if she turned the heads of kings,' Siverac said sententiously.

'Of a Viceroy, anyway,' Régis said, raising his eyebrows with a modest smile.

Cringing with shame, Laura pretended to toy with her pistachio ice-cream . . . It distressed her to see that people envied her her necklace and she longed for the moment when she would be able to caress her Régis' handsome face over and over again.

This night that had been so ardently desired, came at last, but they were overcome with the awkwardness of children when they found themselves face to face. It was as though they were afraid of love. In truth, Régis was embarrassed by the mixture of passion and panic that he inspired. With an unexpected gesture, instead of reaching for Laura's bodice as he had that very morning, he undid the hooks on his dolman and she ran away.

'Stay as you are,' she implored him, from behind the rocking-chair.

The comedy of the situation made him laugh despite himself.

'But, my love,' he said, 'why do you think we are here? I am not going to do you any harm. I adore you.'

She ran to the locked door and tried to open it, but in a bound he was beside her; she panted like a terrified animal. In an attempt to tame her, he spoke gently, holding her hands:

'We will just go to bed like two tired people who want to sleep. Don't you want to sleep beside someone who loves you so much?'

'I am afraid of the dark. You won't turn out the light?'

He promised whatever she wished. After a long debate, full of cunning and tenderness on his part, and love and mistrust on hers, they both got undressed, each on their own side of the bed. She slipped into it first and hid her head under the sheets so as not to see what he was doing. Soon he was beside her.

'You won't put out the light,' she said.

'I promised . . .'

Her heart full of tenderness, she was stroking his cheek, happy and reassured, when suddenly she felt Régis' whole body lying along her own and began to cry out; but he silenced her by putting his mouth on hers and wrapping her lovingly in his two arms like a child.

At dawn, he spoke to her. At first she had been surprised by his long silence, then anxious.

'It hurt a little, Laura, but it's over.'

She whispered:

'Yes, it's over.'

With a little girl's gesture, she stroked his face as if to console him for the pain he had inflicted.

'And then, it gave you pleasure, didn't it?'

She did not want to reply.

'You see,' he said at last. 'Next time, you'll enjoy it.'

She had felt pleasure, like a thunderbolt, in a wonderment of senses that were not expecting it, but she was unable to repress the revulsion that the shock of physical pleasure produced deep inside her. Because of this, she had kept her eyes closed so as not to see him. However, the following night, when he left the bed, she noticed him in a tall mirror as he crossed the room and, confronted with the grace of this supple young body, she understood her inner struggle against total enslavement. She wanted nothing to do with this thing that she desired with all her body and all her heart.

'He will never know,' she thought, when the lamp went out and he slipped, exhausted with happiness, into sleep. 'He will not know, because I love him too much . . .'

At the moment when she was herself about to slide into the abyss, a strange voice whispered to her:

'He who does not love too much, does not know love.'

# 76

*A*fter a few days, his leave ended, he left and she began to suffer.

In love, she thought. Henceforth all my joy — all my life — is dependent on the presence of a single being.

However, she was careful not to let others notice her sadness. Seeing her smile when she was with Siverac and Miss Llewelyn, no one could suspect that she was unhappy. Without taking part in their conversation over meals, she listened attentively to what they had to say. She was interested most of all in the news.

Young Frank also listened more and more eagerly for snatches of sometimes alarming conversations. With his little turned-up nose and big brown eyes, he was the very image of watchful innocence. From time to time he made himself heard, but the order to keep quiet immediately closed his mouth.

'I have to admit,' Siverac said one morning, 'that if our huge American flag were not flapping in the breeze above our heads, I should already have left this place.'

'More plantations burned?' asked Miss Llewelyn. 'It's becoming a commonplace occurrence.'

'The Spaniard is being hunted up and down Santo Domingo, but there's something new: a savannah-priest has been seen with *papas-lois* leading the arsonists, and they are now bands of mulattoes.'

'One cannot be afraid of everything. To me, those Blacks in long, flapping cassocks covered in grigris just look comic. Some of them add a white lace surplice, all in rags, as though a cat had been sharpening its claws on it. Ridiculous.'

'Perhaps, but they have a fanatical following among Blacks and half-castes.'

'So what? Perhaps those English ships sailing just off the coast are there to survey the scenery?'

'I'd like to see a savannah-priest,' Frank exclaimed suddenly. 'It must be hilarious!'

'Quiet,' said Miss Llewelyn. 'Eat your stewed fruit.' Then, noticing the more serious look on the face of the young bride, the Welshwoman said: 'Laura, don't bother too much with what our friend here says. Siverac likes to alarm his audience. We are quite safe here.'

'I'm not only thinking of myself,' said Laura.

'If it's Régis you're thinking of, then you needn't worry about him either. Grande-Rivière is not threatened, or Dondon, or Marmelade. In any event, your husband is there with soldiers acting under his orders who would come to help us, if need be.'

'Do you imagine,' said Siverac, with a hint of irony, 'that they would put their rebuilt bridge there so that they can rush over here with their guns to help us?'

'If their Lieutenant ordered them to do so, certainly. They worship him.'

'Laura, believe me, and put your trust in the star-spangled banner.'

'Monsieur Siverac, I think you are going too far,' the Welshwoman said drily, her eyes shooting fire.

Laura grew pale and, rising quickly to her feet, left the dining-room.

'Siverac,' Miss Llewelyn cried, 'you owe her your apologies, or you are utterly heartless.'

He, in turn, stood up.

'Very well,' he said. 'I'll go. But how irritating she is, this young lady with her nervous sensibilities!'

Alone with Frank, Miss Llewelyn addressed him solemnly:

'Don't say anything about what has just taken place, Frank. I want your word of honor.'

'Word of honor,' he said bewildered, but proud of having been spoken to like a man.

Miss Llewelyn watched him, stirring her coffee spoon in her cup.

'Are you afraid?' she asked.

'Oh, no,' he said, his chest swelling with new-found heroism.

He waited for a moment and asked, 'Is Siverac afraid?'

'I didn't say that,' she said, hastily. 'Siverac is very brave, but he is afraid for Laura. He must have learned something which he is keeping to himself.'

The conversation ended there. Frank went to take care of his pony which belonged to the light, vigorous island breed and climbed like a goat, while Maisie Llewelyn took herself up to her room where the shutters and mosquito nets were tightly closed. In a pleasant half-light that soothed her mind after the argument, she first tossed her two large shoes into the air and threw herself onto the double bed, arms and legs spread out in an X; then she sighed and began to mutter:

'The boy is right, of course, Siverac is afraid. It's obvious. I, too, am afraid. Everybody is afraid, but heavens above, you don't flinch in public, you try to look bold, especially if you have what they call breeding. What about grandpapa's title, Monsieur *de* Siverac? Do you know what it's doing? I'll tell you: it's buzzing around in space like a large black fly above your decomposing ancestors. Maisie Llewelyn, be thankful that you were the daughter of a maid and a blacksmith. You have made your way in the world thanks to your poise and your refusal to let sham aristocrats pull the wool over your eyes. At least Laura knows how to keep up appearances. She is dying with anxiety about her man, with his little cherub's face. I wonder what that idiot Siverac can have told her, the poor dear thing . . .'

In the heat, she suddenly started to snore, not realizing that she was falling asleep.


# 77


*T*hat evening, after dinner, she found Siverac very different from the rather playful and slightly sinister person who had shocked her that morning. She had made up her mind not to speak to him throughout the meal. Laura had stayed in her room and not reappeared. It was nearly ten o'clock and the moon was flooding the plantation with its light, at once dazzling and dead. The cicadas grated in the trees.

While Maisie Llewelyn was coming down the steps of the veranda to take the air in the avenue, Siverac caught up with her and said, with a directness that instantly obliterated any social difference beween them:

'Miss Llewelyn, I was affected by your silence over dinner and led to reflect. I beg your pardon for the intemperance of my remarks this morning.'

'Granted,' she said haughtily. 'What have you to tell me?'

'If you would allow us to move a little further away from the house, I shall feel more comfortable in telling you what I learned last night.'

They took a few steps in silence until they were under the cork-oaks. Rays of moonlight shone through the branches and little silver coins seemed to be sprinkled across the ground at their feet.

'There will always be,' he began, 'problems in relations between the France of King Louis XVIII and Haiti.'

'Mr Siverac,' she said, impatiently, 'there is nothing new in that.'

'Well, then, let's be brief. The Blacks live in terror of a landing of French troops. Seized with rage, they are hunting down the French and three days ago, near Port-au-Prince, they set fire to a house inhabited by French people, who were burned alive.'

Miss Llewelyn stopped dead in amazement.

'I can understand your feelings,' she said.

'That is not all. May I continue? On a board in front of the house could be read these words in large, crudely-formed, red letters: LI SOUVENI MAUREPAS. Do you understand?'

'In memory of Maurepas, I suppose. Do you know what that is meant to mean?'

'It goes back twenty years. Maurepas, a Black, was the commander of Toussaint Louverture's troops in the North against the French. The latter bribed him and made him commander of Port-au-Prince, but they were overcome by yellow fever. Maurepas, fearing reprisals by Dessalines, took his wife and supporters and rowed out to a French ship that was about to set sail. In the Canal de la Tortue there was a scene of terror. One of Maurepas' companions was stabbed and thrown to the sharks. Maurepas himself was attacked savagely, stripped naked and tied to the mainmast. His wife was then hanged from the main yard amid her children. The wretched Maurepas had a general's epaulettes nailed to his shoulders. From that moment on, his conduct was admirable, as if to redeem the honor of his race. He did not utter a sound. To complete the diabolical mockery, they nailed a braided admiral's hat on his head, "to give him shade". Then his body was thrown into the sea. That's it.'

Miss Llewelyn listened to the story until the end, fanning herself with quiet little movements of her wrist.

'The tale is horrible,' she said, 'and does no credit to the French; but your Maurepas made the mistake of switching sides in the middle of a war, and he is what is generally known as a traitor.'

'I will leave you to your definitions,' said Siverac. 'The Blacks are making a martyr of him and the power of a martyr is considerable. He can inspire a whole people.'

'There you are right, but in this case, which affects you so nobly, put the word martyr into inverted commas.'

'May I ask why?'

'Because your martyr is a traitor.'

'Oh, I think you are unjust.'

'I regret, but I do not like traitors.'

'Because of him, and other similar cases, the country is becoming more and more dangerous for anyone of French origin.'

'So, escape while you still have time.'

Siverac smothered an outburst of indignation and replied coldly:

'It is my duty to wait here with you for the return of William Hargove, to ensure the safety of Frank and Laura.'

'Well then, stay.'

The perfidious irony of this retort made Siverac regret having offered his excuses to Miss Llewelyn, and he would have preferred to take them back. It was better to keep quiet, he thought, and re-engage the Welshwoman on ground where she was vulnerable.

The air was growing deliciously cool and they arrived at the end of the avenue of cork-oaks. Between two hills, in the clear fresh air, they could see the reddish lights of Port-Haïtien. Nothing disturbed the calm of the night except the timid song of the frogs, but the ear became so quickly accustomed to the sound as to be no longer aware of it . . . For a moment they were lost in thought, not so much because of the charm of the landscape as about the means of attacking one another in the little secret war that they had been waging for years between themselves. This time, Maisie Llewelyn sensed that Siverac was hopelessly smitten with the lovely Laura. He himself had surprised the Welshwoman as she was glancing furtively at the very handsome Régis.

He instinctively attacked from that direction.

'Would you like us to go back toward the house?' he suggested. 'It doesn't mean that we have to go in, of course.'

She was amused by the gentleness of his tone and could not help laughing:

'Mr Siverac, I love our little reconciliations after our perpetual tiffs. What do you have to tell me?'

'It's about Lieutenant Régis.'

'Well, well!' she said, without batting an eyelid.

He waited for a moment to enjoy in advance the pleasure of demolishing her idol.

'You know he is of mixed blood?'

'Is that all?' she said. 'But one revelation deserves another. Did you know he has a sister?'

He didn't.

'Vaguely heard it mentioned,' he said.

'Oh, I thought you were better informed. She is a Carmelite in a convent which she never leaves.'

Taken aback, he stammered:

'Very good, admirable.'

'A mulatto'

'What did you say?'

'I said that she was a mulatto.'

'Ah!' he said, dismayed. 'That's undeniable proof.'

Hoping nonetheless to arouse her cupidity, he resorted to the most disloyal indiscretions:

'Some friends who saw him bathing naked at Grande-Rivière one hot day assured me that he is snow-white from head to toe.'

'Fancy that!' she said. 'You could just as well have asked our little Laura who must know as much about it as anyone.'

He was left open-mouthed. In a bland voice she continued:

'Moreover, he comes from an excellent family in which there is not a visible trace of black blood, except in that Carmelite.'

Defeated on all fronts, he made an attempt to upset his adversary's conscience:

'Does Laura suspect that there is the shadow of a doubt about her beloved?'

'At last an intelligent question. Now you're not trying to be clever, but to show some feeling.'

'I'll do my best; you do the same.'

'Well answered! It's one of two things: either she knows or she doesn't. Suppose she does know — and who the devil would have told her? It's all the same to her. She takes the boy as he is. In love, don't you see?'

'Agreed.'

'Phew! Or else she does not know and someone will have the sad temerity of going to disillusion the young woman. Will it be you?'

'Naturally, I'd rather die.'

'My word, to hear you, anyone would think you were human.

But, third supposition: she knows that she is running the risk of giving birth to a black baby and, carried away by passion, that is a risk she is willing to run.'

Defeated, he replied:

'Miss Llewelyn, you are right.'

'Women are always right, because the heart is victorious over what you have the weakness to call your intelligence. But we are almost at the house. Would you like to go back and admire the lights of Port-Haïtien: one last walk there and back before saying goodnight?'

'No, thank you,' he said sadly. 'I feel a trifle weary.'

'Then, good night, Mr Siverac; and don't let the amorous problems of our Laura keep you awake too long!'

'Good night, Miss Llewelyn.'

# 78

*T*wice, or even three times a week, Régis managed to spend the night at the plantation. Laura lived only for these moments of happiness, which were, however, troubled by her peculiar mania for seeing them already hasten toward their end when they had only barely begun.

She said nothing about this to Régis, entirely absorbed in the joy of having him to herself in an intoxication of the senses and of the heart. Sleep would have seemed to them a waste of the short time they had together, and they mingled scraps of disordered conversation with sensual pleasure. It was at moments like these that she confided some of her worries to him. She could not forget the discussion between Siverac and Miss Llewelyn which had driven her away from the table one morning: foreign plantations were going up in flames one after the other; the country was in rebellion.

'It will resolve itself,' he said. 'Don't try to understand. It's politics.'

'They are persecuting the French.'

'Because France is asking the country for a huge sum of money as the price of its freedom, and French ships are sailing off our coasts. So, too, are English ones; but everything will be settled, as everything eventually is.'

'Are your soldiers calm?'

'My soldiers are fine Blacks who always obey me. My love, don't think any more about that. The night is ours. Can't you hear the tree-frogs croacking?'

'And after the tree-frogs, the silence of dawn comes so quickly . . .'

'No, Laura. There is only now. Nothing else matters, do you understand?'

Daylight came like a wrongdoer, taking her husband away from her; and her fears revived more sharply than ever. She did not complain, it was not in her nature to do so, but one could tell that she was afraid of the threats looming on the horizon week after week. Because of that, they were careful about what they told her, but they could not prevent the bad news from seeping through the walls in whispered conversations. In the South, at Jacmel, there were riots. In the North, at Cap Haïtien, supporters of the former King Christophe had risen and were controlling a town here, a garrison there.

At other times, she heard the name of President Boyer. He was against all Whites without discriminating between nationalities. In vain, she begged Régis to explain these things to her.

'Laura,' he said one night, in an almost severe tone of voice which she had not heard from him before, 'they will never touch an American plantation. France and England are a long way away, but America is much closer, and she is strong. Just remind yourself that the star-spangled banner flying over this piece of earth has the strength of an army. And then, your Régis will always be there to protect you, he and his Blacks. Do you believe him or not?'

'I believe everything you tell me, my love.'

# 79

*L*aura did her best to believe that Régis could not be mistaken, and as long as she was beside him, nothing troubled her happiness except the lurking awareness that every second brought them closer to the moment when he would get dressed again and leave . . .

As if this were not enough, a minor detail threatened to spoil her happiness. She refused to think about it, but this minor detail entered her mind at certain unexpected moments: the bed in which she tasted the delights of love was the double bed that Maisie Llewelyn usually slept in when William Hargrove was traveling, and which she would relinquish to them on the nights when Régis was there. Easily a prey to disgust, the young woman felt as though she was drinking out of the Welshwoman's glass. What would she have thought if she had known the whole truth? If absolutely necessary, she could have slept in her own room with her husband, but there were two objections to that: the bed was too narrow for more than one person; and the huge painting of the Madonna, hanging on the wall, would have appeared to be watching them. She could not have borne that.

All around her, however, daily life was changing little by little . . . Reconciled once more, Siverac and Miss Llewelyn stopped treating the young bride as a little girl and did not hesitate to discuss the news of the day, which was all bad, in front of her. To them it was one of the pleasures of breakfast. They had all the newspapers and all the gossip.

'This time the Army is doing something,' said Siverac, unfolding his napkin.

'You have taken your time noticing that. We're already at the second pronunciamento, yesterday evening in Port-de-Paix. A black general has seized power. If he stays put for more than three days, he will be lucky.'

'No doubt one of King Christophe's former followers. It will end as it always does.'

'I hope so,' she exclaimed sarcastically.

'Don't worry. The insurgent general arrives, wearing a large hat decorated with a bunch of feathers. He reigns without bloodshed. Then suddenly the regular army appears. The encounter takes place peacefully. The rebel general is given a new bunch of feathers to add to his hat, together with a rank above the one which he had already awarded himself, and he withdraws.'

'The pronunciamento in Port-Haïtien caused more of a stir.'

'What! There was a good deal of shouting. Long Live Christophe! Down With Boyer!'

'In any case, the President is doing nothing to restore order.'

'The President couldn't care less. He is not a bad man, but he's too cynical. You know what he says every time: "What's dis? 'Nudder rebel! I got tree enemy already; when number four come 'long at same time, dey can make a hand at cards!"'

'So, none of this is serious,' said Miss Llewelyn, rather disappointed.

'No, but it is becoming too frequent: disorder is becoming a way of life. The *naked congos* are active.'

'The naked congos!' Frank exclaimed.

'The naked congos, my young friend, are formidable. They oil their machetes with grease from the brains which they take from the corpses of their enemies. These poisoned weapons inflict dreadful wounds.'

'Fatal ones, in fact,' Maisie Llewelyn added. 'Septicemia. It's very clever. The cruelty of these Blacks is proverbial. And where can they be found, your naked congos?'

'I can't tell you exactly; they scatter into the bush. They hide behind waterfalls, in the caves.'

Turning to Frank, he asked:

'Satisfied, young man?'

'Yes,' said Frank, a little pale.

'Well, at least they have more character than those generals with their feathers,' said Maisie Llewelyn.

Starting to get carried away, Siverac decided to add one small detail:

'Do you know what a *maringouin* is?'

'A horsefly?' said the Welshwoman.

'Just so, but a horsefly whose sting sinks into the flesh and stays there, causing unbearable pain. Our naked congos can go through clouds of *maringouins* unharmed. The flies leave them alone, as if they could sense the presence of infernal beings . . .'

'I must admit,' said Miss Llewelyn, 'that one does learn a thing or two when one takes breakfast with you.'

He acknowledged the compliment with a pleasant smile and a bow.

Laura managed to overcome the disgust she felt at these remarks and, to show how calm she was, took some more stewed fruit. The gesture was enough to dispel a more or less artificially created atmosphere of horror, but inside the young woman felt herself dying of fright. In her imagination she saw her Régis struggling with savages . . . However, it had been arranged that her husband would come and spend the night with her, and she was comforted by the thought.

# 80

*L*ike a bad dream, it was William Hargrove who appeared at dusk. Much surprise. No one had been expecting him, and his satisfied expression contrasted with the more or less general confusion in the household.

Laura, who had been at the window looking out for the arrival of her beloved, had to clasp the curtains to prevent herself from falling when she recognized the traveling coach from which her father leaped as though trying to look like a young man. Her terror was all the greater since she was in the room with the double bed, which Miss Llewelyn had once again put at her disposal.

The Welshwoman came in hurriedly:

'Look out!' she said. 'He's back. Go to your room — and remember: he must know nothing. I'll help you carry your things.'

The whole operation took less than two minutes, while downstairs they could hear the exuberant voice which he no doubt considered appropriate to the circumstances of a traveler returning home from afar:

'Ho! Is there anyone there? Where are you all? I come back home and find no one to greet me!'

Siverac emerged from a little drawing-room where he had been dozing, with his hair still ruffled.

'Calm down, William,' he said. 'You can see that everyone is rushing to meet you.'

And, giving in to the desire to instil a little fear into the man, just for fun, he added: 'You are home, no one denies it. I just hope that you don't wish you had stayed over there, or somewhere else . . .'

William Hargrove's face fell and he listened open-mouthed. Siverac could not help laughing, and continued:

'Where have you come from? Don't you know that Haiti has become the land of fear, where fires rage and the earth is slaked with blood?'

Hargrove had put down a small suitcase which he had been carrying. Instinctively he picked it up again.

'Do we have to leave?' he stammered.

'Oh, perhaps not this evening, or even tomorrow morning, but it would be wise to be aware of it.'

Hargrove took off his panama and slumped into a chair without letting go of his case.

'If I had known,' he moaned. 'I could have taken refuge in Jamaica where I've just bought a plantation.'

'And what about us?' Siverac asked.

'You would have joined me. I would have waited for you.'

Suddenly becoming serious, Siverac went over to him and leaned down. Seizing him by his sideburns to shake his head, he looked him full in the eye and said under his breath:

'You really are a dreadful coward, my poor William.'

The silence that followed between the two men had the intensity of the moment following a murder. Siverac had stood up, but Hargrove remained motionless.

A servant came in. He was carrying two lighted lamps which he set down on a long table at some distance from one another, then left.

Laura's voice came down the stairs:

'Good evening, Papa,' she said calmly.

'My little Laura!' he exclaimed.

At the same time he tried to stand, but could not. Siverac put a hand on his shoulder.

'Rest, William,' he said. 'No strong emotions after the fatigue of the journey. Think of your heart.'

Miss Llewelyn appeared behind Laura and said simply:

'So you're back, Mr Hargrove. You must be pleased to see your dear plantation again.'

He nodded to show that he did indeed feel happy, but said nothing.

A few seconds passed in an increasingly awkward silence while no one moved, expecting the traveler to say something. The huge, ill-lit room had the appearance of a painting, a silent still life. The light from the lamps did not extend beyond the few people who were there and did nothing to dispel the great masses of shadow covering the ceiling and the top of the stairs.

It was Maisie Llewelyn who broke the silence and the general immobility. She took a chair and sat down beside William Hargrove. Full of pity for this man stricken with terror, she asked him in a gentle voice:

'Are you unwell, Mr Hargrove? Would you like me to help you to your room? You must be in need of a good night's sleep.'

He turned toward her with the look of a wounded animal and whispered:

'Thank you, Maisie.'

He may have been about to say something else when the sound of a horse's hooves in front of the house stopped him. From his anxious look one could see that everything scared him, as though the universe were changing around him.

'What's that?' he asked.

Siverac crossed the room and at almost the same moment, the door opened. It was Régis.

A single glance was enough for him to take everything in, and he entered without hesitation . . . His arrival had an immediate effect on William Hargrove who tried to stand up; but Maisie Llewelyn prevented him with a forceful hand. Anger, which he had long repressed, suddenly aroused him

'Régis,' he asked, in a muffled voice. 'What are you doing here?'

The young officer took off his shako.

'I came simply to bid you good day, Mr Hargrove.'

'At this time of night?'

'My soldiers saw a coach in the distance making its way toward your plantation. I wanted to make sure that it was you, returning, and I jumped on my horse. I hope that you had a good journey.'

William Hargrove did not answer.

'Sit down, Lieutenant Régis,' Maisie Llewelyn commanded. 'Tell us what's new in the country.'

'Very little. Some disturbances in Port-Haïtien, as usual. Uprisings in the South: some settlers in Jacmel have been butchered. And a confused situation among the Spaniards.'

He hesitated to take the chair that she offered him and remained standing. Siverac came over.

'Would you like something to drink?' he asked. 'In this oppressive weather, a glass of champagne . . .'

'My champagne,' Hargrove grumbled.

'Of course,' said Maisie Llewelyn. 'To celebrate your return.'

'No,' he answered.

'William,' Siverac asked, 'did you notice anything in Port-Haïtien? Commotion, shouting?'

William Hargrove answered irritably:

'I noticed nothing, because I came into Port-Dauphin on an English ship.'

'Frank,' Siverac said, 'go and ask them in the pantry to serve us some champagne. Laura, why are you hiding there in a corner? Come and say good evening to Régis.'

Laura had indeed been standing to one side, her heart pounding. She was dressed in white chiffon because Régis liked to see her in that. Controlling herself, she came over and gave him a sad smile.

'Good evening,' she said.

'Good evening, Laura.'

William Hargrove erupted:

'Miss Laura!' he snapped.

The Welshwoman instantly went over to him and said forcefully:

'Lieutenant Régis and your daughter have known each other for long enough to dispense with such polite formalities.'

At that moment, Frank came running back from the pantry.

'The champagne is on ice,' he told Siverac. 'But they'll bring it in a few minutes. Can I have a glass?'

'Certainly,' Siverac said. 'William, don't sulk. Drink a glass with us.'

'No,' said Hargrove. 'I'm going up to bed. My cases, as soon as possible!'

He managed to get up, but had to lean on the back of the chair to prevent himself from falling. Maisie Llewelyn supported him.

'Come, come,' she said. 'If you want to go up, do so, but I will help you.'

Without listening to his protests, she grasped his arm and led him toward the stairs. He let her lead him up the first steps.

'Maisie,' he muttered, leaning on her, 'what is the matter? I can't stand up.'

'That's because you are no longer twenty years old and all this excitement has been too much for you; but you've behaved very badly this evening. I've never seen you so impolite.'

'That Régis is hovering around my daughter. I don't like it. I'm sure he came to see her.'

'So? We're all here, aren't we? What can he do?'

'I'm suspicious of him.'

'You're quite wrong. His behavior is impeccable.'

'I hate him. I abhor him. I despise him.'

'Oh well! Is that all? Would you like to sing an aria? Take care not to stumble and hold the bannisters tightly. We're almost there. Maisie is going to pamper you.'

'Oh, Maisie,' he said, reaching the last steps. 'Maisie, I'm so unhappy this evening.'

'Willy,' she said, as they went into the room where a light was burning at the head of the large double bed. 'We'll see what can be done about that in a moment.'

As soon as William Hargrove had vanished with Maisie Llewelyn, Régis motioned to Siverac and went to the long table where a bottle of champagne was waiting for them in an ice bucket, surrounded by glasses. The two lamps gave a festive air to the scene, but the young Lieutenant had other things on his mind. The crystal glasses were immediately filled and they each took one, not forgetting Laura and Frank. However, these last two were asked, as politely as possible, to be so good as to move away from the table. Régis wanted to talk about some important matters with Siverac. So Laura, feeling very anxious, and Frank full of curiosity, sat in a corner of the room from which they could see everything, without hearing, and sipped the champagne which neither really enjoyed.

Régis began without any preliminaries:

'I came this evening to tell you that you must leave Haiti. The country is no longer safe. You must go, and go quickly.'

Siverac shuddered.

'Heavens, Régis. I'm a bit taken aback. What do you mean, quickly?'

'Ideally, as soon as possible, but I imagine nothing is ready.'

'I can't believe this. Explain.'

They were standing opposite one another, either side of the table, and the two lamps cast an amber light on their solemn faces.

Simultaneously, they raised their glasses.

'To the future,' Régis said.

'To the happiness of us all,' Siverac replied.

'You're asking a lot,' Régis said, putting down his empty glass.

Taking two maps out of a little pouch which he wore on his belt, he unfolded them and spread them out on the table, after moving aside the bucket with the champagne.

'I shall be brief,' he said. 'Even if you should leave tomorrow afternoon, I must show you the quickest and least exposed route to Port-de-Paix.'

'Port-de-Paix! Why not Cap-Haïtien?'

'Cap-Haïtien is now in the hands of a black general who captured it yesterday and has had the harbor closed . . . General Alexis, who is in charge of the port, has had the buoys removed and because of the reefs, the port is dangerous.'

'And the English vessels?'

'The English squadron is offshore, but cannot approach because of all the reefs below the surface. Moreover, the forts and the Customs are crammed with weapons. It would be impossible for you to reach an English ship. Forget about Cap-Haïtien.'

His finger moved across the map to Port-de-Paix.

'Your only hope is here. Two routes are possible. Now listen: there is the Bay of Manceville, but you have to cross a plain that is unsafe and, if you go across the hills on the Spanish side, then down along the River Massacre, there is a danger of meeting uncontrolled elements of the population. So, let's reject that way.'

'If there is danger on all sides, how do you expect us to escape?'

'I am about to tell you, but listen carefully and remember what I tell you: you must go this way, through the hills near Marmelade and afterwards make for the little empty fortress called Fortin Paradis. It's a long way, but offers no danger for the time being. You can wait for me there; I shall come with my men to help you. As it happens, there are troops of mulattoes who are coming up from the Artibonite. We shall go down Trois-Rivières as far as Port-de-Paix. There, we shall find a boat which will take you to the Ile de la Tortue. English ships stop off there. You will be safe.'

'Very well. I'm going home. Hargrove asked me to take his place while he was away and to look after his children, but I have neglected my own home. I have to see my managers.'

'Don't stay long. Hargrove came here by a dangerous road without realizing. The northern plain is unsafe. He must have been traveling at full speed; no one had time to stop him.'

'No doubt. He hired a coach with four horses at Port-Dauphin.'

'How much can that have cost him!'

'Oh, he always has his pockets stuffed with gold. Good night Régis. I am going home to pack my bags.'

'Good night. Be quick about it.'

# 81

*H*ardly had the door shut behind Siverac than Miss Llewelyn appeared and went straight up to the young officer who was folding his maps. She appeared at once calm and resolved.

'Don't be surprised at what I am about to tell you,' she said. 'I heard almost all of your conversation with Siverac. I was listening on the stairs. I know it's wrong, but that's how it is. I am utterly with you and for you. We must leave.'

'Obviously, it breaks my heart because of Laura.'

'Where is she?'

'There, at the back of the room.'

'Let her stay there for a moment. Laura,' she called. 'Don't move, I have something to say to Lieutenant Régis.'

Laura, who had stood up, remained motionless.

'And me?' said Frank.

'You, go to bed at once.'

'Already? Can't I stay with Laura?'

Maisie Llewelyn made a stride toward him and he took to his heels.

'I understand,' she told Régis, 'that it is hard for you to separate from Laura; but you give us what — two days?'

'Yes, at the most.'

'So, at least spend tonight with your wife.'

'Where? Here it's impossible.'

'Listen. William Hargrove has of course taken back his room, which I occupy when he is not there and which I leave to you when you come to spend the night with Laura.'

'I know that and thank you for it, but you, tonight . . .'

From the battery of deceptions that she carried around in her head, Maisie Llewelyn picked the most appropriate and subtle reply:

'Oh, it's easy as far as I'm concerned: I have my room. From there I can watch everything. Laura's room on the ground floor is isolated and you will be undisturbed.'

'But Laura would not want me to spend a night with her in her room.'

'Why on earth not? I know the bed is narrow, but love can make do in spite of that, surely?'

'Oh, it's not that,' he said, a trifle embarrassed. 'But Laura has certain prejudices — because of the large painting which she can see from her bed. She explained to me . . .'

'Prejudices! Well, I never! Against who or what?'

Her imperious voice rang out:

'Laura!'

The young woman came over calmly.

'It appears,' said Miss Llewelyn, in an ironic tone, 'that Madam does not want to spend the night in her own room with her husband because of the large painting she can see from her bed . . .'

Laura and Régis made the same gesture of irritation.

'Please,' Laura said.

'Well, now! Perhaps you would be so good as to hear what I have to say on the matter. Let's talk religion. It doesn't happen often here, and it will do us all good. What bothers you is that the Madonna should see you while you are busy making children, as the Church requires you to do, in the sacrament of marriage.'

'Miss Llewelyn, I beg you!' said Laura, blushing.

'And you imagine,' the Welshwoman said, 'that Mary hides her face to avoid seeing it. Well, then, let me tell you that Mary has better things to do than to watch you, she is looking at the Lord God, but she knows that you are there and she protects you.'

Now it was Régis' turn to say something:

'Miss Llewelyn,' he said, clasping his hands, 'please stop. We are agreed! Aren't we, Laura?'

'Yes, a thousand times yes, Miss Llewelyn.'

'Good. Then I shall go back to my room and all is for the best,' the Welshwoman said, making the sign of the cross.

Then without losing any more time, she plunged into the darkness of the stairs. And, with infinite caution, she slipped into the room with the big double bed, where William Hargrove was waiting for her, trembling with impatience and desire.

In the ground-floor room, dimly lit by a single lamp, the top of the large picture vanished into the half-light. One could hardly make out head and shoulders.

'You see,' said Régis. 'It doesn't bother us.'

'But she is there.'

He took her in his arms.

'Don't think about it.'

With a speed that astonished the young woman, he took off his clothes and in a moment was beside her. The two fell into each other's arms as though meeting again after a long journey. Joy carried them body and soul into a country where fear no longer exists. Panting, she prayed that this oblivion would never come to an end, but the return to her familiar surroundings left her with the inexhaustible pleasure of caressing his handsome face flushed with love.

'I hope nothing ever happens to you,' she said, letting the tips of her fingers wander across his eyelids and his mouth.

'Have no fear, there is no real fighting around here. Just a few skirmishes. They don't count.'

In a few words he gave her an idea of the journey which she would have to make.

'It will seem long, but you will be brave.'

She gave a long, little girl's moan.

'But we'll be separated!'

'No, I'll come and join you when you get there.'

'Swear that you will, Régis.'

'I shall never leave you, do you hear? Even if . . .'

'Even if what? Say it, say it!'

'Even if you cannot see me, I shall be there.'

'You mean if we are living far apart from one another?'

In a sudden burst of feeling, he clasped her against him.

'You are mine for ever, Laura, for ever, until the end of life.'

With both hands, she imprisoned his head by holding its mass of black hair.

'I'm frightened,' she said. 'Don't leave me. Death is everywhere. Ask the big painting to stop them separating us.'

'You ask. I don't really know how.'

He took her again and again until she lost all consciousness of the world around them.

Dawn tore them apart.


# 82

The day had scarcely dawned in a reddening sky when Régis left the plantation on his piebald gray and set off down the road for Marmelade.

Maisie Llewelyn was the first up in her mauve robe, she took it upon herself to wake everyone except William Hargrove, whom she let sleep because she found him more a hindrance than a help when awake.

She hurried to make sure that all the preparations for their departure were completed that morning to avoid a last-minute rush. No doubt she had started a little early, but she knew what she wanted to do and did it with infinite obstinacy.

Out of humanity, she was careful not to disturb Laura, who had been stricken with a fit of grief in the dreadful solitude of her room.

An hour later, bags and cases had started to accumulate in the large room on the ground floor. Under the guidance of the Welshwoman, Betty in her red shift, ran this way and that, like a mouse, fetching the most urgently needed things. Frank, overexcited, was bustling around with an air of importance, bringing his adventure novels, together with a ball and some rackets which he considered indispensable for the occasion.

Abruptly, at around eleven o'clock, Siverac appeared and was at first struck dumb by the appearance of the great hall in this meticulous organization of their flight; then he flung his hat on the ground.

'Too late!' he cried.

'What is it?' Miss Llewelyn asked.

'All this,' he said, with a wave toward the pile of luggage. 'You don't understand the situation. When I got home last night, there was no one to greet me. This morning I called and looked for my managers. They had all left. All that remained were four loyal Blacks too terrified to move. At daybreak they saw some *papas-lois* brandishing their cow's-tail rattles near the house. Do you know what I found nailed to the front door? A white cock, its wings spread, all bloody. You know what that means? All is lost. I went round the house room by room taking the most precious objects I could find, and filled my traveling bag; it is here, at the door. Two of the Blacks followed me and are now in the kitchen. They will come with us. As for the carriages, they will stay in their coachhouse. We must leave on horseback. Where is Hargrove?'

'Upstairs,' said the Welshwoman.

She had turned quite pale at Siverac's story, but she held herself erect, supported by one hand on the back of a chair.

'Frank,' she said. 'Go and knock on your father's door.'

The boy, who was living through a wonderful tale of brigands, leaped up the stairs like a mountain goat.

'He can't still be sleeping?' said Siverac.

'Oh, no. I went up to wake him a moment ago. He took time recovering from yesterday, got washed and now he is dressing.'

'And Laura?'

'She is in her room.'

'Régis was right. We should have started out yesterday. But he had to have his night of love.'

'He didn't ask for it,' Maisie Llewelyn said keenly. 'I was the one who insisted on it.'

'You were right. It will be a long time before he has another. But whatever is Hargrove doing?'

As if in answer to this question, they heard William Hargrove's hesitant step coming down the stairs, his hand grasping the bannister. Unaware of the danger threatening them, he had dressed in black as if for dinner in town, and perhaps also to correct the unfortunate impression he had made the evening before.

Seeing the pile of luggage and parcels in the middle of the room, he gave a cry:

'What! Have we reached that stage already?'

'Don't let it upset you too much, William. All that jumble can stay until the last judgement.'

'Are you mad?' Miss Llewelyn exclaimed. 'We'll need a lot of things for the journey.'

'Wrong, if you'll excuse me. You still don't know what it means to flee. I have one bag. That's all. You do the same. We must leave within an hour. Would you go and tell Laura? I'll ask my Blacks to saddle the mountain ponies.'

Without waiting for any response to these words, he went to the door and vanished.

William Hargrove slumped into a chair.

'Mad,' he said, putting his head in his hands. 'The man is mad.'

'I don't think so,' the Welshwoman said suddenly. 'We are the ones who are still living in an illusion of security because of that star-spangled flag which the Devil will carry away if he feels like it. Be prepared, Mr Hargrove. I shall speak to Laura.'

To her great surprise, Maisie Llewelyn found the young woman sitting on a corner of the bed, on which she had placed a small suitcase.

Her face, in which something of the child still lingered, was drawn with fatigue and sorrow.

'I know,' she said simply. 'My husband warned me. When do we leave?'

'Soon.'

'I would prefer to leave this room at once,' she said as she stood up.

Miss Llewelyn kissed her without a word and left. Before following her, Laura did something that simultaneously expressed all her distress and her hopes. Turning toward the large picture, she made an emphatic sign of the cross.

# 83

The sturdy Haitien ponies were grouped in their stables. With their hard little hooves they could climb mountains without difficulty. Everyone was ready, but Nature stood in the way of their departure. A burning heat seemed to rise up out of the earth and, in a misty light, the leaves hung on the trees like lifeless hands. The air was still, as if the wind was holding its breath.

Around midday, the sky grew suddenly dark, presaging a storm. There could be no question of leaving for the time being, and heartache at leaving the house gave way to horror at being forced to remain; the presence of danger was becoming more and more disturbing.

Siverac walked back and forth on the road in front of the house, stopping, then coming back, agonized by a yearning to go and see what was happening at his home, but restrained by a superstitious fear that fate might be setting a trap for him.

Not knowing what to do, he returned to the great hall, where Maisie Llewelyn, Laura and Frank were waiting patiently. Hargrove was slumped in a large wicker chair with his back to them. He had long ago taken off the black coat which he held, folded on his knees, and was sweating in a shirt with its sleeves rolled up above his elbows. His sulky silence contrasted with the Welshwoman's efforts to keep everyone's spirits up.

'If I had some cards, I would have told your fortunes. Women in my country always have the gift of being able to see through the darkness of the future. Laura, I can see you already somewhere across the sea . . .'

'And me?' Frank asked.

'You, too, of course, with your sister.'

'Happy?' asked Laura.

'What does that mean in times such as these? Alive and at peace. That's a great deal already.'

'And me?' Frank asked.

'Oh, you! Boys always manage to get by.'

'When will all this be?' Siverac asked, coming over.

'Don't you be in too much of a hurry, Mr Siverac. You will soon be in the land that awaits us over there.'

He shrugged his shoulders.

'With a reply like that,' he said, 'one can pull the wool over a lot of idiots' eyes.'

'Find something better to amuse you,' she retorted with a humorless laugh.

He gave a kick at the bundles which had been piled up there to no purpose.

Hargrove's hands were deep inside his frock coat and he stood motionless.

The minutes passed with alarming slowness in an atmosphere of mysterious hostility toward these listless creatures.

Suddenly, Betty came running in. She was panting for breath and spoke in a confused manner, the red knot of her bandana slipping down over her ear.

'On de ro',' she said.

Siverac ran out and looked in the distance, toward the trees, where he could see nothing. Yet quite close to them, Blacks in blue uniforms with red trimmings were marching down the avenue toward him behind a white officer on a horse. He recognized Régis and gasped with surprise. Under the sky, which was turning dark gray, this great patch of color had the intensity of a scream and the landscape seemed to move with the men.

Régis cupped his hands to his mouth:

'Don't go home,' he yelled into the thick, humid air. 'Bands of looters are taking everything and are going to set fire to the house.'

Siverac, pouring with sweat, ran toward him and cried:

'What will you do if they come in this direction?'

Régis pointed toward the west where they could see the green hillside, whose crest was shrouded in darkness. Around its base, they could still distinctly make out the yellow stones of a steep road.

'Go that way,' Régis said. 'But go quickly, go now. I will stop them in the avenue.'

At his orders, the soldiers deployed themselves in extended order around the plantation. At that moment, Hargove appeared at an open window on the ground floor. He had thrown his coat over one shoulder and, with his free arm, was gesticulating. His eyes, popping out with rage, turned toward the Lieutenant whom he recognized.

'Who asked you to come here?' he yelled. 'We shall not move.'

Régis did not reply. Jumping down from his horse, he joined his men. Already, gunfire was crackling on the road and bands of mulattoes were attacking the black soldiers. The Lieutenant gave the order to fire, but the assailants were hurling themselves furiously at the Blacks. On each side of the road and quite near the house, tall, flowering black-wood hedges, formidably armed with their long thorns, forced them to close ranks as they arrived in large groups. Drunk with tafia, they had no fear of death and on their fanatical faces their mouths were open wide as they howled their cries. Behind them could be seen cows' tails, furiously being waved by *papa-lois.*

The black soldiers' guns caused a dozen of the attackers to stumble and fall, but the return fire left almost as many Blacks lying prone. In the livid darkness torn by the rip of gunshots, bodies fell abruptly or staggered in the midst of growing confusion. The clear voice of Régis sounded above the tumult and his soldiers fell back on his orders, slowing down the thrust of the mulattoes at the edges of the plantation.

Inside the house, the inhabitants had all taken refuge together, apart from Siverac, who was firing at the attackers from behind the lattice of a shutter on the upper floor. Hargrove, petrified, had remained crouching in the corner of one of the large drawing-room windows. His features were drawn with fear, but his eyes, like those of a hunted animal, twitched from right to left, tears mingling with the drops of sweat which were running down his sideburns. In his hand shone a pistol which he had concealed in his coat.

At one moment he thought he saw the ranks of the Black soldiers wavering and Régis waving one arm, shouting brief commands. Hargrove recognized him by the whiteness of his face. The bursts of gunfire increased. At the end of the avenue where the trees were smothered in purple passion flowers, the attackers had halted, no longer protected by the sandy area in front of the plantation, while Régis' infantrymen were fanning out from the storage sheds, whose roofs were covered in banana leaves, to the veranda surrounding the house. With two of his men, the Lieutenant jumped over the balustrade so as to ward off any attack. At once, shots rang through the deepening gloom.

On his knees now, and almost entirely hidden by the folds of a green curtain, Hargrove could make out the silhouette of Régis surrounded by rapidly moving shadows. In a fit of panic, he fired at random. At random? This was a question he would ask himself to the end of his days.

# 84

At the other end of the veranda, hidden like Hargrove in the corner of a large window, Laura was standing beside Maisie Llewelyn. The latter, with a mother's authority, had her arm round the shoulders of the young woman who was trying to see what was going on in front of the house. Protected by one of the half-open shutters, all she could see at first was a confused mass of soldiers without understanding what they were doing. They seemed to be struggling violently, but on the same spot. However, she soon realized, to her horror, that they were retreating and that the battle was approaching the part of the veranda where she was standing. Her body shuddered with revulsion at the proximity of death: she leaned against Miss Llewelyn as if against a wall. Peering forward, she looked for Régis, but could not make him out among the soldiers. Finally, his white face appeared in the midst of all the dark ones around him. The gunfire was becoming more rapid and, she thought, getting closer. Suddenly, the white face reappeared once more and then, almost at once, was no longer there. She felt a large hand cover her eyes and, without a cry, she slipped to the ground.

Maisie Llewelyn took her to a bedroom as far as possible from the veranda.

Outside, drops of rain were starting to fall, widely spaced, heavy, as broad as a man's open hand.

The mulattoes had managed to make their way as far as the three long buildings near the house. They had chosen the highest, from which they could direct their fire on their enemy: the huge warehouse where bails of cotton were kept, a large amount of indigo was stored, and where the tobacco leaves dried. The men could not see this wealth. It was revealed to them by the first flashes of lightning and they were surprised to find themselves confronted with the black infantrymen who had been stationed there to protect the house.

The skirmish was instant and brutal. The guns fired almost simultaneously from both sides. The battle soon moved to the interior, into the darkest corners, while flashes of lightning continued, as though to inscribe the fate of the combatants in the heavens; stray bullets would sometimes bury themselves in the heaps of cotton. Soon, long flames were leaping up through the darkness with a kind of savage joy. The roofing of large dry banana leaves caught fire. The men fought furiously and their frantic commotion in the midst of the storm attracted the lightning: the shed was struck by lightning. Almost immediately the fire had spread everywhere. The survivors fled in panic, the mulattoes first, pursued by a few blacks firing after them.

Suddenly the sky seemed to open. Hot rain poured in torrents, direct and violent, on to the earth and, far from putting out the fire, seemed at first to fuel it. The *papas-lois* fled down the avenue.

Isolated at the corner of the house, the traveling coach contemptuously extended its shafts toward the opulent passiflora, which looked phosphorescent in the flashes of lightning. The fire continued to crackle dimly. Finally, the sheets of water drowned it and an acrid smoke of burned cotton and tobacco swept over the surviving mulattoes who took advantage of the screen to disappear.

The black soldiers gathered their wounded.

The house resembled a person recovering from an attack and trying to understand what had happened. The gunfire had ceased and the flashes of lightning were becoming rarer, but the rain drummed on the roof of the verandas with an obstinate monotony that came eventually to mean something; but what? People were coming and going from one room to the next and somewhere in the house a voice kept on calling, over and over. Here and there, on a table, a little lamp was trying in vain to hold back the darkness; but there was too much of it: it was everywhere, hiding the ceilings and the walls.

Maisie Llewelyn remained in her room, sitting in front of Laura whom she had put in a rocking chair. Both remained silent, but from time to time the Welshwoman gently fluttered a palm fan near the young woman's face, and Laura looked at her without seeing. For the first time Maisie Llewelyn felt intimidated. She expected wails and torrents of tears, not this silent immobility which eventually began to disturb her. In the same way, she could read nothing in the large black eyes that seemed to be looking at something over her shoulder near the door behind her. What could she say? What words can one speak to a young woman of sixteen, who has been a widow since five o'clock in the afternoon? So she just continued to wave the fan . . . But, in the long run, it was becoming as cruel to say nothing as to say something — anything, but something.

Leaning forward a little, she raised her voice in order to be heard over the sinister chattering of the rain:

'The danger is past,' she said. 'They have gone.'

It took a while for these words to reach Laura. In her dead-white face, her mouth half opened:

'Where is he?' she asked.

Maisie Llewelyn took Laura's two icy hands in hers.

'His soldiers are with him,' she said.

Laura did not reply. A conflict was going on in her mind, on which her whole existence depended. She must find the courage to ask the only possible question and she didn't dare: was he alive? She waited for a minute or two, then said in a toneless voice:

'Where with his soldiers?'

Taken aback, the Welshwoman looked for a plausible reply and said at length:

'He is very tired and is resting with them after the battle.'

'Where is he resting? I want to see him.'

'For the moment that's not possible.'

This time Laura looked straight at her and said nothing. Something in her was shouting: You will not see him again. But she did not want to hear it said aloud, because the silence offered her, as one last hope, uncertainty.

Determined to put an end to this trying conversation, Maisie Llewelyn forced herself to smile:

'Laura,' she said, 'I have to tell you of our plans. Will you listen carefully?'

Laura nodded faintly.

'Well, here you are. You know that we must all leave the country, because it is very dangerous here. You saw that today.'

She paused for a moment.

'Everything is ready. We leave at dawn when the rain stops.'

'The rain . . .'

'Yes, you can hear it.'

Dull, deep and even, the long sound continued beneath the windows.

'It must be eight o'clock,' Maisie Llewelyn continued. 'You would do well to take a little rest in the bed I have prepared for you.'

'No,' said Laura. 'The noise . . .'

'As you wish, but the journey may be hard. You must take care of yourself.'

There was a pause, then she continued gently:

'I don't know how well versed you are in these matters, but I have been counting the days and the weeks. A child is on the way.'

Laura did not answer.

'You will ride side-saddle and we shall go as slowly as possible. But you must remember: the little stranger you are carrying inside you, is a part of him.'

Saying these words, she got up and kissed the young woman, who did not move.

'I should like to be alone,' she murmured. 'Excuse me.'

'I shall leave you. Try to close your eyes, in spite of the noise. I shall not be far. I will look after you.'

She glanced at the bed to make sure that everything was in order, turned up the wick of the lamp a little and, with a last — and unrequited — smile, she went out.

The Welshwoman left the room, waited for a few minutes, then crept back on tiptoe and put her ear to the door. She did not have to wait long . . . Sobs, held back for a whole day, suddenly burst out with terrible violence. They went on endlessly, broken by gasping breath. 'That's for the best,' thought Maisie Llewelyn. 'Let her have her crisis now, before the journey; but I am sorry for you, little Laura. You control yourself in the presence of others, you have guts. A real Englishwoman.'

After a short while, she went away for decency's sake. As she was coming down the stairs to go to the veranda, she met Siverac. In the half-light, they almost ran into one another.

'Have you seen Laura?' he asked. 'How is she?'

'Don't go and see her, she knows and she has to be alone with her grief. I left before it erupted, but I heard. It is terrible and it is normal and it breaks my heart.'

'You were right to leave her. Hargrove was vile.'

'What do you mean? It was he who killed Régis,' she said in a whisper.

'I guessed as much,' he said in the same voice. 'But why? He knew nothing of their marriage.'

'Yes, but he didn't want her to get married.'

'To a Catholic, of course.'

'No. He didn't want her to marry at all.'

'What an idea! In general, fathers think of nothing else: anything to marry off their daughters.'

'Mr Siverac, I'm amazed at your innocence.'

'Kindly explain, Miss Llewelyn. I am anxious to know.'

'Very simple. He wanted her all to himself, for ever.'

'Odd!'

'Sometimes, Mr Siverac, you pick on just the right word. Let's call it the last word in this case and say no more.'

But she added, in a sarcastic voice:

'I find that this staircase on which we are standing, neither at the top nor at the bottom, and decidedly closer to the bottom than to the top, is the right place for such revelations. Even the half-light favors them. So, let what we have said never emerge from this half-light.'

'I think I understand . . .'

'You are intelligent, Mr Siverac.'

'But I shall have no further dealings with Hargrove.'

'Only what is strictly necessary during the journey, perhaps.'

Around midnight the rain slackened, then suddenly stopped. A few stars appeared, the breeze drove away the clouds and the constellations shone from one end of the sky to the other.

In the bluish light of dawn, the soldiers harnessed the carriage. They piled their dead into it, then went to fetch Régis' body from the veranda; he was lying where he fell. The shot had hit him in the jugular.

They left accompanied by the other soldiers. The black NCO who had taken command in the dead Lieutenant's place, strongly advised Siverac not to lose any time, but to leave at once.

'De others, dem come wid reinforcemen'. If you go by mountain at once, you safe. We go down big road to cem'try, find priest. Poor Lieutenant!' he added, shaking Siverac's hand.

Without delay, Siverac had the horses and ponies saddled.

Maisie Llewelyn hurried as fast as she could up to Laura's room and found her asleep; but she got up at once when she sensed the Welshwoman's presence. Fleetingly, Maisie had the sense that she was seeing someone she could not recognize. It was not that the young woman's face had aged or grown harder while she was asleep, but simply that she had become someone else, without her appearance changing. The last astonished glimpse of childhood behind the eyes, the look that had attracted Régis, was no longer there.

Without hesitating, she said:

'Are we leaving? You go down, I'll follow.'

On the ground floor, everyone was bustling around in silence as if the house was in the process of dying around them. There had been times when they had hated it because they had been afraid here; but suddenly it reminded them of wonderful moments, the memory of which now became unbearable. They gathered outside with a suppressed feeling of relief.

# 85

*B*y the time they were all mounted, the darkness was slowly lifting. Siverac led the party, with Maisie Llewelyn and Frank on either side of Laura, who sat expertly on a horse with a flowing mane. You could see that she was determined to keep up appearances, in the English way, at all costs. The same could not be said of Hargrove, who had refused the honor of leading the little band at Siverac's side and chose to protect the rear, next to Betty, protected by his six Blacks.

The road, carpeted with pebbles and moss, was broad and rose, at first imperceptibly, toward a hillock crowned by a pale cloud, while the mist lingered below them in the valleys. The ponies and horses kept up a gentle trot, only slowing to a walk when the road climbed sharply. The air was soft, and there were still some stars fading from the timid blue of a sky which was barely light.

The hill they were skirting let them glimpse here and there, through its covering of stumpy little trees, as though through holes in a dark green coat, the bright red fruit of the mancenilliers. No one said anything. The only sound in the silence of first light was the hard, sharp sound of the horses' hooves. Now the road they were following dipped down into a valley along a succession of gently inclined slopes. They continued almost constantly at the same pace, by the sides of the mountains, one hill after another; and, as they were traveling toward the West, remained in the cover of the shadows which hid them from enemy eyes. As exhilarating as it was dangerous, the itinerary spared the fugitives a journey along roads which would have been transformed into quagmires by the previous day's storm and which, ordinarily, might be used as cover for ambushes by rebel groups. Siverac guessed that the mulattoes would return with reinforcements to the place they had left, but the distance between them and the fleeing Whites was getting greater.

Cradled by the steady pace of their mounts, they were all deep in their thoughts and only saw the landscape through the veil of their dreams. For Laura, the child she was carrying inside her was joined with the soul of the lost beloved, and she already gave it all the love that was in her heart.

Miss Llewelyn watched her out of the corner of an eye, admiring her for recovering her poise. She could surely not be aware of the source of the shot that had killed the lieutenant, and she must never know; but what kind of figure was the vile criminal cutting, at the end of the line, as they rode on in single file?

Other thoughts were buzzing in young Frank's head as he rode along beside his sister. Irritated by the cautious pace of the journey, he wished he could spur on his horse and gallop across the mountains. With a bit of luck, he might find a tribe of Sioux dressed in eagle's feathers, which had strayed here by some accident of history. In his own way, he was dreaming too, and the previous day's events mingled with his reveries.

At the back, surrounded by Blacks and protected but not reassured, because nothing in the world now could restore his peace of mind, William Hargrove felt he had escaped from one nightmare into another, into which fate had pushed him with such gentle deceitfulness. No one suspected anything, no one had seen, and he had thrown his pistol under a cupboard; so he could rest easy, while turning a well-trained eye on the features of the landscape; but he had the unpleasant sensation of silent laughter coming from he knew not where.

Meanwhile, the little band was crossing a ridge and on each side you could look down into deep valleys, bristling with scrub. A light flickered on the horizon and almost in a single instant daylight flooded the sky, revealing a chain of mountains of a deep, dull blue, its softness giving an impression of velvet. A unanimous gasp greeted this eruption of beauty into a world ravaged by hatred, and the hearts of the travelers beat as if a song of hope were rising out of the earth.

Instinctively, they stopped for a moment to contemplate the great message and afterwards set off down small paths, some way away from the main roads where hostile forces might venture. The land rose and fell gently enough for them to travel quite quickly, but they were careful not to speak for fear of echoes.

Sometimes, vultures circled above them in country that had grown wilder. They began to feel slightly anxious again, but hours passed without incident as they rode beside empty prairies. Everything in this solitude spoke of fighting and flight.

They soon found themselves having to ride through a pine forest where they vanished in the midst of shadows broken by long rays of light. The pine needles made the ground slippery, even dangerous and difficult, but the sturdy Haitian ponies knew where to put their hard little hooves. Suddenly, the path dropped toward a valley in which the silence was so deep that it seemed audible.

They came to a deserted plot of land. Banana plants trailed their huge leaves on the ground up to a house with a broken roof, its doors and windows, like empty eye-sockets, opening on an orchard overgrown with weeds. Here peach trees dropped wild fruit over which an army of green budgerigars squabbled in a great flutter of wings and tiny cries. It was ten in the morning. Siverac suggested they stop. Betty at once set to work. She had thought of everything. In a few moments, with capable skill and energy, she had spread out a cloth on the grass with an array of biscuits and slices of cold meat. Two Blacks set out to look for drinking water and soon found it in a mountain stream running lower down the hill.

They spent an hour beneath the trees.

When they set out again, the light was dazzling. The road was winding, but the altitude varied little, ranging between six and seven hundred meters. The hills to the West were covered in thicker forests. Little by little the paths were leading them through a paradise. Between the enormous trunks of the mahogany trees, they could see on an opposite slope the white shimmer of a river falling from waterfall to waterfall, sometimes flowing over a bed of creepers and sometimes entirely hidden behind them. From tree to tree hung garlands, festoons and draperies of live flowers. The shadows in the forest through which they rode appeared blue. From time to time, in the thick fabric of greenery, broad openings appeared, full of orchids, where the humming-birds hovered.

Without realizing it, the travelers slowed down as if they were themselves part of the dream of nature itself.

As the afternoon advanced, the light softened. Once more they paused, this time beside a waterfall.

'Do you realize,' Siverac asked, 'that we still have two full hours to go before we arrive at the little fort where we will be safe for the night? We shall have done in twelve hours what can hardly be done in a day, ordinarily.'

'Hey-ho!' said Maisie Llewelyn. 'At times, we were going at breakneck speed.'

'Would you rather we had burned in the house?'

'And after the fort, what?' she asked.

'We'll try to get to the coast, avoiding small towns and the plantations of small settlers who may not be trustworthy in this region.'

'But they are white!'

'So what? Personal interest, politics and fear have no color.'

'Let's go.'

'Come on everyone. In the saddle!'

The Welshwoman took her place on Laura's left and they continued their route through the greenery. Nothing could surpass the beauty of what they had before their eyes: a torrent dropped from one escarpment to another and its waters were smothered in foam on which a rainbow shimmered; giant roots, clasping basalt rocks as dark as they were, served as the starting-point for aerial plants which leaped from one trunk to the next, enveloping them in a deluge of flowers; there was a tumble of corollas, a battle of wild colors behind which one could glimpse flashes of silver tremors of water; on the hillsides, paths ran and suddenly turned back on themselves as if afraid of plunging down a precipice. The brilliant clouds massed on the summits cast their shadows across part of the distant view, but the upland breezes cleared the air and a whole valley could be seen, exposed in every details as though through a spyglass. Where a moment before only a few spots had been visible, one felt one could reach out and touch the yellow wall of a hut sunk in the midst of the greenery, near the dark mirror of a solitary pool. And everywhere, the length of the iron slopes of the mountain, the forest extended like moss, deep green in the ravines where the wild jasmin exploded in flowers. In the course of their flight, and almost subconsciously, they saw places whose names would soon become memories: Le Dondon, with its milk-white church and its cluster of cabins clinging around the *morne*; and, toward the Northern Plain, beyond Marmelade, the long flat tiles of ruined sugar factories; and they cut across the roads leading to Plaisance, Le Gros Morne, Babiole, or toward the West. The hills were sometimes pitted with black holes, which were caves, and sometimes the dazzled eye could not bear to look at the great crevices, which were quarries of alabaster or chalk, that blinded one in the sunlight.

Their shadows lengthened in front of them, covering the fiery disk of the sun. A forest of little trees extended down into the valley. Often they were held up by spiky bushes or cacti blocking their paths, but the mere mention of Fortin Paradis revived in them the hope of a night's rest safe from all harm. Siverac did not stop searching the horizon until, at last, a building in bluish stone appeared in his spyglass. In the distance, he could only distinguish the outlines of the cubic pile, but as they drew nearer, he thought he could make out sentries in the bushes on the road leading to the fort. A few moments later and he was certain of it. He called one of the Blacks and was the first to try to verify what he had seen. He called out to them in vain: they did not move . . . At closer range what he discovered made him shudder with horror, even more so the black man he had to restrain. The sentries were scarecrows. Posts had been dressed up in uniforms, surmounted by a severed head which had almost completely dried out in the sun. A kepi hung over the corner of an empty eye-socket gave the grinning globe a mocking and aggressive air. At once, Siverac and the Black cut down these macabre dolls to prevent Frank and Laura from seeing them, and the travelers were soon able to arrive at the courtyard of the little fort, built of bright blue volcanic rock which still showed beneath its covering of moss and lichen. Casemates, their doors torn off, stood wide open, facing one another, filled almost to door level with stagnant water in which a pile of munitions was rusting.

However, a wide canopy roof, extending down quite a long way, provided a kind of shelter under which the travelers could lie down and sleep on long banana leaves, cut that same afternoon by the Blacks in the orchard with the green budgerigars.

The men took it in turn to stand guard on the stone rampart, protecting the safety of the whole group, but the task was made easier by the enchanting beauty of the landscape. The summer moon in all its glory spread silence across the hills and bathed them in a supernatural light in which everything seemed like a vision. It was easy to believe that, in a waking dream, these masses had become luminous and were ingeniously floating beyond the world, in that silence which the moon renders even more silent.

Dawn put an end to these delights. At daybreak, the ponies and horses were saddled and the travelers set forth. They had a whole day's journey in front of them, but they felt refreshed by a night of real sleep.

At first, at least, everything appeared to be working in their favor. The road sloped down between two hillocks and, when the sun began to warm the air, they were riding between rows of plane trees whose long branches curved above them; but long before midday they had the impression that they were being swallowed up by a furnace which was there to block their way by depriving them of the spirit to continue. Yet on they went, nevertheless, looking out for a patch of shade in which to rest. Every now and then, hidden behind the trees, plantations belonging to French settlers seemed to offer them shelter, but Siverac was cautious and would not hear of it. They were obliged to skirt past them as far away as possible, their hearts heavy and their clothes stuck to shoulders and backs.

Finally they reached Trois-Rivières, a stream formed by three torrents which did exhale a suggestion of coolness. They rode beside it convincing themselves that they were suffering less.

However, the landscape was changing. The hills were getting lower and lower, giving way to mere foothills. For two days, they continued their exodus, climbing and descending difficult paths, only too happy when they found a wood and could take cover under the trees, since it was better for fugitives not to attract attention; then, on the second evening, they were able to make a kind of resting camp behind some giant rushes on a river bank. The next morning, suddenly, a breeze brought them the salt smell of the sea. Their journey was nearly at an end, but now the road was flat and they were crossing a plain in which the heat had become humid and exhausting. They stopped.

'It would be a pity to die in the port,' said Maisie Llewelyn to Siverac. 'I'm not so much afraid for myself as for the girl. She has not said a word since we left the house. There are times when she frightens me.'

'The smell of the sea means there must be a beach close by. At least we can lie down there for a while. Port-de-Paix is at the end of the road, ahead of us.'

They set out again, saying nothing as in a bad dream, and soon they reached the creek — but, to their great surprise, it was covered by an army of crabs. Luckily this multitude, hidden under the strands of seaweed, vanished at the sound of their approach, and the travelers, their legs shaking with exhaustion, were able to flop down on to the sand beneath the shade of the pines.

Only Frank could not keep still. With the impetuosity of his age, he ran after the crabs who tried to escape him, their backs covered with bits of seaweed. In a narrower cove, a trap for silt-laden water, the tide had left behind all kinds of jetsam — rotten wood, shells — and the boy disturbed some hungry little crabs gnawing at the corpse of a sea pelican. The smell of rotten flesh drove him away and he walked back to his sister, who was resting, looking out to sea, dead to all around her.

Both more robust, Siverac and Maisie Llewelyn were standing under the trees looking at their sleeping companions.

'Dirty, smelly and in rags,' said Siverac.

'Like us,' the Welshwoman remarked.

'Like highway robbers.'

'Or quite simply like poor people. We carry on our persons all the stench of poverty. These wretched people are exhausted, but they are out of danger now.'

'For the time being, perhaps, but the most dangerous part of the journey is still to come: reaching La Tortue.'

Someone pulled at his sleeve. He turned round and saw no one, then recognized Betty, who scarcely reached his shoulders. She was decked out in torn clothes knotted around her little body with string, but around her neck hung the modest gold cross which she had been given by her late mistress, Laura's mother.

'Massa' Siverac,' she said, full of excitement. 'Betty go find boat for La Tortue. Betty know Port-de-Paix well. Two of Betty's cousins in Port-de-Paix.'

'Let her go,' Maisie Llewelyn said to Siverac. 'I know her. She will help us.'

'Also need one black man,' said Betty.

'Take Ezechiel.'

'Very well,' said Betty.

And putting her hands to her mouth she called:

'Zikiel!'

A minute later, Zikiel appeared. He had fallen asleep at the foot of a tree, some way apart from the Whites, and came running. Thickset, smiling, in linen clothes which were almost in rags, he went straight up to Siverac and said:

'Yassa.'

Siverac motioned toward Betty.

'Do as she tells you.'

Both of them set out in the direction of the town.


In one way or another, all the streets ended at an avenue which led to the Place Louis XVI. There was a gilded statue there, which might represent a naked woman with some confusedly allegorical significance. The one-storey wooden houses stood next to one another, but not aligned, all their windows open.

It was the hour when the whole town was outside. An orange light added splendor to this late afternoon, as it did to the promenade of fashionable ladies in white chiffon, accompanied by their beaux in red or royal blue jackets with embroidered trimmings. Among the women some were of astounding beauty; their daringly plunging necklines revealed enough to play havoc with the young dandies circling around them. Many of the latter had let their curls grow until they could make a pony tail, adorned by a scarlet bow, which hung down their necks. A loud murmur rose from this crowd, the charming chatter of black voices. Betty was walking along, looking to right and left, when a young fop in a blue jacket with red collar accidently bumped into her.

'Can't you see straight?' he cried. 'Where you goin'? You lookin' foh summun?'

She stared at him in bewilderment.

'My cousin. She live here.'

The boy seemed friendly enough.

'And what she called, your cousin?'

'Ida 'icou.'

'Ida 'icou! She live right here in de avenue. Ever'one know Ida 'icou.'

Betty thanked him and started down the avenue. Little one-storey houses, some in wood, a few in brick, were all covered in honeysuckle and its heady scent was perfuming the approaches of dusk.

On their doorsteps, ladies spread their ample limbs across luxurious, fan-backed rattan chairs and smoked their pipes while watching the fashionable young people parade up and down. They talked among themselves, called out to one another, mocking, in the know . . .

When Betty appeared with her Black, there was a moment of surprise, because the stranger was striding forth boldly. A flute-like voice rang out:

'Oh, la, la! Madam in chiffon think she a p'incess!'

Without hesitation, Betty replied loudly and clearly:

'Madam in chiffon has come to call on her black brudders and sisters for help.'

'Help? Who gonna help you, den?'

There was the sound of merry laughter, and the one who had spoken rocked back and forth in her chair.

'My cousin, Ida 'icou.'

'Ida 'icou! Why din' you say so?'

And, clasping her pipe, the lady sat up a little and called:

'Ho, dere! Ida! Ida-a-a!'

From almost opposite, on the other side of the avenue, a resounding voice came from beneath a veranda:

'What you wan', now, Lili? Ida is here, so what den?'

'Your cousin lookin' for you.'

'I hab got no cousin here, Lili. Dat's not true-oo-oo!'

Betty crossed the avenue and went toward the place from which the voice had come. The house, which was quite small and hidden by honeysuckle, seemed even smaller because of the enormously fat woman sitting in front of the door, dressed in mauve cotton with puffed-out folds. The exceptionally wide sleeves left her superb primadonna's arms free. Her hair, a mass of curls, hung around a face whose flesh, held taut by fat, showed no sign of wrinkles. Her whole body exuded that peculiar benevolence possessed by so many black women. As soon as she saw Betty coming toward her, she cried:

'What you doin' here, den? You in some kinda trouble?'

'Oh, yes, my poor Ida. I'm here wid Zikiel. He's good and he help me a lot.'

Ida got up immediately.

'Well, come in, both of you!'

Going ahead of them, she led them into a room which was so dark that at first they could see nothing except a huge bunch of dahlias which appeared to be emerging from the darkness to examine them as they came in, like huge open eyes.

'I gonna make you a good strong coffee, to revive you,' said Ida.

She bustled around a good deal and vanished into the interior from which her voice could still be heard.

'You sit down. I'm in de kitchen.'

They did not move. In order to explain as briefly as possible why she was there, Betty remarked:

'The house done burn.'

'Oh, my poor girl!' said the kitchen in unison.

Like a sort of mauve cloud, Ida reappeared and, hurrying to the door, cried out in a powerful voice:

'Betty house done burn!'

Cries of lamentation arose spontaneously from the neighboring doors:

'Oh! Oh! Oh!'

Ida turned back to Betty:

'Who done burn your house?'

'Bandits. They done shoot at little Laura's husband and he dead,' said Betty, suddenly bursting into tears.

'And bandits done kill little Laura's husband,' Ida repeated at the top of her voice, to bring the neighborhood up to date with the news.

No one knew who little Laura was, but the choir of lamentations echoed loudly in the gathering dusk.

'Oh, de poor girl! Oh, oh, de poor little girl!'

'So she goin' 'way,' Betty continued, 'wid her family. And she need a boat.'

'How dat: a boat?'

'To go to La Tortue.'

'Betty wanna boat to go to La Tortue wid her fam'ly,' Ida announced in a singsong.

Suddenly she muttered:

'My coffee!'

The back of the room seemed to swallow her up and Betty found herself alone with Ezechiel. Their eyes were growing accustomed to the half-light. They could make out a bench in front of a little table and sat down on it. Outside the wailing was resumed, but the tone was slightly different.

'A boat, poor girl! Of course, to go away. A boat, a boat, dat not so easy to find!'

'Have to ask Commandant Thomas.'

'Ho, ho! Commandant Thomas don't let everybody leave the

harbor! The harbor's shut, fear of French ships.'

Ida returned with a large metal coffee pot which she put on the table.

'Commandant Thomas!' she exclaimed. 'You leave the harbor only if the drum sounds . . .'

She leaned out of the window. In the last rays of a reddish sky, the pipe smoke was rising directly upward in blue spirals outside every house.

'Is there drum this evening?'

'Not if the commandant see something.'

'The commandant only see what he believe he see, like his patron saint.'

'But it's all backways, what you're saying,' Betty said. 'He believe what him see.'

'Not Commandant Thomas. He believe first, then he see it.'

'He believe whatever you want if you give him Creole water.'

There was a burst of laughter.

'Zikiel,' said Ida. 'Go fetch the cups. Under the bed; but mind, you can't see a thing.'

She vanished once more and came back a minute later with a lighted candle which she stood up in the middle of the table in a drop of molten wax. At first the little flame flickered, hesitantly, then revealed a room decorated with shirts, laddered stockings and undergarments on a string which was hung across one corner, half hiding a white wood wardrobe. High off the ground, a huge metal bedstead occupied a distant corner under a pile of red eiderdowns. By lying flat on the floor, Ezechiel managed to reach the large porcelain cups lurking in some murky corner.

Meanwhile, Ida had established herself in a rattan chair and was giving Betty her instructions:

'You go'n fetch de family and tomorrow morning we'll have de boat.'

'How will you manage that?'

'You do as Ida say or you'll stay here. Understood?'

Betty nodded and Ida continued:

'You bring all the orders here. They'll sleep in the garden: there are hammocks on the trees.'

Leaning out of the window, she said in a deep and ringing voice:

'Tonight they'll sleep in my garden and we'll take care of the boat. Agreed, girls?'

A unanimous 'yes!' came back, with a puff of 'Oh! Oh! Oh!'

'Betty,' said Ida. 'Go quick and find 'em and bring 'em here.'

Without a moment's hesitation, Betty left at full speed. Between Ida and the rest of the avenue, the dialogue continued in the heroic tone adopted for days of great activity:

'Tomorrow, is Saint Thomas' Day and the commandant's feast.

We lucky, girls, we can make music. We'll all go to the port.'

'Then you . . . music? Oh, oh!'

'Drum, trumpet and bamboulas, understand?'

'Oh, la! Understand! Long live the commandant's feast day and the drum, drum, drum!'

'Now, now: tomorrow girls! Don't be too hasty.'

'All to the port and boom! Boom!'

'But first we must paint them all!'

'Paint them? What do you mean?'

'Paint them black with soot! That way he no believe anything because he no see anything!'

'Oh, la! Ah, ha, ha!'

The rest was lost in an explosion of merriment while the moon rose on the horizon above the terraces of the town.

At that very moment, Betty was returning to the group of fugitives who were already growing concerned at her prolonged absence. Instinctively, they all counted on the little black woman. She reached them in a state of over-excitement which made it difficult for her to talk, but she quickly gave them to understand that they had to follow her and spend the night in her cousin Ida's garden, and that the boat would be ready the next morning. As usual, it was the Welshwoman, standing in the shadow under the pine trees in the creek, who took the most immediate decision. She listened to the panting messenger until she had finished and announced:

'It's mad but it's our only hope. Betty, we'll follow you.'

In order to avoid the square, which was full of over-curious dandies and ladies, Betty took them on a roundabout detour through deserted streets and, less than half an hour later, they were making their way up the main avenue. There, by the light of the lamps in the windows, they were greeted with an unexpected ovation from the local pipe-smokers.

Ida welcomed them like a mother, offered them dinner and then took them to a spacious garden where the hammocks were waiting for them. There were not enough for everybody, but the Blacks asked nothing better than to lie down in the grass.

A warm feeling of security allowed every eye to shut almost instantly. The songs of the birds and the cries of the budgerigars awoke them from a pleasant sleep. Only Laura had been unable to sleep, but she mentioned it to no one . . .

While her companions were performing their very summary ablutions, Maisie Llewelyn, who was up before everyone, went to look for the mistress of the house:

'Ida, we shall not forget what you are doing for us . . . You are a woman of feeling and action. All our horses, outside, are yours. Twelves animals for a boat!'

'Oh, la, la! Ma'am!'

They began to laugh and the two women embraced.
'You take care of my Betty,' said Ida.
'I promise, I swear! We love your Betty.'

# 86

*A*t daybreak, the promised sailing ship was swaying gently in the waters of the harbor. Meanwhile, Ida and her accomplices smothered the white travelers' faces with soot, carefully applied in several layers, because it would have to last. Maisie Llewelyn and Siverac submitted docilely to this; Frank, who still preserved a sense of adventure, was enthusiastic, and Laura was resigned.

The harbor was quiet and empty; facing each other at each point of the crescent were two forts, armed with cannon. Along the quay-side, under the coconut trees, black barrels and piles of wood waited to be loaded. Clouds of iridescent pink floated in the early morning sky over this austere scene.

A little to one side stood what was called the Commandant's Office, a brick house with arcades covered in pink tiles. It was almost entirely surrounded by coconut palms, shading it from the sun.

Sitting on a chair at the office door, a sentry with his legs wide apart was chewing sugar cane; his gun was propped against the wall. On the door, in large capital letters, was a notice with the following inscription:

STRENGTH TO THE LAW
Tranquillity and order reign here.
Every person leaving must have a passport.
Every person entering must have a passport.

Several minutes went by and nothing disturbed this peaceful picture, when suddenly a distant rumble seemed to emerge from the deep silence. One had to strain to hear it and the sentry was dreaming of something else entirely as he chewed on his length of sugar cane.

However, the noise came closer, dull and regular, though the rhythm was hard to pin down.

The sentry got up and, just in case, picked up his gun.

It was then that he saw coming from one end of the square, about forty large women with multicolored cotton scarves, dressed in light-colored skirts and blouses — lilac, pink, pale green, sky blue, white, and one in bright red, like a shout in a flowerbed. All of them were black, but their coloring varied from coffee to ebony; and all were humming softly, their arms laden with all sorts of instruments for making noise: drums, bamboulas and conch shells.

The sentry instinctively raised his gun, but they laughed in his face and began to form a semi-circle around Commandant Thomas' door at a respectful distance, not without waddling very slightly . . . The sentry himself began to smile without taking any notice of a group of uninteresting and shabbily dressed Blacks who were slipping past behind the musicians in the direction of the sailing boat.

The door of the office opened sharply and Commandant Thomas appeared, peering aggressively. Very imposing in his gold-braided, high-buttoned uniform, he seemed nonetheless to be wavering ever so little on his long legs, while managing to preserve the proud and dissatisfied demeanor of a man who has been drinking — because he was a hard drinker, Commandant Thomas . . . And it was at that moment that, in front of him, from out of a mauve cloud, a magnificent arm emerged offering him a large glass full of Creole water. Without a word he took it, sniffed it and brought it to his lips, while wily Ida raised another glass, full of pure water, and in an enchanting voice sang softly to him:

'Happy feast day, Commandant! To yore reddy precious 'ealth!'

Saying which, she emptied her own glass, while he did the same with his; and knocked back by this unexpected tumblerful, he swayed and had to support himself with one shoulder against the doorpost.

A simple nod was enough for Ida to give the signal to the women, who all began to sway, at first with a stealthy slowness, while at the same time tapping their fingertips over the flat drums and bamboulas, which they were holding with one arm against their bodies. The hum filled the whole square and grew louder little by little as the swaying of the hips grew ever more rapid. And suddenly these huge bodies were swept away in the voluptuous tide of a compelling dance, to the sound of the dull thunder of the drums, and voices of exquisite purity raised melodious nonsense to the blue heavens:

'Is yore feast, Comm'dant Thomas.
We gonna catch great big lobster
For yore feast day, Comm'dant Thomas.'

Already the little band of true and false Blacks had crept into the boat when Ida, with her energetic arms, beat out on an army drum the official drum roll that signaled the opening of the harbor.

Commandant Thomas, almost knocked out by a second glass of Creole water, saw and heard all this in the euphoria of a waking dream.

# 87

Now outside the port, the sailing boat skimmed across the foaming waters, plunging, then rising at the mercy of the waves. Haiti appeared and disappeared by turns, because there were dangerous currents in the stretch of water separating them from the Island of La Tortue, moving unpredictably beneath the surface as if storms were brewing down below. Shadows of sharks prowled around the ship. None of the fugitives moved or said a word, leaving the Blacks to manage the sails. After several minutes, the happy noise of singing and dancing from the harbor square could only faintly be heard, like a fading memory, and their hearts ached. The moment came when they had sailed far enough away to see the island, which seemed to grow flatter as they drew away from it, but as they saw it then, remained strangely beautiful and attractive. The magical enchantment of Haiti reawakened in each of them joyful hours for ever lost. Frank could not reconcile himself to losing the immense possibilities for adventure that the island had promised. Even the Welshwoman, always so imperturbable, could not repress a few sighs. Laura had slumped in a corner of the boat. The wind was tossing her hair and it was hanging down in strands over her face without her noticing. In the depth of her soul, a voice murmured to her that after the disappearance of the man she had loved, the world could never again have any meaning.

And the Blacks, in silence, gazed with eyes full of love at their native land as it slowly faded away.

La Tortue approached like a huge forest rising out of the sea. When they were quite close, the sailors tilted the sails to set course for the port of Cayonne, of which nothing could be seen, though numerous sandy creeks were appearing in the forest which extended right down to the water's edge.

There was a crowd at the landing bay. The arrival of a boat was the great entertainment of the morning. Their heads covered in knotted handkerchiefs, the women came out wearing aprons of every hue, while the men, barefoot, chattering, laughing, dressed in trousers that ended above the knee, commented on the display of seamanship.

The welcome was far from hostile. On the contrary, the travelers were greeted with smiles. They immediately made for what was described as the town. It was as simple as could be: little narrow streets with wooden houses covered in palm-leaves instead of roofs. Seeing that these strangers had no idea where to go, an old black woman offered to serve as their guide. It was not far. She took them to a shed with second-hand clothes, crumpled but clean. Maisie

Llewelyn and Siverac joked and soon found what they needed, as did young Frank, always ready for the unexpected; but Hargrove scowled at them, decking himself out in a cloth suit which was far too big for him and wounding to his dignity. Laura obediently put on a cotton skirt and blouse: its multi-colored appearance was in contrast to the young woman's solemn expression, which would have been better suited to mourning clothes. As for Betty, she was satisfied with a little blue dress which Miss Llewelyn chose for her. The Blacks soon pulled on trousers of coarse white cloth, while the fake Blacks, with their soot-covered faces, looked suspicious, but no one remarked on it.

Several houses were empty. Siverac rented as many as they needed for all of them. A lot of water was poured into tubs and, in less than two hours, the fugitives, restored to their natural color, left their temporary accommodation for a meeting under the trees, to examine their situation. In their second-hand clothes, they looked like a troupe of actors who had been hired to play in a farce, and the inhabitants of Cayonne, curious to have a look at these newcomers, ran away when they saw them, giggling with laughter. Maisie Llewelyn, Siverac and Frank shared their good humor, but Hargrove was pained by it and Betty took Laura to one side to protect her from the high spirits of the others.

When tranquillity was restored, Siverac announced:

'For the time being, all is turning out for the best. We may look a trifle ridiculous, but what does that matter? We are escaping from tragedy into healthy laughter, except . . .'

He looked around and, not seeing Laura, concluded gravely:

'Except the young victim, who has been so cruelly smitten.'

As he said these words, he glanced at Hargrove, who was staring into the distance.

'Betty has been considerate enough to take her into the woods,' Maisie Llewelyn said.

Siverac continued:

'An English frigate is due to stop off at Cayonne, it seems, in four or five days' time. We can wait. Nature has provided for all our needs. There is a superabundance of fruit. The creeks seem to be paved with the best red crabs in the world. Moreover, the local people have welcomed us kindly. Let us wait patiently in this little paradise.'

The first day was peaceful, with pleasant moments for some. The natives, who had little to do, asked nothing better than to introduce these foreigners to the beauties of their island in which they took great pride. There were walks through woods of grapefruit and lemon trees. This is where Betty brought Laura in the hope of taking her mind off things, because she loved her and could not bear to see her eaten up with grief, and saying nothing about it. Humming-birds flew around them, their piping notes following them through the solitary woods. Sometimes the young woman would smile, but she asked no questions because nothing interested her any longer. From time to time she would touch the emerald necklace which she wore hidden beneath her dress.

For his part, Frank set off on adventurous explorations of the rocks above the sea. His head full of exciting stories he had read in books, he desperately hoped that chance would lead him to the mysterious grottoes where old time buccaneers had hidden fabulous treasures. So he wandered off through forests which stretched right down to the edge of the water, deep blue like a fragment of the night sky.

After an hour of fruitless comings and goings, he was returning sheepishly in the direction of the town, but had decided to take a new route to get there. At another end of Cayonne were little houses, set at some distance from one another, one of them in particular seemed to be set distinctly apart at the edge of the water, near a dry stone jetty. To distance itself still further, it was painted red. Frank's heart began to beat. With his sense of adventure, he instinctively felt that he was on the brink of something exciting, and made his way furtively toward the half-open door. A notice stuck to the post brought him up with a start. In capital letters, it bore the following inscription:

WHOEVER ENTERS HERE WITHOUT PERMISSION
DOES SO AT THE RISK OF HIS LIFE

and, instead of a signature, two crossed bones.

He withdrew, unsure of himself. It was too good. He recognized the rhetorical language of pirates and was tempted to doff his little straw hat, but he felt frightened in the way he had always dreamed he might, and shrank back a step. The moments that followed were unforgettable. To run away would mean losing face. He would gain nothing by staying where he was. He decided to walk round in front of the red house, giving it quite a wide berth. When he was exactly opposite the half-open door, he had a pricking sensation in his scalp but, being at the very height of his adventurous excitement, he swore he would not move. At first he could see nothing; then, suddenly, a clear, firm voice came out of the house:

'One more step and I'll fire.'

Frank summoned up all his courage and pride. He reminded himself that heroes had to remain firm in such circumstances. In a slightly choked voice, he called out:

'Why? I am not doing anything. I have the right . . .'

There was a sinister laugh and the voice replied:

'You are on my territory. One!'

Frank did not flinch, but he thought, I am staying, I am staying, I am staying. An inner voice adjusted this: Between two and three, you must cut and run.

He waited, his ears buzzing with terror. 'Two' never came, but the voice said:

'Come here.'

At the same time, the door was kicked open and he saw a tall man sitting on a chair inside the house, near the entrance. His dark-red, tousled hair, stood up above a mocking, sunburnt face, with rough, though regular features. Long trousers, dyed blood-red, covered his powerful legs and there was a cutlass shining in his belt. His large hand was idly toying with a pistol. He did not take his green eyes off the young boy who did his best to hold the man's hard gaze.

'Who are you and what's your name?'

'I have just arrived from Haiti. My name is Hargrove . . . Frank,' he added.

'French?'

'American.'

'So much the better for you.'

The gravelly voice betrayed the man's Scottish origins.

'So, what are you doing on La Tortue?'

The answer came like an explosion:

'There are caves on the island.'

The pistol flew into the air and was caught immediately.

'Well, I'll be damned! Are you looking for pirate treasure?'

The man burst out laughing, 'There is only one person who knows the caves here, and that's me.'

Frank blushed . . . Suddenly getting up, the man slipped the pistol into a holster on his belt. When he stood up, his head seemed to touch the ceiling.

'How long are you staying on my island?'

'Only a few days. We're going to Jamaica.'

'Too bad. You were not afraid when I threatened to shoot, so one might get along with a lad like you.'

With his hands on his hips, he considered Frank and smiled.

'I would have taught you to fish with a harpoon and to shoot like a real buccaneer,' he said.

A strange unease swept over Frank as though he had been on the point of landing in one of those unknown lands described in his books, while at the same time a hand was dragging him back.

'Buccaneer . . .' he repeated, without thinking.

'You are talking to a pirate, my boy.'

And, without giving him the chance to catch his breath, he said:

'Captain Kidd — does that name mean anything to you. The Prince of Pirates.'

'Oh, I've read about him!'

'I could tell it to you better than any book . . . I should have shown you the caves where the pirates stowed their booty. What do you want to be later on in life? They'll send you to school, you'll be like all the rest.'

Frank was disturbed by this incoherent speech and he had a vague suspicion that the man might be mad.

'You are young and sturdy,' he went on. 'I could have made a man out of you.'

And looking at him with a sudden burst of anger, he shouted:

'There, now, go away! Begone from here!'

Frank left instantly and, once outside the house, he felt a growing anxiety which made him walk faster; then, shamelessly, he began to run.

Back in his room, he lay down flat on his bed, his heart thumping. The buccaneer's guttural voice was still ringing in his ears and he wondered if he had not escaped being murdered; but this retrospective alarm was mingled with the vague feeling that he had touched upon the great dream of adventure, which had been devastated by an incompehensible outburst of rage.

A few houses away, Maisie Llewelyn was standing opposite William Hargrove in his room. The door was wide open. Sitting on the edge of his bed of leaves, he was bent double, his head in his hands, while the Welshwoman lectured him:

'In heaven's name, Willie, make an effort. Stop looking like someone who has been sent to the galleys. In a few days an English ship will take you to some peaceful country. So? At least try to appear like a man when there are other people around. Perhaps you have problems: well, who doesn't?'

He looked up at her in despair:

'Oh, Maisie! If only you knew how dreadful it is to be me!'

The Welshwoman had not been expecting this remark and it went to her heart. Overcome with pity, she adopted a jovial tone:

'Come, come. One day you'll tell your Maisie all about it; she's heard much worse. Meanwhile, I'll shorten your sleeves and hem your trousers so that you look a little less ridiculous in that giant's costume.'

'Maisie, I want to die.'

'No, Willie, don't start that. No grand notions. We are all capable of everything and those who think themselves better are not worth much. Have some guts, Willie Hargrove. Pretend — like everyone else.'

He grasped the bedpost and managed to get to his feet.

'I want to ask you to do something for me.'

'Willingly.'

'Call my Blacks. I want to talk to them.'

'What's got into you? Are you going to make a speech to them? But I will call them if you like. It's not hard. There are two in front of the house.'

She went out and motioned to the Blacks who came at once.

'Yes, Ma'am.'

'Go and find all your friends and tell them to come here. Mr Hargrove wants to speak to them.'

'Yes, Ma'am. We'll fin' 'em.'

'Be quick.'

'It will take a while,' she said, returning to Hargrove. 'They have to be found first of all. So be patient.'

In the little room, furnished as crudely as could be imagined, there was at least a white wooden rocking chair. She sat down in it.

'I'll try to take your mind off things,' she said, crossing her hands over her belly, and she began to rock.

Hargrove was now walking to and fro, somewhat consoled by the rough but well-intentioned words of this woman who, he told himself, knew nothing.

'I should also like  . . . .' he said, in a rush of self-pity, 'I should very much like to talk to my dear little Laura.'

'Oh, Laura!' said the Welshwoman, rocking forcefully. 'You'll see her later. Betty has taken her for a walk in the woods and it will be hard to find them in those mysterious depths . . .' (she admired this conclusion).

'I want to see her. I think she's been looking unwell the past few days.'

'It's this journey, Willie.'

'I should never forgive myself if she were to fall ill.'

'You are so kind. You're a model father.'

He look at her anxiously:

'Do you think so, Maisie? Are you serious?'

'Can you doubt it?'

There was a moment's silence. The chair creaked with irritating regularity on the uneven floor.

'It's taking a long time,' said Hargrove, sitting on the bed.

'No its not. Try and take your mind of thing by thinking about your plans. Anyway, they're coming, your Blacks . . . I can see them at the end of the street. What eagerness!'

They were indeed arriving, all six of them. They stood at the door, vaguely anxious, expecting a reprimand. Hargrove reassured them with a smile.

'The room is too small for you all to come in,' he said. 'One will be enough.'

There was a long pause while these heads, with their dark good looks, turned to one another, followed by some whispering. Finally one of them emerged, tall, broad-shouldered, his eyes fixed.

'Yassa,' he said

In a gentle voice, Hargrove began:

'You have served me for many years, you have never disobeyed me, you are like my children. If you want to go back to your home, you may leave, I shall give you twice what I owe you. If you wish to follow us to America, you will be in my service over there, but you will remain free. It is for you to choose.'

There were new consultations between the black heads and more whisperings, but this time distraught ones; then suddenly, in a single voice:

'We'll leave with you and the family.'

'Very well. I am happy at that. The boat will be here in a few days. That's all.'

Wide smiles were exchanged. All of them bowed slightly and retired, at first backward, then dispersing into the street where they had already made friends.

The chair was no longer rocking and Maisie Llewelyn, with a finger to her lips, was looking thoughtfully at William Hargrove.

'Well, I must say, that's something very fine you did there, Willie,' she said at last.

He looked at her with the same anxiety as before.

'Do you think so?' he asked.

'I do. Sometimes the heart speaks. I shall leave you now, but I'll be back in a few minutes. Wait for me.'

She went off to look for Siverac, and found him in the shed.

'I'm dressed absurdly,' he said, rummaging through the second-hand clothes. 'If by chance I were to find something better . . . Just imagine: going to speak to the captain of an English ship in this get-up . . .'

'We have only to give him a hint of our story and he will understand, you may be sure of that. But let's leave that for the moment, may we? We have to make up our minds about William Hargrove.'

'I'm not interested in Hargrove.'

'Perhaps not, but there's still Laura . . . We must tell Hargrove that she is married.'

'Why, since her husband is dead?'

'But the marriage might have consequences . . .'

'And can you imagine his fury at having been duped?'

'I can, very easily, but I'm not frightened by it. Are you?'

'No, but first of all let's get away from Haiti and La Tortue, and speak to him when we are out to sea.'

'And have a scandal on board? Don't think of it. We must do it now, Siverac. I think he's in the best mood to take the shock. You wouldn't recognize the man: he's tormented by his conscience.'

'By what? Hargrove! His conscience . . .'

'I don't like long speeches, so I'll make it short. He lives in terror of what he has done. He is trying to persuade himself that it's
not true, that a mulatto killed Régis, not he. If you bully him, you
may well cause him to lose his mind . . . And then . . . I must admit
I feel sorry for him.'

'You're a woman.'

'And not likely to regret the fact when I see how men behave.'

'Does he suspect that we know who killed Régis ?'

'He suspects that you have guessed . . . As far as I'm concerned,
he's not sure. Come on, Mr Siverac, courage. Let's go.'

Hargrove was expecting Maisie Llewelyn to come back, but the
arrival of Siverac made him shudder. He rocked himself so violently out of the rocking chair that it seemed to throw him on to the
floor.

'Siverac, he said. 'I don't think we have anything to say to one
another since our last conversation.'

'Excuse me,' Siverac said. 'Miss Llewelyn and I have some news
which will surprise you. It's about your daughter, Laura.'

'First, let's sit down,' said Maisie Llewelyn. 'I'll take the chair.
Mr Hargrove, I advise you to sit on the bed. Yes, please believe me,
it will be better, sit down.'

Hargrove sat. Siverac remained standing, his legs apart and his
hands behind his back.

'Your turn, Miss Llewelyn,' he said.

'William Hargrove,' she said calmly, 'you must know that when
you were away in Jamaica and America, your daughter was married.'

Turning red in the face, Hargrove leaped up and cried:

'It's not true!'

'It's perfectly true,' Siverac said in a cold voice. 'The marriage
took place in front of witnesses.'

'I don't believe you, Siverac.'

'That point of honor can very well be settled tomorrow morning,
Hargrove. There must be a field near here; I have my pistol, and
you, I believe, have yours.'

This speech made Hargrove change color, but the Welshwoman
intervened with good-natured authority.

'Come now,' she said. 'You're not going to play at killing each
other when little Laura's happiness is at stake. I can understand
William Hargrove's feelings on receiving such unexpected news,
but let's first of all consider the future of his daughter. You can
settle your differences in America — or in hell! There was a marriage, before witnesses, but you should also know, William
Hargrove, that your daughter is a widow.'

'A widow?' Hargrove repeated, with a stunned look. 'I don't
understand . . .'

'Don't you understand the word?' Siverac asked harshly. 'Her husband was killed by a pistol shot, fired at random.'

Hargrove nearly collapsed, but Miss Llewelyn went over to him and helped him to sit down on the bed.

'Régis . . . ,' he murmured, without knowing what he was saying.

'Well, well!' said Siverac. 'How did you know?'

Maisie Llewelyn, with one hand resting on Hargrove's shoulder, shot a look at Siverac, raising her eyebrows.

'William Hargrove thinks it was Régis and he has guessed correctly, that's all. I think that enough has been said about that matter. We will leave Mr Hargrove to collect himself. Later I shall go and look for Laura, so that he can say something to her and embrace her. Isn't that right, Mr Hargrove?'

'Never!' he exclaimed. 'I never want to see her again.'

This time, the Welshwoman could only raise her eyes upwards.

'Let's go,' she said to Siverac. 'We have done what had to be done, but it breaks my heart.'

'I have to admit that I would happily have shot the man,' said Siverac when they were outside.

'I can't help feeling sorry for him,' she said. 'It's more than I can bear.'

'I think you're sublime, Miss Llewelyn. Why didn't you stay and console the murderer while you were about it?'

'Be quiet, Siverac. You don't understand a thing.'

By tacit agreement, they promptly went their separate ways.


# 88

Meanwhile, young Frank was inconsolable at the idea of leaving the island of La Tortue without at least getting a glimpse of a cave. And despite the terror that he felt of the buccaneer in his red house, he decided to visit him on the off-chance. The pull was too strong.

As on the previous day, he found the door open and, as before, kept at a respectful distance. When no threat was offered, he went forward a few steps. He was greatly disappointed: the house was empty. Since he had not found a cave, he would be daring enough to go inside the strange hut. There were guns hanging on the walls and, at the back of the room, wild animals' skins piled on a wooden trunk in iron straps.

Suddenly, a hand fell on his shoulder. For almost a minute, he was shaken silently, until he could not breathe. When he was at last able to turn round, he saw first of all the legs in their blood-colored trousers, then the whole of the red-headed man looming above him like a colossus, naked from the waist up.

'Little idiot,' he said. 'Did no one ever tell you that a lad of your age should not go looking through people's things while they are away, and fall into the clutches of a pirate?'

With both hands he grasped the boy's head and began to tousle the hair, dragging it this way and that.

'Let this teach you that you don't just walk into a buccaneer's house like that. Now, what do you want?'

His mind reeling from his punishment, Frank could not say a word. The man looked at him with a cruel smile.

'Since you have lost your tongue, I'll tell you. You still want to see a cave. You halfwit, you won't find one at the back of my hut. So, come on. I can't show you one just like that, but you will understand.'

Together they left the town and followed a path which led to the woods which ran down to the sea. Both of them plunged into the foliage with its acrid, penetrating odors, the man pushing the branches aside while Frank followed in a joyful stupor, as if moving through a familiar dream.

When they reached the shore, the man looked in silence at the stretch of ultramarine on which the sun picked out points of light. After a moment he said curtly:

'At your age, I chose between the sea and the land. I continually look at it still from my hut and I can hear it all night long. You don't know what it means.'

'I love the sea, too,' Frank assured him.

The man shrugged his shoulders.

'When you love something, you choose it. It's either her or the land. If you had stayed on La Tortue, I would have taught you to sail and to use a harpoon. Twenty years ago, I was already on a boat with my companions. You attacked ships, fought with a cutlass, and grabbed gold, jewels and precious silks. That was the bounty we hid in the caves.'

With a smile and a slight hint of contempt, he added, as though no longer speaking to Frank but, beyond the boy who stood before him, to the boy he had once been:

'They were rough lads. A merry band of thieves. Nothing on their backs but some rags of cloth or leather, with diamonds in their ears or gold rings. The spray ran off them. Married they were, but married to the sea! Apart from that, no nonsense! On dry land, they had . . .' (he thought better of it:) ' . . .they had dogs for hunting, as many as thirty-five each . . . Savage creatures, too, real devils determined to bag their prey. And when they were out at sea . . .'

He looked at the sea for a moment, as if something might at last emerge from it. Eyes wide, Frank said nothing, but his heart beat faster.

' . . . at sea,' the man with the red hair continued, 'we were the dogs, chasing the big ships which tried to get away like wild cattle or wild boars, over there in the valley. We caught them on the run. We took everything they were hiding, precious furniture and gold plate, everything . . . And we hid it all in the bellies of the caves.'

'Here?' Frank asked.

'You'd like to see, uh? Well, there was no road leading to them. Only a dangerous footpath: below it the slapping of the water, above the blue bite of the sky. But they slaughtered us. In the name of morality, they sent ships after us with hidden guns to deceive us. Only Lafitte has managed to hold out up to now. And there were fights. The French and the English both needed the 'Brothers of the Coast' for their own wars. They started to be very useful, the Brothers of the Coast! For us, the enemy was now this one, then the other. But always, in addition, the Spaniards. In three centuries, the great gold fever was never as great as this little fever that lasted three months. The French took it with them everywhere, the yellow death! At the end, I was fourteen years old! The age of folly . . . There are still a handful of us, here and there on the islands, who managed to escape. Free. And one day . . .'

'What will happen one day?'

Once again the man seemed to be seeing ghosts out to sea.

'That life is not for you. Dreaming was made to be happy. Go, go back home. I've had enough of you.'

'Just now, you told me to stay.'

'I said that like that. Off with you.'

'So I won't be able to see a cave?'

'They have all been emptied, except the treasure cave which is untouched. You will never manage to discover it behind its thickness of creepers. You would walk past a thousand times without seeing anything.'

'Do you know where it is?'

'I'm not saying I do, but when I was your age, they showed me everything. They had stolen great mirrors from the rich ships, and they are there, standing up against the walls. They light everything up when you go in and then you can see everywhere chests full of gold, great heaps of silk cloth, rubies, emeralds, diamonds in boxes, and piles of precious objects.'

'Suppose one did find the cave?'

'You can always go on looking.'

'Have you looked for it?'

'I'm not saying that either. Come, you're too clever for your age. I'll leave you here. I have to go fishing.'

He suddenly grasped the boy's hand and crushed it in his own.

'Little rascal,' he said, with a huge smile. 'I would willingly have taken you with us, we would have licked you into shape. That's enough now, go back to your parents and don't think any more about pirates.'

Frank hesitated, but the man pushed him toward the path.

'Are you going, or not?'

The boy took a few steps, then turned round.

'Goodbye,' he said.

'What do you mean goodbye? Be off with you! Don't let me see you again!'

Filled with regret, he turned back through the trees which brushed against him as he went past, climbed to the top of the path and reached the wide open space behind the houses. Here again he looked back, but the woods hid the shore and he could see only the sea and the thousands of little darts with which the sun pricked the dark blue ocean as it stretched away to infinity.

Heavy in heart, without quite knowing why, he returned to the wooden houses where his fellow-travelers were staying. He could not shake off the impression of having skirted alongside a great adventure, and he felt frustrated. From now on, a character of some import would accompany him in his dreams, rough-mannered and red-headed, the companion of the sea rovers wreathed in wild poetry.

He did not breathe a word of this escapade, but every night he left valiantly in search of the treasure cave.

# 89

The following day was melancholy. No one was any longer speaking to anyone else — at least, this was one's first impression; but on closer examination, the quarrel was confined to Hargrove, Siverac and Miss Llewelyn, who did not even look at one another. Laura remained locked in the silence of grief. Frank was burning with the desire to ask everyone questions about buccaneers, but except for his sister, who discouraged him with a sad little smile, a glance was enough to keep the pest at bay.

The atmosphere was still heavy when, two days later, in the

morning, a three-masted frigate appeared on the horizon. Rocking almost imperceptibly, she seemed to have an airy lightness, but as she appraoched, she revealed a far less benevolent appearance, with her wide ports lowered and the light cannons visible in silhouette on the foredeck. She was a graceful vessel, nevertheless, and she dropped anchor a short way outside the port of La Tortue. A moment later, she put out two sloops to fetch provisions from land, because it was impossible for foreign ships to stop over in Haiti where the ports had been closed because of a French threat to re-establish order there. While the sailors were taking on provisions of fresh water in barrels and buying cured boar's meat from the natives, and fresh meat of musk ox, Siverac spoke to the officer in charge of the landing party, who suggested that he come on board with a first cargo of fruit and water.

Siverac's explanations were accepted unhesitatingly by the Captain, a phlegmatic gentleman who had heard many stories of this kind in recent years. The sloop was sent back to pick up the rest of the group, who were shivering with impatience. This was the moment thay had been anticipating for days and, suddenly, relief meant a temporary truce in their quarrels. The travelers were settled in the stern under the mizzenmast, and the Blacks, more summarily, in the hold. And the *Quarrelsome* raised anchor.

The whole group leaned over the rail when the frigate set sail and said farewell to what was, despite everything, a paradise. Their hearts were heavy. Frank in particular hoped against reason that his buccaneer might appear in the harbor or on shore and wave goodbye to them, but there was no buccaneer. However, he could see the red hut and tears flowed inexplicably. One does not cry over a hut. Was it for the whole island? Of course, why hadn't he thought of it?

Laura was also weeping, standing motionless, apart from the others. Once more she felt that indescribable rending of the soul.

On the rear forecastle, a sort of canvas pavillion had been erected, where the Captain entertained his passengers. A lunch was served, accompanied by Spanish wines, and Maisie Llewelyn had the place of honor reserved for Mrs Hargrove. The wine was a little heavy, but it loosened their tongues and the whole situation on Haiti was explained in great detail to the Captain. Having become the masters, the former slaves had in turn established a military state which ruled through semi-terror despite the gaiety and the naturally care-free attitude of the race. From there, the guests soon turned to the situation in Europe, intoxicated by the wine and by the wind beating against the sails. Frank, however, was only listening inter-mittently to this general conversation, which was becoming increasingly confused. His thoughts were elsewhere, and as he was sitting at the far end of the table and said nothing, he was able to slip away unseen, after the dessert.

He would have liked to have walked around the deck, but his balance was uncertain because of the slight lilting of the ship and he preferred to keep close to the rail. No doubt the effects of the Spanish wine also had something to do with this decision. He felt happier than at the moment of leaving. The sea, in its way, was going to his head. A source of great adventures, it lent a nobilty to the most simple of voyages. In its hidden unsuspected depths were ships sunk by pirates. How respectfully had Frank's buccaneer uttered the name of John Kidd, prince of pirates! In the boy's fevered imagination, sailors were classed in the same league and he looked around him, but there were only three or four washing the planks with great mops and buckets of water: there was nothing heroic about the job. There were certainly sailors in the shrouds, but they were climbing around so fast that it was impossible to observe them at leisure. Frank would not have dared say what it was he was looking for, for it would have seemed absurd: he was seeking in the eyes of these men the eyes of the red-headed buccaneer, the way that man had of fixing his gaze at a distance of 1000 leagues, or so it seemed, and even to the edge of infinity; and there was no imitating that distant gaze  . . .

With a sigh, his gaze fell back on the men washing the deck. He approached them timidly, but they greeted him roughly:

'Mind!' one of them shouted.

This was followed by some ungentlemanly swearing.

Mortified, he went off, back to his place. The conversation had faltered, but Captain de Witt occasionally made some interesting remark or other, in very clear language, which held his audience's attention, so Frank soon began to listen to him with unexpected pleasure. He was listening to the lovely English of England and not the language of the planters which, though not without charm, was a bit casual and had rather a drawl.

Laura, for her part, listened with a sort of hunger to the Captain's accent, to the clipped modulations that took her back to the lost paradise of her early childhood in her parents' house on the borders of Kent and Surrey. She would always remember the parks, with their path lined with oak trees, and the dark brick country houses, with all around her the musical intonation of happy voices. Shortly after she was born, her parents had left Virginia to return to their native England and there, up to the age of five, she knew the irreplaceable happiness of a young life full of love and games, and grown-ups who spoke like this officer in his white uniform, with the same calm and the same good humor. So why had her parents once more left their mother country to go and live in America, this time in the Caribbean, where such an awful fate awaited her? For a few moments, outside time, she was once again immersed in that distant joy. It haunted her for the whole of the following night.

The voyage continued without incident. Toward evening, in a sunset in which everything was drowned in a golden cloud, the *Quarrelsome* sailed past Cuba and the passengers regretted that they could not stop off there, but there was no question of that; and a few hours later they made port in Kingston, Jamaica, just as night was falling over the island. The harbor regulations would not allow them to disembark before morning, and the night on board ship put an intolerable strain on the passengers' patience, since the lights of the town and all the sounds that reached them, in a joyful and provocative din, kept them awake until dawn.

However, there was to be compensation for their exasperating sleepless night in the magnificence of the countryside. Far behind the town rose a chain of mountains of such profound blue that it was almost indigo. In the streets, already full of people, Blacks in pink, mauve, sea-green and purple clothing were going to market in what seemed like a promenade. The group of travelers made for a district which housed the 'great' townhall; but their first consideration was to rush into elegant shops where they could find perfectly cut clothes, because the prosperous English colony of Port-Royal and Kingston was demanding and had trained the local tailors. Our travelers emerged delighted, each rediscovering his or her true self, or rather the idea that they had of themselves, not the humble truth. Siverac appeared as a noble lord with a high, stiff collar which threw back his head; Hargrove looked like a leading planter, self-possessed, proud of what he owned; Frank was no longer a young boy, but a man with understraps to his trousers and — an odd whim — a black scarf carefully knotted, in a casual corsair style. Maisie Llewelyn was dressed as a lady, no more nor less, but elegant, in a light gray dress, with stripes of darker gray, a deception without a single false note. Only Laura did not yield to the temptation to deceive. She chose mauve chiffon, rather more solemn than the colors that she was offered.

Thus attired, they separated into two groups: Frank and Laura, accompanied by Betty who insisted on calling them 'the children', went to visit the town, while Hargrove took Siverac and Miss Llewelyn to his plantation, which he hoped to dispose of at a good price by selling it to Siverac. And, since the two men were no longer on speaking terms, it was the Welshwoman who had to take charge of negotiations.

The plantation was at some distance from the town. A hired carriage took them there. The long, single-storeyed house, in the purest Georgian style, stood with its back to a wooded hill. Its fine proportions, high windows and the imposing double staircase made it a masterpiece of eighteenth-century architecture, and it immediately took Siverac's fancy. He felt himself entirely on a par with this noble residence.

The plantation itself offered almost the same variety as those on Haiti, with a predominance of coffee plants. Covering a considerable acreage, it had an abundance of huge palm trees and everywhere there were coconut palms bent in the wind.

Siverac admired everything unreservedly and asked Miss Llewelyn to find out what price William Hargrove wanted for it; he now called him Mr Hargrove. Miss Llewelyn promptly passed on the price, which was enormous, and the purchaser took it full on the chin without flinching.

They visited the house. The three went up in icy silence. Luckily, the design of the front stairs allowed their mutual hatred to be assuaged as they climbed the staircase: Hargrove took the right-hand stairs, accompanied by Miss Llewelyn, who remained neutral, and Siverac went up the left.

Night was falling. The rooms were lit with sovereign simplicity by hosts of wall lamps making the space seem part of the decor, although this did not prevent richness from abiding where one did not at first detect it. The furniture, at first glance, was in fact exceptionally refined. Woods of fabulous rarity had been used in these straight-backed chairs, topped with fan-shaped decorations so finely carved that one was lost in admiration. In the bedrooms, the uncurtained windows were in contrast to four-poster beds, with columns shaped like strands of rope, and pineapple motifs.

Siverac cast his eye over the place, looked at Miss Llewlyn and nodded as hard as his stiff collar would allow him; then all three went down to the drawing-room where, on a heavy walnut table, a parchment was waiting for the necessary signatures to be added at the foot of a handwritten agreement.

Siverac, who was well-acquainted with documents of this kind, fixed this one with an eagle eye. In large, disdainful handwriting, he wrote the letters of his name and threw the goose quill aside. Miss Llewelyn retrieved it and gave it to Hargrove who signed with the same show of arrogance.

Though the two parties to the contract seemed bound to silence, Miss Llewelyn was obliged to ask them some questions to determine certain essential points.

'How do you intend to make the payment?' she asked Siverac.

'Why, by check on my bank in New Orleans,' he said, in a voice tinged with contempt.

'Mr Siverac will settle by check drawn on his bank in New Orleans,' she told Hargrove.

The reply was immediate:

'Agreed, while reserving the right to judicial proceedings should the purchaser fail to keep his word and his honor by renouncing the agreement which he has just signed before a witness.'

Miss Llewelyn transmitted this message word for word, and the response was not slow in coming:

'Consequent upon this agreement can the purchaser consider himself henceforth at home in this house?'

The reply was conveyed immediately:

'That goes without saying. Such a question is absurd between gentlemen.'

There was an instant reply to the above:

'In that case, between gentlemen, William Hargrove is ordered to leave the plantation belonging to its present owner within the next five minutes.'

The legal formalities were carried out the following morning at the office of Mr Slaughter, who had negotiated the sale of the plantation to William Hargrove less than three months earlier. Miss Llewelyn put her signature to the foot of the agreement as witness and the matter was concluded according to all the formalities required by English law.

# 90

A few days later, a ship flying the British flag, on its way to the United States, put in at Kingston. Hargrove reserved cabins and the whole group from the New World plantation, except Siverac, went on board. Another American ship followed them closely, both escorted when they took to the open sea by the British sloop *Avenger*, formidably armed to protect them against the last pirate at large in the West Indies. Lafitte, known for his daring and sly tactics, had left New Orleans where it had been thought he had settled down, but his presence had been reported everywhere in the Gulf of Mexico, as well as the Cayman Islands, and the shadowy environs of Barbados.

A voyage from Jamaica to Florida could therefore be quite a demanding adventure: after Kingston, one had to cross between the point of Cuba and Haiti, through the Windward Passage, noted for the violence of its gales. Memories, which moved them to different degrees, were waiting there, like other pirates, for our travelers. Off La Tortue, they learned from one of the ship's officers that massacres were still taking place on Haiti and that ships were avoiding Port-au-Prince. Port-Haïtien had been set on fire at least ten times . . . And yet over there, in the distance, hardly perceptible in the heat haze rising from the sea, the enchanted island still retained the same significance in their eyes and in their hearts. Beyond it came the Bahamas, a paradise with magic names that followed one another like rosary beads as far as the coast of Florida.

In the discomfort of the summer weather, the journey seemed endless. For an hour they were followed by dolphins. Then they had nothing else to occupy their minds, except to watch the color of the sea change. Off the islands to the South of Florida, it was pink, a dawn pink above fields of coral. When they were following the coastline, it became turquoise blue, then a green that grew darker and darker as they sailed northwards. Even at several hundred meters from land, the noise of the ship disturbed a blue heron in the silent marshes where it was fishing and they followed its sharp flight above the great cypress trees beside the endless sandy beaches.

The short sunset did not allow them to see much of the shore, but the following morning they observed a long, aggressive-looking stone building which aroused Frank's curiosity. The Fort of Saint-Augustin, left over from the Spanish occupation, seemed to be watching for an enemy to fire at, out at sea. The boy's imagination was stimulated and he was tempted to go and knock on his father's cabin door to borrow his spy-glass, but some intuition held him back and he decided against it.

As it happens, Hargrove had not slept. Still not recovered from the events in Jamaica (though these were a long way away now), he had retired quite early to the large bed in his cabin, which was comfortable, if not luxurious. Already, deeper and deeper snores implied a restorative sleep, when the door quietly opened. Maisie Llewleyn looked round, listened, then went away still more quietly.

On board the *Prosperous*, she had had herself registered under the name of Mrs William Hargrove, and such is the persuasive force of the lies one tells oneself, that she believed it herself, since she did indeed fulfil the functions required in such a case; but a part of herself was amused by it. In short, on water as on land, she shared William Hargrove's bed.

That evening she hesitated and, returning to the deck of the *Prosperous*, began to walk up and down the deck, considering what she should do. Finally, she chose what she called the military solution. Belatedly, both weary and resolute, she went back to the cabin and the conjugal, or nearly conjugal, bed.

Having undressed and perfumed herself, she got into the large bed and displaced Hargrove, who was occupying the whole of the center. He grunted, rolled over and muttered:

'Dearest, is that you?'

'Of course, you idiot. Did you think it was the captain? And then let's have no "dearests" this evening. We have to talk seriously.'

At this, he opened his eyes wide.

'Put on the light,' he said.

'No need. The light from the lamp on deck is quite sufficient. Now, prepare for a shock.'

'Another one!' he moaned.

'Yes, another one. Another is right. You had one already at La Tortue. The second is coming and you had better be lying down for it. I told you at La Tortue in Siverac's presence that your daughter was married while you were away.'

'She's not married,' he exclaimed. 'It's untrue.'

'Not so loud. We have neighbors. Siverac confirmed what I said.'

'Siverac is a liar.'

'It's easy enough for you to say that now that he is a long way away. You already have the promise of a duel in America if he ever goes back there.'

There was a short silence, then Maisie Llewelyn continued:

'I tell you again that she was married. I was a witness, with Siverac, at the chapel of Saint-Michel in Dondon.'

Once again he cried:

'It's not true!'

She moved back a little as if to take aim and landed a noisy slap on that bearded face, struck motionless with fright.

'There,' she said. 'That's for "not true". Now, just listen to me.'

'What?' he said, dazed.

'Can't you hear? They're enjoying themselves in the cabin next door. A domestic tiff is always amusing, so they're listening and having a good chuckle. Can't you hear?'

Some barely stifled laughter could be heard through the wall.

'Luckily your children are at the far end of the corridor,' she said. 'But tomorrow, when you go for a walk on deck, they'll be smiling . . .'

'I shan't leave here,' he muttered

'Well, I can understand that and I'm glad to see that you are calm again. We can discuss this without roaring about it, can we? Agreed?'

He nodded and Maisie Llewelyn went on in a reasonable tone:

'Your daughter Laura . . .'

'Yes, what about her?'

'Have you looked carefully at her?'

'Why . . . Yes.'

'Why . . . No: because you men, who think yourselves so clever, see nothing. She was married three months ago now, to the day.'

'Married? Prove it.'

'Don't let's start that again.'

'I want proof of this marriage.'

'When I tell you I was a witness, at the chapel . . .'

'Maisie, what proof is there that you were there . . . even if there was a marriage . . .'

'Do you mean the slap I gave you a moment ago wasn't enough? Do you want another one?'

Hargrove tried to stand up for himself.

'I'm defending my daughter's honor, Maisie.'

'I like that! If Régis were here, if he hadn't been killed . . .'

'He's dead. Just as well for him!'

'Are you mad? In your place, I'd be careful not to say things like that. Rumors, William Hargrove . . .'

'Rumors?'

'Leave them for the time being and let's get back to our Laura. You may not have noticed, but she is gaining in size. She is no longer a young maiden. Maisie Llewelyn's eye is not to be deceived.'

'I haven't noticed,' he stammered.

'Of course not. Well, understand this, my good friend: your daughter Laura is well and truly a woman. Do you know what motherhood means?'

This time, he looked at her without replying. Now she was talking to him more gently.

'Come, Willy, pull yourself together. In a moment I'll give you your laudanum and you can sleep on this. I can see that you are unhappy.'

He collapsed.

'Oh, Maisie!' he groaned.

She helped him get back under the cotton sheet and began to prepare his laudanum. Everything she needed was in a little box she had bought in Kingston, foreseeing that the decisive interview might take a turn for the worse.

Half an hour later, he was sleeping soundly. The dose had been a strong one. He only woke up the following afternoon. Nothing that he had feared happened thanks to the care and attention of the woman traveling under the name of Mrs Hargrove. Dinner was served in their cabin. They soon became accustomed to this and he undertook the remainder of the voyage as a recluse, not wishing to see anyone except Maisie Llewelyn. Now he bombarded her with questions, but in vain: she refused to answer.

'I've had my share of rebuffs,' she told him one day. 'I'll leave you to think it out for yourself. As far as your daughter is concerned, nature will quietly follow its course, so we have time to think it over. The day after tomorrow we make land. A new life is beginning for all of us.

# 91

*A*t dawn on July 30, they were in sight of Savannah. Such a name, with its sweet sonority, had the magic of Indian poetry and could only belong to a very beautiful town. That is what William Hargrove thought. Since the eighteenth century the magnificence of Savannah had been proverbial throughout the South. Admittedly, there was the financial disaster of 1819, followed by a great fire, but five years had passed since then and the wealth of the State of Georgia had had time to repair everything. However, when he set foot on land with the crowd of travelers, he thought himself in the grip of a nightmare.

His first impression was that of a devastated port in the aftermath of war. A few Blacks were walking idly around, while, more rapidly, some Whites were crossing a large, roughly paved quay with weeds growing out of it. The customs building, in brick blackened by fire, looked out on the river from a façade of broken windows. In this strange dilapidation, the barrels and wooden cases piled at one end of the quayside did still suggest trade, but so miserably that they rather implied a display of bankruptcy and poverty.

In his consternation, he turned to Miss Llewelyn and interrogated her with a silent look.

'Yes, indeed, my friend,' she said. 'I am as astonished as you are. Savannah has not yet recovered, but it's a matter of time, There is no lack of money in Georgia. Now, what do you intend to do?'

'Look round the town for a hotel. We could hire a carriage . . .'

'A carriage! Well, I never! I'd rather go for a walk with the children. They told us on board to leave the port and go directly across the squares. The Blacks could be waiting for us over there, with our meagre belongings.'

Once more Hargrove submitted to the authority of the Welshwoman, who was increasingly coming to regulate his life. The presence of Laura made him uncomfortable, but circumstances did not allow him to escape and he followed Miss Llewelyn obediently.

The advice they had been given was not bad. The streets, with their broken paving stones, made the first steps difficult. A lot of houses were gone, destroyed in the fire, but the squares surrounded by giant sycamores preserved the memory of a magnificent past and, ten minutes away, a stylish house confirmed the notion. It was a two-storey residence with high windows of tasteful proportions, while the dark green door with its heavy bronze knocker was enough in itself to recall the English elegance of former times.

Miss Llewelyn exclaimed:

'Here at any rate is a relic of good omen. Let's knock. No doubt they will give us some useful information.'

With a strong hand, she lifted the knocker and let it fall back twice. A long silence followed, perhaps of outrage, then the door opened and a gray-haired black maid, in a white apron with embroidered flounces, peered out cautiously.

'Who you want?' she asked, through the half-open door.

'If possible, the mistress of the house,' said Miss Llewelyn.

'De mis'ress of the house can't be disturbed at the moment. If you'se looking for room, is full. Dis a boardin' house.'

She shut the door.

After three seconds of hesitation, Maisie Llewelyn announced:

'That reply is unacceptable.'

Grasping the knocker, she let it fall heavily, three times in succession, and said to Hargrove:

'Quick. Your wallet. What price does the Devil put on a conscience?'

The door reopened, as angrily as a door can.

'You 'gain!' said the maid.

'Yes, it is. Just imagine, I found this at the bottom of my purse. It's not yours, by any chance?'

A gold coin was shining between her fingers. The door opened wide.

'Come in, Ma'am.'

They went in, Maisie Llewelyn first, her gold coin still between her fingers.

'I want precise information,' she said sharply. 'We need rooms in a first-class hotel. Where can I find one?'

'Ma'am, the hotels here, not very good; not like before.'

'I don't want that.'

'But up dere, in same street, is fine empty house. The lady sometimes rents rooms. She has several houses in Savannah.'

'What's the number of this house?'

'No number,' the maid said, a trifle shocked. 'Dere's a big sycamore in front.'

'Very good,' said Maisie Llewelyn, slipping the coin into her hand. 'If I'm pleased, there will be more to come.'

'Oh, Ma'am!'

Miss Llewelyn pushed everyone gently outside.

'Let's go and see,' she said. 'If the woman was right, she shall have her second coin; otherwise she'll find out how a Welshwoman deals with a liar.'

'She seems very respectable,' said Hargrove.

'Mr Hargrove, every man has his price, as the regicide* said. Every woman, too, sometimes. Come over here, Frank. You're always hanging around trying to hear what the grown-ups are saying.'

*Oliver Cromwell

— 330 —

They quickened their steps, looking without interest on a row of little houses in pink brick, modest, but not without charm, and decorated with honeysuckle. At intervals, an empty space invaded by wild plants, marked the site of a missing house, victim of the fire, but soon there was a house with a giant sycamore rising before them, entirely white. Its imposing dimensions and proud Georgian façade compelled the admiration of passers-by.

Miss Llewelyn stopped dead and came out with an exclamation that said it all:

'Golly!'

She went up the four steps to the front door and, with a mixture of self-assurance and respect, lifted a bronze knocker in the shape of a heraldic lily. They had to wait for the reply, a courteous lesson in patience. Miss Llewelyn, rather irritated, was about to knock again when the door was slowly opened a little way and a lady of about forty stood in front of the travelers. Small, slender, but very dignified, she was wearing a white cap and a mauve dress which came down to her feet. Her eyes were fixed on Maisie Llewelyn:

'Might I ask . . .?' she said in an icy tone.

The Welshwoman immediately felt herself overcome by something that made her furious, but which she could not control: a sense of social distinction.

'Allow me to introduce myself, and my husband: Mr William Hargrove.'

'Ah! I am Mrs Devilue Upton Smythe . . . But once again, might I ask . . .?'

Hurriedly, and as if burdened with good manners, the Welshwoman explained:

'We have just arrived from Haiti where my husband owns large plantations. While passing through Savannah, we are looking . . .'

'You are looking for what?'

'For very fine lodgings,' said Maisie Llewelyn, resolutely.

'And what makes you think that by knocking on my door . . .?'

At this point, something very odd occurred. Exasperated by this long pedestrian mismatch of minds, the ultra rich man inside William Hargrove emerged and he lost his head:

'What we want, Madam, is to buy your house from you at whatever price, however high it may be.'

At that moment, one had the impression that the door, seized by a violent fit of indignation, was about to swing off its hinges of its own accord and slam in the face of these vulgar foreigners.

'Sir . . . I don't know what . . . How dare you? My ancestral home . . .'

'I believe you have several . . .'

'Is that any of your business? But this conversation has gone on long enough. So good afternoon to you, I think.'

And she shut the door decisively.

Maisie Llewelyn looked at Hargrove.

'Are you out of your mind?' she shouted. 'You spoil everything as soon as you open your mouth.'

'Not at all,' he said. 'I assure you.'

For a minute, unable to make up their minds to leave, they bickered on the steps. Suddenly, the door reopened:

'And just what kind of price were you thinking of?' asked the lady in mauve.


# 92

*H*argrove bought the house for a quite unreasonable price, but this folly allowed him to regain his self-assurance, to breathe easily; and he enjoyed once more the sensation of believing in himself . . . Mrs Devilue Upton Smythe came down from her heights and spoke to him with a sort of respect which he found very comforting — as if, in some inexplicable way, his conscience was leaving him in peace; but what had that to do with it? He did not try to find out, he was determined not to ask any further questions about himself. He was now the owner of one of the most sumptuous and admired houses in Savannah. It was beautiful from top to bottom, from the roof to the basement, and every time the wind blew, the sycamore saluted it. Such was the magic of a fistful of gold. It frees you from who can tell what burdens.

Consequently, the first days in Georgia were pleasant despite the worry he still felt about what he privately called the problem of Laura. One day when she was alone with him, Maisie Llewelyn tackled the matter head on:

'Willy, you're not capable of dealing with such things. Look after your house, it is wonderful, but don't try to settle in a town that has become tragic. Go to Macon, or Augusta, which will give you every opportunity to explore Georgia. There must be plantations for sale. It will be easier for you to start your life over again where no one knows you, and the scenery in those places is magnificent.'

'But Laura, Maisie?'

'Leave her to me. I'll look after the girl. I've made some enquiries. I know what I'm doing. She will be in good hands, but you won't see her again until after the event.'

'I don't want to see her ever again,' Hargrove said softly.

'Then you're an unnatural father.'

'Stop tormenting me, Maisie. It's only too obvious that Providence is watching over me and that I have nothing to reproach myself with. Laura behaved shamefully; she never was married.'

'Yes, she was. Siverac and I told you so.'

'Then I want proof, in writing.'

'Carried by an angel from paradise, no doubt. I'm ashamed of you, William Hargrove.'

'I don't need to take lessons from you. Since you want to look after Laura, I entrust her to you willingly. Consider it a mark of my esteem.'

'I will refrain from saying what I think of you. Haiti is not so far away.'

'Haiti is a past which no longer exists and about which we shall not speak ever again.'

'Let's hope you never run across Siverac, because he might remind you of it.'

'Maisie, there are times when I am no longer pleased to see you.'

'And this just happens to be one of those times. Oh, dear, what a shame! But that Providence you spoke of just now has allowed me to be here with a retentive memory — and we share so many memories, Willy! Moreover, you need your frightful Welshwoman when things get difficult . . . And then, I'm not sure why you are afraid of her. So why don't you kill her? There must be some bullets left in the pistol you had in the drawing-room, in a corner of the window, over there, during that eventful night when the mulattoes attacked . . .'

'Maisie!' he exclaimed, mad with fury. 'How much gold do you want to keep your mouth shut?'

'My love, the treasures of all the pirates in the West Indies would not be enough. Forget that and try to behave yourself, since I am here . . .'

The blood drained from William Hargrove's cheeks.

'Blackmail,' he muttered.

She smiled teasingly:

'Do you realize, my dear friend, that what you call blackmail is at the base of almost all human, social, political, romantic, financial and other relationships? If you don't do this, I won't do that. That is the rule of the world, and no one can escape from it except by leaving the world. Now neither you nor I have any desire to do that.'

'Miss Llewelyn,' Hargrove said icily, 'for reasons which I don't want to go over now, but which I accept, you spoke just now of an absence of several months, perhaps six . . .'

'More . . .'

'Let's say eight if you prefer; so an absence of eight months in the company of a woman who, I regret to say, bears my name . . .'

'Wrong: the name of her late husband.'

'I shall deny the existence of a husband to the day I die; so she will to my great regret have to bear the name of her father and will remain Laura Hargrove as long as she lives under my roof; and, while I am alive, she will not have any other home. Believe me, I shall ensure that. I intend to make her expiate her sin by my side.'

'Hell, you mean . . .'

He did not respond to that, but continued:

'In order to meet all the expenses incurred during this . . . absence, I shall give you the necessary amount within the next forty-eight hours, in banknotes and gold pieces. I shall be generous.'

'That's wise of you, because otherwise I should give you back your daughter, not in forty-eight hours, but in sixty minutes.'

'Miss Llewelyn, I shall not allow you to doubt my word.'

'You see how well the system operates? If you don't do this . . . and so on.'

'I think we have said everything we have to say to one another — for good.'

'Oh, no, William Hargrove; don't you be so sure about committing the future. First of all, you are even richer than I suspected, but you are muddle-headed, as all the rich are. To what address, may I ask, will you deliver the sum destined, etc., etc.?'

'Where do you imagine? The corner of the street? Up to now you have slept in the spare bed which Mrs Devilue Upton Smythe put at your disposal in this house which is mine . . .'

'And which I am leaving this evening. I shall go somewhere else.'

'You will be wrong. Even now, the furniture removers are bringing down some stylish antique furniture — which I bought outright — from the attic of this huge house. A room is being prepared for you and another for Laura, my unworthy daughter — unworthy, if what you say is true. In any case, it will be in your own room that my private secretary will entrust the amount in question to your hands.'

'Well, I never! Everything has already been organized down to the last detail.'

'If you wish. This is only a start, but I beg you not to consider this address, which has become yours, as a permanent invitation. I only expect the two of you to stay here a short — a very short time.'

'No one could be more courteous, you are spoiling us; but have no fear: as soon as we can hire a carriage we shall be gone.'

'I've already seen to that, too. A very suitable carriage, with two horses, will be awaiting you in front of my house, all day if need be.'

'Your generosity overwhelms me . . . Let's say farewell at once, shall we, to save time.'

'There will indeed be a farewell. Just as I don't believe in your story of marriage, so I also refuse to believe that my little girl . . .'

He was suddenly overcome by a violent emotion and he had to regain control of himself before going on, with tears in his eyes; then the rest of the sentence burst out:

'. . . that she could have allowed herself to be seduced by a stranger!'

'What about love?'

'Don't you think I know about love? Paternal love, isn't that love?'

She was about to shout at him that he was shamefully playing with words, but pity kept her silent in the face of the man's suffering.

'Let's say, I lied to you,' she said with a bitter smile. 'When the event takes place, I'll let you know.'

'I shall be there,' he said.

'Then perhaps you will believe me.'

'I'm sure there will be nothing. Her appearance hasn't changed, but you have poisoned my heart with your suspicions. All I know for certain is that that man was pursuing her.'

'And he died.'

'Yes, he died. I shot at random and he paid with his life. Heaven punished him.'

She looked at him, silently this time, not daring to say what was in her mind: The man is a monster, but how can one judge him? He is in love, with the ferocity of a twenty-year old.

'You frighten me,' she said at last, in a whisper.

He did not reply at once, but his face changed and took on the look of perplexed anxiety that he had so often exhibited in the past.

'Am I really so terrible?'

'I'm leaving, William. When I get there, with your Laura, I shall write to you. And you will come, if necessary.'

She said that to leave him a glimmer of hope and went away quickly to avoid the sight of that tormented face.

Without even realizing it, she began to run through the untended gardens where the branches of the trees, no longer pruned, were tangled together and reverting to the wild. Suddenly, a thought crossed her mind:

'He killed his rival, that's all.'

She clasped both hands to her ears as if to block out the words.

## 93

$T$he following morning, she and Laura left early. In spite of all his resolutions, Hargrove could not restrain himself from embracing his daughter, though without saying a word to her. Frank was there, shattered by this departure which he did not understand. She threw herself into his arms, weeping, and whispered:

'Pray for me.'

The little town which Miss Llewelyn had been recommended was a few miles from Macon. A society of Protestant ladies, not unlike a religious order, occupied a kind of hospice where they only accepted people with sufficiently good testimonials, who for some reason or other needed care.

A comfortable house, surrounded by a garden, was rented at the outskirts of the town, well off the beaten track. Life here was a bit like exile, but made easier by walks in the woods or carriage rides in the countryside. The Welshwoman knew the art of distracting and, as far as possible, consoling her charge.

Then came the critical days when Laura's extreme fatigue made it necessary for her to be taken to the Protestant ladies. She was given the finest room and Maisie Llewelyn wrote to William Hargrove.

He arrived two days later. Laura was in great pain. Making a considerable effort to control himself and to appear compassionate, he sat at her bedside and looked benevolently on his daughter. She smiled in reply and thanked him for coming.

'My dear child,' he said. 'Let this trial be a lesson to you. God has forgiven you, I feel it.'

'But, Papa, I did nothing wrong!'

He smiled, got up and went out. He found Maisie Llewelyn waiting for him in the next room.

'There is no doubt about it,' he said. 'People are building a wall of lies around me — I, who live only for the truth . . .'

'William Hargrove,' Maisie Llewelyn muttered audibly. 'The Devil take you and keep you.'

And she swung round on her heels.

Betty and Maisie Llewelyn tooks turns at Laura's bedside, while she tossed in her bed and could not prevent herself from crying out. The decisive moments were long in coming and, from time to time, the young woman, exhausted, fell asleep.

It was during one of these moments of respite that Hargrove once more made an appearance. He had the satisfaction of seeing that Laura was alone with Betty. Putting a finger to his lips, he went over to his sleeping daughter and looked at her. Her face drawn with suffering, she possessed a tragic beauty. Hargrove's eyes looked closer and closer. Already, during the long and difficult journey from the plantation to Jamaica, he had noticed something, though he said nothing about it.

Now, he gently opened the neck of the rather large blouse that covered Laura's breast. Betty stood up at once and held out a hand, as if to prevent him from going any further, but he pushed her aside forcefully.

Not seeing what he expected, he reached out toward the little bedside table and opened the drawer. There was the emerald necklace. Without any hesitation, he took it and looked at it thoughtfully . . .

At that moment, awakened by the slight noise of the drawer, Laura saw her father examining the emeralds.

'Papa,' she said. 'That's mine.'

'My child,' he said gently, 'I don't doubt that, but who gave it to you?'

'My husband,' she said, quickly. 'He gave it to me the day we were married.'

Hargrove was silent for a moment, then announced very gravely:

'In any case, my dear, it is far too precious an object for you to risk losing. It is yours, but I shall put it in my strongbox, for safe keeping.'

In a weak, but indignant voice, she said:

'Oh, Papa! Why are you taking away something that belongs to me?'

'I'm acting for the best, Laura,' he replied. 'Thank God for giving you a loving father who watches over you.'

Having said this, he went out into the next room where Maisie Llewelyn had just sat down in a chair to rest from her duties and await the moment when she should relieve Betty. When she saw Hargrove, she leaped up.

'You again!' she exclaimed.

He showed her the necklace in his open palm.

'Me again,' he said calmly. 'And this is what I find. One lie after another. The poor girl who I thought was pure as an angel admits that she was given this thing by a man whom she dares call her husband. I deserve to be told the truth. It is being hidden from me . . . It has been revealed to me despite every attempt to lie. Do you know what this is, shining in the palm of my hand? I shall tell you, Miss Llewelyn: it is the wages of sin.'

She heard this speech to the end, her cheeks and brow blazing with anger, then all at once she seemed to grow to an enormous height. Coming up to Hargrove, so close that he could feel her hot breath on his face, she shouted at him:

'Thief!'

He shrunk back, thrusting the necklace into his jacket pocket.

'I forbid you . . .'

'What do you forbid me, you filthy thief? The more you forbid me, the more I shall speak and when the Welshwoman wants to make herself heard, she is listened to, believe me. Scandal will pursue you until your death, if I want it, and you will give your daughter back what is hers.'

'When I have proof that she was married.'

'Proof! Always proof! One day, I'll make that word stick in your throat. But that's enough for today. So, out, do you hear me: out!'

'By what right do you dare speak to me in this way?'

'Do you want me to call someone, Willy?'

Women in black appeared, attracted by the noise. Without a word, Hargrove went out of the door.


The day after this scene, some confused fragments of which were bound to reach Laura's ears, she expressed a wish to return to the house that Maisie Llewelyn had rented on the outskirts of town. Without any doubt, the young woman, since she was now a Catholic, did not want to give birth in a Protestant house.

She had never been strong and the birth threatened to be a difficult one. The child came into the world ten days later, in the early hours of January 25. It was a girl. Maisie Llewelyn, who had seen to everything, had a Catholic priest brought almost in secret and he baptised the child Annabel, a name chosen by Laura because it was that of Régis's mother.

Meanwhile, the new mother's condition, though not immediately alarming, was a cause of some anxiety. She took time to recover and the Welshwoman was frightened for her, as was Betty. So the reappearance of William Hargrove, still hankering after his daughter, was not unwelcome. Differences were forgotten and decisions firmly made.

Hargrove would take his daughter to Warm Springs, where the mild climate would help restore her to health. Maisie Llewelyn and Betty would take care of the child. When she was strong enough to leave the house, she would be taken to a first-rate aristocratic institution, not far from the town.

Hargrove had opened his purse and done what was necessary. Maisie Llewelyn could see clearly what this man, whom she considered contemptible, was planning, but for the time being she could only go along with it. He was determined to get his hands on Laura and to keep her for himself. As things were, nothing could stop him, since the Welshwoman, moved with pity for Annabel, the quite innocent victim of these schemes, was firmly decided to watch over her, as Hargrove requested.

In her current state of extreme weakness, Laura suffered from the hard-heartedness of these two people who, for reasons which she did not understand, were separating her from her child, and she began to hate both of them, after making considerable efforts to love them. How could she defend herself? One March morning, she had to say farewell to her tiny daughter and set out with William Hargrove for the spa which gave its name to the town of Warm Springs. Two days later, the Welshwoman and Betty were taking Annabel to the luxurious institution which would take care of her fate.

During the next two years, Hargrove travelled with his daughter in the most beautiful parts of the South, seeking by every possible means to make life pleasant for her and only succeeding in embittering her. He refused to let her see her daughter or even to know where she was.

Finally, in 1827, he heard of a plantation a short way from Savannah which seemed to him an ideal place to live happily with his family. Harold Armstrong, who belonged to one of the best known English families, but had fallen on hard times, gave him a lease on it, on the customary terms, for twenty-five years. Hargrove settled there with his two sons, who had finished their studies, while Frank, the youngest, was just leaving for university in his turn.

A new life now began for Laura, one she might have regarded as a martyrdom.

# 94

*T*he years passed. Laura could never resign herself to not seeing her daughter. Only Maisie Llewelyn and Betty brought her sweets and toys, but they had to observe the cruel silence that William Hargrove had imposed.

At fifteen, Annabel was a great beauty, with a skin like camellias, large violet eyes and a proud bearing. By a disastrous chance, during some celebration at her college, she was picked out by one of the richest men in New York, a millionaire, Old Jurgen, who made her his heiress. 'Old' Mr Jurgen was in fact fifty, but he had the good taste to die suddenly. Nonetheless, Annabel's fate was sealed. She had acquired a love of money and the means it provides to satisfy every whim of a passionate personality.

From time to time, Hargrove summoned Miss Llewelyn into his

library. Raised voices could be heard from behind the closed doors.

'What proof?' the Welshwoman shouted. 'You have only that word on your lips, and you need it in writing, when I told you twenty times that the little church at Dondon was burnt down. Only God knows what happened to the poor priest . . . And there are those emeralds, which you got your hands on . . .'

'To put them in safe-keeping. At least they provide me with proof of lost innocence and a lie . . .'

'You dare speak of lies! You!'

'I speak of it because I live for truth, and these stones, these emeralds which have done so much harm and which, in my life-time, will do no more, these accursed emeralds are the image of an accursed land, green just as they are!'

'Green just like fear and jealousy, Willy Hargrove!'

# 5
# A TREMULOUS JOY

# 95

*I*n the great round hall, the pink of sunset was lingering as if to embellish the final part of the story, for Maisie Llewelyn had not yet entirely finished. She did pause to allow a few moments' silence during which nothing could be heard except the light fluttering of fans; then she continued with a sigh:

'There we are. I think I have told you all that I could decently reveal. But consider the harm that was done by Mr Hargrove's obstinacy in demanding proof that was impossible to supply. When young Frank Hargrove was grown up he heard a gossip in Savannah mention "the celebrated Annabel Hargrove, father unknown." He immediately challenged the man to a duel and was killed the next day, run through the chest with a sword.'

A murmur of dismay ran through the audience, because the storyteller had gained their sympathy for the pirate fancier. Several ladies surreptitiously blew their noses, then the distinguished voice of Mrs Harrison Edwards announced:

'All this is very sad. However, to be fair, one must recognize that the absence of written proof that was so insistently demanded by the late William Hargrove, is a matter for infinite regret.'

These words, spoken with studied politeness, succeeded in creating a low muttering among the gentlemen who were standing behind the ladies. Then one of them called out:

'Excuse me, I beg you.'

And politely making his way through the ranks of astonished ladies, he reached the open space where Maisie Llewelyn was about to finish her speech.

'I have the proof,' he said in a loud voice.

It was young Siverac, Minnie's husband. So great was the excitement that it was as though bolts of lightning were flashing through the air. Maisie Llewelyn smiled like a cat.

'The proof! The proof!' people muttered.

Proud and slender, his eyes shining with indignation, Antonin de Siverac said forcefully:

'My father was at Laura's wedding and he described it all to me. William Hargrove had the cheek to cast doubt on his evidence, which led him to be challenged to a duel, which he refused . . .'

'Or rather,' Maisie Llewelyn interrupted, 'which was postponed until some future date, so as not to complicate our journey.'

'If you wish.' said Siverac. 'The fact remains that the late William Hargrove went green with fear as you told us a moment ago; but there is more. When the brave Régis, known to his soldiers as "The

Angel", was killed, the Black NCO who replaced him took his wallet and a rosary out of his pocket and gave them to my father, "for the young wife". My father, out of respect for the young officer whom he admired, did not look closely at anything until he was left alone on Jamaica. There he found some letters. There were two which touched him deeply. They were from Régis' sister, the nun in Port-au-Prince. The first congratulated him on his engagement, about which he had apparently informed her earlier in a frenzy of love and happiness. The second, written a month later, full of enthusiasm, expressed her joy at knowing he was married. My father told me what was in these letters and offered to let me read them; but my heart was so full that I refused. He could not resolve himself to revive Laura's grief. They are at home, in our house in Charleston. I can have a copy sent to Mrs Harrison Edwards, who regrets the absence of proof.'

Mrs Harrison Edwards burst into tears.

At that moment the doors at the back of the room were flung open and the wave of emotion reached its height when the usher announced in a loud voice:

'Mrs Jonathan Armstong!'

The name, respected among all of them, rang out like a fanfare, but Annabel made her entrance with utter simplicity. Wearing a light gray dress, she was wrapped in a black cape, dramatically austere, and, in startling contrast, the emerald necklace shone insolently around her neck.

With a naturalness that she never lost, this woman, whose beauty endured despite her wrinkles, came forward like a queen in a foreign land. Clearly, most of those present did not expect to see her like this, apart from the ones involved in the conspiracy; Elizabeth, sitting a little behind the front row of seats, stood up instinctively, then immediately sat down again.

Annabel stopped in the middle of the drawing-room and, with an elegance that excited silent admiration, bowed slightly. Not a sound was to be heard.

'Ladies,' she said, 'I know very well that by arriving here among you I am an object of amazement and I understand it all the more since I myself, replying to Mrs Harrison Edwards' very kind invitation, can still not altogether believe that I am here, my mind being full of quite precise, though now very old memories.'

Mrs Harrison Edwards stood up.

'Mrs Armstrong, we wanted to wipe out something that should never have happened and which aroused indignation in us all.'

Annabel bowed again and said, 'I came here this evening to defend my mother's honor.'

The simplicity with which this remark was made moved everyone present and, once more, small lace handkerchiefs appeared here and there. Siverac went over to Annabel, bowed and introduced himself:

'Madam,' he said, 'the honor of Mrs Régis de Lavaur was never at all in doubt in the minds of those who knew her. My father, who was a witness at her marriage, together with Miss Maisie Llewelyn, has given me irrefutable written proof which I shall be delighted to place in your hands.'

In a few words he explained what it concerned and she thanked him, not without making a considerable effort to control the beating of her heart.

'Then the aim of my visit is achieved,' she said, 'and I feel too happy to be able to say more.'

She did in fact remain silent and perfectly still for a moment. As night was falling, the servants lit torches and in the soft light she seemed to recover something of the mysterious power which she had possessed as a young woman. Raising her hand to the emeralds which, as soon as she entered the room, had dazzled and intrigued every woman present, she said with embarrassment:

'Ladies, you must forgive me for drawing your attention to these jewels which hardly suit the person I have now become, but this is the first and last time that you will see me wearing them. These are the emeralds which my mother wore around her neck on the day of her wedding. In their own way, they plead her cause for her.'

As she was speaking these last words in a voice choked with emotion, her eyes began to gleam with anger and were filled with tears.

On the spur of the moment, with a sudden inspiration, Mrs Harrison Edwards rushed over to her.

'My dear,' she said, 'I am sure that I express what we all feel when I ask you to consider yourself one of us and a member of that great family: Southern society!'

This unexpected speech was greeted by a general commotion. The ladies, in amazement, turned to one another in every direction, in the midst of a buzzing of indistinct words, but too many tears were running down too many cheeks and a general feeling came to prevail as if by force, brushing aside any uncertainty or objections. Mrs Devilue Upton Smythe, her head shaking beneath a monument of lace, but with undiminished authority in her quavering voice, proclaimed:

'Yes, for the honor of Laura and to repair a dreadful injustice.'

'For honor!' cried everyone present — and the gentlemen at the back were bellowing at the top of their voices. 'For honor!'

Annabel tottered and had to be supported. But she recovered in a burst of energy, while the ladies felt faint and waved their fans.

She pulled herself together and then, bolt upright, both hands on the hem of her great black cape, which was half-open, she said in a slow, solemn voice:

'Ladies, and you too, gentlemen at the back, my heart is at last beating in time with yours and you have restored to me my pride in our South, whose daughter I am; but the person who is now speaking to you has had her full share of the suffering which the world can inflict on a woman's soul and, last night, in answer to a call which came from beyond this world, she resolved to leave it for ever. Allow me to express my gratitude to you and to bid you farewell, while saluting you as you deserve.'

Taking three steps back and holding aside her cape and her dress with her outstretched arms, she bent as low as she possibly could in the deep curtsey reserved for use in the presence of a queen.

All the ladies stood up. There were sounds of discreet sobbing. Mrs Devilue Upton Smythe, her voice trembling excessively, declared:

'Madam, you are depriving us of a great joy, but we sympathise with you and our blessings go with you.'

Algernon, overcome with emotion, fainted politely in a corner and was brought back to his senses with a few cuffs round the ears from some young officers, while Charlie Jones took Mrs Harrison Edwards' hand to lead Annabel away. Quite distraught, Elizabeth joined them in the little antechamber, her eyes brimming with tears. Annabel turned to her with a broad smile, full of tenderness.

'I was expecting you, my dear Elizabeth, but you have waited a long time to embrace your old friend. I forgive you because I can see that you have round your neck the precious ruby pendant which reminds me of the cruellest moment of my life.'

'Oh, Annabel!' Elizabeth cried, shaking her golden locks.

'Enough emotion for one evening, Elizabeth. Don't you think?' she asked Charlie Jones and Mrs Harrison Edwards.

'A sensitive soul,' said Charlie Jones.

'Young . . .,' Mrs Harrison Edwards murmured, holding a handkerchief.

'Now,' said Annabel, 'enough emotional upsets, Elizabeth. Keep still for a moment.'

Then, taking off her emeralds, she slipped them around the young woman's neck. Elizabeth closed her eyes in happiness.

'How can I thank you?' she asked, putting a hand to her breast.

'Just say thank you and kiss me. That's all . . . There, I've been properly embraced now. I am leaving. Don't forget me.'

And, before they could even answer, she was outside.

# 96

*I*t goes without saying that this gathering at Mrs Harrison Edwards', followed by Annabel's departure, was the great event of the season, with almost endless repercussions. Billy, who was only told about it ten days later, burst out in annoyance when Elizabeth told him about it.

'You knew and you kept it from me. I should like to have said goodbye to cousin Annabel — and you would have heard me cheer and roar louder than anyone. You have let me miss a marvellous occasion.'

'Of course, the ones I can give you don't count.'

'Be quiet! Lock the door and let's waste no more time.'

The usual ecstasy occurred, which Billy's ardor always made into something new.

For her part, Mrs Harrison Edwards found that a less tumultuous life provided charms which she assumed had vanished long ago. The huge success of her reception, graced with the tale of the voyage to Haiti and Mrs Jonathan Armstrong's dramatic farewell, compensated her for her anxieties. Her relief was shared by Charlie Jones who had been as concerned as she was, but his proverbial good humor was overshadowed occasionally. With time, he had begun to take the restlessness of the Northern abolitionists more seriously. Contrary to expectations, the Black, Dred Scott, after an interminable trial, was not released from slavery, but maintained in that condition, by a decision of Chief Justice Taney. Furthermore, the party concerned did not want the freedom that he would have been offered in the North at any price, knowing that it would have been given him in exchange for factory work which was considerably harder than his domestic duties in the South. The Supreme Court judgement poisoned the political climate while an electoral campaign loomed on the horizon.

Charlie Jones travelled to the North quite often on business and came back every time slightly more pessimistic than before. He only spoke of this to his close friends, but he sometimes recalled the great Calhoun's exclamation, on his deathbed: 'Alas, my poor South!' The fact remains that Charlie Jones remained, body and soul, a fervent and loyal friend of the country that had accepted him as a son in his adventurous youth. Nothing could now alter that, but there was mounting anxiety in his heart.

However, life in Savannah went on, apparently carefree. The young were carried away by the dizzying enchantment of the waltz when they were not pining with love beneath the veranda on a summer night, with their fingers on the strings of a mandoline. Sometimes the names of Lincoln and Douglas, the 'little giant', were dropped into the conversation, very quickly. What could be more boring than politics? Much better to be swept away in a whirl of pleasure. Elizabeth could only whirl with Billy, whose jealous tiger slept with only one eye shut; and then there was a child on the way, expected in September. However, she felt happy. She did not believe in war, because Billy had told her that there would not be one. Yet she could not disguise the fact that life was becoming more serious for her. Her little Ned, whom she still loved as passionately, was a cause of odd anxiety for her. She caught scraps of conversation between him and the Irish gardener which alarmed her. They talked nonsense, walking around in woodlands peopled not by living creatures but by voices speaking in some unknown tongue, both imitating these voices, competing for who could speak the faster. Ned excelled at it. Still more alarming for Elizabeth was the fact that Jonathan's name continually recurred. As soon as they saw her, they stopped talking. Ned yawned. Pat took a spade or a rake and greeted Elizabeth.

'Good morning, Ma'am. Have you come to see your magnolias? They get finer every day.'

And the magnolias along the wall, in league with him, stunned the young woman with their scent, heavy with memories.

'The stories you tell each other!' she said, laughing. 'I can hear you from the house.'

'Ireland, Ma'am. I tell him about the Old Country. One day your boy must go on a visit over there.'

'Oh, yes, Mummy! Over there in Pat's country.'

She walked away feeling anxious. Billy must never hear mention of the name of Jonathan. He already knew too much, having witnessed the challenge to the duel under the green oaks at Dimwood. This must never be spoken of, yet now Jonathan's name was on little Ned's lips . . .

A week or ten days later, Celina asked to talk to her mistress. With her somewhat formal good manners and her over-precise foreigner's English, she informed Elizabeth that she was going back to her own country, to Europe.

Elizabeth immediately envisaged the inevitable problems of life without a housekeeper.

'I'm sorry, Celina,' she said, gently. 'Are you perhaps worried about the prospect of war? I can reassure you on that score. I have information from an absolutely reliable source.'

'No, Madam, I'm not afraid of war.'

'My son always treats you well, I hope.'

'Always, Ma'am, and I am very fond of him . . .'

She hestiated for a moment.

'If I might be allowed to make one remark, Ma'am, I go to see him every evening after dinner. He is usually asleep at that time and he talks to himself.'

'All children, Celina . . .'

'Yes, Ma'am, but he is — how do you say in English . . . over-excited — and he speaks in a language which I do not know.'

'Pat must have taught him a few words of Irish.'

Celina shrugged her shoulders and continued:

'I think you should watch little Ned, Ma'am.'

'Very well, Celina. I shall settle your wages and give you a good reference.'

'Thank you, Ma'am. I believe I have done what I could.'

'We shall part on the best of terms, Celina. But can't you tell me why you are going?'

'Homesickness, Ma'am. Nothing more, but it is very strong.'

'I know how you feel. Even now, sometimes, England . . .'

'Yes, Ma'am.'


Celina left the following morning and, burying her pride, Elizabeth wrote to Maisie Llewelyn. She arrived promptly. The meeting took place in the little drawing-room, formerly blue, now the color of blood, since Charlie Jones's decorators had quickly got down to work.

'Well, now,' said Maisie Llewelyn, 'the decor has changed, but we are resuming the scene where it was left off. I advised you to get rid of Celina and she has gone. Just as well.'

'Why?'

'She was about to be denounced.'

'I don't undersand.'

'Still as naive as ever, Miss Lizbeth, if I may venture to say so.'

'What do you mean? A thief?'

'No, inquisitive.'

'You don't mean . . .'

'Yes. Like Miss Pringle in Dimwood: you remember? It was Mr Charlie Jones who chased Celina away. She is now heading for the North with her little package of observations on the state of mind in the South, which she will deliver to her employers.'

'She seemed so honest . . .'

'So she was, according to her lights. She thought she was serving a just cause, the little goose. But enough of that. You have no one to run the household and you are asking for my help, am I right?'

'Oh, Miss Llewelyn . . .'

'Oh, Miss Llewelyn is enough. I want to see the accounts.'

The ledger was brought at once, with the result that henceforth she was permanently installed in Elizabeth's house. Nothing changed, yet everything was different. Now one could feel the presence of an iron will, while in Celina's time one had the impression that everything could give way at any moment, that order only reigned with a sort of flabbiness, through successive strokes of good luck.

One of the Welshwoman's first tasks was to visit the gardener, who seemed to have made Ned his closest companion. It was, above all, the little boy who had intrigued Maisie Llewelyn from the moment she first saw him, busy at his mother's feet, plucking the flowers on the Persian carpet. She sensed an indefinable sense of affinity of breeding between them.

Leaning on his spade, Pat said nothing, while Ned was crouching in front of a bunch of violets looking closely at the tiny flowers which were opening in a ray of sunshine.

'Just one,' he said. 'Just one, Pat, for Mummy.'

'No, not one,' said Pat. 'It's forbidden, they're Celina's.'

Neither of them had seen Maisie Llewelyn who, approaching very softly across the grass, had stopped to listen to them.

'Good day,' she said suddenly.

They turned round and Pat raised his broad straw hat.

'Good day, Miss Maisie,' he said. 'It's a pleasure to see you, but you don't come often.'

'Well, Pat, that is about to change. From now on you are going to see a lot more of me.'

A little mystified, he ventured a huge smile while Ned, standing open-mouthed, considered this very large lady who said such incomprehensible but interesting things.

'So, these violets are Celina's?' the Welshwoman asked.

'Yes . . . My belief is that she has a fiancé somewhere in town and is keeping the violets to make a bouquet which she can wear on her wedding day.'

'You're imagining things, Pat.'

'What do you mean? She's not bad looking, that Celina. She must certainly have a lover, but she doesn't say anything.'

'Does she come here often?'

'Every day. You'll see her in a moment.'

'You think so, do you? Is she talkative?'

'Not very. She prefers to listen to me when I talk to her. I make her laugh; she loves that, especially when I tell her what I hear on the street. I'm good at imitating passers-by — the way they look, the way they talk.'

'Mrs Lizbeth forbade you . . . You do that instead of working.'

'Oh, Mrs Lizbeth says that . . . But I find things out: it's my right to know what's going on, you understand? And then it makes that Celina laugh so . . . One day, without seeming to, she squeezed my hand several times . . . Like that . . . Oh! I'm not saying this to suggest that she wouldn't have said no . . . But she is kind . . . If the child had not been there . . .'

'What? A little flirtation might be allowed, I suppose.'

'Just so, what?'

He approached her with a peculiar look on his face. She shrank back.

'Now, now, my lad! You could be asking for a slap. I'm not another Celina.'

'Oh, come, Miss Maisie! You must have heard a few sweet nothings in your time, back home. You must still like a compliment, don't you?'

Maisie Llewelyn was irritated by this allusion to her age. Without being as young as she once was, she still liked to feel attractive.

'Come, come, Pat. Don't be angry. Tell me what you were talking about with the child. When he is not out for a walk with Betty, he's always with you.'

'He's as much of a chatterbox as I am, you know. I teach him the names of the flowers and talk to him about the Old Country.'

'Ireland,' Ned said, his eyes shining. 'I'm going there. Pat. You promised me.'

'What a strange notion,' the Welshwoman said with a laugh. 'Why not to my home in Caerphilly?'

'It must be very pretty in your country, Miss Maisie, but he's got into the habit of going home to Ireland every evening, haven't you, Ned?'

'Every evening!' Ned exclaimed.

'Well, I never! How do you go there? By boat?'

'No, on horseback. But you mustn't tell.'

'I won't tell anyone, Ned. On the word of a Welshwoman.'

Ned looked at the gardener.

'Can I tell?'

'If you want, young lad, if Miss Maisie gives her word.'

'Well, then. When Celina comes to put out the lamp, I must first close my eyes to pretend to be asleep . . .'

He paused. The very large lady was listening attentively and this always flattered him.

'Then,' he said, catching his breath, 'the horseman gallops up from the back of the room and takes me with him.'

This sentence, spoken in a single burst, had an extraordinary effect on Maisie Llewelyn. She felt that a whole world of poetry was opening up before her eyes, as it did in her native land. She leaned over toward Ned.

'What you are saying is fascinating. The horseman takes you there, across the sea.'

'Oh, I can see the sea, which is quite black.'

'Because it's night,' Pat explained. 'But Jonathan is not afraid of anything.'

Ned gave a great cry of distress.

'Oh, Pat! You mustn't say it! You mustn't say Zonathan, Mummy said not.'

The Welshwoman understood everything, but did not react.

'If your Mummy has forbidden it, you mustn't say it,' she said, stroking the little boy's cheek.

'Miss Maisie has promised she'll say nothing,' said Pat. 'So there's no harm done.'

'Of course there's no harm, little Ned,' Maisie said, encouraging him. 'Besides, it's a very nice name, Jonathan.'

'Oh, yes,' Ned answered, entirely reassured. 'And it's my name.'

'Your name?' Maisie Llewelyn said, innocently. 'I thought your name was Ned.'

'I'm called Zonathan,' the child said, authoritatively. 'But you mustn't tell anyone. Mummy doesn't want me to.'

The Welshwoman felt a shudder of horror, as if the child had resuscitated a corpse, but she repressed it.

'In that case,' she said, 'we won't tell, will we, Pat?'

'Hope to die! I swear it,' said Pat, without really understanding what the discussion was all about.

Together, they put the little boy's mind at rest. However, in the depths of a still unblemished conscience, he made an attempt to put things right.

'Couldn't I give Mummy a little violet?'

'Yes, you can,' said the Welshwoman. 'I give you permission.'

'And Celina?' Pat asked. 'She doesn't want anyone to touch them.'

'I don't know what she has to do with it, but it doesn't matter. I forgot to tell you that she will never again set foot here. I am replacing her. Yes, my fine Pat, your beloved Celina loves the North more than she does the South, and she is on her way there now.'

'The devil! She was spying on us.'

'Not altogether. There is not a war on, but the North just wants to find out, to know if we are ripe.'

'Ripe?'

'Yes, ripe enough to drop into its hands without it having to pay too much for the prize. There you are. Now, Pat, I am the one who gives the orders here, in Madam's name. So back to work. We are friends, but I want work out of you. And you, my lad, come with me. It's time for your walk with Betty.'

She took his hand. He turned round to the gardener and said something that the Welshwoman did not catch. Pat replied in kind. Their speech was quick, confused, with strange sounds.

'What are you saying?' the Welshwoman asked Ned when they were some way off.

'Nothing, that's how we speak.'

'Did he teach you?'

'No, when I'm in the dark, I speak like that.'

'And what about him?'

'Oh, he understands at once and speaks in the same way, though not quite the same.'

'I don't like that very much, Ned.'

'Don't tell Mummy, Miss Maisie.'

'No, I promise.'

'Or Betty.'

'Nobody. But it's odd, this gibberish.'

'It's nice,' the little boy said.

At the end of a day's work, Charlie Jones came to visit Elizabeth in her scarlet drawing-room.

'I hope you're pleased with your new color scheme,' he said, looking around.

'Billy is especially delighted with it.'

'You less so, of course. One of the cruellest tricks life can play on us is to give us what we ask for. But let that be. Dear Annabel gave you a regal gift.'

'I am a little wary of putting it on. What will people think?'

'They will think what Mrs Harrison Edwards and I have told all Savannah. They expect to see you with the emeralds around your neck. They suit you marvellously, but how secretive you are! They were in the box that I gave you at the De Soto. I was dying to know. Has Billy seen your emeralds?'

'No.'

'No need to be mysterious! He would have been delighted.'

'I didn't want to.'

'Why? I'm interested to know.'

'I can't tell you. They are very lovely; I used to put them on when I was alone . . . I don't know why, now they make me . . . afraid. Perhaps it's because of Miss Llewelyn's story. Those stones belonged to Cousin Laura and they did not bring her good luck.'

'Shame on your superstition! Laura gave them to her daughter who put them around your neck with her own hands. You will do me the favor of adorning yourself with them and dazzling Savannah.'

'I'll leave the ruby at home.'

'Perhaps, the two don't go together. The ruby is wonderful, but . . .'

'Tragic, you think — a drop of blood. Annabel told me.'

Charlie Jones gave a start of horror.

'In heaven's name, Elizabeth, be the charming Englishwoman again, whom the whole town loves, and stop thinking you have to mourn everybody. By the way, you will not be sorry to see the back of Celina. She would eventually have become dangerous. Maisie Llewelyn will look after your house as she did at Dimwood. You'll be delighted . . . And Billy? You haven't told me anything.'

'Oh, Billy! He's my whole life.'

'Hurrah! If I can still count on my fingers, you should be expecting a visit from a little stranger in September. It's now June, or almost. There will be a time when Billy will have to behave himself.'

Elizabeth blushed pink.

'Please, Uncle Charlie.'

'Don't worry, I'll talk to him myself. He has as much common sense as a bolting stallion. One thing more and I'll be going. Don't take any notice of the rumors you hear. The Northern abolitionists have been beside themselves since March because of Roger Taney. His decision in the Dred Scott case has become law, much to the satisfaction of the South.'

'Taney? Who is Taney, Uncle Charlie?'

'Splendid. That's even better than I hoped. My dear Elizabeth, forget all this and sleep easy. Take good care of little Ned. He's sensitive and a dreamer. He needs a brother to shake him up and wrestle with him a bit. Let him come and have tea at home one day. My boy is just longing for a fight.'

# 97

*T*he summer settled in, stifling hot, and the pace of life slowed down until it achieved a deathly stillness — although this did not prevent the flowers from splashing their colors triumphantly all over the houses with their closed shutters. Nor did the leaden heat affect Maisie Llewelyn's energy. Calm and swift in spite of her weight, she had made Elizabeth's house into her domain and, as at Dimwood, exercised her strange gift for apparent ubiquity. At once nowhere and everywhere, but always where one was least expecting her, she did not arrive — she appeared.

However, far from spreading disquiet, she was now enjoying the fruit of her dramatic narrative at Mrs Harrison Edwards'. She had satisfied a most difficult audience with shudders of pleasure and terror, by leading it through a paradise in the grip of a revolution. She was admired in the same way as an artist confident in her skill. Even better, she had felt rising toward her a wave of sympathy which was close to love; for, without departing entirely from the truth, she had depicted herself as modestly sublime and the local aristocracy had applauded her. Her breast swelled with pride at this victory. She had respect. At last.

Around her, the world was changing. The heat, usually rather depressing, was powerless against a wave of national pride which was breaking over the South. The fact that Chief Justice Taney had succeeded in defeating the abolitionist fury of the North filled the air with the scent of the morning after a military victory. In Charleston, particularly, there were defiant speeches and a wave of pride spread through the town. Shots were fired in Taney's honor.

Lieutenant Billy and his comrades had their share of this revival of warlike ardor. Elizabeth's husband, bursting with the urge to fulfil his conjugal duties, was no less warlike at home: the two instincts were perfectly combined. Unfortunately, leave was becoming rarer. Beaufort needed to see its defenses consolidated. With Fort Sumter, in Charleston, Fort Beauregard was one of the most important sites for the defense of South Carolina, which claimed it was always ready to go to war. Moreover, as far as Lieutenant Billy was concerned, there was a small matter — of some importance — which stood in the way of his irrepressible natural urges: the Commandant could no longer do without him in his game of whist and referred to the redecoration of Beaufort as an excuse for less frequent leaves, whereas they had once been weekly.

Thus Billy suffered, and so did his wife, both enduring one of the cruellest forms of hunger known to the body. For Elizabeth, the torment was made worse by Maisie Llewelyn adding her advice to Uncle Charlie's: prudence as the weeks went by; though of what use were these instructions, as long as the absent one remained so? An expert in the field, the Welshwoman foresaw everything.

'If it's a daughter,' she said one evening, 'you have nothing to worry about, but if it's a boy, no one can tell how young Ned will take it. I mentioned it to him a month ago.'

'Oh, Miss Llewelyn! What can he understand of all that kind of thing?'

'Nothing, but I told him that in September he might have a little brother, and the look he gave me makes me think that he is advanced for his age. He already knows about jealousy. That young man wants to be alone.'

'Oh, if that's all! I'll arrange everything with affection and tenderness. He knows that I adore him.'

'Then you must dig deep into the treasures of your heart. He will demand to be favorite . . . Your favorite, you understand, like . . .'

Elizabeth looked at her.

'Like who?'

'Like your husband of course. Like his father.'

'Of course. Thank you, Miss Llewelyn. I am going to sleep now.'

The Welshwoman left immediately, but Elizabeth did not go to sleep. What did she mean? she wondered. Why that veiled allusion to Jonathan?

The next day, Miss Llewelyn went for a walk round the garden. It was empty. In the magnolia corner, she paused for a while to drink in the heavy perfume of the flowers which reminded her of the smell of the young men in her own country. She sighed. She had been loved, once.

Putting such memories aside, she went right into the gardener's house, a dark cavern with a door that flapped while Pat was entertaining himself, watching the passers-by on the avenue. In a thunderous voice, she called him, and he emerged almost at once out of the darkness, exclaiming:

'Yes, Miss Maisie. What a grand surprise!'

'You joker! You'll soon be getting the grand surprise of finding yourself thrown out on the street. Would you like me to talk to Madam about it?'

'Miss Maisie, I swear by my patron saint . . .'

'Enough. This time I won't say anything, but I want to see you with a rake in your hand. Your paths are very ill-tended. Where is Ned?'

'With Betty right now.'

'What is that gibberish you speak together?'

'He invented it himself.'

'He also says that he hears people talking like that in the night.'

'That's nothing to do with me.'

'You're lying, Pat. Do you think I don't understand Gaelic?'

'Oh, well, now! Just a word, here and there. The language of the little people.'

'It's very bad for a child of that age. He already spends too much of his time dreaming. I forbid you to encourage him. Do you understand?'

'Yes, Ma'am. But I cannot stop him speaking.'

'In that case, don't answer him. And another thing. The name Jonathan. Let there be no more heard of Jonathan unless you want to be dismissed. I want your word, Pat. If Madam knew, you would be out in under a minute.'

Pat gave his word with a profusion of oaths and invocations to all the saints in the Irish paradise.

'That's enough. Now get down to work!'

The rake miraculously appeared in Pat's hand and was waved in the air.

'Enough play acting,' she said, tartly. 'Work. And remember about Jonathan. If you keep quiet, you stay. Otherwise: out!'

Without another word, she swung round on her heels, leaving him speechless at the importance given to this Jonathan, whom he had thought of as an imaginary being. And, leaning on his rake, he started to dream.

Since her arrival, Miss Llewelyn had occupied Celina's room, the latter having been saved from prison by her flight. It was agreeable, tastefully furnished in the colonial style of the beginning of the century: a four-poster in black wood; a huge rocking chair; a dressing table. A large mirror in a mahogany frame gave depth to an otherwise skimpy little room. The window did not open on the garden, as the Welshwoman would have liked, but on the square lined with sycamores. It was in these surroundings, with their classical banality, that Maisie Llewelyn tried to arrange her thoughts. What bothered her more than anything was the change in little Ned since the day when she had seen him playing on the carpet at his mother's feet. The lisping, laughing child with his baby's gestures had become a visionary full of disturbing fantasies. His mother had brought the presence of the man whom she had loved into this young life. Ned thought he was someone else. It was enough to affect his reason. She thought for a long time about the best course of action to take. Perhaps the birth of a brother or sister would bring things back to normal. For the first time in her life, she experienced the perplexity of a soul confronted with a destiny, the significance of which escapes it. In spite of everything, however, she felt vaguely responsible for the fate of this very young boy haunted by the threat of mental confusion. It was then that an utterly silent, but precise voice asked her a curious question: 'Whose fault?'

Seized with anger and fear, she stamped her foot and cried: 'No!'

But, however much she tried to pretend that she had not heard, she failed. Tiny details came back into her mind. An absurd little phrase rose up in her memory with teasing obstinacy: 'That letter in the fire . . .'

She shrugged her shoulders and began to laugh. All that was so far away. The time came when the things of the past lost all meaning.

Elizabeth had difficulty recovering from her talk with the Welshwoman, who had plunged her into an abyss of anxiety.

What does she mean by her insinuations? she wondered, tossing in her bed. What can she have in mind? That reference to Jonathan, the favorite . . . The child has betrayed me. They have got his secret out of him. He is constantly chatting to Pat . . .

For her part, Maisie Llewelyn, all alone, shared her mistress' anguish. Without knowing it, both were asking themselves the same questions in almost the same terms. Out of an invincible attachment to Elizabeth, the Welshwoman decided to come to her aid.

She waited a further day. It promised to be a fine one. A fleet of white clouds was sailing across an azure sky. The Welshwoman went to see the young woman in her room and addressed her with a kind of affectionate brusqueness.

'Don't be angry with me, Ma'am, if I tell you what is on my mind, without any beating about the bush.'

Elizabeth looked at her in surprise.

'What is wrong now, Miss Llewelyn? You have only been in this house for ten days and there is already something wrong?'

Maisie Llewelyn gave her a broad smile.

'I guess that you are unhappy, and I have come to set your mind at rest, to find again the young Englishwoman of former times with our old friendship reawakened. Let's leap across the years and re-discover one another. We have a thousand things to say which will remove our doubts and uncertainties.'

This little speech, delivered with the charm of a Welsh accent, at first frightened Elizabeth and she said nothing. The Welshwoman waited patiently, then said softly:

'I am not a wicked woman, Elizabeth.'

This phrase, which she had never forgotten, took the still suspicious Englishwoman a long way back in time, to Dimwood, to the Great Meadow in Virginia and, through the magic of memory, brought back Jonathan's face. She owed that man to this woman.

'What do you want?' she asked finally.

'I suggest we take a walk in the Colonial Cemetery where we can talk freely. What I have to say is so simple that it will surprise you. I'll order your carriage and we shall be there in five minutes.'

Faced with the wavering of Elizabeth's will, she rapidly recovered her own imperious manner. She was on the point of leading the hesitant young Englishwoman by the hand.

Less than a quarter of an hour later they were walking slowly under the plane trees in the park, which had nothing melancholy about it apart from a few scattered tombstones green with moss. Here and there, rays of sunshine broke through the heavy greenery of the avenues strewn with pale pink brick. Other ladies were walking about and chatting under their parasols. It was hard to believe that in the early hours of daylight, gentlemen fought one another in duels in isolated clearings at the end of these paths.

Elizabeth felt that the Welshwoman was dominating her as for that matter, she had dominated the whole of Savannah society at Mrs Harrison Edwards'. The charm of the eloquent storyteller was still working. In a soft but clear voice, she said, almost in her mistress' ear:

'How strange children are, Ma'am . . . How did your sweet little Ned happen to hear the name of Jonathan?'

Elizabeth shuddered.

'I really can't tell. What are you implying, Miss Llewelyn?'

'Just this: that he has caught on to the name. It pleased him and he wanted to become a character called Jonathan.'

'What is the significance of this oddity?'

'It has none. Every child has played at being someone else. He has even spoken about him to the gardener, to whom the name means nothing.'

'So?'

'I am the first to understand what memories are stirred in you . . . But the gentleman left no descendants. Who mentions him anymore? Your little boy's whims mean nothing to anyone, except . . .'

'That's enough, Miss Llewelyn.'

'Very well, Ma'am. I merely wanted to put your mind at rest.'

'I thank you for your good intentions. Now, we are far enough from home, so I am going back.'

They walked on without saying anything, until their attention was caught by a man in black walking up and down, a short distance away from them, followed by a few people who were listening to him in silence, for he was speaking like a preacher, wearing a wide-brimmed hat. Elizabeth and Miss Llewelyn recognized him at once. It was Mr Robertson who, after the ceremony on the day of William Hargrove's funeral, had given a speech on the steps of Christ Church. By tacit agreement, Elizabeth and Miss Llewelyn stopped at the sound of this fine, deep, sonorous voice.

'Among these stones, beneath which rest the heroes of the War of Independence, you will notice a more recent one, dating from 1837.'

These words, spoken with feeling, were followed by a pause. Grief suddenly appeared on his pink face, with its frame of white curls, while the birds poured out their song above his head. He took off his hat.

'I loved the man who lies beneath this stone. He was twenty-seven years old. One day, in a saloon in our town, he heard a young fellow from Louisiana speak slightingly of a Miss Laura Hargrove, mother of a daughter "of father unknown". Coming up to him, young Frank Hargrove cut this chatterbox short with a cuff that laid him flat on the ground. The duel that followed the next morning at first light took place here, at the end of the park. I was there, among the witnesses. The swords shone and clashed, whispering the secret name of death. I saw Frank fall, his shirt stained with blood. His adversary dropped his sword and fled.'

He stopped, then went on:

'All this happencd less than twenty years ago, on August 20, 1837, on a morning like this one. And the birds were singing.'

Elizabeth remained motionless, while Maisie Llewelyn lifted both hands to her face to hide her tears.

'Frank,' she whispered.

'That's all,' Mr Robertson said, replacing his hat. 'I asked you to come and you came. Thank you. I have never managed to escape the memory of that absurd death, brought about by an idiot. It has taught me to hate all wars, being itself like a war in microcosm.'

Suddenly his face was distorted with rage:

'War!' he said. 'For years we have been hearing either that it will not come on American soil, or else that it is coming, that it is at our door. How can we be so blind? You are afraid of civil war; but it is here. For the past two years it has been openly raging in Kansas, which demands entry to the Union; but it is up to a population made up of immigrants to choose the type of government it wants. Those from the South are in favor of allowing slavery in the State, those from the North are strongly against. They vote. One agreement follows another. They vote and they cheat. It is impossible to achieve a majority. At the same time they fight one another . . . The number of dead and wounded continues to rise. One fine-sounding orator declared that the knell of the Union was tolled with the first drop of blood. The battlefield can only extend. Cannon shots will mark the entry of Kansas into the Republic. Then the great massacre will begin. Politicians and preachers will have supplied enough patriotic and religious eloquence and, as always, it will be the young who pay the bill, in fine and generous crimson blood. My friends, the North wants its war, and it shall have it; it has already begun.'

Maisie Llewelyn grasped Elizabeth's arm.

'Let's go,' she said. 'When lunatics start to speak like wise men, the sky opens and eventually our world will be rent apart.'

When Elizabeth heard this declaration made in a loud voice, she saw a new women in Miss Llewellyn and had the feeling that the Welshwoman was inspired by some prophetic impulse. Her own imagination was abruptly unleashed and she saw War. She saw it as Maisie Llewelyn saw it. And, gripped by the same feeling, without knowing why, both of them broke into a run. They ran as far as the entrance to the park where the carriage was waiting. There, Maisie Llewelyn burst out laughing.

'What's the matter with us?' she asked. 'Calm yourself, Ma'am. There will always be wars and mankind goes through them like going through a storm; and there will be deaths . . . Come, let me help you up.'

'I don't want Billy to die,' Elizabeth said, her foot on the running board of the carriage.

The Welshwoman pushed her forward, so that she dropped on to the seat.

'Courage! You're English. The English do at least have that.'

'Billy assures me that there will not be war, Miss Llewelyn.'

'He talks to you as he might to a little girl. Believe me: that old loony Robertson knows more about it than Billy does.'

Elizabeth blew her nose and did not reply.

# 98

*T*he next few weeks were trying for all of them. As every year, no one could remember ever having experienced such a stifling end to the summer, but it was not considered polite to complain about it. Savannah valued its reputation as a paradise on earth. After the dreadful years that had seen its humiliation and total ruin, it was once more enjoying the sweet sensation of restored prosperity. As for the rumors of war, they were losing their power to terrify simply because of their frequency. Elizabeth could not accustom herself to them, however; and there was something else. One morning, the mail brought her a letter from Billy, half-loving, half-teasing, which announced that he would be arriving the day after next. How hard it had been for him to obtain this miserable little two-day furlough! But in any case, joy was returning and, then, 'my Lizbeth, make yourself beautiful: pleasure is coming at the gallop . . .'

Pleasure . . . Elizabeth stood in front of the mirror. In her imposingly capacious muslin dress, she could not hold back a few vexatious tears; and, without realizing it as she walked back and forth in front of her reflection, she trod on Billy's letter, two or three times, much to her consternation. Life was too unkind.

At this very same moment, Miss Llewelyn entered discreetly, the corners of her mouth raised in an ironic smile.

'Just so,' she said.

Elizabeth turned round:

'You startled me. What do you mean?'

'That prudence should be the order of the day and, if I guess rightly, that letter which you are brushing around with the hem of your dress . . .'

'You guess everything; one can't hide a thing from you. I know that I am huge and that he will be displeased. Excuse me, but I find you irritating.'

A little knock on the door: it was Ned, coming to say hello to his mother. When he saw her standing in this cloud of muslin, he laughed.

'Hello, Mummy.'

Elizabeth embraced him as usual and the Welshwoman took him back to the door, because she could see his eyes widen as he looked at his mother.

'Off with you,' Maisie Llewelyn said. 'Your Mama needs to be alone.'

'Mummy's eating too much,' he whispered.

The child was born a fortnight later. It was a boy. The Welshwoman took care of everything with such devotion that Elizabeth was overcome with a burst of frantic reconciliation. Billy forgot the cruel disappointments that he had previously had to suffer when, after managing to extort another furlough from his commandant through a daring piece of blackmail at whist, he was finally able to admire the tiny newcomer whimpering with fury at finding himself in a world which he did not know. He was baptised under the name of Christopher, at Christ Church, as one would expect. The ceremony was a quiet one. Billy was bursting with pride, in his dress uniform, and the mother, happy to be no longer in pain, made the best possible impression in her white dress, with the magnificent ruby mysteriously shining on her breast. Young Ned behaved with patience and reserve. On the whole, all went well. However, after the ceremony, there was an incident that nearly caused a drama. The venerable priest wanted to exchange a few pleasant words with those present. Turning to Ned, and gently stroking his head, he had the unfortunate notion of asking him his name. Ned had a moment's hesitation before replying, which alarmed Elizabeth. In a quick, firm voice, she answered for him:

'Edward, his name is Edward.'

Some time later, on one of those lovely autumn evenings when daylight refuses to give way to night, Maisie Llewelyn visited her banker Charlie Jones. For the occasion, she wore a blue dress, bordering on black — a little ceremonious, perhaps, but Charlie Jones was one of the people whom she most respected. He greeted her at the bottom of his garden, in an arbor where the last rays of sunlight caressed a mantle of honeysuckle.

'It's always a pleasure for me to talk to you, Miss Llewelyn. Without wishing to shower you with compliments, especially since that memorable evening at Mrs Harrison Edwards', you have never been known to speak unless you have something to say.'

'This evening at least, I hope to confirm you in that opinion. Will you forgive me if I come straight to the point?'

'Of course, I rather like your style.'

'Well, last night I was unable to sleep. Instead, I read. Does the name Helper mean anything to you?'

'Helper — like a person who helps, you mean?'

'The name is predestined. Until quite recently Helper was one of those poor Whites who are so unjustly despised. Unless I am mistaken, you have always taken a generous interest in them?'

'Schmick House,' said Charlie Jones.

'Indeed. How many poor Whites today owe their honorable positions to you. My Helper, if I may call him that, is Hinton Rowan Helper, the son of a German immigrant who settled in North Carolina and grew rich growing cotton, owning many slaves. Young Hinton had a happy childhood; but his father died and the family was ruined. Suddenly, Hinton was just one among a mass of insignificant Whites while still quite young.'

'That's a sad story. Would you like me to ring for coffee?'

'No, thank you. I suppose you will take some? No. Then I'll continue. Hinton remembers happier days and reflects on them while working hard. Above all, he thinks about the problem of slavery as a source of wealth: the problem as it is assessed in the North, and in the South, and as it appears to that dangerous crackpot Beecher-Stowe, who has never set foot down here or in a black person's cabin. Hinton, too, thinks of nothing else except that. By the time he was grown up, it was an obsession. Then an odd idea came to him. He consulted the United States census on slavery. The result of his research was astonishing. This man, with his passion for statistics, decided that they undermined Calhoun's theory on the undeniable advantages of the slave system. According to Calhoun, you know, slavery made the South the largest and richest agricultural region in the United States. But the figures were there, before Helper's eyes, and the figures said no. Unfortunately, I can't remember those figures.'

'Perhaps I can assist you, Miss Llewelyn. Annual income from agriculture in the slave states: gross 155 million dollars. Agricultural income in the free states: gross 214 million dollars. Slavery is bad business.'

Maisie Llewelyn leaped to her feet.

'Mr Jones!' she exclaimed.

Charlie Jones burst out laughing.

'Forgive me, Miss Llewelyn. You summed up the problem admirably and I am sure that you will not hold it against me, but . . .'

He took a small book out of his pocket and put it on the table:

'*The Impending Crisis,*' he said. 'I, too, spent a whole night perusing it. I admire the seriousness with which you have studied it.'

'But then we are saved!' the Welshwoman exclaimed. 'How can one dispute the figures given by official statistics?'

'We may be saved, if people are able to keep a cool head, but they are not, either in the North or in the South. Clay and Webster are no longer there, and look what we have come to! Everywhere emotion is triumphing over reason. Morever, morality is caught up in it and as a result there is no peace left. The South announces that slavery is a curse for which it is not responsible; the North is against slavery on moral grounds.'

'If you might allow me to express my own opinion on slavery, I . . .'

'You hate it, you too, and you are not wrong to do so.'

'But you have slaves yourself . . .'

'Servants, Miss Llewelyn, servants . . . They know quite well that if they want to flee to the North, they are free to do so. But they are not so stupid. They are very well off with me. They are part of the household, and a little bit part of the family, too. So?'

'I know, I know; but what about the slaves on the plantations?'

'I have no plantations. I have properties which I rent to planters, that's all'

'And Pilate washed his hands.'

'Now, now, Welshwoman! Who began the slave trade in America?'

'The South!'

'Tell me about it. We may learn something.'

'I am surprised that you should have forgotten the Blacks who were landed in Norfolk.'

'Do you mean the ship flying a Dutch flag that brought the first Blacks to the coast near Jamestown in 1619?'

'Just so.'

'How many Blacks, do you think?'

'How do I know? A ship's cargo.'

'The ship was not a big one, then: twenty Blacks.'

'It's a start.'

'A very small one. What is odd is that it did not appear very interesting, because no one has remembered the name of the ship or its captain. The fine little ghostship has been lost in the mists of oblivion.'

'Very well, I accept that. Other ships followed.'

'Ah, now be careful, Miss Llewelyn: *they did not go to James-town*. Most of them unloaded their cargo in Boston. Yes: quite a few great families from those parts owe the source of their fortune to the slave trade. What do you say to that? It has led to a very respectable, commercial aristocracy, which is none the less just as contemptuous as our own . . .'

'Oh, that word: aristocracy . . .'

'. . . turns your stomach, perhaps. And you may be sure that all those fine people sensed it during the reception at Mrs Harrison Edwards'. But that didn't stop all of us being dazzled by you. And I understand your feelings. I only belong to society because of my two successive marriages to ladies whose Scottish ancestors stole cattle in the Lowlands: a fine class of people, in short.'

'You think so?'

'Not at all, but that's what people think over there . . . I am not a member of the nobility. At the very most, I have a grandfather who was granted a title and some land by George II for sinking a lot of Spanish and French ships.'

'Someone of class, in short!'

'As they say.'

'Forgive me, but between ourselves, what a rotten grandfather.'

'A pirate, Miss Llewelyn, a pirate grandfather; but they call him a privateer.'

'Mr Jones, I feel closer to you when we speak like this, but we are straying from the point.'

'As you say. Let's get back to New England. The time soon came when the boats from Boston set sail for the Ivory Coast and took delivery of Blacks who had been abducted, torn from their families — but, what do you expect? It was necessary to establish the prosperity of the great families of New England on a solid foundation. Do you know when and where a ship called *Desire*, the first American slave ship, unloaded its cargo?'

'No, tell me.'

'At Salem, Massachussets, in 1638. It belonged to the town of Salem.'

'Salem! The witches' town!'

'The slave trade appears horrible to us, but it shocked no one at the time. It was acceptable then. Liverpool bought and sold black people. La Rochelle, Bordeaux and Brest competed. You have to wait until the beginning of our own century before the slave trade became illegal in New England. An awakening of conscience, do you think?'

'Why not? They are not all devils.'

'Certainly, but climate became the ally of conscience. The cold in New England killed the Blacks. Morality heaves a sigh of relief — but the climate of the South is just right and the South needs labor to work the plantations.'

'Now we're coming to it.'

'As you say. Yet New England continued to grow rich by dealing in slaves, selling them to the South, which did not prevent the appearance of abolitionist movements . . . Conscience again! It is not surprising that in such a confused general situation someone had the idea of New England seceding. It failed. How is one to understand all this, from the North to the South? One thing certainly is true: until the politicians, throughout the country, settle down, they risk plunging the Union into a fearful war. Poor Helper, with his common sense and his statistics, is powerless against that. In any case, it's not selling like hot cakes, his *Impending Crisis* and, what lies behind his work is the condition of the poor Whites: that's certainly what he has in mind, and slavery in the northern factories. The southern Blacks have to take third place. The truth is not so charming. When it pipes up, people say that it is singing out of tune: they prefer the full-throated tenor of lies. Having said which, even though I consider myself an Englishman, I remain loyal to the South.'

'You could not be more so than I who am a Welshwoman. Good night, Mr Jones. I can hear owls at the bottom of the garden. They have the last word on everything and I don't like what they are saying this evening.'

Elizabeth knew nothing about this book which must have had the effect of a bolt of lightning when it appeared; but people found it more seemly not to speak about it, should they happen to have read it. Miss Llewelyn observed the same silence when she was with Elizabeth, who had not forgotten the shock she had received in the Colonial Cemetery. It needed all Billy's natural powers of persuasion to convince her that all was well and that there would never be a war.

Her strength had returned and she looked after little Christopher, although she did not succeed in finding him beautiful.

The social calendar revived with the first chill of October. The great reception to mark the opening of the season was held, as always, in the Palladian rooms of the Steers' house. Elizabeth did not have pleasant memories of the one evening she had spent there before her second marriage; but now, by some caprice of pride, she felt an urge to blot all that out in a burst of brilliance. Still more profoundly, though she would not admit it even to herself, she was driven by the need for something that would blot out her own anxiety, which had refused to die down ever since she and Miss Llewelyn heard old Mr Robertson's prophetic speech.

However, such a return to the social world of the Steers could only take place on the arm of Billy, a very decorative man, apart from the fact that he was her husband. His furlough had to be fought for and won by the usual means, with help from a pull at the heartstrings provided by the arrival of Christopher, now already three weeks old. Billy made his appearance with military precision . . . He was enthralled by the idea of parading himself at the Steers'. His hussar's uniform suited his figure to the point where he himself could not get over how handsome he was: every mirror told him so, over and again, like a lovesick woman. Added to this satisfaction was another, no less great, of his being introduced with one of the most beautiful of creatures on his arm, her lord and master; in short, her owner.

Everything promised as well as could be. On the evening of the reception, the couple talked briefly before getting into their carriage. Elizabeth had had the idea of dressing in sea-green chiffon which turned her into a water nymph. Billy, ecstatic at the sight of this outfit which went so well with her already famous golden hair, did however risk a rather subtle remark:

'Of course, you will be wearing that marvellous ruby that Aunt Annabel gave you. Are you sure that the flaming red, with this green . . .'

'Count on me, my love. Firstly, I shall have my throat covered with this beautiful Indian silk scarf, which I shall draw back at the appropriate moment, and I give you my word that the jewel will produce the desired effect.'

'How could I but obey you, my beloved? I don't know what is keeping me from throwing myself on you . . .'

She pushed him away with one finger.

'Be sensible, now,' she said. 'The carriage is waiting. Let me go and arrange my scarf.'

She came back a minute later, the scarf, at once thick and light, hiding her bosom . . . And they set out.

A motionless throng of carriages hemming in the Steers' mansion might have made them fear they would arrive after everyone else.

'Don't worry,' Elizabeth said. 'These days it's quite the thing to be fashionably late.'

In the vast expanse of three adjoining reception rooms, all the chandeliers were lit and large crystal candle rings stopped the wax from dripping on to the shoulders of the guests. The softness of the lighting made the rooms look even lovelier, and they seemed larger than they were because of the profusion of huge mirrors in heavy gilt frames. An orchestra, hidden behind some palms, was playing discreetly, not waltzes, for this was not a ball, but soft music.

The usher announced Lieutenant and Mrs Hargrove, causing heads to turn toward the door, and the new arrivals had difficulty in finding a way past the fashionable ladies and gentlemen to reach old Steers, with his Franz-Joseph sideburns, and his wife, in a flounced violet dress, wearing a lace cap in the shape of a tower. They exchanged compliments of warm banality, as custom required, and the young Englishwoman felt that the moment had come for her to make her big impression.

With a careless gesture, which she made as graceful as she could, she parted the sides of the Indian scarf and revealed her throat, on which Annabel's emeralds were shining with provocative brilliance.

It had been learned through Uncle Charlie and Mrs Harrison Edwards that after taking her leave of the world, Mrs Jonathan Armstrong had wanted this ornament, heavy with tragic memories, to be worn by the young woman. Did she want to hide it for ever from the eyes of Sister Laura, who would not have been able to bear the sight of it? This was the accepted explanation. Yet there was general amazement when Elizabeth took one or two steps into the middle of the first drawing-room on the arm of Lieutenant Billy. And he was unable to repress a cry when he saw these emeralds, which his wife had always hidden away from him, and his furious expression was that of a husband who is used to being kept informed.

She gave him a broad smile, at once charming and derisive, and whispered:

'A present from your Aunt Annabel.'

Almost at once a group gathered around them and the orchestra, instructed by Mrs Harrison Edwards, launched into Mendelssohn's *Belle Mélusine*, while a great hum of admiration and astonishment rang in the ears of the beautiful Englishwoman, more lovely and more English than ever. All of a sudden, Billy found himself cruelly isolated and as though driven far from her. In vain, he struck some poses, but the company only had eyes for the lady with the emeralds. He received barely a furtive glance from Algernon, whose attention was then drawn back to the bosom of Billy's wife — something which, in normal times, would have earned him a challenge to a duel; but this evening he had the right, because everyone had the right. And he scorned the god-like creature whose heart was pounding with rage beneath his gold braid.

Billy suffered. This public flowering of his wife made him quite simply disappear and he had to endure this hateful torture and say nothing. His little moment of glory was being stolen from him. The ladies came to breathe on Elizabeth's skin the better to admire her necklace, all in a rustling of taffeta, a whisper of silk, scents, exclamations and gasps of *Oh, my dear*! The men too came over, that whippersnapper Algernon among them . . . Hell.

In the midst of the crowd, which he found stifling, he was suddenly aware of a stocky gentleman insinuating himself, dressed in black, with a fierce appearance, apparently aware of the situation and anxious to put an end to it. In a loud, authoritative voice, he spoke these few words:

'Ladies and gentlemen, it is not given to us every day to see in these rooms a couple of such admirable elegance as Lieutenant and Mrs Hargrove. And at this moment — what a delightful surprise — they are passing around glasses of champagne. I suggest a toast. To beauty and youth!'

There was a moment's panic as the champagne was distributed, some of it spilling on flounced dresses and long coat-tails, but a burst of feeling rose amid the confusion and the cry went up:

'To our Southern youth!'

Billy instinctively put a hand to his forehead. He had recognized his commandant, who had come incognito, partly to support his favorite bridge partner, but still more to take his turn in admiring at close quarters this woman who was so widely spoken about. The Steers, who were part of the conspiracy, came to give a sort of blessing to this unexpected turn of events taken by their reception, while Mrs Harrison Edwards vanished behind the palm trees to ensure that the music was in keeping with the occasion. Abruptly, like a burst of thunder, an irresistible gallop broke out, causing the chandeliers to ring, heads to turn and astonished couples to whirl round. The commandant dashed over toward Elizabeth and, with a victorious wink, carried her off from under the nose of Lieutenant Billy. He had to be content with dancing Mrs Harrison Edwards off her feet; she had been eyeing him since the start of the evening.

# 99

The reception at the Steers did not fail to cause tongues to wag. When the first surprise was over, people pretended to find it amusing, even witty, because it was understood that the Steers could not do anything which was not in good taste. Only Billy had other ideas, but he kept his objections to himself. However, from that day onwards, he gave up blackmail by whist and beat his commandant time and again, without ever granting him the favor of a compensatory victory. At the same time, he began to treat Elizabeth roughly and she, on the other hand, by a caprice of her feminine nature, was delirious about this new approach.

For a time, all this commotion in a world enclosed within itself had the beneficial effect of dispelling an obsession with war.

Elizabeth took advantage of this temporary lull. Bit by bit the memory of old Mr Robertson was fading. Everything in this corner of the South around her gave an impression of invincible stability . . . The colonnaded houses, the gardens, the people coming and going, while speaking in calm voices, most of all laughing: the imagination refused to see the prospect of change in such a harmonious whole, so clearly built to last. It was Billy who was right.

Her only concern was with her little Christopher. She loved him, but without being besotted with him as a mother should be. To tell the truth, she did not feel very maternal. The baby was now two months old and she could not find him pretty. Bald, toothless, with a wrinkled face and startled blue eyes, he was without the charm of the other, whom she no longer dared to call Jonathan. And when Betty took Christopher, Little Kit, into her arms with love, Elizabeth let her. There was sometimes a struggle between the little old woman in the red camisole and the heavy black nanny who took Kit away from her to give him his milk — the mother did not want to feed him herself — and to smother him in affection. As for Ned, he cold-shouldered his younger brother a little; the other looked at him, open-mouthed, and dribbled. A feeling close to jealousy was breeding in the heart of the elder boy, but he had nothing to fear on that score, since Elizabeth still felt her old passion for the child with the secret name of Jonathan, and all the frenzy of her love-making with Billy was powerless against it.

In her husband's absence, she went out more and more . . . Now Mrs Harrison Edwards would accompany her, now Charlie Jones. Without ever admitting it to herself, she avoided being alone because solitude brought fear. The threat of war, banned from conversation, had been replaced by what was in some ways a traditional anxiety. Miss Llewelyn's success had had various repercussions, not all beneficial. In Haiti, everything was as usual going badly. Soulouque, who had believed himself since the age of ten to be Napoleon, was ruling by massacre. Having become Emperor under the name Faustin I, he wore a gold crown. Whites were killed, Blacks were killed, mulattoes were killed. 'Here, at home,' they said in Savannah, 'such things are impossible. There is no question of a black uprising.' This was heard often, even very often. Elizabeth refused to listen. She could not see Betty and her black nanny rising up against her. The Blacks loved their masters and that was the truth, a truth accepted by one and all. And in Kansas, since September, everything continued to enflame even the calmest minds, but Buchanan was leaning toward the South, so there would soon be one more slave State . . .

Drawing-room chatter put everything back in place. They stunned themselves in the whirl and whim of frantic or langorous waltzes. They gossiped, they burst out laughing for no reason. Nothing mattered. That was life. Drifting from one end of a room to another, one sometimes caught a scrap of conversation between older people. Occasionally it was odd: the Emperor of Russia had just declared the emancipation of the serfs. What a notion! But it could be good riddance . . . Elizabeth was not interested in politics. She did not refuse to be admired. Her golden hair made young boys say charmingly foolish things. What was wrong with that?

Billy came less often after the evening at the Steers'. There was an impalpable shadow between him and the commandant; then, all of a sudden, through some underhand means or other, he was obtaining one furlough after another. Now, every kind of pleasure poured into Elizabeth's life. Balls were not out of the question, on the contrary. Billy danced with manly grace. People watched him. Elizabeth felt proud of her hussar and did not disguise the fact. He pretended to be seized with jealousy.

'If you cast your eyes this way and that, I'll bite your ear in front of everybody!'

She laughed in his face.

'I swear it,' he said. 'I'll take off a lobe.'

Then she pretended to be scared, which was delicious, but she scented a joke that was only half funny.

A few hours later, in their room, he became a little rough with her. She had been waiting for the moment, remembering Jonathan.

# 100

C hristmas was gradually approaching. In less favored countries, Our Lord's birth heralded the timid return of the sun and the still distant passing of the cold; while in Savannah the winter went by almost unnoticed. Of course, there were exchanges of greetings and gifts, and the parish bells rang solemnly. Piety there was, but hardly more than usual.

No one was forgotten in Elizabeth's domain. From Betty, Black Nanny, Patrick and Maisie Llewelyn, to Ned and his mother, each and every one gave a joyful cry of surprise on receiving something that he or she might not perhaps have chosen — but the thought was there, and the thought was what counted.

An unfortunate coincidence meant that Uncle Charlie, in all innocence, give Ned a magnificent large black rocking-horse . . . Elizabeth looked worried; but how could Uncle Charlie know? She looked at the creature in silence. Ned merely exclaimed:

'Oh, Mummy!' and leaped into the saddle, whereupon the horse began to rock energetically back and forth, its eye staring wildly, making the floor creak. The boy, delighted, turned to Elizabeth and, in a knowing whisper, murmured:

'Zonathan.'

'No,' she said, horrified. 'You promised me never again to say that name.'

'But there's no one here.'

'That doesn't matter. Don't say that name ever again.'

He gave her a big smile and set off faster than ever.

'Very well, Mummy, ever again,' he said.

While still reeling from this sinister trick of fate, Elizabeth did not have the consolation of a visit from Billy which she had been expecting. A pass for New Year's Day would have seemed quite natural, but the First of January, 1858, came and went, and the irresistible hussar did not appear. It was an ordinary day of tending visiting cards, one half of the town going to pay its respects on the other, and finding most of them away from home, as usual.

Elizabeth left her cards like everyone else and that filled in a tedious afternoon, but in the evening she had the impression of abruptly slipping back into the black pit of solitude.

The brief, joyous whirl of the ball made the solitude which awaited her on her return all the more cruel: true solitude, that of an empty bed, too wide for comfort. What weakness could have made her marry a soldier who was constantly being taken away from her by the demands of the service? It was enough for him to put his arms round her shoulders at the burial of William Hargrove, and she had become his prisoner. She hungered for him, for everything that made him who he was, for that great body which enfolded her. The hunger for a body in love was atrocious. Other women seemed to bear it better than she did, or took a lover, as if all men were interchangeable.

Having no appetite for dinner, she went to say goodnight to Ned. Since her marriage she had somewhat lost this habit which used to be so important to her. It was Betty who went to turn down the wick of the night-light and pull the sheet up over the boy's ears, as though to protect him from some unknown terrors of the night. The little old black woman hummed softly. Elizabeth affectionately gestured her aside.

'Let me,' she said. 'This evening, I'll do it.'

Now, sitting at the head of her child's bed, she felt calmer. His eyelids were flickering in his struggle against the desire for sleep. The emotions of the day had almost overwhelmed him with exhaustion. In a sort of fever, he had got everyone to admire Uncle Charlie's present, though without betraying the secret of his midnight rides. He only regretted not being able to have his confidant, the gardener, up to see him, but he had gone down to the end of the garden to describe his black horse, and then showed it from his window.

Almost asleep, he muttered:

'Mummy!'

'Yes, Ned, it's me. Sleep, my love.'

He stammered:

'The black horse . . .'

'It's very fine. You must thank Uncle Charlie.'

'The other will come . . .'

His eyes closed. She gave him a quick kiss and left him in the darkness. Though not sorry that she had come, she was uneasy.

The persistence of this fantasy in Ned's imagination seemed dangerous to her. He was growing up in the midst of an unreal world, though one of hallucinatory intensity. She would talk to Pat tomorrow. In his Irish way he was encouraging the boy to imagine things. Luckily, Billy knew nothing about it. One night with Billy would wipe out almost everything; she needed him so much that she wanted to scream, and this frightened her. If she suffered like this, she would grow old . . . That was another obsession. She was reaching the point where she would avoid harsh lights when receiving visitors. That night, back in her room, she took a few drops of laudanum, following her mother's recipe.

It was as though, seized with pity, life tried to arrange matters, though not very successfully. A week later, she had a letter from Billy. She sat down to read it in a corner of her room, near one of the windows, then pressed the letter in its envelope against her breast. At last, he would come.

'My beloved,' he wrote, 'a piece of good news, followed by another, not so good; but first of all, be happy: I'm coming the day after tomorrow. It's been hard . . . There is a chill — an icy chill — between the commandant and myself. He played a trick on me at the Steers' by forcing you to waltz with him on his bandy legs. I took my revenge by making him bite the dust at whist, ten times, twenty times in succession. So it's over: diplomatic relations are broken off. He prefers to play whist with the little English sub-lieutenant. Luckily, there is news from the family: my cousin Hilda is getting married at the end of the month in Dimwood to a gentleman from Charleston who had been courting her for six months; a trifle serious, but they are crazy about one another. I asked, in vain, for leave to attend this family wedding, and first of all received a resounding refusal accompanied by a ferocious smile. Then Hilda took it upon herself to write as women know how, in a style garlanded with forget-me-nots and sweet peas, appealing to his better feelings — and he gave in! So: four days in Dimwood, do you realize . . .'

She let the letter fall from her hand. Dimwood. The intoxication of love in the horror of memory, the magnolias beneath the steps of the veranda, but all of Billy to herself for four days . . . She shut her eyes and thought she could see him. It was too beautiful. She continued reading the letter:

'Here is the devilish other side to that infernal coin: we are working harder and harder at doing up Fort Beauregard. This doesn't mean there will be war, but it's as if: I shall be immobilised for a month in Charleston looking for supplies and then supervising the work. The commandant announced the news to me coldly when he was granting me my furlough for Dimwood. There you have it. That's all. The best and the worst, but the best will be good; I dream about it all night. Then . . . Be beautiful. Bring your fine emerald whatsit to dazzle the guests. If I did what my heart tells me, I'd write you a letter like the one you tore up. It was very amusing. So much the worse for you!

Your Billy, who adores you.'

This letter, read and re-read twenty times, made the beautiful Englishwoman's head whirl . . . She went from yes to no and back until she was giddy. It was inconceivable that she should see Dimwood again. It would mean reliving a kind of interior life, the memory of which tortured her. On the other hand, Billy, herself and Billy, body and soul to one another — 'body, most of all' specified the inner voice which she knew well. She shrugged her shoulders. As if she could waver for an instant!

The time dragged by until the minute that a woman in green, motionless beside a window, had been waiting for. Suddenly she left the room and was downstairs at the bottom of the steps.

Billy arrived quite simply from the station in a cab. It was prosaic, but as soon as he set foot on the ground, in his red uniform, he became once more a whole regiment of hussars and despite everything, his smile of happiness made him look like a schoolboy coming home for the holidays. The scene that followed was brief and confused. The servants waited at the door to see everything. Little Ned cried out and hung on his mother's skirt.

'Mummy, don't go!'

She leaned over him to give him a kiss.

'Four days are nothing, darling, you'll see.'

Miss Llewelyn took a step toward them.

'I'll be here, Ma'am, don't worry.'

Elizabeth looked at her as though she had not expected to see her.

'Oh, Miss Llewelyn! If only you had been able to come with us . . .'

'Me, at Dimwood! Never! I'm only happy where I'm in control. I'm no longer anything in Dimwood.'

'Here . . .'

Billy interrupted.

'Hello everybody! Elizabeth, it's nearly one o'clock. Let's not waste another minute. The carriage . . .'

'Is on its way, it's here,' said Miss Llewelyn. 'Joe, take the Lieutenant's suitcase.'

Once more, Elizabeth put on her amazed look as though not understanding. The Welshwoman began to laugh:

'Wake up, Ma'am, and be off! I'll take care of everything here. Enjoy yourselves there. Now be gone, quickly!'

Billy took Elizabeth's arm.

'Miss Llewelyn is right, Elizabeth. We mustn't waste a moment of happiness.'

'Mummy!' Ned cried.

He wanted to run forward, but Betty, who had been just beside him, held him back. In less than a minute the travelers were outside and getting into the carriage.

'At the gallop, to the end of the avenue!' Billy cried to the coachman.

With a flick of his whip, the man roused his four horses which set off at a rapid trot. Pressed into a corner of the seat, as if to hide herself from the world, Elizabeth turned to look at her husband.

'Billy,' she said, 'is it true?'

# 101

Now the carriage was driving through countryside where everything reminded Elizabeth of sights that she hoped to have banished forever from her mind. She was hurtling toward pitiless memories of happiness destroyed, traveling backwards through the tragedy of her adolescent love. Scenes flashed past beyond the windows. Suddenly a horseman galloped up, close to the carriage, and looked directly at her, eyes burning with desire, before vanishing immediately, carried away on his black horse.

'What's wrong, my love?' Billy asked, slipping an arm round her waist. 'You seem upset.'

'Last night, I didn't sleep. I was anticipating . . .'

'But now, here we are together. When we get there, you'll see. I've chosen our room. The one overlooking the gardens. Do you remember the maze?'

'Yes, the gardens . . .'

Unable to continue, she merely smiled at him.

The carriage drew up at the grand entrance door which was not often opened. Elizabeth sighed with relief: she could not have gone in through the veranda.

An old Black in red livery came to welcome them to the house.

'Oh, Miss Lizbeth and Massa Bill!' he exclaimed.

'Hello, Jonah,' Billy said. 'I think we must be very late.'

'Yes, Massa Bill. They servin' dessert.'

'I love dessert,' Billy said with a laugh.

Elizabeth had different feelings, confronted by this hall, the incredible length of which might have made you think of a room seen in a dream. The high windows, the black marble flooring and the walls extending toward a still distant last room: she had known all this, it was all true, while all the years before were no longer true, or never had been. She was entering into the hallucination of the Real and was afraid because, right at the end of a tunnel, down there, there were two men mortally wounded in a wood.

Caught up in the past, she walked forward on Billy's arm without seeing him . . .

At the back of the room, grouped round a table, about a dozen people were talking so loudly that from this distance they did not notice the newcomers, until suddenly Uncle Josh broke away from the group and ran toward them with open arms.

'At last!' he exclaimed. 'We were wondering if you had been lost on the way! The ceremony has been over a long time.'

'We never meant to come so early,' said Billy, jokingly.

There were the usual sounds that accompany the end of an excessively large meal: chairs pushed back, napkins thrown among the plates; and the family hurried toward them. Hilda, wearing a white dress, threw herself on Elizabeth's shoulder.

'Darling, you're an angel for coming! At last!'

Short and determined, she had lost her formerly slender waist, but the merry smile of her youth still gleamed in her black eyes and, in delight, she gave Elizabeth a firm hug, before introducing her husband, a young man so ceremonious that he had great difficulty in keeping upright. Slim and proud, but unsteady, he had the figure of a gentleman of fashion, with rather too pink a face and light blond whiskers. Uncle Douglas stepped in front of him and grasped Elizabeth in his turn.

'Welcome to Dimwood, our lovely Englishwoman! Do you remember the April night when you first came here?'

Leaning against Billy, Elizabeth smiled without answering. Aunt Emma noticed her distress and clasped her hands, followed by Aunt Augusta who guided her to the table and made her sit down in an armchair. There was an immediate feeling of embarrassment.

'That journey is tiring,' said Uncle Joshua. 'Would you like to lie down, or to dine straightaway? It's very simple: we can ask for you to be served whatever you want — and Billy who is dying of hunger . . .'

Elizabeth made a sign to show that she didn't want anything, but her husband hastened to sit down at her side, after handing his shako to a servant.

'You must drink something delicious, to give you back your strength,' said Hilda. 'A glass of champagne . . .'

'Really, no,' said Elizabeth at length. 'I'm already feeling better.'

At that moment, Hilda gave up her place so that Susanna could sit down quietly beside Elizabeth. In a few years, the face of this other cousin had undergone a strange transformation. Without growing old, she had grown into someone else; yet her features still retained the delicacy of her youth. With her long black ringlets making her pale cheeks seem even thinner, she gave an impression of poignant beauty — for, the depths of her dark eyes revealed a hopeless melancholy. Yet she smiled and said cheerfully to the young woman:

'How strange life is, dear Elizabeth . . . Here we are, once more, side by side. I should never have dared hope that one day . . . I mean . . .'

'Nor should I,' Elizabeth said vaguely.

'You remember the night when we climbed up on the bench, you and Minnie and I, in the great avenue, to greet the full moon?'

'And all three of us fell into the field,' Elizabeth said, pensively. 'Do you remember?'

'As if it were yesterday . . .'

'Poor Susanna, you were not happy that evening . . .'

'I shall never be happy.'

'Oh, darling! If only you could get married.'

Susanna did not reply. Getting up, she bent over Elizabeth, until she could feel Susanna's curls on her forehead, then brushing her cheek with a kiss, Susanna left the room.

After Susanna's departure, which aroused no comment, the guests went back to their places, though after a moment's hesitation. They were used to Susanna's sudden decisions and inexplicable silences. Out of habit, eyebrows were raised, but nothing more.

Billy, like his wife, refused the Virginia ham and salads which were offered to them, and began the meal from the other end. But the Englishwoman only wanted a cup of tea, while her husband the hussar plunged into the bewildering variety of desserts that were now being served. One single guest was a little bit thrust apart, into a corner: this was Mike — Mike-Black-Hands — Billy's brother, the terror of ladies in white during Elizabeth's first years at Dimwood. Just back from school, he was almost fourteen, with his round face radiating appetite and exuberance. Red curls were scattered at random across his nose and over his green eyes. They were very fond of him, but had constantly to tell him to be quiet because he voiced his opinions. For the time being he was squeezed between Uncle Josh and Aunt Augusta.

Accompanied by a great chinking of spoons and plates, the conversation began all round the table, while the red-liveried servants poured out some rather deceptively strong dessert wines. Having halted for a moment, the chatter resumed.

'Lieutenant Hargrove,' Uncle Douglas said to his son in a military tone of voice, 'you are just back from Beaufort. What are they saying there about the threat of war?'

Billy cast an anxious look toward his wife.

'Still the same old threat which has been with us for the past six years. One gets used to it, nothing moves.'

'That's one way of seeing things,' said Siverac, Hilda's new husband. 'Even in Charleston, nothing moves, but everything is about to explode.'

'A sulphurous atmosphere,' said Aunt Augusta.

'There isn't going to be a war?' Elizabeth said in a terrified voice.

'If there is a war, I'm going!' said Mike in a shrill voice.

'Douglas, take him out,' said Aunt Emma. 'He's been shouting since the beginning of the meal.'

'It's not his fault: his voice is breaking.'

'He frightened Cousin Elizabeth,' said Mildred. 'If only he could just be quiet and eat like a gentleman; that's all we ask.'

'We should change the subject,' said Hilda. 'There are other things to talk about here, apart from war.'

'Do you think it's any better elsewhere?' Siverac continued. 'Last September is not so far away yet. The country has not come to terms with the massacre at Mountain Meadows.'

Uncle Douglas, strong and somewhat aggressive, stared at his brother.

'Your beloved Redskins, the Paiutes, did that.'

The reply came back like a thunderbolt:

'Stirred up and armed by those Mormons who hate immigrants from the North and want to keep them away from the road to California.'

'The butchery still took place.'

'And who took it upon themselves to scalp little boys and girls — 120 Americans killed? The Mormons all the while giving thanks to the Lord for the sacrifice they were offering Him.'

Elizabeth gave a cry.

'The Mormons! What are Mormons?'

Unwittingly, Billy's voice took on a fierce and bawdy note:

'The Mormons are a sect which is powerful in Utah, who practice polygamy. A man has the right to a whole string of legitimate wives.'

'Not more than five, Billy,' Siverac said.

Feeling a momentary weakness, Elizabeth leaned against the

shoulder of Mildred, her neighbor.

'I wonder if I shouldn't have stayed in England,' she sighed.

Once again, Uncle Douglas roared:

'It's for the federal government to act. With that puppet for a President, I can only wish them luck.'

'But he is acting,' said Siverac. 'He's sending troops to Colorado.'

'And Fred is there!' Aunt Emma groaned.

'You can be sure that he will do his duty,' said Uncle Douglas.

'Fred is as plucky as they come, Papa,' said Billy. 'He's one of the leading cavalry officers in West Point.'

'Fred . . . ,' Elizabeth murmured.

In the flurry of words flying back and forth, she recalled the sad, pretty voice which had sung her a serenade beneath the veranda, then, as she was leaving Dimwood, that declaration, at once awkward and shattering . . .

Billy's clarion tones pulled her out of this reverie.

'Fred wanted us to go for the Northern lads as early as '52. He said that later would be too late.'

'And he was right!' Lawrence's voice suddenly and unexpectedly interrupted. The dessert wine had woken him.

Mike at once chimed in with Hilda's husband:

'Fred was right: go for them!'

'Mike: outside!' Emma said in exasperation.

'No, let him stay,' Uncle Josh said with authority. 'Let him at least learn something. Mike, when you hear people speak ill of the Redskins, just ask them: "Who drove the Redskins out of their homes? Who massacred them? And who is still stealing their homelands?"'

'What about Civilization?' yelled Uncle Douglas.

'Do you think they are savages? What you call our civilization brings with it the curse of the Indian race on the white one. We shall have to pay.'

'Josh, we are capable of meeting the cost.'

'We'll see about that. If there is war.'

The two brothers confronted each other. A deep silence fell over the guests. Uncle Douglas tried to control himself.

'Josh,' he said, 'I don't want to hear you insinuate things that may be misunderstood. We are on dangerous ground. War remains possible, even likely.'

'A punishment from heaven, perhaps.'

'Are you mad? In time of war, you would be arrested for saying that kind of thing. What will you do then?'

'I'll take my gun and leave instantly, perhaps out of self-respect, perhaps out of cowardice . . .'

'Oh, Sir!' Billy exclaimed.

'My boy,' said Uncle Josh, 'you will learn that in any army of heroes there are always cowards, who very properly get killed . . .'

'The admirable effect of setting an example,' Aunt Augusta remarked.

Uncle Josh gave an angry look and finished his sentence:

' . . .but who, in their hearts, until the moment of death, feel ashamed at not having protested.'

Calm and ashen, Douglas clenched his fists and announced:

'After such strange remarks and having been at table for some hours, in my opinion we would all benefit from a walk in the park. The air is warm and it's a fine evening. Josh, your hand.'

Uncle Josh looked at him in astonishment.

'Josh, I want your hand.'

Uncle Josh reached over the table and grasped his brother's hand, which he shook violently, as if to tear it off the arm.

'You've always been pig-headed, Douglas,' he said, laughing, 'and you've never had any philosophical notions, but I'm fond of you. All our excitement this evening was just a continuation of our battles when we were children.'

'Agreed; but what a spectacle we offered our guests! Especially our dear Englishwoman, who must be wondering what it is all about.'

Together, they turned toward Elizabeth.

She was sitting motionless, very pale and upright in her chair, as though in a trance. From the whole scene between the two men she had only caught the one word, *war*, from the jumble of voices, and it frightened her.

While everyone got up, she leaned against Billy who had hurried across to help her. He put his arm round her and asked tenderly:

'Darling, they're suggesting we go for a walk in the great avenue.'

'Oh, no!' she cried, emphatically. 'Not in that direction.'

'Would you like us to go upstairs at once then?'

She wanted what he wanted, happy to escape from the confused sound of chattering voices. People came up to her as they went out and she heard the young women speaking affectionately to her, and her husband answering:

'It's nothing, she's going to have a rest.'

Uncle Josh muttered something in the lieutenant's ear, and he replied:

'I know her, Sir. I can see that she is exhausted, but I'll be careful.'

All at once, she had a pleasant feeling that she was no longer touching the ground and the burden of tiredness lifted from her body. Billy had taken her in his arms and was carrying her upstairs to the first floor. Overwhelmed by sleepiness, she could no longer think of anything, but she recognized the smell of the house with its pine panelling, and a whole world was revived with unbearable tenderness.

She was not aware of the next few minutes. Hands were taking off her dress, she could feel them on her chest. Almost at once she came to herself and murmured Billy's name.

He gave a cry of happiness as if he had brought her back from a nightmare and enfolded her in an amorous rage; but, rather than giving, she abandoned herself. Perhaps he was unaware of it. In delirium he could not manage to satisfy his physical longing for this woman who, while not entirely inert, was still absent. With a voracity to which she submitted without a sigh, he wore himself out with joy.

After a long moment, tiredness opened his arms and he let himself roll beside her. Soon she heard his breathing become more regular. He was sleeping as she had never before seen him sleep. His broad chest rose and fell, his breathing tranquil and slow. Slipping out of bed, she put on a robe. The night was becoming colder and the owls were giving their little hoots in the woods beyond the garden. A three-quarter full moon hung in a black sky and gave this familiar landscape a reality with the outlines of an imperious energy, as if to wipe out the effects of the day, covering even the smallest flowers in darkness. In this violent lighting, the young woman felt very close to a creation which harmonized with her deepest nature.

Returning to the bed, she looked at him and could not help admiring the long, powerful outline of his body which gave the impression of having been deposited at the bottom of an abyss. In dreams, that is how she had seen him, but tonight she was not dreaming. She was walking through a space that had no name, as if it didn't exist.

On tiptoe, she left the room by the door leading to the veranda, but as soon as she took a step, she had a shock. Between the maze and the Accursed Wood, in the great open space, she saw herself together with Jonathan. It was his last night on earth. That night, no light fell from the sky and they were walking in darkness. Neither the murmur of their words, nor the whisper of their footsteps on the gravel reached her. Yet they were coming toward the house and she could see their outlines more and more clearly, then their whole bodies. They were walking slowly and suddenly parted, she running toward the house while Jonathan returned into the depths of the night. Suddenly she found herself alone on the veranda, with one hand on the balustrade for fear of falling, because this vision had nearly caused her to collapse. Imagination was taking the place of memory. She shut her eyes and let several minutes pass. Her heart was beating so hard that she had the sensation of someone hitting her in the chest. She waited, hesitated and then continued her way around the veranda.

When she reached the point from which one could see the entrance to the avenue with the huge oaks meeting at their summits, she risked a terrified glance, then started to run, as though she feared seeing once more the glass of champagne thrown in Jonathan's face. Breathless with emotion, she at last found herself at the far end of the veranda, the place where throughout her years in Savannah, she had dreamed of standing, intoxicated by the scent of magnolias. Wasn't this why she had come? And now that she was here, her face bent toward the flowers opening beneath that same light, with its magic, icy splendor, did she dare think what she was hoping for? She waited. But the occasional cries of the owls around the house did not evoke the liquid song of the tree frogs nor, on this late winter's night did that May night when she was sixteen, return. She leaned a little further over the edge. The greenery did not move. Nothing moved around her. There was no one there.

# 102

*T*he following morning, Uncle Douglas took his two sons along the great avenue, the usual place for talks about politics and love, or the exchange of secrets, since the majesty of the surroundings did not inhibit the most passionate indiscretions. The oak trees were getting thicker and thicker, and now only let through a few shafts of sunlight.

'Boys,' he began, 'the family celebrations are over. Our guests have left, they're on their way to Charleston where I hope you will visit them . . . You will find Dimwood somewhat deserted, somewhat solemn . . .'

'Oh, no!' the two boys protested.

'I'm planning to go riding around here,' said Mike.

'If you don't make him gallop too much, I'll lend you my old Tapageur. He's still a brave beast.'

'Let's talk seriously,' said Douglas. 'You must know that your Aunt Annabel left Dimwood to me after the death of her husband in a duel. I also inherited part of Jonathan Armstrong's plantation, which had passed to his widow.'

'I wonder why she gave up all her possessions,' Billy said.

'She had her reasons.'

'What were they?' Mike asked, without thinking.

A single word from his father shut his mouth:

'Metaphysical.'

'Oh!' Mike exclaimed, dumbstruck.

'The day will come,' Uncle Douglas continued, 'when all Dimwood will be bequeathed to you — not forgetting Fred who is far away on the other side of America.'

'A huge inheritance!' Billy exclaimed.

'Huge,' Uncle Douglas said calmly. 'And burdensome. If there is war, which is quite possible, we may have to worry about some amendments, but all the deeds are safely in Savannah. You will be informed. But for now, Billy, you are eager to get back to your Elizabeth, and you Mike, to dear old Tapageur. As for myself, I shall continue my walk alone.'

'Sir,' Billy said, 'how can I express . . .'

'No,' his father interrupted. 'Don't thank me. It's embarrassing, and it all goes without saying.'

And, turning his back on them he went off with long, slow, authoritative steps. Then, suddenly turning round, he looked at them and called:

'My blessing, even so, boys . . .'

And, very quietly, he added, as he set off again:

'For what it's worth . . . '

Elizabeth had slipped out as soon as she saw Billy vanish. Without losing a minute, she started down the long dark corridors of the old house, until she reached the little, almost vertical staircase which led to the end of a passage to the hideout of Mademoiselle Souligou, the dressmaker.

The young Englishwoman had only to push the half-open door. First of all, directly in front of her, as she expected, she saw the familiar back of the wide armchair in red velvet, surmounted by two points of indigo madras; and from behind this chair back, from all those years ago, came the sharp voice that one could not forget.

'Come in and sit down, Elizabeth. I was expecting you.'

'Expecting me? For how long?'

'For a time, and more, and still more time. Enough questions.'

A single glance was sufficient for Elizabeth to see that, as elsewhere in Dimwood, nothing had changed in the immense laundry-room with its low ceiling, full of recesses; neither the long skylights, like slits, which admitted light in the form of furtive rays, which travelled across the black-painted floor; nor the table which seemed to grow longer the more one looked at it, heaped with linen for darning for the whole household; nor the fourteen chairs; nor above all Souligou, the West Indian, with her head leaning forward and her pointed, prying nose.

'What are you looking at?' she asked impatiently. 'I'm telling you to sit down, there, close to me.'

'It's as though time had been swallowed up,' Elizabeth murmured.

'Always dreaming, always beautiful, always as crazy. Happy to see you again, even so. But you remember the card that I waved out of the window, the day you left? It was a warning from the tarot.'

'What's wrong?'

'Stupidities, as always, Elizabeth. Mistakes. And then, leave those who have departed in peace.'

'What do you mean?'

'You're pretending. You know.'

The young woman leaped back.

'I saw someone last night, outside.'

Souligou gave a laugh that was like a chuckle.

'Apart from myself, everyone here claims to have seen him at least once, around the Accursed Wood, because of the duel; never anywhere else. Every plantation has its ghost. Dimwood made that one.'

'You don't believe in it?'

'No.'

'I could have sworn that he was there, with me beside him.'

'Well, it's what you were wanting . . . And, with your imagination . . . But you shouldn't have come. Shuffle my cards and cut them.'

Her face damp, the young woman took the cards and began to shuffle them obstinately.

'Enough,' the West Indian said. 'They won't be any better for that . . . or any worse. Cut them. Give them to me with your left hand.'

She spread the cards out on the table, looked at them, then with her thin fingers the color of boxwood, she suddenly jumbled them together.

'I've seen it all,' she said. 'If I were you, I'd leave here.'

'But I am leaving Dimwood in three days.'

'Oh, Dimwood . . . It's Dimwood I'm talking about, is it?'

'Where then?'

'You will be told, Elizabeth, but not by me.'

'Why? Is it forbidden?'

'You ask too many questions, but I'm still fond of you. I warned you five years ago, You are often mistaken: the heart, the senses. That's your fate. Once and for all: leave.'

'I cannot leave my husband.'

'Do you love him as much as that?'

Elizabeth blushed deeply and stood up.

'Mademoiselle Souligou, he is waiting for me, I'm going back to him; but I was also pleased to see you.'

To her great surprise the dressmaker also got up and kissed her without a word. A complex odor of old shawls and obtrusive undergarments, attenuated but not obliterated by an under-strength perfume from the islands, swept over the Englishwoman who tried to get away, but could not.

'No, Elizabeth,' the West Indian said to her face. 'Once at least you will hear the truth: you are a sensual and a sentimental person: they are both the same.'

'Leave me alone, Souligou,' Elizabeth commanded. 'I won't be spoken to like that.'

'Alas, no,' said Souligou, letting her go. 'More's the pity. You choose your men with the incompetence of an absolute beginner. Oh, you can play the madam in drawing-rooms, but that's not what will make you happy.'

Elizabeth looked at her, feeling choked. There was a force in this woman's little eyes that immobilized her.

'Your Billy,' she went on. 'I knew him as a little one, here, at Dimwood. He is tall and handsome, he gives you pleasure and the tenderness that goes with pleasure, which is mistaken for love.'

'What do you expect me to do?' Elizabeth cried in exasperation.

'It's the first love that counts, Elizabeth, even when it's as disastrous as yours was. I knew everything. The duel revealed it all. You think you saw Jonathan again. He has never left you. It is not Billy who will free you from him.'

'I love Billy,' Elizabeth protested firmly.

'Of course, but you preferred the other. Someone will make you forget everything, if it's not too late.'

'Souligou, I can't understand a word of what you're saying.'

'Of course you can't. I say what I see, that's my job. I'm only a dressmaker by accident. Over there, in the West Indies, I was valued for my gifts, and our people know about such things.'

'You're worrying me with your stories. I don't want anything to happen to Billy.'

'Don't worry too much. These things look after themselves. It's called destiny. As for the tarot, it's in the card that you didn't quite see. Do you want me to show it to you, the one I was waving out of the window?'

Turning round, she moved the cards around on the table and pointed to one of them.

'The Devil!'

'Destiny. It's the same thing.'

'It may be with you, but not here. I came to ask for your advice and, I don't know why, but I hoped that you might bring me peace. Well, you haven't.'

'Listen. For you, there will be another time. Think about it. Don't fall into the arms of just anyone.'

'I have never fallen into the arms of just anyone, Souligou.'

'No woman would ever accept that she had done such a thing. But in any case, there will be another time. Try to choose.'

'As if one could! Farewell, Souligou.'

Waking late after his first night, Billy had found his wife lying sensibly beside him and did not for a second imagine her melancholy nocturnal escapade.

Similarly, after the talk with his father in the grand avenue, he hunted around for Elizabeth in the house and gardens, then went to wait for her in their room while taking a siesta.

'Well now,' he said in astonishment, when she came back from seeing Souligou. 'I've been looking for you everywhere.'

'So have I.'

'Where have you been?'

'Here and there, the plantation is so huge. I went for a walk, as they say — into the past.'

'We might have been searching for you for ages. When will you stop dreaming? Darling, do you want to have a rest with me, or would you like us both to go for a trip into the past?'

She looked at him.

'Oh, not everywhere,' he said quickly. 'Not outside, only in the house.'

She nodded without saying a word.

'You see,' he said, leaping out of bed, quite naked. 'Give me ten minutes and I'll join you downstairs.'

Avoiding looking at him, she got up from her chair.

'Downstairs?'

'Yes, in the drawing-room near the door, where I saw you for the first time with the family. There we'll start our own little trip into the past . . .'

'Very well, if you wish,' she said without enthusiasm.

He gave a schoolboy laugh which affected her more than his nudity.

Downstairs — in the deserted drawing-room which she imagined as it had been on that April night, seven long years ago, full of people: uncles, aunts, cousins, and Billy's damp lips on her cheek:

'I'm your cousin, Billy Stevens . . .'

There was feeling and poetry in all this, in that rather dramatic arrival . . . But, since her recent discussion with Souligou, she had felt an ironic indifference toward everything. There was poison in some of the words spoken by the old West Indian: 'Your choice of men . . .' — her men! And above all that question, subtly and casually destructive: 'Do you love him so much?' However, whether naked or in uniform, he swept her off her feet. Wasn't that love? The dressmaker's dry voice echoed in her ears: 'Sensual and senti-mental . . . tenderness of desire . . . That's all.'

She got up and began to walk back and forth to free herself from the unpleasant memory. Around her, on console tables, in the tall mirrors rising up to the cornices, she saw the reassuring image of this beautiful Englishwoman who was the pride of Savannah, in her pale green dress decked with little apple-green ribbons. Why was Billy not coming down?

The night before she had wasted her happiness, only thinking of the other. Now she again needed Billy, she was falling in love again. There were four mirrors. If she stood at a particular point, she could see two complete Elizabeths and two half Elizabeths, which made her laugh.

I'll show Billy that, she thought. Stand there and see four hand-some young officers at once!

She laughed again.

'That damned old Souligou!' she said aloud.

In a clatter of boots on the stairs, he appeared, radiant as ever, with no suspicion of anything: the model husband.

'Where do we start?' she asked merrily.

'Surprise, surprise! In your room.'

'But Billy, I'm not sure that I want to. Why should we?'

'For memory's sake. Please let me. To see the bed where you slept, my treasure, in your first night in Dimwood . . . Come, I'm going to carry you up there in my arms.'

'We're not in the Chinese pagoda at Bonaventure . . . and you'll crease my lovely dress . . .'

She hung on his arm and looked up into his eyes.

'Well, too bad. If I said no, you might ask for a divorce,' she said.

'Oh no,' he said. 'They would have to shoot Billy through the head before that!'

She cried out. 'Why do you say that? You shouldn't joke about such things.'

'Silly goose, you know I couldn't live without you, not for an hour!'

He swept her off the ground and carried her in his arms up to the first floor. It was a little harder than at Bonaventure, but they managed. Three more steps and he gently set Elizabeth down in front of the room where she had spent her first months in Dimwood. They went in. She had returned a thousand times to this room in her dreams, because a whole part of herself had never left it: the four-poster bed, the rocking chair, the dressing table, the pale light filtering through from the veranda . . . For an instant, she was struck dumb with emotion. The present was not distinct from the past, but once more became past. She was sixteen . . .

Billy's reaction was considerably less complex.

'I say, Grandpa put you up pretty decently.'

She felt as though this remark was dragging her back, as if to wake her up.

'So, your first night there . . .' he said, suddenly taking on a strange look. 'When you were sixteen . . .'

He looked at the bed, then at Elizabeth.

In a single jump, she was instantly back in the present.

'No, no, emphatically no! Tonight.'

Her voice was so forceful that he merely turned his languorous eyes toward her.

'That was my first thought when I saw you, that night.'

'Perhaps,' she said. 'But all that is long ago now.'

He sighed.

'Do something for me,' she added. 'Go over there to the corner of the veranda and the steps. You'll see . . . The magnolias . . . The scent . . .'

Her voice was begining to be choked with emotion, and she finished the sentence with an outstretched hand, its index finger pointing to the place where memory was torturing her.

'I know,' he said. 'Come with me.'

She shook her head and murmured:

'Please, I beg you.'

'All right,' he said, with a disappointed smile. 'But how odd you are, my love!'

She saw him going away and was once again struck by his elegance, which combined well in that large body with his quiet self-confidence and strength; but when she saw him close to the place where Jonathan's voice had come up to her, a shudder of revulsion clasped her shoulders, as though in self-defence.

'Not bad,' Billy remarked. 'Especially with that mass of magnolia.'

She moved stealthily a little further away along the veranda toward an open door.

It was Laura's room which had been left empty with no furniture except the bed with its linen and blankets neatly arranged, just as she had left them. Above that, quite high on the wall, was a nail and the outline of a cross.

'Laura,' she said under her breath. 'You were in love; but why am I saying that? Why have I just acted as I did?'

Billy's voice was calling her insistently, then she heard him running along the veranda. Immediately she appeared at the door of the room.

He laughed with obvious relief.

'What are you doing there? Do you know where you are? It's Laura's room!'

'Yes.'

'Are you interested in her?'

'I used to know Laura.'

'So what? Everyone knew her. Nice enough. She was kind to me, but not amusing . . . What a fuss they made when she left! I wonder why. She never said anything.'

'I was fond of her.'

'Come on, let's continue our walk.'

This time he took her hand.


They walked slowly round the house along the veranda and, overcome by a sudden sadness that was unlike him, Billy began to speak in a serious tone, very different from his normal voice:

'Elizabeth, I can't get used to the idea of leaving you in less than three days.'

'But you'll be back, Billy.'

'Not for a whole month, perhaps two. At least one month in the arsenal at Charleston, then . . .'

'Won't they give you any leave?'

'Some chance! I'll be there to supervise the despatch of munitions to Beaufort. In the event of hostilities, Beauregard has to be well-defended. Of course, don't worry, there won't be any hostilities, but we must be prepared. In any case, we'll see the state of the federal army over there and what are its means of defense. All the officers in Charleston are very interested in that.'

And, in a satisfied tone of voice, he added:

'Because all the officers come from the South.'

Elizabeth did not grasp the significance of the remark.

'But it's still the American Army.'

'Of course, of course, but you don't understand. Anything might happen.'

'Not war, Billy!'

'For the time being, Charleston is peaceful, but there is already war elsewhere, in the West. You know that. They were talking at table about what is happening with the Mormons.'

'Yes, I know, the immigrants who were killed . . .'

'The federal troops are blocked by the snow in the mountains, but the Mormons have to be brought to heel. At Mountain Meadows . . .'

'That terrible massacre . . .'

'We've learned more about what happened there. It's worse than anyone thought. Up to now the Mormons would attack all the convoys and, when the federal government threatened reprisals, one of their people, John Lee, was chosen to find a settlement. They were foolish enough to trust him. But I'm afraid I'll upset you . . .'

Elizabeth's curiosity overcame her.

'You've told me too much to stop now.'

'Last summer, the largest convoy of immigrants, wagons and cattle, was traveling right across America to settle in California. When they went close to Mormon country, the latter decided to attack as they came out of the mountains. They roused the Indians and, what's more, even disguised themselves as Indians. At dawn they surrounded the camp and fired at it. The immigrants defended themselves, thinking that they were being attacked by redskins. Then John Lee arrived with a white flag and told them to throw down their arms: the Mormons would protect them and allow them free passage to the Pacific and California. They believed him and were soon all disarmed.'

'What happened then?'

'Then John Lee yelled to the Mormons to get to work with their revolvers. The Latter-Day Saints — as they call themselves — fired point-blank on everything that moved, men and women.'

'And the children?'

'They were offered up as a sacrifice to the Lord, with lots of pious prayers. All massacred and scalped. As you can imagine, when the snows melt, the Mormons as a whole are going to have to pay for it. As for John Lee in particular, I wouldn't give much for his hide. There you are, since you asked.'

The young woman collapsed into one of the chairs on the veranda.

'It's better,' she said. 'One can't always shut one's eyes to things, but horrors like that . . .'

She held out a hand toward the maze garden, where the first flowers were blossoming in a pale amber light.

Further away, at the edge of the great meadows, were dark woods of slightly disturbing magnificence — since they were said to be haunted by the spirits of Indians. It was there that the girls of Dimwood had discovered the magic place which they had made into their peculiar paradise. Her memories, combined with the beauty of the landscape, were in sharp contrast to the horror of the story which she had just heard, so she said nothing. Equally moved by what he had just said, Billy remained thoughtful, and it was in silence that they completed their walk through a time that could never return.

At dinner that evening, a fresh quarrel broke out between the two brothers under the anxious gaze of their wives. With Elizabeth and Billy, as well as young Mike at the end of the table, the family was so reduced that it made the dining-room seem enormous and their voices resounded powerfully. At first, Aunt Emma lamented the departure of everyone, some to Charleston, the rest to

Savannah. Never had Dimwood known the loneliness that was awaiting it.

'But we're still here,' the husbands protested.

'And I'm not leaving until the end of the week,' Billy exclaimed.

'I'm sorry, Billy,' Emma said, 'but I like the house full of people.'

In a sarcastic voice, Uncle Josh announced:

'You still have the steward, the overseer, Elisa Carp, Miss Souligou and twenty very devoted servants. They furnish the place.'

'Furnish, as you say,' said Emma like an echo.

Aunt Augusta made an effort to put an end to this awkward misunderstanding.

'It seems that the Mormons,' she said, 'impressed by the number of troops sent against them, are secretly trying to negotiate.'

'Where did you see that?'

'The newspaper arrived by mail this afternoon.'

'Tittle tattle,' said Uncle Josh. 'The Indians won't give in.'

'The Indians?' said Elizabeth.

'Yes, the Indians,' said Uncle Josh. 'Don't they tell you anything, Elizabeth? By underhand means, the Mormons have succeeded in winning over the Indians in Utah, who were persuaded to take part in the massacre at Mountain Meadows because they were told that the American immigrants were coming to attack them.'

'They scalped them,' Uncle Douglas said, calmly. 'Their ferocity exceeds all bounds.'

'What are we doing on their lands?' Uncle Josh asked. 'And the Mormons and the immigrants also scalp their victims.'

'Josh, let's not start that again.'

Uncle Josh turned to Elizabeth:

'Elizabeth, it is time for someone to explain the situation to you clearly. We are on a continent, I don't say a country, but a continent, from which we have already partly dislodged a race of incredible antiquity, heirs to a noble and proud civilization. And by what right are we here?'

'By right of conquest,' Uncle Douglas said imperturbably.

'By right of pillage.'

'That's untrue. Eventually we paid with our money for the territory we occupy.'

'To which the unfortunate Indians answered with a cry that can still be heard: "What does your money mean? Can you buy our lands and our waters? Can you buy the birds, the clouds and the passing wind?" This cry of a people whose homeland is being torn away from it rises continually like a lamentation to Heaven, which will not hear it in vain: we shall feel its wrath.'

'Josh, you're waxing lyrical. You should take a potion.'

Uncle Josh got up and threw his napkin on the table.

'Douglas, I'm ashamed of you.'

'Might I point out to my dear brother that he is speaking like a traitor, before an officer of the American Army?'

'Hardly a traitor!' Billy exclaimed.

'What, you too?' said Uncle Douglas.

'Long live the Indians!' Mike cried on the off chance.

'Oh, I wish I'd never said anything!' Elizabeth groaned.

'So do I!' said Aunt Emma. 'I suggest a reconciliation.'

'As far as reconciliations are concerned,' Uncle Douglas said, pointing at Mike, 'we shall settle this between the two of us, in my library, with the doors shut.'

'What have I done?'

'I hope to let you know with the flat of my hand, my boy.'

Elizabeth was indignant.

'I'm taking him back with me to Savannah,' she said forcefully.

'Of course, he's not going with you on Saturday,' Emma said. 'He goes back to boarding school on Monday.'

'No,' Elizabeth insisted, in a sudden burst of generosity. 'He's coming to stay with us. Isn't that so, Billy?'

'Fine by me.'

'By what right do you dispose of my son?' Uncle Douglas asked, all at once perplexed.

'By right of conquest, Douglas,' Uncle Josh exclaimed. 'Can't you see that the boy is radiant with joy? He hates his school.'

'Ghastly school!' Mike muttered under his breath.

Uncle Douglas gave a sigh like a stifled roar.

'Very well,' he said. 'Once more I'm giving way in order to have peace. My boy will go to your house, Billy, that's natural enough, but you must rule him with a rod of iron.'

'I'll make a soldier of him,' said Billy.

Elizabeth smiled at Mike. 'I'll be there,' she said simply.

Quite reassured by this the boy could not help bursting out. 'What luck! No more school!'

'You'll carry on with your lessons and your brother will see your reports,' Uncle Douglas insisted savagely.

But nothing could suppress the boy's enthusiasm; he was almost bubbling with a sort of effervescence of happiness and, seized by an inopportune bout of zeal, wanted at any cost to demonstrate his historical erudition:

'On the subject of Indians,' he announced loudly, 'it was Christopher Columbus who . . .'

'Silence!' Uncle Douglas roared. 'I forbid you to criticize that man.'

'Why not?' asked Uncle Josh. 'He was the real guilty party. Without him, there would have been no conquistadors, no massacre of the Aztecs . . .'

'The Aztecs, with their human sacrifices,' said Uncle Douglas.

'The Spaniards, with their religion and their stake.'

Aunt Augusta's grave voice interrupted:

'It would have been better to send them a few good preachers to show the pagans that they were wrong and to convert them.'

A worried silence underlined the ingenuousness of this little speech and, by general agreement, everyone got up as if to end the meeting.

Happy to have re-established order, Aunt Augusta was the first to leave, with her head held high.

'We'll continue this discussion later, my dear Josh,' Uncle Douglas said, pressing his brother's arm a little too tightly when they were alone.

'Agreed, Douglas, after the war.'

'Are you mad?'

'No, I'm just one of those who refuse to wear out their eyes, the better to see what they want to see.'

# 103

An invisible cloud hovered in the sky over the last days that Elizabeth and Billy spent at Dimwood. The disagreement between the two Hargrove brothers erupted too often for it not to suggest a civil war in miniature, a prelude to the real one that one could vaguely feel approaching.

For Billy, the real problem was to kill time until nightfall and the moment when he would tear off his uniform to take possession of Elizabeth. Before reaching it, he had to endure the desert of those fine afternoons in the country, in which happiness mingles with a very subtle form of boredom which could not be acknowledged.

Deadly excursions by carriage were organized to give a holiday feeling to the space between meals. They felt an obligation to visit neighbors who didn't expect them and, in dreary conversations, they studied all the possibilities of having a good cotton crop. They avoided speaking about the news and congratulated themselves on living a long way from the hubbub of crowded cities. Smiles remained fixed on faces which grew stiff with impatience. Once the hour had finally passed, the visitors took their leave with all the politeness required by the dictates of etiquette.

'That was charming,' said Aunt Augusta. 'I'm delighted that they saw our Billy in uniform. He gives a fine impression of the strength of our people.'

Her head thrust into the wings of her cloche hat, she could not see the killing look that the exasperated hussar cast in her direction.

Only Mike had escaped the trial of these necessary courtesies. A free child of nature, he scampered along the road, singing tunes of his own invention at the top of his voice. Poor Tapageur did his best to obey frenzied kicks from his heels but, when the boy rode off into the fields, his mount lay down gently in the grass and rolled Mike off to one side. In this way they both rested, each in his own way enjoying the vast solitude which hid them from all eyes. Mike, lying on his back with his hands under his head, abandoned himself to the happiness of being fourteen years old and watching a slow armada of white clouds drifting above him across a blue sky. His body exhaled a simple joy in existing, and his insatiable eyes filled with light.

Far from insatiable, Elizabeth felt weary with everything in the midst of the little family group. She was pained to find that Dimwood was not the Dimwood of her dreams. Only the surroundings were there, but they did not tell the same story, the first trembling of love at the sight of a man's face, or even the despair that followed the moment when he was no longer there, and the tears of wasted tenderness that suffused the rest of the night in her empty room. In the whole house, only that corner of the veranda mattered to her. Now she understood that she had come only for that, to be both happy and unhappy there. By what strange misapprehension had she hoped that Billy's presence at that place on the veranda would exorcise a memory that was killing her? Never would she be able to banish Jonathan from her life. The certainty struck her like the brutal revelation of a fact.

That night she was Billy's. Even though her mind was elsewhere, her senses obeyed with a frenzy which she could not control. If she had thought she would embrace a ghost, her hussar husband quickly cured her of that mistake, and she fell deeply in love with him again.

On the eve of her departure, around the middle of the afternoon, taking advantage of a time when Billy was having his rest, she went for a last solitary walk around the great house. She compared herself to a shadow, the shadow of a younger Elizabeth who would never again appear on earth. This sentimental view of her own self amused and saddened her at the same time. Because of the horror of the memories she attached to it, she did not venture near the wide avenue where Jonathan had said farewell simply by speaking her name.

The chance meandering of her melancholy walk took her to the edge of the river beside the meadows. From the opposite bank one could hear the wind murmuring in the tops of the pines, and this soft and confused voice seemed to whisper secrets in an unknown language. Elizabeth listened, watching the ripple of quiet little waves in a sort of lattice, always the same, which diverted her attention, when all at once she recalled that Susanna had one day left a mysterious note under a stone beside this river which suggested that she was about to drown herself: what a commotion there had been at Dimwood! Except for Fred.

Fred . . . She decided to go back to her husband . . . At the bottom of the staircase she met Susanna.

'I saw you from the window of my room,' she said. 'I often look out. I admit I was watching out for you a little.'

'Dear Susanna, why are you never with us at dinner?'

'I dine alone when there are people here. People bore me. But not you!' she added with a smile. 'I came for you the day before yesterday.'

She seemed very young in her pearl gray dress which reached halfway down her legs, despite the solemnity of the color; even her melancholia could not age her. Her large dark eyes were fixed on Elizabeth.

She went on:

'You stopped not far from the place where I left a message. Do you remember?'

'Of course, everyone was scared.'

'You must know, that day I really wanted to die. Not there, a little further on where the water is deep. I didn't have the courage.'

'You wanted to die, Susanna? But why?'

'You cannot possibly understand. I wonder what I'm doing on earth. I'm not here to be happy.'

'Of course you are, you have everything you need.'

'No, you'll never understand. It's as if on the day I left the message by the water's edge, I really did kill myself. I killed someone . . .'

Her voice was so calm that the Englishwoman remained silent, taken aback, disturbed. She had begun to wonder if the woman was in her right mind.

'You're leaving tomorrow,' Susanna said. 'Tomorrow I shan't have the courage to say goodbye to you, so I must do so now.'

'But why are you unhappy, Susanna?'

'I'm unhappy because I'm Susanna and because I am as I am, that's all.'

Elizabeth remained motionless, but her heart was beating a little faster and she felt an uneasiness that she tried to disguise with a smile.

In the silence that followed, Susanna's voice was raised again, but distorted with anguish.

'Let me look at you, Elizabeth.'

'Just as I am looking at you, Susanna, with affection.'

To her great surprise, Susanna merely shook her head slowly, then went up a dozen steps and turned round:

'Elizabeth,' she said simply; and, taking one more quick step upstairs, she disappeared.

The young Englishwoman remained confused, strangely moved herself . . . Her name, spoken in isolation, but with poignant sweetness, immediately recalled Jonathan's last farewell. She did not know what the association was, but she recognized the inimitable tone.

'Goodbye, Susanna!' she called.

The sound of a door closing was the only reply.

The following day promised to be even more lovely than those that preceded it: warmer, more luminous, as though to heighten the sadness of departure. Nature scoffed at outpourings of emotion. Billy and Elizabeth's farewells were little short of tragic. On the point of leaving him for long while, Elizabeth rediscovered the Billy she had once adored, without escaping into a dream world, while he was furious at the idea of being deprived of the source of his greatest happiness on earth. Both exhausted, they kissed without restraint in front of a family smiling with tenderness, matters of morality unquestioned. Only Aunt Augusta raised an eyebrow and lowered her eyes.

With renewed energy, Billy leaped onto his chestnut horse, his traveling case attached to the saddle, and heroically dug in both heels. Elizabeth's departure was more prolonged. She was terrified of having left something behind and used this excuse to go up three or four times for a last look at the room where she had shared her love, while a large fourteen-year-old lad was stamping his feet impatiently in the coach.

However, at the very last minute, a surprise awaited the young woman. Just after she took her place in the carriage in front of the house, she looked up, sentimental to the last, toward the colonnaded façade. Behind a window, she saw the livid face of despair, framed in long ebony ringlets.

Dumbfounded, she could only wave and call out:

'Susanna!'

At that very moment, a whip cracked like a pistol shot and the team set off down the great avenue. Elizabeth kept her eyes shut until they were quite far from the house. Mike, over-excited, was talking endlessly, but she did not understand anything that he was saying, pursued by the memory of that face watching her at a window, a prey to some inexplicable distress. What should she have said to that enigmatic person when they were together at the foot of the stairs? What did she want? What on earth did she want? The thought obsessed her to the point of obliterating the landscape. Mike's voice numbed her senses. Turning toward him, she put a hand on his arm to try and calm him. With his hard little straw hat tilting forward onto his nose, he could not seem anything but charming and she imagined him four years older, a fine young man . . . How would he get on with Ned?

This question and many others occupied her mind. Was she right to take the boy into her house? Ever since childhood she had always acted on impulse and never looked into the future.

It all went better than she had expected. At home she rediscovered the reassuring banality of everyday life. Miss Llewelyn was there, ensuring that everything was in order, at once respectful and dominating in Elizabeth's presence:

'Nothing has changed, Mrs Lizbeth,' she said. 'Mr Ned is in excellent health and the baby has been surrounded with maternal care by Betty and the nanny whom he adores.'

She looked at Mike and gave him her tiger's smile which widened the corners of her mouth, without expressing a shadow of human feeling.

'I find myself,' she said, 'in the presence of an old acquaintance, if I may dare apply that term to a gentleman in the flower of youth; but I also recall a chase with a broomstick under the dining-room table.'

Mike shot her a darting look with his green eyes.

'I don't know what you mean,' he said.

'Without wishing to offend you, Master Mike, I was referring to a certain Black-Hand-Mike, terror of white dresses most of all . . .'

'Leave him be, Miss Llewelyn. Mr Mike Hargrove is going to live with us. Where is Ned?'

'I'll call him for you. At the moment he is under the magnolias, talking to Pat.'

'I see that nothing indeed has changed,' said Elizabeth.

With her great stride that put everything back to rights around her, the Welshwoman went out onto the back porch.

'Mr Ned,' she cried. 'There's a lady asking for you. Guess who it is.'

'Oh, Mummy!' he exclaimed.

The young boy arrived at full speed and threw himself into Elizabeth's arms, for her to hug him and cover him with kisses. His hair disheveled, he was laughing with pleasure when suddenly he saw Mike and stopped dead. His face clouding over, he considered the newcomer and, without hesitation, Elizabeth placed herself between them, taking both by the hand and saying firmly:

'Ned, this is Mike, your Papa's brother. Mike, this is my son, your nephew Ned. So shake hands like two men and two friends.'

Ned remained open-mouthed and perfectly motionless, while Mike, with sudden warmth, grasped his hand and shook it, laughing:

'In life, in death, Ned,' he said.

His hair cascaded across his forehead in curls of red gold and there was so much good humor in his freckled face that Ned eventually smiled. In relief, Elizabeth stroked Mike's cheek. To her amazement, the boy looked up at her and smiled in his turn with a softness that was more revealing than could be suspected, and she immediately took her hand away as if it had been burned, while he continued to look at her entranced.

But how much innocence there was in that round face and those lovely eyes, devoid of mystery or malice . . . Quite clearly, he was entirely unaware of his growing strength. With his gentle ogre's smile, he had the power to overwhelm her. Terrifying thoughts shot through her mind. 'I shouldn't have . . . If Billy had been here he would speak to him . . . I want to send him to school . . . No, I can't, I don't want to . . . Very harsh, very strict . . . That's how I must be with this child, because he is a child . . . No . . . My God . . . Cousin Laura . . .' Why Cousin Laura? She could not have explained it, but she saw herself once more in the empty room where Laura had lived, suffered and prayed . . . The trace remaining of a cross on the wall, the austerity of that naked room . . . What did all this have to do with her, Elizabeth? Nothing, except that Laura too had been deeply in love — and had rid herself of love by shutting herself in a cell. How had she done it? And what about the memory of her great love, of her handsome Régis, who had been killed over there in Haiti? Forgotten? Destroyed? The Welshwoman had recounted everything. She would ask her . . .

This tangled meditation was interrupted by the voice of Ned, the happy voice of good days.

'Mummy, I'm taking him to see the garden and the magnolias.'

Apparently a sudden friendship had been born. Mike gave Elizabeth a rather intense look and went out.

'If he's starting to make eyes at me,' she thought, 'I'll have to get rid of him.'

In the garden, the magnolias were in blossom and did their best to impress the young visitor. However, Patrick, standing in front of his door, had seen him coming from afar, guided by Ned who wouldn't let go of his companion, and the Irishman had already formed a summary opinion of the boy.

'Mike is the brother of my Papa, the Lieutenant,' said Ned.

'A tough boxer, your father . . .'

He pushed back his shapeless straw hat, the better to examine the subject.

'My lad,' he said, 'you'll be like your brother when you grow up: solid and well-built. Do you know how to box?'

'No,' Mike said aggressively. 'But I can defend myself.'

'You defend yourself with your fists and that's the noble art of boxing. Do you want me to teach you straightaway? Come on: get 'em up!'

'Tomorrow,' said Mike.

'You mustn't hurt him, Pat,' Ned warned. 'He's my friend. Take him to Ireland. We go to Ireland every evening,' he explained to Mike.

Pat took his pipe out of his pocket and fixed it between his decrepit teeth.

'That's another story,' he said. 'You must lend him your horse.'

'No,' Ned said firmly. 'I won't lend my horse, but he can sit behind me.'

'Ned,' Mike said, 'your mother is going to show me my room. See you soon, Pat. Do we shake hands?'

The two hands met with virile strength.

'What a fist already!' Pat exclaimed. 'You've got promise, my young lad.'

'I like fighting.'

'Then come and see me; you won't be bored.'

'Will you tell him about the witches?' Ned asked, anxious for Mike's education.

'Witches and all. My Ireland.'

There was too much that Mike did not understand in this conversation and he instinctively caught a hint of madness, so he preferred to go back to Elizabeth.

At the house he found himself dealing with Miss Llewelyn who was waiting for him on the steps.

'Follow me,' she told him. 'I'm going to take you to your room, Master Mike!'

In her eternal gray dress, she chose to wear an inexorable look of serenity. This was the stance she affected in her relations with the young, her smile being reserved for certain adults.

'Young man,' she said, 'you are here in our house. I don't know how you managed in Dimwood, and I prefer not to know.'

'I have no intention of telling you,' he said, appalled at this insolent tone.

In silence, at a brisk pace, they crossed a room on the ground floor which was connected by a communicating single door to another room. Mike looked round. There was nothing surprising about the decor: the narrow bed, the rocking chair, the table with a chair upholstered in slightly worn, garnet-colored velvet, and, on the red-painted floor, a woven rug beside the bed of indeterminate, dark color. Enhancing the seriousness of this furniture, a window opened on a long garden, the same one in which Mike had been talking to the Irishman a few moments earlier.

'You have Mr Ned as your neighbor. You cannot get into your room without going through his. A word of advice. Don't wake him when he's asleep. I might add that you are sharing a bathroom.'

With a nod, she indicated the place in a corner of the room.

'And that's all,' she concluded. 'I should add that this room where we now are is not the guest room.'

Stung to the quick, Mike instantly replied:

'Being one of the family, I don't consider myself a guest. I'm at home here.'

She blinked in surprise. As an experienced adversary, she secretly admired his repartee and, swinging round on her heels, left without a word.

Elizabeth, for her part, was with Betty at the side of the bed where her newborn son was sleeping, gazing at him with the desire to feel some pang of maternal love; but the good intention was fruitless. In vain she tried to arouse her imagination by saying over to herself: 'Come on, it's Billy's son. So . . .'

She found it impossible to discover the slightest hint of a resemblance, even a distant one. This little being, mysterious in its simplicity, with its tiny breath, moved her by its very weakness, its absolute lack of defenses, its fragility. But she was forced to admit to herself that she did not have what are called a mother's guts, not for this child. With the other, with Ned, it was different: he was the child of a great passion. With this one, she hesitated . . . Billy hadn't wanted him, because . . . But she was resolved she would love this tiny little Christopher. To begin with, she wanted to put her lips to his minute face, which reminded her of a flower. Betty made a shy movement to stop her.

'Miss Lizbeth, You'll wake him up.'

'You're right, Betty. You must be careful never to leave him, even at night when he's asleep.'

'Betty always here, Miss Lizbeth, or Mammy, and Mammy adore him.'

'I do too, I adore him, Betty, but I'm afraid.'

The conversation continued in very low whispers:

'Mustn't be 'fraid, Miss Lizbeth. The door is locked.'

'Yes, but someone might come through the window. There are demons in the world.'

Betty made the sign of the cross.

'Why do you do that, Betty? Are you afraid, too?'

'No, Miss Lizbeth. The good Lord protec' the baby.'

'But if a madman were to come in here, at night, when you have not been able to stop yourself falling asleep . . .'

'Oh, no!'

'Yes. If you didn't hear him and he were to go over to the child and simply put his hand over the baby's mouth so that he could no longer breathe, and then . . .'

Betty suddenly sat bolt upright, her black face distorted with horror.

'Oh, Ma'am! Why you say that?'

'I don't know, Betty. It's my nightmare. We must make sure the shutters are properly closed on all the windows and double-lock all the locks.'

As she said this, Elizabeth had gone dreadfully pale; and, speaking so low that she could hardly hear herself, she said slowly:

'You must pray for him, Betty. You know how to pray. I don't any longer. No one listens to me, do you understand? Because . . . I don't know why. I have the impression that I'm talking to myself.'

'Oh, Miss Lizbeth. You mustn't say that.'

'When I was younger, I believed there was someone there, but I'm not sure any longer.'

'Oh, Miss Lizbeth, you mus' be sure.'

'Then ask him in my place, for me.'

She stood up sharply and went out.


Finding no one in the hall, she called Joe.

'Have you taken my luggage up to my room?'

'Yes, Ma'am. As soon as you arrived.'

'Where is Mr Mike?'

'I don't know, Ma'am.'

Miss Llewelyn promptly appeared.

'Mr Mike has gone out for a walk along the avenue.'

'His room, Miss Llewelyn. Have you thought about his room?'

'Of course. He's sleeping in the room next to Mr Ned's.'

'Whatever are you thinking about? It's only ever used as a lumber room.'

'I had the bed made up there. He will be very comfortable, Ma'am.'

'I repeat: what are you thinking of? There is the guest room.'

'Not far from yours, at the end of the corridor. Where I put him, he can only leave his room by going through Mr Ned's — and Mr Ned notices everything. In the same way, no one can enter his room.'

Suddenly flushed with anger, Elizabeth raised her voice:

'I demand an explanation of what you have just said.'

By one of those natural gifts which made her so unusual, the Welshwoman drew herself up and puffed out her chest, so that she appeared huge.

'Do you want banal excuses, or the truth? Allow me to tell you that you would not be given any banal excuses . . . So you are left with a choice between silence and the truth.'

'How dare you? Well, tell me your truth. You don't frighten me.'

'Mrs William Hargrove, you are in danger.'

'I forbid you . . .'

'And the day will come when you will thank Maisie Llewelyn for warning you in time.'

Elizabeth did not answer.

'Do you realize that you have upset someone?'

'If that's the case, it's quite unintentional.'

'I believe you, but he should not be here.'

'You haven't always preached morals to me, Miss Llewelyn.'

'At that time, the lover was in Vienna, but today, if you were given a chance, he would be at the end of the corridor.'

'Be quiet. I find you impertinent.'

'Not at all. It's common sense speaking to you in the rough accents of the people. Will you listen to me? It is two o'clock and Mr Mike will be back in a moment. You have in your household three strong black men. Have lunch quietly with your brother-in-law — because he is your brother-in-law. When Mr Mike goes back to his room, he won't recognize it. I'll look after everything.'

'You won't . . .'

'Yes. What has been done in one direction can be done in the opposite one. For those colored boys, it's child's play.'

'Who authorized you?'

'It may be that you say, before going to bed: "Lead us not into temptation . . ." I'm putting aside that temptation.'

'Why don't you leave my soul alone?'

'I understand your irritation, because I've never had many principles, but today you scared me. You are defenseless against love.'

'So? What harm is there in love?'

'None, but love for you is in the plural.'

'Miss Llewelyn, there have been times when I felt close to you, but there are others when I hate you.'

'Well, well.'

'For example, just now, when you are right in a provocative sort of way. Your lack of tact would try the patience of a saint.'

'Very true. Welsh, you understand? But I can't stand by and see you going directly . . .'

'To hell. Say it, since that's what you're dying to say: to hell.'

'Not quite, Miss Lizbeth. One can stop halfway. That's what happened to me.'

Suddenly more attentive, Elizabeth took a step over to her.

'How was that?'

'Laura.'

'Could you be more plain? I, too, think of her sometimes.'

'You remember the day when I told you about her story on Haiti?'

'As everyone else in Savannah does, Miss Llewelyn.'

'I saw it all over again, that afternoon: I was there. At her wedding in the little church, then in the plantation under attack from the mulattoes. I saw Lieutenant Régis fall from a shot fired out of the house. Laura's face followed me . . . I have never had the courage to visit her in her convent since Annabel joined her there.'

'How does Annabel's presence affect the situation?'

'In no way and in every way. Annabel is loyal and will not talk about you, but it's because of you . . . that she left the world. The ruby I can see at your neck looking like a drop of blood describes the story, your story . . . '

She thought again and said:

'Our story, because I have my share of responsibility. Annabel doesn't know that, but I do and she is there with her mother. She has forgiven everything, but she is there. I understood, I felt that, for my part, I should arrive at the point of no return if I took another step. I was afraid, I backed down, I gave myself up. You are speaking to a different person.'

She paused for a moment and asked:

'Did you burn my letters?'

'Of course! And you: did you burn mine? They were no less dangerous . . .'

'This very morning.'

'What!' Elizabeth cried in indignation. 'You kept them all that time!'

'Yes. I liked money. They were worth a lot and you were becoming rich.'

'What a foul scheme!'

'Yes, foul. But I've confessed everything . . . I've told you and I have got rid of that and all the rest of my past. I'm a different person, at peace with myself. But you, Elizabeth, you are close to the point of no return. You should not touch that boy.'

'Are you mad? Who says I have any intention of touching Mike?'

'Everything proclaims it when I see you together. Mike is too easy a prey and already consenting.'

'In short, I am lost.'

'No, saved! Maisie Llewelyn is there like an angel with a fiery sword. You don't know what a Welshwoman is when religion takes her.'

'Miss Llewelyn, we are going to have to part if you continue in this tone.'

'Not on any grounds: I have a mission to watch over you.'

At that moment they heard the sound of furniture moving above their heads. Objects were being lifted and then dropped heavily on the floor.

'Don't be alarmed,' said Miss Llewelyn. 'It's your Blacks. They have taken down the bed in the guest room and are carrying it along the fatal corridor.'

'The fatal corridor?'

'The one down which that poor fool would have gone to join you at night.'

'You're talking like the devil.'

'But it's absolutely true! See how the enemy of our souls takes advantage of the purest intentions to assist his sinister plans! Behind me, Satan!'

Hardly had she finished these words than the noise of the removal men increased with remarkably appropriate timing. Elizabeth looked toward the Welshwoman who nodded with an air of extreme satisfaction and, almost at once, a bed, minus its columns and canopy, appeared at the top of the stairs. Two Blacks running with sweat were bringing it down in fits and starts, striking their heels on the staircase and emitting harsh groans.

As though to increase the confusion, there was a ring at the front door and, since no one went to open it, Elizabeth did so herself. She found herself face-to-face with Mike, stunned by the noise and with a host of questions on his lips.

'Don't pay any attention to it,' Elizabeth shouted. 'You'll discover later. Go to the dining-room.'

He said simply:

'Betty.'

She was indeed following behind him with Ned, whom she had taken for a longer walk than usual. A glance at the stairs made them open their mouths wide with astonishment, but Elizabeth cut short any questions:

'Take the child to the dining-room,' she ordered.

The dining-room was sheltered from the hustle and bustle of the removals. The table was laid and the lowered blinds softened the urgent February light. Elizabeth sat between Ned and Mike. Outraged by the Welshwoman's attitude, she had recovered all her British aggressiveness. The large clock, in a corner of the room, showed a quarter to three.

'Wait,' said Elizabeth. 'They should know that we are here.'

At that moment, Miss Llewelyn appeared at the door.

'Miss Llewelyn,' Elizabeth said brusquely, 'kindly ensure that we are served immediately.'

Spoken in the tone of the mistress of the house, these words seemed to restore everything to its place and put an end to the discussion.

'Yes, Ma'am, at once,' said the Welshwoman.

When she had gone, Elizabeth turned to Mike.

'You'll soon have a chance to see the improvements to your room. I hope you'll be pleased.'

'I liked it very much,' he said with the smile of an obedient child.

One felt that he wanted to approve of whatever she decided for him and was unable to avoid looking at her with a naive admiration that betrayed his complete innocence. Elizabeth would not have been a woman if she had not been sensible to the sincerity of this tribute, but it made her uneasy.

A servant in red livery brought a plate of snow-white, steaming rice, then another of pink meat, finely sliced. Elizabeth served her young guests herself and the conversation during the meal was very simple. Ned was the most talkative, describing his dreams of the night before without leaving anything out. Miss Llewelyn once more made a discreet appearance to oversee the serving of the meal. Without seeming to, she narrowed her eyes and looked sharply but furtively at Elizabeth and Mike before going out. The Englishwoman controlled herself as best she could.

Mike proved delighted with the transformation to his room. Furniture in pure George III style had replaced the jumble which had been moved back to the next door room, which had been so sparsely furnished that it still left space for a six-year old child to romp in. Moreover, Ned did not complain: an extra bed and armchair offered new elements to furnish his imaginary tales. He was also pleased to be so close to Mike, whom he saw as an accessible listener, and a change from Pat who had become slightly ordinary. And Mike had developed an affection for the imaginative little storyteller. He listened patiently, giving all the necessary signs of amazement, but he had to go back to school the day after tomorrow and was less sorry about it than he would have thought on the first day, because he was starting to be bored at his sister-in-law's.

He only saw her at meal times and, when he looked at her, she made a show of lowering her eyes. For all that, she did not seem to him any the less strangely beautiful, but he experienced confused feelings of guilt. The incredible abundance of her golden hair was what first attracted his attention, then above all — and here began the revery of the senses — the fresh brilliance of her pale pink skin and what he could surmise of her bosom beneath the chiffon scarf.

She said very little to him; that wild animal look peculiar to young men disturbed her, though she would not admit it to herself. 'A mere lad,' she thought. 'And to be warned against a schoolboy by that dotty woman who has just rediscovered religion . . .' But the Welshwoman had been right and it was better for the young man not to sleep at the end of the corridor. 'Fatal!' Elizabeth added to herself, with a silent laugh. Oh, how she wished Billy would come back and put an end to this uncomfortable situation! But how to 'put an end'? She didn't know. Billy would arrange it all.

Meanwhile, everything in the house seemed to be running smoothly. Miss Llewelyn had calmed down after her spectacular crisis of conscience and had regained control over Elizabeth's world. The two boys got along famously. Mike sometimes listened at night to his young neighbor giving little cries of terror in the nightmares which he, Mike, would have to endure listening to the following morning, in stories that were full of confused details.

Usually he dined alone, because Elizabeth had again begun to go out and would come home late. So Miss Llewelyn, while not actually keeping the boy company, would watch to ensure that he was properly served and would linger for a while in the dining-room. With a strange mixture of delicacy and brutality, she asked obscure questions whose significance he did not grasp. She would go a long way, then stop just in time. She was curious about conditions at school, his teachers, above all his school-mates, and worried about the state of morals in the college; and, why not? about his own morals in particular. The boy was embarrassed and would not answer. He sensed this large woman behind his chair, heavy, graying, breathing a little too heavily. What did she want? Her language was obscure. He would have liked her to go away, but she stayed. She stayed until the dessert which, of course, she did not touch. That sort of dessert did not appeal to her.

# 104

*T*he season was as brilliant — if not more so — as any preceeding year and was at its height from March to mid-April. Under the great chandeliers, an elegant and loquacious crowd forgot the petty irritations of the age and of history. It was wonderfully easy to plunge into this timeless world. It was merely a question of cutting a dash and not being boring.

In Mrs Harrison Edwards' vast circular drawing-room, Elizabeth's appearance always excited a moment's admiration, which she ensured by varying her outfits and more especially by never wearing the same hair style on any two sucessive occasions. She played with her hair as one exploits one's wealth. The subtlety of the result was akin to the skill of an artist from Paris who restricted the number of his clients. The secret of the surprise was in the simplicity of the unexpected. The abundance of the gold made it simpler to devise new effects with it.

It should be said that Elizabeth never lost her awareness of a natural shyness which she shamefully exploited. Her lack of confidence excited in men the noble instinct of protection: she had learned this for herself after only a few excursions into society. So the young black jackets flocked around her like a shoal of fish in tail coats. The irresistible Algernon, who had never given up hope of conquest, was not the least charming of them. And, of course, there was Lieutenant Hargrove — Billy terrorized Algernon beyond words, but that evening, by an accident which Algernon did not dare call providential, Lieutenant Hargrove was not there. Finally, he approached the beautiful Englishwoman and, with languid eyes, said simply:

'Elizabeth, remember . . .'

She turned sharply toward him.

'Remember what?'

'Our evening at the Schmicks'.'

'Are you mad, Algernon? I'm trying to forget that nightmare!'

He shrank back a step, crestfallen, and his place was instantly taken by a personable young man with a gardenia in his buttonhole, which he took out to offer to Elizabeth. She took it, sniffed it with her eyes shut and was tempted to stroke it against the face of her admirer, whom she found to her liking, but she managed to restrain herself . . .

That evening, Algernon vanished.

Returning home after a cruel period of deprivation, Billy found the house as he had left it, or almost. A little world which seems motionless does move, even so, in a way that is impossible to analyze. Perhaps the Welshwoman seemed more peremptory in manner and Mike had put on weight . . . They ate well in Oglethorpe Square. But was that all? Every furlough gave Billy an Elizabeth who was more lovely and more passionate: this time, she threw herself into his arms like a fury in love. He had never known her like that and he assumed that she must have missed him a good deal, so everything was for the best.

On the second day, a shadow fell across them. Billy would not have known how to describe it. An uncertainty perhaps, but so slight a thing that he thought at first that he must be mistaken. It was particularly in evidence at table, when he saw Mike, pink and rounder in the face, next to Elizabeth. He was looking at her surreptitiously, the innocent, much as a child looks at a Christmas tree on Christmas Eve. And now ridiculous thoughts ran through Billy's head which he put aside; but ridiculous thoughts have a habit of coming back. Why? Precisely because they are ridiculous.

From another corner of the table, a six-year-old boy, always slightly mysterious, sat gravely observing these grown-ups, and longing for Ireland, but he too gazed at Elizabeth with an adoration which he did not try to hide. Sometimes he smiled at Mike and Mike responded with a merry wink.

For Billy, as for Elizabeth, the days passed at a dreadful speed. The furlough had been generous, thanks to a reconciliation over whist between the commandant and the cleverest of his hussars, but its last hours were in sight. In Billy's universe only Elizabeth existed, but one day he went to tickle his little newborn child in his cot, until the baby cried with irritation.

'A fit of the giggles,' said Elizabeth.

Betty stopped the game by taking the child in her arms and the happy parents withdrew.

'I had a thought as I was looking at him,' said Billy. 'He'll get more handsome as he grows. Meanwhile . . . We're not a bad-looking family. Take Mike. He's starting to fill out. He's a sturdy young boy. The kind we need most in the Army.'

'In Heaven's name, Billy!' Elizabeth exclaimed.

'Why, does it bother you?'

'Not at all, but we're all used to having him around the house.'

'Are you very fond of him?'

'He's a good boy.'

'They teach him nonsense in his school. I'll take him away and have him admitted to the military academy at Charleston. I know almost all the instructing officers. What do you say?'

Elizabeth swallowed heavily and tried urgently to think of what she should say, the only possible reply.

'Wonderful,' she said, her heart beating.

He quickly took her in his arms and hugged her until she was gasping.

'I've been pondering my plan these past few days,' he said, gaily. 'You can go and tell him in a moment to get his cases packed; or would you rather I did it?'

She could not hold back her tears and blew her nose.

'He'll be sad,' she said, pulling herself together. 'Perhaps I should explain to him.'

'Perhaps. I'm only able to talk like a soldier.'

Mike was in the garden with Ned. She took him aside under the magnolias, their perfume seeming to imprison them in tenderness.

First of all, Elizabeth could only mumble some phrases which he did not understand. She had lowered her head and put both hands on the astonished boy's chest. Finally, she found the words she needed to inform him of Billy's plan. When he heard the words 'military academy', Mike's eyes began to shine.

'You leave there with a commission,' he said.

'I believe so,' Elizabeth sighed.

She hadn't been expecting this joyful tone, but had hoped for something different, anything that might express some hint of feeling . . . She had thought that, in the looks which he gave her at table, she could detect some shy declaration.

Suddenly, he kissed her gauchely, a kiss planted on her forehead.

'Don't be sad, I'll come back.'

She stood upright, stung by this hint of masculine vanity.

'But I'm not sad at all, my dear Mike. Go and tell your brother that it's agreed.'

He ran to the steps. Miss Llewelyn was there, hands on hips. She had been watching from afar, without hearing anything.

'And where are you going in such a hurry?' she asked Mike, smiling.

'To find my brother,' he blurted out. 'He's taking me to Charleston. I'm going to the military academy.'

She stood aside to let him go and remained motionless, leaning against the door, as though he had struck her.

'Military academy . . .,' she murmured.

Mike was already in his brother's room. The latter, in shirt sleeves, was hunting for clothes in the drawer of a long dressing table.

'So, did you speak to my wife?' he asked.

'Yes, she agrees. She was very kind.'

'Of course. Women arrange everything with their tenderness . . . We'll take the morning train the day after tomorrow. Elizabeth will help you pack. Are you pleased?'

'Oh, yes, Billy! You bet, leaving with you . . . '

'Fine. Now be off. No speeches in the Army.'

Mike ran out like a young animal and leaped down the stairs. At the bottom, Ned was waiting for him, in a blue linen suit with short trousers.

'Aren't you coming into the garden?'

The clear voice rose like a call from happy childhood itself . . . Mike walked more slowly down the lower steps. When he came close to Ned, he sat down in front of him and took hold of both his arms.

'Ned, I've got some news for you. I'm going to be a soldier, like Billy.'

Ned didn't understand at once, but his eyes widened with anxiety.

'When?' he asked.

'Soon. But we'll still be friends, won't we?'

'When — soon?'

'Listen, if I could take you with me; but I can't . . . It's the day after tomorrow.'

Ned's mouth opened and let out a cry so powerful that it seemed larger than he was. Miss Llewelyn ran to them, then Elizabeth, and Billy himself appeared at the top of the stairs while Mike was trying to calm the boy whom he had taken in his arms; but Ned was struggling and his cries came one after another, interrupted by frightening gasps. Alarmed faces appeared all round, especially from the kitchens. Betty and the black mammy tried to get near the child. More resolute than any of them, the Welshwoman grasped hold of him and took him into Mike's room where she laid him out on the large four-poster bed. Here, she eventually calmed him by quietly singing him songs in a language which he didn't understand. After a while, the little body, worn out with weariness, stretched itself out and the brown eyes closed, drenched in tears.

Elizabeth crept in, but the Welshwoman at once showed her the door.

'If there is any sign of tenderness,' she said in a severe whisper, 'it will start all over again.'

'But he's my son.'

'Do you want him to have a nervous breakdown, Ma'am?'

And she pushed her out. Elizabeth, dumbfounded, heard the key turn twice sharply in the lock.

In the hall there was at first a dismayed silence, except for Billy, who agreed with Miss Llewelyn.

'Full of common sense, your Welshwoman,' he told his wife. 'A strong hand, you see: the only way. And then, what's all this about? Do you understand it?'

She didn't answer. She settled into Ned's room with Betty and Black Mammy. No sound came from the neighboring room in which the cause of all this commotion was sound asleep.

The evening soon took on a strange atmosphere of mourning. Elizabeth and Mike took it in turns to sit at Ned's bedside. He refused to eat anything, but succumbed in spite of himself to the treacherous temptation of a bar of milk chocolate which Mike slipped him at nightfall.

Ned flopped against Elizabeth's shoulder, asking continually why Mike had to go, and she eventually managed to console him by promising that he would come back very soon. The lie was delivered to him in a gulp. Mike, whom he clasped like a drowning man, only received a single appeal, always the same:

'Don't go, Mikey, don't go!'

It was as though the violence of the first shock had exhausted the strength of a despair that was reduced to a groan. Little by little the child grew calm, but a resignation beyond his years was more distressing than his cries and his rebellion against the incomprehensible whims of life. The next day was even more difficult, although the drama unfolded almost in silence. Ned followed Mike wherever he could, afraid that he would escape him at the turn of a corridor or behind a door. In order to spare him the distress of parting, which seemed likely to unleash another storm, it was decided that the Lieutenant would leave the house with his brother at first light. Billy agreed, but not without grumbling.

In the dawn light hovering behind the tops of the trees everything went as smoothly as possible. Joe, in red livery, held a lantern to light the little group on the steps. A carriage was waiting to take the travelers to the coach station.

It was just as the servants were taking the luggage to the carriage that the inevitable confusion of all final moments took place. Billy hugged his wife forcefully several times, the fury of love mingling with the exasperation of departure, and the buttons on his dolman crushed her lightly covered breast. Seized by a sudden impulse, Mike clasped Elizabeth in his arms and their two mouths touched in a rapid kiss, permissible between relatives; wasn't he her brother-in-law?

Infinitely more reserved in her attitude, Miss Llewelyn showed a face hardened by the pain of sadness. She could only smile at the boy, who thanked her politely for looking after him and his comfort.

It was all over in less than three minutes. The whip cracked and the carriage went off while the first rays of sunshine were sliding across the rooftops. There was a pained silence, then Miss Llewelyn accompanied her mistress as far as the hall. There, when they were alone, she allowed herself a bitter remark:

'What an idea of yours, bringing that boy here! With his lovely green eyes, like a young animal, he made everyone fall in love with him.'

Elizabeth did not answer, but went up to her room. Raising her voice, so that she could be heard, the Welshwoman continued:

'I'll have the guest room refurnished as it was before . . . at the end of the corridor.'

A few seconds went by, then she could not prevent herself from adding:

'From now on you can have whoever you like to sleep there.'

From the top of the stairs, the stinging reply came back:

'Thank you for your permission, Miss Llewelyn, but that's enough.'

'Yes, Ma'am,' said the Welshwoman, quite satisfied that her English mistress still had her normal British reflexes.

## 105

*T*he calm of the following weeks was slightly artificial, since too many hearts had been troubled and could not find peace. The hardest hit was Ned who could not even forgive his mother for having deprived him of the sad pleasure of seeing Mike for one last time, on the morning of his departure. Young as he was, he vaguely sensed a general conspiracy of all adults against all children, allegedly for the good of the latter, who made up a little nation apart. These still very confused ideas came to him through one of those intuitions that enter the minds of all young people on the brink of going to school, where education will methodically deprive them of their instinctive and just opinions.

Miss Llewelyn, who doubtless understood better than the rest, thought of putting Christopher to sleep in the room which had belonged, for too brief a time, to Mike. Betty and Black Mammy would keep the little baby company. She realized how awful it would be for Ned to have that room, empty but already full of memories, next to his own.

The ball at Mrs Harrison Edwards', during Billy's long absence, had revived Elizabeth's taste for society. Did she realize that the passing of time had something to do with it? When one is twenty-four and still considered the most beautiful of all the beauties in Savannah, one cannot get used to being alone. One wishes to be seen and to enjoy oneself. Now, especially, since Billy's departure and the almost equally heart-rending departure of innocent young Mike with his dangerous charm, she needed at any cost to sink herself once more into the noise and light of great, luxurious reception rooms. So, quick, Joe, my carriage!

Despite the first breath of summer heat, social life was unusually brilliant, as if the threat of what was to come had spurred on the flower of society.

What made Elizabeth's life still more exciting was the increased frequency in the number of Billy's furloughs. As he always warned her of his arrival, he never risked the horrible disappointment of finding her absent, because with the blind confidence of husbands who are at the same time very jealous and very sure of themselves, he encouraged Elizabeth to go out, fearing that boredom might lead her into mischief. That said, he did have one particular enemy: Algernon; but he had so often in his dreams run the man through with a sword that this had finally put his mind at rest. However, when he held Elizabeth in his arms, he never failed to ask her, in a tone that she knew well, for news of 'the little whippersnapper', as he called him; and she could always reply, with some sincerity, that she had none . . .

In the pauses between their lovemaking, he told her what she needed to know. For example, that he had obtained permission from his father, by a simple exchange of letters, to allow Mike to enter the military academy at Charleston. Similarly, to keep her informed of the few events that interested her, he told her that in Utah the snow had melted, and the Federal troops had come down from the mountains to march into Salt Lake City, the Mormon capital. The latter had immediately sued for peace and delivered to the Federals the men who were suspected of responsibility for attacking the immigrants. The vile John Lee, some Mormons and a few Indians were hanged on the spot where the massacre took place, in Mountain Meadows, and their bodies left to the coyotes and the vultures.

Elizabeth gave a fitting little shudder, but could not help feeling some satisfaction. The victims were avenged! And then, repeatedly, Billy reminded her that this had taken place a long, long way from Savannah.

Alone once more after Billy's departure, she consoled herself by looking at the invitations stuck in the mirror above the chimney. There were many of these pretty cards on elegant paper, because she had truly become the queen of the most fashionable *soirées*, the favorite of young Savannah society! She stifled a weary little yawn: the demands of one's position . . .

That evening, there was a ball at Mrs Harrison Edwards' which could not be missed. They were celebrating the inauguration of the fountain in Forsythe Park, the loveliest in the United States, according to the newspapers. Throughout the duration of the work, there had been fences all around it, but there were chinks through which you could catch a glimpse. In the last few days especially a lot of people had been to the site. Miss Llewelyn had decided to join the crowd to find out, she said, but returned with a very off-hand air, saying she had seen much more imposing fountains at home and on Haiti. Elizabeth hadn't made the trip. So: off to Mrs Harrison Edwards'.

She called for Miss Llewelyn who appeared immediately, smiling but already sarcastic.

'Mr César?' Elizabeth asked.

'Mr César, again, and as ever . . .'

'I can do without your observations, Miss Llewelyn. I'm asking if Mr César is here.'

'He lives some way away and he has all his customers in the town to cope with. However, since you are making him a fortune, rest assured that you will always be the first to be served. He's on his way.'

Scarcely had Elizabeth had time to throw the appropriate robe over her shoulders than there was a knock at the door. Miss Llewelyn, who was still there, opened, then stood aside to give way to a gentleman of medium height, elegantly thin, pressed into a dress coat as if for a society evening. What remained of his ink-black hair, plastered to his scalp, crowned a broad expanse of forehead and, under a beak-like nose, a slender, equally black moustache seemed to have been painted on the light brown skin. The eyes, which at least were naturally black, shone remarkably under elongated eyebrows carefully drawn as in the portraits of Persian princes. Where did he come from? No one could have said, but his accent could only be Parisian, even in English. The mystery surrounding him dissipated in part when he opened his mouth, because he was talkative and asked nothing better than to pour out all the secrets in the world, except his own.

Putting a flat suitcase in red morocco down on the carpet, he gave a great bow and exclaimed:

'Already fully prepared, Madame, with that royal golden gown over your shoulders. May I?'

Plunging his long fingers into the heavy golden hair, he lifted it abruptly on one side, while letting it gently fall on the other.

'There!' he said. 'Your hair is done!'

'But Monsieur César, not for this evening. It's frightful!'

'Frightful? Look at yourself in the mirror and turn a little toward me.'

'Ah!' she said.

'Windswept: you are caught up in a storm, and I shall fix that storm, I shall immobilize it.'

From his bag, which he opened with one hand, he took out a vaporizer which let out a misty stream. Elizabeth glanced in the mirror and did not recognize herelf. He had changed her into a Fury, but she found it beautiful, though the beauty was frightening.

'Magnificent,' she said. 'But perhaps not for this evening. Everyone will be there, and they are so stiff, so formal . . .'

'Perfect. I'll take it all to pieces and find something else.'

'Something simpler, perhaps?'

He gave a gently reproachful look.

'I only know simplicity, Madame; that's the height of our art.'

Without asking her opinion, he walked round her waving his comb in the air like a magician's wand.

'All I ask is to be beautiful,' she said, slightly anxious. 'But I don't want to alarm people.'

'Alarm them! In Paris, you would have been considered sublime and altogether fashionable. Since the twentieth of January, Paris knows all about fear. She lives in fear.'

'I don't understand you, Monsieur César.'

'Orsini, Madame.'

'Orsini? I think I vaguely heard speak of him here, but you know, I don't read the newspapers.'

'Madame,' he said, pityingly. 'Their Imperial Majesties are going to the Opéra . . . It's a singer's farewell performance . . . At the moment their carriage turns into the boulevard, one, two, three bombs explode. Napoleon III is scratched on the hand and Eugénie has blood splattered on her white dress. One hundred and fifty wounded, eight dead. Italy only just missed them.'

'How terrible.'

'Isn't it? The Emperor was superb. He arrived in the middle of an act. They had heard the explosions in the theater. The orchestra stopped and played 'Partant pour la Syrie,' (he hummed softly) 'then the performance continued. What do you think: life and its pleasures go on. However, the Emperor slipped out of his box to go and see one of his guards who was dying in a pharmacy that was still open nearby in the Rue Le Pelletier. And he pinned his own Legion of Honor on his chest.' (He lowered his voice). 'All France wept. What madness it all is . . . Would you turn a little this way, please. The Opera House attracts murder. It was built with what remained of the walls of its predecessor, where the Duc de Berry was assassinated. The shadow of the first opera house had settled on the second.'

'I didn't know.'

'What matter! All Paris spoke only of that and all Paris still knows by heart the programme which Their Imperial Majesties was going to listen to. Destiny was inscribed as clearly as may be in that program. Shall I tell you what it was?'

'I'd be delighted.'

'The second act of *William Tell*: the conspiracy of the Swiss patriots against the Austrian governor. Does that mean anything to you?'

'Well . . . vaguely.'

'No matter. It's about a man who has to be killed.'

In a fair baritone voice he hummed 'Dark forests . . .'

'Wonderful Rossini!' he exclaimed. 'Then Donizetti's *Maria Stuarda*. The Queen is not beheaded on the stage, but we know that she will go under the axe.'

'Oh!'

Elizabeth gave a groan of horror.

'Indeed so. Then there was the overture for the ball in Auber's *Gustave III*. Another successful assassination of a crowned head.'

'Ah!'

'Indeed so. And to end with, the second act of *La Muette de Portici* . . . Revolution in the Kingdom of Naples.'

'But, Monsieur César, you'd think that the choice was deliberate.'

'Indeed. Destiny, fate. Oh, you'll be pleased with it, just wait. Afterwards, there was the wrath of the government. The Emperor was bewildered — Orsini was a remarkable man — but eventually decided to act. The guillotine was awaiting the guilty man, and suddenly the whole of Paris was full of suspects. In three months, two thousand people were arrested and four hundred deported, sent to Toulon and from there to Algeria, and the press was gagged . . .'

'Monsieur César, I'm chilled to the bone by your story, but I forgot to tell you that I don't want any spit curls.'

'What are you thinking of? Spit curls are for chambermaids.'

He began to caress her hair with his comb, and his hand became so light that it made Elizabeth shudder.

Then, instantly, he stopped and said simply:

'It's done. If you would like to get up and hold this mirror so that you can see your back in the cheval glass.'

She took the mirror and examined herself.

'But, Monsieur César, my hair isn't dressed! You've done nothing to it!'

'Madame . . .,' he said in a pained tone of voice.

'Well, here I am with my hair down my back. Is that all?'

'Allow me . . . The only ball anyone is attending this evening . . .'

'. . . is Mrs Harrison Edwards',' she said, with slight irritation. 'So?'

'To inaugurate that fountain of which I, like everyone else, have stolen a glimpse. Journalists are stupidly writing that it is an exact copy of the fountains in our own Place de la Concorde in Paris. There is no comparison. In our fountain, tritons and naiads of provocative beauty display themselves without the slightest embarrassment for the admiration of passers-by. Their fountain here lets you see nothing, through the planks, except some reeds and, I believe, a scornful heron as well as a few tritons — but no naiads. What a country!'

'What has all that to do with my hair, Monsieur César?'

'Don't give me that severe look, Madame, and be patient, I beg you. What is the theme of this ball? A fountain. Hurrah! You appear, queen of all naiads, dressed entirely in white, your hair flowing like a waterfall in the sunshine, dripping with shining droplets, like . . . like what? But like diamonds, Madame. Fix a few diamonds here and there, in this divine hair of yours. Eugénie will die of jealousy when she hears tell of it and, believe me, it will be heard about.'

'But diamonds . . . I really don't know! Of course, I have some: what lady doesn't have diamonds in her jewel box? But will I have enough?'

She walked across the room and opened the door of a large dressing table, out of which she took a little bunch of keys, then vanished into the adjacent room. A few minutes passed and she came back with a little shagreen box which she put on the table to open. When she raised the lid, Mr César, who had been standing discreetly a little way off, saw enough for him to raise his hands in a gesture of amazement, with a sort of dance step backwards.

'Sublime!' he exclaimed.

'It's a present from my father-in-law, Mr Charlie Jones. But I have never been crazy about diamonds; I much prefer emeralds and saphhires, and I have few of them.'

'Your splendid emerald necklace would not be suitable for this evening, Madame, if I may venture to say so. For this night, let us remain with the divine simplicity of the diamond.'

The fervor with which he spoke these words convinced her at once and the hours that followed were devoted to carrying out his suggestion.

For this ball among all the others in the season, Mrs Harrison Edwards had decided to do things on a grand scale. Every drawing-room in her huge mansion was open. People would dance everywhere. The preparations demanded no less than three days.

Emerging from the hands of Mr César, who had looked after every detail, Elizabeth made an entrance that would be forever memorable in the lives (some long, some short) of the guests. They thought — as they said at the time — that they saw enter the fairy of lakes, rivers and waterfalls. Her chiffon dress, pleated with a skill that was almost that of an illusionist, imitated the movement of water at every step she took, and her hair, spangled with diamonds, reflected the light of the chandeliers in little multicolored flames. What might have been ridiculous, had she herself not possessed such radiant beauty, struck everyone dumb with amazement and wonderment. To perfect his masterpiece, Mr César had even gone so far as to put between her fingers a glass wand at the end of which he had fixed a star of brilliant stones. With his gift of the gab and the self-assurance of an undoubted master in the field of hairdressing, he had managed to entrance his victim, who was all the more compliant since he assured her of a triumph. However, when she reached the center of a circle of admirers, she heard the first notes of an invisible orchestra and was seized with a panic at the idea that, if a waltz was about to begin, she would cut a strange figure. It was most of all the wand, of which she had been so proud, that now bothered her and she decided to get rid of it as quickly as possible. And then, dancing in this vast white chiffon dress was unthinkable; but here, Mr César had anticipated her difficulty. The waving chiffon was only a veil from which she could liberate herself whenever she wished once the effect of collective enchantment had been achieved. In a great murmur of flattering exclamations and exaggerated compliments, she saw approaching all the elegant young men with their ecstatic smiles. Almost at once she observed bold Algernon and, suddenly inspired by feminine malice, she gave him an encouraging nod. When he managed to get close to her, he gave her the tenderest look, and as on the last occasion, simply said:

'Elizabeth.'

To which she replied:

'Algernon.'

And she held out the diamond studded wand to him; he took it with a long sigh.

'And above all,' the fierce Englishwoman added, 'keep a good hold on it and don't let it go. It's my sceptre.'

He raised up eyes full of wild gratitude, which made her feel guilty. But what of it? The handsome Algernon got on her nerves.

Turning in the opposite direction, she gave a smile all round, to all of them and to no one; and in a soft voice, asked:

'Would one of you be kind enough to help me?'

'One of you': ten of them almost tore the fragile chiffon into shreds as she removed it. Now she appeared in a white silk dress, less fairy-like, but more real and dangerously more attractive. She could almost feel the breath of these young men on her shoulders and the situation was becoming awkward, when a fanfare of trumpets shattered all conversation. The ball opened with 'Roses of May', a beguiling little waltz by Josef Strauss. Elizabeth instantly chose the most handsome of her admirers, whom she had noticed a few minutes earlier, and let herself be carried away in the deceptive slowness of the gathering storm. As the music accelerated, she felt her head grow lighter and did not try to escape the charming face which dared to approach her own and seek out her mouth. There, it found quite feeble resistance. Her unknown partner swept her off the ground and — as if by chance — their lips touched. Almost at that moment, she noticed her sceptre waving in the distance, in the joyful throng of dancers, hesitantly, this way and that, clearly trying to escape from the crowd, and she had a pang of conscience. No doubt people were smiling at the efforts of gorgeous Algernon as, with a heavy heart, he tried to escape from being carried away by 'Roses of May'! After another moment, she looked for him again and, to her great surprise, was unable to find him. Perhaps he had reached the drawing-room from which ladies of a respectable age could shelter behind their fans and watch the young people dance. However, far from ending, the tireless waltz was increasing in tenderness and the beautiful Englishwoman and her admirer had reached the point of exchanging those trivial remarks that sometimes go on forever; and now she had an even greater surprise than the first. She had stopped thinking about Algernon when suddenly she saw him, barely two couples away from her. Their eyes met. He was on the arm of a young blonde, whose pretty little face was giving him an alluring smile. He gave Elizabeth a gracious bow and she called:

'My sceptre!'

'In the cloakroom,' he replied, with an ironic smile.

For a moment she was speechless, then she burst out laughing:

'Well played, Algernon!' she said.

A turn of the waltz drew them away from one another, while 'Roses of May' faded in the last shudderings of love.

There followed a polite bustling in the direction of the refreshments, which were in a long room, its walls clad in blue silk with tables under white cloths vanishing beneath piles of fruit, canapés and an astonishing variety of delicacies. Bottles, three rows deep, were standing in ranks like regiments of soldiers.

The ladies in their exquisite dresses showed a healthy appetite and may even have been the most adept in the rush toward this gourmet's paradise. They were unaware of the delicate tapestry of colors that their taffeta and satin dresses were making. Against this gently multicolored background, the black tail-coats contrasted with a beauty that was equally unsuspected by the batallions of the smart young men who wore them.

However, retreating into a pleasant little drawing-room where they had permission to smoke their cigarillos, some rather older gentlemen were exchanging views on the present state of the Union and commenting on the latest news. Among them, Charlie Jones's white waistcoat seemed to be speaking prophetically.

'In any case, the Illinois elections will put the spotlight, as on a stage, on two men upon whom the fate of the country may depend. Douglas has a following wind and, if he is re-elected, believe me, he will want to leap into the presidential chair, three years from now. Can you see the country governed by the Little Giant? But that's Stephen Douglas!'

'The nickname serves to his advantage as much as otherwise. People believe in his small stature more than in the vast dimension that his party attributes to his intellect — and of which he himself is convinced. He thinks that he represents the South, and the South is wary of him.'

This was the reply of old Dr Appleton, Professor at the University of Georgia. His white hair fell in curls around a face pitted with scars, and he wore a bitter look.

'Not without reason,' Charlie Jones said, approvingly. 'He may be an aristocrat, a Scotsman and a member of the Douglas clan, like my wife, as well as a fine speaker who can dazzle the innocent, but he is two-faced . . .'

A sallow-faced gentleman with a cravat reaching up to his ears spoke in a disdainful voice:

'Circumstances drive him to it. The Democratic Party in the South has seen its counterpart arise in the new Democratic Party of the North. That means that even though your Douglas exhibits his eloquence here, he will still have an eye on people up there, who represent a greater number of votes. Polticians are aware of such details!'

'He is lucky to have as his opponent someone who has failed before he even starts,' said Dr Appleton. 'That beanpole named after a patriarch . . .'

'Allow me to disagree with you,' said Charlie Jones. 'I accept that Abraham Lincoln doesn't make a very good first impression. He's a son of the people and of the poor people, and he has common manners. One can't imagine him in a drawing-room . . .'

There were a few laughs at this remark.

'Or in the Senate!' added Mr Sallow, the gentleman with the high cravat.

'Or in the presidential chair,' Dr Appleton said, spluttering with laughter. 'They do say he's thinking of it!'

General hilarity encouraged Mr Sallow to take the floor: 'He is preoccupied by the problem of slavery, because this is a slippery pole. It seems that he declared that the real solution was, as Henry Clay suggested, to send all the Blacks to Africa, to Liberia. So: no more Blacks, no more problem. Brilliant for a lawyer, don't you think?'

'He also said,' Dr Appleton added, 'that if he were in the South's place he really would not know how to resolve a situation as dangerous as ours.'

'What an admission of impotence for a politician!'

'Those are truly Northern ideas!'

'Gentlemen,' Charlie Jones said, 'I wonder if you have read his speech of June 16, three days ago?'

'No.'

'Yes, I've skimmed through it.'

'Let me read a few words from it,' Charlie Jones said, taking a copy of *The Mercury* out of his pocket. 'Here we are: " 'A house divided against itself cannot stand' (*Luke*, XI, 17). I believe this government cannot endure permanently, half slave and half free. I do not expect the house to fall — but I do expect it to cease to be divided." Gentlemen, I think I hear the sound of a voice which I fear is prophetic.'

No one felt like replying to that and the cigarillos were finished in a heavy silence.

From the large drawing-room now came the first insidious notes of another Viennese waltz, muffled, but quite clear. The gentlemen got up to 'join the ladies,' as they said: though this was a sort of coquettry, because 'joining the ladies' meant sitting sensibly with the mothers along the walls and watching the young people swirling around under the lights.

Charlie Jones, still thoughtful, had stopped for a moment in the little drawing-room when he saw, approaching him from the back of the room, a man of about fifty, leaning on a stick. Tall, casually, but still quite elegantly dressed in a black suit and white tie, he had a look in his dark blue eyes that was striking because of its furious energy: everything in his face and bearing indicated a military man. He bowed slightly toward Charlie Jones.

'You don't know me, Mr Jones,' he said. 'My name is Miles Edward Achison and I am here with my daughter. I was wounded in Mexico where I fought in '33 under the command of Colonel Lee — who was later to describe that expedition as a war of conquest; but no matter . . .'

'As a British subject,' said Charlie Jones, 'I cannot allow myself to express an opinion on that, but I do understand your colonel.'

'A while ago I heard you talk with those gentlemen. You quoted a few words from the speech by Abraham Lincoln . . . He touched on a topic which has preoccupied me since my adolescence. I come from Charleston in South Carolina. You said that you had the feeling that a great voice had been heard. Contrary to what you might suppose, I too found some grandeur in the tone of those words, but I have been asking myself the same question since I was fifteen. Do you want to know what the question is?'

'Please.'

'Why does he want the Union?'

Without waiting for an answer, he bowed again and went out with a stiff, slightly cautious step.

Charlie Jones paused for a moment longer before going back into the main drawing-room. Far from being irritated, he felt moved by the controlled violence that he felt in the words of Lee's soldier, and the fine, fearless look followed him.

'That sounds very like a lesson,' he thought while laughing out loud. 'But in two words, the South has made its protest: this is not a matter of one house, but of two.' For a few moments the words sank into him as though across an unexplored tract of land.

Meanwhile, the triumphal din of the waltz was inviting him to think other thoughts and, still sharp enough, despite a hint of a paunch, he hurried toward the ballroom. Here he almost bumped into Mrs Harrison Edwards and, carried away by the demon of the waltz, he clasped the lady in her peach silk dress and made her pivot and float through the air like the rest. Their mutual astonishment was equalled only by their mutual delight.

They danced. Everyone danced, and the great circular room itself whirled as if the walls wanted a share in the general folly. The impression was so powerful that Mrs Harrison Edwards had to close her eyes: she liked her ballroom. All around them, in a delirium of the senses, arms stretched and legs were thrown back.

'Have we ever danced a polka together?' Uncle Charlie asked his partner.

'Never.'

'How much time we have wasted!'

At that moment, the music stopped dead — three seconds — and then suddenly a huge noise made everyone start and the chandeliers shuddered above them. The whole orchestra, drums and bass drums united, was imitating a roll of thunder.

'The Explosion Polka,' said Mrs Harrison Edwards, smiling like a bacchante.

'Well, then: off we go!' cried Uncle Charlie.

They plunged with renewed energy into the waves with their all-powerful eddies. Enchanted once more, they were both twenty years old. Leaning forward, tossing their heads backward, their hands joined at the end of outstretched arms, touching the ground, their heels scoffing at the void, they abandoned themselves umrestrainedly to the dizzying dance.

'I'm going to die,' Mrs Harrison Edwards panted.

'So am I,' her partner replied.

'A sweet death.'

The orchestra softened in the last light of evening. The dancers, exhausted, looked at one another with lunatic eyes; and suddenly thunder exploded in the gardens and the sky burst into flames.

'It's the end of the world.'

'It's war.'

'It's my fireworks,' asserted the piercing voice of Mrs Harrison Edwards.

Night had now fallen completely and the sky was full of multicolored stars. Blazing clusters flung out bouquets of scarlet roses which scattered across the black sky and, from the other end of the gardens, all along the avenue, an 'ah!' rose from the crowd.

The continued rolling of the bass drums accompanied the spectacle with the thunder of a canonnade. From one end to the other, the sky was covered in fiery signs in the shape of flowers, and the guests flocked, jostling each other to reach the balustrade on the terrace from where they could see better, far from the lights in the ballroom. In the half-light, the noise of cries and laughter suggested a riot.

Elizabeth behaved badly. Two glasses of champagne had turned her head. Too many young men were pressing around her, too many hands were adjusting her scarf on her neck when it insisted on sliding off her shoulders. She was no longer quite sure what she was doing, and her defences were down. Young men dared to make coarse jokes and she laughed with them without understanding a word. The slightly slower rumble of the bass drums was making her heart beat a little faster. Smiling, or serious, eager faces appeared and disappeared beside her and said things which the noise prevented her from hearing, but she laughed and said no, without knowing why.

Suddenly an unexpected apparition sobered her. At first she thought it was a waking nightmare. Miss Llewelyn was in front of her, forcefully pushing everyone aside. She had a black cape wrapped around her which reached down to her boots, and her head vanished inside a wide hood, no less black. But her stern face could be seen and her eyes stared directly through Elizabeth's, so that the latter could only open her mouth and say hesitantly:

'Miss Llew . . .'

'Yes,' a high-pitched, precise voice interrupted. 'Yes, Miss Llewelyn, who has come to tell Mrs Hargrove that her husband has just arrived back from Charleston and is waiting for her at home.'

At that moment, as the drums doubled in frenzy, a comet shot directly into the sky where it exploded, then, in a second explosion, covered the black vault with blue, white and red stars, covering the sky above the town with the national colors. This was an initiative of the head artificer, who had thought it would make a fine climax to the display. The crowd roared.

Enthusaism among the guests was not unanimous. There were differences of opinion and arguments which threatened to disrupt the party. Mrs Harrison Edwards was nervous, but the conductor, a prudent fellow, resolved the problem in his own way. One of the favorite tunes of the South drowned the threatening rumble of discontent and every voice was soon singing *Twinkling Stars*. The atmosphere became joyful and heroic.

> *Twinkling stars are laughing, love,*
> *Laughing on you and me;*
> *While your bright eyes look in mine,*
> *Peeping stars they seem to be.*
> *Troubles come and go, love,*
> *Brightest scenes must leave our sights;*
> *But the star of hope, love,*
> *Shines with radiant beams tonight.*

Outside the crowd took up the song:
> *Golden beams are shining, love,*
> *Shining on you to bless;*

*Like the queen of night you fill*
*Darkest space with loveliness.*
*Silver stars how bright, love,*
*Mother moon thronely might,*
*Gaze on us to bless, love,*
*Purest vows here made tonight*
*Twinkling stars are laughing, love,*
*Laughing on you and me . . .*

The orchestra, Mrs Harrison Edwards' guests and the crowd in the avenue, the whole night of Savannah, sang.

Meanwhile, the Welshwoman had seized Elizabeth's hand and, with a purposeful step, was leading her through the drawing-rooms toward the exit. They had reached the front hall when they saw Algernon running after them with the diamond sceptre that the beautiful Englishwoman had given him. He was pink with excitement and was holding the rod above his head.

Still recovering from her astonishment, Elizabeth looked at him open-mouthed. He held the object out to her, but with a swift movement Miss Llewelyn seized it.

'What is this?' she asked Algernon roughly.

Instantly brought back to her senses by this brutal action, Elizabeth ordered her in a peremptory voice:

'Give me that sceptre immediately and go and fetch my white cape which must have been put in the cloakroom.'

The two women's voices were raised and several people who had been getting ready to go out, paused inquisitively.

'I'll go myself,' said Algernon. 'I should have thought of it.'

He vanished while Elizabeth and Miss Llewelyn, seeing that they were about to make some kind of scene, retired to a corner of the antechamber. They sat down and considered it sensible to remain silent; but they looked each other directly in the eye, each challenging the other.

Suddenly, in a calm voice, and almost an undertone, Miss Llewelyn began to speak:

'Mrs Hargrove, you are going to your ruin.'

Amazed, but determined not to engage in an argument in a public place with a woman employed in her service, Elizabeth merely shrugged her shoulders.

'I saw you from a distance with all those young men,' Miss Llewelyn continued on the same note. 'You are dishonoring yourself and you are headed for a place from which no one returns.'

'Save your sermons, Miss Llewelyn,' the young Englishwoman replied in an icy voice. 'I have just decided that from this evening onward you are free to go.'

The Welshwoman did not flinch.

'No, Ma'am,' she said.

'What do you mean: *no*?'

'I am in your house and I must never leave it again, for your good. I've always known you. To be more exact: since the evening when for the first time you set foot in Dimwood, right up to now. In short, I know you too well not to be there, to keep silent and to make everyone keep silent.'

The fine pink color drained from Elizabeth's cheeks, leaving her as white as paper.

'Miss Llewelyn, I can hardly believe what I am hearing. There is a word for what you are doing.'

'Don't say it, Ma'am. It makes the dead speak.'

'If you're referring to my letters, you assured me that you had burned them.'

'Did I say that? Well, let's say that it's true and I'll give you some advice: let's both keep quiet and try to put up with one another. But here is your charming gentleman carrying a large quantity of chiffon.'

Algernon was coming; in fact, he was almost running.

'A thousand pardons, Elizabeth; they're fighting in the cloakroom, the guests are starting to leave. Here is your wonderful snow garment. Can I help you to put it back on?'

Elizabeth stood up.

'I should be most obliged, Algernon.'

The maneuver was accomplished far too quickly for the liking of the eternal admirer, but the lady was in a hurry.

'Your sceptre, Elizabeth.'

'Keep it.'

Less than a minute later she was outside, her head wrapped in a shawl that covered her hair and the stream of diamonds.

Miss Llewelyn followed at a respectful distance while Algernon ran ahead, the magic wand in his hand, looking for her carriage.

Back in the house, Elizabeth already had her foot on the bottom of the staircase when Miss Llewelyn took her arm.

'One word more,' she said softly. 'You hate me, Mrs Hargrove, and I can understand why.'

'This evening, I must admit . . .'

'Very well. I used unfair means to impose my presence under your roof. You will thank me . . .'

'I doubt that.'

'Because you will always need Maisie Llewelyn. I am unbearable, but I am loyal, I shall fight for you if need be. And remember this . . .'

'My husband is expecting me, Miss Llewelyn.'

'Remember this, I say: I am not a wicked woman and I have a lot of affection for you, Elizabeth.'

Elizabeth went upstairs without replying.

She found Billy lying down, asleep and half undressed. He woke up as soon as he heard her come in and leaped toward her:

'At last! At last!'

'Yes, at last. I have just come back from the ball at Mrs Harrison Edwards' — a huge ball.'

'You must tell me about it . . . But what's that I see?'

'Oh, some notion of Mr César's. Help me to take it off . . .'

'Not at all: you're sublime, you must keep it on. To bed, quickly, my love.'

'With all this on? Don't think of it, Billy.'

'I want you to.'

She had to give way to his demands, but when the sun rose, the diamonds were glistening here and there on the carpet around the marital bed.

Even before breakfast, Billy left again for Fort Beauregard. His furlough had been highly irregular, but he was counting on the commandant, for once, turning a blind eye, cards in hand.

Elizabeth breakfasted alone with Ned, who told her in every last detail about some exceptionally confused dreams; and, after the events of the previous evening, she was herself wondering if she had not dreamed it all. What disturbed her most was the presence of the Welshwoman, who appeared from time to time under different pretexts wearing the smile of an attentive housekeeper . . . Could it be that this woman, eight or ten hours earlier, had threatened her with hell, then impudently refused to be dismissed by using blackmail, only to assure her finally that she was her friend?

This morning she was particularly attentive and even made an attempt at conversation, cut short when a servant brought a letter on a tray.

'By hand, Ma'am, a moment ago.'

Elizabeth took the letter and, not to her surprise, recognized Mrs Harrison Edwards' writing.

'There is also a packet of newspapers,' the servant added.' The mailman has just been.'

'I don't want to see them on this table while I am eating. Put them in a corner of the drawing-room.'

The servant bowed and left.

'If you will allow me,' said Miss Llewelyn. 'I'll go and read them.'

'As much as you wish. I shan't even open them.'

The Welshwoman went out at once and her mistress seized upon Mrs Harrison Edwards' letter. It covered no less than four pages, in large, undisciplined handwriting, and the style was elevated:

'Elizabeth, my dearest,

'I am penning these few lines at dawn in the vast silence that follows a joyful celebration and thinking of you, who were the ornament — no, the jewel of my whole ball. My gratitude is boundless and I am yours for ever; but after this immersion in the intoxicating seductions of the world, my soul aspires — as I am sure yours does also — to escape, distracted, into the bosom of nature and to breathe the ocean breeze. In short, tomorrow I am abducting you — it is tomorrow already — at ten o'clock precisely to spend a few hours on Tybee Beach where we can contemplate infinity in silence together, soul sisters.

Your Lucile.'

Elizabeth folded the letter again with a smile. The Englishwoman in her revealed itself in its entirety.

'When people talk about soul,' she thought, 'it means that there has been one glass of champagne too many. Or something else.'

Something else?

'Why are you laughing, Mummy?' Ned asked, holding a spoon.

'Nothing, Ned, darling. Sometimes I do laugh to myself, just like that.'

In fact, she could see Mrs Harrison Edwards dancing a frenzied polka with Uncle Charlie . . . and from there to imagining the unimaginable . . . She imagined it: hence her mysterious hilarity!

'Mummy,' Ned said softly. 'When there is no one there, why don't you call me Jonathan, like you do in the evening?'

She got up quickly.

'You've finished your cherries. Come on, let's go for a walk in the garden.'

# 106

While they were out, there was a ring at the front door. It was Mrs Harrison Edwards even though it was not yet ten o'clock. A splendid soft wide-brimmed straw hat, tied under the chin by a green ribbon had replaced the hat with the feather. Without asking the servant, she went straight to the drawing-room where she expected to find Elizabeth.

Standing in the middle of a disordered pile of newspapers, the

Welshwoman lowered the *Savannah Morning News* which she was holding in her outstretched hands.

'Good morning, Miss Llewelyn. I should like to see Mrs Hargrove.'

'She is no doubt in the garden. I shall go and inform her, Mrs Edwards; but have you seen the papers? They are full of astonishing news.'

Mrs Harrison Edwards now knew Miss Llewelyn, as did all of Savannah, but she had never seen her face so animated or her little green eyes shining so brilliantly with excitement.

'What? War?'

'Not yet, but things are happening. I am not talking about the arrests in France: that is the daily bread of journalists.'

'Rather stale now. If that's all . . .'

'From next month, the American continent will be linked to Europe by a submarine cable, between Newfoundland and Ireland.'

'There was talk of that, indeed.'

'Here Western Union is sending messages from the North to the South by telegraph.'

'Bah!'

'So much for the United States as they are called. On Haiti, there is a bloody and spectacular uprising. I quote the *Petersburg Express*. I know Haiti, it must be a nightmare: hell in the midst of paradise . . . In China . . . look out!'

'In China . . . Let's sit down. I love talking to you, Maisie Llewelyn, the conversation has real style. You muddle everything together. So: in China?'

'A Franco-British squadron off Peking.'

'Good heavens! What are they doing there?'

'Demanding the opening of the ports for trade.'

'By what right?'

'The right of the strongest — the only right politicians recognize. Coming nearer to home with the *Charleston Mercury*: in Mexico, war has broken out between two generals, Miramon against Comonfort, one for the secular cause, the other for religion. When religion is involved, the Devil can open his maw wide — I'm sorry: the abyss.'

'Oh, Maisie Llewelyn, you make me shudder, but you are always interesting. Always just that little bit subversive: I like that.'

'A little bit!' the Welshwoman cried. 'Don't you mean from head to toe?'

'Oh, how terrifying you can be! I love it. You have all the daring I wish I had myself, were it not for convention . . . What else is there?'

'Nothing. The German Emperor has gone mad . . . Yes . . . It's in here.' (she tapped one of the Charleston newspapers). 'In Europe, there is the eternal problem of the Orient. The Sultan, massacres of Armenians by the Turks, all the peoples of the Balkans on the brink of revolt . . .'

She had reached this point in her dramatic exposé when Elizabeth appeared, held firmly by a six-year-old hand determined not to let her go.

'Dear Lucile, your letter . . .'

'Dear Elizabeth, my heart had much more to say.'

They kissed.

'If I were you, ladies,' said Miss Llewelyn, 'I should not delay. It'll be hot on the road.'

'I'm coming with you, Mummy,' said Ned.

'Well . . . of course,' said Mrs Harrison Edwards.

She hadn't anticipated this and it somewhat disrupted her plans, but how could she refuse?

'He'll play on the beach,' said Elizabeth. 'He's already fully dressed in white . . . Betty will do the rest: sandals and straw hat . . . As for me, there's my hat . . . I'm not sure where I put it.'

She went to the door and called Betty.

Everything happened very fast. When all three were in the carriage, the idea of an outing made them laugh and joke for no reason, and Ned was not the least talkative among them. Sitting between his mother in her pale green, and Mrs Harrison Edwards, now simply Lucile, entirely in mauve, he waved and gestured, while the ribbons on his little round hat floated merrily in the breeze.

The journey was not long. Coming out of the popular districts where Whites watched gravely as the Good Life swept past in a shiny carriage with large black and yellow wheels, they went through an almost deserted area. The occasional clapboard house stood beside the road, the sandy surface of which slowed the horses down. There was an increasing number of palm trees, waving their fronds around white villas with narrow verandas. At last the first houses of Tybee appeared, quite a long way behind the beach which they enclosed; and suddenly the shifting vastness which for a moment silenced the travelers like the presence of a terrifying force. Beaten by the wind, the dark green mass cast a wide, foamy edge on the sand, then drew it back with a soft roar. Elizabeth felt her heart beating in her breast.

Beyond all this water, she thought, days and days away from here, is the country from which I was taken when I was sixteen. Why am I still an exile on this foreign shore, to which I shall never accustom myself?

Ned clapped his hands and cried out. He wanted to jump out of the carriage immediately, but it only stopped a little further on, near a path covered in planks.

They got down. Lucile, less touched than Elizabeth, found some affinity in herself for the ocean with its tumult hidden beneath a slightly ruffled surface. She liked to persuade herself that underneath the first lady of Savannah society, there was a barbarian with wild passions and an all-consuming appetite for life. The 'Explosion Polka' had, if only too briefly, freed her instincts, but there was no question of that, here, with this nostalgic Englishwoman and her little boy, who had to be kept amused.

For the time being, he was bothering no one. Running along the beach where some boys and girls of about his age were romping around, he quickly joined them. No need for introductions. In less than a minute, he was rolling around with them in the sand, laughing as he fought with boys who took off his hat and pulled his curls. Small blows were exchanged without anger; he was happy for the first time, with a boisterous joy that relaxed his limbs.

Elegant wicker cabins furnished with cushions would allow the ladies to watch the waves and the clouds in the greatest possible comfort. One of these cabins was particularly spacious and accommodated two people. Mrs Harrison Edwards had reserved it for the whole day, because her communion with the ocean did not deprive her of her ever-watchful common sense. She took Elizabeth's arm and led her to this double cabin sheltered from people and from the wind, and they settled in there, soul sisters, hand in hand, to give themselves up to the joy of contemplating infinity in a silence that lasted a full three minutes, before their tongues were untied.

'Darling,' Mrs Harrison Edwards said, 'this is a choice spectacle for which we should both be very grateful.'

For an instant, Elizabeth was afraid that she was about to deliver some improvised, pious sentiment, but she was reassured almost at once.

'We'll think about it this evening, of course,' Mrs Harrison Edwards went on. 'Meanwhile, nature reminds us of our human condition.'

A number of lengthy and amusing reflections followed and their chatter was only interrupted later by a sudden:

'Are you hungry?'

'Yes. The fresh air . . .'

'Perfect. I've got a little surprise for you. Early this morning my Blacks came here to prepare a very simple lunch, hardly more than a snack, in the pine grove a few yards away from here behind us. I know there's a restaurant nearby, but what dreadful things would they have offered us?'

'Indeed, I'm much afraid . . .'

'We'll have to call your little Ned in a moment. But first, let's watch him playing in the sun, with his hair blowing across his pretty face. He is charming. Uncle Charlie tells me that he is already just like his father, your poor dear departed . . . Your . . .'

Elizabeth cut her short by calling loudly for Ned. Leaving his new friends who were fighting with spades, he ran up dishevelled, covered in sand. The magic sound of his mother's voice had made him run as fast as his legs would carry him and he wanted to throw himself at Elizabeth, but she gently pushed him aside. Mrs Harrison Edwards had something to say on the matter:

'One of my Blacks will clean him up and brush his hair. Let's go, dearest. I love these heart-to-heart conversations with you, but I too am fainting: this sea air has made me terribly hungry.'

They left the cabin and went across to the carriage which put them down, three hundred yards further on, on the outskirts of a pine grove. Ned, who had not stopped jumping up and down on the carriage seat, was laughing through his curls which hung over his forehead and cheeks. In an entirely novel excess of energy, he was stammering as he tried to describe his games on the beach. Elizabeth could not recognize him and was relieved when a young black servant carried him off to make him more or less presentable before lunch.

The place had a fairy-tale charm. In the mysterious shadow of the pine was a green-striped canvas tent, high and wide, allowing one to walk easily around a table covered with a white cloth. The three guests sat down and a liveried waiter brought, first, a lobster salad, none of which remained after five minutes in which conversation was brief and forks busy. The odd sip of champagne had hardly had time to ease the passage of the crustaceans. Ned drank a glass of lemonade. Once the first hunger had been appeased, the ladies could allow their eyes to scan the ocean, with its mesmerizing expanse, and Mrs Harrison Edwards was making some high-toned remarks when an imposing salmon pie was served and honored with several glasses of champagne, as well as a gulp of lemonade. Spirits lifted, life became rosier and rosier. Mrs Harrison Edwards, politeness itself toward Elizabeth, regretted that Billy was not there to join them and risked making a rather daring joke about hussars. Ned laughed without understanding. Everyone was happy and a fresh bottle of champagne was drawn from the ice bucket.

The sky clouded over. Fringed with white, threatening looking waves rolled in and the children deserted the beach.

Then the dessert arrived, a huge lemon meringue, which was greeted as a masterpiece and which promptly vanished, as if by magic, from the plates.

The liveried servant ventured to remark that a storm was imminent.

'Very well,' said Mrs Harrison Edwards. 'Serve the coffee.'

She remarked modestly that she could never see the elements disturbed without feeling a hint of rebellion rising in her, as if by some obscure association between them: 'a simple observation . . .'

The piping hot coffee had been standing ready for some time. It was poured into two china cups, while a delicious herb tea was offered to Ned, who smiled, delighted by everything. Elizabeth had been looking at him uneasily for some time. Not that she hadn't looked at him often enough since his birth . . . But she realized that today she was discovering him as he truly was, and not as she had forced herself to see him over the years. 'The image of his father . . .': Mrs Harrison Edwards' phrase ran round in her head. How could she deny it? But the resemblance had burst upon her this very morning when she was watching him playing on the beach, his hair flying, intoxicated with a new kind of happiness, and she experienced the odd feeling of having lost someone.

As if in a dream she heard Mrs Harrison Edwards giving orders.

'Put up the hood of the carriage at once. Unfold the large umbrellas. Take Massa Ned to the coach, I don't want him to get soaked. Collect everything and take shelter under the tent.'

Now she was outside with Mrs Harrison Edwards; and the first heavy drops were resounding as they struck the vast green umbrellas that the Blacks were holding above them. The kind manservant who had washed little Ned was carrying him in his arms, both of them wrapped in a wide cloak the color of earth.

In the carriage which seemed to have been transformed into a coach, the travelers took shelter just in time, so pleased at escaping the storm that it still seemed like a party. However, Elizabeth felt sorry for the Blacks who were left behind and would be drenched.

'Don't worry. The canvas is waterproof. I think of everything.'

The team set off at a trot, the sand slowing their pace: they were only able to break into a gallop when they reached the road. Beneath the huge leather hood which covered the carriage like a lid, the travelers could hardly see anything; but it was a question of either darkness or of light and rain: one or the other. Any gap that might have admitted light had been filled and the darkness gave mystery and a scent of adventure to this pleasure trip which had started so peacefully.

Ned was greatly enjoying himself. The rain fell directly downward, drumming against the hood, and suddenly a flash of lightning rent the half-light, followed a moment later by a roll of thunder that seemed to fill the sky from one end to the other. The two women held each other's hand . . . Ned pretended to be afraid and shouted out, hiding under the seat.

Through the clatter of the rain, they could hear the hard, sharp hammering of the four horses' hooves — reassuring, since it told them that they had reached the hard cobbled road; but further streaks of lightning flashed, and inside the carriage, enclosed though it was, something of their brilliance entered, like steel blades slicing through the darkness, and struck them with horror for less than a second. The two women saw each other as if in a vision, open-mouthed like tragic masks. As darkness closed around them, their self-respect was restored.

'I do hope you're not afraid,' said Mrs Harrison Edwards. 'Personally, I find this fury of Nature quite grandiose.'

'Of course I'm not afraid,' Elizabeth said calmly. 'I've seen just as impressive storms in England; but, if you'll forgive me, I was wondering what would be left of the tent in the pine grove.'

'Nothing. I shall have it replaced.'

'Here in Savannah?'

'Oh, darling! What a question! From New York, since everything comes to us from the North. It's absurd. But I just have to send the order by telegraph and in less than a month I shall have a new tent precisely the same as the other. They have my model.'

'And the Blacks who stayed behind there?'

'Oh, the Blacks! They always get by somehow. And then, what can I do? After all, Providence . . . Where is Ned? It's some time since we heard him.'

'Ned!' Elizabeth cried frantically.

A voice rose from beneath the seat.

'Mummy, are we going to be home soon?'

'Yes, my love. You mustn't be afraid.'

'I'm not, but I want to go home.'

'We'll be back in no time. You'll see. Why are you staying under there?'

There was a plaintive note in his voice:

'Tummy-ache, Mummy.'

'Come and sit with us.'

'I'd rather stay here, Mummy.'

'What can we do, Lucile?'

'Nothing. Nothing at all. It will work itself out . . . badly, but it will work itself out.'

Once more the carriage was invaded by the pitiless flash of white which searched their faces before instantly plunging them into darkness again.

'Oh, Mummy, are we there yet?' moaned the seat.

A deadly fifteen minutes later, they were passing through the suburbs of Savannah. The rain was gradually stopping and the last rolls of thunder were dying in the distance. When the carriage reached the house in Oglethorpe Square, Elizabeth herself got down and rang the doorbell.

Miss Llewelyn was waiting in the hall.

'Quickly,' Elizabeth said. 'Have Ned fetched urgently.'

The Welshwoman understood immediately and called Betty and Black Mammy, who ran, shouting and waving their arms, toward the carriage. Ned was hauled out from beneath the bench where he had been hiding like a criminal. Black Mammy wrapped him in her white apron and carried him into the house. He was weeping, both hands pressed to his eyes. At the moment when he passed close by the Welshwoman, she smiled maliciously and said:

'Don't let it bother you, Mr Ned. It happens to the best kind of people.'

# 107

*I*n her room, Elizabeth mulled over her day at Tybee Beach. The storm had bothered her less than the behavior of her son. She now searched in vain for the chatterbox, with his occasional moments of meditation and silence, who she was accustomed to seeing every day.

'It's nothing,' she thought, to reassure herself. 'Two or three hours rough and tumble on the beach with some playmates . . . A good night's sleep and he will recover.'

She dined alone. Seeing her still a little uneasy, Miss Llewelyn ventured to express an opinion.

'Nothing could be more trivial than this little accident which seems to be preoccupying you. Your child ate too much, nothing more. It's even quite salutary: one must occasionally mistreat one's habits.'

'Mistreat one's habits . . .,' Elizabeth repeated, thoughtfully. 'You have a way of saying things . . .'

'Welsh, Mrs Hargrove, I am Welsh.'

'Is he asleep?'

'Certainly, at this time, and he will wake as fresh as. ..'

'A daisy.'

'A little fighting cock, rather.'

The conversation ended here. Elizabeth went to bed very early. For the first time, in the solitude of her bed which she compared to a desert, her thoughts turned not to Billy but to Ned. Quite obviously, on that day at Tybee, he had become 'other'. This was the only word she could find to describe the change. And a small thing had struck her: he no longer lisped. It seemed normal to her, even desirable. She fell asleep.

The following day she was relieved to find him as he usually was: full of loving impulses and merriment; but he kept asking when they would be going back to Tybee; her replies were evasive. Of course, no one referred to the unfortunate accident of nature. Moreover, Elizabeth did not have to endure the story of his journey through the labyrinth of his dreams.

All day she thought of these things, waiting for nightfall. When it came, she went into her little boy's room. Eyes wide open, he was lying in bed, a light on his bedside table with Betty sitting on a chair beside him. She got up when she saw her mistress and gave a smile which lit up her face. Like a light from some other place, profound benevolence radiated from this black face, scarred by age and fatigue.

'My dear Betty,' Elizabeth said. 'leave me with Ned. This evening I'll stay with him for a moment as I used to.'

Ned gave a cry of delight:

'As we used to, Mummy, long ago . . .'

'Not so long, was it, Betty?'

'Nearly a month, Ma'am.'

'Oh? Very well, Betty, good night.'

Alone with Ned, she kissed him and said:

'I'll stay here beside you until you fall asleep.'

'Yes, Mummy. Will we go back to Tybee soon?'

'I don't know if it will be soon, but we'll go back.'

'Promise?'

'Yes. Now you must sleep. As soon as you feel the dream coming . . . Your dream, you know?'

'My dream, Mummy?'

'Of course, Ned. The horseman . . .'

To her surprise, he said nothing.

'Well?' she asked anxiously.

'There is no more dream, Mummy. Yesterday, it wasn't there.'

Suddenly Elizabeth's heart began to beat as if at the approach of some misfortune. She let a minute go by, stroking her son's face, then leaned over him and, with a tightening of the throat, whispered in his ear:

'Listen, we're alone. No one can hear us.'

'Yes, Mummy.'

Close to his ear, she said under her breath:

'From the back of the room, Ned: the horseman on a black horse.'

'Not yesterday, Mummy. There's nothing there now.'

'Ned, listen.'

She hesitated. Ned said nothing. Finally she murmured:

'Jonathan, Ned.'

He didn't answer.

'Why don't you say anything?' she asked, almost aloud. 'I thought that you loved me.'

'But I do love you, Mummy.'

'Jonathan,' she said, frightened now.

'There's nothing any more, Mummy. Nothing at all,' he said, tenderly stroking her cheek.

His eyes were partly closed.

'You're sleepy, darling.'

He had suddenly fallen asleep. Elizabeth waited a moment longer. The light breath, peaceful and regular, seemed to fill the silence. Trembling, she got up, turned down the light and went out.

In her own room, she threw herself on her bed without lighting the lamp. The darkness was a refuge for her. In it she could hide her shame and cruel disappointment. The ghost which still tied her to her first love had vanished from the moment when it no longer haunted the boy's dreams; but how foolish of her to have become attached to a ghost! She had known this for a long time. She had let herself succumb to the temptation out of weakness: this obsession, this strange consolation . . . Tonight, she could not escape the feeling that Jonathan had died a second time, and for ever.

More bitter than the rest was something that she did not admit to herself: the increasingly clear resemblance of Ned to his father. There was some kind of coincidence about the disappearance of Jonathan and the reappearance of the other Edward. The father had taken back his child . . . The cruel irony of this situation drew a burst of nervous laughter from her which she couldn't stop even though she tried to suppress it. Her face pressed into her pillow and her shoulders heaving spasmodically, she laughed until she was breathless.

Suddenly a shaft of yellow light shone diagonally across the room . . . The surprise put an end to Elizabeth's laughter. She looked up and stared around her before she understood . . .

The lamplighter was coming up the avenue and had ended his round with the great bronze street lamp near the house.

# 108

No one would ever know about this very personal drama. Normal life resumed in Savannah, interspersed with minor local events. Balls became rarer. After Mrs Harrison Edwards' reception, which had been an occasion, there were only a few modest dances. Even the newspapers were less closely read in the general somnolence of summer. People were very much put out, however, on learning that the famous underwater cable linking America to Ireland had ceased to function in July, after only three weeks.

Another awakening of interest came with the news from Haiti. People were aware of the latest uprising, but there was something to add . . . Soulouque I, Emperor of Haiti, who wore a stepped gold crown especially made for him in Paris, had been driven out by a general. They learned a new name: General Geffrard was now master of the island. With Miss Llewelyn's colorful story still fresh in the memory of Savannah society, they were quite eager to learn all the horrible details, but they had to wait.

What else? Not much, it appeared. At the height of summer, it was as if History was dozing. That is, unless one was interested in the drone of political speeches, the rhetorical duel of Douglas the Democrat and Lincoln the Republican, as to who would represent Illinois in the Senate; but Douglas was losing the confidence of the South. He was too undecided between the rights of the South and the ideas of the North . . .

Elizabeth did not bother with such things. Beneath her eyes, she witnessed her dead husband growing in the young child, and a whole past of forbidden life sank under the look of that innocent face.

Just once or twice a month, Billy came and restored her sense of joy, but the relapse into melancholy was hard. Uncle Charlie had left with his wife and children for Virginia, where the air was cooler. Because of the sometimes unpredictable visits by the only man who could console her, Elizabeth did not move out of Oglethorpe Square.

August passed in a mood of torpor. They slept naked at nights, and panted by day. Boredom reached its height. In the vast empty avenue, at dusk, a lady walked slowly, a beautiful Englishwoman who was the prisoner of a hussar.

With the first smiles of September, everything improved: the thermometer dropped a little and, toward the end of the month, fashionable people returned, prudently, as though following some disaster. Then, in the last days, something happened. A very grand carriage stopped in front of Elizabeth's house and a lackey in royal blue livery, who had been seated beside the coachman, leaped off his bench and rang authoritatively at the door. Joe opened at once, wearing a red livery: a horrible clash of colors. Behind him was Miss Llewelyn, intrigued by the effrontery of the ringing.

'Does Mrs William Hargrove live here?' the royal blue lackey asked in a marked English accent.

On hearing that she did, he ran to the bottom of the steps and rushed across to open the door of the carriage. At that, with the help of the model lackey, a large, straight-backed lady descended from the carriage, wearing a beige traveling costume, her head thrust into a cabriolet hat, the two sides of which enclosed the face like two walls. From the depths of this lair shone two eyes like those of a bird of prey.

With a rough gesture she pushed aside the lackey, who was offering a hand with a white cotton glove, and ascended the steps to confront the Welshwoman. The understanding between aristocracy and ordinary people was immediate; each, as it happened, was prepared for hostilities at the least provocation.

'We have already met,' the lady said with regal condescension. 'You know me. Go and inform Mrs Hargrove that her mother is waiting. And bring me a chair, quickly. I can't wait standing up.'

'Yes, Ma'am,' said Miss Llewelyn, pushing one of the large chairs from the hall toward her.

Lady Fidgety sat down and the Welshwoman, spurred on by a sort of invisible goad, climbed the stairs with youthful agility. She knocked on Elizabeth's door.

'Your mother is waiting for you downstairs,' she said.

'You're imagining things, Miss Llewelyn.'

'I'm not imagining it, and I might add that in her one can recognize true quality, not at all like this so-called local aristocracy.'

'Another remark like that and you're dismissed.'

'You know very well that you can't dismiss me. Meanwhile, I advise you to go downstairs. The Quality's patience is limited.'

Pink with anger and emotion, Elizabeth threw a light, white woolen shawl across her shoulders and went down.

Lady Fidgety was sitting motionless.

'Your mother! Yes, it's your mother! Oh, what a surprise! I'll spare you the exclamations and we can cut short the emotional outbursts. You are young, you can stand.'

'Miss Llewelyn, another chair.'

'Not bad,' said Lady Fidgety. 'You still have your pride. I was afraid of finding some spineless creature, softened by the moral and physical climate of this America of ours.'

Miss Llewelyn brought up a second chair, just like the first, and bowed respectfully to her mistress.

'Here you are, Ma'am,' she said.

'Very well, you may go.'

Miss Llewelyn bowed again and at once vanished from the sight of the two ladies, who were seated facing each other.

'I think,' Elizabeth said in a loud, casual voice, 'that we should be better in the drawing-room, with the doors shut.'

'Let anyone listen who has ears to hear,' Lady Fidegety remarked. 'The precaution is unnecessary. I have nothing secret to tell you. We'll stay here for the time being.'

'Mother, you are at home here.'

'I imagine I am. I detest the hotels in this country; their vulgarity is only equalled by their discomfort. A carrier should be arriving shortly with all my luggage. I am, naturally, going to put up here.'

Elizabeth drew herself up.

'But Mother, you should have warned me. Nothing is ready.'

'An obedient daughter is always ready to welcome her mother. Even so, I did inform your father-in-law of my arrival by means of the miraculous American invention, the submarine cable. I learned later that this wonder of science had failed pitifully. Whose fault was that? I am here.'

'Well, we shall manage. You will have two large rooms over-looking the veranda from the upper floor with a view across our garden and the neighboring ones.'

'One floor up? I very much hope your Blacks will carry me.'

'My Blacks . . . ,' Elizabeth said dubiously. 'Yes, of course.'

'I understand from Mr Charlie Jones that you are remarried and that you have married one of the Hargrove boys.'

'That's right.'

'Didn't I advise you to choose a husband of respectable age who would not have to go to war?'

'Mother, we're not at war.'

'We will be, as surely as day follows night . . . Whom did you marry?'

'Billy.'

'Listen to me. If your first marriage had not made you rich and safe from maternal reprisals . . .'

Cut to the quick, Elizabeth challenged her with her blue eyes which began to flash.

'Well, Mother?'

'I should disinherit you, my girl.'

'I never wish to owe you anything except respect. I don't want any of your possessions.'

To her surprise, she thought she could see a broad smile in the depths of the black hat.

'My opinion of you is unchanged,' said Lady Fidgety. 'You are an idiot, but in your place that is the reply I should have given. At last I hear the voice of the blood. And what is your husband's situation?'

'Lieutenant of hussars in a regiment in Carolina.'

Lady Fidgety burst out laughing.

'That's all we needed! Go and see if my luggage is coming.'

'Miss Llewelyn!' Elizabeth called.

As if by magic, the Welshwoman rose out of a dark corner. With-out even looking at her, Elizabeth passed on her mother's order. Miss Llewelyn went out onto the steps, then returned.

'A hired wagon loaded with trunks and suitcases, Ma'am.'

'Let them wait,' said Lady Fidgety. 'I want to see if these rooms on the upper floor suit me; otherwise you can give your mother your own. Didn't you say that I was at home here?'

'Miss Llewelyn, go and tell Joe and Toby to come and help Lady Fidgety upstairs.'

'Who are Joe and Toby?'

'The strongest of my servants, Mother.'

Transporting the new arrival was no easy matter. Miss Llewelyn had told the cook's assistant to put on white gloves: he was a black colossus who simply picked the noble lady up in his arms and managed to take her where she wanted, despite cries and insults from his precious burden. Joe, dressed in red livery, did no more than open the doors.

Downstairs, Elizabeth slumped into her chair and sighed:

'I should have gone up with her.'

'That's what she was expecting,' Miss Llewelyn remarked, having stayed with her mistress.

'I know. But I lost my nerve. If she's not satisfied with those rooms . . .'

'Have no fear, Ma'am. She cannot settle into your two rooms without your husband's consent. If she insists, I shall make it my business to let her know that . . . She doesn't frighten me and she knows it. It took just one look for her to realize that.'

'Oh, Miss Llewelyn, how pleased I am to know that you're here.'

'At last!' said the Welshwoman.

'Mother does seem a little hard,' Elizabeth continued, as if talking to herself, 'but she is kind at heart. Everyone knows how hard things were for us, over there in London. I shall never forget that one night, in the icy room of our wretched lodgings, she took her coat off to cover me with it while I was asleep.'

'One could forgive anything for that!' said the Welshwoman.

'I have nothing to forgive her, but I hope that she won't come back down too soon.'

Against all expectations, she only came down two hours later, in the arms of the assistant cook, satisfied.

After being gently set down, she appeared majestic in a plum-colored taffeta dress which rustled loudly at every step she took.

'To the drawing-room,' she said to her daughter.

Elizabeth took her to the little scarlet room.

'What frightful taste!' Lady Fidgety exclaimed. 'It reminds one of the Lucknow massacre . . .'

'Lucknow?'

'You don't know a thing. I'll tell you about it some other time.'

She immediately sat down in the largest chair in the room and smoothed out the folds of her dress, which she spread out around her. Emerging from the dungeon of its hat, her face was remarkable for the nobility of its sharply etched features, its long, thin nose, its narrow mouth and its piercing gray eyes, in which from time to time shone a flash of tenderness when she was talking to her daughter. A lace bonnet, with flaps, partly disguised a thick but graying head of hair.

'My dear girl,' she said, 'for the second time you have made a dangerous mistake, even worse than the first. You have married a hussar. Was he so handsome, then?'

This unexpected question amazed the young woman, but she replied at once:

'He's the most handsome man anyone ever saw.'

'In that case, I understand. I had the same weakness when I was your age.'

'You, Mother?'

'Yes, me. Don't look at me like that. I'm human. As a young man, your father was splendid. But, enough of that. Do you know that there is going to be a war?'

'I don't believe that.'

'It will break out without your permission. Where will you go?'

'Where? I can only stay here. The South will manage to defend itself.'

'The South is brave because it is English, but the balance of forces is dreadfully against it. The North will crush it. Everyone in England is sure of that. Listen to me. Despite your marriage, you are an Englishwoman. Uncle Charlie, who gets what he wants, has done what was necessary. Your British passport will never be taken away. Come back to England with me. Come home.'

'Leave Billy, Mother? Never.'

'If you had answered any other way, I should have been ashamed — ashamed of you, but I should have been delighted to take you with me, even so. Kiss me, my child. We haven't embraced yet.'

Elizabeth threw herself in her arms.

'No tears,' said Lady Fidgety, covering her face with kisses. 'An Englishwoman never weeps.'

She said this, the words broken, in a hoarse voice, with tears streaming down her cheeks.

After a while both of them calmed down and Elizabeth resumed her seat.

'When I think,' Lady Fidgety went on, with a furtive sniffle, 'that England is swarming with handsome men and that, beautiful as you are — because you are very beautiful, my wretched Elizabeth — you would only have needed to take your pick. So . . .'

'Perhaps there will not be a war.'

'In any event, a piece of advice: if hell should break loose, go to Uncle Charlie's and don't move from there. Charlie Jones is a very important person and as English as can be. In wars, foreigners are respected.'

'Yes, Mother.'

'But I want to see your Billy. I am hard to please. We shall see if the two of us have the same taste.'

'You'll see him in a few days.'

'Your housekeeper told me that Charlie had come back from Virginia. I have a message for him from Liverpool. Send word for him to come and see me.'

Lady Fidgety, an inquisitive lady, had to be shown the house from top to bottom, and she admired everything, except the drawing-room where she no longer wished to set foot because of the blood-red walls. A meeting took place in the garden between her and young Ned. For a few seconds they considered one another, then there was an exchange of rather forced smiles, a brief attempt at reciprocal charm which achieved nothing. Lady Fidgety did not like little boys, and Ned found the lady stern and distant.

They waited all day for Charlie Jones. He appeared after dinner when they had given up expecting him. Elizabeth suggested that they go and sit on the veranda. Lady Fidgety attached herself to Charlie Jones's arm which lifted her at every step, and she laughed quietly, as if playing a game, instead of pouring out insults as she had that same morning into the ear of the assistant cook.

They took their places in spacious chairs with cushions. The night was pleasantly mild. Only a faint and distant sound of traffic pass-ing along the avenue disturbed the silence from time to time. They felt happy for no reason, because the air was good, full of scents which came in puffs of breeze from the neighboring gardens. Lady Fidgety took a roll of papers tied with string out of the long bag of black linen which she kept at her elbow, and held them out to Charlie Jones.

'Your shipyards in Liverpool,' she said, in a very official voice.

He took them with expressions of retrospective terror.

'You brought them like that?'

'You know as well as anyone that in Savannah you can come and go as you please.'

'In Charleston, the government keeps an eye on everything,' he said, lowering his voice.

' Which is why I was not foolish enough to go through Charles-ton,' she said in the same tone of voice. 'And then, you have the right to order trading ships if you want to.'

'Not any longer. I owe you a debt of thanks, my dear Laura,' he said, reverting to his familiar friendly tone.

Both of them were whispering like conspirators.

'For the South, which remains English,' she said, 'even though it rebelled against us.'

'Solid, peaceful merchant ships,' he said.

'Capable of being put to any useful purpose,' she added, stifling a malicious laugh.

'Hush, in Heaven's name!'

She put her mouth to his ear:

'Who can hear us?'

Adopting the same device, he answered:

'The owls!'

As if to confirm what he said, some owls hooted softly. Elizabeth thought they were kissing each other.

'If I'm in your way,' she said coldly, 'I can leave.'

'Forgive us, Elizabeth,' Uncle Charlie said aloud. 'We are boring. We are exchanging some very confidential remarks.'

'About the war.'

Uncle Charlie gave a jolly laugh which put everything to rights.

'My dear girl, there is no war. Peace reigns in our beloved Savannah.'

'Hm!' said Lady Fidgety. 'But let's leave your hemisphere. Do you know what's happening in India?'

'Everyone does. Britain has been grappling with an attempted uprising for more than a year. There is fierce fighting around Delhi. The Sepoys . . .'

'The Sepoys, yes. The revolt of the Sepoys. We had details of what happened at Lucknow and Cawnpore. Elizabeth, go away if you don't want to hear about horrors.'

'I'm not a softy. I want to know why my drawing-room looks like Lucknow.'

'Well, not Lucknow itself, but in the countryside around, hundreds of Sepoys were attached to the mouths of cannons which blasted their bodies against the town-walls instantly transforming them  into walls of bloody flesh.'

'Shame on us!' exclaimed Uncle Charlie.

'Not on those who fired the cannons, who only did as they were told, but on the officers who were not afraid to give such barbarous orders. Gladstone protested against it. He is expected to make a speech in Parliament. The public is furious and humiliated. How do we look to the rest of the world? We are barbarians ourselves.'

'I'm going to have my drawing-room painted green,' Elizabeth said resolutely.

'Have you just woken up?' asked Uncle Charlie. 'Were you asleep?'

'Charlie, you don't follow,' said Lady Fidgety. 'What Elizabeth said makes a lot of sense.'

'Here at least such atrocities are unknown,' said Elizabeth.

Charlie Jones nearly leaped out of his chair.

'Unknown!' he shouted. 'And what about the extermination of the Indian race? Elizabeth, you're still talking like a little girl. And, of course, that's why everyone adores you,' he added, quickly. 'But you must know that there is not a single so-called civilized nation in the world which has not indulged in horrors of the kind you have just heard. Spain, Italy, France, Prussia, all of them, man is everywhere the same, an animal only partially emerging from his prehistory. The deepest instincts are the same. The Gospel changed nothing. The Assyrians were no worse than we are.'

'A history lesson by moonlight, my dear Charlie,' said Lady Fidgety. 'Did the Assyrians have convertible ships?'

'I know,' Uncle Charlie said merrily. 'I'm quite ridiculous. But I'm right. Basically, I'm right.'

'But of course,' said Lady Fidgety. 'I agree with you, Charlie. . . . How the moon glitters at our feet!'

Through the trellis, silver lozenge-shaped spots lit up a luminous veranda.

'It is late,' Lady Fidgety continued. 'And this journey has made me quite exhausted, but we shall see one another again. I am here for at least two months. My dear husband is pinned to his chair in Bath by his gout. Port!' she added merrily. 'But he is expecting me back for Christmas. Good night, Charlie dear. Elizabeth, I am delighted with my two rooms and already settled in my splendid four-poster. Until tomorrow, my dear child.'

Having pronounced this little speech in her precisely articulated consonants, she vanished in a headlong rustling of taffeta.

Charlie Jones went downstairs slowly with Elizabeth.

'A remarkable woman, your mother,' he said pensively.

'Who is the poor husband immobilized in Bath with his gout?'

'One of the best-established fortunes in the United Kingdom.'

'If he doesn't come here, I may never see him. Does Mother love him? Why did she marry him?'

'If I might parody a fine writer whom you will doubtless never read: the heart has its reasons which only the wallet knows . . . But here we are at the foot of the stairs. Keep what you have heard this evening to yourself, my dear and lovely Elizabeth.'

# 6

# THERE WILL BE NO WAR

# 109

$D$aily life arranged itself agreably enough in the house in Ogle-thorpe Square. Ned was sent to school at an institution formerly attended by Mike. The former little Jonathan, who now only responded to the name 'Ned', found some merry companions in the infant's class with whom to fight. Endowed with rather similar psychological tendencies, and the imperious nose of an English aristocrat, Lady Fidgety forged a path into society — which offered no resistance. Far from it.

Public attention was now concentrated on the battle of words over the seat of Senator for Illinois. Douglas, the 'little giant', was predicted to be ahead, but could only truly count on the Democrats of his state supported by those in the North. The South no longer had confidence and the Democratic Party was threatened with a split. As a very moderate abolitionist candidate, Abraham Lincoln played his hand without much emotion and still remained a mystery.

On November 2, a cold, rainy day, Douglas was elected, but Lincoln considered his personal failure as a sort of victory, given that the Republicans had gained a large number of votes. From the few public and private statements he had made, two were noted which seemed of particular importance to people in the South: he refused in advance the principle of citizenship for the Blacks (who, moreover, were still forbidden to settle in Illinois), and secondly, he supported the old humanitarian idea of Henry Clay to send all the colored people to Liberia, to restore their freedom, their customs and their own land. As for becoming a senator, he was not interested in that: he was looking to the future and higher things.

More disturbingly, Seward, the Senator for New York, a man of fanatical violence and full of his own importance, demanded an immediate confrontation. 'The conflict cannot be stopped,' he bellowed. He was urging war with all his forces: total war, in order to settle the matter once and for all. Many people thought him an imbecile, but he was only a politician and it has occurred before that a catastrophe has been instigated by this particular type of imbecile. He aspired to Buchanan's chair in the name of the Republicans — like Lincoln — but in any case, his program was well-known: the extermination of the South. He belonged to the little band of fanatics (Garrison, Wendell Phillips and their kind), to whom were attached the moralizing and maniacal tribe of the Beechers.

Oddly enough, in spite of this political ferment, 1859 was heralded as a year of appeasement. By one of those chances which defy analysis, a wind of optimism was blowing, perhaps the product of a long weariness with fear. Dreading war, without it ever breaking out, people had managed to convince themselves that it was merely an empty threat. The future, in the life of a whole nation, could not for ever remain blocked. People were determined to hope, and the spiritual climate changed.

Charlie Jones still continued his rather mysterious journeys to New York and abroad, but he came back as quickly and as often as he could, not only to look after his business in the port of Savannah, but also to oversee the completion of his Tudor house, which was the talk of the town. The roof was still not in place, but the greater part of the house was already habitable. The beauty of the proportions, which were very imposing, was much admired, notably the oriel windows — in the purest Elizabethan style, projected outward, overhanging like little crenelated cages.

Lady Fidgety went to cast a curious eye on this monument, which she accepted was architecturally correct.

'But what is this Tudor latecomer doing,' she asked Charlie Jones, 'in a largely eighteenth-century town?'

'Because,' Charlie Jones replied, with his most winning smile, 'I prefer our glorious Henry VIII to the four Hanoverian Georges who never learned to speak English.'

'So how would you explain to our irascible Henry VIII the presence of these palm trees, casting their shadow on those fine red bricks?'

'English brick, of course. I shall reply to your perfidious question: I want to build a corner of England in this distant land and under this hot climate, as a refuge in the event of war.'

'Oh, bravo! Our Elizabeth is safe. I take back all my objections.'

This slightly teasing camaraderie with the most influential man in Savannah greatly facilitated Lady Fidgety's stay: she had everything she wanted. She was invited everywhere and, since she adored company, her imaginatively British elegance, her haughty bearing, her incisive wit and the subtlety of her apparently innocuous, yet cutting remarks, all promised her a brilliant career in society. She only regretted that she could not join the young people whose fresh faces and well-turned figures she appreciated with the eye of a conoisseur as they whirled around the ballrooms.

To her great regret, she could not manage to drag Elizabeth with her on her social outings. How could she guess that the young woman, whom she assumed to be unassailably faithful, wanted her freedom and her share of excitement? And what could interfere more with that than the presence of a mother?

Lady Fidgety was also occupied with more serious matters. One morning she went to the docks in Savannah, those same docks where Elizabeth had never once set foot since the death of Jonathan. Her carriage took her there and she had herself taken to Charlie Jones's office. It was not the first time she had been here. She liked the bustle of the employees and secretaries in the long room with its walls covered in huge sea charts. She had the impression that all these people were talking at once in the stimulating hubbub of business. Names of boats and distant ports crossed with figures in an atmosphere colored by the pale smoke of cigarettes. She did not find Charlie Jones here. Warned of her visit, he was waiting in a room with two padded doors, sitting behind a vast rosewood desk. He got up from his chair when she came in and pointed to a comfortable seat in tropical wood, but she would not sit down. Turning to the veranda which overlooked the port, she watched the ships for a moment, their masts bending gently under a sky crossed by light clouds. Heaps of cotton bales wrapped in cloth were piled at one end of the port and half-naked Blacks were slowly loading them into the hold of a ship. A crowd of idlers was walking around the quay, sometimes pushed aside by luggage porters or workers, and a murmur of voices rose up to the great open bay windows.

Lady Fidgety did not stop long to contemplate this landscape, even though it meant far more to her than the squares and long avenues of Savannah.

'You'll never guess why I came here this morning,' she said, sitting down. 'First of all, I warn you that I shall accept no objection.'

'So I'm muzzled,' said Charlie Jones. 'You must do the barking.'

'I shall, but beware of my bite. When I left for England...'

'Eight years ago,' Charlie Jones remarked, sensing something.

'Eight years, I've calculated everything . . . My debt to you and Hargrove was considerable.'

'What do you mean? All that's forgotten, you surely don't intend . . . You cannot . . .'

'Be quiet, you're muzzled! The interest has continued to accumulate and I couldn't contemplate even a progressive settlement; then I married Lord Fidgety who has himself continued to get older and to see his relatives and friends die, leaving him their heir. Indeed, my venerable spouse is the inheriting sort. So, give me a pen and some paper.'

Shrugging his shoulders, he offered her a sheet of white paper and a goose quill dipped in ink. She put the paper on the desk and, with a little scratch of the pen, wrote a figure.

He took the paper and said simply:

'You're mad.'

'Do you need the accounts? You can have them.'

'I refuse. I refuse all of this.'

'I shall bite,' she said. 'I had thought you a gentleman, but one can be mistaken, can't one?'

'What are you trying to say, wicked woman?'

She took a bill of exchange out of her bag, carefully wrote out the amount, and handed it to him.

'How can I accept this?' he sighed.

She leaned toward him, both hands on the desk.

'For the South,' she said, looking aggressively right in his eyes, and adding softly: 'For the Assyrian fleet.'

Suddenly on his feet, he cried:

'For love of the Assyrian fleet!'

And, leaning across the desk, they embraced. Neither of them had for a second doubted that the check would first be offered, then refused, then accepted; but the little play-acting had covered the friendly brutality of the transaction.

Lady Fidgety could not have been more comfortably settled than she was at Elizabeth's that sunny late November, visiting friends and already thinking of her solitary return home. What pleasure was there for her without the daughter whom she hoped to take away from the South to her magnificent house in Bath, where her seventy-two-year old loving husband awaited her, pinned to his chair by gout? She had played and lost.

'But I shall return,' she said one day, aloud, to herself.

When, my Lady? The answer to that question could not be framed, or even admitted to herself under her breath, but it hovered somewhere in the darkness: When the war has relieved her of her Billy. This wicked thought did no more than flit through her mind, and she swept it aside with a noble gesture, but the gesture did not get rid of it any more than it would have gotten rid of a fly.

At last, surprise! Billy appeared on an unexpected furlough like the last one. The English lady and the hussar found themselves face to face, alone, in the hallway, while Elizabeth was grasping her slippers and her bathrobe.

The interview was a trifle short, but decisive, the introductions as brief as the yapping of a puppy dog, but it was followed by a silent scene which was not without interest to observe. Lady Fidgety considered the hussar as one might admire a landscape; then, making as if to retire, she was not ashamed to walk round him as if around a monument. One might imagine that he would have tried to avoid this indecent proceeding, but one would have been wrong. At first falsely indignant, he acceded to it out of vanity, even taking up poses, content to give a little cough once or twice. The English lady found him handsome. After all, he was used to these situations which he had never found unpleasant.

Suddenly Elizabeth was there like a wild bird that had escaped from a cage and, without a word, she threw herself into Billy's arms.

Lady Fidgety preferred to vanish in the direction of the garden.

'What! She's gone,' Elizabeth cried. 'Did you speak? No? Do you realize she is my mother?'

'Your mother?'

He burst out laughing.

'Why are you laughing?'

'I don't know,' he said as he kissed her. 'We'll see her later.'

Without a further word, they went up to their room.

As the date for her departure approached, Lady Fidgety became increasingly attached to the house in Oglethorpe Square. She was getting used to it, she was comfortable here. Two reasons, which she considered imperative, justified her presence in Savannah: the first was to settle Charlie Jones's naval affairs; and the second, not the least, but less overt, was a new attempt to bring her daughter back to England. Successful in the first of these, she was less so in the second.

Where Billy was concerned, her heart was divided, like that of a tragic heroine. She hated him because he was keeping Elizabeth in America, yet she weakened cravenly when she saw him parading around the drawing-room. Was that all he could do? The wretch guessed the unreserved admiration which he aroused in this proud woman's gray eyes. Limited though his furlough was, it lead to a polite relationship nevertheless between him and his victim. The latter suffered, but took a mysterious pleasure in it. Alone at night, she gave free rein to her imagination and was shamefully jealous of her daughter.

Consequently, she was relieved when her dear tormentor disappeared from the house one day at dawn, taking with him a whole world of dreams and desires.

She consoled herself as best she could and, as they say, argued herself out of it. In her fifties, barely past that age, she could not yield to impulses of the heart and body for a handsome soldier, like a scatter-brained twenty-year old . . . That did not alter the fact that by nature she was almost as much in love with him as her daughter was.

Two days before her departure, she went down to the garden to say goodbye to Ned. That morning she had seen him at a distance through the window and thought him lovely . . . He, on the other hand, had so far found her repulsive. She sensed this and consequently was given an unpleasant little shock.

At that moment, he was humming to himself, playing with a ball which he was throwing above his head and catching awkwardly. When he saw Lady Fidgety coming toward him in her plum-colored dress, he stopped, petrified. She herself was seized by a ridiculous feeling of shyness and began by producing one of her most engaging smiles.

'Hello, Ned,' she said.

'Hello, Ma'am.'

At that, she reverted to the most treacherous weapon in an adult's armory, the one used by all child abductors, because it is usually infallible. Rummaging around in the bag which she was carrying on her arm, she took out a large box of Lousiana sweets. Savannah boys, without exception, know these, and the oldest desire of child-hood longings shone in Ned's eyes.

Lady Fidgety opened the box and asked him to take a sweet. They were mixed and Ned lost his head when confronted with the problem of choice. Suddenly, she shut the box.

'They're all yours. Take the box, I'm giving it to you because you're the best little boy I've met in America. And I'm going away, Ned. Will you give me a kiss?'

Without letting go of the box, he offered a face radiant with hap-piness. She picked him up in her arms, lifted him off the ground and covered him with kisses, as though in a storm of affection.

'I love you very, very much,' she said.

The child laughed, the box held tightly to his chest.

Then came the final morning when, in the port of Savannah, with one foot already on the gangplank up to the ship, she pressed her streaming face to that of her daughter, unable to utter a single word.

Half an hour later, Elizabeth was back in her room, looking at the furniture and the walls around her with a strange feeling of bitter-ness. She had to come back and live once more live in these banal surroundings while the ship was still there, expecting its last pas-sengers! For a moment she dreamed of taking her carriage to the port, but she knew only too well that she would not leave her rock-ing-chair and that her mother would leave on her own, taking Eng-land with her.

A memory, still more agonizing, haunted her. In vain she tried to drive it from her mind, but it returned ceaselessly, and she gave in, living again a delicious torment: she was sixteen and she was there, on the quayside, almost at the same spot as just a short while ago, the crowd shouting with joy around her and hailing the boat which was slowly coming into port. Little Miss Charlotte was standing in front of her, her arms raised, and there he was, just beside her, the man, pressing her in his arms, his lips brushing hers; then she heard his voice in her ear once more, assuring her of his love over and over, until finally the awful moment came when he said farewell, in the midst of the cheers and cries of the crowd, and the little flags flapping in the wind, and those words which she would keep inside her for months: 'I shall return.' Then suddenly she was alone among all those shoulders and loud cries, and when she turned, she could see the light suede leather jacket going across the square, running toward Annabel's carriage which was waiting, down there, at the end of the quay . . . I shall return. He did return. And after his death in the duel, he had returned a hundred times in little Jonathan's dreams. No more. Never again would he return. There are deaths of the soul as there are deaths of the body, and the former are no easier to endure.

After Lady Fidgety's departure, the house seemed empty and too large. This turbulent woman, with her somewhat disordered manner of speech, brought a whole country with her: her voice and accent by themselves gave you London, Bath and all of British society.

The year '59 opened grandly as though for a celebration, with a superabundance of presents and smiles. The roses flowered and young people waltzed until they were dizzy. They were emerging from a bad dream: one might almost have thought it was the day after a victory — and it was: a victory over the prophets of doom, a victory of what they considered eternal peace; death had been despatched.

The euphoria lasted until May. Then everyone talked about war. Where was the war? A long way, a very long way off, in that Europe with all its myriad nations which were so hard to place. This time, it was France fighting with Austria; and where? In Italy. The newspapers talked a good deal about it, but did anyone want to read the newspapers when everything was going so well at home? Let Europe battle out its incomprehensible quarrels, and, out of habit, but without apprehension, people were rather inclined to turn their eyes northwards, where a bomb had just exploded.

The book, by the German writer Helper, *The Impending Crisis*, a book that was now two years old and which had been passed around a bit in the South and was now forgotten, had been rediscovered by the North which was making short work of it. What a lot of fuss about those prophecies bristling with statistics! The South was heading toward its ruin. Slavery was slowly going bankrupt. In the long run, the forced labor of the Blacks in the plantations would not pay. The opulence of the slave States might be deceptive, but what a catastrophic future awaited them! The author demonstrated all this with amazing clarity . . . Figures, figures and more figures. The North was jubilant, its conscience at ease. The special institution, so deeply immoral, had finally suffered its death blow. 'We shall settle the question ourselves,' the South replied. 'We can do without anyone's help, however well-intentioned.'

Shortly afterwards, at the beginning of June, Mrs Furnace gave a dinner in her house in Monterey Square. She had inherited this very remarkable home, as well as a sizeable fortune, on the death of Mrs Devilue Upton Smythe, whose faithful companion she had been for many long years . . . ever since the wedding of Ned and Elizabeth. Elizabeth was among the guests, as were Algernon and his mother, Mrs Steers; the lawyer, Harry Longcope; Mrs Harrison Edwards, without whom the party would have lacked a certain *something*; the venerable Mr Robertson, always listened to in awed silence; and finally Major Crawford, the loud-voiced moving spirit of the town.

It might be worth mentioning that Mrs Furnace had miraculously become Lady Furnace by a more or less intentional slip of Mrs Devilue Upton Smythe's tongue, she having introduced her under that name at a large reception at the Steers'. No one had been vulgar enough to correct the mistake, so the title of nobility remained without its owner making any attempt to rectify it.

As for the magnificent house which had come to her, it was the very same one that William Hargrove had bought from Mrs Devilue Upton Smythe on his return from Haiti; but, as soon as he had settled in Dimwood, he resold his house in Savannah, whose original owner had been only too happy to repurchase the ancestral home. And the money flowed.

Everything within its walls was designed to impress. Thus, the dining-room ceiling was so high that it was lost in semi-darkness, but the round table, laden with candles, managed to restore an appearance of intimacy thanks to their gentle and flattering light.

Gardenias were scattered across the white tablecloth between the silver gilt cutlery and the Bohemian glass. The older guests recognized on the fine porcelain plates the arms of the heroic Devilue family, which had protected the unfortunate King Harold in 1066 at the tragic Battle of Hastings which delivered his kingdom to the rule of William the Conqueror. In short, one took a journey through history while partaking of the most delicious food. Servants in dark violet livery trimmed with gold thread wandered around this dream dreamed by a lady's companion who had suddenly gone completely mad.

However, Lady Furnace still retained her wits when it came to some things. An incorrigible storyteller, she had promised herself that she would take her guests to no more than two exotic countries. She shone chiefly in the Orient among the sultans and the emirs; and, from the outset, she transported everyone to Kashmir, where she dazzled them with the evocative and sonorous names of princes.

Elizabeth, her cheeks bright as a pink-and-gold statue, smiled silently and carefully observed this lady, dripping with jewels, whom she had known well in Virginia and who this evening appeared to her as beautiful as she had then. There was a ghost between them that the young Englishwoman could not forget. Lady Furnace was grateful to her for never having divulged her sad secret. For that reason, there was a bond of affectionate complicity, of feminine complicity, between these two very different women.

When Lady Furnace had completed the description of Kashmir and her close relations with several maharajahs from that country, the conversation at once became general and, by common agreement, they launched into *The Impending Crisis*. Everyone began to speak at once — and it took the courteous authority of the venerable Mr Robertson to restore calm for a moment.

'Not everything the North says is untrue, but the sting is in the tail, that is the conclusion. It suggests, for the sake of humanity, that, for the good of the South, slavery should be abolished without delay.'

Major Crawford, his brick-colored face even redder than usual, raised his familiar voice:

'And they are right!' he exclaimed. 'But if they intend to mobilize their troops to cross our frontiers, we shall be there, to give them the welcome they deserve.'

'Fix bayonets!'

This loud and clear cry came from Algernon and, coming from him, was found very surprising for indefinable reasons. There was some applause.

'We've not reached that point yet,' Mr Robertson said softly.

'Perhaps,' Algernon retorted, 'but there are two ways of reading a text, and I have read this particular one.'

At that, every eye turned toward him. Transformed by genuine feeling, he seemed to turn into a purple-colored Greek statue. Elizabeth looked at him admiringly.

'You can read a page from top to bottom without leaving out a line, and you can read the same page, covering half of it with your hand, so as not to see what upsets you.'

A deathly silence was their response to these words, and every whisper ceased.

'Helper establishes, with figures to support him,' Algernon went on, 'that the annual work of the slaves brings in markedly less money than agricultural work in the so-called free States. With tireless patience, he goes many years back in time. The fall is uninterrupted and the ruin of the South is inevitable. He calculates, State by State, in the South as in the North, and in the North acre by acre, bushel by bushel, wheat, oats, rye, with diabolical perseverance . . .'

Here Mr Robertson raised a hand and interrupted him.

'Young man,' he said, 'you speak well, but you are forgetting two very important things. The first is that Helper was for many years a poor White, and a poor White in the South, which means he was despised.'

There were a few dull sounds of protest.

'Do you think the word *despised* is too harsh?' Mr Robertson asked. 'Then find a better one. You call them the dregs of the White race.'

There followed a sombre silence.

'For that reason,' Robertson went on, 'Helper hates the Southern aristocracy. The second important thing is that slavery exists under another name and in other forms in countries where an excess of wealth leads to the formation of castes. The man who works hard in a factory or an office will never rise to join the caste of the wealthy unless he succeeds in making a fortune himself. To succeed is to get rich. You can't escape from that. The factory worker will never sit at the rich man's table. Helper knows what he is talking about. He enjoyed wealth as an adolescent, and he was thrust into poverty at the death of his father. The problem of black servitude only interests him in relation to the problem of white servitude.'

Here Major Crawford roared once again.

'But the North distinguishes the problem of black slavery and turns it into a moral question. *Uncle Tom's Cabin* is its Bible. It doesn't matter that the good lady Beecher has never set foot in a black man's cabin: the incendiary text supplies the pretext; morality is allied to lies!'

'And if there is a war,' the lawyer Longcope said gently, having up to now managed the heroic feat of not opening his mouth, 'it will be interesting to see what the Blacks' attitude is, compared to that of the poor Whites.'

'Sir,' Major Crawford asked him, 'what Northern state do you come from?'

'From Louisiana, sir. At your disposal at whatever time and place you wish.'

Mr Robertson stood up.

'Gentlemen,' he said warmly, 'you're not going to fight over a misunderstanding. Mr Longcope's question is full of good sense. No one can tell what the three million Blacks and the five million poor Whites will do in the event of a conflict. We are all asking ourselves the very same question.'

'You are right,' said Major Crawford. 'Mr Longcope, I spoke hastily.'

'Major Crawford, it is because all of us, in the North and in the South, are speaking hastily that war is likely to break out. I also spoke hastily in my reply to you.'

To everyone's surprise, Mrs Harrison Edwards raised an arm in a gesture at once perfect and prophetic.

'Gentlemen,' she said. 'what we must retain in what you have said, is that the North is trying to get its hands on the whole of the South.'

'Never!' exclaimed Lady Furnace. 'And, while we're on that

subject, let me tell you what I saw in Anatolia. You,' she said to the black servant standing motionless at the door. 'Don't just stand there like a post. Go and tell them to serve the turkey.'

# 110

Ned's seventh birthday had been celebrated in the simplest manner and the one most to his taste. A few presents, first of all at home, but above all, instead of sending him to school, Elizabeth took him to Tybee Beach where, from morning to evening, he had been able to fight and run around as much as he liked. He returned to Oglethorpe Square delighted with his day, but a surprise awaited him, of which he could not yet have the slightest idea, and life resumed, ordinary and easy.

He was no longer a little boy. Longer trousers reached halfway down his legs and he wore a straw hat with a hard rim, like the one he had seen on Mike: he too could balance it on the end of his nose. A black ribbon, floating in the wind, helped to make this the most fashionable headwear imaginable. In short, little Ned was becoming a little man.

One holiday, shortly after the dinner at Lady Furnace's, a carriage stopped in front of the house and a lackey in dark green livery came and asked for Mr Charles-Edward on behalf of Mr Charlie Jones. Very astonished, Ned put on his cheeky hat and came down the steps. The carriage was empty. He got in and allowed himself to be taken to the great Tudor house. For the first time he saw it without its scaffolding and, to all appearances, completed.

Jumping out, he went up to the front door, which at once opened wide. Dressed in black, as if for a reception, Charlie Jones held both hands out to him. Ned took off his hat and could think of nothing to say, except:

'Good morning, Grandfather.'

'Welcome, Charles-Edward,' his grandfather said, with a fine smile. 'For reasons which you will discover a bit later, I want you to be the first person to visit my house. It still does not have a roof on it, but you will see it is altogether habitable.'

As if immersed in the strangest of his childhood dreams, Ned followed Charlie Jones, but hardly understood what he was saying. Both of them walked through a hall which seemed to the young visitor as wide as a street, bordered here and there by marble statues standing on truncated columns. Connoisseurs would have recognized Venus, Apollo, Diana, Hermes and Dionysus, all in the chaste nudity of the Ancient World, while Ned, whose education had not advanced so far as that, wondered if he was going mad.

Charlie Jones, seeing his astonishment, laughed, took his arm and led him into a huge drawing-room which opened directly onto the hall. Very high windows framed in dark wood rose almost to the heavily worked cornices on the ceiling. Because of their shape they seemed narrow, but that very fact gave the room an air of unusual majesty. In a corner, a vast red sofa with contours that were at once rounded and twisted, prevented the whole from appearing too severe. Chairs and armchairs, in purple wood and in the same style, finally ensured that there was no gravity in a decor that was more friendly than imposing.

Ned turned right, then left, open-mouthed, and said nothing, which made Charlie Jones laugh aloud. Suddenly, he put a hand on the boy's shoulder and asked:

'Do you like it, Ned? Do you like my house?'

'Oh, Grandfather!'

Ned could find nothing else to say, but his brown curls jumped from one side to the other of his astonished face.

'Let's go a little further,' his grandfather said, taking his hand.

They went back up the hall and Charlie Jones' voice echoed strangely in the empty house. But everything in this visit seemed odd, almost as though they were visiting the place by moonlight — yet the sun was shining brightly, filtering through three thicknesses of white net curtains.

To the left, a long library decorated with Roman busts looked out over a garden path alongside which young sycamores were growing, and a still tiny palm tree.

'When the house has its top on,' Charlie Jones explained, 'it will be surrounded by trees. But it is too early now.'

'All these books . . ., ' Ned said suddenly, pointing at endless rows of volumes with gold lettering shining softly on the dark leather bindings. 'How many are there?'

To this naive question, Charlie Jones replied:

'Thousands and thousands of friends, the only ones who never let you down.'

Ned listened without understanding: everything his grandfather said seemed wonderful to him. Advancing further without looking too closely at the completely naked men and women, they reached a spiral staircase, which seemed almost miraculously light to Ned, so that he wondered how it could stand there in empty space; but that's how it was.

'It looks as though it's dancing,' said Charlie Jones. 'Don't you think?'

'Oh, yes, Grandfather.'

'Graceful, isn't it?'

'Oh, yes: graceful!'

'So you like the house?'

'Yes, very much, Grandfather.'

'Well, listen carefully, Charles-Edward. I haven't given you any-thing for your birthday.'

Ned had a rush of politeness:

'It doesn't matter, Grandfather, really it doesn't.'

'Well today, Charles-Edward Hargrove, I'm giving you this house. When you are grown up, you can come and live here with your family. Are you glad?'

Ned didn't answer. His eyes misted over. He took Charlie Jones's hand and held it in his own without a word.

'That's the best thank you anyone has ever given me,' his grand-father said, leaning over him and giving him a kiss. 'Now listen,' he added, standing up again. 'If it should ever happen that, before you are of age, the North should come to Savannah, you can all take refuge here, because my house is English and you will be safe in it — as safe as in God's own pocket.'

The little boy laughed at the idea of God's pocket.

'Very well, Grandfather,'

They retraced their steps toward the front door, then stopped in front of a huge picture set into a stucco frame with a rounded top, very ornate and elaborate, imitating a band of leaves full of birds and flowers. In this alabaster frame was an unexpected painting: the Virgin Mary in a blue-tinted dress, wrapped in a cloak of dark blue, holding the Child in her arms and bending down toward him. The background looked like a cloud of pink-ish gold.

'Look, Ned, this is by a very great Spanish painter, Murillo. A Daughter of Israel, she is holding against her the Child who saved the world. You will hear a good deal of ill said of the race to which both of them belong. You must never speak any such ill. You will remember this painting.'

'Yes, Grandfather.'

'Is that a promise?'

'I give you my word of honor, Grandfather.'

'Very good. You are a good boy and a gentleman. That's all. We shall say goodbye here, but we shall see each other again soon. The carriage will take you back to Oglethorpe Square — unless you would prefer to return on foot.'

Ned replied with a smile:

'I'd prefer the carriage, Grandfather. My head's spinning.'

'I understand — and so it should.' (Charlie Jones burst out laugh-ing). 'Put your hand in mine.'

A minute later, a still dumbfounded boy was on his way back to Oglethorpe Square.

Life went on without any significant events, and the simple pleasure of living revived the happy days of former times which old people recall sentimentally. Parties, receptions and balls followed in a continual stream and took them through pleasantly until Summer when the town sank into a stupor of heat and tranquillity.

For Elizabeth, Billy's appearances, sudden and increasingly unannounced, varied this rather monotonous extended period of happiness. He told her that he liked to surprise her with a furlough decided at the last moment. Far from complaining, the young woman delighted in this without asking for explanations. Billy was always the same, perfectly fulfilling his role as a loving husband. However, he was more likely now than before to ask his wife questions about her life during his absence. This curiosity flattered Elizabeth and she described visits, balls and receptions to him to satisfy the soldier's desire to follow her in his imagination and 'in my heart, too, my darling, in my hours of solitude'. Thus, there was something more to him than an immoderate taste for pleasure — which she shared. A more sensitive Billy was hiding beneath the dolman of the savage warrior.

For his part, he tried to amuse her with the rumors circulating in the mess, some of which might make a change for her from the eternal society gossip.

'Have you heard about the latest scandal in Washington? No? I'm not surprised. All America is talking about it. After all, Washington is the capital and my gossip is still fresh! It concerns an important figure, the District Attorney, a gentleman of barely forty years, with neat little mustaches, very elegant and a prominent member of fashionable society. One fine Sunday afternoon, on February 27 last, to be precise, he was walking, like everyone else who is anyone in Washington, near the White House. A warm southern breeze was blowing. The attorney was walking along slowly, up until the moment that he found himself alone on the far side of the avenue, opposite the house of an honorable member of Congress; and there, he took out of his pocket a white handkerchief which he waved three times, round and round — as a signal.'

'Oh, Billy!' Elizabeth interrupted. 'How romantic! What then?'

'Does it amuse you?'

'I'm thrilled. I adore these love stories.'

'How do you know it's a love story?'

'Come, come! What else could it be?'

'You'll see. So, he waved his handkerchief three times, looking up toward a window, and waited. No one appeared, but suddenly . . .'

'Suddenly. . .?'

'Just when he had raised a pretty little opera glass focussing on the empty window a few yards away, bellowing with rage like a bull at the sight of a red rag . . . came *the husband*!'

'The husband?'

'The husband of the lady who did not reply to the call of the handkerchief. At that same moment, she was in bed suffering from nervous prostration, because the honorable member of Congress Daniel Sickels, her famous husband, had forced her to admit her affair with the District Attorney. He had a revolver in his hand . . . He fired . . .'

'Oh, no, Billy!'

'And missed!'

She gave a sigh of relief.

'The attorney ran off as fast as his legs would carry him. The husband went after him, firing. In self-defense, the attorney threw the case of his opera glasses in his face, shouting: "Murder! Don't fire! Don't kill me!" Then he managed to reach a large plane tree and hid behind it. Almost immediately, the honorable member of Congress caught up with him. There was a short struggle and, suddenly, another shot. The attorney fell, bent double, on the pavement, and rolled around in agony while the husband fired two more revolver shots at him which finished him off.'

'But that's frightful!'

'Passers-by ran over toward the murderer. Some knew him well and pulled him to one side. "He dishonored me!" he shouted.'

'The dreadful brute!'

'No, no, darling, and his career won't be affected at all by it. On the contrary. The trial has made him a prominent figure: he emerged the victor and justified. Come, I can see that you are shocked by my little story. Let's talk about something else. For example, about Algernon.'

'Algernon, Billy?'

'Yes, don't put on that odd expression. When did you last see him?'

He asked the question in an offhand manner.

'At a dinner at Lady Furnace's. Why do you ask?'

'Did you speak with him?'

'No.'

'I want the truth.'

'I've just told you the whole truth. What more do you need?'

'I want the real truth.'

'Are you mad?'

'Were you close to him?'

'Well, if you must know, we were placed next to each other at table.'

'And you didn't say anything to each other?'

'No. The conversation was about politics, to do with some book by . . . I can't recall who. Major Crawford said that if the North crossed the frontier, it would be met as it deserved. And Algernon shouted: "Fix bayonets!"'

'Algernon?'

'Yes, Algernon Steers. You have gone quite red. What's wrong with you? You're not the same. Billy. You're not Billy any more.'

She got up brusquely and went across to the door of the adjoining room. Seized with panic, he ran after her and grasped her in his arms.

'Yes, I am!' he cried. 'I am!'

She struggled a little, without conviction.

# 111

Autumn suddenly brought something new which disturbed the South, then the whole of America. On October 16, at ten o'clock in the evening, twenty armed men crossed the metal bridge at Harper's Ferry and seized the federal arsenal; the night was pitch-black, as though the darkness were necessary to hide the folly and the blood.

It was a young English architect from Oxford who, at the beginning of the eighteenth century, at the junction of the Shenandoah and the Potomac, between the States of Maryland and Virginia, struck by the beauty and importance of this spot which allowed the construction of a road westwards through Indian country, established a ferry across the river, then a bridge which was given his name: Harper's Ferry. Later, George Washington, impressed by the driving force of the waters and their particular suitability for the treatment of iron, set up the government arms factory and even bought the mountains of Bolivar and Loudon, so that he could group all the necessary installations together in the same place.

From the heights of Maryland, on the far side of the Potomac, the view extends almost to infinity, but when you go down to Harper's Ferry, through the vapors that rise out of the two rivers, the hills rise up like ghosts, and one can sometimes make out the dishevelled silhouette of a pine tree, like a madman dancing in the mist. Down below is the covered railway bridge crossing the Potomac and, on the other side, Harper's Ferry itself, a long road beside the Shenandoah. Here it was that John Brown, arriving from Maryland, carried out his coup. The few federal soldiers guarding the arsenal were bound up, as well as some twenty people who were passing nearby on their way home. A free Black who wanted to cross the bridge and refused to obey John Brown's order to stop was shot — ironically, since his killer was a man who claimed to be freeing the Blacks.

A moment later, the mayor of the town came forward to talk to these unknown attackers who had fallen back into the dark brick building where the steam engine was. He was killed with a single shot. The body remained on the same spot for hours, because no one could come near without drawing deadly fire from John Brown. The barman from the only hotel in the town did however succeed in reaching the dead man, to close his eyes; and, as a reward for his courage, was captured by the men who were holed up in the arsenal.

At dawn, a small group, sent by John Brown into the surrounding plantations to rouse the slaves, returned with hostages: Colonel Lewis Washington and fourteen of his Blacks. The latter were regarded as prisoners by Brown since they refused to take up arms in the cause of what he described as liberty. To his amazement, Colonel Lewis Washington saw that his attackers had stolen a family relic from his house: the sword that had belonged to his ancestor, George Washington. They had given it to Brown who did not hesitate to attach it to his own belt.

The town awoke to thick fog. No one knew who the invaders were who had already killed two people, so all the inhabitants, men and women, armed themselves to set the soldiers and hostages free. At this point Brown realized that he had not made provision for food for himself and his men. After some discussion, he agreed to let the barman out to find enough to feed at least fifty people. He had an hour, or the hostages would die.

Who exactly was this John Brown, already known for his bloodthirsty career in Kansas? A man sick in mind and body. His mother had died insane, as had his maternal grandmother, and — something which might have been thought a sinister joke — one of his aunts, five of his cousins and two of his sons had died, or would die in the asylum.

His own madness took the form of religious fanaticism. A tall thin man with sharp lips, he called himself the instrument of God. Twice married, he had twenty children whom he was incapable of bringing up, but he enlisted some of his boys in his band of killers. He was a sadist; and yet, before killing, as afterwards, he read psalms aloud to his followers, in an over-excited voice. Music made him weep.

The idea arose in this tragically deranged mind that he alone could free all slaves. He dreamed of arming them and, helped by the abolitionists in the North, setting up military forts defended by Blacks in the mountains of Virginia.

For some months, he retired to Canada. There, he had another idea: an independent Black state, south of Washington, with himself as its president. To this end, he assembled a convention of fifteen Whites and thirty-four escaped slaves. They drew up a Constitution and formed a government of five members. Wendell Phillips, a fanatical and well-intentioned millionaire, Gerrit Smith and a few other wealthy and honorable citizens, whose families had grown rich in the slave trade, granted him $3,800. A few anti-slavery campaigners were suspicious of him: the famous Garrison, a recognized agitator in the North, knocked the ash out of his pipe and said: 'No'. Other influential figures refused, purely and simply. With the money he had accumulated, Brown hid in an abandoned farm eight miles from Harper's Ferry, but on the other side of the river in the State of Maryland, to spy out comings and goings and prepare for his attack. He assembled his troops in this abandoned spot and paid an old mercenary soldier of the Federal Army to train his men.

Finally, on the night of October 16, the pitiful idiot crossed the Potomac into the South.

Meanwhile, in the arsenal, in exchange for ham and eggs for fifty hungry people, the barman was granted his freedom.

Hours passed. At midday, the inhabitants of the little town and its environs competely surrounded the building and shots rang out from all directions. Two of Brown's sons were mortally wounded and four of his men killed. Another of the besieged party managed to reach the river and tried to swim away. His body was riddled with shots by the townspeople, firing from the bridge, and was carried away on the current.

When evening fell on the 17th, Brown realized that the Blacks would not rise up. This was demonstrated by Colonel Washington's slaves, who announced to him that they were very happy with their master. The latter, sitting with arms folded on a fire hose, was consumed by a furious rage.

At dawn, a party of marines arrived, led by Commandant Green under the orders of Colonel Robert E. Lee. He had been personally chosen by the Secretary of State for War and immediately sent to Harper's Ferry by General Scott, commander in chief of the Army. There followed a night of waiting, wrapped in fog. At first light, a courier appeared in front of the arsenal, carrying a white flag and asking for talks. Brown was told to free the hostages and to give himself up. He refused. Less than an hour later, Colonel Lee blew open the door and the hostages were freed. On the Federal Army side, one soldier was killed. Brown was wounded and lost almost all his men, except three who were arrested with him. The following day they were sent to the prison at Charlestown, Virginia.

A week later, the trial began. They were charged with treason, murder and attempting to cause a rebellion. The trial divided America — not only North from South, but even across the North, where many people condemned this raid against a federal arsenal. Throughout the five days of the trial, the little Virginian town was placed under martial law, while troops were sent from Washington and Richmond to ensure law and order. A host of lawyers came down from the North and correspondents from all the newspapers in America made the courtroom into a battlefield for all the ideologies in the Union.

# 112

*A*t the beginning of November, Billy was surprised to receive a letter from Fred. It was waiting for him at Oglethorpe Square, where he took advantage of one of his more or less regular furloughs to console Elizabeth while keeping an eye on her. Raising his eyebrows in an effort to understand, he read as follows:

Charlestown, Va.
November 1, 1859.

Dear Billy,

We never write, letters not being your forte or mine. We are tending to lose sight of one another, but we are never far. The memory of Dimwood does not fade. I learned that you were in Charleston, in South Carolina, while I, for the time being, am in a place called Charlestown, in the west of Virginia, and I should willingly have exchanged my Charlestown for yours, but nowadays this sleepy little town has suddenly moved into the forefront of the news.

I'm not telling you anything you don't already know. John Brown was judged by the court in Charlestown and condemned to death yesterday. As a captain of cavalry in Colorado, I am among the troops who have been entrusted with keeping order in the town for the duration of martial law, and, as aide de camp to Colonel Lee, I was able to attend the trial. We are some ten miles from Harper's Ferry where the events (about which you know) took place. The newspapers are full of accounts, all more or less exact. No sense in going back over them. After being wounded in the leg during the attack on the arsenal, John Brown was half-laid out on a stretcher transformed into a chaise longue, and bellowed considerably at every sitting of the court. He is not an old man, as the papers say. He is fifty-seven and has the hardest face it has ever fallen to me to see, either in the Army or in civilian life. His features are sharp and his look is remarkably cruel. The first and most lasting impression is of a madman, nothing more nor less. This fact alone pleads strongly both in his favor and against him . . . In the North and in the South, the cruelty he showed during the atrocities at Pottowatomie has left an indelible impression of horror. Yet no one can deny that throughout the three days of the trial, he never lacked courage. On the contrary, he challenged society in a stream of insults and imprecations, but his mental debility is so evident that it gave me pause for reflection.

There is not any doubt that he conspired against the State, that he killed — or rather massacred — quite a few people and that, if one is in favor of the death penalty, he would doubtless have deserved it had he been of normal, balanced mind. But that is not the case. I am sorry for him, and for us, that he was not killed during the fighting at Harper's Ferry, because we now have a homocidal maniac to execute.

I am also sorry that the Federal Government which has accused him and had him arrested did not require that he should be tried in Washington; but the rights of the States had to be respected, and they demand that he should be tried and executed in the one where he carried out his rebellion by seizing a government arsenal.

Like you, I am a son of the South, ready to fight for the rights of the States and the Constitution which guarantees them, and I am dismayed by the fact that, by hanging this imbecile in Virginia, they will supply the anti-slavery lobby in the North with ammunition to make him a hero and, far worse still, a martyr. You see: the name of John Brown will become the rallying cry of all the enemies of the South, and the hypocrisy of the abolitionists will put down its trump card — Morality — which it always keeps up its sleeve. As far as I can see, we should put the man in an asylum, because hanging him is an irreparable mistake from which we shall all suffer.

Just before the trial, Wise, governor of Virginia, went to see him in his cell and tried to get him to talk. Before making his move at Harper's Ferry, John Brown had hidden in an abandoned farm in Maryland. It was searched and there, apart from a certain amount of money, they found documents showing that the madman must have been commissioned by the Northerners. Wendell Phillips was particularly suspected. Wise made great efforts to get Brown to give him the names of his accomplices, but failed — to the prisoner's credit. It goes without saying that the journalists from the North have said nothing about this fruitless interrogation. Too many important people would have been implicated in this matter, which has stirred up the whole abolitionist cause. As for the President, Buchanan has refused categorically to intervene for a pardon, but the agitation has only just begun.

Enough of that. Let's talk about Dimwood. Under the provision which our father has made for the future, you, Mike and I will become the owners of the plantation. I don't know what you intend to do with it. As far as I am concerned, I feel no wish to go back there. Painful memories drive me away — and yet, on some occasions, how much nostalgia I feel for those gardens, those woods, the old house . . . Isn't it strange that in the depths of our hearts we can sometimes long for the places where we have suffered the most? I was the unhappiest of men in that paradise, which haunts me. Don't try to understand. You couldn't; but I wanted to say that to you, without saying it altogether. I hope with all my heart that you will be happy with Elizabeth. You can tell her that Fred wrote to you. It might amuse her.

As far as the war is concerned, we are heading straight for it. You know my views on that matter. Remember the '50s and what I kept yelling about at that time: it was then that we should have attacked and gone for them. We would certainly have won . . . Remember the morning when, at breakfast, we cried: 'Long Live the Secession!' You were yelling it too, very loudly. The moment has gone. We have lost ten years. We are going to fight, and we shall win, but the struggle will be harder.

So long, Billy. You will always be my favorite in the family; and then, since once is not a habit: I hug you.

Fred.

Still in shirt sleeves, with his long legs stretched straight out in front of him, Billy read this letter sitting in an armchair while Elizabeth, in a white robe, was doing her hair and enjoying a pleasure of which she never tired. She heard the soft crackle of the sheets of paper between her husband's fingers and wondered who could have written him such a long letter, because he had not told her anything about it. He had not been quite the same with her since the rather ridiculous scene when he allowed his jealousy to emerge, and then had asked her forgiveness. She felt he was becoming mistrustful, even suspicious, but with the naive guile of a child, he asked her stupid questions, some of which were so close to the mark that they had to be quickly evaded. In any event, she found him still as enthusiastic when it came to fulfilling his conjugal duty. He even endowed it with a quite new kind of fury; she didn't complain of this, but assumed that it was a means of getting her to forgive him more fully.

'It's a letter from Fred,' he said, when he had finished reading. She shivered.

'Oh?' she said, continuing to comb her hair.

'Yes, he goes on endlessly about the trial of John Brown who has been condemned to death. Have you heard about it?'

'A little. Maisie Llewelyn reads the papers and told me something, a day or two ago. He killed a lot of people.'

'That's it, broadly speaking. Fred tells you everything with so much detail . . . We're good writers in the family, but it's a bit long.'

She lifted up her hair to make a chignon at the back of her neck.

'Greetings to all of us, I assume,' she said, with no interest in her voice.

'Vaguely. He talks about Dimwood. Oh, he gets so mixed up there that you realize he must be tired. He must have been falling asleep. You can't understand a word of it. He says himself that he doesn't know what he wants to say. Just listen.'

Elizabeth finished tying her hair and sat in the rocking chair.

Stumbling a little, because Fred's handwriting was less clear toward the end of the letter, Billy read the passage about Dimwood and the contradictory feelings that it aroused. Sometimes Billy would add an irritated comment.

'One moment he's happy, the next he's not . . . My dear brother must have been drinking that evening.'

Elizabeth shut her eyes and felt her hands go cold. These allusions, which were so obvious to her, brought a lump to her throat: 'painful memories . . . the unhappiest of men . . .' And that little phrase at the end, cruelly ironic, like a reproach . . . She swallowed and bit her lips.

Billy burst out laughing.

'He hugs me! He's a good fellow all the same, dear old Fred. But what's wrong, darling? Aren't you well? Look at yourself in the mirror. You're quite white.'

'I'd like to lie down,' she said. 'I'm very tired.'

'It's my fault,' he said, grasping her in his arms; and he carried her to the bed. 'Rest, my love. Last night I was like a madman, you understand? Beyond myself with desire.'

She stroked his face.

'It's fine,' she said. 'It's nothing.'

'Do you feel better?'

'Yes, already. It's nothing, Billy. I'm going to put on my dress and we'll go down. Some tea will do me good.'

Delighted at seeing everything put to rights, Billy got into his dolman and, five minutes later, they both went down to the dining-room.

# 113

*O*n December 2, John Brown was hanged. His companions suffered the same fate a short while afterwards . . . The governor of Virginia had refused to pardon them and President Buchanan had similarly refused to intervene on behalf of a man whom he considered a traitor. On the other hand, the abolitionist press ranted and raged as never before, but public opinion was not with it and some newspapers were even burned in Cincinnati and Chicago, as the northern Democratic Party approved of the execution. In New York, agitation against the abolitionists themselves was so violent that it became likely that even this part of the Union might secede.

Meanwhile, what Fred had predicted in his letter to Billy proved resoundingly correct. Two of the most prominent writers in the North, Emerson and Longfellow, were foolishly hastening to talk of John Brown as a national hero. People forgot the massacres and the plan for an insurgent government hostile to Washington: the madman was becoming a martyr. Voices were raised in protest against this deification, but it was impossible to fight a view that was at once simplistic and striking. It was specious, but it went with the current of History and the enemies of the South, though their judgement was wrong, were calculating correctly.

In Savannah, the event was discussed heatedly. In general, people regretted that the man had not long since been captured and confined to an asylum, or quite simply shot down by mistake. Moreover, there was increasing talk of a conspiracy. The South was unanimous in accusing the whole of the North, without realizing that a small handful of agitators in the North were, like squids, ejecting a cloud of ink over what people really thought.

Journalists became overheated, insults flew, and the Beechers and their followers staged more and more of their carnival productions: fictitious slave sales, sermons in which hell burned with a fire fuelled by the purses of their fellow citizens. In the House of Representatives, in sitting after sitting, they were ready to come to blows once the verbal arsenal had been exhausted. The Congress chamber was almost like a boxing ring.

Christmas came, and once more warlike thoughts were put aside. Buchanan was about to enter the final year of his presidency, and the coming elections were already taking shape. In Savannah, certainly, as in Charleston, they had nothing against the President still in office, whose entourage was mainly composed of Southerners, though they did not take sides openly. On the threshold of 1860, the future yawned.

At Oglethorpe Square, Elizabeth spent Christmas alone with her children. In view of the political situation, the troops had been kept on duty: in Fort Beauregard, Billy suffered from this as much as his wife did; and she, no longer able to endure it, took the risky decision to go and join him. She got Joe to drive her and, one fine January evening, her carriage arrived at the entrance to the fort. Her daring worked to her advantage. At first they did not want to let her pass, so she began to rage as a woman can when deprived of her mate. A young officer appeared at the guard house, gave a cry of surprise and stammered with emotion. It was the young British sub-lieutenant who served as Billy's courier when required. Elizabeth gave him a huge seductive smile.

'I wish to see my husband, Lieutenant Hargrove,' she said imperiously.

The sub-lieutenant saluted and went out. In her carriage, Elizabeth took off her hat, spread her hair across her shoulders and waited, but not for long. A distraught Billy emerged from a doorway and dashed over to the carriage:

'You adorable little goose,' he cried, jumping in beside her. 'What are you thinking of? But I shall arrange everything: the commandant has been informed . . .'

And, almost immediately, he arrived on his bandy legs.

'At your service, Ma'am,' he shouted from a distance.

Elizabeth felt that her cause was won when he came and leaned on the carriage.

'In all my career,' he announced, 'I have never seen standing orders violated in such a reckless manner. But we shall violate them to the end, you and I. Don't try to explain. I understand . . . A beautiful Englishwoman before my eyes, on the arm of one of my officers! Lieutenant Hargrove, come down and present arms to allow Madam's carriage to drive onto the parade ground.'

Jumping down, Billy obeyed. The soldiers of the guard, amazed, did the same, while the team of four horses entered the courtyard, drawing behind them an Elizabeth who was at once full of dread and delight at her incredible rashness. The news of her arrival spread immediately. In less than a minute, the windows of the barracks were full of hussars, then emptied just as quickly. There was a thundering of boots down the stairs, and everyone ran into the courtyard buttoning their dolmans.

It was as though the threat of war had given way to rejoicing. Elizabeth was housed in the apartment reserved for distinguished visitors, usually arrayed with stripes and medals. The commandant gave precise orders:

'All officers are invited to take their places at table where they can admire our charming guest of honor from a respectable distance. The soldiers can gather in the courtyard and will be exceptionally permitted to ogle the windows in an orderly fashion.'

As for Billy, he took him aside and gave him a dressing down in a voice of terrifying severity:

'You, Lieutenant Hargrove, because of your innumerable examples of irregular behavior, I order you to spend the night guarding the lady, this duty to be carried out in her apartment. Understood? Dismiss!'

Since they correctly assumed that the beautiful Englishwoman would be dying of hunger after her ride, a small supper for twenty-five persons was improvised in the mess, while Billy, with zeal beyond the call of duty, was guarding his wife.

Properly dressed, if slightly dishevelled, he appeared with her in the vast refectory where a table had been set up with a white cloth. All the officers and some NCOs were standing, waiting for the couple as if at a wedding feast. Tightly buttoned into their uniforms, they stood as if on parade, but when Billy went past them, they gave a friendly whisper in his ear — always the same:

'You rascal, you have all the luck!'

The menu was simple. The reserves of the fort and those of the commandant had been raided for the sake of Elizabeth's lovely eyes and the amazing golden hair which made all these warriors stare. Six Virginia hams were the main victims, washed down with forty bottles of champagne. Hastily prepared by harassed cooks, delicious corn fritters enlivened as best they could this makeshift supper, in the course of which two dozen officers were continually proposing toasts when they were not devouring the supply of food intended for the week. Pancakes, flambéed in brandy, appeared twenty at a time for dessert, which was completed by a mountain of fruit.

Elizabeth only sipped the champagne, knowing that its effect on her was devastating, but accepted without false modesty the lavish compliments of these soldiers on the appropriate parts of her person: the sapphire of her pupils, the incredible gold-mine of her hair, her alabaster hands, and a little way up the arm, but no further, because the commandant was there to ensure good manners and Billy occasionally turned a ferocious eye this way or that. Though entirely in command of herself, the young woman was enjoying the noisy evidence of her power over the stronger sex. Secretly, she considered herself guilty and vulgar; a shudder of pleasure ran through her at each round of cheers; but she clasped Billy's hand to reassure him and smiled with the condescension of a sovereign.

The banquet ended quite late. Regretfully, they all dispersed and the greedy eyes glued to the windows vanished like extinguished fires. Elizabeth was conducted to her room with the consideration usually shown to a general. Grasping Billy's arm, the commandant dragged him almost by force into a little room next to the mess and there, both of them seated in armchairs, he made a speech appropriate to the size of the place:

'Lieutenant Hargrove, my friend,' he said, 'I am enchanted by this amorous escapade of your wife's. You are young, she is beautiful and you are enjoying it while you can: this is fine, and it amuses me to cooperate to some extent in your happiness, because, make no mistake about it, war is coming; it is at our door. When you go to Charleston, you realize that. Don't say too much to Elizabeth who prefers not to know. As I told you just now, I am giving you four days' freedom. Go where you wish with her, to Charleston — anywhere. You will always find somewhere to stay, but on the morning of the fifth day, I demand your presence here, or else, no more furloughs. And now, one moment. You owe me a return match at whist. This very evening, at once, pronto, we shall settle it at this table. The beautiful woman must wait. We shall not be long.'

He took the cards out of a drawer and the game began. The commandant played with a sort of frenzy as if he wanted not only to have revenge for the defeats he had suffered, but to punish his opponent for the night he was about to enjoy, a delicious night about which he was already dreaming, as were all the men in Fort Beauregard. Impatient to finish as soon as possible, Billy let himself be shamefully overwhelmed and his conqueror, delighted, wished him a good night's rest with only a hint of lewd irony.

They were woken by the bugle. Billy's orderly came in to open the wooden shutters. Dawn flooded the room, bathing everything in rosy light, including the mosquito net which barely hid the untidy bed. At eight o'clock they were back in the carriage and Joe was merrily cracking his whip in the sharp air.

Still somewhat dazed, the travelers watched the pine trees beside the road shake off their coverlets of morning mist; for Elizabeth, the red-walled fort was already no more than a memory. With her ears full of the cheers at supper and the good wishes for their journey which Billy's comrades had heaped on them, the Englishwoman could see in her mind's eye the barracks yard at first light, with men carrying buckets or bustling about at all sorts of other tasks, the stables from which emerged the stamping of hooves and powerful breath pouring out above the open stalls, and, in their little casemates of dark brick, the bronze cannons lined up, overlooking the sea.

They went through forests, passed beneath avenues of palm trees, followed the Broad River estuary to Beaufort where they crossed over on a ferry and then resumed their journey toward Charleston. New forests, new rivers: the Indian river Combahee, with its rust-colored waters; the swifter Edisto; and broad muddy waterways sweeping along treetrunks which still had all their foliage.

On a bare promontory, they stopped briefly to take lunch. At their feet, the forest stretched away in breaking waves, while to the east, on the other side, the sea, stormy gray, seemed motionless.

By the afternoon they were north of Charleston on the main road toward the ocean, but still felt themselves lost in their dreams of the previous night. Elizabeth pressed herself against Billy. Dozing a little, then opening her eyes again, she wondered if the dream was not continuing in this journey through an unknown country, where rows of pines followed one after the other in the silence of a vast solitude. Savannah was vanishing from her memory. She was forgetting everything so as to live entirely in the present, and she felt happy, with an almost animal happiness. Nothing mattered except the man whom she held in one arm, his head in the hollow of her shoulder.

Thinking of him, being near to him, revived in her a sense of repletion that went beyond the yearning of the flesh, and her heart swelled in a love that exceeded the bounds of human language, which frightened her. She felt, briefly, a terror of losing him. At one point she tried to talk to him, saying the first thing that entered her head about the forests and the clouds, just to hear a word, but he hardly answered, astonished that she should admire a landscape in which he could see nothing.

'Do you find that beautiful, darling? It bores me, but you're there, so everything's all right.'
'Perhaps you're sleepy?'
'No, but wait until this evening. In the carriage — do you see . . .?'
'I wasn't thinking of that, Billy.'
He whispered in her ear:
'Joe can hear what we're saying, you understand?'
'Yes, of course.'
To calm her, he stroked her face. She liked that, but put his hand gently aside.

'Behave yourself,' she said mockingly.

Seagulls flew above them, calling, and their wild voices abruptly drew her out of herself. It seemed as though the Elizabeth of the first days in America, with her insecurities and ignorance of life, had come back in some inexplicable way. That was her; and this woman leaning against a young officer, in a carriage, was also her. A rush of common sense told her not to embark on these fantasies. Now she was the wife of the man they called handsome Billy — who was, indeed, a splendid creature. She hoped that he would always remain as he was now. He ate far too much . . . Suppose he were to grow fat. The little voice she sometimes heard asked: Would you still love him? She struggled against the thought, which seemed to her absurd; it was not possible to freeze time, but the present filled her with joy.

'Those gulls, Billy, over there . . . Isn't it magnificent to see them flying in all directions?'

'Dirty creatures,' he said. 'Dirty creatures. There must be some carrion around somewhere. Their call gets on my nerves.'

She began to laugh, then was silent. Something was no longer right in her life. Nothing had changed, yet nothing was the same. Instinctively she held back from discovering what. By simple reasoning one could manage to understand, but one was in danger of reaching dreary conclusions which would cloud the pleasant state of things. Where could she find a more handsome, more ardent man than Billy? 'Or more expert,' the voice whispered. This detail disgusted her and, on a sudden impulse, she squeezed Billy's arm as hard as she could.

'I love you, Billy,' she said.

Startled out of his half-sleep, he turned to her with a surprised look:

'What? What?'

She looked up with eyes full of tenderness.

'I love you, you're my Billy.'

'Of course.' He touched her cheek. 'You must be good and patient. This evening, you see . . .'

'Oh, Billy,' she sighed. 'I'm not always thinking of that.'

'I am,' he replied. 'But I can control myself, darling.'

Seeing that she was put out, he added:

'We shall find an old, almost abandoned plantation where they put up travelers for the night. The commandant pointed it out to me. So, don't worry. We shall be happy.'

Tucking himself into a corner, he nodded off again, his hands along his thighs. What a disconcerting boy, Elizabeth thought, and she too found a corner of the carriage. She had the impression that the hooves on the road were trampling on her marriage. She recalled the morning when Billy had read Fred's letter, mocking what he considered a meaningless jumble, when the sentences, utterly clear to her, tore at her heart. How could he not have understood, the poor hussar, that what he was reading in that mocking voice was a declaration of love to his wife? A desperate declaration, like the cry of a man when a gag is taken off him. And how much intelligent sensitivity there had been in everything Billy had read from that letter! She dreamed of the conversation she might have had with someone of that quality . . . She had received the dagger thrust of memory when once again, deep down, sounded the melancholy serenade of the mocking bird on the tomb of the beloved. Finally, crueller still, the dreadful 'no' she had indicated, shaking her head, when he had simply declared his love for her. Oh, why, why? It was indeed time to ask herself why, now that she belonged to a man who could only see in her a delicious instrument of pleasure . . . But no, she was being unfair; he loved her in his way, with his flesh, and he would have died for her. Fred also said that. That had been Fred's phrase, the last. She always came back to him.

At that moment, behind a pine forest, an immense, blazing red sun appeared. In the midst of hundreds of black trunks, it glowed with all the glory of a motionless fire, and the young woman was so moved by it that she shook Billy's arm.

'Look!' she exclaimed. 'Oh, look, Billy! How wonderful!'

He shook himself and yawned.

'I was fast asleep,' he said. 'Oh, I see. A sign of dry fine weather for tomorrow. In any case, we're nearly there. Joe, follow the pine wood until you come to a crossroads. There is a signpost there. And there you can light the lamps. Night falls fast here. Elizabeth, come close to me.'

She obeyed as she had always done. In the half-darkness, his authoritative hand felt her breast under her fur-lined jacket. She had no intention of moving away.

At the end of the road, Joe lit the two lamps and took a somewhat wider, but rocky road and soon, as darkness fell, they saw lights through the forest. The horses were almost walking. A few minutes more went by, then they could make out a whitish house in the middle of low oak trees with twisted branches, hung with Spanish moss in long, torn, gray veils, the fringes of which were moving in the evening breeze.

A dim lamp lit up the porch and an old black maid showed the travelers into the hall. Almost immediately after that, a gray-haired man appeared. In his worn frock coat, he recalled times gone by, and the impression was confirmed by his rather ceremonious manners.

'Welcome,' he said. 'We shall be dining in an hour, but expect a very frugal repast.'

Elizabeth and Billy assured him that they wanted nothing more.

'Ada will show you to your room,' the old gentleman continued.

He clapped his hands and the black servant returned. The travelers followed her to the top of a steep staircase. In her hand she had a little oil lamp and she guided them to the end of a corridor where she opened a door.

As soon as they glanced inside the room, they both had the same thought: 'Let's leave!' But at the same time, without saying it, they were reluctant to hurt the old gentleman who had greeted them and so they indicated that the room was suitable. The lamp was set down on a table and the black woman went out, apparently quite at home in the darkness into which she disappeared.

Large and empty, the room had no amenities except a wide and battered bed. A muslin cloth, torn in places, served as a mosquito net. In one corner of the room, a basin and a large jug of water were provided for all their toilet needs. The only window was protected from daylight by shutters missing some of their slats.

'We might as well take it all with a laugh,' said Elizabeth, merrily. 'It's a refuge for the night.'

'Tomorrow we can go to our cousins in Charleston,' Billy said. 'There you will find luxury and one of the finest tables in the South.'

Suddenly hurling themselves at each other, they clung together, standing up, while on the wall, the lamp cast fantastic shadows of their two imprisoned bodies.

As their host had announced, the dinner was simple . . . Some country bread dunked in a thick soup dampened their hunger, while they waited for slices of ham with salad. A plain apple was their dessert and the water, which they were told came from a nearby spring, flowed freely from a tin jug. The gentleman with the gray hair presided over the meal and, at the beginning as well as the end, said the usual old-fashioned grace: he did so with a simple elegance that Elizabeth found touching, but which made Billy, who had no time for religion, grit his teeth in irritation. His commandant had told him that the plantation had once been prosperous but had fallen into ruin twenty years ago, leaving only traces of its past glory. He could see none of these, while Elizabeth noticed, on the dilapidated dining-room walls, some fine mouldings in the style of the preceding century, before the Revolution of '76. She said nothing, but the gray eyes of the old gentleman followed her sharp look and a fine, melancholy smile thanked her without a word.

The night was spent as it always was. Commonplace and frenzied, it differed from all the rest only because the bed collapsed.

They left early.

The gardens of the plantation, once renowned for the richness of their colors, were abandoned. The old black woman had shown Joe the avenue that he should follow to go there. The dark foliage of the oak trees met above their heads, giving them the illusion of passing down the center aisle of a basilica hung with tattered flags. Suddenly the vault above them vanished and they were traveling between two walls of yellow and red azaleas which the morning light seemed to be offering them. Joe had slowed the team to walking pace. Next came crumbling masses of gardenias leaping out of the dark foliage, stunning them with their scent, at once fresh and undisguised. Finally they stopped in a clearing beside a pond. A few planks formed a landing stage where flat-bottomed boats were moored, trapped among the water-lillies. Billy jumped down from the carriage.

'Let's go for a row!'

At first they were proceding along a passage in the water between banks of flowers, Sometimes Billy pushed them back with his oar, because they almost blocked the way . . . At last they stopped beneath some gigantic cypress trees which looked as if they were bathing in ink.

A light mist hung over the surface of the dark lake. The boat moved forward slowly, its wake vanishing almost at once beneath the high columns of the trees. Behind the heavy curtains of white vapor shone a sickly sun. The motionless air stifled the fearful cry of distant birds and the waters shone darkly beside monstrous roots which they did not reflect. Overloaded with rags of blackened moss and greenish lichens, a tree extended its titanic arm across the marsh, from which rose a stench of death. Nothing moved. It had been many years since any canoe had cut through this decaying water, or any human word had broken the silence of this place, which had doubtless been forever awaiting the murder for which it vainly supplied the setting, because horror lurked above the obsidian surface of these waters. The swamp seemed intent on suffocating and strangling creepers hung uselessly along a few of the branches. In this corner of jungle inhabited by a nightmare, nature, patient as an Indian, was waiting for the White man, its old enemy.

After a while, without saying a word, they turned back. The journey was not an easy one. The silence around them seemed to be full of secret menace, when suddenly they heard once more the cries of birds in the far distance. The last roots, twisted in motionless violence, vanished beneath the calm fan of the ferns, then, like a sudden smile, they were greeted by a mass of white camellias and roses.

'There,' Billy said, when they were once more on the road. 'You've seen one of the curiosities of the place. The commandant told me not to miss it. What do you think?'

'Well . . . I don't know.'

'Even so . . . Going out of our way just to see that filthy place . . .'

She didn't answer.

'Huh! You'll be more talkative this evening on the pillow. And now, off to Charleston.'

He helped her to get into the carriage and sat close to her. Joe set his team off at a brisk trot. Since it was understood that they would not talk to each other in the carriage, Elizabeth was at leisure to escape into her dreams. The first strokes of the oars had carried her away into a world where everything seemed strangely familiar. Already, six years earlier, on a first journey from Dimwood to Savannah, she had passed briefly not far from a swamp where there were trunks of dead trees floating; and this place, merely glimpsed, had filled her with the sense of a solitude that wrung her heart with fear, yet nonetheless exercised an invincible fascination for her. Souligou, the dressmaker who was a devotee of sorcery, had told her that she possessed what she vaguely called 'gifts'. Elizabeth preferred not to have any more precise information on the point, because it frightened her, and in the boat, just now, she had thought of it, there where the sound of birdsong had died. In the center of the swamp, life was engulfed by a silence of indescribable depth. Billy had gone across without being at all aware of it, but she was seized by panic and had to hold on to avoid falling off her seat. Without moving, she endured the horror of complicity with the invisible and, once back on dry land, she had breathed a sigh of relief.

Bewitched by this bizarre interior journey, she had not noticed the palm trees lining the road or the masses of poinsettias and camellias in the gardens of the houses — quite small gardens around properties that were moving closer and closer together. Toward one o'clock, they were passing through the outskirts and into the town. 'Sweet watermelons, sweet watermelons . . . crab fish, crab fish . . .' The soft voices of the black fishmongers and sellers of watermelons rose from all sides, taking her out of herself with a reminder of Savannah, but soon this kind of chant, at once joyful and plaintive, stopped dead. The heavy sound of hooves on paved streets rang through the silence. Before Elizabeth's eyes there rose magnificent dwellings with superimposed verandas decorated with white columns. No house was contiguous with its neighbors: one might have thought that they were ever so slightly cold-shouldering one another. Giant sycamores shaded the avenue, but not the gardens. The gardens extended behind the walls and the sugary scent of magnolias was carried along on a breeze wafting in from the sea.

This was Charleston.

# 7

# THE RED WING

# 114

*N*ine o'clock in the evening. In the round room where the shaded gaslights cast a soft, golden light on the ceiling and the peach-colored walls, nine people are sitting around a table, all talking animatedly in a conversation punctuated by bursts of laughter and exclamations. Crystal decanters circulate from one end to the other of the white surface on which the family silver is shining. Glasses are filled and miraculously emptied. Hilda is shaking her black ringlets: the heat of the discussion has caused her to rise halfway up on her chair to make herself heard. A siblings' squabble is taking place with her sister Minnie, whose auburn tresses make her pale and delicate face more slender.

'Susanna is obstinate,' she said. 'She doesn't want to move from Dimwood. She'd be a lot happier here, with us.'

'You know nothing at all about it. She confided in me. She has the right to live as she pleases.'

'No, she's wrong,' Minnie cried. 'If she were here, this evening, the whole family would be at Dimwood, apart from the parents.'

'And Fred,' Mildred snapped, her blond curls flapping. 'If he was here, we should already have seceded instead of marking time over politics.'

'I'm on Fred's side,' Billy roared. 'Since '50 he's been saying that we should go for them. We've lost ten years.'

'Does Fred say that?' yapped Mike, in a high-pitched voice. 'They say the same thing in the fortress: go for them with bayonets, but it's not too late.'

A dull, hoarse voice rose above the hubbub. It was Minnie's husband.

'Better late than never, if we go at once,' he said. 'The South is strong enough to sweep away that hybrid bunch of shopkeepers who think they are a nation.'

'Oh, Antonin, how well you speak,' said Minnie. 'If Fred could hear you . . .'

'He wrote me a letter,' Billy interrupted, taking on an air of importance. 'A letter of at least eight pages . . .'

'To you?'

The incredulous voice is that of Lawrence Turner, a heavy drinker who is sitting more and more upright and articulating more and more clearly as he imbibes his white wine.

'Without wishing to offend anyone,' he went on, 'I wonder what he could have to say to you.'

'It's none of your business,' Billy answered. 'Except his account of the trial of John Brown after Harper's Ferry, which is everyone's business.'

'No longer, Billy,' Lawrence retorted sharply. 'That's already ancient history; he was hanged in December.'

'Unfortunately,' said Antonin de Siverac. 'The North dug him up and mummified him into a hero. That's one corpse that has a long life in front of it.'

'What was our Fred doing at Harper's Ferry?' Hilda asked.

'Aide de camp to Colonel Lee.'

'Colonel Lee,' Millie exclaimed. 'Someone had to say it. Billy . . . do you realize?'

A great shout from all round the table.

'Lee! Let's drink to Colonel Lee!'

Everyone leapt to their feet and glasses were raised in outstretched hands. A great 'hurrah'! made the black servants shudder and flee the room.

'In college, everyone loves him,' Mike shouted, spilling half his glass over Elizabeth, who was trying to sit down beside him.

She laughed as she wiped herself and stood up feeling perplexed, because she was not following at all and the name 'Lee' meant nothing to her. Since the start of dinner, she had been dreaming, happy to be beside Mike. He filled a glass, held it out to her and whispered:

'Shout hurrah for Colonel Lee!'

She cried hurrah, and put down her glass, which had barely touched her lips. She thought of the camellias around the marsh where the silence deadened the song of the birds. Her mind was wandering.

'All the officers at Beauregard are for the South,' Billy thundered. 'And at Beaufort and Pinckney.'

'Lee is wholly for us,' cried Mike. 'And all the officers. What are we waiting for to secede?'

'Long live Secession!' Lawrence said distinctly, leaning with all his weight on Minnie to avoid collapsing.

'You're shouting so loudly that you will be heard in the street,' Antonin de Siverac cried.

'So what?'said Hilda. 'Do you think Charleston is not shouting just as loudly?'

'Lawrence, that's enough, if you don't want a slap. Do you take me for a piece of furniture? Sit down, you're drunk.'

Minnie forced him to sit down, and the noise abated somewhat.

'Lawrence, pull yourself together,' said Antonin de Siverac. 'You are the only one of us here who knows Colonel Lee, and all you can do is shout: "Long live Secession!" You must have more to tell us.'

'I've seen him, too,' Hilda cried, getting up. 'Lawrence took me three times to Virginia, to his uncle's at Kinloch in his old house in

Fauquier County where the Colonel goes to rest.'

'Yes, Kinloch,' Lawrence murmured, his furred tongue struggling to get round the words. 'Up there in the hills, far from everywhere . . . Huge trees . . . all round . . . '

'Enough,' said Siverac. 'We've understood. And the Colonel?'

'A splendid man,' Hilda said, emphatically. 'Tall, very handsome, clear eyed and always very calm.'

'Calm?' Mike interrupted. 'Are you sure?'

'Yes, yes,' said Lawrence. 'He talks softly.'

'Very well-mannered,' Hilda went on. 'Very serious. He reads . . . a lot.'

'His horse, Traveler . . .,' Lawrence tried to say.

'Oh, yes! He goes riding in the woods on Traveler, his friend — he calls him his friend . . . He doesn't want to hear about Texas. You only have to look at him to love him: everyone loves him over there; he smiles and you have the impression he's telling you all sorts of things.'

'Your wife's in love with the Colonel,' Siverac remarked.

'She's like everyone else,' Lawrence said, emerging from his inner fog. 'He's one of those men who say practically nothing, yet one would die for them.'

'That's right!' Mike shouted. 'The officers say the same.'

'So, he's for Secession!' William Hampton cried, standing up suddenly.

'He never mentions it,' said Lawrence. 'In Virginia, people are much calmer than here.'

Mildred exclaimed triumphantly:

'His family is fabulously old.'

'Not so fabulous as that,' Lawrence Turner said, correcting her. 'His ancestors fought beside King Harold against the Normans.'

'Hastings, 1066,' Mike trumpeted.

To everyone's suprise, Elizabeth spoke up, with a hint of irony:

'Charlie Jones's were there, too, in 1066. Everyone claims to have defended King Harold. What a bunch of aristocrats . . .'

'You're laughing at us!' Mildred said, standing up, as aggressive as her husband, William, the handsome, bad-tempered blond.

'Not at all. I've been told the same about my own family, but I don't believe it. There's no proof.'

'Where Lee's concerned, there's ample proof,' Lawrence Turner said. 'But he doesn't want to know about it. I heard him say myself that he was not interested in ancestors and that he was bored by genealogy.'

'He really is unlike anyone else!' William Hampton exclaimed.

'Yes,' said Hilda. 'And that's why they like him. He's a great man. One doesn't want to argue with him: he silences you with a smile.'

'But one never knows what he thinks,' said Lawrence, now quite sober. 'Even though I'm a relative, he doesn't confide in me.'

'What does that matter?' William Hampton said, aggressively. 'He's the South itself.'

'So, one more toast for Colonel Lee!' shouted Mike, climbing up on his chair.

In his blue uniform, his hair tousled, he waved his arms toward the ceiling, the picture of youthful enthusiasm. The air was pitted with champagne corks and the foam spilled out across the table-cloth. With every glass raised high, the evening ended in deafening cries of 'hurrah'!

They went their separate ways regretfully. The house was vast and there were many rooms. The first floor echoed with 'goodnights'.

A few minutes later, in the empty dining-room, the indescribable chaos on the table suggested a battlefield after a bitter struggle of bottles around a red fortress, savagely torn down. Fans lay among wide open cigarette cases.

Now, as cautiously as a couple of mice, two old black servants in gray jackets appeared . . . Without a word, they grasped the bottles, some lying on their sides, half-empty, and drank directly from them, in silence, with an almost professional ardor, to tidy things up. Then came the turn of the gigantic raspberry cake, devoured in thick slices. This took some time, and nothing could be heard except the busy working of lips and tongues. Not a crumb remained; now came the delicious moment of digestion in the deep armchairs. The delicate odor of cigarettes taken from tarnished silver cases rose through the heavy atmosphere of a great dinner washed down with champagne, and their ideas began to stir, confusedly, in a murmur.

'So, then,' said one of the two graying, curly-haired heads. 'This Secess'n: d'you understan'?'

'Of course,' said the second curly-headed man. 'All de Whites will fight and we'll make our 'scape.'

'You silly ole ting: where you go? Me, not so stupid, stay here, 'cos here, we with the Madams who want eat. You not well off here in de kitchin?'

'Of course. You're right. The Ma'ams are always good to respectable colored folks.'

'If you 'scape, you'll be caught and sent to the plantation. You want to work in the sun on the plantation?'

'What if we go to the North?'

'Oh, there, you goin' to the Devil. They make you work in a fact'ry and that's hell . . .'

'I'm too old for fact'ry.'

'Come, don't be a fool. You stay here. Nothing happen to you here . . . Now, we mus' clear the table, so that everything clean and nice for tomorrow mornin'.'

'Of course, Hilda would be mad.'

'You mustn't say Hilda; say "mistress".'

'Oh, between us: no one can hear us!'

'Well, well, hark at you! So: for Hilda, for Hilda.'

'For Hilda!' echoed the second curly head in reply.

Both of them began to clear the table and the room soon returned to normal, but the gray-headed man who dreamed of fleeing, suggested opening a window to let in the fresh air. As they did so, they saw black birds with outstretched wings flying between the houses and both men cried out:

'Bustards! Close the windows, quick!'

They were overcome by superstitious fear of these scavengers: to them, these sinister birds were the servants of death, precursors of disaster. They quickly extinguished the lamps and vanished into the darkness.

The same guests gathered for lunch the next day, but the meal promised to be a lot less animated. Echoes of their secessionist clamor secretly induced a sense of discomfort, except within Mike and Billy, who were always ready to bellow.

In daylight once more, the room lost the slightly theatrical appearance that the gaslights had given it and suggested someone who had calmed down after a regrettable nervous outburst. Its charm came from an elegant simplicity in the choice of its English furnishings. Huge bunches of multi-colored flowers on the console tables added to the happy tranquillity that reigned between these walls.

The conversation began with a promising lack of excitement and took a long time to get started. They talked rather vaguely of the Conventions which were due to be held in the Spring and about the respective candidates of the Democratic and Republican parties for the presidential election. Lawrence Turner made some disparaging remark about President Buchanan, who would not be missed in the South:

'It's not enough to be a pleasant gentleman to rule a country, and Buchanan's wavering was dangerous.'

Not a single voice was raised to defend the incumbent president, and the crayfish were pronounced delicious.

'Isn't it odd,' Lawrence Turner went on, 'to think that today, like a forewarning, the invisible man on whom all our fates will depend in a year's time is already sitting in the presidential chair?'

'We haven't reached the point of electing ghosts,' Siverac remarked. 'But there are several names floating around, even though the Conventions only take place in April: Douglas for the South, Seward for the North, but neither of them . . .'

William Hampton's slightly irritated voice broke in:

'Douglas has already been rejected by the South. He betrayed us in the Kansas business. And as for Seward, even the North is suspicious of him. He's an unregenerate warmonger, he wants war, he wants, quite simply, to crush us.'

'Even so, that rascal Seward has some chance,' Antonin said. 'He has Wendell Phillips and company behind him, and money.'

'What we need is a man like Toombs,' said Lawrence. 'Toombs is a thunderer. He would be the herald of the South. Imagine him coming out with one of his favorite statements: "Slavery — we'll solve that problem ourselves. Let the North concern itself with the slaves in its factories!"'

'Bravo!' Mike shouted. 'I'm for Toombs!'

This declaration was greeted with laughter.

'Even if he did run,' Lawrence Turner said, 'it would not be easy to win. Douglas is surrounded by his own people, whom he has bought, and some of them are powerful.'

There was a break in the conversation while they brought in a sturgeon stuffed with mushrooms. This marine creature was of impressive size, and greedy murmurs of admiration greeted its appearance. There were the pistol shots from champagne bottles, without which there can be no festivity. Everything was tasted in that meditative semi-silence well known to gourmets. Politics eased its way back when the plates where empty. Antonin de Siverac remarked:

'Perhaps the most interesting of today's political figures is someone we haven't mentioned: the redoubtable Abraham Lincoln, who is not a candidate.'

'Even if he was for us, I wouldn't find him too appealing. There were photographs of him at the time of his battle with Douglas.'

'He's not for us, certainly,' Siverac said. 'But he does come from the South, from Kentucky, and is proud of it, apparently. As for his defeat in his debate with Douglas, he thinks that it was a success; it earned him all the Republican votes.'

'He's a lawyer,' Lawrence said. 'One of the most formidable.'

'A Republican, and so an abolitionist,' observed Hilda.

'So many contradictory things have been said about him,' Lawrence went on. 'You make me want to read you some lines from a speech. Excuse me, I kept the cutting in my desk. I'll go up and get it. I won't be a minute.'

He left them at once.

'How your husband loves politics!' Minnie said.

'You don't know how much. And Lincoln interests him especially, I can't think why.'

'Oh, that lanky, badly dressed, vulgar fellow . . .'

Mildred broke in to sketch in the portrait of the mysterious Republican.

'They say that, at home in Illinois, he amuses his lawyer friends by imitating a preacher in full flow: he puts on a nasal voice, rolls his eyes, reaches out his hands and talks nonsense in a pious voice . . . a perfect Beecher!'

She was about to continue when Lawrence reappeared, holding a sheet of paper. He adopted an orator's voice:

'Here we are. This is a speech he made in Charleston, Illinois, in '58: "I am not now, nor have I ever been, in any way a supporter of the social and political equality of the white and black races . . . There is a physical difference between them that means they can never live together in social and political equality. There is naturally a situation of superior and inferior and I am inclined to ascribe the position of superiority to the white race."'

'An amazing declaration on the part of a Republican,' William Hampton said. 'We were told he was an abolitionist.'

'But he doesn't say he is hostile to the Blacks,' Lawrence said. 'He's just against equality for the two races.'

'Meanwhile, here's the mud pie,' Hilda announced.

The mud pie was smooth and dry on the outside, but dissolved into flakes of delicious chocolate at the first touch of the spoon. It was eaten in silence and followed by a burning hot coffee in the New Orleans style.

Everyone was in good humor. The discussion had been less violent than the evening before, but no less interesting. All politicians seemed interchangeable and the young people felt secretly powerless against this wave of dangerous and useless information.


Around four o'clock they dispersed, each free to spend the time as they chose. Lawrence Turner announced that he would go to his architect's office near Broad Street.

'I'll join you,' said Willam Hampton. 'I'd like to talk a little.'

'I warn you, we're going on foot. After a luncheon like that . . .'

'Fine.'

As soon as they were outside, they once more exchanged some words on the political situation.

'One can never tell the whole truth when there are ladies present. They get carried away at once. If it were up to them, we'd have been at war long ago. All the time you feel that it's getting nearer and then receding again.'

'Believe me, it would be a great relief to see it break out,' said Hampton. 'Nothing is more paralyzing than uncertainty; but enough of that. I thought Elizabeth's attitude throughout the luncheon was odd.'

With his hands clasped behind his back, he turned an emotional pale face toward his companion. Turner, calmer, gave him an amused look.

'As long as I've known her, she's been odd, as you call it, but I should say I've seen little of her, only on the day of my wedding in Dimwood. She has silences that are unlike those of a woman: is that what you mean?'

'I agree about the silences, but her outburst against the nobility . . . I almost said something.'

'You couldn't because she included herself. She's not stupid.'

They were walking slowly beneath the sycamores, and the sunlight scattered pale gold reflections on their dark blue frock coats.

'I don't know about that,' said Hampton, with a trace of impatience. 'But I find her mysterious.'

'Mysterious is the right word. I don't know if she thinks a lot, but she does daydream.'

'What of? I have my own ideas, but perhaps it would be wiser to keep them to myself.'

'William, we know one another too well to play polite games. Tell me what you think.'

Hampton's face suddenly took on an appearance of extreme displeasure:

'If you will permit me to say so, she looks at her husband with . . . well, with a kind of greed.'

Turner burst out laughing.

'So what? If anyone has the right, she has!'

'I don't deny that, but one shouldn't behave like that in company.'

'William,' Lawrence said with a smile, 'you're not in love with her.'

'Heavens above! I saw her yesterday for the first time . . . I'm quite indifferent to her.'

'All right, all right. Don't you find her, let's say . . . pretty?'

The question drove Hampton to the brink of exasperation.

'What's that got to do with it?' he said, crossly. 'She behaves badly that's all.'

'She's my guest, under my roof,' said Lawrence, who pretended innocence to tease him still further.

'She's not my guest, any more than her husband is with those overweening airs.'

'It's the husband's turn, is it now?' said Lawrence, with gentle irony.

Hampton stopped dead and looked directly into Turner's face.

'Lawrence,' he said, 'I'm afraid you don't understand at all.'

'Yes, I do, William. Elizabeth is well-known for the irritating effect she has on some men. I've experienced it myself. Believe me, you soon get over it.'

Hampton shrugged his shoulders.

'What can I have to get over?' he said brusquely.

Then he suddenly exclaimed:

'Let's forget this foolish talk, Lawrence. Here we are in Broad Street. I'll leave you. I have only to thank you for your fascinating hospitality. I'm staying at home this evening with my wife.'

Grasping Turner's hand, he pressed it strongly.

'Friendship above all,' he said. 'Don't pay any attention to my momentary irritations. Goodbye.'

He swung round on his heels, crossed the street and strode off. Turner watched him go.

'Bitten,' he thought. 'Like all of us, one after the other. That little English woman spares no heart, though she doesn't even realize it. I shall be relieved to see the back of her, much as I shall miss her.'

He sighed. Broad Street restored his good humor. This great street full of bustle restored him to a humanity that had no mystery. Blacks were running hither and thither on various errands, most of them messengers wearing bright colors — pink, sky blue, green and a gray that was almost white — which drove out melancholy thoughts.

The afternoon sun cut the street in half, and the colors were either glimmering in that golden sheen, or else, by contrast, in the shadow of the trees, momentarily more intense, before vanishing into ashen shadows. The hubbub increased. Banks and shops were plunged in the feverish activity of late afternoon as if to justify the hours of siesta, the scents that danced in the air, the beauty of the town, in short, the joy of being alive . . .

The hours passed quickly, bearing away with them what remained of Billy's furlough. Joe took him back to Beauregard, traveling at night to reach his destination at dawn. Elizabeth decided to stay a bit longer in Charleston as Hilda, taking responsibility for entertaining her, urged her to do.

The fine weather was conducive to any activity: to war, or to celebration. For the time being, it was a case of neither of these, but of the simple happiness of showing the Englishwoman some of the town, which prided itself on being the loveliest in the South.

A carriage ride to the Battery seemed essential. At the meeting-place of two rivers, the Ashley and the Cooper, the walk along the boulevard culminated in gardens celebrated throughout the whole country: White Point Gardens. It was here that, on the terraces overlooking the port, people came on warm evenings by moonlight to hear the boys playing the guitar and watch the glimmering surface of the water. Here, too, at dawn, the vultures settled before picking the streets clean. Oak trees, with monstrously thick trunks, gave ample shelter on hot days and contrasted with the youthful curves of the palm trees that greeted the sun in the bay. Everywhere, myrtle, jasmin . . . masses of flowers with provocative scents were crammed along the borders of the footpaths. Hilda knew every corner of these enchanting gardens and chose an itinerary that would take them to the place where one could see the full extent of the estuary, the port and the whole bay, its strategic importance obvious even to Elizabeth's innocent eyes. In the middle of it, she could see what looked like a long dark red vessel with a dozen square openings in its sides. A the end of this strange boat was what she assumed was a wheelhouse.

'Fort Sumter,' Hilda said. 'Whoever holds that fort holds the South. At the slightest emergency, a cannon will emerge from each of those openings. There is no more deadly a fort in all America — which is why the federal government is solidly ensconced there.'

She said these words in a firm tone which made her into a Hilda whom Elizabeth did not recognize, all the more so since this military speech was accompanied by precise gestures, her index finger pointing toward different parts of the bay.

'This is not the only fort. There are three more, each almost as fearsome: Moultrie, Johnson and Pinckney, without counting the fortress and the arsenal.'

'Are they in the hands of the North or the South?' Elizabeth asked.

'Let's say, in the hands of the government.'

The young Englishwoman understood nothing, but kept quiet. There was a long silence which allowed them to hear the trilling of a bird in the oak trees. The ocean breeze carried this tiny voice, which sometimes stopped, then resumed a little further on.

'Do you ever think of Dimwood?' Elizabeth asked.

As if roused from a meditation, Hilda turned round abruptly:

'Often,' she said. 'It was one of the good moments in my life . . . Adolescence . . . The evening of your arrival with your mother . . . We all loved you straight away. You brought a breath of fresh air . . .'

'I was a little frightened, but you were all kind to me: you, Mildred, Susanna. Do you remember the little paradise hidden in the wild garden . . .'

'The hidden paradise?'

'Yes, near those giant ferns and the forbidden corner where the Indians slept . . .'

'Yes, vaguely. It's all so long ago. We hardly ever go there now.'

Elizabeth began to laugh merrily.

'And our lace pantaloons which we had to show off, but I didn't dare.'

'Oh? I don't remember at all, dear. Your memory's better than mine. Why don't we go on a few steps . . .'

They got up and started down the long pathways running around the gardens. The sun was shining full on the thick foliage of the white oaks and, despite the half-light, they sheltered beneath their little parasols. The heavy scents of the flowers followed them and they felt happy.

'You did well to marry Billy,' said Hilda. 'We all knew from the first that he was madly in love with you. It was a secret throughout the family, and we told him to declare himself, but he didn't dare. He was still too young. We were so amused . . . And then you left for Virginia and everything changed . . .'

'Yes, everything changed,' Elizabeth repeated mechanically.

'Now he's as happy as could be. It's plain to see. And are you happy, darling?'

'Oh, yes, very — dear Hilda.'

'You make everyone fall in love. Fred would have liked to marry you, too. Everyone knew, it was obvious, but no one mentioned it.'

Elizabeth blushed.

'Fred?' she said.

'You never realized. We love him, but you made the best choice without realizing it. Fred is so serious. We used to say: "He will be our great man." And then he had that accident which made him become rather melancholy, when he fell out of the window.'

Tears were running down Elizabeth's cheeks.

'What's the matter?' Hilda asked.

'Poor Fred.'

'Yes, of course, you're so sensitive, darling. But he has recovered very well after his operation. He hardly limps now. You have to know about it to notice. They told ridiculous stories, about an attempt at suicide. All that's forgotten. I love to hear him sing, myself. He has a charming voice, a real Southern voice, which one doesn't often hear. Look, from here you can see where the waters of the Ashley and the Cooper meet, all brown and ruffled by the wind. You look tired; do you want to sit down?'

Elizabeth nodded. They took a few more steps until they reached a bench. It was a delightful time of day. The light was becoming softer and the sky on the horizon was growing pink. Naturally a bit of a chatterbox, Hilda talked on affectionately, happy to inform her cousin from England about every detail and little secret of the family's life; but, for a moment, Elizabeth had stopped listening to her. Troubled in her heart and her mind, she was coming to terms with the revelation of an oddly misdirected life: a Jonathan in the shadow of her husband, then Fred, romantic and chivalrous, in the shadow of Billy, whom she could not do without. And Jonathan was under the earth, as was Edward, who had killed him.

'I'm cold,' she said suddenly.

'Cold! Then let's go back, darling.'

# 115

*E*lizabeth did not stay on a day longer in Charleston. Billy was not there and she couldn't stand the sight of their now empty room. She was hugged until she could hardly breathe as the women covered her lovely pink cheeks with kisses. Joe, back from Beaufort, was waiting for her in front of the house. She leaped into the carriage and set off for Savannah.

At first, she could see absolutely nothing new in Oglethorpe Square . . . While she was away, nothing moved, she thought. Out of respect, perhaps. She still had to learn that everything changes, surreptitiously, at every moment.

Miss Llewelyn greeted her in the hall.

'I hope,' she said, 'that I packed everything you needed.'

'Everything. You're perfect, Miss Llewelyn.'

'Yes, Ma'am. That's my job.'

Ned appeared at the door. He was coming in from the garden and crossed to see Elizabeth.

'Hello, Mummy.'

'Is that all?' she said, laughing.

What counted for her was the obvious impulse, the leap forward, in his voice and in his face, lit up with joy; instead she received a calm and well-bred 'hello'.

She gave a sad look.

'My little boy doesn't love me any more,' she said.

At which, with a groan, he threw himself toward her, grasped her arms and forced her to bend down to his face.

'It's not true, Mummy!'

She had the cry she wanted.

The Welshwoman observed this scene with an amused smile.

'You left very early,' she said coolly. 'And you forgot to say goodbye.'

It was the young woman's turn to cry out.

'I didn't want to wake you, darling. You know I love you.'

'Oh, Mummy, of course . . .'

Full of emotion, they sat down on the stairs and clasped hands. The love scene was becoming a little embarrassing. Miss Llewelyn left.

'I'll give orders for your luggage to be taken upstairs.'

And, on her way out, she let fly:

'When you've finished and you can tear yourself away!'

Everything was reverting to normal.

In his blue suit with the long trousers, Ned, now seven-and-a-half, was imperceptibly taking on the look of the young man he would one day become. His mother alone could still make him burst into tears, but his eyes were acquiring a more reflective gaze. Night rides seemed to have gone out of fashion. On the other hand, he had started to read stories about Indians. Betty complained that Massa Ned no longer wanted her to accompany him on his walks. After all, he was as tall as she was now, so how would he look? But the large black eyes watched sadly as Massa Ned set off without her for school, his little hat with the ribbons tipped forward over his nose as fashion demanded among his young contemporaries.

He had not yet told anyone that his grandfather had made him a present of the most astonishing house in Savannah. It had taken him some time to believe in himself, and he had decided that it would be a great secret between him and his grandfather, a secret between men; but that partly helped to explain the cocky angle of the little hat.

Savannah tried to get back to a completely normal way of life and, above all, a peaceful one. It was bad form to talk politics. After the shock the country suffered with Harper's Ferry and the execution of John Brown, calm gradually took over the great Southern town. On the principle that whatever is not mentioned ceases to exist, silence brought peace. Let the North bray if that helped it feel self-righteous.

However, a secret idea was brewing in Charlies Jones's mind. After a visit to New York, where he was constantly obliged to go on business, he returned with a grandiose plan which, at first, he confided to nobody. Around the end of January, and not before, he decided to lay the first foundations of a spectacular rapprochement between some members of Northern and Southern society.

To this end, he invited three of his usual accomplices in his Georgian circle: Mrs Harrison Edwards, Josh Hargrove and Algernon.

There was a conspiratorial atmosphere. The three guests were asked to arrive at ten o'clock in the evening at the side entrance to the Tudor house which, apart from Ned, had not so far had any visitors. Of course, they were sworn to the utmost secrecy. It was a dark night. Charlie Jones stood at the door which opened into the passage between the dining-room and the kitchens. He was alone in the empty house. All the servants had the day off until the following morning.

From their first steps into the huge house — as yet quite new to them — the guests sensed a mood of mystery that promised a magical evening. Five or six burning torches lit a huge open space in which marble statues gleamed, seeming to watch over the silence. Deliberately obscure, this light shone dimly, on the right and the left, on rooms which in their vastness were plunged into utter darkness.

The guests' reactions varied. Mrs Harrison Edwards gave a great cry which left no need for words, while Algernon swooned at the sight of the Greco-Roman nudes. Josh, after a short silence, declared:

'My dear Charlie, it's an undeniable success. My compliments.'

'Ah, old chap, this house is a long way from my dreams; but who has ever solved the problem of the unattainable ideal . . .'

'Don't be too modest, Charlie. It's really not bad.'

'Perfect. Now, my dear friends, let's get down to business: are you hungry?'

Polite silence. They were all expecting a fine supper.

'I understand,' said Charlie Jones. 'Please follow me.'

He took them to a room which they had not noticed before and which struck them by its modest size. An oval table and six heavily ornate chairs occupied the whole center of it. This made it hard for servants to pass behind the diners, but this evening the problem did not arise. Everything was ready. An impressive venison pâté, oysters, puddings, meringues, fruit and, in a decanter, a ruby-colored wine. The guests immediately set about helping these choice delicacies disappear and their enthusiasm reduced them more or less to silence, which allowed Charlie Jones, above the clinking of forks, to explain his plans:

'Dear friends, what a pleasure to see you so generously partaking of this little improvised snack . . . I would not spoil your appetite for anything in the world by reminding you that war is not altogether unlikely. We must prevent it. We must say 'no' to it. Here is my plan: next April, this house will be opened officially and, that very same evening, there will be a reception of a kind that Savannah has not seen since the last century. As it involves public figures, I have already sent the invitations and had some formal acceptances. You may perhaps be struck by a few of the names: among those who will certainly come are Mr Breckinridge, our Vice-President, and Lord Lyons, the British Ambassador. My friend Jefferson Davis is also invited, naturally.'

'Now, there's someone,' said Algernon. 'Have you seen how he defends our rights in his speeches to the Senate . . .?'

'Ferociously,' said Mrs Harrison Edwards, digging her fork into an oyster.

'I might mention that he is fanatically in favor of the Union,' said Uncle Charlie.

'It's hard to reconcile that,' said Josh. 'Everyone is for the Union, and everyone is against it. Only a few fanatics in the North demand the separation of the States as quickly as possible. You saw what Greeley is writing in New York.'

'On the subject of New York,' said Charlie Jones, interrupting, 'I have a story. But first, let me recommend this Château Yquem with the pâté . . . Lucile, may I? It's a bit of a change from the usual champagne, don't you think?'

'Oh, Charlie!' she said. 'You know about everything . . . Cooking, politics — and isn't it the same thing? Quickly, tell us your story. We can't wait.'

'I've just come back from New York. It's freezing cold there, but the theaters are full. Do you know what one of the most popular plays is?'

No one answered, so he carried on, knowing he would impress them:

'A play based on the novel by the Beecher woman, with her blessing. Of course, I went to see it.'

There was general exclamation.

'Oh!' Mrs Harrison Edwards cried. 'It must make those simple souls weep.'

'Simple souls? In New York?' Algernon said sarcastically.

'Algernon, you're impossible!' said Charlie Jones. 'You're sabotaging my story.'

'Sorry,' said Algernon. 'Shut up, Algie!'

'On the stage,' the narrator went on, 'the black extras kept on giggling. At the end of the first act, the curtain fell and you could hear the director of the company shouting: "You swine, if you carry on like that, I'll have you properly whipped on the stage and you can weep real tears: it'll be in the play!"'

'Splendid!' said Mrs Harrison Edwards.

'I always said there were slaves in the North,' Algernon remarked.

'That's not all,' Charlie Jones went on, exasperated by these interruptions. 'The play continues. The Blacks showed the whites of their eyes and pretended to be scared, and the pitiless New York audience latched on to every line. They had to send the play off on tour in the towns of the North. But the fact remains that this woman's rantings are doing a great deal of harm.'

'And what about the Indians?' Josh asked.

'Leave the Indians for the moment, Josh. Do you know what they're saying in New York? "There are three kinds of human beings: saints, sinners and Beechers."'

The Bohemian crystal glasses were raised at once.

'Cheers!' they all said, together.

As for Charlie Jones, who had become serious again, he took a sheet of paper out of his pocket, so that he could let his guests know the list of those he had invited.

'Toombs!' he said.

'The dear man!' exclaimed Mrs Harrison Edwards.

'The heart of the South,' Algernon announced.

'Yes,' Charlie Jones said. 'The heart of the South: extreme, stentorian, but generous, brave as a lion, wonderfully eloquent, capable of magnificent rages. In short . . . I'll continue: Courtenay of the *Times*. We need good journalists who favor the South, and he is clear and incisive. Then, several proprietors of our own newspapers: the *Mercury*, the *Petersburg Morning News*. And then some people from the North, in particular Simon Cameron of Pennsylvania. I think he's running as a candidate against Seward. Then, Alexander Stephens and Governor Brown, and Julian Hartridge, and everyone who is anyone from Charleston, Augusta and here . . . I might add the Senator for Kentucky, John Crittenden, and some Northern Democrats, plus a surprise . . . and also some businessmen from New York and Philadelphia . . . I want to show them what our South really is in all the magnificence and hospitality. And it will be here, where we are now, the first party to be given in this house . . .'

This rhetorical flourish was drowned in a resounding cry of 'cheers!' and the glasses were emptied.

'I'm counting on you,' he continued. 'Let all Savannah celebrate that evening!'

'I'll have everything lit up,' said Algernon.

'Would you like me to bring some Indians?' asked Josh.

'You will have everything, everything,' Mrs Harrison Edwards promised.

'Of course, not a word about this!' said Uncle Charlie.

'Count on us. We'll be as silent as the tomb,' they answered.

After a last 'cheers!', they crossed the dark, deserted house through the dimly lit hall. Charlie Jones, a torch in his hand, accompanied them to the front door. There they went their separate ways, wishing one another good night softly beneath the moonlight, like real conspirators.

# 116

*I*t was April 30. Charlie Jones wanted a celebration that would exceed all expectations. He had at first seen it as a diplomatic attempt at national reconciliation; then, on reflection, he had eventually persuaded himself that it would be like an apparition of Peace, triumphing over all fears at the decisive moment. Day and night he lived in a grandiose dream that he was working to realize with a dedication that was close to fanaticism. He had no anxieties as to the magnificence of the decor. With all the means at his disposal, he was sure to surpass the unimaginable; but he did have some lingering doubts about the choice of guests. He had taken risks, admittedly carefully calculated ones, as a very experienced financier might do with stocks and shares, but from time to time there were fleeting anxieties. He was not worried about England — Lord Lyons would assist him with all his strength. It was known that Queen Victoria and all the British aristocracy favored the South, which in their eyes remained English — despite the opposition of Prince Albert, a rather narrow-minded fop. There was still hope that the Crown would support the Southern cause; even the majority of the British press was on their side.

Charlie Jones's worries lay just where he was most sensitive to them, because they concerned a long-standing friendship with Jefferson Davis. Neither the man's moral rectitude nor his political opinions were the problem. On February 2, he had just introduced, and had passed in the Senate, very clear bills defining the States' rights, which were entirely consistent with the Constitution. This stand was all the more important since the whole of the South was willing to fight for it. So far everything was clear-cut. It remained to be seen which way Jefferson Davis would go. Charles Jones admired him unreservedly. The Senator from Mississippi was exceptionally cultured and a man of very wide reading. A scholar? Much more than that: an idealistic philosopher whose weakness — this was the point — was that he mistook words for solid facts. Convincing one's opponent with irrefutable arguments seemed to him the guarantee of certain victory. Natural powers of persuasion hid this blind faith in the power of words, and that made it dangerous. The finest moral qualities could not resist this. There was something of the visionary in Jefferson Davis: hence the shadow that hung over the man which tormented his friend, Charlie Jones.

His incurable optimism lifted him out of these dreary thoughts and he set to work. Teams of experienced servants were commanded to transform the house into a palace out of *A Thousand and One Nights*. A light, at once soft and powerful, rained down on the great gallery, bathing the long space in the splendor of dawn. No woman could fail to become more beautiful as soon as she entered here. When one crossed the threshold, one had an indefinite sense of well-being, due in reality to the mysterious lighting of numerous chandeliers which formed a shining vault cunningly filtered by globes barely shaded in pink. The secret of the miracle, which only a few would guess, was gas, then as prestigious as it was novel.

There were so many guests that invitations were required to be shown at the main door. All Savannah was invading the Tudor house — and in a sense all the South and all America. Dressed in silk, taffeta and satin, the ladies appeared, showing astonishing ingenuity to distinguish themselves from one another by some unexpected touch to their hair or their jewelry. Many had their hair done up into a crown with a pearl, coral or diamond tiara on top. A few, slaves to the latest fashion, had arranged their ringlets in such a way as entirely to hide their foreheads — Paris decreed this idiotic, with pitiless irony; but they all gleamed with precious stones on their necks, ears, wrists and throats. Embroidered light scarves hid what was required by decency, but only just. Gloves came right up to the elbow, while generously cut sleeves permitted a friendly glimpse of lovely naked arms. There was a surprising variety in the delicate shades of colors which aroused the admiration of male escorts. Like blackbirds in their coats, they strutted impertinently in this gigantic flower-bed of monstrous ambulant flowers.

A great hubbub arose from the crowd, intoxicated by an almost childish pleasure at being there and being seen at this unique event. Without pausing from their chatter for a second, the ladies surveyed every corner with eyes that missed nothing. Monumental mirrors in heavily gilded frames cast back the reflection of this grand aristocratic parade in which not one of them failed to admire herself in passing. Fanning themselves and confronted by the noble marble nudes, they threw back their heads in an attitude of pleasant surprise combined with amused interest.

Meanwhile, an orchestra in the library was attacking the first bars of a piece that displayed both joy and good taste: Gottschalk's *American Suite* — something that would make hearts beat faster without awaking antagonism. There was a hum of approbation and the guests spread along the large rooms to the right of the gallery where they exclaimed at the splendor of the furnishings. Long sofas and spacious armchairs upholstered in crimson embossed velvet were twisted in astonishingly bold curves. Was this a new fashion, or just Charlie Jones? 'Rich, heavy and entwined' might have summed up his ideal where decoration was concerned. People might smile at this rather naive approach, but it would surprise even the most demanding connoisseurs. The dark purple wood, preferred by this fanatic of ostentatious perfection, was the pretext for numerous twisting wreaths of fruit and flowers in minute detail running up and down the backs, the feet and the arm rests of all the chairs. It could have been grotesque, but was in fact full of charm.

Charlie Jones was standing in the middle of the hall to receive his guests, but flinched slightly at the number of them and eventually slipped away . . . Besides, for socialites as they invaded the Tudor mansion, the main thing was to get inside. The servant announcing the names was hoarse from giving due credit to the best-known names. The important guests had deliberately been invited for later in the day, so that they would be spared the discomforts of the crowd. Charlie Jones awaited them near the library.

The first to arrive was Lord Lyons. He walked straight up to

Charlie Jones with a broad smile. Nothing in him betrayed the professional diplomat, but his distinction was evident in the simplicity of his manners. Slim and tall, he immediately impressed one with his elegance and bearing. What struck you first, in his regular features, was the high forehead and the depth of a direct gaze which could only be avoided by turning one's head. In the midst of this American gathering, he could not have been confused with any other of the guests, so strongly did he personify England. Charlie led him to a corner of the drawing-room where the patriotic outpourings of the orchestra were less audible, and there they immediately tackled the main purpose of the evening.

'Avoiding war at any price?' said Lord Lyons. 'The generosity of such an ideal is in keeping with your taste for grandeur. You see everything in large terms.'

'We are wagering against fate. We cannot afford to lose by being tripped up by details.'

'The Prime Minister's opposition to the South is not a negligible factor.'

'I hate Lord Palmerston.'

'But unfortunately it is he who fashions British policy with the consent of Her Majesty — which means, above all, of Prince Albert, who continues to exercise a decisive, and perhaps fatal influence over her.'

'And what do you think?' asked Charlie Jones, cut to the quick.

'Can you doubt my attachment to the South? But here is something to cheer you. People at home are increasingly talking about Gladstone as the man of tomorrow. He is entirely for the South and he has a strong influence on public opinion.'

'Could it be decisive at a critical moment?'

'Yes, if he has time, and yes, if fate wishes to wait for the fall of Lord Palmerston . . . Have you invited any journalists?'

'Courtenay of the *Times* and several others from London, New York, Florida and here.'

'I shall speak to them. Count on me, Charlie. This evening I came immediately you called. You can be sure it will ever be thus.'

They were taking leave of each other when notable guests arrived; introductions were unnecessary, since all knew one another. As one might expect, Senator Toombs caused a sensation as soon as he came in. All he wanted was to be heard, but the orchestra drowned everyone's voice and made it difficult for him to achieve his rhetorical effects. Already his famous Apollonian physique was starting to get heavier, but he shook his fine head of hair and called out at the young men who had come to greet him:

'We need nobody's good offices to settle our problems in the South. Let those gentlemen from up North stop poking their abolitionist busybody's noses across our borders.'

Charlie Jones hastened to intervene and take Toombs' arm.

'Robert,' he said, 'in heaven's name, you are the voice of the South and we all love you, but this evening we have met here for the sake of peace. Remember Henry Clay: "A Union of Hearts". That's what we are looking for this evening. Try to understand me, Toombs. We must prevent war. Help me.'

By talking to him and looking directly into his eyes, he managed to calm him down.

At the back of the gallery, the guests were besieging one of the largest rooms, the doors of which remained obstinately open, held by two strong black servants who laughed and resisted the pressure. In the middle of this room, with its bright gilding, one could see a monument like a pyramid laden with candied fruit which covered it with a sort of shining, multicovered chasuble. A great number of tables and chairs were set out in front of piles of plates and hundreds of bottles of champagne. Without the slightest restraint, the ladies vied with one another in daring and strength to reach this alluring edifice. In vain did servants in white jackets try to press plates and spoons on them: like furies in frills, they descended on their favorite delicacies and tore them off with such energy that the edifice was pitted with long scratches, revealing its tender depths of marzipan. This patient demolition work ended in a progressively faster collapse which produced general hilarity without spoiling the insatiable harpies' appetite.

The men gallantly joined in this childish female behaviour, and pretended to enjoy it, but they were more interested in the bottles of champagne, and soon the corks began to fly.

'Here's a well-organized range,' exclaimed a military-looking gentleman. 'At the Alma, at Inkermann, at Malakoff the cannons would not have rivalled . . .'

There was laughter at this neat comparison and the conversation became more lively. The sound of exploding corks attracted an increasing number of wine lovers and the voracious beauties were quickly imprisoned in a circle of men raising their glasses at every opportunity. An atmosphere of comradeship was settling in, when a smiling figure discreetly appeared. He listened with an air of faintly malicious indulgence. The face was one which immediately struck you by its sharp features and calm, self-assured intelligence. His thick, graying hair covered his skull like a cap.

'Simon Cameron,' someone said. 'We are happy to have you among us.'

'A friendly visit from a Northern neighbor,' he said. 'But I am not alone. I see Noah Brooks of the *Tribune*, who is dying to send a sensational report to his newspaper.'

'That would be news indeed,' said James Butler, a correspondent of the *Savannah Morning News*, famous for his perpetual irony.

'In any case, let us admire the dependability of these journalists, always here, there and everywhere. Mr Cameron,' proposed Senator Hunter, 'will you join a Virginian in drinking to their health?'

'It is my turn to admire the dependability of champagne, always ready to serve the cause. Let's drink to journalists, gentlemen.'

They drank to the journalists who were delighted and astonished.

'But,' Simon Cameron continued, 'I see the Senator from Alabama whom I am happy to greet. Mr Clay, will you let me borrow the finest phrase ever coined to celebrate peace from that great man of the South, your uncle?'

'Mr Cameron,' said Clement Clay in a loud voice, 'I was going to suggest it to you myself.'

Simon Cameron looked very serious and, in a voice that attracted the attention of everyone present he cried:

'Gentlemen, as a great servant of our country has done before me, I propose a toast to the Union of Hearts.'

The glasses were raised toward the ceiling and a massive cheer caused the crystal pendants high above them to vibrate.

Charlie Jones appeared at once.

'Mr Cameron, this is better than I hoped,' he exclaimed. 'You have given a powerful boost to our hopes.'

'I am just passing on a message. If anyone had listened to Henry Clay and Daniel Webster, peace would have been established in 1850, for good.'

For a moment even those faces most lit up by their libations took on a serious expression.

'It is the scheming of politicians that defeated a possible ideal,' said Governor Wise of Virginia.

'And yet,' said Senator Hunter, also a Virginian, 'there are honest politicians.'

The tone was changing, edging toward the bitter-sweet. A determined journalist from the *Petersburg Express* managed to reach Simon Cameron:

'Mr Cameron, according to you, what is an honest politician?'

Simon Cameron looked him up and down.

'An honest politician, my friend, is one who, when bought, stays bought.'

This quip was greeted with a burst of laughter as loud as the hurrahs and a crackle of applause. Even Lord Lyons, who was quite close to the group, could not repress his merriment.

'You have a golden tongue, Mr Cameron,' he said. 'Your definition will survive: it is valid for all countries and all times.'

Simon Cameron gave a slight bow. He caught sight of a gentleman of medium height who, without making an effort to push through the crowd, had gone to stand near Charlie Jones. The fine peaceable face of Jefferson Davis gave an indefinable impression of being surrounded by silence, even in the midst of this crowd that had gone back to its chattering. A sovereign sense of ease emanated from his whole being and his absent look might have suggested someone lost in a revery, but a word from Charlie Jones, at once jolly and affectionate, soon brought him back to his senses.

'Jeff, you're not worried, I hope?'

'Sometimes, perhaps, but not this evening,' said Jefferson Davis, with a smile. 'Your presence drives many shadows away, but no sooner have I been re-elected senator than I have a few minor anxieties about my health.'

'Nothing serious?'

'No, the eyes, as usual . . . But it'll sort itself out.'

Even as he spoke with him, a little way from the ruined pyramid, Charlie Jones kept asking himself a question, always the same one, as he examined the face of this man he admired: A leader. Could he become one if circumstances demanded it?

As if he had been reading his thoughts, Jefferson Davis gave him a look like that of a mocking schoolboy:

'Well, Charlie, are you questioning who I am?'

'Forgive me, Jeff, I was astonished to see you still so spry.'

'Vile flatterer. Take me to Simon Cameron: I have a word to say to that Republican.'

'No provocation, please, Jeff.'

'You'll see.'

When he was close to Simon Cameron, he held out a hand which was grasped warmly.

'Mr Cameron, I congratulate you on your toast to a Union of Hearts. If I were not afraid of casting a shadow over such a fine evening by spreading discord here, I should have proposed a toast to union, pure and simple.'

'Thank you, Mr Davis, I think that we have a good deal in common, but I can only answer with a sigh: alas.'

A few people heard this exchange and there was a murmur of voices. Suddenly, a man's voice declared loudly:

'Believe me, gentlemen, you would not have been the only ones here to drink to union, and I am a Southerner, first and foremost.'

In his turn, Charlie Jones took the floor, as he knew how in such circumstances, wielding the authority conferred on him by a wealth that was already proverbial throughout the land

'My dear friends,' he said. 'I can see that we are about to have a fascinating political discussion, but it will soon be ten o'clock, which is the time when I plan to offer you a quite different kind of entertainment, which I am sure will unite us all.'

With surprising agility, he vanished. Already there was a stir among the crowd of guests who had started to move slowly toward the end of the long gallery, clearing the space around the entrance.

Here, the Blacks, with an almost mechanical speed of movement, were installing a dais hung with red velvet.

Their curiosity had reached its height and the murmur of voices had grown so huge and so deep that it sounded like a public demonstration. At this moment, standing on a chair in the middle of the hall, they saw Charlie Jones waving an arm to demand silence. When this proved unsuccessful, he suddenly transformed himself into a sort of public orator, articulating very clearly:

'Ladies and gentlemen,' he exclaimed, 'excuse me if I raise my voice in this unacceptable way, but I want to announce a wonderful surprise. Right until the last minute I was afraid that it would not be possible, but the miracle has occurred and I shall have the great pleasure of introducing to you a young girl of barely seventeen whom everyone is already fighting over . . . She has agreed to come here from New York so that you can hear the loveliest voice that human ear has heard since . . . since . . .'

'Since the flood,' said a joker at the back of the gallery.

Charlie Jones corrected him:

'Since Adam and that unfortunate incident with the apple.'

This speech, which entertained the public while awaiting the entrance of the glamorous stranger, allowed her to climb the steps to the dais with the help of a few attentive gentlemen. A long murmur ran through the audience. While not conventionally beautiful, she possessed irresistible charm. The fine, if slightly prominent nose — an adventurous nose — did not detract from a small face, swallowed up by two fine Italian eyes, loving and warm. The women already felt a lump in their throats and all the men had fallen in love. Charlie Jones announced in ringing tones: 'Ladies and gentlemen, I present Adelina Patti, who will sing us one of the most heartrending arias from the opera by the great Donizetti, *Lucia di Lammermoor* . . . The madness aria.'

The singer's name was whispered like a magic charm from one end of the gallery to the other, then silence fell while the orchestra in the library gently tuned its instruments. Jumping down, Charlie Jones disappeared and the young singer, frail but self-assured, waited for the first bars. Her black hair, held by a single comb and tumbling over her shoulders, was adorned only with a rose above the ear; and in her white, full-length gown, she still retained something of the delightful awkwardness of adolescence.

Her face changed in a flash as soon as the orchestra struck up. Her mouth opened wide and the sound flew out to the far end of the room with the imperious limpidity of a birdsong, rending the air and making her enchanted listeners shudder with joy. Then, in an outpouring of scales to the accompaniment of the flute, madness was unleashed after the murder of the husband she had been forced to marry, and the dream of marriage to the man she loved. All the resources of the coloratura soprano lifted this story with its heightened romanticism to the summit of emotion. When the last sounds of this other wordly voice faded, the audience was seized with an unbounded delirium. Fans flew, ladies embraced without knowing why, perhaps to console one another, and men stamped their feet and shouted like idiots. The lovely child had to be protected from the hands reaching out to her, and was hurried from the hall.

Outside, the crowd, which had heard everything through the open windows, was screaming with joy and demanding an impossible encore. Ever ready to please, she would have liked nothing better and, in delightfully inaccurate English, said so to Charlie Jones who was serving as her bodyguard. He was holding her in his arms in such a way that the Italian's feet hardly touched ground.

'Your safety first.' And, in his most powerful and roughest voice, he cried: 'Gentlemen, do your bit. Help me pass and hold back your charming wives who are threatening to suffocate the signorina!'

By some means or other, he managed to carry her to the foot of the stairs. 'Go straight up,' he said. 'Go in and lock the door behind you. All the rooms are lit. Don't be afraid. I am keeping guard. We shall come and get you when calm is restored.'

Trusting and elated by her triumph, she seemed to fly up the steps. Almost at once, Charlie Jones heard a door shut behind her. Standing at the foot of the stairs, legs apart, wearing a ferocious look, he was ready to act if need be.

A few minutes passed and the uproar in the gallery and outside was slowly subsiding, when suddenly the magical winged voice could be heard, soaring above the noise . . . La Patti, from a window open on the square, sang a few notes, then stopped, and at once silence fell, in the house and in the avenues. They waited for a miracle, and *La Paloma* rose into the starry sky. The effect was no longer the same as a moment earlier: this time the music went straight to the heart, in a flood of tenderness. From the library, beneath the window, the guitars in the orchestra were quick to accompany her. Everyone knew the tune, but not this indescribable quavering in the voice which seemed to come from the throat of a nightingale. To that was added nostalgia for a legendary country and the wresting of powerful feelings from the ever vulnerable audience. They were happy, they were in pain, tears flowed unashamedly from every woman's eyes.

Outside, meanwhile, a carriage had stopped near the main door and in it Elizabeth was sitting motionless, allowing herself to be thrilled by a voluptuous sadness. At first, she had not wanted to go to her father-in-law's reception, because she knew that they would be discussing the politics of North and South, and she was restrained by a panicky fear of everything to do with the threat of war; but the discovery that all Savannah would be on display there had given her an itch to exhibit herself, to arouse admiration. At the last moment, she gave in to it, and now this voice, with its divine purity, was gluing her to the seat of her carriage. Caught in the crowd, unable to move forward, not understanding nor trying to understand, she abandoned herself to this fairytale enchantment.

The last notes of *La Paloma* and the silence that followed descended like a shock over everyone in the avenue, in the square and inside the house. The release from the spell was expressed in a prolonged 'ah!', then the applause rose, deafening, to such an extent that the signorina stepped back from the window.

Below, in the gallery, waves of affection drew sensitive souls together as before, but now with a greater degree of tenderness in their unexpected vows. The union of hearts would have been perfect if the men had taken part, but they were content to howl like animals.

Mrs Harrison Edwards, in a far corner of the hall, had caught hold of a slightly bewildered Algernon and, clasping him in her arms, she let her head roll on his shoulders, groaning:

'Algernon, aren't you moved? Why are you so timid with the fair sex? Your face and your name would justify the most extreme boldness. What am I saying? Look how I am laying myself open. Oh, do not take advantage of a weak woman.'

The irony of this speech disturbed him and emboldened him to the extent that he planted a kiss on Mrs Harrison Edwards' moist cheek.

'Is that all?' she asked. 'But — enough . . . Don't imagine that la Patti came here just for the sake of Charlie Jones's pretty eyes. He went to New York and a thousand gold dollars flowed from his hands into those of the enchantress, or anyway of her impresario, and he almost came to blows with her managers who did not want to let her go. I discovered all this . . . But nothing is proof against money, even the conscience of New York managers . . . What is happening at the front door? A fight? The people are invading the hall. Be a man: go and see what's happening. Defend us!'

Only too pleased to escape from the seductress' voluptuous arms — which she daringly exhibited as she laughed to herself — Algernon vanished into the crowd which was drawn by curiosity toward the main door, but it was not just the swarm of people. It was Elizabeth, entering with some commotion; shuddering with indignation, she was protesting at the obstacles she had had to overcome to get into her father-in-law's house. People had tried to reach the hall with her and she had been pushed . . . Some gentlemen came to her aid and tried to cool her temper, while the main door was shut behind her and triple locked.

A billowing dress of black taffeta with dark golden highlights made the beautiful Englishwoman look absolutely splendid and the effect was accentuated by the red tint of anger in her cheeks. She demanded imperiously that Mr Charlie Jones should be informed of her arrival. Unfortunately Mr Charlie Jones had disappeared, and she had to go herself to look for him. Her golden hair, in artful disorder, and the emeralds shining at her throat, produced the usual effect even on those who recognized her, but above all on a tall gentleman who had never yet made her acquaintance. Well-built and solid, he advanced toward her like a ship under sail. Hair in crows' wing style framed a high forehead beneath which two clear eyes directed an eagle's gaze, full of admiration, at Elizabeth. Stopping a few paces away from her, he bowed ceremoniously.

'My compliments, Madame,' he said. 'Allow me to introduce myself: John Breckinridge.'

The only reply was a forced smile. Elizabeth was looking for Charlie Jones. This stranger was merely getting in her way. Suddenly Uncle Josh, who had seen her come in, ran over, turned to John Breckinridge and said:

'Mr Vice-President, Mrs William Hargrove is English, but her husband is an officer in South Carolina.'

'Oh! Ah!' said Mr Breckinridge.

Vice-President . . . Elizabeth felt her head swim. Already Mr Breckinridge's presence seemed less of a nuisance to her. His face was not without nobility. He earned another smile, more courteous this time. In truth, Elizabeth did not know what to do with a Vice-President. She could better manage a handsome young soldier.

'Mrs William Hargrove is Mr Charlie Jones's daughter-in-law,' said Uncle Josh.

'Oh, what an unforgettable evening he is giving us! What did you think of *Lucia*, Madame?'

Lucia? Frankly, she thought nothing of this person.

'*Lucia di Lammermoor*,' Uncle Josh prompted.

She shook her head.

Mr Breckinridge smiled subtly.

'Oh, connoisseurs like yourself are sometimes a little strict. I must humbly admit that for my part I was carried away by *La Paloma*.'

*La Paloma*! Oh, yes! Elizabeth was about to say that she had heard it outside in the square; but how would that make her appear? She was confused. The Vice-President's eyes turned to the splendid emeralds and furtively slid down to Mrs William Hargrove's bosom. Uncle Josh was not at his best in diplomatic situations, and awkwardly suggested that one of the less crowded rooms might be better suited to a conversation on music. He gestured toward one nearby. Elizabeth gave him an anxious look.

'I'll go and look for Charlie,' he said.

Mr Breckinridge offered Elizabeth his arm and both slowly made their way toward the drawing-room that Josh had indicated. There were a few people in it, standing beside the sofas. As the young woman and the Vice-President came forward under the lights, she was horrified to see that people were standing back to let them pass, out of respect.

In the drawing-room, Elizabeth sat down on a sofa. Not having been invited to sit beside her and following the customs of the South, he chose an armchair. His manners were perfect; she recognized that, but it did not alter the fact that the Vice-President's pale blue eyes were those of a bird of prey when they looked at Elizabeth. In contrast, he spoke to her with a scrupulous regard for convention without ever risking a hint of a compliment. In fact, while he gravely spoke of nothings, his eyes were saying something entirely different. Did he realize it? Elizabeth eventually forgave him. She had never yet been unfaithful to her Billy, but she found it hard to resist the pleasure of letting herself be adored just a bit. She answered with cautious little smiles, nothing more, but she was not unhappy about it. The others present in the room discreetly looked elsewhere while keeping up entirely natural conversations; and the minutes passed.

Meanwhile, Uncle Josh was searching in vain for the master of the house among the crowd and in every room. Charlie Jones was on the upper floor, talking to la Patti. He was full of advice, and their conversation was entirely about practical matters. She replied with astonishing volubility and the understanding between them was perfect to the end . . . The Italian wrapped herself in a black cape, which Charlie Jones had brought for her, and they were coming silently down the staircase just as the guests gathered at the front door.

Like two characters from an opera, they reached the hall near the little dining-room beside the kitchens and went out. No one saw them, except Mrs Harrison Edwards who, plotting as ever, was observing events.

Outside, la Paloma in her black cape was immediately taken in charge by two bodyguards sent from the New York Opera, who conducted her to her carriage, then to the De Soto, and finally to the station, to tear her away from the dangerous lure of the South.

In the gallery the guests began to disperse, and the party seemed to be over. They were serving ices in the dining-room and some black servants were walking around with trays laden with glasses of champagne, which were almost immediately emptied. Charlie Jones reappeared suddenly, all smiles, to announce in his public speaker's voice;

'Ladies and gentlemen, let's not part so soon. Our divine nightingale has just flown. Let's seek consolation elsewhere. After the delights of the soul, after a voice direct from Paradise, I offer you . . . Hell!'

Hardly had he said these words than the orchestra launched into the elder Strauss' *Mephisto Waltz*. Everyone's breath was taken away, but the appeal was irresistible and couples formed more or less haphazardly. Not altogether, though. John Breckinridge, also electrified, stood up, but Elizabeth had taken flight as soon as she heard the first bars. She was afraid. With cat-like agility, she avoided the dozens of arms that reached out for her and slipped through the crowd until she found Algernon, who was struggling politely with Mrs Devilue Upton Smythe's heiress, the new Lady Furnace.

'My turn,' she said impudently, grasping his hand.

Flabbergasted, he obeyed, but with an anxious look.

'It's your opportunity, idiot,' she told him. 'Take it. Remember the conversation under the streetlamp.'

He enfolded her and began to whirl around with her, while she laughed in his face, shouting at him.

'Don't be afraid, Billy's not here. My word, you dance like a sylph. Lift me off the ground. Be amorous, Algernon, or pretend to be.'

'I'm not pretending,' he panted, red in the face.

'I am, frankly, but I want to get away from Breckinridge who freezes me with his eyes. You're not bad this evening. The *Mephisto Waltz* is very amusing. Do you believe in the devil?'

'I don't know,' he said. 'Yes . . . in the dark . . .'

'I don't, but I'd rather people didn't talk to me about him. Come on, make me jump in the air. Follow the music. Here's the great wave . . . Off we go! Hup! Ah! You're killing me!'

Suddenly, and as though driven to the limit, he kissed her.

'At last!' she said. 'But how badly you kiss! Don't be afraid of the devil! It's just for fun at the ball.'

'There are those who might think otherwise.'

'Oh!' she said, laughing. 'You're afraid of Billy. But I forced you to dance with me. That's what I intend to tell him.'

'Angel!' he said, relieved.


While the music invaded the gallery, some Southerners took the opportunity to slip away and shut themselves up in Charlie Jones's smoking room. Most had left the Democratic Convention in Charleston, slamming the door behind them. They still carried this atmosphere of discord around with them.

'Douglas was quite simply staging a take-over of the gathering,' exclaimed young Julian Hartridge with all the passion of the South. 'He put his men in every job; he imagines we're children. His theory about the squatters in Texas is untenable. In Savannah, no one will have it . . . He even dares to attack President Buchanan, accusing him of weakness toward the South.'

This outburst seemed particularly addressed at Governor Wise. Sitting in a wide armchair with leather upholstery, the latter was listening with the calm of a true Virginian, smoking his cigar.

'Do you know,' he said softly, 'that at the time of the attack on Harper's Ferry I received within the hour the following message from the President: "End this matter as soon as possible and let justice be done".'

There was a pause. Some had settled into the black leather chesterfields to right and left of the chimney; others remained standing. Toombs was leaning against a bookcase, his thumb in the opening of his white ottoman waistcoat. They were already surprised by his silence, when Jeff Davis said in his clear and precise voice:

'Our friend Hartridge is right. No purpose was served by Charleston. Our delegates left before the final vote. The South is united, but the Democrats no longer are. The lesson is clear: if we want to keep the presidency, we need a single candidate.'

'Of the South,' said a powerful whisper.

It was Toombs.

'Yes,' Jeff Davis went on. 'If you wish. Or in any case someone who will defend the rights of States under the Constitution.'

'The eternal apple of discord. We always come back to that,' muttered Governor Brown.

Slim, tall and broad-shouldered, he had the intimidating look of a man who cannot be deceived.

'Howard Cobb,' suggested a voice from near the window.

Toombs' retort came like a burst of lightning.

'Oh, no! He advocates Union before everything. Excuse me,' he added, seeing a pained smile on the faces of Stephens and Davis. 'Not Cobb. In any case, he himself withdrew his candidacy when he saw the opposition which it aroused.'

'You mean your personal opposition and that of your journalist friends?' Brown asked in a tone of friendly irony.

'I speak for public opinion,' Toombs replied proudly.

'So, along with it, we are sailing toward the unknown,' Governor Wise objected.

It was as though they were all doing everything they could to provoke the full force of Toombs' oratory.

'Even that is better,' he burst out, 'than to entrust oneself to a right hand that doesn't know what the left is doing. We are virtually on the brink of civil war.'

His resounding voice shook the window panes. There was a general protest at these last words.

'Virtually, I said! In the Senate, opposite me, I have secret enemies of the South. I declared as much a few days ago and repeat it now: they are using their authority to attack and demolish the rights of the States, contrary to the oath they swore on the Constitution. They don't care about their obligations. They have lost all feeling of shame as well as all virtue. Even though they represent millions of people in the North, I denounce them as enemies of the Constitution, and so as enemies of the Union and of the South. Peace and tranquillity are incompatible with such people . . .'

While they were listening to this much-loved, deep voice, and moved by its grandiloquence, all those present had in their minds a picture of the Senate: the solemn immobility among the rows of seats, Toombs proudly shaking his locks in a gesture that recalled Mirabeau, and his fiery words piercing the hostile silence like arrows. No one would have dared to interrupt. 'Don't listen to idle chatter,' he cried, 'to fallacious babble about obvious acts: they have been committed and we have moved on! Defend yourselves, the enemy is at your door, don't wait until he is at your fireside, meet him on the threshold and drive him from the temple of your liberty, or you will be reduced to pulling down the pillars of that temple yourselves and burying yourselves in the general ruin. Today, the greatest danger is that the Union will survive on the corpse of the Constitution . . .'

'Incompatible . . .,' muttered Governor Brown. 'So, there will be a break,' he added, aloud. 'Do you really want us to separate from the North?'

'No,' said Stephens, who until then had not moved on the sofa.

'No,' said Jefferson Davis.

'No,' they replied from all sides in the room.

'And you, Toombs?' Governor Brown asked of the man who was still standing with his back to the bookcase.

'You know my feelings . . . Unless the North ends its aggression against slavery and the States' rights, I am in favor of disunion. Let's not wait until it's unavoidable. We must take decisive action. It's up to us, and us alone, to settle our problems peacefully, in our own time, and to deal with our own institutions.'

'Very true,' said Jeff Davis.

'So you hope that we'll reach a breakdown.'

This statement, made by the youthful voice of Julian Hartridge, gave the illusion that they were in a court arriving at the end of its deliberations.

'Well, no,' Toombs replied, so softly this time that all heads turned toward him simultaneously. 'I hope that they will pause for thought over there . . . as long as Buchanan is present.'

Pursuing his line of argument, Julian Hartridge asked:

'And if their attacks continue, in the press and in Congress? The State of New York is even talking about secession for itself.'

'If the South's rights are threatened, it is my turn to ask you,' Toombs continued, cleverly. 'Would you put up with it?'

'No.'

The answer was unanimous.

'Even to the point of Secession?' the great orator went on pitilessly.

'With a breaking heart,' (Alexander Stephens' soft voice knew how to command attention) 'with a breaking heart, I should abandon the idea of Union, because my heart will always remain entirely with the South.' (He paused for a moment, then continued). 'But I hope that the Union will survive in peace and prosperity, and that the Constitutions, those of the Nation and those of the States, will remain intact, continuing to give happiness to the thousands of men who will be born on our soil, as they have brought happiness to us, who are now alive.'

Toombs said simply:

'Alexander, we all have ideals at heart. May God hear you.'

After a long silence, they all stood up and left the room to go back to the reception. Scarcely had they opened the door, than the world with its tumultuous music closed in around them.

Waltzes, quadrilles and polkas had followed one after another. Feet were ceaselessly tapping the floor.

Finally, in a great, triumphal burst, a quadrille ended and the couples separated.

'Thank you, Elizabeth,' said Algernon. 'I shall never forget . . .'

But already she was somewhere else. Throughout the whole of the last dance she had noticed a man among those who were not dancing. In fact, many men were looking at her, but this one seemed different. Without being what she considered a handsome man, he appeared much more than that. Something in him attracted her very strongly, though she could not explain. Slender and of medium height, he had that grave and thoughtful air of people who have not been spared physcial suffering. His black eyes drew her with an intelligence and goodness that set him apart from all the others present. One might have wondered what he was doing there. He was observing Elizabeth with such profound attention that she had briefly the impression that he was reading her. When the music stopped, she saw him trying to approach her and instinctively moved a little toward him. When he got near, he bowed and said:

'Madam, allow me to introduce myself: Alexander Stephens, from Georgia. I am a friend of your father-in-law, Mr Charlie Jones.'

Elizabeth could not stop looking at his dark eyes which seemed to say so many things to her with a mixture of tenderness and compassion, as if he were sorry for her. She said simply:

'Sir, I am happy to meet a friend of my father-in-law's.'

'So,' he continued, 'might I ask you to introduce me to your husband, whom I do not have the honor of knowing?'

'I shall willingly do so at the first opportunity, sir, but this evening, he is not here.'

'Oh, I am sorry! Excuse me, I thought at first . . .'

She realized the misunderstanding and quickly replied:

'No, sir, my husband is a cavalry officer at Fort Beauregard.'

As she said this, her color heightened a little. Once more, the black eyes plunged into the blue ones as if looking for the answer to an unspoken question.

'Forgive my error,' he said softly.

'It was quite natural,' said Elizabeth, suddenly on the defensive. 'With all these people . . . the hazards of the dance . . .'

'Of course, madam. A confusion on my part . . .'

She gave a slight nod and turned on her heels. He also moved away, but his eyes followed her for a moment.

The party was almost over. There were a few more cheers for the orchestra and people took their leave of Charlie Jones with congratulations that warmed his heart.

'You have served the cause of peace,' they said again and again. 'Served peace, saved peace.'

But he still had his doubts.


# 117


*E*lizabeth went home as quickly as she could. She felt weary and was irritated to see that Miss Llewelyn was waiting for her in the hall, upright and massive in her ash-colored dress.

'I'm not surprised to see you coming home so late,' she said with that humorless smile of hers that crossed the lower part of her face in a thin, malicious line. 'The sound of the party even reached us here. I thought the crowd was demonstrating about something.'

'Applause for a young singer. I hope the children are asleep.'

'I think so, but your young Ned did something odd. He wrote a letter to Mr Charlie Jones, sealed the envelope and wants it to be delivered tomorrow.'

'Why?'

'He refuses to say anything about it.'

'He'll tell me everything. Good night, Miss Llewelyn.'

'Thank you, Madam. I hope you will sleep well and long. You look very tired.'

Reaching her room, Elizabeth immediately looked in her mirror. 'Tired' sounded to her like an attack on this face which had been so abundantly admired in the drawing-rooms of Savannah. A shadow furrowed the corner of the eyes and her features — the little oil lamp cast an unflattering light — the nose and the mouth seemed hardened.

She put away her emeralds, quickly got undressed and slipped into the large bed which was so wide, when she was in it alone, that she felt she was lost in the night. She was utterly weary and sleep would soon come; but she had to look for it, first on one side, then on the other. She pushed aside her pillow: too soft; but the bolster was too hard. Lying flat on her belly, she covered her head with her blankets so as not to see the yellow light of the street lamp shining through the shutters. She would ask her father-in-law, who could do anything, to have it moved. But she could not manage to lapse into sleep, as she usually did, when all was well.

What bothered her that evening was her absurd conversation with Alexander Stephens. First of all, just what did he want? The name meant nothing to her, but he seemed so patient and almost affectionate, without courting her . . . He had thought — or pretended to think — that she was the wife of that idiot Algernon. And Algernon, as they were dancing, had said such an odd thing about the devil: in the dark, he believed in the devil . . . What nonsense people talked while dancing . . . She pushed aside the blankets and lay on her back. The long shaft of light cut the room in half, coloring the ceiling with a dull yellow and leaving the lower part of the room in darkness. She shut her eyes. She did not dare get up and draw the curtains.

She remembered the first nights in Dimwood. Nobody told her then that she was the most beautiful creature in the world, no one went into raptures over her. The song of the tree frogs would keep her awake. At that time of her life, she used to say her prayers, but less now. She said the Lord's Prayer as a formality, yet when she was younger she had wondered what it meant: 'Deliver us from evil.' Was she the prisoner of someone? Evil could only mean the devil. The waltz came back to her in haunting snatches of music, in wheedling tunes, in amorous pleadings; then suddenly the triumphant thunder of Mephisto. It was odd, but there were places in the Bible better left alone. Her mother was not here to ask about the Scriptures, so the black-bound volume could stay there on her bedside table, like a talisman on which nothing must be placed, because after all it was the Bible.

Her memory evoked the hours spent in Dimwood like a series of pictures. From her last visit she recalled the empty room where Laura had lived. There was nothing in that empty room except the outline of a cross on the wall, but the silence there had seemed deeper than anywhere else. One felt at peace and oddly far from everywhere. Elizabeth liked Laura. The silent woman who sometimes smiled with a sad look had given her advice which the young Englishwoman could not recall, but she wanted to see her again for no particular reason, except that in those distant days she had given her an impression of reassuring tranquillity . . .

Now the street lamp had gone out and, without even being aware of it, Elizabeth fell asleep.

The following morning, she woke at ten o'clock. Life had resumed its normal course. Ned had already left for school. Miss Llewelyn had Madam's breakfast served in bed and then came to take her orders for the day. Characteristically, the Welshwoman hovered on the very borderline between insolence and respect, which was like a frontier that she passed over, back and forth, with her disturbing smile.

'I prefer to see you looking as you do today, not like last night, if I may say so.'

'You've said so, with or without my permission. That will be all, Miss Llewelyn.'

The Welshwoman nodded and went toward the door.

'No,' Elizabeth said. 'One moment. I want to see the letter that Ned wrote to his grandfather.'

'Too late, Madam. At eight o'clock, Ned gave it to Joe and told him to take it at once to Mr Charlie Jones.'

'Without my permission?'

'Madam, you were so fast asleep . . .'

'That's no excuse. But too bad, I don't think there can be any secrets between Ned and Mr Jones. Just one moment more. I have something to say to you. Last night, I thought of the woman we all call Aunt Laura.'

Miss Llewelyn nodded.

'Laura,' she murmured.

'I should like to see her.'

'It will be difficult, but not altogether impossible.'

'I know. An enclosed nun . . .'

'Oh, that doesn't matter; but she's no longer in Georgia. Thanks to Mr Charlie Jones, she and her daughter, with all their community, went and settled in a convent that was built for them in the heart of Maryland, some thirty miles from Baltimore.'

'Why?'

'He thought, correctly, that they would be happier in a Catholic region.'

Elizabeth opened her eyes in astonishment. The Welshwoman looked at her defiantly.

'You must know, Madam, that the Church is at home in Maryland. There is nothing austere about the landscape where these nuns live: just green fields and hills. The convent itself is universally admired. Mr Charlie Jones does things on a grand scale.'

Elizabeth pushed away her tray. She had not touched the food.

'I admit that it distresses me. I don't even know why; I don't know what I would say to her, but that's how it is.'

'As far as I am concerned,' the Welshwoman continued, in a suddenly inspired tone of voice, 'I went to say farewell to her — do you know with whom? With little Betty, who was weeping like a child. Laura and her daughter Annabel hugged her and covered her with kisses. They would have been delighted if you had come. But what is done, is done.'

Elizabeth looked at her without replying. Neither of the women moved. It was as though they were expecting something.

'It's strange,' Elizabeth said at last.

'Yes, Madam, like everything else . . . like life . . .'

The conversation had taken an unexpected turn and the Englishwoman felt herself floundering.

'I am going to have my bath,' she said, smiling. 'Thank you, Miss Llewelyn.'

'And I shall take care of the house,' said the housekeeper.

Alone again, Elizabeth felt an unease that she could not explain. For some time she had been feeling less happy and less sure of herself. She had the feeling that something had happened which she could not grasp.

'Perhaps I should not have said anything,' she muttered.

A moment later, sitting in front of her mirror, she was confronted by an Elizabeth once more beautiful and rested, but troubled. One of the most dizzying tunes from the *Mephisto Waltz* kept running through her head, and it seemed ridiculous to her.

# 118

Charlie Jones was at home, sitting in front of his tea and his plate of bacon and eggs; and, as he ate breakfast, he was reading in the *Savannah Morning News* a fiery speech by Julian Hartridge, the young and already famous public speaker. There was nothing new about the theme, but the tone had the energy of the great revolutionaries of 1776. 'Fanaticism, emboldened by impunity, has called treason, murder and pillage to its aid, crossed the frontier and, advancing to the threshold of the South, has spilt blood and stirred up trouble. Georgia is ready with its brothers, the States of the South, to take part in any action needed to ensure their common rights under the Constitution and within the Union, but if that is no longer possible, then to ensure their independence and security, outside the Union.' Such were the unending repercussions of John Brown's raid, and the North was still waving the rope that hanged him.

Charlie Jones gave a grunt of approval and was preparing to drink his tea when his servant handed him a letter on a tray, delivered by hand.

He gave an astonished look at the envelope. The writing, very uneven, resembled that of a drunken man. Yet another appeal for help, he thought, with an urgent request for money . . . What he read took his breath away. Only three lines, each falling away at the end:

Dear Grandpa,

You gav me your hous and didnt invit me to the party yesday evening in my hous. Which is not fer. Im not plesed.
Lov
   Ned
     (not plesed).


Charlie Jones folded the letter and, laughing heartily, slipped it into his wallet. After that, he skimmed through some more newspapers, finished his breakfast and left for the office.

It was here, at the end of the day, that he penned his reply to his grandson's letter.

My dear Ned,

You did well to write to me and next year, on the same date, you will give a party in your great house in Madison Square. You will invite all your friends, there will be an orchestra and mountains of cakes. And if you want to invite me, I shall come, but if you don't invite me, well, I shan't come, but I shall write you a letter in my turn. Meanwhile, come and spend the summer in Virginia from the end of May onwards. There is a surprise awaiting you there. No one yet knows that my house in Savannah belongs to you and I expect you to keep the secret as a man of honor.

A strong handshake to a loyal friend.
   Your grandfather.

This letter was immediately taken to Oglethorpe Square with firm instructions that it should be delivered to the addressee personally. Only too happy to enter into a little conspiracy, Miss Llewelyn went to find Ned who was still in the garden, and personally supervised the transaction, which remained secret.

# 119

*I*n Charleston, the Democratic convention broke up on May 2, without taking any decision about the candidate for the presidency. There were motions and emotions. They voted endlessly, and for what? For nothing. They would meet again in June: the date, the 18th, and the town, Baltimore, were chosen. The Southern delegates who rejected Douglas had left the Convention the day before Charlie Jones's reception, led by Yancey, the representative from Alabama. On their side, they intended to hold a Convention of all Southern States in Richmond a few days after the one held by their brotherly opponents from the North, who supported Douglas.

The pace of events began to quicken. The little constitutional Union Party, which chiefly defended the rights of the States, held its own Convention in Baltimore like the others, and without any fuss chose a senator from Tennessee, John Bell. The history of the United States was slowly shifting. Then the Republican Convention opened in the middle of May in Chicago. The heat on the shores of the lake was stifling, as if forewarning of the difficulties that would arise. The situation was a repetition of what had gone before: as with Douglas for the Democrats, Seward thought he could dominate the discussions without opposition. However, a majority of delegates did not want to speak about abolition and preferred Secession, pure and simple, advocated by Horace Greeley in his newspaper with the support of the representatives of New York. Politics lurked on all sides.

At the first vote, it was clear that the delegates were stalemated and that Seward would not carry the day. Among the other candidates, Simon Cameron retained the large vote of his own state of Pennsylvania. He remained thoughtful. Around him, it seemed that a ditch was being dug, dividing the Republicans as the Democrats had been divided. Seward thought of Douglas, and reminded himself that the specter of civil war hung over the political world.

Remembering the evening at Charlie Jones's and the feeling that had caught hold of everyone when he had raised a toast to a Union of Hearts, he decided to give his votes to the unknown candidate, the stranger in the house: Abraham Lincoln. In exchange, he would be offered the post of Secretary of State for War, which for him meant peace, if the Republicans grasped their opportunity. So Lincoln was chosen as candidate, on the third round of voting. At this, some extremists were seized with fury and Wendell Philipps, his sideburns ruffled, a solemn and fine speaker, cried out amidst the politicians who were exasperated at seeing their candidate thrown out: 'Who is Lincoln?'

# 120

One warm evening at the end of May, Elizabeth was sadly packing Ned's suitcase. She did not want anyone to help her in this task which she found heartbreaking, but Miss Llewelyn was nonetheless standing by, occasionally offering advice.

'The little woolen cardigan perhaps. It may be chilly there in the evenings.'

'I thought of that, Miss Llewelyn. I do know Virginia.'

This was the first time that she had been separated from her son, and she was putting a great deal of tenderness into the choice of clothes and all the things that the young traveler might enjoy.

In a voice that she tried to make sound affectionate, the Welshwoman murmured:

'You should have gone with him, Madam. Together with Betty and Black Mammy, I would have taken care of little Kit.'

'Impossible, Miss Llewelyn. I'm intending to take Christopher to Dimwood where he will at least have some fresh air.'

'He would have even more in Virginia. Did you consider it?'

'I know, but it's not possible.'

'A pity, for him and for you.'

'Thank you for your kind thoughts, Miss Llewelyn, but I have my reasons. Bring me two more shirts, will you.'

The Welshwoman hastened to obey, but could not stop speaking.

'The *Savannah* sets sail at ten o'clock. Mr Charlie Jones will be here at eight.'

'Why so early? As if his own boat would leave without him! But we shall be ready.'

'We shall be ready': the words, said without thinking, re-opened a wound. For a second, she saw herself setting off with Ned, happy to feel him close to her on board ship. She was so overcome that her legs gave way and she slipped into a chair. Miss Llewelyn leaned over her.

'I can see that you're upset, Madam. It is not at all too late to change your mind. It would be simple. Mr Jones would be delighted.'

Elizabeth gave her a pained look.

'What are you thinking of, Miss Llewelyn? One can't go back on one's decisions. I'm expected at Dimwood. Leave me.'

She spent a bad night, but the next morning, at eight o'clock, she was standing in the hall, with Ned's hand in hers, waiting for Uncle Charlie who arrived punctually a few seconds later. The farewells were swift. Everyone feared last-minute emotional outpourings. Ned kissed Mummy twice, three times, assuring her that he loved her very, very much, then leaped toward the carriage, mad with joy, and frenziedly waved his hat with the long ribbons just as the wheels began to turn.

Her face hardened by her determination not to weaken, Elizabeth swung round toward the Welshwoman.

'Now, my turn,' she said. 'Tell Joe to have the carriage harnessed at once. All the suitcases are packed. Bring them down. I am entrusting the house to you, Miss Llewelyn. Keep an eye on Pat and the servants. I think we've said all that's needed to be said. I shall be waiting in the drawing-room. Please hurry.'

In the scarlet room, for the hundredth time, she went over the reasons that justified her behavior: 'No chance of seeing him in Virginia. The journey is endless. He came to Dimwood, he can come again; Charleston is not that far.'

Less than half an hour later, she was on her way. In a humbler, but comfortable carriage behind her came little Christopher, settled into the folds of the huge white cloud which enveloped Black Mammy. Beside her, Betty seemed tiny in her red jacket, and at their feet was a whole world of huge bags, cases and parcels.

The journey seemed very long to Elizabeth who did not like being alone in carriages. She had the impression that her adolescence was accompanying her all the way down the road, and there were places where she closed her eyes to avoid reliving unforgettable moments. The hard noise of hooves on the ground brought back cruel memories and made her groan with despair. Once more, she had the feeling that she had wandered through life like someone wandering through an unknown land. Jonathan passed like a ghost so close to the carriage that she expected to see him, and her hands clasped together in horror. She wondered what was awaiting her in the plantation where she had been foolish enough to take refuge.

At one moment, the marsh with its black waters full of dead trees appeared to her as it had done years before, speaking to her in the same incomprehensible language in which she thought she could hear a cry for help. It lasted only the duration of a lightning flash, but she was afraid and crouched in a corner of the carriage trying to sleep.

At last, the avenue of huge oak trees appeared, majestic as a procession of kings, to lead her toward the site of the disaster where her happiness had foundered. Her heart beating wildly, she put both hands over her face and stayed like that until the carriage drew to a halt.

Emma and Douglas Hargrove were waiting for her in front of the main entrance. They were alone, strikingly so. There were too many people missing around them.

She came forward without a word, like a sleepwalker, but Aunt Emma caught her in her arms.

'What a pleasure to see you for the summer in Dimwood,' she said, with an unexpected burst of affection. 'You know how happy it makes us both, Douglas and me.'

'Yes, indeed,' said Uncle Douglas.

'The house is empty,' Aunt Emma continued.

'Empty, but full of memories,' Elizabeth said in a faint voice that she did not recognize as her own; then, pulling herself together, added: ' . . .full of good memories.'

'Oh!' Aunt Emma exclaimed. 'You've come with your youngest and his black nanny — and Betty, I'm so glad to see her again! Hello, Betty.'

The kindness of these words warmed the atmosphere a little. To satisfy every delicate nuance of the laws of Southern hospitality, the young Englishwoman was given the room formerly occupied by her mother. The child would be put up with its black nanny in the next-door room, the same one occupied by Elizabeth when she arrived. In this way, a kind of sentimental symmetry was established although it seemed an anomaly that the Black Mammy should sleep with the child; but how else could they ensure that Elizabeth was left in peace? In any case, Christopher was well-behaved and did not cry.

Alone in her room before lunch, Elizabeth looked around her and wondered by what irony of fate she was there; but whose fault was it? From top to bottom, the house was haunted, like the road that led to it. The four-poster bed and, on the bedside table, the inevitable Bible bound in black leather, next to a glass in a saucer, with a teaspoon and a little jug of water — all that was needed to prepare the laudanum which was certainly to be found in the medicine chest in the bathroom — everything was in place and the setting perfect; and she was there, ten years later . . . The house was haunted and there was no doubt that she was the ghost.

Lunch was served in the dining-room where she had formerly tried to escape from the eyes of William Hargrove behind a bunch of flowers. The room seemed much larger than she remembered and, in fact, the whole house miraculously seemed to have become enormous and voices echoed louder than they used to, resounding off the walls.

Emma and Douglas made an effort to enliven the conversation.

'The house is not entirely empty,' he said, laughing. 'Souligou has stayed upstairs. You must remember Souligou?'

'And the Blacks, needless to say,' Emma added. 'There are not many now, but one has the feeling that they are everywhere. You see: it's odd.'

'And Hilda? And Mildred?'

'Didn't you know? They are at Limestone Spring in a county in the north of the State, with their husbands, though the men are coming back home at the end of the month. They are pining for Charleston. That's their real paradise.'

'And Susanna?'

Emma adopted the look that everyone in the family wore when talking about Susanna — at once affectionate and reserved.

'Susanna is very well. She's spending the holiday with some friends of her own, in Georgia, in the hills.'

'She is distancing herself a little from Dimwood,' Douglas observed. 'She's a very independent girl.'

'We are very fond of her,' Emma said.

'So am I,' said Elizabeth. 'I'd very much like to see her.'

She suddenly had a vision of the tear-stained face behind the window.

There was a brief silence, then Douglas suddenly said:

'I hope our Billy comes to see you from time to time in Savannah.'

'Oh, yes, of course. But his furloughs are so rare.'

Douglas went 'tut, tut', in a sympathetic way, and smiled:

'When the situation in Charleston is a little clearer, he will come more often.'

'In any event,' said Emma, 'everything will work itself out. It must. Don't listen to pessimists.'

'Billy knows I am here. I wrote to him. He may come.'

'Of course,' said Douglas. 'He came with you before.'

They served sweet potatoes, which Elizabeth loved, but she hardly touched them. She had no appetite. However, so that she would not give the impression of rejecting a delicious meal, she tasted the dessert and accepted a small glass of champagne . . . She suddenly realized that she was a source of concern for Emma and Douglas: what could they do with this daughter-in-law who was so obviously unhappy at finding herself there? So, having finished her cup of coffee, she announced that she was tired after the journey and wanted to rest. They strongly approved and she went straight up to her room, looking anxiously into the hall and up the stairs. She felt like a prisoner in this nearly deserted house, a prisoner of a house that was too big. What would she do with her time: waiting for Billy who might not come? Outside, the crickets wove their curtain of scraping sounds which her mother could not stand. She sat down in the rocking chair and rocked as her mother had done, feeling, like her, disgusted at being there.

The door opened very slowly, admitting Betty whom Elizabeth did not see at once. Now barely taller than a little girl, she came in silently, thinking her mistress asleep.

'Betty,' she said. 'What are you doing in my room?'

The reply was a smile that never failed to touch Elizabeth. Pointing, the old woman indicated the still closed suitcases.

'Are you pleased to be in Dimwood, Betty?'

'Pleased with you, Ma'am.'

The kind eyes seemed to laugh as they looked up toward her.

'Is the baby next door? I can't hear him.'

'Mammy put him to bed.'

'I'll go and see him. Open the cases and put everything away wherever you wish.'

Slipping out of the chair, she went into the next room, the room of her sixteenth year. The bed, with its white canopy, the commode, the mirror: she saw it all in a glance and, although she had been expecting it, she got a slight shock at seeing the black mammy near a child's bed in which Christopher was sleeping. It was as though two pictures placed next to each other did not fit. In the white cloud, the black face smiled like Betty's, full of a simple benevolence that comforted the young Englishwoman.

The child had opened his eyes in which his mother saw Billy's blue irises but they were expressionless apart from a look of astonishment and profound innocence. Now two years and a few months old, he was still not what Elizabeth would call beautiful, but the blue eyes rescued everything. The features were crumpled and would have given the little face an unattractive look had it not been for that gaze with its dazzling limpidity. She leaned over him a little and he studied her without moving, then his half-open mouth split into a smile that devastated her. Though the child did not have the looks of his brother at the same age, he already had the more mysterious gift of charm. In a sudden burst of affection, she kissed his forehead and he started to laugh, waving his hand: 'Mama.' this was followed by some incomprehensible words. She then began to kiss him everywhere — on the head, the cheeks and the ears, enchanted. Someone to love . . .

The black mammy was also laughing heartily.

'Pretty,' she said. 'Pretty baby, Ma'am.'

'Very pretty, Mammy.'

He's frightful, but I adore him, she thought.

And, brushing lovingly against the little laughing face, she caught a scent which recalled those wild flowers to which one seeks in vain to give a name.

'Have you put perfume on him?' she asked.

'No, Ma'am. Never perfume.'

'So, is it soap?'

'No, Ma'am, pretty baby smells good.'

'How much I am going to love you,' Elizabeth murmured in the child's ear.

Why hadn't she discovered it earlier? But Billy was not really interested in him; and there was Ned . . . The memory of the little boy jumping into the carriage, then waving goodbye, came back at once and brought a lump to her throat. But now she felt less pain at being away from him — or at least, not the same pain: someone was living in Dimwood, someone to love.

'Happy, Ma'am,' said Mammy.

'Yes.'

Suddenly she found herself wondering where this imposing creature was going to sleep. In the bed with the canopy? It seemed, if not shocking, at least slightly incongruous . . . This would have been unheard of in the South, but if it was necessary for Christopher . . . The name suddenly seemed to her very long for such a tiny person.

'We must call him Kit,' she said to the nanny.

'Yes, Ma'am: Kit. We always call him Kit . . . Massa Kit.'

'Just Kit,' said Elizabeth with a smile. And she asked: 'Mammy, where do you sleep? In the bed?'

'Oh, no, Ma'am,' said the nanny, quite shocked. 'Not in the bed. Mammy sleep on ground.'

She pointed to the bottom of the bed under which Elizabeth noticed a mattress.

'Do you sleep well on that?' she asked.

'Mammy always sleep on that, Ma'am.'

In fact, the mattress was thick. One last kiss for Kit and the loving mother went back to her room. Everything was in order, the cupboards were full, the cases had vanished and Betty was there, smiling and waiting.

'Betty, my little boy is an angel.'

'Yes, Ma'am.'

The following day, as soon as she got up, she went back into Kit's room. He was still lying on his back in the bed which had belonged to all the Hargrove children. When she leaned over him, he turned his face round, opened his right eye wide as if to see her better, and smiled from one ear to the other, making her his prey and his slave. From now on, Elizabeth's presence in Dimwood had some meaning.

Emma and Douglas quickly noticed the change, and the whole house seemed to throw off its depressing solitude. It was as if the drawing-rooms and corridors were overflowing with memories like radiant shadows. Elizabeth was cautious enough to avoid certain specific places: the spot where Fred had confessed his love and, most dangerous of all, at the end of the veranda where Jonathan, through the magnolia leaves, had brought his face close to hers . . . Here, however, the temptation was too strong for her to resist it for long and, at night, in the silence filled with the croaking of the tree frogs, she slipped out to relive those moments which were lost for ever. Her heart beating fast, she went back to bed, distraught as though she had spent a night of love with a ghost. Black Mammy pretended to sleep, imagined everything, understood nothing and kept quiet. By day, Elizabeth consoled herself by running her mouth across Kit's face while he showed her his tiny teeth and stroked her cheek, her eyes and her nose, haphazardly, laughing and blabbering a rush of words for her.

Billy's absence often came close to torture. Sometimes she had a letter which spoke bitterly of furloughs that were impossible to obtain, maneuvers made more frequent by the political situation . . . In her bed, unecessarily wide, she fought against insomnia and dreamed of a new escapade to the hussars' barracks, a sadly lewd dream that was soon expunged when she awoke by a broad smile from tiny teeth of bluish white.

The weeks passed with a dizzying slowness; it was as though time seemed not to move even as it destroyed itself. Newspapers arrived from Savannah and elsewhere which she did not even glance at. People tried not to talk about anything except the weather, the delicious meals which followed upon delicious meals in the same usual rhythmic immobility of happy times. The distant song of the Blacks in the plantation added a melancholy note to this reassuring monotony.

## 121

While Elizabeth was discovering a new passion at Dimwood in the person of little Kit, Ned was traveling with Charlie Jones on his boat toward Virginia. As soon as he set foot on the red earth of the country roads, he felt that they were in quite a different country, with a quiet and powerful magic. The great green expanses exhaled peace under a gray sky and the landscape, with its perfect simplicity, spoke to the heart of the boy from Savannah. Here, anxiety ended and, for the first time in his life, he felt the appeal of a happiness beyond this world.

Charlie Jones did not stop to dream. He made his grandson climb back into the four-horse carriage which took them off at a gallop, his main concern being to arrive at Great Meadow as soon as possible; and Ned, still feeling the surprise of his unfamiliar surroundings, did not dare ask him anything, because his grandfather was trying to read a newspaper which he had taken out of his pocket and folded in half. From time to time, he gave a groan that might be interpreted as one wished, but which intrigued his young companion as if the noise of the town were following them all along the rusty highroad.

Here and there, solitary houses appeared, all of white or pale yellow painted wood and, after several hours, they passed near a village where there was a long store which was full of people. Charlie Jones put down his paper.

'That's the grocery store around here, where everyone meets. They sell everything and talk about everything. There is one near us. You see, we're not very far away now.'

They carried on for a further half hour, then slowed down and stopped in front of a gate. One of the two coachmen jumped down from his seat, lifted the wooden bar across the road and opened it wide. The carriage set off down the long avenue which curved gracefully around a field in which there was a cedar with gigantic branches. Ned had a shock, because his mother had talked to him about this, and he sighed; he even recognized the gray wooden house with its dark red roof, its two pointed lodges on each side of a façade with high windows, surrounded and partly hidden by chestnut trees and pines. Despite his mother's tales, he was vaguely expecting a grand house with columns, as in Georgia, instead of which he discovered a huge, rather countrified house, but one which instinctively attracted him. 'One falls in love with it as soon as one sees it,' Elizabeth had told him.

The carriage stopped in front of a veranda over which an elm seemed to be watching, its branches bending like a tent of greenery down to the horses' heads. Black servants greeted Uncle Charlie with cries of welcome and grasped the luggage. As Ned was crossing the threshold of the door behind his grandfather, a little woman, old but sprightly, came toward them. In her black dress with its white collar, she was hardly bigger than the boy, but above her was the full height of a tall cloth bonnet decorated with lace and muslin crowning a finely lined face in which shone two delightfully merry gray eyes. She gave him a wide smile.

'Ned?' she asked.'How he has grown . . .'

'You guessed before I told you, Charlotte. My poor Ned's son. Ned, kiss Aunt Charlotte.'

The old lady offered him a cheek and he placed a kiss on it.

'I know your Mama very well,' she said.

Anticipating a long chat, Charlie Jones said to Ned:

'We still have an hour before lunch. How would you like to go for a ride around the place?'

Without waiting for a reply, he took his hand and pulled him toward the left of the house.

'In Savannah I promised you a surprise. It's waiting at the stable door behind the house. You run on, I'll follow you.'

Ned did not ask for an explanation, but ran round the house at full speed. Then suddenly he stopped dead in amazement: at the stable door, a young black stableboy was holding the bridle of a white pony which was shaking its abundant mane. With its slender but sturdy joints and its silver tail, it looked as though it had come straight out of a fairy story. The boy cried:

'He's mine!'

'Yes,' Uncle Charlie said, coming up behind him. 'He's called Whitie and if you talk kindly to him, he will be very obedient.'

Ned went across and stroked the pony's neck. It turned its great black eye toward him.

'Whitie,' whispered Ned.

This was not the first time he had had dealings with a pony and this one bent down a little. Giving way to an impulse, Ned kissed him, even though the stableboy motioned to him to be careful. What affinity drew the boy and the animal together? The pony did not move, but shook its head every time Ned put his hand on it.

'You're good friends already,' Uncle Charlie said with a laugh. 'Joe, don't bother to saddle him. From now on, Whitie belongs to Master Ned, who will ride him bareback.'

'Oh, Grandfather!'

'Very well,very well, you're happy. When you come on holiday to Great Meadow, you will always find your friend Whitie here. Meanwhile, go for a ride in the field.'

Ned mounted the pony and set off at full speed. Although he was not yet fully grown, Whitie galloped with astonishing speed. Ned uttered cries of pleasure and yelled out compliments which the wind tore from his lips. Mad with joy and sure he would not be heard, he poured out innocent declarations of love:

'Whitie, you'll be my friend. We'll be happy together, you'll see.'

Whitie set off at a gallop for the pine wood to which Ned directed him. As soon as they reached the first low branches, they slowed, then Ned jumped down and walked forward in the half-light. In the mysteriousness of the darkening wood, the pony did not leave him. Ned looked over his shoulder to keep track of the great white mark in this darkness shot through with shafts of light, and from time to time he said:

'Whitie, I'm here.'

At one point, he stopped, seized with a vague anxiety, then he retraced his steps, turned round, and passed a second time over the spot where his mother's lover had forcibly planted that first kiss on her. Like so many boys of his age, with their heads full of pirates and brigands, young Ned had a passion for the unknown, but he had found nothing strange and secret here, so he left the wood with his pony, disappointed, the dead branches cracking beneath their feet. Back in the meadow, they set of at a gallop. The grass was so high that Whitie's legs were entirely hidden by it and you might have thought they were crossing a river.

Ned arrived just in time for lunch and sat down to the left of Charlie Jones, with Miss Charlotte on the right. Emmanuel, with whom Ned had once come to blows, was sitting next to Miss Charlotte because she knew how to keep him quiet, while John, the one with the long blond hair, was demurely seated between Ned and his brother, but closer to Ned. Emmanuel was already challenging his 'cousin' with a look, after aggressively shaking his hand. The plates were filled with rice and rare roastbeef, when Charlie Jones, turning to Ned, announced:

'You won't see my dear wife Amelia today. For some months she has been living at The Coppice, a charming house very close by here, with our little twins and our daughter whom she wants to keep always beside her.'

Ned vaguely remembered a large, solemn woman; and Miss Charlotte took advantage of the silence to continue her train of thought:

'Your dear mother and I used to read the Psalms together. She can't have forgotten. I hope that you read the Bible regularly, Ned.'

Emmanuel gave a quiet chuckle and looked mockingly at Ned, who was nonplussed.

'Charlotte,' said Charlie Jones, 'one doesn't talk religion at table.'

The white bonnet protested:

'Wrong!' said a very high voice from under it. 'Religion is every-where.'

'Ned,' Charlie Jones asked, 'are you and Whitie getting along well?'

'Friends for ever!' Ned cried.

'Friends for ever,' John repeated tenderly, not having said anything up till then.

'Whitie is at Great Meadow,' said Emmanuel. 'He belongs to everyone.'

Charlie Jones turned on him:

'Now, you, don't start that. Once and for all: Whitie belongs to Ned.'

Emmanuel gave Ned a withering look.

'We'll have this out later,' he whispered across the table.

Ned's cheeks reddened, but he said nothing. His open collar and his tousled hair already made him into a slightly dishevelled country boy. He looked all the better for it.

'Ned,' Miss Charlotte said, 'you look like your father.'

'I was going to say the same,' said Charlie Jones, smiling. 'I've given you his room, on the top floor.'

He looked so sad as he said these words that silence fell until dessert.

Ned went up to his room as soon as the meal was over, accompanied by a Black carrying his bag. High-ceilinged and spacious, the room struck him by the severity of the dark furniture, the long red curtains with their heavy folds and the mirror in its walnut and mahogany frame.

'Here you are, Massa Ned,' said the Black, putting down the case. 'With Massa Charlie's room, this is the finest in Grand Meadow.'

As his back was to the door, he had not seen Emmanuel who slipped in behind him and shouted in his ear:

'You! Outside!'

The Black jumped in the air and took flight, aghast. Emmanuel shut the door.

'Ned,' he said, 'you're here for the whole summer, so listen: we'll take turns riding the white pony, with me first, or else I'll take him from you by force.'

'Over my dead body,' said Ned, shaking with fury.

'Then let's start now.'

He put his head down and rushed at Ned, knocking him on his back. A ray of sunlight lit up the aggressor's red hair and his face was contorted. Ned felt his hot breath on his face.

'I'm the son and you come after. Understand? Otherwise you'll get my fist in your eye.'

Mad with rage, Ned suddenly arched his back, rolled over on one side and dug his knee into whatever part of his adversary he could reach. He had not forgotten the advice of the gardener and, taking advantage of Emmanuel's confusion, grasped hold of his shock of red hair and banged his head several times against the floor. The boy cried out.

Charlie Jones, who had guessed something, entered abruptly at this point. Calm, his hands behind his back, he said simply to Ned:

'Don't kill him for me, even so. He must have understood by now.'

The two boys stopped.

'He hurt me,' Emmanuel groaned.

'I guess so. One has to defend oneself.'

Ned leaped up. Emmanuel pulled himself up, at first on all fours, moaning.

'Stop that,' his father ordered. 'It'll wear off. I'm ashamed of you. What's the problem?'

'He wants to take Whitie,' said Ned.

'No one apart from you will touch Whitie. The stable boys have their orders. Now, shake hands.'

Ned stepped forward holding out his hand. Emmanuel put his hands behind his back.

'Emmanuel, you must learn how to be a good loser,' said Charlie Jones.

Emmanuel did not move.

'Very well, you're stubborn. I'm putting off for a year the present I intended to give you on your birthday.'

Emmanuel's hand shot out toward Ned's like a knife. The reconciliation was swift and short.

'Is it Agenor, Papa?' asked Emmanuel.

'We'll see, it depends on your behavior from today on . . . I'll be watching you.'

Without a word he went out, closing the door. Emmanuel looked at Ned.

'You!' he said, stamping his foot.

The door re-opened.

'Do you want me to put everything off for a year? Ned, you must be wondering who Agenor is. He's the prettiest bay in my stables and the highest spirited.'

He vanished again. Emmanuel just turned his back on Ned, but there was absolute silence until the future owner of Agenor went out in his turn, furious, but without making a sound.

No on knew anything of this outburst. Miss Charlotte expressed delight at the peace in the great house and tried to draw the new arrival into fine, edifying discussions, but Ned showed some reluctance. He was fond of this busy old lady who looked at him with a hint of affectionate malice, but she embarrassed him as if she was making heaven knew what pious demands on his soul. What were they? At the age of eight he knew nothing of that, but she wanted his well-being and he evaded her without hurting her feelings, their two forms of innocence failing to concur.

Elated with happiness, he plunged across the fields on Whitie's back and vanished into the surrounding woods. The pony seemed to know even better than he did which paths to avoid. One morning when they were trotting in the chiaroscuro of a forest, Whitie suddenly stopped and would not budge. Ned jumped down and only then noticed that he was on the brink of a ravine hidden by undergrowth. He stroked the pony's forehead and it put its head with its tangled mane against his shoulder. This unexpected gesture delighted the boy who put his arm around the horse's neck and began to talk to him as to a friend.

'We're well off here. At home they don't understand anything, they make a fuss because of you.'

In spite of everything he was still shaken by the idea of falling into the ravine where Whitie might perhaps have broken his legs. He decided to take a different route home and lost his way.

There were anxious Blacks posted along the road. In the house they had waited for him before starting lunch. Charlie Jones did not scold him, but raised an eyebrow as he told him to sit down, and there was a heavy silence of disapproval. It was a hard lesson and Ned had no appetite for the Smithfield ham which he loved.

After lunch, he went alone for a walk across the huge lawn in front of the house. Running behind him, Emmanuel caught up with him. With a roar of laughter, he gave him a powerful, but entirely friendly thump in the ribs and said:

'So, it seems we have to make peace. Papa demands it. If we do, then I can have Agenor for my birthday. What's wrong? Did I hurt you?'

Ned had his hand flat on his side.

'Sorry, so sorry,' said Emmanuel. 'It's my manner, I'm like that. And then, what about you, the other day, huh? Forget it. When you see me on Agenor, you can trot behind us on your little horsey.'

'Whitie goes like an arrow.'

In Emmanuel's piercing eyes shone the desire to grapple with Ned and throw him down on the grass, but he thought of Agenor and restrained himself. His locks, walnut red, fell over his forehead and gave him a kind of savage beauty.

'In any case, tell Papa we're good pals.'

'Pals . . .,' Ned said dubiously.

'At least, pretend to believe it. Don't be a cad.'

Ned held out a hand which was grasped eagerly.

'Swell! That's for ever.'

'For ever,' Ned repeated with a smile. 'I prefer that.'

'Me, too! And I've got Agenor!'

With surprising agility, he turned a cartwheel on the lawn.

'If you like, one day, we'll have it out behind the house.'

'One day, but not right away. Can you box?'

Emmanuel's face changed.

'A bit,' he said cautiously.

'Oh, I learned with a really strong Irishman.'

Emmanuel shrank back imperceptibly.

'Ah, I see!' he said in a quieter voice.

Then he put his hands in his pockets and asked:

'Are you staying here long?'

'Until September. What about you?'

'Me? For good. I live here. One day the house will be mine.'

'Oh?'

'Yes,' said Emmanuel in an ironic tone of voice that made Ned's heart sink. What would happen to Whitie when he was no longer there? But the conversation stopped and, after walking in silence back to the house, they went their different ways.

Long rides on Whitie occupied almost the whole of Ned's days. He went as far as possible, up to the banks of a river where he stopped to rest. The water ran through the bottom of a wooded valley with a murmur, at once calm and busy, which delighted the child. There was a rustic bench where he sat down to rest while Whitie cropped the grass a few feet behind him. These expeditions into the countryside were the best times of the holiday. In the far distance, he could see the crests of the blue hills, so pale they merged with the sky. How could he have guessed that nine years earlier, his mother had sat here? A dreamer, like her, he imagined wonderful adventures on those mysterious mountains — meetings with Indians wearing head-dresses of eagles' feathers, prepared to welcome him among them.

He was bored in the great house. Vast and silent, it seemed empty, and his footsteps echoed disturbingly. At meals, he found himself with the same people, saying more or less the same things. Very often Charlie Jones would not appear and Miss Charlotte would then make the usual announcement:

'Uncle Charlie is dining at The Coppice.'

This Coppice, where no one entered except Charlie and the servants, became a mysterious place, even though it was quite near. Miss Charlotte would chatter on in a low voice. No one thought to listen to what she was saying, because they realized that with age she was growing accustomed to talking to herself about the housekeeping or religion, though she still waited for the moment when she would have an opportunity to grasp the hand of the boy from Savannah (whom she liked, of course but who, coming from that suspect place, at least deserved an attempt at reform). Unfortunately for her, he ran off as soon as he had swallowed his last mouthful.

Emmanuel had adopted a jovial attitude toward Ned, tapping him on the shoulder with the authority of an elder — and an uncle.

'As soon as war breaks out,' he said one day, 'I'll jump on Agenor and charge.'

'War . . .,' said Ned.

'Papa says it will break out one of these days.'

However, Charlie Jones did not say this at table when he appeared there. In fact, he hardly spoke at all, embarrassed by Miss Charlotte's monologue which he pretended not to hear as he did not want to hurt her. Always good-tempered, he smiled at the boys and ate with a healthy appetite, but he was in a hurry to get back to his wife, his little daughter and his twins. Their presence was his reward for a life of toil and strife in Savannah. In the little house at The Coppice, he played out his sentimental dream of the ever-loving husband of a wife who consoled herself with purely heavenly expectations, but submitted with sublime resignation to her marital duties between each new birth.

Unnoticed by almost everyone, little John, just six years old, sat next to Ned at table. With his bright golden hair down to his shoulders, he was the very image of a well-behaved, dreamy child. His brother Emmanuel could terrify him with a single sideways glance. A soul of an almost unhealthy shyness shone out of his pale blue eyes. One guessed that he would instinctively flee the world of loud voices and inflexible wills. All the delicacy of this self-effacing boy was revealed in features so fine that they reminded one of a pencil portrait by a hand that was careful to touch the paper as lightly as possible. He kept as close as he could to Ned, looking at him from time to time with an air of confident affection which his relation did not always notice — and which plunged him into confusion whenever he did become aware of it. Both of them exchanged smiles: a short smile from one and a long one, indefinably grave, from the other. This was the extent of the mysterious dialogue which never took any other form, except once only, when it was betrayed by a cry from John, echoing one of Ned's: 'Friends for ever!'

# 122

While Virginia was basking in the half-sleep induced by a fine summer, the little world at Dimwood, dozing no less profoundly, was woken with a start. Toward the end of July, two carriages stopped in front of the house and, with a kind of rush, under their parasols, Mildred, Hilda and Minnie stepped down, followed by the much calmer figures of Aunt Augusta, helped by Uncle Josh. William Hampton got out last of all and ran over to greet Douglas.

'We've come without warning you, Mr Hargrove. Forgive us. These ladies had had enough of Limestone Springs and, at their urging, I went to fetch them.'

Josh also shook Douglas' hand.

'Surprised to see us, Douglas? Augusta was dying to come back to Dimwood.'

'Delighted to have you all here, Josh; but where are the others? We appear to have some husbands missing.'

'Oh, Siverac and Lawrence? One month at Limestone Springs was enough for them. The truth is that one dies of boredom in these spas and they could think of nothing except Charleston, their paradise . . . In short, that is where they are, engaged in their usual pursuits, especially politics.'

Augusta finally appeared and kissed her sister-in-law.

'Emma, you're back at dear Dimwood, at last!'

'How lovely for us to see all of you here, darling,' said Emma.

'Josh and I are staying but the others will go on to Charleston. Yes, they're setting us down here, and then — off to the town! That's youth! At the same time, they're taking Elizabeth away with them.'

'Really! But let's not stay in the sun.'

She called:

'Elizabeth!'

Elizabeth appeared, on the stairs, when they reached the hall. In her eau-de-nil green dress, with her hair tied up at the neck, she looked radiant.

'Am I dreaming?' she asked.

There was a general burst of laughter.

'Come, Elizabeth,' Hilda said with a little malice, welcoming her with open arms. 'You certainly managed to make a great entrance. Come down and kiss us.'

Her cheeks slightly pinker than theirs, she went from one woman to another, then turned to Josh. There was a smile for William Hampton, whom she had always considered elegant.

'Elizabeth,' Hilda said. 'You thought you were dreaming just now, but the dream starts here. Pack your bags, we're taking you with us to Charleston.'

Elizabeth's face fell.

'Impossible . . . The baby: I can't leave him.'

'Why not?' Douglas asked, surprised. 'He's got his Betty and his black mammy to look after him.'

'It's not the same,' Elizabeth groaned. 'I want him close to me.'

Douglas, anxious to see her go, would not give in.

'You can't take him with you to Charleston in July. At his age the heat would make him ill. He needs the cool air here — here, at Dimwood . . . And then, heavens above, let me enjoy my grandson a little!'

Hilda gave a diabolical smile.

'In Charleston, you'll have Billy. Think of that, darling.'

'But he's not in Charleston, he's at Fort Beauregard.'

'From there to Charleston is only two hours on horseback. He must surely be able to get a furlough for a day . . . or longer.'

Racked with uncertainty, Elizabeth asked for a few minutes to reflect and went straight to Kit's room. She knew quite well that she would give in, but she wanted to clasp the child in her arms, giving him one last chance of keeping her there . . . You would have thought he was doing everything he could. Sitting on Black Mammy's knees, he waved his hands as soon as he saw her and gave incomprehensible cries. Falling to her knees in front of him, she covered him with kisses, weeping.

'I'm going away for a few days,' she said to the black woman, who could only open her eyes wide and say:

'Oh, Ma'am!'

'Goodbye, my love,' she repeated, her face shining with tears.

It was then that, by some intuition or other, the child turned his head to one side, looking at his mother with blue eyes full of malicious merriment. 'Mama, Mama,' he chanted. She thought she was going to weaken, but she pressed him to her, gave him back to Black Mammy and went out.

Betty hastily packed her bag and a few minutes later she was getting into one of the carriages with William Hampton and Hilda, while Mildred and Minnie took their places in the other. The goodbyes were exemplary in their brevity, cutting short the usual endearments and speeding their departure.

The horses set off at a cracking pace, Dimwood vanished and the beautiful Englishwoman managed to make a good impression on Hampton, whom she hardly knew. He tried to console her by describing the attractions of Limestone Spring.

'You wouldn't believe your eyes. It's the most romantic landscape in the world. We went everywhere, right to the borders of the State. Waterfalls forty feet high tumble down wooded hillsides, creating rainbows that only vanish at sundown. You can walk in the delightful shade of trees so old that no one even knows their age. Everywhere are prodigious masses of flowers with dizzying scents and every color imaginable, from dark violet to the most delicate shades of blue, competing in rowdy confusion . . .'

'The hotel close to these splendors,' Hilda added, 'has every modern comfort: gas lighting in all the rooms, hot running water.'

'You would have enjoyed it for a week, Elizabeth, but one has to admit that the uniformity of daily life in that paradise does not make up for the enchanting scenery and tries human patience to the limit.'

'But what about the pure air?' Hilda said, laughing.

'And what about the smell of the sulphur baths? Pooh!'

All three burst out laughing.

Day was starting to fade when they reached the outskirts of Charleston. Elizabeth had more or less recovered and the silent immobility of Dimwood was driven further and further into the distance by the noise of the town.

'You'll find changes in our Charleston since you were here last,' said Hilda. 'Except in our house, and even there . . .'

As soon as she was in her room, the same as the first time with its large double bed, Elizabeth wrote a short letter to Billy which was like a cry for help . . . After that, she resolved to be firm and patient.

Hilda was right. The atmosphere in Charleston was different. There were more people in the streets and they seemed to talk at a higher pitch, while the young newsvendors ran faster, crying their wares which were snatched up as fast as in times of crisis. One sensed a dormant, profound disquiet. In Lawrence Turner's house Elizabeth missed the happy atmosphere which had raised her spirits on her previous visit and the merriment of mealtimes as nine people gathered around a table laden with delicious dishes and wines. Though dinner was no less good, it was shorter, with continual comings and goings. It was as though the public highway had become the real meeting-place and news was debated there whatever the time of day. Shut up at home, one risked missing the latest rumors . . . Politics invaded every corner.

Hilda sometimes took Elizabeth out walking on the pretext of showing her some of the finest houses in town, but above all because she could not keep still. In this way they caught snatches of the latest news, which Elizabeth did not understand at all. Patiently, Hilda explained. They spent their time paying visits. One morning, with Mildred, when all three were coming back from a walk through the town, they ran across William and Lawrence sitting on the front steps engaged in drawing up a veritable plan of campaign.

'We must have Union, Union and more Union,' Lawrence was saying.

'What's the matter with him?' Hilda exclaimed.

'Don't worry,' William said, waving a hand without looking at her. 'We're doing the election.'

In front of the three women leaning on their parasols in the shade of the wisteria, the debate continued.

'I'm withdrawing Bell,' Lawrence said. 'He hasn't a chance and the only sensible thing is for him to support our candidate.'

'How can you withdraw Douglas? He's a leading player,' William remarked.

'The neatest solution would be for him to have a heart attack.'

'Oh, oh!' said the chorus of women, suddenly more interested.

'You don't beat about the bush.'

'What else is there? Remember what Julian Hartridge said yesterday in Savannah: "Three tickets for three different directions, and the train never arrives anywhere." He is right: the Democratic Party is going off the rails.'

'The Republicans don't have a majority,' said William. 'Their candidate is an unknown.'

'Don't say that, William,' Lawrence answered. 'Abraham Lincoln is formidable. He's a lawyer, a clever and tricky man. Do you recall the Armstrong affair two years ago? The murder?'

He was talking to all of them and, since the story concerned a crime, they listened even more attentively.

'Oh, it was vaguely mentioned at the time,' said William.

'I'll tell you the whole thing briefly. In August '57, after a fight, two men were accused of homicide leading to the death, two days later, of their victim. One of the accused, Armstrong, was the son of an old friend of Lincoln's. The main witness for the prosecution gave his account of the affair so clearly that the jury was convinced, as was the judge. Lincoln cross-examined with a detached air, with questions that seemed to support the prosecution: how far away was the witness, what was the precise time and, since it was dark, how could he see clearly? Without hesitation, the witness replied that he was fifteen yards away, that it was precisely eleven o'clock and that there was a full moon, so bright and so high that it might have been the sun at ten in the morning. Lincoln asked to be given an almanac for the year of the murder, 1857. The moon that night had been low in the sky, covered in clouds and about to vanish in the West. The whole court burst out laughing. The witness was disproved. But that was not the end: all the evidence was against his client when Lincoln began to speak. His speech, in my opinion, showed what a great actor he could have been. He appealed directly to the jury, speaking of his poor upbringing, the help and comfort given to him by the parents of the accused, their struggle to survive, the recent death of the father, the mother's tears and her distress if her son were to be taken from her. Tears were running down the speaker's face, and then the jury and the whole court began to weep with him. And the defendant was acquitted.'

'Well, I never!' Hilda exclaimed. 'If he was ever President, he couldn't do that!'

'Why not?' said William. 'He's a Republican!'

'In short: Breckinridge must be elected at all cost.'

With this, Lawrence was about to stand up when they were all surprised to hear Elizabeth's voice.

'Breckinridge!' she exclaimed. 'A wonderful man! He will entrance the crowd with his eagle's eyes.'

'What, Elizabeth?' said Hilda. 'Have you seen him? But you've never been interested in politics. Do you even know that he's our Vice-President?'

'I know him.' Elizabeth took on an air of importance. 'He was at my father-in-law's, the night when Patti sang. We had a long talk. He's fascinating. He's a conqueror.'

'Ah-ha!' Hilda said, since Elizabeth added nothing further. 'Let's go and have lunch, if these gentlemen will let us through.'

Lawrence and William stood up and followed them, but they looked at Elizabeth with new eyes. For the first time, she had made a considerable impression on them.

That same evening, they were with Minnie, Mike and Antoninus in the Battery gardens. The whole town was walking there, listening distractedly to the band of the cadets from the fort: Mozart's *Turkish March*, a favorite with the public, burst out with childish joy — and much support from the cymbals — in the silent light cast by the moon. The paths were full of young people, whose high, clear voices blended in happy confusion out of which from time to time emerged, not Patrick Henry's famous cry of 'Freedom or Death!', but its more timely variant: 'Secession or Death!' Under the dark shadows of the plane trees, these linked silhouettes passed across the large silver patches of the pathways, their presence given away occasionally only by peels of laughter.

Along the esplanade, Elizabeth and her little group were leaning over the balustrade from which one could look directly down into the port. There, on the quayside, a little lower, some Blacks were playing the banjo, and these sharp notes seemed like little claws scratching at the triumphant Turkish march raised by the cadets.

A light breeze was blowing in from the sea and the reflection of the moon danced on the waves. The friends, usually so talkative, said nothing. Suddenly Mike broke the silence:

'The lights over there,' he told Elizabeth, 'come from Fort Sumter.'

'And much further,' said Lawrence, 'though we can't see it, is the mysterious Fort Moultrie. Let's take a walk beneath the trees.'

'Why mysterious?' Elizabeth asked; but they were already talking about something else and a dance tune now seemed to be distracting everybody . . .

The night was mild. In a vast and indistinct murmur of anxious conversation, the crowd continued to stride up and down the gardens even after the band had left. Some hangers-on could not make up their minds to go home, but at first light the vultures descended on the town as far as the esplanade, insolently screeching to drive off the last night owls and establish their rule over the streets. These dark refuse collectors, hopping on their red feet, had come to reclaim their empire. Resisting any attempt to drive them away, they stretched their bluish necks and spat at the loiterers, beating their heavy wings.

The days, at once the same yet different, succeeded one another in a bubbling of ideas, and music faithfully filled the gardens by night. Billy galloped in for a brief furlough and then galloped out. All the young people of Charleston knew exactly how many guns, munitions and canons were held in the fortress and the smaller forts. One of these, Fort Moultrie, facing the sea on a tongue of land across the bay, became a favorite spot for the townsfolk to ride and picnic beneath the ramparts, now covered in sand and scarcely protected at all by its defenceless garrison. As the presidential election drew near, talk became more and more heated and Charleston proceeded from one speech to the next, as if from one holiday to another — the speeches becoming more and more enflamed under the ever clear sky.

In September, Elizabeth at last considered returning to Savannah. The schools were re-opening and she could not leave her boys any longer. And then Billy, as a soldier garrisoned in South Carolina, would have to vote in Charleston; therefore, she thought, he would have a furlough. This seemed an ideal excuse for returning at the end of October. No one corrected her mistake — because in South Carolina, nothing was done as elsewhere. The Carolinans had already chosen their electors, and since their vote was secured for Breckinridge, the State of South Carolina would be following events from the sidelines on the day when all the rest of America was seized with electoral fever. On September 6, Elizabeth left the Turners' home and all of them, particularly William Hampton, who had now succumbed to her charm, made her swear that she would see them again as soon as possible.

That same day, in the late afternoon, a six-year-old boy was crossing the great green space separating Charlie Jones's house from the long low building formerly known as the House of Chaos. He was making his way slowly through the undergrowth, which came almost up to his shoulders, and the setting sun cast a soft light around his pale blond head. Though he did not know it, his father was watching him through a window at Great Meadow, and paying particular attention to the boy.

Finally, he reached the door of the low house and raised his arm to grasp the knocker, which he let fall twice. Was it a signal? The door opened at once. A lady in black, still beautiful despite having put on weight as she grew older, gave him an affectionate smile which did not entirely cancel out the unhappy look on her patient and resigned face.

'Come in, Johnny. I saw you coming some time ago from my chair. Go and say hello to the commodore, like a good boy.'

John went over to a man with graying hair and a nose like a beak, whose clear eyes seemed to be searching a distant horizon. Sitting in a huge rocking chair, he was holding a pipe.

In a corner, near the fireplace, a large yellow dog was gently snoring on an old cushion. Woken by the sound of the door, he opened one eye and his long tail, oddly twisted, wagged two or three times when he saw the little boy.

'Welcome on board the *Quarrelsome*,' said the commodore. 'What news from Great Meadow? Still sulking?'

'Great Meadow will always sulk,' said the lady in black.

'Quiet, Maisie. Go down to the galley and prepare some refreshment for the cabin boy.'

Maisie simply went into an adjoining room.

'Now, you,' the commodore told John, 'answer me and speak like a man.'

John's high-pitched voice replied without hesitation:

'There's nothing to report.'

'Your father?'

'Papa says nothing.'

'You can tell him that I take the air on the poop deck every day at eleven o'clock. For his information.'

'The poop deck, the road,' Maisie explained under her breath, coming back with a glass of iced tea in her hand. 'Take this, child, and don't drink it too fast.'

'Understood, sailor?' asked the commodore.

'Yes, sir.'

'Yes, captain,' the commodore corrected him in a thunderous voice.

John, holding his glass in both hands, almost dropped it. Maisie took it from him and put it on a table.

'Yes, captain,' he said timidly.

'Sit down beside me,' said Maisie, 'and don't be afraid. My husband shouts, but it doesn't mean a thing. We're very fond of you.'

'When you grow up,' the commodore went on, rocking in his chair, 'we'll send you to sea and you'll cruise around the West Indies, as I did.'

And again he began to rock, silently turning over his memories.

'How is Ned?' Maisie asked.

John's eyes clouded and he looked up at Maisie with despair:

'He's never at home, always on his pony.'

And suddenly he burst into tears.

'Come, come, child,' Maisie said, stroking his hair. 'That's not sad. I see him go past sometimes. He seems very nice.'

'Very nice,' John repeated.

She gave him a handkerchief to wipe his eyes and blow his nose.

'What's up with the cabin boy?' the commodore asked.

'Nothing. He must have a cold.'

Bending over little John, she put her lips to his forehead.

'We're always delighted to see you. Once the house was full of people. It was merrier, you can't imagine . . . But night is falling. Go home before it gets dark. And don't forget to tell your Papa that the commodore would like to talk to him on the road.'

'Can I say goodbye to the dog?'

'Of course. He knows you. But don't touch his cushion: he is possessive about it and will growl.'

John went and stroked the head and ears of the old dog, whose broken tail immediately began to thump the floor beside his bed.

'What happened to him?' John asked.

For the first time Maisie gave an amused little laugh.

'Oh, his tail? It was caught once too often under my husband's rocking chair . . . Hurry off, Johnny, it's getting dark. And come back soon.'

The child ran off without further delay. A faint light still lit the meadow and the tiny, pale, golden head could be seen in the half-light, bravely cutting a way through the undergrowth.

Charlie Jones was sitting at his desk in a room on the ground floor. Green curtains hung beside the windows and the walls were almost entirely covered by colored views of the various capital cities of the world. In these surroundings which stimulated his appetite for work, he caught up on the latest news. A large pile of newspapers rose like a wall around his chair, while still more had spilled over onto the table, and he was unwrapping them with an increasingly nervous hand. Some he read very carefully. 'The port of Peking blockaded by the Anglo-French fleets and the city surrounded by the troops of the two countries.' All at once, the Chinese Empire was spread from top to bottom of the front page. In Vienna, nothing. They were waltzing in Vienna . . . France had annexed Savoy after a heavily rigged vote, the newspaper said. In Paris, they were dancing. One dance was all the rage: the Cancan of Hell.

Cancan of Hell . . . Charlie Jones cast an amused glance over the mountain of newsprint. 'What a splendid definition of the press as a whole!' Casting aside Europe and Asia, he embarked on America. Savannah first of all: The *Savannah Morning News*, Democrat, of course; as was the *The Express*; then finally the black sheep, the Republican's *Republican*.

All three papers had a lot to say about Mrs Harrison Edwards, Algernon Steeers and Julian Hartridge. Charlie Jones looked more attentively, giving credit first of all to his faithful accomplice. Since the beginning of September, while summer was still triumphant, she had given one ball after another. Everyone rushed to her to express their Southern beliefs and to admire her latest ornament: a bird of paradise sent direct from a Parisian fashion house, with a very large blue diamond for its eye.

As for Algernon, he was enthusiastically raising a subscription to buy guns and if need be to arm the militia of Georgia. Governor Brown was giving him full moral support. Some Northern governors were going much further: Andrew and Buckingham were stockpiling large quantities of arms and military equipment in their arsenals for a war they considered imminent.

As for Julian Hartridge, he poured more and more scorn on the divisions in the Democratic Party and called insistently for the immediate withdrawal of Douglas and Bell — because, he said, if one does not want a Union with the North, one must have a Union of the South. From Mississippi to the Carolinas, many supported him. Charlie Jones agreed entirely.

Once more, he considered the piles of newspapers which were not diminishing . . . The Democrats shouted, the Republicans yelled. Their murderous cries seemed to echo across this room, sheltered as it was from the world. The press of both North and South contained an equal share of noise, din, tumult and clamor. The unrest during June, the dramatic events, the apparent calm of summer: all this lay dormant or seethed forth from these sheets. 'Me, me!' each of them proclaimed. 'Only I am right!'

Douglas had just criticized the South and had only succeeded in uniting it against him. The Republicans, who were not in the majority anywhere and whose party included people with widely different views, could see their chances increasing; and, even though they, too, were not in a majority in the South, the Secessionists watched the Union slowly dissolve. The Republican Seward and the Democrat Douglas still hoped to come to a secret arrangement: each thought he held the reins of his own party, but their plans were overturned by the skill and political intelligence of their adversaries: Breckinridge, combative and eloquent, rallied the leading figures in the South behind him; while Lincoln, who rarely showed his lanky figure and slack suspenders except in his electoral meetings, turned out to be obstinate and inflexible.

Every newspaper gave its opinion on everything. In the South, the papers competed in vehemence. From the Petersburg *Express* to the Augusta *Constitutionalist*, via the Richmond *Dispatch*, all of them — the Charleston *Courier*, the Atlanta *Constitution*, the *Lynchburg Virginian* — not forgetting the *Alexandria Gazette* and the Richmond *South*, together with all the rest, cried: 'Secession!' The New Orleans *Abeille,* consistently refusing to use the English language, called in French for *'la Séparation immédiate!'*

Things were not quite as simple in the North. The Democratic paper in his own town, the *Illinois State Register*, openly mocked the candidate Lincoln and his electoral campaign: 'Cost of the match: two hundred dollars; goal: a presidential chair; result: nil.' In the *New York Herald*, the paper's founder and owner, Gordon Bennett, supported slavery, and the paper enjoyed great success; while in the pages of the *Liberator*, Charlie Jones could perceive the shadowy figure of Garrison, in a cloud of opium, calling for an insurrection of Blacks. Seward waved his large yellow handkerchief in the *New York Tribune* and Horace Greeley had the moralizing impudence to write: 'I have taken a definite decision to be more intelligent today than I was yesterday, and much less than I shall be tomorrow.' Charlie Jones burst out laughing: in the article that followed, the same Greeley preached disunity and violence.

He rummaged through this pile of newspapers for a little while longer, throwing them down on the ground beside him, and the great rustling of paper was like the mutterings of a mob.

'Here we are, in the City of Confusion,' he muttered.

Night was falling. With a sigh of irritation, he stood up and lit a lamp. At that moment, there was a knock on the door.

'No one's to come in,' he said. 'I'm working.'

'Papa,' said a little voice.

He opened the door at once.

'Johnny, what do you want?'

The child looked up: the lamp shone on his silky hair, tousled by the wind, seeming to add light to light.

'I went to see Aunt Maisie,' he said; then continued more rapidly, as if reciting a message he had learned by heart: 'Commodore wants to talk to you on the road at eleven o'clock tomorrow morning.'

'Did he say that?' Charlie Jones exclaimed. 'By Jove, I'll go there in the morning. He must have read my thoughts. Thank you, Johnny.'

The next day he walked over to the House of Chaos, smoking a small cigar. Wearing a large check cap, he adopted a nonchalant air and pretended to be looking at the clouds without taking the corner of his eye off the yellow door with its knocker. Suddenly it opened rather violently and the commodore emerged, offering his powerful hand.

'Charlie, we'll have to put an end to this. We see one another once a year on the poop deck. But we haven't fallen out, despite that.'

Charlie Jones opened a cigar case and offered a small cigar to his old comrade.

'Thank you,' the commodore said. 'But at sea, we usually smoke this . . .'

He took his pipe out of his pocket and thrust it into a corner of his mouth, even though it was not alight.

'News,' he said. 'I don't get the newspapers. How do things stand?'

'Everything depends on the election in November.'

Walking together along the road that separated the House of Chaos from Great Meadow, they went over the events of the day. In the event of war, the commodore was determined to rejoin the fleet, just for the pleasure of sinking the Northern Navy.

'Teddie,' Charlie said brusquely. 'I want to see your wife.'

'As you wish, but we're better off here, between men. Women, you know . . .'

They turned round and Charlie Jones, cap in hand, went into the House of Chaos. The old dog barked, as if to salve his conscience, feebly and dully: a bark that had been over-used.

Maisie cried with joy:

'Charlie!'

'Yes, Charlie. Just because you quarreled with Amelia fifteen years ago, that doesn't mean I can't come and see you. These family quarrels are ridiculous.'

'Ridiculous,' Maisie sighed, her head on his shoulder. 'But Amelia never forgives.'

'Holy women never forgive,' the commodore said sarcastically.

Charlie Jones and Maisie sat down beside one another.

'Maisie,' he said, clasping one of her hands, 'when I saw my boy going across the meadow to see you . . .'

'Johnny is an angel,' Maisie said, her pained face hidden beneath a smile.

'Just so,' said Charlie Jones. 'Do you remember the *still, small voice*? I heard it. That's why I came.'

'You did well, Charlie. I have also heard that voice, here, in this empty house. All the children have gone, the girls married in California and Mississippi, Clementine, Elsie, Fanny; and the boys are far away, at sea, Dick, Harry, Daniel, the best-looking of them all, a naval officer. Everyone said he was as handsome as a god, and do you know why he left suddenly? Because of the beautiful Englishwoman . . .'

'I guessed as much, Maisie, but Elizabeth never said anything.'

'She didn't want to marry him; so, one morning, he kissed us all very quickly and set off. We haven't seen him since. He is on the West coast. He never married.'

'Poor Daniel . . . But one day he will forget all that and get married. In any case, there is now peace between the House of Chaos and Great Meadow. I shall ensure that my wife accepts the fact.'

'Are you sure?' Maisie said with a sceptical smile.

'You'll see. Now I intend to go back to Savannah, but I shall return from time to time. You're not thinking of going away?'

'Where to?'

'How should I know? Don't listen to rumors . . . In this quiet corner of Virginia, you will be safe whatever happens, as we shall in Great Meadow.'

With these comforting words, they parted. There was a manly handshake at the door with the commodore, concluding a visit that had put an end to years of silence.

Charlie Jones spent the night at The Coppice and the next morning, having opted to take breakfast at Great Meadow, announced with a broad smile that his holidays were over and that business called him back to Savannah. Within twenty-four hours, he and Ned would be on their way to Norfolk where one of his boats was waiting. This news, which took them all by surprise, affected the boys in different ways. Emmanuel was stoical: he had his Agenor; but Ned let out a heartfelt cry:

'Whitie!'

'You can't take him with you,' said his grandfather, amused. 'You can come back to him next year. We'll take care of him for you, don't worry. And be a man, please. No crying at table.'

John's anguish was much less open and wrapped in silence. His cheek against Ned's arm, without a word he drenched the older boy's sleeve with his tears.

Miss Charlotte's sharp voice provided the comment she considered appropriate to the occasion.

'My children, you must accept joyfully whatever each new day brings us. Ned, some more jam?'

But Ned did not want any jam. He wanted Whitie. As soon as he could, he ran to the stables and clasped the pony's head in his arms; then, jumping onto him bareback, he set off on a crazy race through the countryside where he knew every wood, every field and every stream.

As for Johnny, he took refuge in the children's room and, his face in his pillow, sobbed, endlessly repeating Ned's name. By one of those cruel ironies of fate, the bed in which his heart was breaking was the very same one in which, nine years earlier, in this innocent-looking little room, Ned had been conceived.

The day was spent in a bustle of packing, while Miss Charlotte kept an attentive eye on everything.

Night passed. The sun had scarcely risen on the new day — which promised to be radiant, as though to prevent the travelers from departing — when two carriages set off at a brisk trot, one carrying a red-cheeked gentleman wearing a black and dark green coat, and a solemn-faced young boy, who said nothing, while the other was laden with a huge pile of baggage. Until the moment night fell, Virginia displayed its song of peaceful happiness before their eyes. At Norfolk, they stopped to sleep in the only large hotel in town, and the next day they were on board one of Charlie Jones's most comfortable boats, sailing toward Savannah.

In Oglethorpe Square, Ned climbed the steps followed by a servant carrying his cases. In the hall, Miss Llewelyn was waiting for the young traveler, for she only had to hear the sound of a carriage in front of the house to rush to the foot of the stairs, full of quiet authority in her black dress. Ned looked at her like someone who was having trouble awaking from a dream and found himself confronted with a pitilessly dull reality.

'Mama is back from Charleston and will be happy to see you,' said the housekeeper.

Elizabeth was coming down from her room at that moment and cried:

'Darling!'

'Mummy!' he said.

It was like a well-learned lesson, but they embraced each other tenderly, even though neither was entirely the same person they had been two months ago. There was a hint of banality in their greeting: even they themselves were vaguely aware of it. With Dimwood, Charleston and Billy behind her, lovelier than ever in her white outfit, Elizabeth felt matured by a new experience of life. Ned, oddly disoriented in surroundings he knew only too well, was still living somewhere else, riding with Whitie through the fine open spaces.

In spite of that, they soon returned to their old habits, as they must, and the house in Oglethorpe Square became the same old house for both mother and son . . .

After the heat of summer and the over-excitement of the electoral campaign, Savannah gradually slumped back into a kind of lassitude where news was concerned. They had heard the same things too often from the candidates: Breckinridge, Douglas and Bell. The theme never varied: electing a Republican meant Secession and war; but did anyone really believe in war? This eternal phantom was imperceptibly losing its power to terrify. What threatens to happen and never does, ceases to exist. When it came down to it, Mrs Harrison Edwards had shown great common sense in offering society the opportunity to forget its troubles by dancing and enjoying life which was still beautiful and joyful.

Charlie Jones's irritation, sitting among his newspapers in Virginia, would have seemed odd in Savannah. So much excitement over a mere speech . . . Good taste required one to speak of such things calmly and not very often. Breckinridge was theoretically favorite. Little or nothing was known of the Republican opponent, Lincoln. Every prominent politician has his myth, and Lincoln's was unappealing. Too tall, badly dressed, even vulgar, he spoke little: an enigmatic, even rather sinister figure.

There was something gloomy about that long wait for the November day when America would learn the name of the victor. There was nothing brilliant about the contest. One felt that the event, however it turned out, would bring relief, like a man threatened by illness who, after years of uncertainty, examinations and tests, finally learns the name of his disease. At last he can act; it was not knowing that was intolerable.

In this atmosphere of muted exasperation, Algernon became more and more active. His fundraising exceeded his expectations, and Mrs Harrison Edwards supported him as though for a charity bazaar. The money was entrusted to Hodgkins & Sons of Macon, Georgia, who would order rifles from New York and dismantled guns from Manchester. There would be no problem about anything that came from England in ships flying the British flag under the auspices of Charlie Jones, who was a British subject. However, he had to be requested to ensure that the cargo of rifles was loaded on the New York docks by the *Monticello*, a vessel from his personal fleet which traded with the great Northern city.

September was drawing to a close. The time was near when the electoral machinery would be set in motion, and there was no end to predictions. One day when Mrs Harrison Edwards was conversing in her drawing-room with Algernon, they had the pleasure of seeing Charlie Jones come in, just returned from Virginia, wearing his usual smile.

'I have news,' Algernon said at once.

'I know everything,' said Charlie Jones. 'If you think that the newspapers have been quiet on the subject . . . Your plan is splendid, I accept. My ships are requisitioned in advance to go to Manchester, agreed, agreed. We'll look into it together.'

'We should have done nothing without your permission, Charlie.'

Charlie Jones shrugged his shoulders.

'Well, let's act quickly now that I am here and while we still have time.'

'Do you truly think there will be war?' asked Mrs Harrison Edwards.

'I know nothing, absolutely nothing, but I act as if I knew.'

'In any event,' Algernon said, 'Secession is likely.'

Mrs Harrison Edwards threw back her head defiantly.

'In Charleston, it happens virtually every day.'

'And what are they doing in Virginia?' Algernon asked.

'Virgina is calm and keeping its head. It is never in a hurry, it thinks carefully before it acts.'

'It's holding up everything!' cried the ebullient Algernon.

Charlie Jones suddenly adopted a graver look.

'Have patience,' he said simply.

October slowly went by without changing anything in their everyday lives. The climate of optimism was not perceptibly altered. Perhaps people were more often inclined to say, soberly: 'If a Republican is elected, there will be Secession.' Some would then remark: 'Yes, but Secession is not war.' This statement made wise heads nod: 'One can't exclude the possibility of a peaceful Secession.' On the face of it, there was a universal yearning for tranquillity and for the satisfaction of being able to live in harmony with one's neighbors. In just ten more days, on November 6, America would vote. Between now and then . . .

On October 28, French and British forces captured Peking.

# 8

# DIXIE

*I wish I was in de land ob cotton,*
*Old times dar am not forgotten,*
*Look away, look away!*
*Look away! Dixie Land.*
*In Dixie Land whar I was born in,*
*Early on one frosty mornin,*
*Look away, look away!*
*Look away! Dixie* Land.

# 123

O n November 6, America voted. That evening, in Charleston, the little group of Hilda's relatives were in her drawing-room, seized by an excitement that had them all talking at once. The men in their coats, the women in their best dresses as if they were about to go to a ball, they could not agree on the route for their nightly walk. Elizabeth, wearing a white dress, with her hair in artful disarray, did not even try to put in a word, since she was still not fully acquainted with the town; but when everyone else was shouting, she did the same in order to enjoy the pleasure of over-excitement. Suddenly, she felt as though she were sixteen again.

Hilda's voice rose above the general din:

'It's already ten o'clock. We can't stay here when everything is happening outside . . . Let's go anywhere.'

'To the Battery.'

'Later. First to the corner of Broad and Meeting Street.'

'Why not go straight to the Hamptons?'

'Papa's giving a reception,' said William Hampton. 'But once you're there, you'll never get out.'

Suddenly, in a jumble, they were all outside. The mild Indian summer lingered under a blue-black sky, teeming with stars. Along the streets, buzzing with noise, the crowd moved this way and that, as if looking for the place where the great news would erupt with the greatest force. It was an historic moment, not to be missed. More or less everywhere they were saying the same thing: 'If it's Breckinridge, we shall gain a President, a real one; if it's Douglas, we'll see how to contain him; if it's Lincoln, then it's Secession and long live Secession . . .' Elizabeth caught snatches of these confusing remarks, though the name Breckinridge made her vaguely hope that her admirer would win. When they reached the front of the courthouse, whose columned façade displayed a monumental notice-board with mobile panels, they stopped as the central panel showed the first votes received and the corresponding number of electoral votes. From time to time, the notice vanished to reappear with new results. The telegraph was constantly tickering in news from the most distant States. There was no excitement at the struggle between Douglas and Breckinridge. Bell, the third Democratic candidate, seemed to be fading, only winning the marginal States, but the figures showing a slight advance for Lincoln aroused a sense of anxiety.

'Lincoln doesn't look at all like a winner,' said Siverac. 'He's climbing very slowly, and there's not one vote for the Republicans in the South.'

'Obviously the North has not rallied behind him as a whole,' said Turner. 'I've never seen such a dull election.'

'We'll have hours of this,' Hilda exclaimed impatiently. 'William, let's go and see what's happening at your father's party: that's always sensational.'

They could see the house a little way down Broad Street, lit up like a huge lantern with dazzling lights. On the upper floor veranda, an elegant crowd could be seen through the tall windows thrown wide open to give a glimpse of the gilded drawing-rooms with their glittering chandeliers. An orchestra was pouring out the latest European waltzes into the night air and the dancers whirled round, as though carried away by a furious desire to live at a new pitch of intensity.

Outside, men and women were caught up in this music and, clasping even the waists of strangers, they swung round and round in the street. The sound of singing got louder and louder: from the neighboring streets, bands of young people were hurrying, armed with lanterns on the end of poles, which they raised above their heads with shouts like the sibilant war cries of Indian braves.

In the midst of this tumult, Hilda and her friends cheerfully struggled to make a path through the throng. People stood aside a little to let them pass with the inbred good manners of the South, but, as always, Elizabeth caused a stir and attracted barely veiled compliments. Some young people murmured as she passed: 'Put me down for the next dance, Miss.' She blushed and, feeling herself blush, felt even more beautiful. Being happy, she was prodigal with her smiles. She had never been able to resist the instinct to please and breathed in their admiration like someone intoxicating herself with the scent of camellias.

After a while, they managed to reach King Street through an alleyway between the gardens. There were fewer people trying to reach the Battery by that route, but the rare open spaces were filled with noise and laughter.

'A bench under the trees,' Minnie sighed, tired of walking. 'Oh, if only we could rest! You're tireless.'

All around them the crowd was almost as thick as in front of the notice-board, and there were more ordinary people, though the general excitement abolished all class distinctions. Workmen in loose overalls were talking freely to gentlemen in coats and even to ladies in evening dress. The mood was one of fraternization in an open struggle for independence. As around the Hampton house, people were dancing, but in a more spirited way, accompanied by popular songs. Here, as elsewhere, Elizabeth was the object of much flattering attention, bordering on familiarity, so that Hilda, who ran no such risk, thought to throw her white silk shawl over the beautiful Englishwoman's head.

'You are laying yourself too open,' she said, arranging the folds of the material so that they entirely covered Elizabeth's hair. 'One shouldn't exhibit oneself like that in public.'

Elizabeth held back the reply that was burning on her lips. One couldn't argue in a town that was prey to such patriotic fervor: the excitement was becoming a riot. More and more lanterns were waving above their heads and the singers' voices drowned any conversation. A taste for violence and struggle was mingled with the furious merriment. Siverac, Turner and Hampton instinctively grouped around the ladies to serve as their bodyguards; but what were they afraid of? Everyone was everyone else's friend.

'We shall be quieter at the Battery,' said Minnie.

However, as they progressed, this hope faded. The crowd had been holding back its enthusiasm while it was surrounded by the tall, disdainful houses of the great families, but in the Battery Gardens it felt freer to express itself. Bands of young men were running aimlessly around under the trees, cheering for their South as though after a victory. Many were shouting to be given guns.

Hilda thought they should go back. The men wouldn't hear of it, and Elizabeth felt bold, aroused as she was by this feverish mass of young people.

'Let's try to get to the terrace,' Hampton suggested.

'Good idea, we'll have a view over the whole bay and what's happening,' said Elizabeth.

This idea seemed so sensible that the little group, shoving with elbows and shoulders, tried to carry it out. Could they have guessed that the view across the bay interested the Englishwoman less than the sight of the cadets who were there, close by, along the terrace? In their dark blue uniforms, they were as excited as the civilians, singing warlike songs at the top of their voices and cheered by the whole crowd, which was trying to sing with them. Elizabeth did not take her eyes off them. As they were marching up and down, she finally saw them so close by that she lost her head. They were so handsome in their tight-waisted uniforms and they looked so gallant that, in a wave of irrepressible admiration, she did something very strange: furiously, she tore off the silk shawl covering her head and her hair gleamed provocatively under the lights. Astonished and delighted looks were cast in her direction. Several cadets smiled and waved, and she loved them, she loved them all, she was for Secession, she was for battle . . .

Hilda pulled her back:

'Elizabeth, are you mad, you're indecent — can't you see that these young men are making eyes at you?'

Could she see! Siverac and Turner had to stand in front of her to protect her from this amorous fusillade.

'Stop dreaming,' said Hampton. 'Think of Billy.'

They forcibly pulled her away from the cadets to the edge of the terrace, where she could admire everything, the port and the bay. Still dazzled by the sight of the uniforms, she forgot them at once when with a single glance she took in the hundreds of boats, each lit from prow to stern as if for a festival, ringing the port with lights. In the distance, the coastguard ships were also fully lit, their reflections moving gently on the water, with only the dark mass of the paddle wheels in the center. Boisterous, joyful music rose from the quaysides below: the Blacks were dancing wildly to the sound of banjos. Why such merriment?

'Everyone is happy, so they, too, are joining in this jollity,' Turner explained.

She watched them for a moment. In their bright clothes, they moved with the natural elegance of their race, and she was touched by their leaps and shouts. Thinking of Betty, she felt at one with them.

She searched for Fort Sumter beyond the ships. She had seen it in daylight, but Turner, who followed her eyes, told her that it was no use: hardly more than a tiny light shone on a rock to light ships into the open sea, and you had to know where to look for that; while Fort Moultrie, on the other side, was plunged into total darkness.

'Yet another mystery,' she said, with a laugh. 'The South is full of them.'

'Does it frighten you?'

'You must be joking; but I have the feeling that tonight the world is changing — or perhaps I am . . . Where is Billy?'

It was his turn to laugh.

'I was expecting that question. Billy's at the arsenal.'

'Is it far?'

'Between the port and the fortress, west of town; but Billy is sure to come along later.'

'So much the better for me!'

'So much the better for you!' he said, like an echo, in which she failed to hear the irony.

'Let's go back to the gardens.'

'Take my arm, will you?'

Of all these people, Elizabeth would have preferred to do without his help, but already the little group was reforming around her. She suddenly guessed that, without appearing to, they were flanking her. They were looking after the eccentric, beautiful Englishwoman. She dropped Turner's arm in irritation and set off alone, walking directly but haphazardly toward the darker end of the gardens which she did not know. Hilda and her husband followed close behind her, but her free flowing hair was a challenge to them. The crowd got bigger and bigger while the latest voting results flew through the air, carried on the voices of the people. When Lincoln took a small but steady lead in the North, it was greeted with mocking cheers. Everyone agreed that with Lincoln as President, Secession would be easier, but no one felt any greater love for the Republican beanpole with his hanging suspenders and stovepipe pants. Elizabeth could not altogether grasp the paradoxical subtleties of this reasoning. In any case, without knowing where she was going, she was satisfied with the simple pleasure of teasing her bodyguards. Guided by the light of the lanterns wandering through the darkness, she marched resolutely toward the least frequented part of the park, dragging the others after her, in spite of themselves. At last the husbands intervened authoritatively. Siverac stood in front of her.

'Elizabeth, it's time to rest a little.'

'Where?' she asked.

'Near the bandstand. There we have a chance of finding some chairs or a bench.'

She laughed in his face.

'You're imagining things, but I'll follow you, Mr de Siverac.'

Once again they made a path through the throng, in the opposite direction. In truth, they were all tired and had had enough of waiting for the curtain to rise on the sensational event; but you would have thought that some playful fate was in league with the adventurous Elizabeth. They were still a long way from the bandstand when, between two rows of oak trees, she saw a group of men dressed in an unusual way, their leader wearing a military cap and bandoliers crossed over a short tunic. Trousers as wide as those worn by ordinary folk completed a form of dress that intrigued the inquisitive woman. She stopped.

'Not at all interesting,' said Hampton impatiently. 'It's the town militia.'

'Without guns?'

'Their rifles must be stacked behind the trees,' Turner replied in a precise voice.

'Come on, darling, let's go,' said Hilda. 'They're country boys and rather unappealing.'

'Perhaps, but I want to see the militia.'

'Elizabeth,' Hilda insisted. 'Think of Billy: what would he say?'

'If Billy was here, he would go right across to talk to them. What are you thinking of, Hilda?'

'Let's all go and look at the militia, then,' Hampton cried with a laugh. 'In any case, we won't be the only ones.'

Passers-by were indeed pausing for a moment in front of these young men who asked nothing better than to chat with the civilians. They had orders not to go far from their guns, but they were allowed to move. Followed by Siverac and Turner, Elizabeth went across to the boys, who looked at her incredulously: they were quite evidently intimidated by her. She immediately sensed it, and felt a shudder of pleasure. Almost all of them appeared at once smiling and resolved, as Southerners do, some were of striking beauty and almost all blond. Without hesitation, Elizabeth went over to them with a smile that was immediately returned by some of the bolder among them, but Siverac cut short any chance of dialogue by asking the usual questions himself:

'Are you waiting for the result?'

'We have orders to stay here, sir.'

'Where do you come from?' Elizabeth asked a boy who seemed to her a little smarter than the rest.

'From Charleston, Miss,' he answered, looking her straight in the eye and adding mischievously: 'But you don't, Miss.'

'How do you know?'

He was about to respond, when Hilda pulled Elizabeth back.

'Elizabeth, please come with us,' Turner said taking her arm. 'We're all going to rest near the bandstand.'

Mildred and Minnie came to the rescue to help drag the English-woman away from the soldiers, and she was so struck by the anxiety in their faces that she relented.

'How fearful you are!' she said. 'What are you afraid of? A scandal? Here?'

'You were about to encourage that boy to say things that he shouldn't say,' Hilda explained.

'You don't realize what a disturbing effect you produce on these men,' Minnie added.

Vaguely flattered, Elizabeth conceded, ironically:

'I didn't imagine so, but if it bothers you . . .'

After some efforts to pass through the crowd gathering around the soldiers, the little group finally reached the Chinese pavilion occupied by a military band which was temporarily resting, surrounded by a solid phalanx of old ladies sitting on chairs — all the chairs.

'And now?' said Elizabeth, sarcastically. 'What do you suggest?'

Hampton took his watch out of his waistcoat pocket.

'It is midnight, or thereabouts,' he said. 'We can't go on this way. I suggest we go back . . .' And, as if he had just thought of it, exclaimed: 'To my father's! That's it!'

'Hurrah!' said Turner and Minnie. 'To Meeting Street, everyone!'

With the exception of Elizabeth, the whole group cried unanimously:

'Everyone to Meeting Street!'

Exhausted, but suddenly enthused, they set off, back toward the center of town, with no less difficulty than they had found in leaving it. All around them the crowd was cheering as a new gain for Lincoln was announced. He still did not have a majority, but the Democrats were weakening, split down the middle. Both men and women were applauding as loudly as they could and, as though the defeat that they so ardently desired was already certain, the band struck up one of the most popular songs of the South, 'The Bonnie Blue Flag': 'We are a band of brothers . . .' Lincoln was not yet victorious, but this did not prevent people from singing at the top of their voices, asking the band for a dance tune and throwing themselves frantically into quadrilles that made the ground shake beneath them.

In Charleston itself, the excitement was almost at fever pitch, even though the shadow of a doubt remained on the billboards. It was so close that a disappointment was still possible and would have been dreadful. Elizabeth and her companions finally reached the house of William Hampton's father and had to struggle again to make their way inside, as a great mass of people was blocking the door which only opened after extraordinary precautions had been taken: they were afraid that the crowd would burst into the house. William had to send his father a message scribbled on a scrap of paper and thrust into the hands of a terrified Black who did not recognize him. Finally, the group managed to get in through the garden door. When all seven of them found themselves inside, in the hall at the bottom of a magnificent staircase, they gave a grateful whoop of joy. Hilda, the most sensitive, decided to faint. A glass of water in her face restored her, and Elizabeth added two or three slaps delivered with firm British resolve.

In the drawing-room, dazzled by the lights, they were disoriented for a moment and put the young women on the sofas while the men were assailed with questions: what was happening in Battery gardens, what did they see, what was being said in the street . . . They were like travelers returning from the other end of the world. Glasses of champagne brought them back to their feet and they became loquacious, except for the beautiful Englishwoman who allowed herself to be admired, and said nothing.

'My word,' said Hampton senior. 'We did well to remain here, away from that crowd, which is beside itself.'

He was a slender man of slightly outmoded elegance, with iron gray hair and a goatee beard.

'Father,' William told him. 'Tonight, the whole of Charleston is in that crowd, from the humblest to the highest. All distinctions are abolished.'

'Truly?' his father said, with an incredulous look. 'I must say that I am not fond of such blending, but no matter . . . we are well-placed to get all the news here. The large billboard on the court-house is twenty yards away, or thirty at most. Also, we can hear the crowd clearly enough. Some music, please.'

A Viennese waltz drifted out of a back room, slipping in slyly with its caresses and sudden outbursts. Hampton senior went over and bowed to Elizabeth, whom he had been watching out of the corner of his eye.

'Would you do me the honor . . .'

She could have said that she was feeling weary, but in the eyes of this gray-haired gentleman there was a flame of youth and a hint of adoration. She did not resist. The whole room turned around her. In the clamor of the musicians as they attempted to drown the noise rising up from the street, she pretended not to notice that the men were looking only at her and once more experienced the exhilaration of a happiness which never palled: that of being admired.

Suddenly, thunder broke in the room and the dancers came to an immediate halt. A cry seemed to fall from the heavens and cover the earth: carried by the roar of massed humanity, it abolished all other noise. For several minutes it unfolded in space, across the whole illuminated town like the very cry of light itself. Everyone ran to the veranda.

The cheers of the crowd pounded against the darkness. The flag of South Carolina, the 'palmetto flag', appeared and there were soon thousands of them waving above the heads of the crowd. Every time the numbers changed on the billboard, a cheer rose from a single powerful voice into the sky. Then, all at once, bursts of gunfire tore through the noise as if ripping a sheet of cloth. The cadets and the militia, all along the Battery, were firing one salvo after another. The crackling of fireworks joined in. The sky was lit up like the town and one sparkling burst followed another, as if leaping from the heart of the crowd. Down below in the street a man in shirt sleeves shouted up to the veranda: 'Lincoln is in the lead, it's over!' Someone else cried: 'Secession!' — and the word ran from mouth to mouth along the streets, in the gardens, in the lanes and in the port, like fire along a fuse.

At four o'clock in the morning, Billy arrived. Outside, the excitment continued. Not without difficulty he managed to make his way into the house and his red uniform seemed to harmonise with his happy face. What he had to say caused a sensation.

'We've done good work in the arsenal. Let them come: we'll give them a proper welcome. Do you know the vultures are mad as anything?'

'What do you mean? How's that?' they asked.

'The noise and light upset them. These fellows had gathered in the trees in the cemetery, on the far side of the arsenal. When we went too close for their liking, they tried to spit on us.'

'They're Lincoln supporters!' Mr Hampton exclaimed. 'The only ones in the South.'

At dawn they were forced to think of resting a little, even though the townspeople seemed tireless. The Hamptons offered hospitality to their cousins and, while they sank into their beds, with all curtains drawn, in the town, on the front of the *Mercury* building, the palmetto flag was raised and fluttered in the sharp morning air.

# 124

C harleston celebrated for the next three days. Fireworks conquered the sky. Multicolored bouquets exploded endlessly through the night, accompanied by cheers and songs.

The following morning, November 7, everyone at Hilda's and the Hamptons' was caught up in the general mood of gaiety. They had eventually fallen asleep like the rest of the town, when something occurred that woke everybody up. An officer of the Federal Army had disembarked at Fort Sumter intending to remove the arms from the Arsenal in order to forestall any attack, but men and women, constantly on guard, were waiting for him on the quayside, their flags fluttering in the breeze, and blocked his path. The officer went back empty-handed . . . The affair caused a tremendous stir.

That morning's *Mercury* announced in huge letters:

THE TEA IS OVERBOARD
THE REVOLUTION OF 1860  HAS BEGUN

As clear as daylight, this was an allusion to the famous Boston Tea Party of December 16, 1773, when the American settlers seized three British vessels in the port of Boston and threw their cargo of hundreds of tea chests into the sea as a protest against the iniquitous taxes imposed by London. Thus began the uprising in the colony and, a few years later, for a few cups of tea, Great Britain had lost America.

Thinking that the officer who was in charge of Fort Sumter had handled the matter badly, the Washington headquarters changed commander on November 15, and the fort became the focus of every eye in the Union. The new commandant, Major Anderson, was married to a woman from Georgia and, while he secretly sympathised with the South, still remained loyal to his duties. A brilliant, highly cultured and thoughtful man, he soon realized that Fort Sumter, on its tiny rock in the middle of the bay and commanding the straits that led into the open sea, was one of the strongest positions. It would be even more so if its neighbors, Fort Moultrie and Fort Johnson, were repaired: though more vulnerable, they could prevent any approach to the fairways with their cannon. He decided to begin the repairs at once: builders and carpenters were requisitioned in town and every day boats took them out to the sites. Of course, the builders talked and the whole town followed the work with interest. 'They're repairing the forts for us,' most people said.

However, Charleston continued to dance and the fireworks lit up the sky, but the cadets vied in political ardor with the militia which was training energetically.

# 125

*E*lizabeth's joy was not unalloyed as she listened to news, the significance of which she did not always understand. She found the complications of politics excessive when it meant that people applauded the victory of an enemy of the South; but she was furious at the reminder of the Boston Tea Party, which she considered outrageous as much for the vulgarity of the act as for the waste of good English tea.

'Unfortunately, there's nothing to be done about it,' Hilda said with a mischievous smile. 'It's all at the bottom of the Atlantic, for ever and ever. And I doubt if the fish enjoyed it . . .'

Elizabeth turned her back to her.

'I'm English and remain English,' she said.

In a quiet voice, Laurence Turner remarked:

'We're all of English stock in the South.'

The shocked Englishwoman's only reply was a faint smile. For the past few days she had felt a vague sense of unease with her Charleston cousins. Her friendship for them had not wavered, but from time to time she was amazed at finding herself here in this feverish town. As soon as England was mentioned, she was transported there in spirit, in a rush of emotion, and it seemed to her that her native land was pulling her with all the strength of its fields and quiet little villages. And, fate being what it is, that is to say, teasing and slyly intriguing, this idea was confirmed by a laconic remark of Charlie Jones's: 'I have news from your mother. Don't wait too long before coming home.'

News from her mother . . . She shut herself in her room with every intention of thinking hard. How did one go about it? She had never known: one thought chased another like a magpie scaring sparrows. What was keeping her in Charleston? Billy. Yet, on the one hand, he had become one of the busiest officers in Fort Beauregard, so she rarely saw him in this time of crisis; and, on the other, he could always come and see her in Savannah: it was not far, he had often done it. In a burst of honesty, she tried to analyze herself honestly. The cadets in the Battery gardens with their delightful uniforms, those copper buttons and all that lay behind the copper buttons, yes, she could finally admit it, she loved them all, those boys . . . And the militia with that slightly untidy, unbuttoned look, so elegant and, moreover, revealing the neck . . . The blood rose to her face. She looked at herself in the mirror: she was blushing and this always made her look more beautiful still. Abruptly, as she struggled against her mental confusion, a remark returned to her like a shaft of ice — Miss Llewelyn's sharp voice saying one evening: 'You are going to your doom, Mrs Hargrove.' What right had the Welshwoman to say that to her? But sometimes people spoke in place of someone else who was using them. She closed her eyes and did not move.

That night, Billy arrived and this calmed her. He, in himself, was worth the whole army and his frogged jacket was finer than all the cadets' copper buttons. She kept these thoughts to herself, but with that instinct peculiar to jealous men, he appeared to have sensed something. And she told him that she was going back to Savannah.

'Excellent idea,' he said. 'I'll always manage to see you somehow. Here, the atmosphere is unhealthy for a woman as highly strung as you are. All these people waving flags and shouting Secession: I don't want it to upset you. And then there are those rowdy young militiamen everywhere . . . Leave tomorrow.'

So it was arranged. Her cousins said their affectionate goodbyes, extracting a formal promise to come back, and come back quickly, but they could not retain her. This was an odd thing that she could not help noticing: no one ever retained her; anywhere.


The journey home passed without incident. Alone in her carriage, Elizabeth abandoned herself to all the dreams that constituted the web of her life and, as she expected, she was welcomed back by the impassive Welshwoman who was waiting in the hall.

'Pleased to see you home, Mrs Hargrove,' she said coldly. 'There is some disturbance in Savannah, but nothing comparable to the frenzied demonstrations in Charleston. We heard some reports of it . . .'

'The children?'

'The children are fine. Mr Jones would like to see you.'

'Tell him I'm here.'

Ned came in from the garden and hugged her with the usual protestations of love, but she quickly left him to go up to Kit's room, where she found the child on Black Mammy's knees — as if the intervening time had been wiped out and she had only left him five minutes ago. He looked at her with his big blue eyes, his head on one side, as if searching his memory for who she could be. She threw herself upon him, smothering him with kisses, while he gabbled words in the unknown language that young children invent from the words they hear. Carried away on a wave of tenderness, her heart was filled with him, his freshness and the scent of his milky flesh, rediscovering love in its most primitive form. Black Mammy gently took the little boy from her arms. For the first time for many days, the mother felt at peace, reconciled with the Elizabeth of Charleston who had been a prey to such dizzy flights of fancy.

Charlie Jones came to visit her that evening.

'Your mother has written to me from London,' he announced almost immediately. 'She'll be in New York at the beginning of December. She's expecting you there. Let's not stand around looking at each other. I have a lot to tell you.'

They sat down opposite one another in the scarlet drawing-room. He began in the cold voice of a businessman.

'Your mother has reserved a room, or rather an apartment, for you in the newest and most luxurious hotel in the city.'

'But what would I do in New York, Uncle Charlie?'

'She is certain that you will leave America and go back to England with her. I'm telling you this plainly. Why beat about the bush?'

'Go back to England?' said Elizabeth.

He gave her an icy look. He was no longer the same Charlie Jones.

'Exactly. To begin with, you would have a whole floor of one of the finest and most admired houses in Bath all to yourself. Doesn't that appeal to you? You could start a new life in that very fashionable town, quietly, far away from the rumblings of war.'

'But there is no war.'

'Your mother can see it coming and she wants to help you escape a dreadful fate. Your cabin for New York is booked on one of my own ships, the *Queen Mab*, leaving Savannah in ten days.'

'And Billy?'

He went on imperturbably:

'Oh, Billy! Yes, she's thought of him. You will go back to him after the war, which will be a short one, she claims.'

'So, is she serious?'

'I haven't even considered that. I'm passing on her message, her appeal. Her letter is slightly hysterical.'

'Show it to me.'

'No.'

'You have never spoken to me in this way.'

'I am trying to be honest. You'll understand later.'

'So, I'm to leave Savannah, to leave Billy. And what about the children: Ned and little Kit?'

'Yes.'

'Well, I've thought it over, I'm staying.'

'But you haven't thought it over.'

Elizabeth got up, her eyes blazing, and stamped her foot.

'I'm staying. Staying, staying. I won't leave Billy.'

Charlie Jones also stood up and took her in his arms.

'Elizabeth . . . That was the answer I hoped you would give, though I was not sure. She has played and lost. She was wagering on your fear and your nostalgia for the old country. I, too, could leave with my family to settle in a large house in Cornwall, but I owe everything to the South, so I'm not moving. In our hearts, we have become Southerners and our children come from here . . . Your mother's letter is heart-rending . . . It's an underhand appeal from a mother's heart.'

She bowed her head and said nothing. With an affectionate gesture he took her hand.

'I spoke roughly to you just now and it was unlike me, but I had to do so. Remember: Secession does not necessarily mean war. And if war should break out, remember this: you can bring your children to me. There, in Virginia, you will be safe. At Charlie Jones's house, you are on British soil. You have nothing to fear.'

'I'm not afraid.'

'Another thing. In Charleston, I understand that there is a wave of enthusiasm and fraternisation which has abolished class distinctions?'

'I witnessed it myself: society and the workers.'

'The militia would be recruited from the common people and they are hurrying to volunteer . . .'

The militia . . . She recalled the young men in their charmingly casual dress, with their collars undone.

'Yes, that's right. And it's very good,' she said.

'In Savannah, there is still prejudice among the upper classes. When you come from Dimwood, you must have seen the men and women in the suburbs, in rags. Some find work and barely earn enough to survive. That's poverty. In America, you must be rich.'

'I know, I know. When I first came to Savannah, I saw those people by the roadside and I was outraged.'

'No one thinks of them. I try to help them a little, but it's a drop in the ocean. There are too many. Do you remember the Schmicks? They managed to escape from it, by hard work. I sent Algernon to them in an attempt to interest them in my efforts. That's where you met him, I think?'

'Algernon . . . Yes, yes.'

'He's going to come and see you shortly, if you would be good enough to receive him with me.'

'Of course.'

'He's a good boy, but he's never known cold or hunger, and so he's impervious to the problem of the poor.'

'I was cold and hungry,' she said, 'in London, with Mama, when I was fifteen.'

'I experienced it as a child in Shropshire. Believe me, there's no better school. Algernon has a different kind of heart. He is fanatical about an armed South.'

'This is a long way from the question of the poor!'

'That's where you're wrong. If war comes, there will be surprises. Let them be given bread and guns and they will march side by side with our Algernons and our planters' sons.'

'Seriously, Uncle Charlie, you don't believe in war, but you're unintentionally spreading panic.'

He looked her directly in the eyes.

'Do you want me to send your mother a message by telegraph to say that you are coming?'

'Don't start that again,' she said irritably. 'I'm not a little girl, but let's talk about something else, for heaven's sake!'

Charlie Jones gave her his most appealing look, with a smile that made him ten years younger.

'I'm sorry, Elizabeth. I must admit that Lady Fidgety's letter disturbed me a little, but I have the feeling that a "no" from you will upset her, and at the same time make her proud of you.'

'I should like to have seen her.'

'Then let her come here. If you go there, she may talk you round.'

'Enough of that. I'll write to her myself.'

'I can hear the bell. It must be Algernon.'

'Would you like me to call for champagne, to cheer us up a bit?'

'One never turns down the offer of a glass of champagne when it comes from a lovely young woman.'

Algernon entered. Dressed in a black jacket, his fine head perched on a collar wrapped round with a white silk tie. This rather formal dress was suitable for a late visit, he thought, but did not favor idle chit-chat. He bowed to Elizabeth and kissed her hand.

'Well, Algernon, you look like someone bringing news?'

'No news,' he said. 'Except that the ten thousand rifles I ordered in New York will be delivered in the first days of January.'

Elizabeth shuddered . . . Algernon and his ten thousand rifles . . . She thought she had misheard and chose to say nothing.

'My office had confirmation yesterday evening; but this is of no possible interest to a lady,' Charlie Jones said gallantly. 'Of course, Elizabeth, we're talking of hunting rifles for . . . hunting partridge.'

'Big partridge!'

Algernon burst out laughing and the young woman looked reproachfully at her father-in-law.

'You mentioned news,' Algernon went on. 'I'm dying to hear Mrs Hargrove's news from Charleston.'

'Oh, call me Elizabeth, Algernon. What's wrong with you today?'

A servant brought a tray with three glasses of champagne, then withdrew.

'Elizabeth,' said Charlie Jones, 'whose toast shall we drink?'

Without hesitation, she answered:

'Let's drink to peace and the happiness of all.'

'What a delightful toast, Elizabeth,' Algernon said, giving her the adoring smile for which she had been waiting.

Since Algernon's arrival, she felt especially beautiful, with her hair piled up in a crown on her head, and her previous conversation with her father-in-law made her feel like asserting herself; she wanted to shine. She put down her glass, casually gathered the folds of her Isabella taffeta dress and incautiously began:

'How can I describe the follies of Charleston to you? Where to begin . . . Enough fireworks to set the stars on fire, the deafening cries of the crowd, the enthusiasm, a thousand flags in the air, especially the one they call there the 'palmetto'; and soldiers running in all directions around the Battery gardens . . .'

'Soldiers?' asked Algernon, raising an eyebrow.

'Yes, or anyway cadets, young cadets in uniform with lots of brass buttons, and elegant, too, all of them . . .'

'Nothing unusual about that,' Charlie Jones interrupted, embarrassed by this outburst, but she was already carrying on with the same enthusiasm.

'And others, more simply dressed, in large trousers . . .'

'The militia,' Charlie Jones said, growing impatient. 'The militia, Elizabeth. But what were people saying, what were they shouting?'

'Secession!' she said, waving an arm.

Her father-in-law adopted a reasonable tone to bring to an end a situation which was becoming uncomfortable and, turning to Algernon, who was blushing a little, he said:

'Secession. This cry that we are starting to hear in Savannah was once seriously considered in Massachusetts. It would be possible without violence if the North would only examine it more closely and calmly. Nations of different origin, but living one beside the other, in peace.'

He was expanding on this theme, which his listeners seemed to find boring, when suddenly his tone altered:

'As for the false pretext of slavery which the North uses as a stick to beat us, have you ever thought that there is a very simple way of ending it, once and for all? Instead of having slaves who work for nothing, we could pay them . . .'

Algernon nearly spilled his champagne.

'Pay them?'

'Why not? Like workers. The lure of gold would keep them here instead of leaving for the false freedom of the North. There, it's a case of either work or starve. I'm sure they would stay. The South has ample resources to keep them and those who were born here are at home here.'

'At last!' Algernon exclaimed. 'The voice of common sense. This is the first time I've heard it.'

Charlie Jones sighed.

'I'm afraid it may be the last. After the yapping of speeches we risk hearing the senseless bark of guns. And, on that subject, I have something to tell you . . . But we are boring Elizabeth.'

Standing up, he took Elizabeth's hands in his own.

'Forgive us, dear Elizabeth. I have to go to New York at the end of the month for some business to do with the Customs. I shall use the opportunity to visit your mother when she arrives and tell her your answer. Even though she is English, she is also human. She will understand. May I kiss you?'

Without replying, she offered a cheek and felt herself enveloped in a wave of eau de Cologne.

'I'll write to her,' she murmured.

'Why not leave it up to me. I'm skilled in the art of calming mothers.'

She was reassured by this and, after a further kiss on the hand from Algernon, the two men went out.

In the main thoroughfares, which were quiet once more, they could converse freely.

'I'm doing what I can to put that anxious young woman's mind at rest,' Charlie Jones said.

'She seems very determined.'

'She's brave. She fears for her Billy and she's right to do so. One can feel the inevitable coming, even though one may hope one is wrong. If you want peace, prepare for war, according to the wisdom of the Ancients. That's ridiculous. If you prepare for war, it will come.'

'You're dreadful, Uncle Charlie!'

'Don't be naive, Algernon. I have no illusions, that's all, but when war does come, one has to fight it, and I want to help the South to defend itself. I'm going to New York to arrange for the shipment of guns which I ordered in Manchester. My ships are waiting in Liverpool to bring them, as I explained, in separate parts, directly to Savannah.'

'You're not afraid of being inspected?'

'In peacetime — because this is peacetime — a British ship boarded by the Americans for inspection? It would be an act of war against Great Britain.'

'I must say, your terminology . . .'

'The ships are expected to arrive in Savannah at the end of the year. We still have time to think about it.'

'And my rifles will be here in January.'

'Good. We are moving toward an absurd war. The South is one against three. The North is arming and training.'

'Already?'

'Haven't you heard? The North has its militia, Republican scouts. They already exist in New York and, God knows, people there aren't keen on the Union. A whole panoply of preparations to excite the people. I'll tell you what I see when I come back.'

'Do you understand why the North has this hatred for us?'

'There is something that the South has not grasped, Algernon: the importance of the financial disaster of '57. The North is only just recovering from it. During this humiliating time of trial, it had to endure the spectacle of our prosperity. King Cotton saved us. It was then that they acquired this obsession with taking us over entirely.'

'Entirely?'

'All our wealth, yes. I'm simplifying, but that's the root of it all, Algernon. There was that decisive psychological moment. Whether it is long or short, the war will be dreadful. Buchanan who is still President until March, can do nothing to avert the catastrophe, except sleep in the White House and give parties!'

'But, Uncle Charlie, you already seem to see the South crushed!'

'I didn't say that, and I don't think so. But I don't know. Let's leave it at that, Algernon. It's a clear night, the stars are shining. In a month it will be Christmas. Let's enjoy the good time while it lasts.'

They shook hands and separated in an empty street, where their footsteps echoed on the brick paving with a distinctive noise — a noise that neither of them would forget.

# 126

*T*he following days were hard for Elizabeth. Her scarlet drawing room was invaded by Society, which wanted what it called fresh news from Charleston. Hungry for details, it was not content with generalizations, but wanted color and sound — all the physcial and emotional outbursts of its great, noisy rival. Poor Elizabeth had not been expecting this. Mrs Harrison Edwards and her bird of paradise with the blue diamond eye trapped her in a corner and tried to extract a sensible reply. Behind her, the Steers and Lady Furnace, all the married women, young or otherwise, and all the unmarried ones, young or otherwise, assailed her with precise questions, sometimes indiscreet ones, accompanied by bursts of laughter. Never had so many hats been seen, as jaunty as those of Paris under the Empire, never so many feathers or so much lace, all in a whispering of flounces of chiffon and taffeta. The scent of ylang-ylang, heliotrope and rose water were enough to make you faint, as well as subtler perfumes from Arabia, unknown to Lady Macbeth! Diamonds glittered.

Seized with panic, Elizabeth served this demanding crowd her cadets and her militia, but these were not enough. With a single voice, the ladies demanded a description of the evening at the Hamptons. Mrs Hampton's reception room, famous for its luxury and its chandeliers, was more important to them than all the rest of the town, and they were relieved to learn that Elizabeth considered it as fine, but no larger than those of Savannah. Once the stage had been set in this way, they demanded to know what could be heard, what cries came up from the street, if possible imitating the sounds to have an idea of the atmosphere. The irritated storyteller was on the point of sending her audience packing (in the politest way), when Miss Llewelyn, suffering on her mistress' behalf, suddenly appeared at the door and announced:

'Ladies, tea is served.'

Tea! The Welshwoman had improvised a tea. In an instant, Elizabeth had forgiven her everything, her betrayals, her insolence and even — hardest of all — her kindnesses.

In the main dining-room, the ladies were already enjoying further interrogations as they drank their tea, when under the cold blue eye of the bird of paradise, Mrs Harrison Edwards called them to order:

'Ladies,' she said, standing up. 'We all know more or less everything we wanted to know about the excitement in Charleston. We may be sure that ladies' fashions there are similar to our own; and as for the strange mixing of social classes, let us leave that to them for the time being.'

'Distance or death!' said a quavering voice, crowned by a trembling feather.

There was a short silence, then, by common agreement, the conversation turned to the latest society scandals. Elizabeth breathed again.

# 127

*I*n New York, on December 6, Charlie Jones hurried round to see Lady Fidgety whom he found in a sumptuous apartment in the Fifth Avenue Hotel. Lying back on a long sea-green sofa, she was not surprised to see him, but he noticed that the folds of her dress, with its blue flounces, concealed a cane. Her handsome face, hardened by age, retained its natural nobility and the imperious nose defied time. She did not get up, but smiled with a charm that gave her a flash of youth.

'Forgive me for not moving,' she said. 'One wrong step in my bathroom and here I am, stretched out on my back for two days. But I am better already. Quickly: tell me my daughter's reply. Is she coming or not?'

Charlie Jones shook his head.

She said nothing, but turned her face a little toward the wall. Charlie Jones remained standing, his top hat in his hand, as though before a corpse.

'I expected as much,' she finally said in a faint voice. 'But I am disappointed, even so. Women have these contradictory emotions . . . Will you sit down?'

He took a French chair with rather hard armrests.

'The decision was painful for her,' he said simply.

'I should have been mad with joy at seeing her and I should have felt ashamed at taking her home with me. Do you understand?'

'Very well. You are saying exactly what she herself feels. Leaving her husband . . . She would never have reconciled herself to the idea of having run away, she could not have lived with herself.'

'Well then, everything is settled, let's say for the best. I shall leave in three days.'

These words were spoken as if it had been a question of the most trivial matter, and he admired the courage of this woman whom he had loved.

'Laura,' he said softly.

She looked at him in astonishment.

'You remember...,' she said, and a smile of sad merriment crossed her eyes. 'It is better not to look too deeply into one's youth, it's an abyss.'

Suddenly changing her tone, she waved her hand around the huge room.

'Admire the luxury of the North!' she said ironically. 'They can't find enough gold to stick on the moldings and the mirror frames, but is there any taste? Not a bit.'

Charlie Jones thought this judgement severe. Certainly, the opulence of this room with its great windows was excessive. What it lacked above all was intimacy, but there was comfort everywhere: the heavy, dark leather armchairs, the huge chests covered in ironwork and, in the adjoining room, the monumental bed in its alcove with the heavy curtains, and an eiderdown like a cloud of yellow silk.

'That's the best they can offer,' she said with a mocking laugh. 'At least, there is space.'

'And calm,' he said, walking to a window. 'What can you see from here?'

'Be careful, you'll get vertigo if you open the window! We're on the fifth floor!'

He did not open it, but looked directly down into a rectangular plaza lined with elegant shops. Some closed carriages were passing and people in furs were walking quickly along.

'I chose this floor because I hate noise. The apartment is overheated, but I must admit that you can hardly hear a sound. And yet, there is commotion in town: people are talking of Secession . . .'

'But not because Charleston is calling for it at the top of its voice . . . Most of the South doesn't agree . . .'

'Charlie, I'm not talking about the South. I'm talking about New York! What have I had to do in this room since my little mishap except to read their papers? You wouldn't believe your eyes.'

'It's anti-Southern propaganda.'

'Oh, the abolitionists want Secession with all their hearts, Charlie, and call for it daily, without caring what anyone wants down there. They beg Heaven to deliver them from the slave states, and as soon as possible. Public opinion anticipates a war and is afraid of one. They are frightened that the South will crush the North. Well, you just have to look at them.'

She waved toward the newspapers and periodicals piled on a small table.

'New York is hysterical!'

'More so than you seem to think, Charlie. The Mayor is calling for the town to break away from the Union in the event of hostilities, and to become an open, international city.'

'That doesn't surprise me from Fernando Wood. He must have Italian blood.'

'Don't joke about it, Charlie. The bankers think the same. Believe me, New York is losing its head. I already read that in the London *Times* before I set sail. I thought that Russell was exaggerating. Well, he wasn't. No sooner has he been elected than they turn against the new President. People make fun of his appearance, his manner of speaking, everything. Nations are more inconstant than men . . . or women, as you prefer.'

'Laura, you must be in a hurry to get home to Bath.'

'Without Elizabeth? I'll be dying of anxiety when I get there, if war breaks out.'

'Even if the South secedes, which is by no means settled yet, war is not certain. And tell yourself this: in the event of war, I shall take Elizabeth and her children into my house in Savannah, or to my estate in Virginia, which you don't yet know. Both of these represent a refuge on English soil.'

'In Virginia?'

'At Great Meadow, a country house standing among woods and fields. We'll be quiet there. Those are two absolutely safe refuges; and I can also count on Lord Lyons.'

'Thank heavens, Charlie! You've put my mind at rest. Your visit has done me good, despite your news.'

'Laura, I hate to be the bringer of bad tidings. Pharaoh used to kill his messengers when they bore him bad news. I can understand that.'

She couldn't help laughing.

'Did he really? I will just offer you a cup of tea.'

'Alas, I can't stay. I'm also here on business. My life is incredibly complicated at the moment. The bank, exports and so on . . . I must say goodbye, but we'll meet again soon.'

'After the war.'

'Don't think so much about the possiblity of war, Laura. May I kiss you?'

'In memory of the good times.'

He bent over her and their mouths touched. Then he took his hat and made for the door. As he was about to open it, he turned round and said:

'Of course, we shall meet again . . . in a short while. We're having dinner together.'

'Delighted. In the hotel, if you will. Come for me at eight?'

'At eight, precisely. What a charming and useful evening we have in front of us, because we haven't told each other anything yet. We have business to settle,' he said, opening the door.

'The Assyrian fleet!' she exclaimed.

He began to laugh so loudly that she could hear him still chuckling in the anteroom.

They went down the five floors together, she clasping his arm but only lightly touching the floor with her cane, so that Charlie Jones wondered if the cane was genuine or just a prop, allowing her to receive guests stretched out on her sofa, for example. He had chosen an isolated table, in front of a large window. It was lit by candles, like everything else in this grandly proportioned dining-room. Here and there, the walls were hung with mistletoe and branches of holly. Christmas was in the air.

A sip of champagne accompanied the menu which Laura considered acceptable, and the soft candlelight made the two people look younger as they sat opposite each other, sometimes drawing closer when they had something confidential to say. They also lowered their voices, because a lot of people, very elegantly dressed, had started to come in.

'You will be pleased with the metal,' Lady Fidgety said softly over the soup. 'Trust Manchester.'

'I've been dealing with them for six months,' he whispered, 'for the large items. I can depend on them. As for the smaller ones, the . . .' he further lowered his voice, 'guns, that's Algernon.'

'Algernon?'

'Steers,' he murmured.

'Oh, that's very serious.'

'Very, my dear Laura. Assyria is on its guard.'

These mysterious remarks were drowned by the hubbub of conversation around them. People were discussing politics a great deal, a little about the theater (one had to see Sothern in *Our American Cousin*), a tremendous amount about the latest big financial scandals (the speculations of the sharks, Jay Gould and Jim Fisk, bribery at City Hall, and so on), when suddenly everyone's attention was drawn toward the bay windows overlooking Fifth Avenue where they heard the alarums of war.

'Oh, Charlie! How lucky for you! Look. The Republicans are on parade.'

In serried ranks, each carrying a lantern on the end of a pike, the Wide Awakes were marching. The lights shone on their long capes of black oilskin, shifting at every step, like flames. Broad-peaked kepis shaded their fierce eyes.

'What do you think of that?' she asked.

'Striking,' he said. 'Not without a certain infernal beauty.'

'Infernal is the word. They want to intimidate, to create fear. I find something childish in this demonstration.'

'There is something childish in every American, my dear Laura. Buchanan's message, two days ago, proves it. He thinks he is Father Christmas, handing out kind words like presents: "Everything will be all right, all is well . . ."'

'But that's nice,' said Laura.

'Just what South Carolina thought — and do you know what it did as a New Year's present: it sent him commissioners demanding its forts and arsenals back.'

'I admire such spontanteity.'

They laughed and drank a toast to spontaneity.

'To settle it all — that is to say, to create a real muddle, my dear Laura — the commander in chief of the army, an old fogey, took it upon himself to write to the President and give him some good military advice, all couched in a pompous and confidential style.'

'Charlie, you know the secrets of the gods!'

'Wait, wait. Broadly speaking, he recommended keeping the Southern forts, if necessary by force: the forts in Charleston, Savannah and Florida, and sending in new troops. In short, protecting the present garrisons which were too weak in his opinion.'

'Protecting the troops! What an odd army!'

'Laura, please let me finish. Poor old Winfield Scott had no luck. Buchanan passed the letter from his general on to his Secretary of State for War. Now, John Floyd is a Virginian and a dedicated Southerner. He circulated the letter to his friends. So there is your secret of the gods.'

'But that's incredible!'

'Wait until you hear the rest. Floyd did as we are doing. He took advantage of it to have his reserves of weapons sold to South Carolina.'

'And then?'

'For the time being, the story ends there. Isn't that enough? The rest remains to be written.'

'Charlie, History with a capital H will take up the pen in our place; but isn't it odd that we should be talking of war and rumors of war in a place famous for pleasure-seeking?'

'Yes, those are the little ironies of life. Look outside: what an image of the future . . .'

'Look, you'd think it was starting to snow.'

'Yes, it is. That will disperse our valiant scouts.'

'Between ourselves, I think the Wide Awakes are dreadful. I shall take away a nightmarish vision of them. Charlie, it's not that I'd ever weary of talking to you . . . '

'Laura, you're tired.'

She was about to reply when a waiter bowed in front of them and suggested a dessert — *the* dessert, crêpes Suzette. Both looked at one another and said yes. The waiter, a man of respectable age with white sideburns, gave a fatuous smile.

'No one ever refuses my pancakes. If you will permit me . . . It's starting to turn very cold.'

Passing behind Charlie Jones, he pulled a thick beige curtain with gold tassels, and went away.

'That was an expression of opinion. The town doesn't like the Wide Awakes — and then the good spirits of the customers must be protected.'

'How does that wretch think we could refuse crêpes Suzette? In Europe you only find them in Paris. And here?'

'Nowhere else in America, not in the South, in any case,' Charlie Jones said sadly.

The crêpes Suzette duly made their appearance and were zealously fired by a chef in an immaculate tall hat. A gentle blue flame was still hovering over them on the plates.

'Enchanting,' said Lady Fidgety.

They set about them without further ado and talked for a few minutes longer.

'You are leaving the day after tomorrow, Laura, and I shall be there, on the quay, but tomorrow my day will be taken up with business and I must spend it shut up in banks.'

'British ones, I hope.'

'That's an interesting reaction, Laura! Whatever happens in America, they won't touch an British bank. That's what you mean, I suppose?'

'Being British, neither one of us is a dreamer.'

'Perhaps we are on the point of saying more than we intend. What do you think?'

'I think we must persevere in our efforts. That's all, but you can sense a tremendous strength in the North. Charlie, I'm going up to bed.'

'Don't go on foot, Laura.'

'No, I shall be entrusting myself to that modern machine called a lift.'

'I'm sorry to contradict you, but here it's an elevator.'

'How like them to abandon English and jabber away in Latin. Let's go, shall we?'

As they were walking toward the elevator, she said with a laugh:

'You haven't complimented me on my hat, which is the latest London fashion . . .'

She was wearing a mauve satin poke bonnet, with a little ostrich feather on the side hugging her ear.

'You were more gallant in the Thirties,' she said ironically.

'Dear Laura, in those days I wasn't married.'

'Don't spoil me, will you! But here we are.'

A bellboy in a red livery with gold buttons, forming a triangle from his shoulders to his waist, was standing in front of the elevator, holding the door open.

'I'm pleased to see that you're taking the lift to go up, Laura. Why didn't you take it to come down the five floors?'

'What are you thinking of, Charlie? Going up, perhaps. I think of something else during the journey; but as for throwing myself into the void in this box . . . Can't you see the difference?'

'Of course.'

'Then,' she went on with a smile that would once have been enchanting, 'coming down on foot allowed me to take your arm. Goodnight, Charlie. I'll be waiting for you in one of the hotel's cabs on the quayside, the day after tomorrow.'

'I shall be there at ten o'clock.'

She got into the elevator and shut herself in with the bellboy. Charlie Jones looked at her standing in the walnut and glass box. The elevator rose at a cautious speed. Just as she was about to disappear, he waved and had time to see her quickly touch the tips of her fingers with her lips.

'He was so handsome when he was twenty-six,' she said aloud.

'Please, Ma'am?' said the bellboy.

She did not reply, but gave him half a dollar when they arrived. With the door open, one could hear the dull noise rising from the hall of the hotel through the void beneath the elevator.

In her room, first taking off her bonnet, she looked closely at herself in the gold framed mirror which went up to the ceiling. For a long while, she stayed motionless before this image of a gray-haired woman, then she stuck her tongue out at it. After which, she sat down at her desk where she found a blotter with sheets of writing-paper. Without hesitation her pen began to race across it.

New York, December 6, 1860.

My dear daughter,

As I expected, you did not come. Charlie Jones has tried to explain why, but his reasons are worthless. You would be ashamed to flee a country threatened by war! That's not correct. You are English and you have never thought of the South as a new homeland. You have never ceased to feel homesick for your native country; but you are above all a woman in love and your real native land, in America, wears a hussar's uniform: Billy. That I do understand. One cannot abandon the man one loves. He alone represents towns, parks and castles. It is possible to love a country; some countries have personalities. The South is a person, but you do not belong to her, or only a little, because you are English and the South is made of England as clothing is made of cloth. Your Billy is part of England. Stay with him. Charlie Jones and I will always back the South, which is purely English, while the North is composed of scraps of nations, more or less solidly glued together. You do not belong to that Union.

There is the solution to the problem of your conscience, my daughter. I am not sentimental. I have a cool head and a clear eye. Having said that, I kiss you and bid you farewell. I have never had much faith in the practical value of blessings, but if you think mine can be of any use to you, you have it, as is customary, from a firm and faithful heart.

Your mother,

Laura.

She did not re-read this letter, but slipped it into a long envelope and sealed it. Outside, the city had reverted to silence and it was hardly snowing at all now. She undressed and suddenly fell to her knees at the foot of her bed. She stayed in that position for half an hour, her hair spread in iron-gray braids over the old gold eider-down. When she stood up, her cheeks were shining with a mixture of tears and sweat. It was as though a bowl of water had been thrown in her face. Opening her Bible, she read two or three psalms and a page of a Gospel, then went to bed.

The next day, she went to marvel at the shops which were crowded with ladies eagerly doing their Christmas shopping. On Broadway, one could go into department stores with marble halls, equal to any in Paris or London, which offered six floors of whatever they de-sired to people intoxicated with their own wealth; but there was too much of everything in the overheated rooms. On the avenue out-side, along sidewalks where the shop windows shone with gas-lights, the less fortunate passers-by waded through the black slush. Time passed quickly.

Dining alone that evening in her hotel, she chose the same table as she had occupied the day before with Charlie Jones. She ate, staring ahead of her, into nothingness. For dessert, she ordered crêpes Suzette.

The following day, a little before ten o'clock, she was waiting calmly, dressed in her furs, at the back of a handsome cab on the European quayside. The staff of the Fifth Avenue Hotel, with the respect due to great wealth, had taken it on themselves to take her baggage to her cabin on the *Neptune*. From time to time, Laura's eyes shifted imperceptibly, waiting for Charlie Jones to arrive. Since dawn, the port had been covered in mist which was only dispersing very slowly. Through the threads of vapor, one could see the low warehouses on the far side of the quay. People were coming and going like shadows along the docks: travelers in greatcoats almost down to the ground, porters carrying cases, in an apparent confu-sion interspersed with shouts. All were swallowed up inside the Customs House, solid and black like a prison. In the far distance, beyond this almost white gloom, foghorns were moaning, and Laura felt something of the despair that she was concealing inside her as she listened to their sad call. She would have a luxury cabin for two passengers and occupy it alone throughout the voyage: she had not wanted to change her reservation, crazily hoping for a last-minute change of heart and the impossible surprise of seeing Elizabeth appear there, on the quayside . . . 'I love her too much and life is taking her from me,' she thought, leaning forward, still searching. She couldn't see the driver, sitting high up behind her on the top of the carriage, and wondered if he was cold. The horse hardly stirred under its leather blanket. Through the large window in front of her, she could see the reins above the cab, twitching from time to time when the horse gave any sign of moving.

Suddenly, she saw Charlie Jones standing beside the carriage. She opened the door and he got in, bringing all the winter with him in a blast of icy air.

'Dear Laura,' he said. 'We still had so much to say to one another.'

'Come with me to the gangway.'

He opened the little window in the roof of the cab and gave an order to the driver. Without waiting, Laura opened her bag and brought out the letter.

'This is for my daughter,' she said. 'Let her read it when she is alone.'

Charlie Jones slipped the letter into the inside pocket of his jacket.

'I'm sailing back home myself the day after tomorrow. She will have the letter in five days.'

'You have a huge influence on her. You could make her agree to anything.'

'If she still has Billy . . .'

A movement of his hand dismissed the dreadful possibility.

'We are parting having done all we can for the South. In any case, for the time being,' she said.

'Everything is in order at Lloyds Bank.'

'And the ships?'

'On their way to Liverpool. But Laura, we are almost there. The journey is short.'

He brusquely grasped her in his arms and hugged her, raining kisses on her handsome, tired face. She did not try to stop him.

'My poor Charlie,' she said at last, adjusting her poke bonnet. 'You're thirty years too late for this journey into the past.'

'I was madly in love with you, Laura.'

'And I . . . Can't you guess? London, in '30 . . . at Lady Jennifer's ball . . . Help me down, dear, we're there.'

The air was growing clearer and light snowflakes danced in the sky as if to add a jollier note to their parting after this little burst of belated confessions which, they were both aware, seemed vaguely funereal. They wished each other a happy Christmas, without much conviction, but with an appropriate smile. Then they took their leave of one another. He waved his hat. On the gangway, she did not look back.

# 128

*C*harlie Jones took the boat for Savannah two days later, arriving on December 13. He was strongly tempted to stop over in Charleston on his way, to hear the latest news, but resisted, since he was urgently required at his office. There he spent the morning, after which he rang the bell at Oglethorpe House. Miss Llewelyn met him in the hall, looking even more solemn than usual.

'You've come just at the right time, Mr Jones,' she said. 'Mrs Hargrove has had a letter from Charleston which has upset her. Perhaps you could say a few words to put her mind at rest . . .'

He didn't have long to wait. Almost immediately, Elizabeth appeared at the top of the stairs.

'Uncle Charlie!' she cried. 'How glad I am to see you . . . This very morning I received a letter from Billy telling me not to try to see him in Charleston for the moment. There is too much disturbance there and then there will be changes and he will wear another uniform.'

'Nothing unusual about that,' Charlie Jones said calmly. 'Hysteria has become the normal state for Carolinans. No doubt Billy has been held back in Beaufort.'

'He adds that he will let me know when it is possible for us to meet there.'

'So you see.'

'But it's odd.'

'Everything just now is odd. Things will settle down, because they must. Don't be afraid. Meanwhile, here is a letter that your mother gave me for you.'

Elizabeth grasped the letter and had begun to break the seal on the envelope with her finger when Charlie Jones stopped her:

'She asked that you should be alone when you read it.'

Miss Llewelyn withdrew.

'Forgive me for being so brusque,' Elizabeth said. 'It was that letter from Billy . . . I haven't even kissed you.'

'You are so sensitive, Elizabeth. Do you think I don't understand? While you are reading the letter, I shall go and see Ned and take a walk round the garden. I'll be back soon.'

He kissed her affectionately and went off without further delay. Elizabeth went back to her room and, sitting down beside the window, opened the letter and read it so quickly that she had to re-read it to grasp its full meaning. What did she expect? She could not have said, but she had the odd feeling that a key was turning in a door. The letter slipped out of her hands and fell to her feet. Her emotions were so strong that she had to walk round the room. Outside, the sun was shining on the pink bricks in the avenue. A few passers-by were walking along, talking unhurriedly. The air was mild despite the season. Once more she had the fleeing impression that something in the world was escaping her. Her mother told her that, since she was married to Billy, this was her homeland, her England. Beyond that she did not know. She had said that she would never leave him and that she would stay on and on . . . Fine words, fine sentiments. She was admired; but identifying the South with England was simply a manner of speaking. It was easier for her to see her homeland in the person of Billy, but he mustn't be taken away from her. War mustn't take him from her, but every time they met, he told her there would not be a war. In that case, yes, definitely, she would stay on and on — with Billy. What did her mother imagine? Secession? She had been told that Secession did not mean war. 'One doesn't leave the man one loves.' Of course not, but he mustn't leave her, either. Other than that, she was not interested.

He, too, was talking about change. What change? A change of uniform? There were all sorts of uniforms in the army . . . As long as the new one was as pretty as the old one, with frogs and loops! How coquettish of her to wonder . . . But she was not happy with the letter her mother had seen fit to write. She sensed a kind of trap, but preferred not to know what it meant. As soon as one tried to understand, one was caught, the trap closed. One thought like everyone else. One shouldn't: that was the secret of everything.

Picking up the letter, she put it back in its envelope, and slipped it in a drawer of her bureau. Unseen, it had ceased to exist. And she felt strangely reassured.

But what was Charlie Jones doing? He had been gone for half an hour. She went down to wait for him in the drawing-room.

Charlie Jones had gone to the garden where he thought he would find Ned. The boy was talking to Pat, and ran over immediately.

'Good morning, Grandfather. You're back at last. Have you any news from Great Meadow?'

'You mean about Whitie. No, but I found a letter from Miss Charlotte waiting for me and there may be something in that. I haven't yet read it. Good morning, Pat. So what were you talking about with my grandson?'

Pat only knew Charlie Jones from a distance, but even an Irishman was impressed by this tall gentleman with the fresh complexion.

'About what people say as they walk along the street, sir. We exchange ideas. People chatter a lot.'

'What about?'

'All the rumors. At one time, it was about war.'

'What war? There won't be a war.'

'That's just what they say now, but at one time they said differently and I was ready to leave with the army. I am prepared to fight, right away, all the time.'

'Well, it will be some other time. There is always some war or other simmering in the Devil's kitchen.'

Pat shook his red head and gave a furtive wave across his face that might have passed for a sign of the cross.

'Let's not speak of that,' he muttered. 'English is his favorite language. It's what you might call his natural tongue.'

Charlie Jones burst out laughing and took Ned's hand. As he was going away with him, he said cheerfully:

'You'll see him again, your dear Whitie. In the first days of next summer, when school shuts, I'll take you there, to Virginia. You can gallop around the fields all day, but don't listen to your Irishman's gossip about war. It's by talking about wars that people make them happen. Remember that.'

'But I'll go to war one day.'

Charlie Jones let his hand go.

'My dear little halfwit,' he said. 'You don't know what it means. But I'm not worried, you'll never see it happen. I must leave you to go and see your mother. What are you up to now?'

'I've arranged to meet a friend to eat ice cream at Solomon's.'

Uncle Charlie took a small gold coin out of his waistcoat.

'There: this will turn your ice cream into an ice cream soda.'

'Oh, thank you, Grandfather!'

Ned skipped off with his hat askew.

Charlie Jones found Elizabeth in the drawing-room, lying on a chaise longue.

'I beg your pardon, I've kept you waiting,' he said. 'I wanted to take a closer look at that Irish gardener. Don't you think he chats a bit too much with Ned?'

'Oh, they used to talk a lot more at one time. They lived in some fantasy of Ireland, but that's over now. Ned doesn't go there often. Here's my mother's letter. Tell me what you think of it.'

He opened it at once and put on his glasses to read. His brow knitted more and more as he progressed toward the last lines. Finally, with a pleasant smile, he handed it back.

'It's a pretty letter of the kind that women write when they don't quite know what they want to say.'

Elizabeth sat bolt upright.

'A pretty letter! But there are dreadful insinuations in it. Running away from a country at war. And Billy?'

'Dear Elizabeth, let's stop talking about a war that will doubtless not take place. What's wrong with you all? What does your mother say? Be loyal to your husband and stay by him. Don't you agree with that?'

'Oh, Uncle Charlie, it does me so much good to hear you assuring me that there won't be war.'

'I said "doubtless".'

'That's the same thing. Quite simply, Billy won't have to fight.'

'Do you have Billy's letter?'

'It's upstairs, but I know it by heart. It is so short. Dear Billy, he's not a man to write long letters — except once, an enormous one.'

'You mustn't tell me your love secrets! But in his latest one, doesn't he speak about changing uniform, or something like that?'

'Yes. Can you believe: it amuses him. I find that so sweet.'

'Very. He doesn't give any details?'

'No. Just: "I'll be wearing another uniform." There are so many uniforms in the army. I just hope Billy's will have gold braid like the last one.'

'We'll see. In any case, don't worry. I repeat: there is no threat of war.'

These words fell on Elizabeth's soul like a promise of supreme happiness. She would have found it natural to dance around by herself singing, had not Uncle Charlie's face taken on a worried expression that she did not like. She was careful not to ask any questions. Charlie Jones embraced her a little more affectionately than usual and returned home.

A few days went by. Life continued around her uneventfully, with that sort of goodwill that makes things resume their accustomed appearance. Christmas was not far off. Elizabeth knew that there was a ball at the Steers's after the New Year. Unfortunately, Monsieur César would not be there to do her hair: a family matter, he said, had called him back 'unexpectedly' to Paris. She would have to manage by herself. Perhaps Billy would come on Christmas furlough, in his new uniform . . .

# 129

On Thursday, December 21, something dramatic happened. While Elizabeth was taking breakfast with Ned in what was called the morning room, Miss Llewelyn came in silently, holding in her hands a special edition of the *Charleston Mercury:*

THE
UNION
IS
DISSOLVED!

*Passed unanimously at 1.15 o'clock, P.M., December 20th, 1860.*

AN ORDINANCE

*To dissolve the Union between the State of South Carolina and other States united with her under the compact entitled "The Constitution of the United States of America."*

*We, the People of the State of South Carolina, in Convention assembled, do declare and ordain, and it is hereby declared and ordained,*

> That the Ordinance adopted by us in Convention, on the twenty-third of May, in the year of our Lord one thousand seven hundred and eighty-eight, whereby the Constitution of the United States of America was ratified, and also, all Acts and parts of Acts of the General Assembly of this State, ratifying amendments of the said Constitution, are hereby repealed; and that the union now subsisting between South Carolina and other States, under the name of "The United States of America," is hereby dissolved.

Ned leaped up and read the huge letters of the headline aloud. His clear voice rang out as joyful as a clarion call:

'It's war, Mummy. I'll see the war.'

Elizabeth, white as a sheet, clenched her teeth. The Welshwoman, having created a more dramatic effect than ever before, gave the boy a secretive smile, put down the newspaper and went out. Cheeks red, eyes shining, Ned launched into a flood of words:

'That's all anyone ever talks about at school. The big boys say that if South Carolina leaves the Union, all the South will follow like a single man, and then the North . . .'

'Ned, be quiet!' Elizabeth commanded. 'You don't know what you are saying, you don't understand anything, you . . .'

Her voice stifled, she seized the paper and held it up in hands that were trembling so much that she could only read the large print. The brutal headline hit her like a wave.

She, too, leapt up and left the room.

'Mummy, where are you going?' Ned called.

Without answering, she reached the stairs and went up painfully, one hand clasping the bannister. When she was in her room, she resisted the desire to lie down on the bed and instead sat in a chair by the window. Through an effort of will, she sat upright, but she felt as though a hand was gripping her throat, and the blood pounded in her temples. She had only one thought: They were lying to me. Everyone . . . Billy, Uncle Charlie . . . All of them. And she had believed them. How foolish she must have seemed, like a little girl who mustn't be told certain things. A voice insistently repeated Billy's name to her. She looked out of the window and saw women going past unhurriedly, with measured steps, in their dresses of subdued colors, gray, beige or dark brown, with short, fur-lined jackets. It was the hour for the morning walk in the fine winter weather. They still didn't know. The voice said 'Billy', but Elizabeth refused to go any further. Nothing could happen to Billy. Her mind fastened on this thought until it became a certainty. Leaving her seat by the window, she walked around the room and into the adjoining one: their own rooms, husband and wife. The sound of her feet on the floor restored life to normal, with the surprise of Billy coming in unexpectedly, his fingers already on his dolman to unbutton it, to tear it off.

Suddenly, downstairs, she heard a sound of quarreling. The voices of Charlie Jones and Ned mingled, both sounding furious; then there was a great blow on the table and silence was restored. Almost at once she heard heavy footsteps on the stairs and the door was pushed open. Without even saying good morning, Charlie Jones, red in the face, planted himself in front of her.

'Elizabeth,' he said, 'listen to me. There is no war and no one in the world knows if there will be one. Don't pay any attention to your bird-brained son: his mind has been poisoned by the boys at school who are fantasizing about Secession. I terrified him by threatening not to take him this summer: no Whitie! So he shut up.'

'Oh, thank you, Uncle Charlie. I admit he did worry me this morning with all that talk of war, and you have restored peace. But Billy . . .'

'Billy is serving in Beaufort. That's as it should be. The situation has changed and his presence is required, but everything will return to normal. If he doesn't come on furlough at Christmas, I'll take you there myself. Are you satisfied?'

'Yes,' she said, without conviction. 'Yes.'

'Trust me,' Uncle Charlie told her, his smile returning to his still scarlet face. 'You'll see. Be patient.'

'When are we going to Charleston?'

'Well, the day after Christmas.'

The young woman immediately returned his smile, imagining herself already in Billy's arms. As for Charlie Jones, he went out, a good deal less satisfied by his policy of appeasement than she was. His fury could be explained by the fact that he did not believe it, but that he thought it essential to put a stop to the enthusiasm that might drive Georgia to Secession, when it was so ill prepared, so improvised, and he was infuriated at seeing Ned challenge him for the first time — a Ned who knew he was right.

In fact, no sooner had Charlie Jones left Elizabeth than the talk of the town reached him, giving him the most resounding snub. People had just heard the news, and they were delirious. As if rising out of the ground, the crowd was everywhere, screaming with joy and cheering its impetuous neighbor's rebellion. Ned escaped from the house and rushed to the square where he vanished into a group of young fanatics whooping and calling for separation from the North. An effigy of Lincoln was burned amid frenzied applause. In the distance, the canons roared: no doubt Fort Pulaski was acclaiming the new era in its own way. In less than an hour, Savannah had become like a town in the aftermath of a victory. Ned, pushed this way and that by the crowd, was tired, so a well-built man of humble origin raised him on his shoulders; the boy was beside himself with pride. The aimless comings and goings brought him in sight of the Tudor house, 'his' house, which he greeted with a triumphant wave of the hand and the cry: 'I was right, Grandfather!'

He waited for them to make another circuit of Madison Square and, letting himself slip back to the ground, wove his way through the crowd toward home. No one asked him any questions, everyone was at their windows.

Along the avenues and the squares, the crowd, growing more and more dense, continued its parade in a hubbub of cries, cheers and songs. From the first hint of dusk, processions formed. They lit torches, at first some individuals here and there, then more and more of them. When night fell, the flames rose above people's heads like red flowers, and in this bright, shimmering light the rows of houses seemed to dance on the spot.

The whole South exploded in thunderous joy. In Atlanta, the canons sounded from dawn to dusk, almost uninterruptedly, unsettling the commanding officers who (though they said nothing) deplored the waste of munitions that might be needed one day. For its part, having paraded him through the streets to the shouts of a mocking crowd, Augusta burned the newly-elected President in effigy, while cursing the present tenant of the White House.

Washington, too, experienced a bizarre event. In one of the most luxurious houses in the federal capital, a reception was being held which President Buchanan had honored with his presence. He was still a fine figure of a man and, since he liked the company of young women, many milled around him prepared to sacrifice flirting with eligible young men for his sake. From the neighboring drawing-room could be heard the old quadrille of the lancers, and heels were beating time with the orchestra. Through the wide-open doors you could see the dancers and Buchanan was smiling at the young ladies who fought to get the seats nearest to his. Suddenly there was a commotion and noise in the hall. One of the young women went out to see what was going on. A representative from South Carolina was waving a telegram in the air.

'It's like being expelled from school,' he shouted to those around him. He had not even taken off his greatcoat.

'What's the matter with you, Mr Keitt?' said a man dressed entirely in black.

'South Carolina has seceded.'

The young woman at once went back to tell the President. He went very pale and, in an instant, his face dropped and became like that of an old man.

'Could someone call my carriage?' he asked in a weak voice. 'I am going back.'

Once he was home, in the White House, nothing was heard or seen of him for the whole of the next day.

He was reflecting on the strange fate that, in the last months of his presidency, was putting the pen in his hand to sign the decisive instruments of government when, no sooner was the ink dry, he would no longer be in office. In a week, he had to receive the three commissioners sent from South Carolina to negotiate the hand-over of the federal forts to the State militia. His successor could be of no help to him, being engaged in forming his cabinet and tied up in lawyers' quibbles — almost as if to ensure that History would forget him! The hostility within his own cabinet was now open and every meeting was stormy: the Secretary of State for War and the Secretary of State for the Treasury were both ardent Southerners and could not stand the presence or even the physical appearance of the Attorney General. This Edwin Stanton, self-satisfied, insolent and cowardly, even crawling when he was dealing with someone powerful, was an insufferable runt. However, Buchanan had chosen him for his team and was not responsible for his snooping eyes or his infuriating prophet's beard. Thus he would have to face some more difficult meetings, when nearly four years earlier his presidency had begun with applause and embraces, and he might have left the White House now in a shower of expressions of regret and rhetorical flourishes. These thoughts were like a funereal toast.

In the solitude of his office, studying the dispatches that were continually brought in to him and the stories in the newspapers, he found out how Charleston had lived, hour by hour, through that fatal Wednesday: at 1.15 in the afternoon, the vote on the ordinance of Secession; *The Mercury* composing and distributing a special edition in twenty minutes, a remarkable achievement in itself; Institute Hall invaded by the social elite and the people who had come to see their joint delegates sign; Governor Jamison at the stand to proclaim the breach with the Union; the men raising their top hats; the deep hurrahs, broken by silences; and, everywhere in the avenues, when the ceremony was over, the bands and the processions, while the young people planted a tree of liberty and sang the *Marseillaise* 'as fast as the French', according to witnesses.

Then all the Southern States were caught up in the fever and the Abolitionists in the North satisfied, while the silver paper garlands were dripping with Christmas stars in the shops. In New York, it was snowing and Chicago was able to skate on its lake, while in Charleston, in Savannah and in Mobile, the roses poured out their perfume like an escaping murmur, in this South that was, nevertheless, replete of cries . . . It was a matter of saving the Union and the President felt himself burdened with a responsibility that was too great for him. If only he could wait for everything to return to calm and order, temporize, let the enthusiasm cool . . . he would save the end of his term!

In Charleston, everyday life continued with parties, dances, military parades and fireworks that spread their glitter from one end of the heavens to the other, as though mocking the real stars.

Christmas Day was gray and mild. In Savannah, Charlie Jones invited Elizabeth and Ned to lunch in his Tudor house. The beautiful Englishwoman felt at home in this place where the very walls spoke to her of her native country in her native tongue. Her son, immune to such nostalgia, looked around him with a proprietorial gaze, while keeping the secret as he had promised to do. The meal was served in the small dining-room with its rosewood paneling. The conversation was jolly and, at the same time, calm, not touching on any current affairs that might stir strong feelings. Uncle Charlie maintained his policy of appeasement, while mentally following the voyage of his ships loaded with gun parts ready for assembly. This explained his presence in Savannah when one might have expected him to be with his dear Amelia, but he had promised himself he would see her at the New Year when his artillery was safely in harbor, in the warehouse in front of his offices. A series of succulent dishes arrived at the candlelit table: the day was dull and the dining-room quite dark. Peace was restored between the grand-father and his grandson, and toasts were exchanged.

At dessert, the presents appeared. From Lady Fidgety, for her grandson, there was a pirate ship with all its sails and rigging, its boarding boats and guns, more than a meter long in all, and su-perbly finished. Elizabeth had to make do with a sapphire bracelet, which her father-in-law put on her wrist himself. And it was Christmas. A telegram came from Billy: 'Lots of love and see you soon.'

The next day, Charlie Jones kept his word and at nine o'clock came to fetch Elizabeth to take her to Charleston. The weather was magnificent, the sky royal blue. The journey didn't seem very long to the young woman who enjoyed the peace of the countryside after the days of ferment in Savannah. The pinewoods concealed in their depths a peace and silence that would have comforted her much more than Charlie Jones's optimistic little speeches; but in spite of that, she felt happy every time her eyes turned to the sapphire bracelet, which she did not want to take off. Billy would love it.

Reaching the suburbs at two o'clock, Charleston seemed empty to them, as on the day after a holiday. When they drove through the center of the town, they had the same impression of emptiness and this quiet Charleston struck them as odd. No one was in the streets, but a dazzling blue sky presided over the solitude. The town was not dead, simply empty; and yet one could still feel the presence of its inhabitants in a sort of provisional disorder everywhere. They went directly to Hilda's where they had a further surprise. They rang the bell. A voice reached them from the veranda, and a rather disshevelled black servant leaned over the balustrade above them, trying at the same time to put on his jacket with the sleeves inside out.

'All gone,' he called.

But he recognized Elizabeth and, under his curly gray hair, his face broke into a smile.

'Oh, Missie Hag'ove,' he said, chuckling. 'Happy Christmas! Ever'body at Fort Mout'ie, ever'body. With your carriage, must take the ferry, not go round the long way.'

'The ferry?' Elizabeth said in astonishment.

'Hurry,' the black man went on. 'Ever'body there. Happy Christmas!'

Getting back into the carriage, Charlie Jones gave directions to the driver and they set off.

As they were crossing the bay, both of them were struck by the calm and silence. Not a single sea bird was flying, not a boat was moving, apart from their ferry.

'What on earth have they gone to Fort Moultrie for? It's the end of the earth,' Charlie Jones muttered. 'There's nothing there except sand dunes facing the sea, clumps of dry grass and a few trees. I can't believe that the commander of the fort is giving a ball.'

The three o'clock sun was making the sand gleam around them as they arrived at Fort Moultrie. The most unexpected sight met their eyes. All Charleston was having a picnic. Some were even taking lunch right beneath the walls of the fort, in the shade; others had set up parasols further away on the beach; the thickets had been invaded and there were groups reaching as far as the horizon. People had settled everywhere, on the short grass, on the dunes. At the highest point of the latter, some men were looking through spy-glasses, not at the flight of herons or seagulls over the waves, but at what was going on inside the fort, the silent center of this fête. In sheltered hollows, young men were playing the guitar, singing love songs and war songs. Some ladies had planted their easels on one of the forward casemates which the wind had covered with sand up to its roof, sketching the scenery. Children were riding around the walkway on their cycles, or playing at soldiers with Sioux war cries at the entrance to the fortifications, which echoed with this din. And the officer in charge of the detachment had to chase them away, then have the doors shut and confine his men to their barracks, after doubling the guard.

Elizabeth and her father-in-law at last discovered Hilda and her guests under some pine trees. Stones were holding down the four corners of a cloth, even though there was no wind, and trunks in leather and wickerwork, with inner compartments, provided plates and cutlery. They were all enjoying themselves. Empty bottles seemed to sleep off their wine poured on the sand. However, Charlie Jones understood in a flash the tension beneath this party which had brought out the whole town. There was no sign of either Billy, Hampton or Mike . . .

The new arrivals were dying of hunger and were allowed a blanket where they could make themselves as comfortable as possible. Champagne and liver paté went to Elizabeth's head less than the open air, the light reflected from the beach and the conversations that bounced from one group to the next.

When the sun went down, they could hear the sound of the waves once more. Suddenly, in a few minutes, everyone packed up and the children's shouts faded. The boats, and the carriages of those who had come across on dry land, set off . . . Charleston went back to Charleston.

Now began the story of Fort Moultrie.

When the dunes were deserted, when the last boat had left the shore and the dusk had drowned the shadow of the fortifications, Captain Doubleday, the Union commander, loaded his men into two long boats and, rowing quietly across the evening water, they went past the coastguard and reached Fort Sumter. It was the time the workmen were packing up. They were just putting aside their tools when they were unceremoniously bundled into the boat which took them back to the town, and night fell over the sea.

But no sooner had the boat reached the quayside than these workers, who had been hijacked by military force alerted the inhabitants and were taken to the Governor. At once the whole town was put on a war footing. In the port, the sirens hooted, flares went up to watch over Fort Sumter lying silent and dark in the bay and, at dawn, the militia seized the abandoned Fort Moultrie. The same builders and carpenters who had labored to prepare Fort Sumter for the federal army, eagerly got down to clearing the walls. The cannons were unpricked. During the morning, the coast and Fort Johnson were occupied and the cadets installed batteries facing the sea, transforming the low dunes of Morris Island into a fearsome and invisible bastion against any approach to Fort Sumter from the open sea. History was arranging its pawns on the board.

# 130

*B*ack at Hilda's with Charlie Jones, Elizabeth looked around her as if seeing the rooms for the first time and kept a silence that seemed ill-omened to her father-in-law. Even though he spoke softly, any attempt at normal conversation failed, and she had the fleeting idea that she might be losing her mind. She answered his questions with a smile. In fact, she was not listening to him. As soon as she could, she went up to her room, prepared her laudanum and fell asleep. All reality was wiped away.

The following morning she took breakfast with Charlie Jones who was relieved to see her, if not entirely serene, at least much more actively present. But she was still grave. They spoke a little as usual, entirely avoiding the news. In an instant, that had been suppressed; it no longer existed.

'I still haven't told you,' Charlie Jones said, 'that I'm leaving for Virginia tomorrow. I'll arrive there in time for the New Year which I always spend with dear Amelia. Just now, she must be shut in by snow. In any case, she never goes out . . .'

'I love the snow,' Elizabeth said dreamily, suddenly imagining herself in England.

At that moment the gray-haired servant put some buckwheat cakes on the table. Talkative, but almost one of the family, he was allowed considerable liberties.

'Oh, Missis 'Lizbeth not happy,' he said. 'Everythin' will be better, with the good marm'lade. There wasn't much in the kitchen, but we manage . . .'

'That's right, Tommie.' Charlie Jones was irritated. 'It'll be enough. Now you must go, I'm talking to Miss Elizabeth.'

'Ver' well, Massa Charlie, I go tell de kitchen that Massa Charlie say all is well. Good, bitter marm'lade,' he added, to Elizabeth.

Once more alone with his daughter-in-law, Charlie Jones went on:

'I shall be back in Savannah around January 15th.'

'So much the better.'

It was a strange morning. The regular inhabitants of the house came in, stayed long enough for a cup of tea, then left. Newspapers were thrown on the table and Charlie at once made them disappear. Lunch time came. The meal was brief: everyone seemed busy and anxious to get outside as soon as possible.

While Tommie was serving coffee, the door burst open and Billy appeared.

Elizabeth got up with a cry as if she was seeing a ghost. It was Billy, yet it wasn't. He was wearing a gray uniform with bronze buttons, two by two, right and left, on his jacket. Amazed as she was, she noticed every detail.

'What's wrong now?' he said, laughing. 'I warned you we should be changing uniform since we are no longer in the federal army.'

'The federal army . . .,' she stammered. 'And what about your gold braid?'

'If I were Billy,' Charlie Jones told him gravely, 'I should take Elizabeth to her room with me for a rest. Do you have a little time?'

'Two hours, Uncle Charlie. Come on, Elizabeth. That's an order.'

She ran into his arms without a word. Before leaving the room, he announced:

'Our batteries have occupied the whole coast. We're going to instal them as far as North Carolina. As for Fort Sumter, it's surrounded . . . completely! Colonel Beauregard will come here. There's a man, a real one! Fortune favors us. We're going to seize the arsenal, for a start.'

'Oh, Billy,' Elizabeth groaned, her arms round his neck. 'You're not going to fight?'

'Don't worry, my darling, the Federals will run like rabbits.'

'Whew!' Charlie Jones exclaimed when they had gone.

Everyone burst out laughing.

This brief encounter with Billy only made the following days harder for Elizabeth. She had been happy for too short a time and felt abandoned as never before. Charlie Jones's departure for Virginia accentuated her feeling of sadness. He had left on December 27. Who did she have to talk to now? Who could she confide in? Admittedly, Hilda and her little group of friends said they were delighted to have her with them, but except at mealtimes, they left her alone. All of them constantly had some mysterious business in town, and she was told nothing. A quick note from Billy raised her spirits, then immediately worried her: 'My beloved, I love you more than ever, but for at least a fortnight, I shall not be able to see you. Duty calls. We'll meet again in Savannah. Your Billy.'

Two days later, driven mad with boredom, she called for her carriage and set off for Savannah.

Back in Oglethorpe Square, she was almost pleased to see Miss Llewelyn. The Welshwoman was waiting for her as usual in the hall.

'Welcome back, Mrs Hargrove,' she said. 'Is there still as much disturbance in Charleston?'

'No, calm seems to have been restored.'

'The calm before the storm. Things are moving here.'

'And the children, Miss Llewelyn?'

'In fine fettle.'

Elizabeth went up to see her youngest and, on an impulsive gesture, silently smothered him with kisses. At least he did not abandon her.

'Oh, Ma'am,' Black Mammy said, the lower part of her face bursting into a huge smile. 'Mustn't eat him all up, Kit, the angel!'

The angel, for his part, gave her an enchanting look from his blue eyes and added a little speech in which she could make out the words: 'Lo, Mummy, Kit love mummy lots.'

Her heart full, with tears in her eyes, she left him and went up to her room. It was nearly dinner time, but she was not hungry. Her only desire was to go to bed and sleep. Before that came the usual ritual of a moment's admiration in the mirror. As night was falling, she looked at herself by the light of the oil lamp on the dressing table, with a close, critical eye. For her, this was one indisputable reality. By a sort of deliberate replication, she examined herself as though she had been someone she did not know and demanded that her judgement should be pitiless. At first, she was as delighted as usual, but a closer look disturbed her. Something in her face had changed. Perhaps the curve of the cheeks was not as pure, but there was something simpler than that: the insolent freshness of a sixteen-year old girl, which had stayed with her for so long, had vanished. 'You are getting old,' she said in horror to the image which was staring at her wide-eyed. 'Well, not old . . .' said the inner voice. 'But, even so . . .' She turned out the lamp and went to bed in the dark. Sleep was her only true refuge, even without laudanum.

# 131

*O*n January 4, 1861, the Steers gave their great winter ball.
Elizabeth was there, not in white as before, but in almond
green taffeta, her hair drawn up into a crown on top of the head in
the latest European fashion. She was beautiful, certainly, but no
longer so much that she turned every head. The slight difference in
the way she was greeted was impossible to define, yet she sensed
it. People bowed to the beautiful Englishwoman as she passed, but
now they didn't rush toward her. In any case, they were dancing.
She made her entrance to the sound of one of those slow waltzes,
which Vienna was endlessly exporting. Under the crystal pendants
of gigantic chandeliers, the couples were turning round as they
talked, the ladies more dazzling then ever, covered in sparkling
jewels. A young man with black eyes hurried over to Elizabeth
who he noticed was alone and was looking around her, and ceremoniously asked her to dance. His face, pinkish brown in color,
suggested his native Lousiana, and she found him charming . . .
smile, nose, eyebrows, everything. Any woman would be flattered
to have such a partner. She was not yet the dethroned queen.

As she danced, she listened somewhat distractedly to the sweet
nothings he murmured, because remarks were being made all around
them which she caught in passing as they waltzed by.

'With John Floyd and Howell Cobb gone,' a young man was
saying, 'Buchanan has no more ministers from the South.'

'Oh, him!' answered the young woman, who was leaning backward in his arms. 'He's going to fall straight into the hands of those
scoundrels from the North.'

Elizabeth did not understand, but the ironic tone of the remarks
reassured her. Yet she did notice that the dancers spoke of nothing
except politics. Where were the usual silly trifles that one used to
hear at balls?

'The North can only come by sea,' said a handsome masculine
profile.

'They wouldn't dare,' his pink-cheeked partner assured him.
'We've got batteries everywhere.'

'We have?'

'Yes: we — the South.'

The same conversation seemed to be going on everywhere around
Elizabeth. She felt she was at a dance in a barracks.

'South Carolina's appeal to all its brother states is absolutely
admirable. Oh, good evening, Mrs Hargrove.'

Elizabeth recognized one of the young women who had come to
Oglethorpe House when she had come back from Charleston.

'Good evening, Mrs Ryker.'

'Weren't they wonderful in Charleston, Mrs Hargrove?'

'Oh, yes,' Elizabeth said with a smile.

But the waltz swept her along. She just had time to hear Mrs Ryker exclaim to her partner:

'Mrs Hargrove was there. She described it all to us. It was dazzl . . .'

The rest was lost in a sudden whirl of acceleration which brought her close to Mrs Harrison Edwards and Algernon. Curiosity overcoming anxiety, Elizabeth paused for a moment near them as the last chord separated her from her dancer.

'You have no news, but I do. Nothing has come from New York, if indeed the Liverpool ships are in.'

These cryptic words came from Mrs Harrison Edwards, and Algernon replied:

'The Convention of every State in the South must take up its own position. Do we know the dates of their meetings? Here it will be on . . .'

They were so absorbed in each other that they took no notice of the young woman. She seemed to be overhearing two conspirators and felt herself caught up in a huge plot without knowing what it meant or what its aim was. She suddenly had a disturbing thought: for some time she had been living like a sleepwalker on the edge of an abyss. Below her was war . . . perhaps madness. She was afraid and went home.

There, as she was going upstairs in a rustle of the taffeta dress which she was wearing for the first time, she imagined several voices saying incomprehensible things to her. A dose of laudanum calmed her down.

The following morning she had the feeling that she had gone to the extremity of her fear, because she felt ashamed of it. Pride woke her: an Englishwoman could not live in dread, but she shuddered for all that and when Miss Llewelyn brought her the papers, she instinctively pushed them aside.

In town, the word Secession was on every lip, in an unending hum, and was concealed in more or less every sentence. One morning, Ned appeared before her oddly disguised. An old cap out of the attic covered his head and he had twisted it around so as to give himself what he considered a military appearance, while his waist was held by a metal buckled belt.

'I'm going to be a soldier,' he said simply.

For the first time in a long while, she found the strength to laugh.

'At your age, you've got plenty of time.'

'My turn will come. Soon.'

She wanted to scream, but restrained herself. War was everywhere already, it breathed in the air. 'What about Billy?' she thought from morning to night.

At breakfast, on January 10, Miss Llewelyn as usual brought her the newspapers which she put down on the table, saying:

'Today, Mrs Hargrove, you would be wrong not to cast an eye on this, because something odd happened yesterday, involving someone . . .'

'Not Billy?' Elizabeth exclaimed.

'No, no. May I sit?'

Without waiting for permission, she sat down and adopted her favorite pose, that of the storyteller.

'*The Star of the West*, a merchant ship from the North, was sailing off Morris Island quite innocently, it seemed, at dawn on the 9th, aiming to make Fort Sumter and, surprise, surprise, put down two hundred soldiers and some munitions there.'

'So? Please come to the point.'

'No, I'm not going to spoil a good story . . . Unfortunately for *The Star of the West*, its captain sailed on a course not usually taken by merchant ships, the southern approach which passes close to Morris Island; and he did this in order to avoid exposure to the guns on Fort Moultrie on the other side. Well — don't be impatient, Mrs Hargrove, I'm getting to it — well, Morris Island had been fortified with batteries manned by cadets. And among them was Mike.'

'Oh, no. Dear Mike!'

'More wily than foxes, don't you think? The cadets guessed that the good old merchant ship was suspect. They fired a warning shot. The gun . . .'

'It's war!' Ned cried.

'Hush!' said Miss Llewelyn. 'I haven't finished. The gunshot went too high. So the boys adjusted their weapons and aimed for the waterline. At the second shot . . .'

'They sank her!' Ned yelled.

'*The Star of the West* preferred to turn about .'

'Bravo!' Ned applauded.

'And Mike?' Elizabeth asked anxiously.

'You can be sure he was magnificent.'

'Wonderful.'

'Superb, Mrs Hargrove, I am pleased to see that you are waking up, but you will hear more such tales in the days to come, and news to make the ears of Northerners ring. I feel it, I know it. Long live the South, Mrs Hargrove!'

'Long live the South, long live the South!' Ned cried.

After this statement, Miss Llewelyn went out, as satisfied as could be at the direction History was taking.

From now on Elizabeth kept abreast of everything. She had become as eager for news as everyone else in the town: she had fallen into the trap — the trap of reality. And reality was Secession. Each day brought a new one, in a well-ordered avalanche: Mississippi on the 9th, Florida on the 10th, Alabama on the 11th and, finally, Georgia on the 19th. Elizabeth was carried away by the general mood of exultation. Savannah became another Charleston with its processions, its songs, its fireworks. Five stars, four red and one blue on a white background, surmounted by an eye, replaced the federal flag. A new dawn was rising on the country, 'fresh and joyful'.

Charlie Jones had still not returned to Savannah. Undoubtedly his affairs must be getting more complicated in New York. Presumably he had to keep a watch from Virginia on the voyages of his ships.

# 132

Since the start of the year, Toombs had kept relatively quiet. While Georgia was still debating the question of breaking all ties with the Union, and what form to give to some future association, he took a disturbingly moderate line. Which is why declaration appeared all the more sensational. His was the best way of uniting supporters of different policies in the South. His subtle and unanswerable way of dissecting opposing ideas had the result of winning over Unionists, like Jefferson Davis and Alexander Stephens, while gaining the fanatical support of all Southerners, governors, senators, representatives, soldiers, planters, young society idlers, workmen, adolescents, schoolboys and, of course, women.

'I would recommend waiting until March 4, the day when the new President takes office. Then we can consider the will of the Republicans to act *honestly* toward the South.' In his quietest voice, he went on: 'I do not wish to fear, but I do fear, that the Northerners are about to prepare new, sly laws against the plantation owners to assist future John Browns, paid by people who are always happy to display their *Christian* sentiments. No, no: no one will make me say that I am trying to allude to criminal conversations and correspondence. I shall not throw those blazing papers on a smouldering fire.' And with what was for him unexpected geniality, he asked: 'Is there any means of saving the sick Union?' After a silence, his most rhetorical voice concluded:

'Yes, there is one cure, only one: new constitutional guarantees. Let the Republicans offer them as a sign of good will. And if they refuse? Well, we shall see if that will is a *malevolent* one and we shall have to exorcise it. So let us give them one final opportunity to restore this tottering Union.'

And the Union tottered.


# 133


Charlie Jones had not vanished. On leaving Great Meadow, he had made a detour via Washington, because he wanted to be present at an extraordinary session of the Senate, and that is where, on January 21, he found himself.

At nine o'clock in the morning, in a Capitol still under construction, the Senate is full. Scarcely are the doors open, than the crowd floods in. The stairs and passages are black with people.

A row of very tall Corinthian columns gives the vast semi-circle the full majesty of a monument dedicated to oratory, and everything even the capitals, soars in a flight of eloquence. Women are pushing and shoving in the gallery set aside for them as are the gentlemen of the press in theirs. Under the President's desk, ready to carry official documents, stand the 'pages', boys of fourteen, elegantly dressed, with their heads in the air and looking more self-confident than veteran politicians. On the floor of the Senate, to one side, at the left of the Speaker, are padded leather chairs reserved for some distinguished guests: Charles Jones and Lord Lyons remain silent, while to their left, the very conceited Comte de Paris is in full flood.

There is a lot of talking, but it is subdued, except for the women; then, little by little, even this noise abates and fades away as the time approaches for the session to start. Everyone is waiting for this moment when their world, in this very room, will change. The Senators from the States which have seceded are due to address the House for one last time and Jefferson Davis, the Senator from Mississippi, even though he is unwell, has let it be known that he will speak last.

When he finally appears, he will be greeted by profound silence. His whole person possesses a natural dignity, with no sign of the affectation so common among politicians. Slim and elegant, he strikes one with the seriousness of his expression on a finely molded face, with prominent features and well-marked cheekbones. From time to time, he wipes an ailing eye, an eye that is almost lost.

Now, standing at the front of the room, leaning on the podium, he delivers the first words of his speech in a weak voice. He has come despite his high temperature and he is listened to with all the more attention by those eager to catch every word. 'I rise, Mr President, for the purpose of announcing to the Senate that I have satisfactory evidence that the State of Mississippi, by a solemn ordinance of her people, in convention assembled, has declared her separation from the United States. Under these circumstances, of course, my functions are terminated here. It has seemed to me proper, however, that I should appear in the Senate to announce that fact to my associates and I will say but very little more. The occasion does not invite me to go into argument; and my physical condition would not permit me to do so if it were otherwise . . .'

In an increasingly assured voice, he explains that he considers himself a partisan of the State which he represented, even though always desirous of saving the Union, but only within the limits of the rights of each State. 'I am sure,' he goes on, 'I feel no hostility toward you, Senators from the North. I am sure there is not one of you, whatever sharp discussion there may have been between us, to whom I cannot now say, in the presence of my God, I wish you well; and such, I am sure, is the feeling of the people whom I represent toward those whom you represent. I, therefore, feel that I but express their desire when I say I hope, and they hope, for peaceful relations with you, though we must part. They may be mutually beneficial to us in the future, as they have been in the past, if you so will it. The reverse may bring disaster . . .'

He is speaking from his heart, without hurrying, and he ends amid a deathly silence. The gas lamps cast a dramatic light on this America, frozen in horror at seeing the nation fall apart.

'In the course of my service here, associated at different times with a great variety of Senators, I see now around me some with whom I have served a long time; there have been points of collision; but whatever offense there has been to me, I forgive and forget; I carry with me no hostile memories. Whatever offense I have given which has not been redressed, or for which satisfaction has not been demanded, I have, Senators, in this hour of our parting, to offer you my apology for any pain which, in the heat of discussion, I may have inflicted. I go hence unencumbered of any injury received and without bitterness. Mr President, fellow Senators, it only remains to me to bid you a final farewell.'

He steps down from the rostrum and leaves the room, followed by the Senators from the South. On the great marble staircase, and later in the hall, the crowd parts and only silence accompanies them.

# 134

*I*n the days that followed, Washington was rapidly abandoned by the Southerners posted there and a large number of Army officers resigned.

Charlie Jones returned to Savannah to find Elizabeth transformed. The young woman was reading the newspaper in her scarlet drawing-room, in a purple dress, her hair in ringlets on top of her head. She came toward him eagerly.

'Well, you're back, then, Uncle Charlie,' she said merrily. 'Where were you?'

Amazed at this unexpected tone of voice, he repeated the question before answering:

'Where was I? Why . . . in Washington.'

'It must be interesting just now, isn't it?'

'Interesting? Yes. I wanted to be present at the farewell session of our friend Jefferson Davis.'

'In the Senate. It must have been moving.'

'But, Elizabeth, you seem to know all about it. Are you reading the newspapers now?'

'Like everyone else. But do sit down.'

She sat on the sofa and, with a sweeping gesture, spread out her dress like a flag.

'It's Louisiana today,' she said with an air of importance.

'And it's not over. But I see you are much less uneasy about the turn of events, and I am glad of it.'

'What do you expect: one gets used to the turn of events! Have you seen Miss Llewelyn?'

'Yes . . . No . . . She wasn't standing at the door as usual, but sitting in a corner of the hall, apparently engaged in doing something. We greeted one another from afar.'

'Would you like to see what it was she was doing?'

Without hesitation, he got up and went out. Sitting a little apart, between the staircase and the garden door, the Welshwoman was sewing, with a white cloth on her knees.

'Excuse me for not getting up, Mr Jones,' she said. 'I am just adding a star to the five previous ones. Louisiana this time. It's becoming fascinating. Would you like to see?'

She stuck her needle in the cloth and unfolded it, holding it at arm's length. There was a partial circle of red stars boldly outlined on the improvised flag.

'I see,' he said. 'You have got to work quickly. Louisiana added its star last night.'

'We need another ten for a perfect circle, but they'll come.'

Her normally stern face lit up with a smile.

'Happy, Mr Jones?' she asked, putting the cloth back on her knees and leaning over her new star.

'Yes, I think,' he said. 'If all goes well.'

'If all goes well,' she repeated, drawing her needle. 'Mrs Hargrove is convinced all will be well.'

'Astonishing. What happened?'

'We shook her out of her dreams, Mr Ned and I. And then, recently, she has been carried away by the enthusiasm in town. There is nothing so contagious as these waves of popular feeling. Your daughter-in-law may be English, but she still has a heart.'

He burst out laughing.

'Caustic as ever, Miss Llewelyn, but I'm grateful to you for bringing her back to the real world. What a relief for us all.'

The Welshwoman looked up with a wily expression.

'I don't want to spoil your pleasure,' she said more softly. 'Mrs Hargrove is for the South and quite ready to stand up to the North, but she can't believe in the eventuality of war. If by misfortune . . .'

'Let's not speak of misfortune, Miss Llewelyn.'

' . . .the shock would be severe,' she concluded, adding simply: 'Billy, Mr Jones.'

Charlie Jones turned his back to her.

Five days later, Miss Llewelyn was sewing the star of Texas on her flag. The State had seceded on February 1st.

Until now the Confederation of the South had no common frontier with the North: Virginia, Kentucky and North Carolina even formed a bloc between the adversaries. The secessionist States proposed to elect Jefferson Davis as President and Alexander Stephens was chosen as Vice-President. One might hope for a *status quo*, but the most utter confusion reigned in the political headquarters, each temporizing, each having the solution for the future, launching an appeal to Union — a word that changed its meaning from one place to another. Lincoln, who was to take office at the beginning of March, was as hesitant as Buchanan and, in public, kept quiet, while among his own people he declared his obsession: Union at any price. On every other matter, the future President's ideas were vague; his main preoccupation seemed to be a careful balance in the choice of the politicians whom he would put in place around him. With his long, greenish face, he looked more and more like a phantom, entirely decked out in black, something which was not altered by the beard that he had started to grow. Only a a skilled psychologist could have detected in his look a greatness of which he himself was not yet conscious.

On February 4, John Letcher, Governor of Virginia, called for a peace conference of all States in the Union, except the six States of New England, which he didn't trust. They had themselves tried to secede several times in the past and would only have brought feelings of discord into the discussion. A former President of the United States, the Virginian, John Tyler, was to preside over this assembly of twenty-one States, in the private rooms of the Willard Hotel in Washington. All of them, especially the frontier States between North and South, hoped to find a basis for an agreement. On the same day, in Montgomery, Alabama, the seven States which had seceded elected their President: Jefferson Davis. The man and the moment had come together.

In Savannah, Mrs Harrison Edwards and Algernon Steers met every day in Oglethorpe Square at Elizabeth's. She was now party to all their plans. The discussions were long and led to action. The British guns had been delivered and handed over as a gift to Governor Brown, while he had seized control of the State arsenals and, at Fort Pulaski, which commanded the entrance to the Savannah River, the hussars from Georgia were now mounting guard. However, there was still one black spot: using the Secession as an excuse, the Governor of New York had embargoed the cargoes of weapons on the *Monticello*: boxes of guns and cartridges.

Throughout the month of January, he refused to reply, then did so evasively after repeated requests from the Governor of Georgia. The latter, claiming that the contracts had been entered into correctly and the merchandise paid for in cash on the nail, responded in February by seizing in turn five merchant ships from New York sailing off the Georgian coast. New York cried: 'piracy!' There was a struggle between the two governors who fought one another by telegram. The authorities of the Northern State — Governor, Mayor, police — passed responsibility from one to another, resorting in turn to the most complete bad faith.

'By what right,' Governor Brown roared, 'do you lay hands on our goods? This is an act of interference in the private affairs of a sovereign State.'

From one day to the next, he was promised that the *Monticello* would be freed. New York claimed to give way, then, when its own captured ships had been released, went back on its word in the name of morality. Finally, at each new lie from the North, Brown replied by new seizures and the ultimate threat of selling by auction, in Savannah, the cargoes and the ships themselves by way of compensation . . . So February went by, the whole of America captivated by the successive episodes of this maritime tale.

Algernon considered further purchases. As Elizabeth was English like Charlie Jones, the transactions could be made in her maiden name and the British trading posts in Jamaica would be free to send Miss Escridge, a British subject, whatever Algernon, Mrs Harrison Edwards, Governor Brown and Julian Hartridge, Representative for the town of Savannah, might order, for better or worse.

Elizabeth took part in this dangerous game, without knowing what she was letting herself in for.

Billy breezed in briefly from time to time, fully immersed in his regiment and in instructing the militia. On each of his short visits, he grasped his happiness like a godsend, only too well aware of the threat hanging over his future. To Elizabeth, of course, he said nothing except words of love. On the days when he was in the house, as on those when Mrs Harrison Edwards and Algernon met there, Elizabeth sent Ned away. He alone was more disruptive than a whole army.

# 135

On March 4, at dawn, Captain Fred Hargrove was in command of a brigade of light cavalry. Washington looked like a city under siege. There had been rumors of a plot and General Winfield Scott had used this as a pretext to recall the troops stationed near Harper's Ferry and in the neighboring counties of Maryland. The soldiers gave the general the nickname 'old bluffer' and muttered that he was drumming up this whole circus simply to flaunt his own importance through his pessimistic views; and so that, if there really was a Southern conspiracy and it succeeded in its attack on the capital, he could then put down his commander's baton on the desk of the head of state.

The town was full of soldiers and yet crowds of people poured in at all hours of the night out of the Republican trains. On every roof down Pennsylvania Avenue there were armed men and everything was under guard right down to the official platform underneath the national flag.

As the sun began to climb, the Capitol rose before Fred's eyes against the stormy sky. There was scaffolding around the columns of the unfinished dome, making it impossible to use the room where the President should have taken the oath.

As an image of the State, the Capitol sustained its illusion from afar, thought Fred. And while the men were waiting patiently in the cold, he recalled the last few years: his flight from Elizabeth, the need to restore and impose order on the Mormons, the years spent in the West in Indian territory, Harper's Ferry under the orders of Colonel Lee, and the trial of John Brown . . . How he had loved Colonel Lee, and what a wrench for all those around him when he was appointed to Texas . . . Fred, who had been promoted to Captain, had to join another regiment. When Georgia had voted for Secession, he hesitated over leaving the Army, fearing that if he went back to Savannah he might see Elizabeth again . . . And now what would he do? He had just learned that Colonel Lee, recalled by headquarters in Washington, was at home in Arlington on the other side of the Potomac. What would he do if his Virginia, his native state, were to secede in its turn?

The morning passed. Under heavy gray clouds, the immensity of the architecture would have seemed melancholy had sudden gusts of wind not added a dramatic note. The ceremony began at noon. It was under the East Portico that the President took the oath of office on the Bible presented to him by Roger Taney. The latter had been Chief Justice for twenty-five years and, one after another, the incoming Presidents of the United States had sworn the oath to this profoundly religious Catholic. Now sick and very thin, he trembled as he walked, and the tall, lanky man dressed entirely in black who faced him showed a no less ravaged face. Once the formality was accomplished, Lincoln stepped forward onto the platform.

The clouds were racing above the Capitol, there were sudden bursts of bright light and the wind made the canvas on the scaffolding flap. Lincoln took his papers out of his pocket with an awkwardness that betrayed the depth of his feelings. In a hesitant voice, he began to read his speech, the wind taking the words out of his mouth and dispersing them across the heads of the noisy crowd. Fred caught scraps of phrases: he had no intention of interfering directly or indirectly with the institution of slavery in the States where it already existed; he considered he had no legal right to do so, and no desire . . . One of his sheets of paper was snatched away by the wind at this point and Senator Douglas, his old Democrat adversary from Illinois, who had stood near him in order to be seen, had the good fortune to catch it in flight. The crowd was not listening.

'The power conferred to me will be used to hold, occupy and possess the property and places belonging to government.'

'So much for Sumter,' Fred thought.

The speaker went on: 'Physically speaking, we cannot separate. A husband and wife may be divorced, but the different parts of our country cannot do this. Union cannot be dissolved . . .'

This lawyer's eloquence in defense of a fiction seemed derisory in the face of the soldiers' guns, the mob of people and the massing of clouds that the wind was tearing apart above the unfinished monument. One single, burning question kept coming back into Fred's mind: 'Why do these Northern Republicans want Union at any price?' And he recalled Toombs's visit to Dimwood on the day when Susanna had disappeared. 'The ambition of the North is to increase the power of its factories with money from cotton and to seize the riches of the South by legally imposing its customs tariffs. As for their protectionist policy, slavery is only a pretext. It will be obsolete in a few years, but these people want to take advantage of it; their consciences must always be appeased.'

The new President's speech was full of such contradictions. He told the Southern States: 'the government will not attack you. There will be no conflict unless you are the aggressors' . . . , while at the same time speaking of carrying out 'the laws of the Union in all States.'

Power, at all times and in all countries — power and the lust for power led directly to contempt for individual freedom; and every State could be considered an individual. Fred decided to leave the Army.

His squadron was now following the open coach from which Buchanan was waving in response to the cheers of the crowd for Lincoln on the way to the White House, while the new President remained calm and motionless. All the officers were invited to the official reception after their regiments were relieved. Fred found himself being pushed by the crowd. Everyone was going in.

In the reception rooms, foreign ambassadors were rubbing shoulders with woodcutters in flannel shirts and farmers in their Sunday best, but not a single Black except for the servants. A delegation of workers from a factory in Chicago in their best clothes were admiring the decor open-mouthed, some of them even stroking the gilding on the door frames, happy to verify the reality of their votes. In the coming and going of the crowd, Fred noticed that some squares had been cut out of the silk curtains and the backs of the sofas near the walls, no doubt as souvenirs. Lincoln was standing at the entrance to the blue drawing-room and looked uncomfortable. White leather gloves made his enormous hands seem even larger. Fred wanted to take a closer look at him.

At that moment, a very young boy approached the President who listened to him for a short while, then replied with a smile that transformed his face like a ray of sunshine. Fred watched more closely. 'This man,' he thought, 'is no more all of one piece than I am, or anyone in the world. Human affection draws us toward one another, but his ideas drive me strongly away from him. There is nothing more for me to do here.'

Without further ado, he left. Outside, his brigade had been replaced by other cavalry guarding the approaches to the White House. Walking through a good-humored crowd, many of whom had been drinking heavily, he went back to his barracks and there he wrote his letter of resignation.

On the 10th, he was back in Savannah.

# 136

Ameeting took place at Mrs Harrison Edwards' to discuss the problem of the *Monticello* once again, and to look for a quick and lasting solution. Joseph Brown, Governor of Georgia, was present, as well as Charlie Jones and Algernon, with Elizabeth who was very anxious to demonstate her loyalty to the South. Brown was a little under forty years old, but what immediately struck one was the direct and resolute gaze of a born fighter: his Irish roots (he came from Londonderry) were the key to his personality. The family had fought often and valiantly. His face was handsome with its regular features, but elongated by an exceptionally high forehead. The hair, thick and black, was cut straight on each side with no hint of vanity, and a thin beard framed his boxer's jaw. Because of this unforgettable face, as well as his liking for argument and the energy he brought to it, he had often been compared to Toombs, one of his best friends, with whom he got on wonderfully — except when they held the same opinion on something. Then would begin the great rhetorical duel which delighted their audience, especially Charlie Jones who admired them both.

Elizabeth, despite herself, could not take her eyes off this person, who was for her the very image of a great man.

In a deliberately measured and quick voice, he spoke:

'The organization of our troops,' he said, 'is proceeding rapidly. Officers are constantly rallying to us, many of them West Pointers. The latest to arrive seems to me the very man to take charge of this matter of arms from the military point of view. His mission will be to recover them. I have asked him to wait in the antechamber; if you agree, he can take part in our discussion.'

They all agreed. They rang for the servant who was ordered to admit the young officer waiting outside.

A minute passed and Fred appeared.

Elizabeth instantly leaped to her feet.

'Fred!' she cried.

Without a second's hesitation, he went directly up to her and kissed her. She blushed.

With a smile, Joseph Brown said simply:

'Captain Hargrove.'

'This is Billy's brother,' Elizabeth explained. 'We have not seen each other for eight years.'

Charlie Jones laughed.

'Her brother-in-law, Brown: the heart, the family, you understand.'

'Very much so,' said the Governor of Georgia. 'Now, Captain, if Mrs Harrison Edwards agrees, will you join us?'

'If I agree!' Mrs Harrison Edwards exclaimed. 'Fred, come and sit opposite me.'

He obeyed and she, delighted at her own importance, described the misadventures of the *Monticello*.

'Quite right,' said the Governor. 'Now, let's get to work. The Northerners are taking us for a ride — or, more precisely, a sail! The ships I've taken are luckily good catches. I intend to sell them at auction at the end of the month, this time without prevarication, and so attract merchants who have dealings with the New England ports. We shall invest full authority in Captain Hargrove and he shall have every power to search on board and to seize any goods belonging to these people from New York in the name of the State of Georgia. We shall start with the port of Savannah and continue at other points along the coast, such as Darien or Brunswick, where ships call. I think there is nothing more to be said today and I have the honor to bid you farewell.'

He stood up and they all followed suit. After a last look at Elizabeth, Fred followed the Governor.

The practical measures taken by the two men must have been effective: ten days later, New York gave way and the *Monticello* left the snow-bound, muddy docks of Manhattan for Charlie Jones's sunny quays. They had the arms, war was only a word, the peace conference continued its obscure work in Washington at the instigation of Virginia, and the speeches there had one thing in common: they ignored reality.

# 137

Seated once more beside the window in her room, Elizabeth was recovering while wondering what she thought of Fred. He had come back into her life after all these years. What meaning could there be in this — because, to her, everything had a meaning. Her heart overlooked such speculative notions and spoke to her more simply: she loved Fred. She knew only too well the dizziness of love, the first minute . . . Nothing of the sort had happened when he spoke to her at Dimwood. She had felt nothing then, yet today . . . By what whim of the spirit . . . These questions remained unanswered because one simply could not argue with love. And then, there was Billy. She adored Billy. Fred had changed, his face was a little fuller and there was a softness in the eyes, an all-round charm, and that fervor that he had . . . The uniform, too, well cut, a little severe, but it suited him, while at Dimwood he had been too young, it was different . . .

'Wretched Elizabeth!' she said to herself, getting up from her chair. Did the uniform really count for so much? They were settling into a world of uniforms. It was not war, thank Heaven, but there were uniforms to be seen everywhere. Those cadets, so gallant, which people mentioned to her whenever the subject of Charleston came up . . . But she had promised to be a good girl, for Billy's sake.

# 138

*H*ilda had just woken up with a start. The guns! Everyone had been expecting it for some days and the whole town had gone to bed at one o'clock in the morning, disappointed because the days went by and nothing happened. She looked at the time: half past four.

Laurence had also got up. They both got dressed quickly with the same idea of going out onto the terrace from which you could see the whole bay. Major Anderson must have refused the ultimatum from Governor Pickens, when it was learned that the federal government was sending an armed fleet to break the blockade of Fort Sumter. On the pretext that it was carrying foodstuffs, the President had declared: 'They will not dare to fire on bread.' So why deliver it in warships?

Major Anderson had only two days' worth of reserves, so they had to act in reply to the North's provocation. That cannon shot had been the signal for war.

On their terrace, Hilda and her husband were dazzled by the flashes lighting up the sky. A continuous stream of red rockets rose from the coast, as though to illuminate the target. Then the shells exploded. Beauregard had had camp fires lit on all the islands around Fort Sumter. Beyond was the deep black of night above the ocean on which the relief expedition was approaching from New York. The gunners were waiting, hidden in the dunes on Morris Island, controlling the passes toward the open sea with the crossed fire of their guns and those on thc dunes beyond Fort Moultrie and on Sullivan Island.

Once their eyes had grown accustomed to these alternating flashes and the darkness of night, Hilda and Laurence noticed that the terraces all around them were crowded with people. All Charleston was on the roofs.

Throughout April 12th, the town was shaken with explosions. The houses trembled a little under the continuous thundering of the cannons. From time to time, mortars barked. When night fell, they organized parties on the terraces. The spectacle of battle became as popular as fireworks. Bottles of champagne were cracked open and sofas brought out so that they could rest while watching the fire in the sky.

They were kept informed, hour by hour, of what was going on. The cadets from the fortress had opened fire and were solidly installed on Morris Island. They were the ones shooting all the time: they had the largest artillery pieces and some short mortars which had inflicted damage on Fort Sumter. The fort was replying only against Fort Moultrie; what use were all its cannons? It was said that only the gunners were left. The door had been broken open and a powder magazine was burning (that was the trail of smoke drifting up into the clouds) . . . How long would Anderson hold out? At sea, the Northern ships had tried to come close, but without a tug they had no chance of breaking through the bar . . . And even then there would be our guns. Officers from the Navy had had floating batteries brought up to close the circle around Fort Sumter.

Hilda said to Minnie,who had joined them on the terrace:

'It's lucky Elizabeth is not here, We'd have to tell her that Mike is on Morris Island and that Billy is in charge of the artillery in Fort Johnson. She'd be impossible.'

'Poor Elizabeth!' Minnie replied. 'Put yourself in her shoes.'

Hilda could not prevent herself from laughing.

'She is worried about the uniforms. She likes them clean and fresh!'

The 13th dawned radiantly. A morning mist vanished at the first rays of the sun and the sky across the bay was so clear that one could see the whole horizon as far as the distant dunes with topographical precision. The smoke from the guns hung around like light flakes of lovely weather. One could see the canvas of the tents and follow the young officers galloping along the foam-flecked shore as they carried messages from headquarters. In the transparent air one might have heard the dull sound of their horses' hooves and the shouts of command had it not been for the predominant voice of the guns.

The afternoon passed in the enthusiasm of an outing, as though war were a game with no dangers. Night and day, the guns continued to growl, so that one might have thought they had no other aim except to keep the defenders of Fort Sumter from sleep. The Battery gardens and the sea shore were invaded by enthusiastic spectators. They sang, or rather shouted:

'Cannon and mortar,
Musket and shell,
With Beauregard
We'll greet the North well.'

And the crowd passed on the names which the young regiments of Carolina had given themselves: Tigers, Lions, Eagles, Savages. They also circulated the text of the message sent to the commandant of Fort Sumter in the night of the 12th at 3.30 a.m.: 'We have the honor to inform you that our batteries will open fire in one hour.' Beauregard had been honorable, as Anderson was in defending himself. In the afternoon, moreover, the major's guns had suddenly, for a short while, fired back, salvo for salvo, and the watching crowd cheered wildly. War seemed a jolly business; there was no red except the trace of the shells across the sky.

Another evening rang with the music and songs of the South. In spite of the warm and overcast weather, they settled onto the roof terraces to watch the spectacle above the heads of the magnolias and the oak trees, and not miss a second of it. Trains from everywhere in the State and from neighboring Georgia brought groups of over-excited young men, who had come for a sniff of powder.

On the 14th, Fort Sumter surrendered.

The garrison was handed over with the honors of war, and the federal soldiers, who were to be carried on board the Union ships still lying off the coast, raging but powerless, struck their flag. During the ceremony, one soldier was killed when a box of ammunition blew up just as his comrades were firing a farewell salvo. He was buried inside the fort, and a clergyman from the South said the prayers. This accidental death had a somewhat demoralising effect on the men who were leaving.

Thousands of shells were fired without a scratch, noise or blazing of lights: the operation had been easy. The uniforms remained as brand new as the enthusiasm of those who wore them; the youth of the South had no idea what it would be like, this coming war, nor what lay behind simple words like 'campaign', 'night march' or 'skirmish'. Death did not exist. No one could imagine his solitary death agony in a ditch; they were all together for glory.

When the seven-starred flag finally rose above Fort Sumter, the whole town rose – on the terraces where it had been following the events of the battle through spyglasses, in the Battery gardens, on the quaysides in the port and in the boatloads of onlookers which filled the bay – and sang Dixie:

'In Dixie land I'll take my stand
To live and die in Dixie!
Look away, look away!
Look away down South to Dixie!'

Once the fort had surrendered, Major Anderson, red-eyed, was conducted to the confederate headquarters and kept . . . to have dinner. It was he who had taught Beauregard the art of ballistics while the latter was a cadet at West Point, so he became the guest of his former pupil.

A long night began in Charleston, noisier than ever. Bands marched tirelessly through the streets. The restaurants and bars were full to bursting, everyone offering drinks to the gray uniforms with their yellow trimmings. There was dancing everywhere, in the houses, in the streets, and everybody drank everything, champagne corks popping in honor of a recovered Fort Sumter. People's faces were bursting with happiness and everything was swept along in an orgy of fraternization.

The following day, while repairs began on the fort, President Lincoln launched an appeal to all the States of the Union, asking for 75,000 men from their militias for the federal army, to bring the South back to its senses. Two days later, considering this as an act of aggression, Virginia seceded. Events were gathering pace, as though the gunshot at half-past four had suddenly released them after months of expectation and speeches. The Virginians at once seized the arsenal at Harper's Ferry, which had acquired symbolic significance since John Brown's failed attack on it. The Federals had set fire to everything, but the Southerners saved the machines for manufacturing weapons and sent them at once to North Carolina, which was about to vote for secession in its turn. Twenty-four hours later, Lincoln decreed a blockade of the Southern coasts. In reply, the Virginians took over the naval dockyards and seized a fair quantity of cannons, together with the most modern warship, the *Merrimac*, which had been ineffectively scuttled by the Northerners and which was at once put back on the stocks for repair.

Passions mounted, artifically fuelled, and all young men, from both North and South, had already started to see enemies in those whom they had considered their brothers only a day earlier. Enemies: the word did not make sense . . .

# 139

*O*n April 18, Colonel Robert E. Lee, on leave at his estate in Arlington, was called to the federal capital. He had been expecting his new posting since the beginning of March and was resting in the large colonnaded house overlooking the banks of the Potomac, from which he could see in the distance the unfinished Capitol building and, on the other side, his beloved hills of Virginia.

So, on the very day that his native State had just opted for Secession, he was received by Francis P. Blair, semi-official spokesman for President Lincoln, and Simon Cameron, the Secretary of State for War, who offered him the command of the Federal Army. He refused. He could not take part in an invasion of the South; even though he was opposed to Secession, he was also opposed to war. When he left this interview he went, out of friendship and respect, to call on old General Scott, who saw him as his successor. He told him of the offer and his refusal. The general tried in vain to make him change his mind.

Returning home to Arlington, to that house which had once belonged to the family of George Washington and had been inherited by his wife, Lee considered the peculiarity of his position as he continued to belong to an army which he refused to command in a civil war, even though he still wanted to believe such a war impossible.

Who was Robert E. Lee, this man who won everyone over with his handsome face and calm, direct look? Though he came from a fine family, his simple manner and natural courtesy made it easy for him to mix with anyone. One of his ancestors, originally from Shropshire on the Welsh border, had built Stratford Manor in the county of Westmoreland, Virginia, in the seventeenth century. Here Robert was born. His father, Harry Lee, an enthusiastic cavalry officer and companion in arms of George Washington, was then forty-nine. His birthplace was not far as the crow flies, but throughout the anxious moments of that April day, under the sycamores in Arlington, Robert Lee had other things on his mind.

He was alone with himself. Leaving the Union meant leaving the army, and the army had been his whole life since adolescence: West Point, his friends, his memories . . . even memories of the Mexican War, that war of conquest of which, in his heart, he disapproved. However, wearing a uniform obliged him to accept constraints, but in this submission a passion for duty and obedience kindled something inside him. He had the greatest respect for those with whom he had served over the years, subordinates as well as generals. It sickened him to break such bonds of comradeship in an instant.

Saying goodbye to the army meant saying goodbye to his entire past life. Did God want that?

He would resign and return to civilian life, never again to wear a sword, unless Virginia itself was attacked. From his porch he could see the hills unfolding like motionless waves breaking against the huge expanse of fields. The wind was furrowing the corn. This countryside was streaked with long roads the color of rust: the soil of the South.

He went into his room. As a true Christian, he asked God for guidance.

He knew that the Lord is a hidden God and that his language is silence. Ask and it shall be given. The promise of the Gospel is straightforward, but one must wait and wait again, perhaps for hours, in faith, in the confidence of Love. For the man on his knees at the foot of his bed, only God counts, because the man on his knees at the foot of his bed loves God. This is the central fact of his life, but he is not one of those who speak of such things.

When the night was over, he made his decision, convinced that the Lord had answered him. Had he correctly understood the message? Anything will do when speaking to men: sudden inspirations or events. But Lee was sure of what he was doing.

Composing his letter of resignation, he sent it to the Secretary of State for War and, by the same messenger, had a letter brought to General Scott, once more expressing his terrible dilemma: he would leave the federal army, which might one day invade Virginia, for it was quite impossible for him to fight against Virginia.

Now he thought of going to Kinloch to his cousins, the Turners, to rest, since two of his daughters were spending their holidays there. But on April 23rd, the Governor of Virginia asked to see him in Richmond. The North was massing its troops on the far side of the Potomac and threatening to cross. This, then, was the true reply to his long prayers.

He saddled Traveler, his old dappled gray horse with the black mane, and set off for Richmond.

Already, the whole of the South was marching behind him.

# 140

*E*lizabeth was gradually recovering from her meeting with Fred. She had been excessively disturbed by the encounter at Mrs Harrison Edwards' and it had temporarily deprived her of any desire to meet people. She was discovering the charm of solitude. She firmly rejected the idea of going for a walk in town, in Bull Street, for example. There was too much agitation in Savannah. Processions gathered and young people paraded past, shouting songs which she did not know. If she absolutely had to take the air, did she not have her own garden, with its row of flowering magnolias? She preferred to go there at the times when Ned was in school. Recently, he had adopted warlike attitudes and a tone of voice which irritated her, though she did not want to admit it. She could no longer entirely recognize her Ned of former times, but he still displayed surges of affection that warmed her heart.

One morning she went down the steps and took a short walk along the path beneath the trees, where the breeze was scented by the magnolias which she loved. Patrick was not there. Perhaps it was just as well. He was no doubt chatting with the passers-by, but she would tell him off some other time. She carried on toward the Irishman's house, and suddenly stopped. A hum of conversation was coming from it: two people were talking and she was amazed to recognize the voices of Patrick and Ned.

Without hesitation, she went in. At first she could see nothing. A cellar would not have been blacker; but from the darkness there was a cry, not of love so much as anxiety:

'Mummy!'

'Ned, what are you doing here?'

Now she could see her son and the gardener sitting on something. They both got up at once.

'We're not doing any harm, Mrs Hargrove. I'm teaching him some things he should know.'

'Stand aside, both of you,' she commanded.

They obeyed and she saw a metal tube shining on a table.

'My gun,' Patrick said. 'Master Ned has never before touched a gun, so I'm explaining it to him.'

'One day I'll have a gun, Mummy,' Ned said confidently.

Now she understood everything: the light coming from the garden, this weapon and these two accomplices she had disturbed. For a moment, struck dumb with horror, she said nothing. She briefly sensed that some sort of image was being shown to her, but she could not guess its meaning.

'Patrick,' she said at last, 'I want this weapon removed from my home.'

The man put his hand on the gun and announced:

'Ma'am, I shall put it away in its corner and you'll not be seeing it again, but it has been here all along. It's my gun.'

She felt the blood rise to her face but managed to keep her temper.

'My husband will talk to you, Patrick. I forbid you to let my son enter your house. Ned, come with me.'

There was such authority in her voice that the man said nothing and Ned, without a word, followed her. But after a few steps, he tried to protest. He suddenly stopped before they got to the steps.

'Mummy,' he said. 'They teach drill to the big boys of thirteen, with wooden guns. I, too, will be a soldier.'

'You don't love me any longer, Ned.'

He grasped her hand.

'Oh, Mummy!'

The adoring look reassured her, but she did not give in so easily.

'If you continue to play soldiers, we shall no longer speak to each other.'

He said nothing, but he took her hand and they went silently up the steps. Near the door, Miss Llewelyn was sewing a star on her flag.

'One more,' she said. 'Tennessee. Yesterday it was Arkansas. You see, I'll have my thirteen stars.'

Elizabeth looked at her absent-mindedly. All those stars: it was like some absurd game, sewing a home-made flag. How could one take it seriously? She let go Ned's hand.

'Go for a walk in Forsythe Park,' she said, 'if you want, but don't mix with the crowd.'

He promised and set off. Miss Llewelyn shrugged her shoulders. Elizabeth was unsure what to do with herself until it was time for lunch. The house bored her, especially the red drawing-room. For a change, she went up to the veranda, perhaps because there were all those steps to climb, but today, once she was there, she sat in one of the great wicker chairs and looked at the trees through the trellis. The profuse greenery seemed to color the light, and, in a nearby courtyard, a bird let forth a series of notes, stopped and then resumed, as though perfecting its scales. She was suddenly overwhelmed by the memory of the delicious moments she had spent there in Billy's arms . . . Why was there always sadness attached to any memory of the past? Everything came to an end. Billy had not been home for the last three weeks and, even though he sent her a hurried note from time to time, she was starting to worry. Why? He was in no danger. The very word troubled her thoughts, and she recalled things unconnected with the present. She saw herself in

Dimwood, with Laura's face smiling at her. Why Laura? Why now? She hardly ever thought of her.

She went back downstairs. The day passed, like every other, but the noises from the town were getting closer every day, with that new popular song, joyful, rousing, like a march. Ned sometimes hummed it.

'"Dixie",' he said. 'Would you like me to sing it for you?'

No, she wouldn't.

'But it's fine. Everyone sings it: the song of the South.'

The last words were spoken with a pride that she found charming, so she said, with a condescending smile:

'All right, let me hear your song.'

At once, the pure, clear voice rang across the scarlet room, making Elizabeth tremble with emotion. Something inside her was stirred by that joyful, belligerent appeal. When the boy had finished the first stanza, she said:

'Teach me the words.'

Delighted by his success, he made her repeat after him those phrases, each of which was an impassioned cry, and she was soon able to sing it herself.

Attracted by this patriotic outburst, Miss Llewelyn appeared and pretended to applaud.

'What a pleasant surprise, Mrs Hargrove. Now you are a Southerner entirely.'

'Not so fast, Miss Llewelyn. These popular songs amuse me, that's all. Now, now; I don't want to keep you.'

The Welshwoman bowed and went out, her completed flag under her arm.

With this distance restored, the monotonous routine of everyday life resumed its course, but Elizabeth felt herself being drawn a little further toward an unknown future. There was nothing savage about the good humor of 'Dixie'. On the contrary, the words chased away dark thoughts. She considered them childish and enjoyed singing them around the house in her fresh and fragile voice. She promised to sing them for Billy and to laugh at his astonishment, but he still did not come home and his love letters became rarer and rarer. Whenever she felt one of her temporary crises of anxiety coming, by some reflex which she could not explain, she would see Laura's face appearing and disappearing. She had only good memories of this woman with the grave and friendly smile, whose tragic story had been told by the Welshwoman. Sometimes Elizabeth regretted not having known her better. She saw herself once more in the empty room, at Dimwood, thinking of her . . . It was far away now, like everything that had happened at Dimwood . . .

She suffered more and more from Billy's absence.

A few days later, at Mrs Harrison Edwards', she learned incidentally, in a casual conversation with Algernon, that Captain Fred Hargrove had left for Richmond to join General Lee. Lee? She had heard the name at Hilda's. They were talking about a Virginian army. Elizabeth did not ask questions. Around her, the chatter went on. She heard the name of Missouri. There the federal troops were fighting the militia. It was war. She told herself that Missouri was a long way off, so the war was a long way off. Someone near her said that regiments had been raised in all the States. Why had Fred left Georgia? Here, again, she could not understand. Suddenly, she had the idea of asking Charlie Jones what had happened.

At six o'clock in the evening, he was in his office above the cotton warehouse by the harbor. She had still refused to go there, because it reminded her of Jonathan, but this time she did not hesitate: she got into her carriage and told the coachman to drive to the port. As soon as she arrived there, she was amazed by the sight of all the ships: she had never seen so many and the almost motionless masts in the light of the setting sun seemed numberless to her. At the shipping company building, they told her that Mr Jones was not available for anyone at all, but she had her card sent up and he received her at once.

'What is the matter? You seem devastated,' he said, offering her a chair.

'Fred has gone and Billy doesn't come home,' she said without hesitation.

'Fred has gone to join General Lee who is now commanding the army of Virginia at Richmond. Fred wanted to serve under him. It will be the second time.'

'But Billy . . . He hasn't been home for a month . . .'

'Billy can't leave his post because of what is happening. That's the army, Elizabeth. You should realize.'

In a flash of memory, she saw Laura's face.

'Uncle Charlie, I'd like to go and see Laura.'

At once he leaned forward as if he had not quite heard.

'Don't you realize anything, Elizabeth! Laura is safe in her convent, but you can't get into Maryland. The President has had it occupied by the federal troops, to prevent Secession. In Baltimore, they threw stones at the soldiers from New York. The troops retaliated and there were riots and deaths. Lincoln may be sincere, but power has turned his mind. Miss Llewelyn will explain it to you, but have no fear, Laura will be safe.'

She stood up and leaned on the chair as if about to faint.

'Laura . . . ' she said.

Charlie Jones also stood up. 'Elizabeth, you must excuse me, but

I'm overworked and I have a host of urgent problems to deal with. You see all the ships in harbor? Washington is blockading the entire Southern coast. Now do you understand? I'll have you taken back to your carriage and you can go home. Don't worry. There is no danger. Billy is where he must be. So don't fret. Drink a glass of champagne; it'll restore you.'

He rang and someone came to escort Elizabeth. She refused to be shown out.

'I'll go on my own,' she said with a gesture as if to push the importunate stranger aside.

Suddenly she felt angry. She was being treated like a child and found herself confronted by an Uncle Charlie whom she did not recognize. She thanked him curtly and left.

'Another time you can kiss me,' he called out as she went through the door.

She was tempted to turn back, but did not reply and continued on her way. Back in Oglethorpe House, she found Miss Llewelyn standing in the hall, with her hands clasped together and a counterfeit air of discontent, like a schoolmistress.

'Miss Llewelyn, make me a strong cup of tea.'

'I should have advised something tastier and sparkling!'

Elizabeth held back her cry of surprise.

'Why did you say that?'

'Just like that: I have gifts. I followed your train of thought. It's not hard, you are not a complicated soul. You are frightened.'

'That's not true. I'm not frightened.'

'We'll see. At one time you wanted to keep abreast of the news. Then you stopped because it scared you.'

'No, because it bored me!'

'If you wish. Now, a new twist. You went to see Mr Jones to find out what's happening. And he always recommends champagne as a tonic.'

'I wanted above all to visit Aunt Laura. He told me about riots in Baltimore and said that one can no longer get into Maryland. That's all. Why?'

'Because the people of Maryland are almost all for the South and have blown up the railway bridges. That will prevent the Northern troops from reaching Washington and no doubt invading Virginia.'

'But we are not at war.'

'We are not far from it. The distance in such cases is that of a sheet of paper: an ultimatum. You wanted to see Laura?'

'Yes.'

'Shall I tell you why?'

'I have my reasons.'

'Please sit down, Mrs Hargrove.'

Elizabeth did as she was told.

'At Mrs Harrison Edwards' house I described how Laura's young husband was killed in battle in Haiti. Because of that, you think she will understand you better than anyone.'

Elizabeth held out an open palm as though trying to prevent her from continuing. The Welshwoman went on without paying any attention.

'And you imagine your husband suffering the same fate.'

Elizabeth did not answer. Her face froze and the color drained from it. There was silence and the two women each sensed an unknown presence in the room. They looked at one another and Elizabeth said, in an oddly calm voice:

'You do not have the right to say that to me, Miss Llewelyn.'

'I have told you only what you are hiding from yourself.'

'I'm not hiding anything from myself. Do you think that I have not imagined the worst in this very house? You speak about your gifts. Do you have the gift of second sight?'

The Welshwoman remained silent for a moment, then murmured:

'You hate me at this moment, Elizabeth, but I have always been loyal to you and I shall be beside you when you need me.'

Without a word, Elizabeth left her and went up to her room.

# 141

On May 24, the North committed its first act of aggression by crossing the Potomac and occupying Virginian territory along the river, from Arlington to Alexandria. Within the hour, the secessionist States had sent men to reinforce the Virginians. The Southern army had come into being.

From Mississippi, Alabama, Georgia and the two Carolinas, whole regiments moved up toward Richmond. Day and night, the railways were requisitioned to transport soldiers of every age, but mainly young men, who were eager to drive out the invader. The poor Whites flocked to join, thereby answering the question posed by Charlie Jones, and the whole of the South:'If war comes, what will the poor Whites and the Blacks do?' The Blacks continued to work in their own way and, along the coasts of Georgia, they kept watch on the blockading ships, preventing certain attempts at a landing by the Northerners.

Throughout the South, there was a tremendous surge of patriotism.

Boys lied about their age to enrol, but there were not enough weapons and the administration could only offer them a cap and a bandolier. They set out in their worn clothes, with a bayonet instead of bullets for their guns. However, they came in waves to serve, in any capacity — whatever their social origin — as drummers, as auxiliary gunners . . . with the enthusiastic generosity of youth.

In this war, which was to some extent improvised on both sides, the South was defending its land. The capital was transferred from Montgomery to Richmond and President Jefferson Davis called on General Beauregard to confront the invading army at Alexandria.

# 142

$S$ tanding alone, her hand resting on one of the corner posts of the large double bed, she tried to pull herself together. Miss Llewelyn's words had shaken her and she was trembling as though she felt cold. A trite phrase insistently returned, like a refrain in her mind: 'in the face of death.' That was the presence she had felt downstairs. For a long time she remained motionless, her eyes fixed on the white expanse of bed, which she called her desert. Someone knocked: dinner was served. Ned was waiting for her. She went down. He kissed her as usual and as usual began to tell her stories which she did not listen to. Everything went on as before. Miss Llewelyn appeared from time to time, as she always did, to supervise the service. Everything had to be done properly. Elizabeth looked at her with astonishment. Was this the same woman who had just said those terrible things to her? She dismissed the idea that she had been dreaming. Now she was dining, or pretending to. One must pretend in order to regain one's balance.

The following morning, a letter was waiting for her on the breakfast table. A glance was enough for her to recognize Billy's handwriting, but she did not open it until she was alone in her room. Finally, he was going to tell her he had leave . . . Standing by the window, she read the following:

'News, my beloved. I am leaving this very day for Virginia with General Beauregard's troops. The Federals have occupied Alexandria. We must see these people off, with our sabres or bayonets in their . . . backs. Three regiments are going, by railroad. Everyone is leaving, the enthusiasm is indescribable.

Turner and Hampton are leaving with us, Mike with the cadets. We have changed color again, now we are in gray. Uncle Josh came, he is joining the Indians as a liaison officer. All the Indians are for the South, except one poor misled tribe. The Northerners must have got them drunk!

By railroad, it's three long days' journey. It seems we're going to Warrenton, not far from the place on the map where Uncle Charlie's estate is. Perhaps we'll meet there. Above all, don't worry. Everything is fine. Yours body and soul for life.

Your Billy, who smothers you with kisses.'

In a flash she had a vision of what she called 'the worst' and fainted. Smelling salts brought her back with a start. Miss Llewelyn was leaning over her and saying with a smile:

'I was sure of it, so I came up behind you. I did say that I should be there when I was needed. We're starting from today.'

With one hand she put her ashamed and very displeased mistress back on her feet.

'Leave me,' she said. 'I am coming back down to finish my breakfast.'

'Do you know who's waiting in the drawing-room? Mrs Harrison Edwards. She must have got up at dawn, but everything is topsy-turvey today.'

Elizabeth put a hurried comb through her hair and went down on the Welshwoman's heels. Mrs Harrison Edwards was pacing up and down in the scarlet drawing-room. She ran over to Elizabeth.

'My dear girl, what a business! Algernon has left. Our Algernon — in the cavalry! He is joining Jeb Stuart. Can you imagine Algernon, so refined, so elegant . . . But it's for the good,' she said, wiping her eyes. 'And your dear Billy?'

'He's left.'

The word was said with all necessary firmness, to make the point. The Englishwoman was in her element again. 'Let's have a good strong cup of tea.'

Ned had vanished. Escaped to town, no doubt. Elizabeth no longer kept an eye on him. A cup of lapsang souchong helped Mrs Harrison Edwards to gain control of herself, and she announced that she was going to volunteer as a nurse — a nursing officer, she emphasized — and follow the war.

For her part, Elizabeth was determined to leave. Plans formed quickly in her head. The children would be sent to Dimwood with Black Nanny and little Betty. She would go as soon as possible to Virginia, to Uncle Charlie, who would surely be leaving for Great Meadow if his ships did not keep him here in Savannah. Miss Llewelyn would stay in Oglethorpe Square to look after the house. Good riddance! The Welshwoman was becoming unbearable.

Everything was turning out for the best, without panic. The gardener's wages had to be paid and he must be told what she expected of him. With his gun, he could assist Miss Llewelyn in the defense of Oglethorpe House, if necessary.

With the money in hand, she ran down the garden to Pat's house. The door was open. She called. No answer. He must be outside in the avenue, chatting with the passers-by. Once more she called, but in vain. Very annoyed, she was just about to leave and slam the door behind her, when she noticed a sheet of paper nailed on the door with the words: 'Gone to war.' He, too — and without his wages. She burst out laughing and, in spite of herself, felt admiration for him.

Back home, she was confronted by Miss Llewelyn who was waiting, this time with the flag which she unfolded gravely:

'With Virginia and North Carolina, I have my thirteen stars.'

'Very good,' said Elizabeth. 'You know the gardener has left.'

'Like everyone else.'

'Even so, he's no youngster.'

'They're not turning back any volunteers — above all, none who have their own guns. Pat's thirty-eight years old, which is fine. I'd like to tell you straight away that I, too, am leaving.'

'But Miss Llewelyn, you can't. You promised you would be there . . . Who will look after the house?'

'The Blacks. Count on them. They won't budge. It's war, Mrs Hargrove. I shall organize first-aid posts in Virginia.'

Too amazed to answer, Elizabeth said simply:

'I'm going to see Mr Charlie Jones. Have the cabriolet harnessed.'

'He must be still at home at this time.'

'Very well, hurry.'

A moment later, she was at Charlie Jones's, being welcomed, to her great relief, with open arms.

'I was going to send word to you that I am taking you with me to Great Meadow. This is the loveliest time of the year in Virginia . . . You must obey. I am your guardian.'

'Not any longer, Uncle Charlie.'

'Yes, I am. You need a guardian. They are requisitioning all the railroads. I have given my wagons. I am not going to wait, we'll go in the carriage. I shall be alone in mine — I always travel alone. You and Ned in the other.'

'Miss Llewelyn has declared her intention of going there.'

'She will be very useful to us. I'll take her.'

'Not with me, if you please.'

'In a separate carriage with . . . with Pat?'

'He has set off to fight, with his gun.'

'Three cheers for Ireland! How many Blacks do you have at home?'

'Five. One of the cooks is a colossus.'

'Excellent. Your Blacks will protect the house. So, quickly, pack your bags. Of course, your youngest can stay in Dimwood with his Black Mammy and Betty. They will leave today without delay. Hurry. Now, I'm showing you the door. I'll come to pick you all up tomorrow morning at seven o'clock with my carriages.'

'That's not a departure,' she said. 'It's a flight.'

'You still don't know what war is, Elizabeth. See you soon — I mean, tomorrow.'

She hurried away. Reality was confronting her with a force that took her breath away.

The excitement had affected even the calmest members of the household. Only the Welshwoman was entirely in control of herself and gave orders, pointing her finger. The baggage started to pile up. Betty was weeping because she would not go to Virginia, but was put in a carriage with Black Mammy and Kit, who laughed at everything, even the huge, smothering kisses from his mother. He tried to sing like Ned with words he had invented. In a second, they had gone; Elizabeth felt a great void. Stunned, but only able to think of seeing Billy again in Warrenton, she obeyed all the orders given her by the Welshwoman, who was taking revenge for years of forced respect. Ned jumped with joy and ran everywhere, as swiftly as his 'Dixie', which he was continuously humming or singing out loud.

The following morning at seven o'clock, the three travelers climbed into Charlie Jones's carriages.

The journey was uncomfortable, except for Mr Jones. He was taking with him his valet who sat beside the driver. Elizabeth, who thought she had not slept a wink the whole night, was fast asleep in a corner of the carriage next to Ned, while he was more awake than he had ever been in his life. He was wearing his little soldier's cap, which was intentionally crumpled up to give it the appearance of use. All alone in her carriage, Miss Llewelyn had on her black bonnet which, she thought, made her look like a lady. Around her was a heap of packets containing all the drugs she could find, which she intended for the soldiers. One last carriage completed the train, a simple and solid vehicle for the baggage, pulled by a powerful Norman cart-horse.

At first, the journey was swift and eventless. The carriages kept a certain distance between them because of the dust, particularly since the hoods had been raised as the morning became warmer and warmer. They passed well to the west of Charleston and went through endless pine forests. Only a few rare houses broke the monotony of the countryside. At nightfall, finally, they reached Lake

Marion on the edge of which they were able to find a woman who lent them some bungalows, which were very primitive: wooden beds with nothing more than very flat mattresses and thin cotton blankets as if to defy any attempt at sleep. But, 'there's a war on,' Charlie Jones said, and they were so tired that they fell asleep fully clothed. An army of mosquitoes came and buzzed around them. Luckily, Miss Llewelyn had brought some lemons which she rubbed on their faces, but despite that they could not get rid of the obstinate humming of the insects around them.

The next day, before they left, they threw themselves at the food hampers. Uncle Charlie made them get back into the carriages as soon as the Blacks had harnessed the horses.

Ned had expected a joy-ride, but his enthusiasm began to wane. The journey was becoming dismal. After a further stop, leaving South Carolina, the route they followed through North Carolina was no less deserted, passing through the eternal forests. At times, they crossed over empty railroad tracks extending to the horizon, and the carriage wheels suddenly rattled over the rails. Then, by chance, they were forced to wait near a station full of songs and shouts. Crowds of people were waving flags from a halted train and 'Dixie' was bursting enthusiastically from every chest. Taking advantage of the stop, people were bringing fruit and cool drinks to the soldiers, who were leaning out of the unglazed windows shouting even louder while waving their caps and the flags which the onlookers gave them. All these young faces, laughing and flushed with patriotic fervor, hung down in clusters over the mass of delirious civilians, and a deafening roar rose up into a clear blue sky.

No sooner had the train left than Charlie Jones gave the signal to move off, without wasting time, and the stages that followed immersed the travelers once more in the irritating noise of hooves and wheels. They slept more or less comfortably in small towns, but Charlie Jones was uncompromising as to the quality of food they were served.

On the fifth day after they had left Savannah, they entered Richmond into the bustle of a city that had been entirely garrisoned. The government had just taken up residence here, together with the headquarters of the Southern armies. Everywhere one saw nothing but uniforms. There was no room in the hotels. Anxious to reach home, Charlie Jones gave the order to carry on without stopping, prepared to sleep in the carriage. On several occasions they drove past soldiers along the way, marching in single file toward the North, in the setting sun.

Now, with the end of the journey in sight, the exhausted travelers felt their spirits lift and, on a radiant June morning, the old house rose before them at the end of the avenue that circled the field.

Elizabeth put her hands to her breast and said nothing . . . Here peace reigned in the indescribable silence of the fields.


# 143

*A*fter the noise of the towns and the rumors of war, life took on some meaning again. The young woman was so moved that her eyes glazed over: memories good and bad came back at once and she had to make an effort to return to present reality. The horses had pulled up in front of the porch. For a few minutes, no one appeared. As before, as always, the house seemed to be asleep. Charlie Jones took it upon himself to rouse it from its dreams. Opening the front door, he went into the hall and shouted loudly. Little Miss Charlotte came trotting toward him, her arms in the air.

'What a surprise!' she cried. 'What's the matter, Charlie?'

She smiled pleasantly and her large bonnet, sitting askew, seemed as astonished as she was.

'Don't you know anything? You haven't heard the news?'

'No, they say so many things . . . I don't meddle with all that. We're quiet here.'

Elizabeth came in and bent over Miss Charlotte to kiss her without saying a word:

'Why are you crying? Is something wrong?'

'No, no, Miss Charlotte, I'm happy to be here, that's all.'

The little woman burst out laughing.

'Still the same beautiful, crazy Elizabeth. Go and drink a large glass of water to recover.'

Outside, the Blacks were making a lot of noise unloading the baggage cart and Charlie Jones was directing operations. All at once, Miss Charlotte found herself face-to-face with Miss Llewelyn. The two women looked at each other for a moment like two animals of different species, wondering what the other will do. The Welshwoman, monumental in her black dress and hat, produced an effect of amazement, but the old lady was not going to let herself be intimidated and, throwing back her head, challenged the intruder. Elizabeth stepped in and made the necessary introductions.

'My housekeeper, Miss Llewelyn. Miss Charlotte: Miss Charlotte is Mr Charles Jones's sister-in-law.'

A brief nod. The two women had summed each other up.

At that moment, a furious redhead ran through the room without stopping and rushed outside, where he found Charlie Jones coming from the hall.

'Papa!' he cried. 'They're taking the horses. We must hide Agenor.'

In the sun, his hair seemed on fire.

'Who says?'

'There's a rumor . . . people from Warrenton. I don't want them to touch my Agenor.'

'Calm down. You have forgotten to greet me, Emmanuel.'

'Hello, Father. If they take Agenor, I'll take Whitie.'

'I forbid it. Go and brush your hair and say hello to your cousin Elizabeth who has come to spend the holidays with us.'

The boy went in and said hello to Elizabeth.

'How tall you've grown!' she said.

'Not tall enough,' he said savagely. 'If there's a war, I'll enlist.'

'Be off with you,' said Miss Charlotte. 'There's no war here.'

'May I know where I shall be sleeping tonight?' Miss Llewelyn asked with affected politeness.

'I beg your pardon,' Elizabeth replied. 'My father-in-law will tell us; but do sit down.'

'No, thank you.'

She preferred to stand, motionless, annoying or embarrassing everyone. She did not like Great Meadow, and this was her way of protesting.

'Miss Charlotte,' Elizabeth said. 'Let's go and sit in a corner of the drawing-room.'

'Indeed, yes. To celebrate your arrival at Great Meadow, I suggest we read two or three Psalms of gratitude together. I always keep my little book in my pocket.'

Elizabeth sighed and followed her into the drawing-room.

'Who is that woman?' Miss Charlotte asked.

'My housekeeper? A Welshwoman. A little difficult, but loyal.'

'I know that sort of person. She'll try to take charge of the house, but I am here. Now, the Psalms.'

'No,' Elizabeth said firmly. 'Later, this evening, for example.'

Charlie Jones swept in.

'I have had them give Miss Llewelyn the lovely room on the upper floor with the gable. A servant is taking her there. Now, Charlotte, it's time for you to be told about the situation which, in any case, has nothing to alarm us here. The North has occupied Alexandria.'

'What impertinence!' Miss Charlotte exclaimed.

'Perhaps, but that's how it is. The troops of the Southern States are under General Beauregard's orders to contain the Federals. They hold the land and all roads leading to Washington.'

'And Billy?' Elizabeth asked anxiously.

'I've already told you. For the time being he is at Warrenton. That's not far. You are at peace in our little corner of Virginia. To reassure you, let me tell you that General Lee has sent his wife to the other side of these hills, to our cousins in Kinloch. You can rest assured.'

'All the more so since the Lord is protecting us,' Charlotte interjected.

'Of course. But above all, we can defend ourselves,' said Charlie Jones. 'In Alexandria, a little colonel from the North, a show-off from New York, a lawyer by profession and one of Lincoln's protégés, tried to show his mettle. He was in command of the Zouaves, whom he had disguised "in the French manner". They were marching through empty streets when they saw a Southern flag flying above the main hotel, Marshall House. Can't have that, thought the greenhorn and, with three of his men, he climbed up on the roof and cut down the flag. At the foot of the stairs, he met the owner of the hotel. "What are you doing with my flag?" "It's my booty." "Very well, then you're mine!" A shot, and thus Colonel Ellsworth ended his fine military career on . . .'

'Bravo!' Elizabeth cried suddenly.

'That's not all. The toy soldiers threw themselves on their opponent, killed him and stuck their bayonets in him to make sure of their revenge. And in Washington, the President weeps and arranges a national funeral!'

'Ridiculous,' said Miss Charlotte. 'So, it's war then.'

'Yes, such things happen quite suddenly. Don't worry, here we are far away from it all.'

At that moment, a servant came to tell him that an officer wished to speak with him.

'I know what it's about; it's already arranged. Ladies, please excuse me.'

He went out briskly, to talk to an officer in a gray uniform. The two of them walked away and disappeared behind the house.

'My dear girl,' said Miss Charlotte. 'You may be sure nothing will happen. I think you will have your old room on the second floor. I'll have your baggage taken up.'

A moment later, Elizabeth was in the room which she had once occupied with Ned, her husband Edward Jones, and the memories flooded back. Her husband, yes, but before that there had been her secret correspondence with Jonathan. Ten years later, the name still retained its magic, in this room where her story was preserved. In Savannah, it had gradually faded, but here, between these walls, she was once more the Elizabeth of former times. Only Billy could make her forget an unforgettable past.

Someone knocked on the door. For a moment she had a wild hope. She called:

'Come in.'

Miss Llewelyn entered. With her little black hat, which Elizabeth could not abide, this woman whom she saw every day now presented an odd, disturbing appearance. With one hand stretched out, she went directly toward her mistress.

'Excuse me,' she said. 'I've come once more to make my peace with you and offer you my friendship, all my friendship.'

In spite of herself, Elizabeth took the hand which she never shook and felt its exceptional strength.

'I never speak lightly,' Miss Llewelyn went on. 'And today less than ever. If I have come to see you, it is because here, in this very house, you will need me.'

Both were standing a little way from the big double bed and the Welshwoman tried to smile, but Elizabeth remained quite still and serious, not knowing what to reply.

With a more emphatic smile, which was supposed to be affable, Miss Llewelyn adopted an almost familiar tone:

'Might I take off this bonnet which is rather tight?'

'Of course.'

The housekeeper removed the bonnet and, not knowing where to place the austere head covering, threw it on the bed. Elizabeth gave a horrified look at the frightful black hat with its flat brim, making a sinister blot on the white expanse of the quilt. Ancient superstitions surged up in her memory. Miss Llewelyn's voice seemed to be coming from very far away.

'In this vast house where it is possible to lose oneself, you must feel calmer than you were in Savannah. For my part, I like silence and the peace of the countryside. We shall live here, it appears, for the whole summer and I hope with all my heart that everything will be well between us. Do we agree, really agree?'

'Yes, of course, yes,' the young woman said, staring at the black hat.

'Thank you, Mrs Hargrove. When I see you still so beautiful, I remember our timid effort to get close to one another when you were sixteen and had the charming illusions of that age. The good days, I'm sure, will return. Meanwhile, patience — and courage.'

'Yes, yes,' Elizabeth murmured. How she hated this discussion behind which she suspected a hidden motive . . .

'But I can see that I am tiring you,' the Welshwoman continued. 'With your permission, I shall retire.'

She went over to the bed and put the hat smartly back on her head.

'Remember,' she said. 'Maisie Llewelyn will always be there to serve you and help you, faithfully and . . . loyally.'

'Thank you, Miss Llewelyn. I shall not forget it.'

A last smile and the housekeeper left the room. Elizabeth waited for her footsteps to fade in the corridor, then on the stairs, before going down.

Downstairs, in the hall, she could hear cries coming from an adjoining room, but Charlie Jones came rushing to meet her and reassure her.

'It's nothing,' he said with a laugh. 'Emmanuel is giving rein to his coleric temperament in the library. They came to requisition horses for the army. I offered them twenty-five and kept five for my own use — the most serviceable, of course. And they took Agenor, Emmanuel's horse. Hence the outburst you heard.'

'I hope they left Whitie.'

'A pony! They didn't even see him. No sooner was Ned here than he jumped on Whitie and went off for a ride on his friend.'

# 144

Life soon settled into a routine at Great Meadow, and all was for the best. Miss Charlotte supervised everything conscientiously, with the sort of fervor that she reserved for the fulfilment of a duty. The coolness between her and Miss Llewelyn had not diminished, particularly in view of the latter's courteous, but firm refusal to read the Protestant Bible — the old maid having smelt a whiff of Catholicism about the Welshwoman. They did say good morning to one another, in spite of everything, but nothing more.

Elizabeth went for walks by herself in the country, going as far as the edge of the wood where she dreamed of seeing a victorious Jonathan gallop triumphantly toward her. This ghost consoled her in the absence of Billy.

One evening, there he was. He had been allowed a few hours and, without a moment's delay, he went directly up to Elizabeth's room; she nearly fainted with surprise. The hours of tenderness and love that followed seemed to them stolen from fate and were all the more intense for that, but the young woman no longer felt the delirium that she had experienced in Savannah. The memory of the ridiculous little black hat on the bed was probably plaguing her. She said nothing, but Billy guessed that all was not well and, to distract her, said merrily:

'You haven't noticed that I have an extra stripe. I'm a captain.'

And, without giving her time to reply, he added:

'I hope that doesn't alarm you.'

'No, there aren't any battles.'

'Even if there were, you should not be afraid. A captain's wife is not frightened.'

She did not insist. They had to separate at first light, but she held him against her as though to prevent him from leaving. He forcibly separated the hands that were locked behind his neck.

'I've only just time to get back to Washington at a gallop,' he said.

'Will you come back?'

'Of course, my love. I promise.'

When he had gone, she leaned out of the window and saw him galloping along the little road beside the meadow, then disappear beyond the gate. And now she was seized with a dreadful anguish. That's how it must be when one is going to die, she thought.

The following days gradually restored her equanimity. She did not try to discover the news and no one gave her any. Billy had promised to come back. That was enough.

Young Ned only appeared at mealtimes. The rest of the day he was off into the countryside on Whitie. Elizabeth knew he was happy and allowed him his freedom. These were his holidays.

At Great Meadow, nothing occurred to disturb the lovely somnolence of a magnificent summer. Only Miss Llewelyn and her namesake, Maisie de Witt, were actively engaged in a task which seemed to them of the greatest importance. In the village grocer's, they installed a first-aid post for use in the event of fighting in the area. The Welshwoman was the active party in this scheme, which they did not discuss in the house for fear of causing panic, both convinced that one must prepare for any eventuality, because the opposing armies would not be happy for long parading around their camps, as they were at present.

But at The Coppice, Amelia and her children remained detached from everything. She spent the time reading edifying novels, and her husband's visits brought her perfect happiness. Given a brief summary of the already stale news of events in Alexandria, she decided that nothing had happened for weeks and she stopped worrying.

At the end of the month, a further lightning visit from Billy made Elizabeth utterly radiant. For a whole night she held him in her arms and felt herself restored to the happy life of former times. He explained briefly that he had left Warrenton for Fairfax on the road to Alexandria. There were troop movements to ensure the defense of Virginian territory against any renewed aggression from the North. She could sleep easy and, as on the previous occasion, he departed at dawn — but left her satisfied in body and soul.

Nothing stirred, not even the clouds. On July 2, Charlie Jones had his carriage harnessed and set off for Richmond where he was immediately received by his friends, President Jefferson Davis and Robert Toombs, Secretary of State in the Southern government. On his return the next day, he had a talk with Miss Llewelyn giving her his instructions. He meant to sail for England on a British vessel to acquire ships, no more or less.

'And you realize what I mean,' he said, 'if I add, ships capable of forcing the, blockade.'

She was delighted and thoroughly approved. Charlie Jones left easy in his mind, the failure of Federal attempts to advance further into Virginia completely reassuring him. To calm Emmanuel, who was in an emotional state loudly demanding the return of his Agenor, he spoke to him as a man and entrusted the house to him in his absence: he would have to look after the whole family, The Coppice as well as Great Meadow.

'And Ned and Whitie as well?'

His father asked him to be serious. Suddenly Emmanuel felt puffed up with a new sense of importance and gave his word that he would obey.

On July 4, Charlie Jones hastily said goodbye, got into his carriage and set off at full speed.

That summer an exceptional heat hung over the cornfields, meadows and woods; the whole of Virginia seemed to be drowsing in the glaring light. Plump white clouds remained motionless in a sky of unfailing blue. They suffered. People slumped down in every corner of the large rooms on the ground floor where a scrap of nocturnal coolness lingered behind the closed shutters. Maisie Llewelyn held firm, ready to bring aid to any eventual cases of sunstroke outside. In a few days she had managed to assert an increasingly stronger authority over the house and its surroundings; without even realizing it, she was adopting the habit of marching like a soldier.

One morning, a flock of birds of every species crossed the sky, spread out like a multicolored screen. This frantic flight struck Elizabeth as a bad omen. Charlotte attempted to calm her by suggesting a few minutes' prayer, but the Englishwoman recoiled from the good lady's pious advances. In any case, the birds vanished. Then, in the afternoon, there were some sounds of cannon fire in the distance which might have been mistaken for a grumbling storm.

Billy came that evening. His joyful voice drove away all dark presentiments, and once more they drowned in happiness. When she asked him about the gunfire that afternoon, he said it was nothing. He spoke playfully of shooting 'to stop the guns getting rusty'. She had never seen him more merry or more unrestrained in his pleasure. At daybreak, just before leaving, he suddenly said in a serious voice:

'No one will ever have loved you as I do, my love.'

When he galloped by on the drive in front of the house to reach the main road, she waved both arms wildly and he replied by putting his fingers to his lips.

During the day, Mrs Harrison Edwards appeared. She had come from Sulphur Springs where the whole of of society was taking the waters, and she wanted to surprise Charlie Jones with her visit; for a moment she was in despair at his departure. Elizabeth was not sorry to see her. She was an unexpected confidante and friend, so she was well received at Great Meadow, which always seemed empty, and she quietly settled down. The real reason for her presence here was Algernon, serving in Jeb Stuart's cavalry which was due to join Beauregard, but she said nothing about that. Instinctively she tried to take the life of the estate in hand, but here she came up against the Welshwoman's iron fist and Miss Charlotte's obstinacy, so she contented herself with living like Elizabeth.

Little Johnny, forgotten by everyone, escaped all the time from The Coppice, where he was bored, to take refuge in the House of Chaos. Maisie de Witt always received him with a smile. She was now alone in the house which seemed enormous because of the absence of her husband and all her children; for, at the first threat of invasion, the commodore had presented himself in full uniform to enlist in the Confederate Navy, at Norfolk. The poor woman pined for her dear tormentor and a visit from the boy with the pale golden ringlets seemed to her providential. He spoke timidly, but continually, and she heard only scraps of his long stories. She pretended to follow them with a smile which lit up her martyr's face, and she rewarded the storyteller with a mint or two. She was enchanted by his gentleness, but astonished even so by the questions he asked her about his 'own nephew', Ned. Where was he? No one ever saw him. At one time Johnny used to sit next to him at meals, but now his mother wanted Johnny with her at The Coppice and Ned remained, unseen, at Great Meadow. In short, he was suffering and mint sweets were of no help to him. Like most adults, Maisie de Witt knew nothing of these first pangs of love which can be so profound in a seven-year-old heart.

# 145

On the 18th, in the morning, they heard more gunshots: real cannon, louder and more malevolent than the first, a dull, continuous rumble that brought everyone to their windows in that part of Virginia, in Prince William County. This time they could recognize the voice of war, low and threatening. At Great Meadow, they went down to the lawn. Even Amelia had left her ivory tower to join them. No one said anything, the guns having shut the most voluble mouths. Nearby, other groups were gathering. Above the woods, in the distance, a thin column of gray smoke rose directly upwards. Time passed, at once slow and rapid. Lunchtime came unexpectedly, for only the children were hungry. They ran to the table as soon as the servant appeared on the porch. The grown-ups sat down, simply to show willing, but ate nothing, contenting themselves with glasses of cold tea; then everyone returned to the lawn. The cannon was still rumbling in the distance. Outside, near the great cedar, Elizabeth was standing beside Mrs Harrison Edwards, both with a different name in their heads and the same thought. Miss Charlotte, drawn up to the full height of her diminutive figure, seemed carved out of stone, but Miss Llewelyn walked backward and forward, looking toward the horizon already battle-scarred by her memories of fire and blood in Haiti. The children got used to everything, so the sound of war did not disturb their games. A boy ran, his kite rising behind him, then soaring above the prairie, almost motionless in the warm air above all these anxious figures, standing around like groups of statues.

Eventually, the firing stopped, though it was still quite early in the afternoon. Finally, at dusk, when a magnificent light lit the sky and bathed the tops of the trees with its reddish gold, news arrived. The Northern troops, twice as numerous as our own, were suddenly moving down the Alexandria road, intending to seize control of the railroad fork at Manassas which led in one direction toward the South and in the other toward the valleys of the West. Beauregard had already been forced to fall back on the far side of Bull Run, a deep river running through tangled woodlands, but crossed by at least ten fords and a bridge. That very day, the Federals had tried to make the crossing. The Confederate cannon, hidden among the trees — the ones they had heard — had driven back the attack. However, Beauregard was calling for assistance from Johnston's Army, in the west of Virginia, on the far side of the Blue Ridge Mountains, because Washington was sending further regiments to General McDowell with strict orders to advance on Richmond.

Johnston was endeavoring to arrive in time, before this planned massed attack. He had ordered Jeb Stuart, whose daring and exuberance were well-known throughout the South, to get his cavalry to entertain the Northern general who was facing them and to advance cautiously down the Shenandoah valley, as if frightened by the fact that he had twice as many men as his opponents.

How could one transport 8,000 soldiers quickly across so many miles? A fortuitous initiative had already provided the key to the problem. At the end of May, when the Virginians, immediately after Secession, had seized the arsenal at Harper's Ferry, which was on their territory, Colonel Jackson, the leader of their militia, had not hesitated at the same time to requisition the locomotives and wagons of the Chesapeake and Ohio Railroad whose lines passed along the south bank of the Potomac, within reach of his troops. He cleverly induced the railroad company authorities to bring back as many trains as possible so that, toward the end of June, having to abandon his position at Harper's Ferry which was in danger of being surrounded by the considerable forces of the Federal Army, and not wanting to leave behind any materials which might be of value to the enemy, he had all the wagons and locomotives which were in poor condition thrown into the river and the others sent to Winchester, then transported from there by road to the nearest Confederate railroad yards. This meant that, between Winchester and Strasburg, forty kilometers on, farmers could see the iron monsters go past, pulled by horses. Now the soldiers were going to look for them after a long march through the mountains in rain that looked yellow in color.

Here is what they were told at Great Meadow: trains of soldiers coming from the West would pass by on the Manassas line the following evening.

When night fell on the 19th, by the light of lanterns, in carriages or on foot, through pathways and across woods and fields, all the women of the surrounding district seemed to have arranged to meet at Gainesville station. This was hardly more than a halt: single brick platform, a canopy and a few signals pointing their iron fingers at the stars. Two trains had already gone by in the afternoon, earlier than expected, and no one had been there. Now, all these women brought fruit, cakes, cool drinks, smiles and flags which they had made themselves with love, sparing nothing, cutting bits out of their silk dresses; and, as if they had guessed what sweat was poured out in those hours of marching in the rain and hours of waiting in the sunlight, they came with baskets full of clean shirts. There was little noise in the expression of their feelings, no doubt because it was night, the light of the lanterns making all the shadows seem dramatically larger, and because the soldiers were heading for what one could only call a battlefield.

# 146

At first light on the morning of the 20th, the countryside was blurred by a bluish-gray mist which promised a hot day to follow. It didn't matter to Ned. Putting on his cap and pulling the peak down over his eye, to look more soldierly, he set off as usual on Whitie. Where was he going? Nowhere and everywhere, as chance took him, happy to be free. As all appeared calm, he took the risk of riding a little further than usual and soon realized that he had lost his way in the fog. Suddenly, like ghosts, he saw the outlines of riders in blue uniforms coming straight toward him. Turning round at once, he set off toward home as fast as he could. Whitie always guessed his master's thoughts and began to gallop flat out not toward the house, but into a thick wood where the two of them had sometimes played. Never had a pony's legs flown so quickly over the ground. For a minute or two a blue rider pursued them.

'Damned little rebel!' he cried.

At the edge of the wood, seeing that he was wasting his time, he fired a pistol shot into the air and turned about, all the more quickly since some Southern cavalry had appeared a short way off in the mist, dispersing at the first rays of the sun.

Both exhausted, Ned and his pony did not move for a while beneath the trees, then came out of the wood on the far side and galloped back to the house. Bathed in sweat, the boy was sent up to the bathroom by the Welshwoman.

'You stink of horse,' she said, ordering him to take a bath and change his shirt.

No one knew about his escapade.

At Great Meadow meanwhile, the sound of gunfire brought everyone to the windows. They tried to peer through the closed shutters. There were horsemen from South Carolina, recognizable by their standard, chasing some Northern scouts. A few shots hit the porch and lodged in the walls of Great Meadow. For more than quarter of an hour the crackling of gunfire broke the silence, then faded. One could almost follow the route taken by the riders as they fled and the people of the house, taking refuge in the rooms overlooking the woods, were relieved to hear the last shots in the distance.

Miss Llewelyn opened the door and took a few steps outside. The sun was now falling full across the meadow and she saw, lying on the road, a man in a light gray uniform. His horse was standing under the trees in the avenue. She called the Blacks to help her. They had been crouching under the kitchen tables and appeared stricken with fear. She took two of them and ran to help the wounded man.

Flat on his face in the dust, he was groaning feebly and she recognized the young English sub-lieutenant who had once served as Billy's messenger. Blood was running from his right side and she lifted him up herself before handing him to the two servants who carried him into the house. They set him down on the library sofa. The Welshwoman sent a Black man to fetch the family's doctor from Gainesville. Meanwhile, she did what she could to comfort the wounded man and care for him with whatever she had in her first-aid box. He was trying not to complain, but in his eyes she could read an agony that distressed her and this woman, usually so rough, showed a maternal kindness to the young soldier to whom pain had given the soul of a child. While wiping the dust and black powder off his face, she spoke gently to him and he regained his courage. Alcohol and bundles of cotton more or less succeeded in staunching his wound.

They had to wait nearly an hour before the doctor appeared. He was a white-haired man who, for many years, had inspired confidence and respect throughout the area. Miss Llewelyn stood modestly beside him, ready to obey. She helped him partially to undress the wounded man, then stood aside and awaited orders.

Outside, in the corridors, Ned was prowling. He had seen the young officer arrive, carried by the Blacks, and with beating heart was staying as close as possible to the door, at once curious and horrified: he had seen traces of blood on the ground. Now he was listening, but the doctor and Miss Llewelyn were talking almost in a whisper and Ned could not catch a word. This lasted a long time. He thought he could hear a cloth being dipped several times in water, then another silence, longer than the first, and at last a voice, young and pleading:

'Doctor, please, don't let me die.'

'My friend,' the old doctor said softly. 'You must die.'

Ned took to his heels.

# 147

*I*n the night of the 20th, part of the Northern army began to march. After a failed attack by an advance party on Blackburn's Forge, knowing that Beauregard's troops had a tight grip on the fords of Bull Run, General McDowell planned to move round from the North against the left flank of the Southern lines by a surprise maneuver to seize the road leading directly to the railroad junction at Manassas. In order to create a diversion, one of his brigades would attack Stone Bridge, the only non-wooden bridge across the river, that morning at six o'clock.

So, the Northern boys advanced under the light of the full moon, a harvest moon, particularly large and bright. They marched forward, sure that they would drive back the rebels as far as Richmond, and that the war would be over. Had they not already known the heady scent of victory in Washington, in front of their President, when they marched down Pennsylvania Avenue to the sound of cheers, while the fanfares of the military band made the heavens shake? All their weapons had been gleaming in the sunlight! The endless bridge over the Potomac was crossed in the same mood of euphoria, but after that they had to march uphill. They quickly found themselves breaking ranks as they passed through a countryside that seemed to be dreaming. The silence of the Virginian hills made their step still more noisy and the heat exhausted them. They could only see a few scattered houses in the thickets and, since these were deserted, even the poorest, they pillaged them. For two whole days they had been ambling slowly through this country that reminded them of summer holidays, and now, at the end, there was this night march through the woods, happily not too long, down an embanked road, by moonlight.

At dawn they stretched out under the trees, then they discovered bushes covered in blackberries and feasted on them. Finally, the officers called them back to their ranks. The boys wiped their hands as best they could, but there were still stains around their mouths.

At six o'clock, the whole countryside was suddenly woken by a violent burst of gunfire. This was the signal. They set off again.

At five o'clock in the morning, Billy, who had slept very little, was walking under the pine trees, thinking of Elizabeth and their last meeting. Never before had they felt so close, and he could still hear the sound of her voice rather anxiously saying goodbye to him, but he soon put aside this memory which he found troubling. His thoughts turned to the young English sub-lieutenant whom he had sent off on reconnaissance the day before and who, alone of the group, had not returned. All that Billy had been able to establish was that a skirmish had taken place with some Northern scouts in the countryside; he was worried. And then, he also wondered, how could one find one's way in the heat of battle among all these regiments, some of them hardly equipped at all? In Colonel Evans's brigade, for example, they, the Carolinans, were with men from Mississippi and men from Louisiana . . . The Louisiana Tigers had a variety of uniforms, when they had any at all, though they did wear the same red scarves around their necks which had given

General Beauregard the idea of asking the ladies of Richmond to provide his soldiers some kind of rallying sign: badges — handkerchiefs, scarves, whatever they wanted — and above all flags. The ladies had immediately sent whatever they had in red: silk, cotton, linen. One might have thought it was deliberate. Billy recalled the remark of a young drummer boy with long hair and the drawling accent of the South: 'That way, it won't show if we bleed.'

Beneath the pine trees, in the cool of the first bluish light of day, the soldiers were drinking their coffee and occasionally exchanging jokes in an undertone.

Suddenly, at around six o'clock, the Federals opened fire at Stone Bridge and their artillery concentrated its fire on the bridge itself. 'It's stupid,' observed Billy, 'to destroy the bridge if they want to cross it.' And accompanied by a lieutenant, he went down the wooded slope to Colonel Evans' command post to receive his orders.

Bold, reckless, casually dressed and with his famous red scarf tied casually, Colonel Evans adopted a 'devil-may-care' pose, but he had an eagle's eye for anything to do with tactics and battle. Well before the first shot, he had positioned his own batteries to rake the bridge with their fire and was keeping a sharp watch through his binoculars at what was happening on the far side of the river, all along the horizon. He observed a thick cloud of dust above the woods, on the far left of his own position.

'What do you see there?' he asked the officers around him.

Like him, they saw all the dust rising into a clear sky and attributed it to the morning mist, with its promise of heat. Billy arrived at that moment and said that one could see even better from the summit of the pine wood.

'They're outflanking us on the North, ' said Evans. 'That's not stupid; and all the racket around our bridge is bluff. They're not even trying to come very close. Get all of your regiments on the two hills opposite, here.'

He showed them on the map, which was laid out on a tree trunk, some high ground called Matthews Hill and more behind them where there was an isolated house among oaks and pine trees: Henry House.

'I'll leave a battery and half a regiment to hold the bridge at all costs. There are two covered bridges over the Young Branch, that's the shortest. Go there, calmly and quickly. A liaison officer must warn Jackson to move up. At the double. I hope we shall all meet again, gentlemen.'

Even as they were saluting, a young soldier ran up with two pennants. He had just received signals sent from the observation post in the far south, on the Manassas plateau. The wigwag confirmed what Evans had suspected: these little flags informed them that some mounted artillery had been betrayed by the sunlight shining on the barrels of the cannons and that part of the Federal troops were crossing the river at Sudley Springs, where there were three wide fords, almost next to one another. No one had thought to guard them, because they were too far north and everyone expected a direct attack on the strategic routes: the Warrenton Road which crossed over Stone Bridge and, further down, at the place called Union Mills, the Alexandria railroad line. The greater part of Beauregard's Army was deployed there, along Bull Run, protecting what was like the moat of a castle against any surprise attack.

At nine o'clock, Evans had taken up his new position and the Confederate guns seemed to be looking out over an empty landscape. The cadets from Charleston were among the gunners. In front of them stretched meadows and fields with the occasional fence, ideal country for maneuvres or a battle. Behind them were hedges covered in hazelnuts and blackberries. As far as the eye could see, the landscape was already shimmering in the heat.

Sitting with his back to a tree, Mike waited. In the distance, down toward the river, the guns were still pounding: in the end one got used to it, like a natural sound. The heat haze made the fields wave and induced sleep. Mike felt torn between the desire to fight and an unconscious refusal to kill. Deep down there was fear; he would have to overcome it. His mind turned to Elizabeth whom he loved without admitting it, and also toward Billy, whom he admired and whose regiment was not far away on Henry Hill.

The batteries occupied a line just above the crest of Matthews Hill, at the edge of the woods, and the hills opposite danced as if in a dream. The rough bark of the pine tree against which his head was leaning seemed to him in his torpor the only real thing. His gaze fastened onto the distance, where the river shone, then onto the silent, wooded hills, which seemed to be shifting in the burning light. How glorious they had been, those rides along the beach on Morris Island, after the taking of Fort Sumter . . . Riding was a challenge! The cadets galloped their horses at full speed across the sand for the simple intoxication of speed and winning. They would return panting, while the mist rising off the sea clouded the light on the dunes and at twenty paces seemed to swallow up both horses and friends, leaving only their happy voices . . .

But wasn't he recalling ghosts from a past life down there? Silhouettes shimmered in the warm air. Coming closer and closer they seemed blue in the sunlight. In an instant, Mike was on his feet.

'Look out!' a boy cried. 'Here are the Northerners.'

Algernon had been galloping for hours on the Virginia roads with Jeb Stuart's cavalry. Behind them, out of the red earth, a pinkish dust rose into the burning air. The sun shone down implacably, devouring everything. The heat was so heavy that one could not even feel the wind created by one's own momentum, and almost had the illusion of going forward without moving. Algernon welcomed the sudden change in his life with a joy close to fanaticism. Overnight, fate had rid him of a person who now seemed imaginary: the Algernon of balls and parties, at once daring and timid, with a drawing-room shyness. Today, his uniform sticking with sweat under his armpits, he felt released from a world of empty worries. War abolished his timidity. Only two faces remained from the past, two names that followed him still: Elizabeth and Lucile, close and at the same time distant, the second quite ready to take him seriously in love, while the other, cruel without knowing it, let herself be worshipped like a teasing goddess. He could not forget the star-studded rod that she had made him hold that evening to the sound of a Viennese waltz, and he could hear once more the music that rose above the couples chattering joyfully and the soft light of the chandeliers . . . He loved them like sisters. And then, suddenly, a man's voice brought him back to himself.

'Halt! Five minutes rest. There's no such thing exhaustion. We must reach Manassas quickly! Now, music!'

Jeb Stuart gave his orders.

They hardly had time to tether their horses to the trees. Sweeney was already plucking his guitar. In two seconds, all these horsemen were in another world. Jeb Stuart walked back and forth, tapping his fingers in time to the music. There was nothing warlike about him any longer, and it was easy to see why men would die for this tall redheaded boy. He wore his uniform jacket open at the neck, buttons undone, as elegant as could be. The feather in his cap was changed every morning and his scarlet-lined cape was legendary. Three other Blacks began to accompany Sweeney with a violin and some castanets. By turns, you might have thought you were in a cotton field, or in a New Orleans dive.

Jeb Stuart sang every song. All at once, he said to Sweeney:

'Right, come on, hot it up a bit!'

The music became more martial. In a minute everyone was on his horse.

'To Manassas!' Jeb Stuart cried. 'We'll chase them away at the gallop, these Northerners.'

The whole troop set off. In his saddle, Algernon continued to dream. Elizabeth must be in Savannah in her cool house beneath the magnolias and Lucile Harrison Edwards had written to say that she was taking the waters at Sulphur Springs. She hoped that a furlough would allow him to come . . .

They passed a station: Gainesville. Cannons thundered in the distance. Wasn't it near Gainesville that Charlie Jones had some land? Manassas was on the horizon. And Billy? wondered Algernon.

Weren't the South Carolina troops with Beauregard? In short, if Jeb Stuart was coming to the aid of Beauregard, didn't that mean that he, Algernon, was hurrying to help Billy?

In front of him, pink horses were galloping, the dust sticking to their coats. The horizon was getting closer.

# 148

Not a carriage, not a horse, not a person was in the silent streets of Washington. Everyone had left for the battle to 'see the rebels run'. It was the ideal opportunity for a picnic on this lovely Sunday in July.

At eleven o'clock in the morning, a jumbled mass of carriages of every description arrived on the heights of Centerville: coaches, tilburys and cabs. A large number of riders added to the confusion by tethering their horses here and there. Eventually, the jostling stopped and it was just a matter of waiting, as in a theater. They looked in vain for an empty space on the huge sloping meadow from which there was a splendid view, but everything had been provided for. Rugs were spread out and hampers full of food were set down wherever there was space, while black servants placed cases of ice for the champagne. The cream of Washington society settled down comfortably, men and women with spyglasses. Mindful of business, shopkeepers had set up their stalls with provisions for a blazing hot day: fruit juice, ice creams and sorbets, and — ever welcome — sausages to work up a thirst.

Among the spectators eager to see the entertainment, some officers strolled in their fine new uniforms, all buttons shining. They explained every trace of fire or smoke in technical terms, pointing to features of the landscape with their sticks, or even with their binoculars which they turned as much on the crowd as on the horizon.

'And there?' asked a woman in bright pink. 'Where the flashes are?'

'Bayonets, Madam. They are being fixed.'

'Oh!'

Despite these easy and learned explanations, the flashes were simply caused by the sun shining off the Cub Run stream, which flowed through the fields to join the Bull Run on the far side of the valley.

'May the rebels be routed!' the lady in pink cried, raising her glass of foaming champagne.

'Hurray!' the army officers answered.

Ladies and gentlemen of a martial disposition raised more cheers.

Further off, under a sycamore, chairs were being set out for members of the Senate and other official personages newly arrived from Washington. These gentlemen on their padded chairs seemed to have been miraculously transported from their offices onto the grass. The impatient crowd was good-humored: they were amusing themselves, the day was growing warmer and at noon, as the 'cannonade' could only, as it were, be 'seen' with the ears, everyone sat down. Before yielding to the excitement, they needed to eat. A few young civilians were stretched out in the shade, with their hats on their faces, alongside their young ladies. They were resting to gather strength, the better to hail the victory when it came.

The lady in pink, who had been joined by several of her lady friends, continued to stare at the horizon, without noticing the beauty of the landscape at the end of her opera glasses: the vastness of the empty land and, in the distance, the purple hills in the sunlight.

'Officer! Officer! Tell us what those little puffs of cotton wool are that have just appeared.'

'That's the breath of our cannons, ladies!'

It was the breath of cannons, but the cannons of the South on Stone Bridge.

# 149

*E*vans' troops had already driven off the Northern attack three times. There was utter confusion, but the Federals had eventually swept forward and Matthews Hill was lost. Lower down, on Bull Run, Sherman had succeeded in crossing a ford with his regiment, above Stone Bridge, and was attacking Evans' Southerners who were falling back. Their batteries could not even give them cover. The enemy gunners had faster cannons and their shells were falling in clouds of red dust. On the road to Warrenton, they couldn't even tell friend from foe because of the all-enveloping dust. The young soldiers of the South began to flee. It was just after half past eleven. All seemed lost.

Only Colonel Evans was still holding out (but for how long?), with a handful of men in Robinson House, a huge wooden pile belonging to a freed slave from Virginia, and which dominated the folds running down to the river from its rocky crest, while General Bee, for his part, was trying to halt and rally those who were fleeing. He galloped as far as Henry House to seek reinforcements. There, Jackson was waiting calmly in the midst of his men.

Without dismounting, Bee, covered in black powder and sweat, cried:

'General, they are beating us!'

'Well, sir, we shall show them our bayonets.'

He immediately formed a line on the edge of a young pine wood where the soldiers could take cover from enemy fire while waiting to attack. Bee rediscovered all his old enthusiasm. Turning tail, he reappeared in the midst of his demoralized troops who were fleeing the field.

'Look!' he yelled. 'Jackson's standing like a stone wall. Let's rally to the Virginians!'

His cry stopped the rout and his men regrouped.

Beauregard arrived with reinforcements of young soldiers who had never been under fire, but who ran almost at a trot, to the rhythm of their heartbeats. The Federals advanced from all sides in a wave of yellow dust. They had now been fighting for four hours and the cannons ceaselessly spat their fire, raising new clouds of smoke.

Algernon looked at his hands. They were as red as the earth. Around him, all Jeb Stuart's other horsemen were turning the same color. One of the boys who had seen his gesture shouted:

'So what? We're true Americans: we're redskins now!'

And he burst out laughing.

Algernon felt happy and light-hearted. As in an ideal world, there were no longer rich and poor. War! Until now, it was just noise . . . In spite of Jeb Stuart's impatience to lead them into battle ever since they joined up with the army at ten o'clock that morning, they were being held in reserve, and three and a half hours of inactivity had been three and a half hours of soft banjo music, music for waiting. 'My God,' Algernon thought, 'suppose it was only pretend: a battle as in college. We would punch one another and then shake hands. But . . .'

A courier arrived through the woods, with a red scarf tied to one epaulette.

'Our turn now!' cried Jeb Stuart. 'It's our turn. Forward, Sweeney! Forward, boys!'

Algernon stood up, carried forward with the rest of them, like a single body. On the slope, a shell knocked him from his horse.

Jeb Stuart's charge cleared the enemy guns from Jackson's left flank. The Northern regiments fled, running across the slope of

Henry Hill, letting themselves be swept along by one another on an irresistible wave of panic, and their guns remained in the middle of the battle field, pathetic, silent, surrounded by dead horses.

However, despite this setback, the Federals continued to bring in fresh troops and came back to the attack. Jackson did not give an inch of ground.

Everywhere else, the Southern soldiers were falling back.

At times, against the dull background noise of gunfire, there was an instance of silence, a break between two bouts of firing; and this was more dreadful than anything else, for at that moment death was flying through space, before falling blindly.

Mike was afraid. With the other cadets — his friends — he had run as far as the thicket covered with blackberries behind their battery. The horses that had been pulling their guns at the moment they changed position had been cut down with the sabres of the Federals who had swept past. Now the young Southerners were trying to get their bearings to save themselves from hell. The smell of battle, the smell of powder, insinuated itself everywhere, and even those under the pine trees had dry throats. They were afraid of being found and captured by the boys from the North. Where could they go without being given away by their dirty jackets, their collars drenched in sweat and the red scarves tied around their necks? Luckily the colors could only be seen from a few feet away, since the dust covered everything. In the open space in front of them, uniforms seemed to be sleeping on the ground and horses lay overturned like houses. A more subtle odor than that of gunpowder drifted across the land.

An officer in gray galloped past.

'Henry Hill is holding!' he shouted. 'Bring the guns here and fire at the woods opposite.'

They went down to the guns and untied the dead horses. From then on they fired continually in the exhilaration of the action, their throats burning, their ears blocked. There was no noise, they had become the noise.

For the first time, at a quarter to three, Jackson hurled his Virginians against the dark blue masses which were approaching Henry House from every direction.

'Wait until they are in sight, then fire! Then go to it with your bayonets. And, as you charge, yell like fury!'

This was the famous rebel yell.

To his left, with the remains of Evans' brigade — Carolinans and young recruits from Mississippi — Captain Hargrove took the head of the charge. As he threw himself forward, Billy recalled what the commandant at Fort Beauregard had told them: 'Head high, upright in your saddle, shoulders back.' The honor of the South was at stake.

Everything was drowned in dust.

'Forward for the South!' he cried.

And he heard the wild yells of his men which seemed to carry him toward the enemy even faster. So he shouted: 'For Elizabeth!' without knowing what he was saying, and plunged into the fire-colored cloud.

There had to be an end to it. At the hottest moment in the day, shortly after three o'clock, a long gray line appeared on the edge of the wood. Suddenly, the hills echoed with a terrible hunting call, then the gray soldiers charged. The bayonets shone. The Northerners took fright and gave way. They rushed down Henry Hill in confusion, protected from complete rout by a few regiments which were withdrawing for the time being in good order.

Beyond the fords at Sudley Springs, the young soldiers slowed down to cut through the woods, thinking themselves under cover; but shells burst in the bushes around them, tearing their weapons and haversacks out of their hands sticky with blackberries, and there was no more regiment. Defeat was hovering in the dust that had floated around them since dawn. It was four o'clock.

The civilians saw nothing. They had drunk a lot and eaten well. The senators in their corner had made thunderous declarations to the waiting journalists, and the famous back-seat officers continued to prove that the smoke covering the horizon was preventing the ladies from seeing the rebels in flight, but insisting that they would be caught, especially for them, so that they could see their own prisoners of war.

Suddenly, Northern soldiers swept past shouting: 'Everyone for himself! They're coming!' The moment of hesitation was brief. Leaving everything on the grass, the cream of society elbowed its way as fast as it could toward the carriages. There was a huge scramble. As it appeared too difficult to escape by carriage, they started to run, together with the ordinary people who had abandoned their carts at the side of the road. Reticules, gloves, hats, telescopes, coats, waistcoats and canes lay with rifles in the ditches. There were no more soldiers and civilians, men and women, officers or soldiers, but only a mass of humanity fleeing, terrified of the enemy cavalry which they thought was on their heels. Haggard and disheveled, they did not stop until they were in sight of Washington. Night was falling and torrential rain fell as they crossed the bridge over the Potomac.

# 150

*T*hat afternoon, Ned left secretly on his pony and once again went further than he would surely have been allowed; but the boy was inquisitive and everything seemed to be calmer after the great noise of the battle which had kept all the inhabitants of Great Meadow indoors. Now one could only hear increasingly distant sounds of gunfire, like a soft bellowing.

The heat was still oppressive, but the light was getting gradually softer as if to bring back the silence. As he rode on, Ned saw that some trees had lost their leaves, as in the depth of winter, while others had been broken and their branches were lying in huge heaps. Though not afraid, he had the strange feeling of entering an unknown land, familiar yesterday, through which death had passed; but what was death? He did not know. The word, sometimes spoken in his presence, always in the same grave tone of voice, struck him as something very black. He had heard nothing more of the wounded man in the library . . .

The river, the Young Branch, was not far away. He could already hear its gentle, almost happy sound among these disturbing trees. The water was singing at the bottom of a valley with a covered bridge across it that looked like a little house with wooden walls painted red. Ned always liked the sound of his horse's hooves on the planks above the cool water. And, a hundred yards further on, was one of those huge barns, red, long and high. It appeared entirely isolated, standing like a person in its solitude. A large dark space was visible through its big open doors.

Nearby, a soldier was sitting on a tree trunk in his torn uniform. He was young, with thick brown hair which fell across the top of a face spotted gray with gunpowder. His black eyes were smiling.

'What are young doing here, kid?' he asked.

'Riding Whitie. I come from Great Meadow.'

'A long way. You'd be better off at home. How old are you?'

'Nine.'

Ned jumped off his pony.

'Can I leave him here? He won't run away. He's my friend.'

The soldier smiled, showing a fine set of white teeth.

Ned walked over to the door where the afternoon light filtered through. He saw everything at a single glance. At the far end of the barn, two soldiers in torn gray uniforms were lying down, side by side, their arms beside their bodies. Closer, at the edge of a shadow, another was lying, one hand clutching the stalks of straw on the ground with a large piece of red cloth over his face.

At that moment, the soldier who had spoken to him grasped his hand and pulled him away from the door.

'I didn't say you could do that. Now go away.'

'Why was that red thing on the soldier's face?'

'Because of the flies. He's sleeping.'

'And the others too?'

'Of course. But you didn't see anything. Understand?'

'I didn't see anything,' Ned repeated.

He was shivering slightly.

'Don't tell anyone about the barn. Promise.'

'Yes, I promise.'

'I have your word.'

This was said in such a serious way that the boy calmed down.

'What's your name?' the soldier asked.

'Ned Hargrove.'

'You're not from around here. Where do you come from?'

'Savannah.'

'Oh, yes! I can hear it.'

'My father is an officer.'

'Do you know in which regiment?'

'With General Beauregard.'

'Beauregard. There's none better. Now listen. Get back on your friend and go home. And don't say anything, remember?'

'Nothing,' said Ned.

The soldier shook his hand.

'We won, Ned. The South won.'

Ned's eyes began to shine and he smiled in his turn.

'We won!' he cried.

He jumped on his pony and exclaimed, laughing:

'Whitie, we won!' He stroked the pony's head and it snorted.

'Go home quickly, kid,' the soldier said, lifting a hand.

Ned set off at a gallop. In the far distance, the guns could still be heard: dull thuds, spaced out.

'We won, Whitie,' Ned said again.

When he got to Great Meadow, he led the pony back to the stable and came in through the kitchen. The Blacks gave him a smile of complicity.

# 151

*A*t dusk, Mrs Harrison Edwards and Maisie de Witt climbed into a carriage lit with lanterns. They had just learned that convoys of wounded were to pass through Gainesville station. Maisie Llewelyn officiously took her place beside them without arousing the slightest objection. Behind the carriage, a Black man followed in a cart with some baskets of fruit and cool drinks, and Miss Llewelyn added linen and bandages.

Elizabeth preferred to stay at home, waiting for Billy to ride back unexpectedly. She had installed herself near the bedroom window from which she could see the road running around the meadow. On each side of the front door were lamps which she ordered to be lit before nightfall, which was never done unless a visit was expected. Though not particularly anxious, she had to struggle against impatience. 'Perhaps he won't come until tomorrow morning,' she thought. 'Manassas is quite close, and I know Billy; even if he is tired, he would not want to wait.'

The last guns had fallen silent long before sundown and, in the approaching night, a breeze was dispersing the heat. The first stars appeared, one by one, here and there, in a deep blue sky. Everything was peaceful, but no birdsong had marked the end of day.

Miss Charlotte had stayed at Great Meadow to watch over the house. She met Ned in the pantry. Gripped with hunger, he wanted to know what they would have for dinner. When he saw the old lady, he was eager to tell her that they had won the battle, but stopped dead at the thought that she would want to know where he had heard the news. He must keep his secret. She walked briskly toward him.

'You're hungry,' she said with a laugh. 'But tonight dinner must wait for the ladies to come back from Gainesville. Would you like to wait with me while I read something to you?'

As he did not answer, she added greedily:

'Both of us in the drawing-room, quietly, in a corner . . .'

He shook his head.

'I must wash,' he said, running off. 'I must smell of horse.'

She adjusted her bonnet which was always threatening to fall forward, and sighed.

'The smell of a pony, what harm can that do? But I'll go alone, as usual.'

In Gainesville they were jostling each other in the waiting room and around the little station. From all sides — villages, local farms and large estates — people had come to help the wounded on their way toward the emergency hospital in the hills, before they were taken down to Culpeper, further south. The train had just pulled in when the carriage from Great Meadow arrived and Miss Llewelyn was among the very first to run forward. Mrs Harrison Edwards held a lamp and Maisie de Witt a basket of food.

Those of the wounded who could remain upright were pressing against the windows and asking for water. In the flickering lights on the platform, very young faces appeared covered in bandages, trying to smile; but behind them, in the back of the wagons, there were groans. The crowd had been expecting a celebration of heroism and was confronted by suffering. For an instant, they remained silent. Somebody began to sing 'Dixie', then immediately stopped. Let the civilians sing about victory at home! War was not fanfares, flags flapping in the wind, great deeds, the heroism of paintings; no, it was young men, mutilated and in pain, shaken about in railroad trucks.

The Welshwoman understood this better than her dismayed companions and climbed up on a step of the wagon, asking simply what she could do immediately: change a dressing, put water on a forehead. She distributed some fruit which was instantly devoured by mouths burning with fever. The soldiers understood her because she was their equal. Mrs Harrison Edwards eagerly followed suit, hurried about, passing out beakers of fruit juice which were almost torn from her hands. The local people brought everything they had, even ham. It was dark in the wagons and one could only see the dressings stained with blood and eyes burning in the dark. During this prolonged halt, they went as quickly as possible from one compartment to another, finding everywhere boys whose faces wore the same horrified amazement at having been wounded. One cadet, with a bandage over his eyes, was quietly complaining like a child: 'I can't see anything, can't see . . .' Maisie Llewelyn leaned over and kissed him.

After a long half hour, the guard waved the flag for the train to leave and the crowd shouted:

'Long live the soldiers! Long live the South!'

The silence that followed the train's departure was terrible. They couldn't understand, they couldn't believe what they had seen. The train was carrying away a nightmare. People looked at one another as if the night was full of moans around them. Someone, an officer, had nailed a sheet of paper on the wall near the door: it was a first list of the missing and those who had been identified. They rushed to read it.

Mrs Harrison Edwards did not dare look, but the Welshwoman, as usual, managed to find a place just next to the long sheet of paper beside which they had hung a lantern. Maisie de Witt was overcome with emotion and sitting to one side on a bench. The Welshwoman looked down the list and remained motionless, standing where she could see best. She read the name 'Steers', paused, then went on until she finally reached the name which she most feared she would find there: Captain Hargrove. Leaving the group of men and women, with their sporadic cries and exclamations, she went back to Mrs Harrison Edwards and said softly:

'Madam, I know that you were very fond of him.'

They left the crowd, found Mrs de Witt, and all three got into the carriage and set off.

Mrs Harrison Edwards hung her head and said nothing. A few minutes passed, accompanied by the sound of wheels and hooves on the road, then they heard the Welshwoman's voice suddenly say:

'Billy's there, too. It's over.'

'Billy!' Mrs Harrison Edwards groaned. 'Poor Elizabeth!'

'We won't say anything to her immediately,' Maisie Llewelyn said. 'Later. The right time will come.'

In what had been Elizabeth's room in Great Meadow, ten years earlier, Ned was unable to sleep. Miss Charlotte had made him eat corn pancakes, alone, late in the evening (without which he couldn't have closed an eye); but, even with his hunger pacified and his head on the pillow, he remembered the visit to the barn where the three soldiers had appeared to be sleeping. He could not get rid of the memory of the red scarf on the face of one of them. 'Because of the flies,' the young soldier had said outside, while preventing him from going further. The straw shone and he had heard the flies buzzing in the warm air, but why didn't the two other soldiers at the back of the barn have red scarves on their faces too? He could only imagine, and that scrap of material frightened him.

First, why that color: why red? A large white handkerchief would have seemed terrible to him, but less, a little less so. The thought of red cloth made him pull the blanket over his head as if to protect himself from ghosts. Who could he ask for an explanation? He had given his word not to talk about the barn and in his mind the secrecy extended to what the soldier had told him: 'We won.' It was part of a whole. He couldn't drive away the images: the branches and leaves everywhere on his path, the noisy wooden bridge, the barn where the light died, the sleeping men, the young soldier's voice . . . Finally, Ned fell asleep, taking the red scarf into his dreams.

# 152

*E*lizabeth had not left her room and from time to time went back to her seat in the chair by the window, but she continued unconsciously to strain her ear to catch the sound of the only horseman she was waiting for on the road. The air grew cooler and the night was clear. Elizabeth never tired of looking at the wonderfully starry sky, and it helped her to remain patient.

The inexhaustible mystery of the luminous vault comforted her because she thought she could read in it promises of happiness and peace. In truth, the great language of all the constellations remained untranslatable into human language and there lay its fascination: it reassured the doubting soul.

The hours passed. Toward midnight, she heard the sound of a carriage driving up the avenue and stopping in front of the house. She leaned out and saw Mrs Harrison Edwards and Maisie de Witt coming back from the station with the Welshwoman. All three came in. She recognized the sound of the bolt that closed the front door from inside. If Billy came that night, he would have to knock and she would hear him. She could sleep easily until morning, so she slipped under the blankets, but could not sleep.

Day broke and the sun rose gloriously in a cloudless sky. Elizabeth got up and ran to the window. It was not yet eight o'clock, but this morning Billy could come at any time, and she wanted to see him galloping along the avenue. Then she would run down and throw herself into his arms; but how much longer would she have to wait? What did it matter? Waiting for happiness was already a happiness in itself, a happiness stolen from the future. She began to laugh to herself for no reason.

Suddenly she heard something. Yes: there was no doubt. Someone was coming, a horse was trotting along the road, then under the trees in the avenue. Her heart beat and without hesitating she ran to the door of her room in her white robe. Two seconds later she was flying down the stairs, hardly touching the steps and, still smiling, opened the front door. A horseman dismounted in front of her. It was Mike.

He took off his shako and let it fall to the ground. His face, usually so pink, was as white as plaster.

'Elizabeth,' he murmured.

'Yes, Mike. What is it, Mike?'

She went down two stairs and stood close to him. At once he let his head rest on the young woman's shoulder. She had the impression he was suffocating.

'Billy . . .,' he said softly. 'Billy.'

'No,' Elizabeth said. 'It's not true.'

She put her arms around him, strangely calm and in control of herself, but her legs were weakening.

'Help me back upstairs,' she begged. 'He promised he would come back.'

As they went into the house, they saw Miss Llewelyn waiting for them.

'Leave her with me,' she said quietly to Mike.

In a painful stupor, he saw this woman take Elizabeth and lift her up like a child, carry her to the staircase, gravely mounting the stairs. When she reached Elizabeth's room, she lay her on the bed and slapped her to bring her back to consciousness. At last, Elizabeth opened her eyes and looked at the Welshwoman.

'You here?' she said. 'I was at the window . . .'

'I'm going to help you to sit up in your chair. Can you stand?'

'Yes.'

She made a faint effort and fell back.

'It's the heat,' the Welshwoman said. 'I'll carry you.'

Once again, she took her in her arms and, carrying her across the room, sat her down in the chair.

'Didn't Mike come just now? I thought he did.'

'Perhaps. Look at the children playing in the field. Aren't they funny?'

Ned was pretending to let little Johnny chase him around the cedar tree. Then, turning round, he caught him and rolled in the grass with him, laughing. Suddenly, they both looked up toward the sky. Very high, so high that one could hardly see it, a lark was singing. Its voice filled the air.

'Elizabeth,' Miss Llewelyn said softly, 'you see how beautiful life is. The children are glad because the South is victorious.'

Elizabeth gave her a long look.

'Remember,' said the Welshwoman. 'Remember what I told you in Savannah: I shall always be beside you in the hard times . . . This is the hardest.'

'Why don't you speak frankly to me? I'm not afraid.'

She got up and stood upright, with one hand resting on the chair.

'I've known for a long time . . . even when I refused to admit it.'

Outside, beyond the lawn, Ned was shouting something in a happy voice. The Welshwoman looked out, standing beside Elizabeth: the sun was shining on the grass and the lark's song was still rising higher and higher in the clear sky.

Mike had gone out on the porch. Part of himself remained in Manassas among his dead comrades. He was afraid for Elizabeth. The trees and fields were misting over before his eyes . . . Then, at once, he heard a high voice shouting his name.

'Mike!'

Ned had seen him from a distance and was starting to race across the meadow toward him. Now, at last, he could tell his secret.

'Mike,' Ned shouted. 'Mike, we won! We won!'

A little voice, higher still, repeated like an echo:

'We won.'

And Mike saw the children running toward him in the sunshine.

# Major Reviews of *The Distant Lands* by Julian Green

'Hypnotic. . . . There is a forgotten ease and dallying here, where there lurks in the shade of each magnolia and is heard rustling in every crinoline the South's impending doom.'
— *The New York Times Book Review*

'. . . a compelling drama of the 1850s South . . . colorful and careful historical fiction, Green's opus is a delicious immersion into time and place, stylish and fluid, with an abundance of characters who attract with their humanness.'        — *Booklist*

'The book covers tantalizing territory. . . . Green depicts the Southern landscape as haunted and beautiful.'
— *The Philadelphia Inquirer*

'The writing, the characterization and sensitivity all combine to foreshadow the doom of the elegant, aristocratic South in this epic and wonderful novel.'        — *The Sunday Independent*

'One feels while reading these pages something of the pleasure that one feels watching *Gone With the Wind* for the nth time.'
— *Harpers and Queen*

'An astute, subtle novel of the old South . . . the prose is deceptively transparent, a lens, not a pane of glass. . . . The memories awakened by *The Distant Lands* are our own.'
— *The Boston Globe*

'. . . I am sure it will give a great deal of pleasure. . . .'
— *The Washington Post Book World*

'Using period misbegotten romance set in relief against a gallery of fascinating, pivotal characters . . . Green indicates that the distant lands are sublime habitations. It is a triumphant novel of pilgrimage.'        — *The Literary Review*

'*The Distant Lands* is no simplistic novel. It lends itself to a variety of interpretations and has more than its share of plot twists. The author creates beautiful images of Dimwood, Savannah, and Great Meadow, and the aristocratic lifestyle of the era.'
— *Richmond Times-Dispatch*